PROMISES

BY

JUDITH ARNOLD

MILLS & BOON

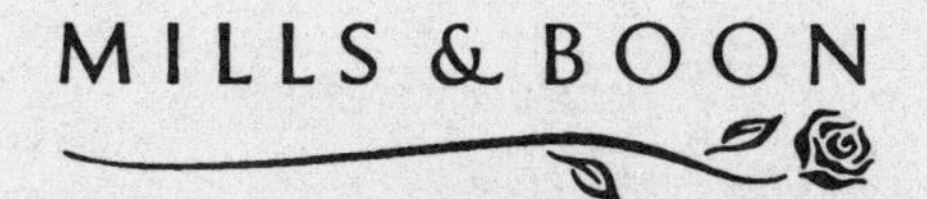

MILLS & BOON LIMITED
ETON HOUSE, 18-24 PARADISE ROAD
RICHMOND, SURREY TW9 1SR

All the characters in this book have no existence outside the imagination of the Author, and have no relation whatsoever to anyone bearing the same name or names. They are not even distantly inspired by any individual known or unknown to the Author, and all the incidents are pure invention.

Published in Great Britain in 1994 by Mills & Boon Limited, Eton House, 18-24 Paradise Road, Richmond, Surrey TW9 1SR

ISBN 0 263 78905 5

87-9406

Made and printed in Great Britain

Foreword

My friends and I were scornful about romance. The word conjured in our minds images of long-stemmed roses, candlelit dinners, midnight strolls with the man of our dreams. It implied a glittering engagement ring, a spectacular wedding, a cozy little house in the suburbs, two-point-two kids and a station wagon.

Romance? What could be cornier?

Besides, what could be more pointless than romance? How, after all, could we be worrying about trying to find Mr. Right and settling down, when there were so many more important matters to take care of? We were too busy changing the world to care about getting married.

There would be time for romance later, we resolved. But for the moment, while we had our youth and our energy, we would right all the world's wrongs.

But romance isn't really about flowers or moonlight. It's about listening to your heart, listening and then obeying what it tells you. Romance involves giving free rein to your feelings, having faith in yourself, believing in what is right and following the dictates of your soul. It means keeping promises, making commitments and chasing dreams. Sometimes romance entails the love of a man and a woman. Sometimes it entails the love of a country, a principle, an idea. But always it entails love.

In this trilogy, I've created six characters who, like me, came of age during the turbulent late sixties and early seventies. Although they lived together through certain universal experiences of the time, each of them has personalised those experiences, adapted to them as individuals and allowed their shared history to affect them in individual ways.

Laura Brodie absorbed from her youth the emphasis on brotherhood. She is in many ways an "earth mother", eager to save humanity, finding pleasure in the simple life. For Kimberly Belmont, reaching maturity during an age of rebellion gave her the strength to distance herself from the constricting conservatism of her family and to pursue a career in government, supporting a political leader in whom she believed. Julianne Robinson drew from the sixties the power of the feminist movement, which enabled her to succeed as a publishing executive who could use her magazine to expound her principles. Seth Stone took to heart the personal freedom celebrated in those days, the joy of "going for it," laughing at the universe and tweaking authority. In Andrew Collins's case, the sixties was a time when being armed with knowledge was considered the best defense; he chose a career with academia, where he could help mold the minds of a new generation. For Troy Bennett, the most significant aspect of the era was the war in Southeast Asia. The choices that war forced him to make both scarred and saved him. Like the other characters—like any of us from that era—he lives every day with the understanding of how his past has shaped his present.

"Is it all right...

...if we go straight to your place?" Seth half asked.

"Why wouldn't it be all right?"

Laura felt his fingers digging through the mass of her hair in search of the back of her neck. He found it and gently stroked the warm skin. "Because...maybe this is an off-the-wall idea, Brodie, but..."

"But...?"

"The God's honest truth is, the minute we get there, I'm going to want to do something very carnal with you."

"Carnal, huh." She laughed quietly. For some reason, the idea didn't seem particularly off the wall to her. Impractical, impulsive, imprudent, maybe, but not outlandish.

"I've been thinking about you all day, Laura, thinking about you and getting turned on."

"That's very intriguing," Laura said, unsure of how to react. At least her words were honest. She *was* intrigued.

"What are you going to do about it?" he asked.

There is a little of me in each of these characters. Like Laura, Kimberly and Julianne, I have struggled to reconcile a career and motherhood. I have lived on a commune. I have seen the difficulties faced by my divorced friends. I have benefited from the variety of possibilities the feminist movement opened to all women. Like Seth, Andrew and Troy, I have tried to "go for it," worked as a college professor and felt the repercussions of our nation's tragedy in Vietnam.

When I was young we used to say, "Never trust anybody over thirty." Now I, like the characters in these books, have passed the thirty-year mark—and survived. Laura, Seth, Kimberly, Andrew, Julianne and Troy aren't the same people they were fifteen years ago, but perhaps they're better people today than they were then. As their stories unfold in *Promises*, *Commitments*, and *Dreams*, they are finally able to acknowledge the romance of their past, and welcome the romances in their futures.

Just as it always has, romance still means listening to your heart and following your dreams. My characters listen, follow and triumph.

Chapter One

"I'm standing in the heart of a dream right now. Or, to be more accurate, the heart of the suite of offices that house Dream *magazine on the seventh floor of the Shelton Publications Building in midtown Manhattan. We're only a few miles from the Columbia University basement classroom where, exactly fifteen years ago today, a group of enterprising students decided to start an underground newspaper they called* The Dream. *But looking around at the elegant decor of* Dream*'s headquarters, I can't help thinking that the distance* Dream *has traveled these past fifteen years is much farther than a few miles."*

Julianne's gaze circled the festively decorated reception lounge. Already the room was fairly crowded. Journalists, luminaries of the publishing world and advertising executives mingled and chattered softly, sipping champagne punch from plastic cups and nibbling on hors d'oeuvres. The guests of honor hadn't arrived yet, and she knew that checking the door every minute on the minute wouldn't make them arrive any faster. Yet staring at the door was easier on her eyes than staring at the glaring white light the television crew had set up.

Connie Simmons, the reporter from *Evening Potpourri*, stood in front of the table where the sheet cake sat, two candles in the shape of a one and a five protruding from its rich butter-cream frosting. Behind the cake a framed black-and-white photograph was on display. It was a picture of a very young Julianne and her fellow dreamers, clowning around outside the campus building where the cellar office that had housed their operation was located. Troy had taken the picture with a timer. Kimberly and Laura had hunched over Troy and the other men as they held Julianne, their editor in chief, across their laps, and in the photo she had managed to look not at all disturbed about the possibility that they might drop her. It had been a real possibility, since they had all been laughing so hard. All six of them had been dressed in the requisite scruffy jeans and shirts. All six of them had peered out at the camera from behind inordinate quantities of hair.

Usually Julianne kept the eight-by-ten photo in her office, hanging on the wall behind her desk. Looking at it, seeing how idealistic and bright-eyed they appeared, ought to have made her feel depressingly old. But aging wasn't the sort of thing that upset her. Time passed. It was something one simply had to accept.

She noticed that Connie was beckoning to her, and after patting her smooth brown page boy and adjusting the lightly padded shoulders of her royal-blue silk dress, she joined the reporter at the table. Standing at five feet nine inches, not to mention the two inches her high-heeled shoes added to her height, she towered over the petite young woman, who tilted her head upward and gave Julianne a winning smile. "Nervous?" Connie asked.

Julianne returned her smile. "About being on television? Not really." If she was nervous about anything, it was about reuniting with her old friends. And no, she wasn't nervous about that, either. Except perhaps seeing Troy...

"With me is Julianne Robinson, *Dream*'s editor in chief," Connie recited, facing the camera. "Julianne was one of those six Columbia and Barnard students who founded the newspaper, which has since evolved into a glossy hundred-page monthly with a national circulation in excess of half a million. Tell us, Julianne, was starting up a newspaper like one of those Judy Garland-Mickey Rooney movies? You know, where someone says, 'Hey, my uncle has a barn—let's put on a show!'"

Julianne peered down at Connie, who was still smiling warmly. "Actually, no," she replied, trying not to sound self-conscious as the television camera recorded her speech. "We were classmates in an advanced rhetoric and composition course, and we decided to pool our energies for a class assignment. We thought it would be interesting to put together a newsletter about a block of brownstones owned by the university in Morningside Heights, approaching that single subject from different angles. One of us wrote about some of the older tenants and one about the kids who used to hang out on the street. Another of our group wrote about the questionable condition of the buildings themselves, one about friction between the residents and the neighboring college students, and so on. Troy Bennett—one of the founders—had a camera, so he took some pictures. We ran off a bunch of copies and distributed it free. It created quite a sensation."

"The original name wasn't *Dream*, but *The Dream*," Connie commented. "How did you come up with that?"

"It was from Dr. Martin Luther King's 'I have a dream' speech. We were all big fans of his."

Connie turned to the camera and said, "To help celebrate *Dream*'s fifteenth birthday, Julianne Robinson and her publisher have invited the other five founders back for this gala celebration. We can't help but wonder, where are they now? What have they been doing since those heady, radical days when underground newspapers were all the rage?" She pivoted to Julianne again. "Any of them here yet?"

"Not yet," Julianne told her. "But they'll be here. At least, four of them will be. They telephoned me to let me know they'd be coming." The only one who hadn't called in response to her invitation was Troy. She wondered if the invitation had reached him, if he had thrown it out without reading it, if he was even still alive.... "They'll be here," she said, as much to assure herself as to assure Connie Simmons. "They wouldn't miss this party for anything."

"YUCK! You aren't gonna wear *that*, are you?" Rita squawked.

Laura rotated from the full-length mirror on the back of her bedroom door. She had rather liked what she'd seen. The Indian print wraparound skirt was a bit snugger about her waist than it had been when she'd bought it back in her college days, but it still fit. So did the lacy white peasant blouse, of the same vintage as her skirt. "What's wrong with what I'm wearing?" she asked her daughter.

"It's flaming bad, Ma. I don't like it."

Laura's gaze skimmed the thirteen-year-old girl who had marched into the bedroom to plop herself onto the double bed. Rita had on a baggy, loose-knit pink sweater that fell nearly to her knees—in Laura's day, such a garment could have passed as a dress by itself—and a pair of equally baggy powder-blue slacks that left her ankles exposed, as if she'd outgrown the pants. Rita's curly black hair was shorn short in a punkish style, and her ears were adorned with brassy triangular earrings. If Rita's attire was good, Laura was more than happy to look flaming bad.

"Do you know how old this skirt is?" she asked, moving to the bureau and reaching for her hairbrush.

"Older than you, probably," Rita mused, tearing her eyes from her mother to examine a chip on her copper-colored nail polish.

"Heavens, if it were *that* old, it would have disintegrated into dust by now," Laura said with a laugh. "I bought this skirt in college. It was the first nonminiskirt I ever bought myself."

"I bet it looked bad then, too. You look like a gypsy or something."

"What's wrong with looking like a gypsy?" Laura ran the brush through her long, rippling curls, then pulled two frizzy locks back from her face and clasped them behind her head with a silver comb. A gypsy. With her unmanageable brown hair and her dark eyes and olive complexion, Laura found herself agreeing with Rita. She put on her silver hoop earrings and a matching silver bangle bracelet. "There," she said, spinning around on the heels of her leather sandals. "I think I look wonderful."

"Yuck," Rita appraised her. The doorbell sounded, and she sprang from the bed to answer it. She returned to the bedroom with Courtney Gonzalez in tow. Courtney lived three floors below Laura and Rita. Half black and half Puerto Rican, Courtney was the product of a background as unconventional as Rita's. The two girls were best friends.

Like Rita, Courtney was wearing an oversize sweater and baggy slacks. "Hey, Laura, you look great," she said.

Laura shot Rita a triumphant look. "No wonder I love you, Courtney," she joked, reaching for her white crocheted shawl and flinging it around her shoulders. "All right, girls, you know the rules. I may not be home till midnight, so if you get tired, just go to sleep. Anything goes wrong, you call Courtney's mom. There's frozen yogurt in the fridge if you're hungry."

"Yuck," Rita grumbled. "Why can't we have ice cream like normal people?"

"Yogurt's better for you," Laura answered.

"I like frozen yogurt. It's good stuff," Courtney remarked. "Anyway, I gotta lose weight. So do you, lardo," she ribbed Rita.

Laura eyed her daughter's friend and then Rita. Both girls were built like string beans. Lord, but thirteen was an awful age to have to live through.

She lifted her purse from the bureau, opened it and counted the money in her wallet. It was still early enough to be safe taking the subway into Manhattan, and she had enough cash on hand for a cab ride home. "Okay," she said, heading for the bedroom door. "Do you want me to give you a call in a couple of hours and see how you're doing?"

"Ma-a," Rita groaned.

"All right," Laura conceded with another laugh. "I'm on my way. Stay out of trouble."

THE JET TOUCHED DOWN with a gentle thump. Seth opened his eyes and stared out the window as the plane taxied toward one of the terminals. It seemed as if they'd been in a landing pattern for hours, and he felt stiff from having sat with his seat in the upright position for so long.

He raked his hands through his short dirty-blond tufts of hair, then reached into the inner pocket of his white linen jacket for his sunglasses. It was nearly seven o'clock and dark outside, but the sunglasses were a gag. Their rounded lenses were one-way mirrors.

He didn't bother to tighten the narrow gray tie at his throat. When you were wearing a wrinkled white suit and a turquoise shirt—to say nothing of mirrored sunglasses—you weren't supposed to strangle yourself on your tie. He watched the much more conservatively dressed businessman in the next seat preen and adjust his collar. No class, Seth reflected.

The party was supposed to start at seven, which meant that even if Seth went straight from the airport to the Shelton Building without checking in at the hotel first he'd still be late. But what the hell, he'd rather be visiting with his old buddies than unpacking. In fact, he couldn't wait to see the gang. Winging in tedious figure eights above Long Island had just about driven him nuts. He'd get to the hotel later.

He was the first passenger to reach the cabin's makeshift closet when the airplane lurched to a halt, and he yanked his garment bag from the rod and bolted down the aisle, nearly knocking over a flight attendant who seemed to think his life depended on her bountiful expression of gratitude for his having chosen to fly United. *Fly United...* He remembered the obscene poster he had hung in his dorm room in college; it featured two mating geese in midair, with "Fly United" printed underneath them. He loved that poster, and the other one he had, depicting a very pregnant woman with the caption "Nixon's the One." And his Spiro Agnew dartboard. Interior design á la hippie cheap.

The white limousine was parked outside the terminal, along with cabs and buses and elongated station wagons that bore signs reading Connecticut Express. Seth had arranged for the limo as a joke. Back home he preferred to drive himself wherever he had to go. But nowadays the New York taxis charged an arm and a leg, and anyway, what the hell. He could afford the limo.

The driver, though—he looked barely out of diapers. He was leaning against the gleaming front bumper, but he rose to attention when he spotted Seth approaching him. "Are you Mr. Stone?" he asked, quickly slipping his uniform cap onto his head.

"Good guess," Seth said, handing him the garment bag and opening the back door for himself. The driver stowed the bag in the trunk, then took the wheel. Seth sank into the plush leather upholstery and sighed. "Skip the Sheraton," he instructed the driver. "Let's go straight to the Shelton Building."

"Whatever you say, Mr. Stone."

Mr. Stone. Seth grimaced, then chuckled. The kid was only being polite, doing his job.

He gazed through the tinted-glass side window long enough to become disgusted with the snarled traffic. Life was as crowded on the highway as it had been in the air above Kennedy Airport. He had a long trip ahead of him. "Are you old enough to drive this thing?" he asked the young man piloting the car.

"Yes, sir. I've been doing it for nearly a year."

"How old are you?"

"Twenty, sir."

Twenty. That was how old Seth had been when they'd gotten *The Dream* started fifteen years ago. What did twenty-year-olds do these days, besides go to the movies and chauffeur limos? "So tell me," he said, figuring that a conversation with the driver would make the trip pass more pleasantly. "What do you want to be when you grow up?"

The driver accepted Seth's question with equanimity. "Actually, I'm studying to become an actor," he confessed. "I take classes at the Neighborhood Playhouse."

"No kidding? Good for you," Seth praised him. "You know, I'm in the film business. I write screenplays."

He glimpsed the young man's thrilled smile in the rear-view mirror. "Do you really? That's terrific," the driver enthused. "Anything I might have heard of?"

"Only if you like junk," Seth said modestly. "I wrote *Victory of the Ninja Women*, *Coed Summer*, cowrote *Return of Ax Man* and *Ax Man: Final Cut*. Right now I'm working on *Ax Man Cuts Both Ways*."

"I thought *Ax Man: Final Cut* was the last one in the series," the driver remarked.

"It was supposed to be. But hey, people keep coming. Why spoil a good thing?"

"But Ax Man was killed in *Final Cut*," the driver protested. "They blew him up with a grenade, didn't they?"

A fan, Seth realized with a smug grin. Everybody was always quick enough to put down the schlock movies Seth wrote, but the theaters had to turn patrons away whenever one of Seth's movies was appearing. "Wait until *Cuts Both Ways* comes out. You'll learn more about resurrection than they ever taught you in Sunday school. So what's with this traffic? Are we going to get to Manhattan before the summer solstice?"

"It's Friday night," the driver said apologetically. "Big night in the Big Apple."

"Yeah," Seth grunted. "Right."

"I'll get you there as quickly as I can."

"As long as you don't break any laws," Seth admonished him. "I don't want to take a tour of the city jails."

THE THING ABOUT REUNIONS, as far as Kimberly could tell, was that it was bad form to attend one if you were a failure. When she and Julianne had attended their five-year reunion at Barnard, each and every classmate they'd encountered had been doing something utterly wonderful with her life. Sally Bolton was into her medical residency; Cathy Beck was a lawyer; Doreen O'Connell had just edited a coffee table book on Ireland; Brenda Slavin was on the verge of opening her second boutique; Melanie Fierberg was a marine biologist and happily married. When Kimberly had commented to Julianne about the exemplary lives their classmates were leading, Julianne had pointed out that the reason all the returning women they saw were successes was that failures weren't likely to attend class reunions.

Kimberly had been a success then, too. Happily married, rising fast at the public relations firm. She didn't consider herself a success anymore, and she was entertaining serious misgivings about having let Julianne talk her into attending this party to celebrate *Dream*.

Cars were backed up for half a mile from the toll booths leading into the Lincoln Tunnel. There was no way for Kimberly to turn around and drive back to Washington. All she could do was wait, creep the car forward an inch at a time, tap her manicured fingernails against the steering wheel and worry about what everyone would say if they found out what a mess she'd made of her life in the past fifteen years.

She lowered the sun visor above the windshield to check her reflection in the vanity mirror. Despite the fact that every gentle blond wave was in place, her eye makeup impeccable, her cheeks smooth and pink and the line of her jaw as clean and taut as it had ever been, she thought she looked old and haggard. *Blame it on the long drive,* she muttered silently. *Blame it on a hellish week at work. Blame it on anything but the fact that you've blown it.*

"Accentuate the positive." That was what Julianne was always telling her to do. "You've got a prestigious job. That's something you ought to be proud of." *Sure,* Kimberly answered her silently. *I work absurdly long hours, I'm underpaid, and so what if I can address the senator by his first name?* Even though Senator Milford had granted her permission to call him "Howard," she felt uncomfortable calling him anything but "The Senator." That was what all his senior staff people called him. And to work on The Senator's staff—well, that sounded exalted, too. But it wasn't as if Kimberly were actually making policy. She was only enunciating it, shaping it into orotund phrases that rolled trippingly off The Senator's tongue whenever he was on the stump. Which seemed to be most of the time.

She was tired. Tired of the Washington rat race, tired of struggling to pay the rent for her basement apartment in

Georgetown on the stingy salary she earned, tired of having to think about dollars and cents. And lawyers. She'd finally obtained a competent divorce attorney to handle her end of things. She had put off taking that step as long as she could, not only because she needed to save money, but, more important, because she didn't want to accept the finality of the situation. But it was final, no doubt about that. Her marriage was a certifiable failure.

Only two more cars to go. She rummaged in her purse for a couple of dollar bills, then moved forward, waiting her turn to pay the toll. Once she had paid, she was able to shift into high gear again, grateful for the sudden rush of humid darkness as the tunnel swallowed her BMW.

At least she didn't look as old as she felt. People kept telling her that. Whitney Brannigan had been constantly pestering her for dates, practically from the day she'd moved out of the house in Chevy Chase. "Good God, give me some space," she'd complained. "I'm hoping that Todd and I can work things out and get back together." *Ha,* she grunted beneath her breath. *As if there had ever been a chance of that.*

The car emerged in Manhattan, and she steered north to Forty-second street. The sidewalks were crowded with throngs of people milling about the rehabilitated pornography houses that had been transformed into Theater Row, an enclave of off-Broadway showcases. The road was clogged with double-parked cars. So many people, Kimberly pondered, each of them a statistic. Just like her. A pretty, well-educated woman for whom the world once promised everything—except that she'd blown it and joined the ranks of the losers, the statistics. The next time she filled out a census form she would have to write "divorced."

She'd better do something about her frame of mind before she reached the Shelton Building. She would walk in with her head held high, as if her entire life were proceeding swimmingly, just as everyone had always predicted it would. Hadn't she been elected "Most Likely to Succeed" in high school?

She would march into the reunion like the conquering queen she was alleged to be. She still had her beloved BMW, she still had her figure—which Whitney, in one of his more expansive moments, had described as luscious—and she still had her pride. Nobody, other than Julianne, had to know about the mess with Todd. Kimberly could pretend she was a success for the duration of the evening, and then, when she returned to Julianne's apartment for the night, she could let down her guard and share with her good friend all the miserable details of her first meeting with the divorce lawyer.

"DON'T FORGET YOUR JACKET," Edith said, rushing ahead of Andrew to the coat closet and pulling the brown corduroy blazer from a hanger. "And here, let me straighten your tie. You look wonderful, Andrew. I'm sure you're going to have a fine time."

"Of course he is," Henry chimed in, hovering behind Edith as she adjusted the knot of Andrew's knit necktie and smoothed the button-down collar of his shirt.

"I love reunions," Edith babbled. "I just love them. And I'm so glad this one gave you the opportunity to visit us. You don't visit us often enough, Andrew."

He smiled faintly. It wasn't that he didn't want to visit Edith and Henry. It was just that whenever he did, they always looked so sad. No matter how much they beamed and laughed and fussed over him, their eyes always shimmered with unspent tears.

They meant well, and he cared for them a great deal. Every time he saw them, he promised that he wouldn't wait so long before the next visit. He knew that they still viewed him as a son, and he didn't mind that in the least.

But their eyes, always brimming, always bravely damming back the tears... It was hard, that was all. Hard seeing them, hard being forced to remember.

"The dinner was great, Edith," he said genuinely, adjusting his aviator-frame eyeglasses and feeling in the pocket of his khaki trousers for his keys. "I'll try not to get back too late."

"Don't be silly," Henry admonished him, pulling a house key from his own keyring. "Here, let yourself in. We won't wait up."

"If you're sure you don't mind..."

"Of course not. You'll probably want to spend half the night talking to your old friends. Come home when you come home. We'll let you sleep late tomorrow morning."

"You're really very generous," Andrew said, a half-hearted protest.

"Don't be silly," Edith echoed her husband. "It's our pleasure, Andrew. It always is. You look very handsome. Have a good time."

He strolled down the front walk without turning to wave goodbye. He knew Edith and Henry were lingering on the porch, watching his departure. He loved them, he really did, but sometimes they could be a bit overwhelming. They doted on him, practically smothered him with affection. He appreciated it, but it made him claustrophobic at times.

Once he'd driven down the cozy street of split-level houses and turned the corner, he began to unwind. Edith and Henry were much easier to love when he wasn't in the same room with them, forced to look at them, forced to acknowledge that, underlining their fondness for him, was that deep, pulsing sadness that would never go away.

He didn't plan to think about it anymore tonight. He couldn't help but think about it when he was with Edith and Henry, but now that he was on his way to the city, he could shunt his grief to the tiny corner of his mind reserved for it and concentrate on renewing his friendship with Julianne, Seth, Troy and Laura.

Oh, yes, and Kimberly, he added with a snort. Cutesy Kimberly, with her coquettish smile and her cheerleader approach to life. The others had all undoubtedly been doing interesting things with their lives. Laura had probably adopted a bunch of Asian orphans and was running a pig farm or something. Seth? If Seth hadn't fried his brains, Andrew would bet that Seth was engaged in some wonderfully frivolous enterprise—running a record shop, perhaps. Troy might be living out of a camper in the Sierra Nevada, taking breathtaking photographs, doing an impersonation of Ansel Adams. And Julianne... well, Andrew was a regular subscriber to *Dream*. He already knew that Julianne had parlayed their little newspaper into an illustrious magazine. But Kimberly Belmont, Southern belle *extraordinaire*... Married, Andrew decided. Mother of two, living in some pillared Atlanta mansion, active in the Junior League, chairwoman of the Red Cross Ball.

Trying to imagine what his old cronies would be like made the drive pass more easily. As for himself, Andrew suspected that the others wouldn't be much surprised by what they saw—except that they would see more of him than they'd ever seen before. None of them had known him before he'd grown his beard, back in his freshman year. He'd shaved the beard off six years ago, when a few strands of premature gray had infiltrated it and given him a Nestorian look that didn't sit well with him. Some gray had permeated his thick brown hair, too, but he wasn't about to shave his skull. He didn't need too many reminders of how old he was. The young, energetic students he faced every day were reminder enough.

He rarely drove down to New York City, but as he crossed the invisible boundary separating Westchester from the Bronx he felt a slight charge. Maybe he was spending too much time in his quiet little corner of western Massachusetts. Maybe he was becoming too remote. The sooty sting of the Bronx air resonated with teeming humanity. Andrew was glad for this excuse to venture back into the messy, disorganized, vital city that had been his home for four years. Returning to the past didn't always have to be a mournful experience.

Grinning, he crossed the bridge into Manhattan.

TROY STUBBED OUT his cigarette and stared through the pane of glass at the boxlike skyscraper across the street. Somewhere inside that building on an upper floor dozens of celebrants were drinking and congratulating themselves. Five of those dozens of celebrants were the special people with whom he'd come of age. One of those five special people was Julianne.

It was nearly eight o'clock. Sooner or later he would have to make up his mind whether to join them or to head back to Penn Station to catch the next train to Montreal.

"Care for a refill?" the waitress asked.

He turned from the window to acknowledge the plump young woman, who was holding a glass decanter full of coffee. He nodded, then reached into his shirt pocket and pulled out another cigarette.

The waitress spoke English, but Troy couldn't shake the feeling that he was in a foreign land. He supposed he was. The United States had become a foreign land to him on July 4, 1972. Independence Day, he recalled with a bitter laugh.

He lit his cigarette, then propped his head in his hand and stared through the window at the Shelton Building again. His overnight bag sat on the chair beside him; he'd already arranged to crash at Peter's apartment that night—if he decided to stay. If he did, if he made it to Peter's place, he might just throttle Peter for having forwarded the invitation to him. If only Julianne had sent the damned thing to his parents, instead, he would never have received it, and he wouldn't be sitting in this dingy coffee shop now, getting wired on caffeine and nicotine and wondering when the next Amtrak left the city.

Julianne wouldn't have invited him if she hadn't forgiven him. He'd left nearly fifteen years ago, and she wasn't the sort to hold grudges, to hang on. She was probably married by now, attached to some straight, law-abiding gentleman. Damn, he should have just telephoned her when he got the forwarded invitation, and saved himself the torment of traveling all this way without knowing what to expect.

He saw an extravagantly huge white limousine pull up to the curb in front of the building across the street, and he quickly turned away. If that was the kind of party it was, Troy was sure to stick out like a sore thumb, in his faded jeans, scuffed Western-style boots and brown leather bomber jacket. He'd worn the heavy jacket because Montreal was a great deal colder than New York in March. He'd worn the jeans because they were comfortable. He'd worn the boots because he always wore boots—when he wasn't photographing a wedding—and because Julianne always used to wear Western-style boots.

But that was a long time ago. Now she probably wore high-heeled shoes, panty hose, designer dresses, lipstick. Now she was a proper executive, writing letters of invitation to magazine birthday parties on fancy stationery with her name and title engraved along the left margin.

Hell, why did he come?

TURNING THE CORNER, Laura noticed the white limousine parked in front of the building and drew to a halt. A shy smile crept across her face as she wondered what famous celebrity would be emerging from the elongated vehicle. When she'd called Julianne after receiving her invitation,

Julianne had assured her that, no matter how resplendent the gala was going to be, as far as *The Dream*'s founders were concerned, the party was definitely a come-as-you-are type thing. Laura didn't feel inhibited by the luxurious car, or embarrassed about her "flaming bad" outfit. But she shrank back a step, awed and curious to see whom the car had carried to the party.

Before the nattily uniformed chauffeur could reach the passenger door, it swung open and a lanky man wearing ridiculous mirrored sunglasses stepped out onto the sidewalk. He had short, fluffy dark blond hair and he was dressed in a wrinkled white suit with a flamboyant turquoise shirt. Laura didn't recognize him, but, then, Rita was always deriding her for not knowing who all the latest stars were.

The man noticed Laura and froze in his tracks. Then his mouth spread in a broad, exuberant grin—an eerily familiar grin, Laura realized. "Laura?" he hooted. "Laura Brodie? Is that you?"

"Stoned?" she shrieked, racing over to him. "Seth *Stoned*? I don't believe it!"

He wrapped her in a lusty bear hug. "What don't you believe? It's me, all right. In the flesh. Look at you," he said, releasing her from his embrace and backing up to give her an intense perusal. "Something tells me this is going to be the cliché of the evening, but you haven't changed a bit."

"You have," she claimed, laughing. The last time she'd seen Seth Stone, his hair fell below his shoulders and his wardrobe consisted almost exclusively of T-shirts with off-color sentiments stenciled onto them and jeans with bizarre patches stitched on: an American flag across the seat of one pair, an appliquéd daisy on the knee of another. And always, even in the bitter dead of winter, he wore water buffalo sandals on his bare feet. Her gaze wandered down the length of his pleated white trousers to discover his feet enclosed in bright red high-tops. She was overcome by fresh laughter.

Seth didn't appear to be at all fazed by her reaction to him. He propped his sunglasses on the top of his head so she could see his sparkling, well-lashed hazel eyes. "Now tell me, Brodie, same eyes?"

She lifted her gaze to his face. "No, Seth," she answered, her laughter replaced by a delighted smile. "They don't look nearly as bloodshot as I remember them being."

"I rarely pull all-nighters anymore," he pointed out.

"All-nighters weren't what made them bloodshot," she reminded him.

He grinned. "I don't do much of that anymore, either. I could pass any blood test in town. But look at you! Man, you look fantastic."

"I love you, too," Laura said, giving him another impulsive hug. "But you're a liar. I've gained weight."

"Two pounds, three ounces," he estimated. "You used to be too skinny. God, look at all that hair," he said, gently stroking the thick, kinky locks that drizzled down her back. "At least one of us didn't get a haircut."

If she'd thought about it, Laura might have been amazed that she felt instantly comfortable with someone she hadn't seen in close to an eternity. She plucked his sunglasses off his head and tried them on. "These are absolutely stupid," she declared. "And that car, Seth—what possessed you to buy a limousine?"

"I didn't buy it," he told her. "Just rented it for the night. I thought it would be a gas. Same with the shades," he said, adjusting them on her nose and then chuckling at how she looked in them.

"You rented the sunglasses?"

"Yeah, right," he scoffed. "Laura, where I live the sun always shines. I've got more sunglasses than Imelda Marcos has shoes."

"Where do you live?" she asked.

"Topanga Canyon. Outside L.A. Listen, pal" he called over his shoulder to the chauffeur, "stick around, get some coffee or something across the street. I've just fallen in love, so I'll be a while." He slipped his arm around Laura's waist and escorted her to the revolving door that led into the lobby of the Shelton Building.

"If it's me you've fallen in love with," Laura said, removing the sunglasses and handing them back to Seth, "I'm very flattered."

"Believe me, my intentions are totally dishonorable." Seth ushered her to the guard posted by the elevators. He produced his invitation from an inner pocket of his jacket, and the guard directed them to the seventh floor. An elevator was waiting, and they entered it. "Let me warn you," Seth continued, donning his sunglasses, "I plan to march into the party and shout, 'I just flew in from the coast.' I want to make a grand entrance."

"You could make a grand entrance with your mouth shut," Laura chided him. "Those shoes are absolutely—"

"Outrageous," Seth completed with an impish grin. "So where did you fly in from?"

"Brooklyn. My daughter and I have an apartment in Flatbush."

"Your *daughter*?" He staggered backward in an exaggerated display of shock. "You have a *daughter*?"

Laura smiled and nodded. If Rita ever had the opportunity to meet Seth, she would probably consider his strange outfit flaming good. She would probably comb the city for a pair of mirror sunglasses just like his, and a weird-looking white suit and a Day-Glo blue shirt.

"So where's your husband?" he asked.

"I haven't got one."

"Divorced?"

Laura shook her head placidly. "No."

Seth's eyebrows rose. "Very interesting. I can't wait to hear about it."

But before he could question her further, the elevator door slid open, depositing them outside a double doorway that led into a reception area mobbed with revelers. Just inside the doorway stood a trio of people: a statuesque brown-haired woman in a classically styled blue silk dress, a curvaceous blonde in a cream-colored suit and a violet crepe-de-chine blouse and a tall, clean-shaven man in a preppy getup—khaki pants, corduroy blazer, loafers.

"Oh, boy," Seth whispered to Laura. "Déjà Vu City."

"Laura! Seth!" Kimberly broke from the trio and collided with Seth and Laura in the doorway. "You're here! Did you two come together?"

"Hardly," Laura said with a chuckle. "He came in a limo. I came on the D train."

"No, no, wait a minute," Seth silenced her. He strode through the doorway and announced, "I just flew in from the coast."

"We know that," Kimberly prattled, Seth's broad pronouncement evidently having little effect on his friends. "Julianne already told us you live in California."

"Is that really you, Andrew Collins?" Laura inquired, turning to Andrew. "Is that really your face? I never knew you had a chin."

"I needed a chin to hold all the hair," he said mildly. "You're looking wonderful, Laura."

"She's got a *daughter*," Seth proclaimed. "Do you believe it? Laura is a mother."

"Of course she is," Kimberly confirmed. "She was always mothering us. It makes sense that she should be mothering someone else these days."

"Let me get you some drinks," Julianne offered. She eyed Seth's sunglasses and suppressed a guffaw. "You," she said, "look egregious. Make sure you wear those when Connie Simmons interviews you."

"Who's Connie Simmons?" Seth asked.

"A television reporter," Andrew replied as Julianne vanished in search of some champagne punch. "Julianne has been prepping us. We're going to be on *Evening Potpourri.*"

"That tacky syndicated TV magazine?" Seth protested.

"It's good publicity for *Dream*," Kimberly explained. "They're doing a kind of before-and-after piece on us and *The Dream*. It's going to air in a couple of weeks. So behave yourself, Stoned."

"I *am* behaving myself," he insisted. "Where's Troy?"

"He hasn't gotten here yet," Kimberly informed him. "Julianne said she wasn't sure whether he'd show. He didn't respond to her invitation. Maybe he never got it. She sent it to him in care of some small-press owner who published a collection of Troy's photographs a few years ago."

"Troy published a book? I think I'm impressed," said Seth. "So, Andrew, what have you done that can top that?"

"I've published a book," Andrew answered before sipping his punch.

"What am I, illiterate?" Seth asked rhetorically, spinning around to Laura. "I haven't heard of any of these books. Have you heard of any of these books?"

"No, I haven't." She turned to Andrew. "What's your book about?"

"It's a text on political economics in Latin America," he answered. "Very dry, very boring. The sort of thing that's supposed to win me tenure down the road."

"You're a professor?" she asked, thinking that that was exactly what he looked like.

"Yes, I teach at Amherst College."

"Oh, man," Seth groaned good-naturedly. "Amherst College. And I thought I was going to impress people with my fancy-dancy sunglasses."

JULIANNE LOCATED a waiter carrying a tray of drinks and secured two cups. Through the swirling throng, she could see her friends clustered near the doorway, talking and laughing.

Kimberly had been the first to arrive, looking ravishing, although her eyes were wide with barely contained panic. She had corralled Julianne, dragged her into a corner and whispered, "Don't tell anyone about me and Todd, okay? We've gotten lawyers and my life's a disaster. But we'll talk later, Okay? Not a word to the gang."

Julianne had dutifully sworn that she wouldn't breathe a hint of Kimberly's marital difficulties to any of their school chums. And then Andrew had entered, cool and quiet, his hair longish but neatly groomed and his manner reserved. The panic in Kimberly's eyes had abruptly vanished, replaced by sedate control, and she'd abandoned Julianne to greet him.

Julianne had learned from Andrew's parents, whose address she'd ferreted out of the Columbia University Admissions Office, that he was an assistant professor at Amherst College, so he had been easy to reach. She'd already known about Seth's career as a writer of raunchy film scripts, since *Dream* regularly ran movie reviews and essays on contemporary culture, much like the "Kulchah Column" Seth used to write for *Dream* when it was a fledgling newspaper. And she'd tracked down Laura's current address from the Barnard Career Office. Julianne had been delighted to learn that Laura currently lived in Brooklyn and that they would be able to see more of each other than simply a formal reunion once every fifteen years.

Julianne was happy, happy to be with her friends, happy to see them having such a good time together, catching up. She was happy that the party—she had long ago come to think of it as *her* party, not the magazine's—was going smoothly. Only one thing would make her happier: seeing Troy.

As if a fairy godmother had heard her unspoken wish, Julianne suddenly spotted the tall, lean man in a worn leather jacket and jeans standing just outside the door. His hair was an unkempt mane of black waves and his upper lip was hidden beneath a thick mustache. His dark eyes were guarded, searching the room as he hung back. A tattered duffel bag rested on the floor at his feet.

Troy had come.

Chapter Two

"Are you sure you don't mind?" Laura asked.

Seth laughed and swung open the limousine's passenger door. "Don't be silly. The thing's already paid for, whether or not I use it. Why should we waste time looking for a cab for you?" He helped her into the car, then climbed in himself. "Besides, when was the last time you got to ride in a white limousine?"

"In a former incarnation, if ever," she said with a smile. She took in her surroundings: the spacious, well-appointed interior, the soft leather upholstery, the tinted windows, the carpet as thick as the carpeting in her apartment. The arm ledges protruding from the insides of the doors were covered with a mystifying array of buttons. She fingered them, but didn't dare to push any of them.

It was all so glamorous, so—so alien. Laura wasn't sure how she felt about traveling in such a ritzy vehicle. At thirty-five years of age, she had never even owned a car. Material possessions simply weren't a major part of her life.

However, riding home in Seth's rented limo beat having to try to flag down a cab at this late hour. And getting to spend a little more time with Seth was an added bonus. Or maybe the chance to spend more time with Seth was the real reason Laura had accepted his offer of a lift, and the limousine ride was the bonus.

The chauffeur set aside the book he was reading and donned his cap. "Where to, Mr. Stone? The Sheraton?"

"No, we're going to Brooklyn," Seth informed him. "We're taking my friend home first." He pressed one of the buttons by his elbow, and a glass panel rose behind the driver's seat, sealing Laura and Seth in privacy. "What do you think?" he asked her, observing her awestruck expression as the limo pulled away from the curb.

"If you hoped to impress me, you've succeeded," said Laura. "Except . . ." She smiled mischievously.

"Except what?"

"I always thought these things had TVs inside them."

"Well, there's just no pleasing some women," Seth muttered, feigning annoyance. Then he chuckled. "A lot of limos do. But I specifically asked for one that didn't. If there were a TV in here, I might feel obliged to use it. And if I turned it on, I might get stuck watching one of my own movies."

"Don't tell me they show movies like *Coed Summer* on television!"

"With extensive editing," Seth told her. "But you know, not everything I write is R-rated. I've done a few made-for-TV jobs—*Black Market Babies*, *Rich Intimacies*, *Barrio Warlords*. . . ."

"What uplifting subjects," Laura teased him. "I hope they pay you well for writing such trash."

Seth accepted her criticism with a lackadaisical shrug. "I ain't kicking. The bottom line is, it's fun."

"I'm glad," Laura said. She meant it, too. Seth had always been one to pursue things for the sheer fun of it. She'd hate to think that he had turned into a mercenary, writing nonsensical film scripts only because he lusted after money.

She nestled into the deep cushions and sighed contentedly. Seth turned to her and absorbed her weary smile. "Tired?" he asked.

She nodded.

"The night is young, my love."

"In California, maybe," she conceded. "We're on Eastern time now. You'd better get used to it."

"By the time I get used to it I'll be on the plane back to L.A."

"How long are you planning to stay in New York?"

"Till Sunday afternoon. I figured I ought to spend at least one full day on the ground before heading for home. But jet lag never bothers me much," he assured her. "I can get by on only a few hours of sleep."

"Just like in college," Laura recalled. She compared the energetic, freewheeling, hirsute young Seth of her memory with the serene, dimple-smiled man seated beside her. Too many years might have passed since she'd last seen him, but his humor was just as infectious as it used to be, and his eyes still glinted with life, and his hair—in its abbreviated length—was still lustrous with pale blond streaks visible even in the darkened interior of the car. "I'm so glad you came tonight, Seth," she murmured. "I've missed you. We should have kept in touch over the years."

He nodded and brushed a stray lock of her hair back from her cheek. The gesture warmed her. She and Seth had always been close, close enough to touch each other without attaching any significance to the act. Sitting with him now in his rented limousine seemed as natural to her as sitting with him on an overcrowded chartered bus to Washington, or on a subway downtown to Greenwich Village, or on a bed in a dormitory room as they plotted a series of essays for *The Dream*.

"I'm a lousy letter writer," he said, responding to her wistful comment. "People who write for a living shouldn't have to write in their spare time, too."

"We could have kept in touch by telephone," Laura noted. "At least, you could have. My budget's tighter than yours."

"Yeah, and how many years were you living on that commune in the sticks? You said you didn't even have electricity up there, let alone a telephone."

"That's true," Laura conceded. "But even so...I wish it hadn't taken all of us fifteen years to get back together. It was so good seeing everybody." Her eyes glowed happily as she reflected on the reunion. "Everybody's doing such exciting things with their lives. You're out in Hollywood—"

"Writing trash," Seth reminded her.

"And having fun. And Julianne's got the magazine, and Andrew's a professor. Kimberly's working for Senator Milford. Troy's got his own photography studio...."

"And you're helping unwed mothers. That's exciting, too."

"No," Laura disagreed. "It's rewarding and it's fulfilling, but I wouldn't call it 'exciting.'" She didn't want to think about her own work. Yes, it was rewarding and fulfilling, but it could also be downright frustrating, and even depressing at times. Although she and Neil hadn't gotten married when she found out she was pregnant, at least she had been fairly mature and well educated, and she had wanted the baby. Most of the mothers she counseled in her job were teenagers, totally unprepared for the difficult tasks that motherhood entailed. Laura's clients hadn't become pregnant because they were bursting with love but for quite the opposite reason—because they were sorely in need of someone to love them. Their actions were grounded not in idealism but in carelessness and ignorance.

Laura knew she was doing something important in her work. But to write speeches for a senator, or editorials for a national magazine, or lectures for the young wizards who attended Amherst College, or, for that matter, screenplays for silly television movies like *Barrio Warlords*—such careers had to be more exciting than what she did.

"Didn't everyone look great?" she mused, preferring to concentrate on her friends rather than herself. "Kimberly is just as gorgeous as ever—"

"Once a prom queen, always a prom queen," Seth summed up. "I've got to admit, I was surprised she's still 'Belmont.' She didn't strike me as the sort of woman who'd keep her maiden name after she got married."

"I always knew she was a feminist," Laura remarked.

"Yeah, but whose initials did they use on the monogrammed silverware? That's the sort of thing that used to matter to Kim."

"You underestimate her," Laura scolded him. "You guys always did. Just because she married her hometown sweetheart doesn't mean she doesn't possess a healthy streak of independence."

"Uh-huh," Seth snorted dubiously. "So, what were you independent feminists cackling about when Andrew and Troy and I were dealing with that Connie Simmons person?"

"About how funny you looked in your sunglasses and about how clean-cut Andrew looked without his beard."

"What about Troy?" Seth goaded her. "How come you weren't laughing at him?"

Laura's smile waned. "He seemed so lost, Seth. Kim and I noticed it right away, that sadness in his eyes. Julianne didn't want to talk about it, though. She just kept saying, 'At least he came. At least he's here.' Did you know Kim's staying at Julianne's place tonight? I'm meeting them there for lunch tomorrow. God, I'm glad they're back in my life. I missed them."

"You must have known Julianne was living in the city when you moved to Brooklyn. Why haven't you contacted her before now?"

Laura shifted slightly in her seat. Why, indeed? It would have been easy enough. She knew that Julianne ran *Dream* magazine; she could have called their editorial office and asked to speak to the editor in chief.

But the move from Buffalo had been exhausting, and beginning a new job and getting Rita settled in at a new school... And then Laura had wondered whether Julianne would have wanted to see her. Julianne was a reputable executive, polished, elevated above the world Laura inhabited. Laura had had enough experience with childless professional women to know that she functioned on a different wavelength than they. When she had lunch with her unmarried colleagues at work, they either spent the entire time talking about shopping at Bloomingdale's, attending singles' weekends at resorts in the Catskills, refinishing antique chests of drawers—activities for which Laura lacked the time, the money and the interest—or else they focused the entire discussion on Rita, as if Rita were the only thing in Laura's life worth talking about. Women in positions like Julianne's didn't seem to understand Laura, and she usually avoided them.

She shouldn't have avoided Julianne, though. She shouldn't have assumed that Julianne wouldn't want to make time in her life for a harried single mother who made a career of counseling other harried single mothers. "Well," Laura resolved, "tomorrow we can start making up for lost time." She turned fully to Seth. "And what were you guys cackling about while we were dealing with Connie Simmons?"

"Mostly about how funny I looked in my sunglasses," Seth joked. "Actually, they were psyched to hear about all the little starlets I work with."

"Sure," Laura scoffed.

Seth abruptly grew solemn. "They've both had kind of a rough time of it, Laura. You're right. Troy isn't all that happy in Montreal. I told him he ought to come home, let bygones be bygones and move back to the States, but he said no, he didn't think he ever would. And Andrew..." Seth drifted off.

"What about Andrew?" Laura prodded him.

"Well, he told us about his wife. Kind of by accident, I think. I got the clear impression he really didn't want to talk about it, but—"

"His wife? Andrew's married?"

"Was. She died a few years ago. The truth was, we weren't cackling much at all."

"Oh, God." For a moment Laura couldn't think of anything else to say. "I wish he'd told me."

"Why? What would you have done?"

Laura ruminated. They'd all grown a lot in fifteen years, grown up, grown old. But to be widowed—were they really old enough to be widowed? "I would have put my arms around him and given him a big hug," she said.

"Why don't you give me a big hug, instead?" Seth suggested.

Laura slid close to him on the seat and he wrapped his arm comfortingly around her. She rested her head on his shoulder and sighed. The solid warmth of Seth's lean body was almost enough to dispel the chilly ache in the pit of her stomach at the thought of Andrew's loss. "He looked so good without the beard, and in those spiffy eyeglasses," she recalled. "Remember how he used to look in his old wire-rims?"

"He looked professorial," Seth remarked. "And now he's a hotshot professor. Don't get all mopey on me, Laura. He's doing just fine. And anyway, you lost a lover, too. I've lost thousands of them myself. *C'est la vie* and all that."

"I didn't lose a lover," Laura disputed him. "If you're talking about Rita's father, I didn't lose him. He just left."

Seth angled his head to view her. She wondered whether he was going to question her about Neil, the dynamic, ruggedly handsome man she'd met and fallen in love with when she was living on the commune. She had long ago stopped loving him, and she had forgiven him for his having fled from the commune shortly after Rita was born. Neil wasn't a bad man, only a weak one. Laura felt sorry for him; he had deliberately chosen to miss out on the special joy of raising a child. She pitied him and she forgave him. Forgiveness came easily to Laura.

But she didn't want to explain all that to Seth. She didn't know whether she could. People who knew about Neil were always getting on Laura's case. "Why don't you sue him for support money? Why don't you get a bloodthirsty lawyer to drag the bastard over the coals?" Laura wasn't vindictive, and she had no desire to force anything out of Neil. She didn't even know where he was living anymore.

She waited for Seth to speak, hoping that he wouldn't demand to hear the entire story of Rita's birth. She would tell Seth about it someday if he wanted, but not tonight, not while she was still savoring the pleasant shock of having seen all her old friends.

Blessedly, Seth refrained from probing. All he asked was "Is Rita going to be awake when we get to your place? I want to meet this daughter of yours."

Laura twisted Seth's arm to read his wristwatch. "It's nearly one o'clock. If she's still awake she's in big trouble."

The limousine had crossed the Manhattan Bridge into Brooklyn, and the driver rapped on the glass barrier with his knuckles. Seth dutifully pressed the button to lower the barrier. "Directions, Mr. Stone?" the driver requested.

"Listen to this guy," Seth whispered to Laura. "He sounds like he graduated from the London School of Genteel Servants."

"You get what you pay for," Laura teased him, once again surveying her plush environment and shaking her head in awe. She provided the driver with instructions on how to reach her address, then snuggled into Seth's shoulder. Perhaps Troy wasn't happy living in Montreal, and Andrew had lost his wife, but Seth at least was enjoying a fairy-tale existence. "Thousands of lovers, huh," she pondered. "Were they all starlets?"

"No," Seth answered with a straight face. "Probably no more than seven or eight hundred of them were starlets."

Laura laughed softly. "Seriously, Seth. Tell me what your life is like. I can't imagine ever having enough money to rent a limousine." If someday, by some fluke, she did have that much money, she doubted she'd spend it on a limousine. But she was awfully curious, in a detached, anthropological way, to hear what life could be like when one was rich and surrounded by starlets.

"I rarely travel in limousines," Seth confessed. "I own a Porsche 944, and I use it to zip around the canyon roads and give myself cheap thrills."

"What's your house like?" she asked. "Do you have a hot tub?"

Seth guffawed. "I don't have a hot tub, and I don't have a water bed, and I don't have a mirrored ceiling in my bedroom. I don't do cocaine. I don't play tennis. I don't kiss strangers. I don't own a sailboat or a tuxedo. And I don't call people 'sweetheart' if I can help it. Anything else you want to know?"

"You still haven't told me what your house is like," Laura commented.

"It's not too big—eight rooms, if you count the breakfast room separately from the kitchen. Modern. Stuck halfway up a hillside. If there's ever a mud slide in our neighborhood, it's Sayonara City," Seth told her. "I've got a huge doghouse in the backyard, where my dog, Barney, lives. And I've got a garage, where my Porsche lives."

"Do you have a garden?" she asked. She was trying her best to picture Seth's home, but it seemed as alien to her as the limousine.

He shook his head. "I thought about starting one, and then in the nick of time I came to my senses and convinced myself that the canyon was too dry. Actually, it isn't—some of my neighbors have gardens—but keeping a garden going is too much effort, so I decided to pretend the climate was wrong for it."

"So what do you have in the yard? Grass?"

"A little. Mostly scrub, ground cover, whatever doesn't take any work to maintain." He drew her more snugly to himself. The lapel of his jacket was surprisingly soft against her cheek, and his neck smelled faintly of a musky after-shave. "You ought to come out to California and see the place for yourself, Laura," he said.

"Do you mean that?"

"Of course I mean it. What do you say? You could go swimming in the Pacific, get a genuine 'It Never Rains In Southern California' tan, and tool around town with me in the Porsche. I'll even throw in the 'Homes of the Stars' tour at no extra charge."

"I'd love to," she said impetuously, not bothering to consider where she'd get the money to make such a trip, or whether she could secure some vacation time, or what she'd do with Rita while she was away. She hadn't told Seth that she *would* visit him, only that she'd love to. Which was the truth.

The driver brought her back to reality by asking, "We're on Ocean Avenue now. Which building is yours, ma'am?"

Laura caught Seth's eye and stifled the urge to giggle. Hearing the driver call her "ma'am" was as jarring as hearing him call Seth "Mr. Stone." "It's the one by the fire hydrant, on the right," she informed the driver.

Seth peered at the massive old apartment building, its entry pillars and rococo embellishments contrasting with the spray-paint graffiti that marred one brownstone wall. The building—like the neighborhood—was clearly long past its heyday, not quite a slum but evolving in that direction. "Are you sure it's all right if I come up?" he asked Laura.

"Why wouldn't it be all right?"

"I don't know. What does your daughter think when you bring strange men to your apartment?"

Laura laughed. "She's a big girl, Seth. And you're a friend. Although you *are* pretty strange, I've got to admit."

He pretended to be offended. "Just for that," he warned Laura as he shoved open the door, "I'm going to embarrass you mercilessly in front of the kid."

"That shouldn't be difficult for you," Laura parried. "Just be yourself."

Seth faked a scowl and jammed his sunglasses onto his nose. By the time he and Laura had left the car, however, they were both laughing. He held the building's outer door for Laura and waited patiently while she dug her key out of her purse and unlocked the inner door to the foyer. A few dusty tables and a horsehair sofa stood in the dimly lit lobby. Laura wondered whether the place looked seedy to Seth. It looked seedy to her, but she was used to it.

That she should care about Seth's opinion of her home surprised her. She'd never been one to worry about keeping up with the Joneses; the fact that her school friends were more affluent than Laura didn't bother her. She was proud of what she'd accomplished, and there wasn't a single thing in her life that she would have done differently if she'd had the chance: not living on the commune, not becoming pregnant, not raising Rita by herself, not leaving the commune and moving to Buffalo, earning her master's degree in social work, then moving to Brooklyn. Not a thing she'd want changed.

Except, perhaps, for a more brightly lit lobby in her apartment building and a less nosy super than Mr. Santiago—who, Laura knew, was spying on her through the peephole in his door as she escorted Seth into the building—and an elevator that didn't wheeze eerily between floors two and three.

Seth removed his sunglasses when the elevator ground to a halt on the fifth floor. The hallway smelled of onions; Mrs. Cobb in Apartment 5-D had a tendency to cook casseroles at odd hours. Trying to ignore the strong odor, Laura led Seth to the end of the corridor and unlocked the door.

Light streamed into the entry hall from the living room, and Laura heard the muffled babble of the television set. She wasn't the strictest disciplinarian in the world, but with Seth by her side, she decided she ought to appear at least a little bit miffed at the girls for having stayed up so late. Pressing her lips together, she marched into the living room—to discover Rita and Courtney both fast asleep on the couch, Rita curled up in one corner and Courtney sprawled dramatically across the cushions, her head balanced precariously against the sofa's arm. An empty container of frozen yogurt stood on the coffee table in front of them, along with two gooey spoons.

"Which one's yours?" Seth asked impishly, drifting into the room behind Laura and evidently finding the scene amusing.

Laura couldn't deny that she was also amused. "I think the one in the corner," she answered Seth as she crossed to the television set and turned it off.

The sudden silence roused both girls, who stirred, grunted and opened their eyes. "Hi, Ma," Rita mumbled groggily. Then her gaze wandered to Seth and sharpened. She sat up and stared at him for a long minute, giving him a detailed inspection before turning back to her mother. "Who's that?" she asked.

"*That*," Laura replied, slipping her hand through the bend in Seth's arm and leading him toward her daughter, "is Seth Stone, a school friend of mine. Seth, meet my daughter, Rita. And this is her friend Courtney."

Seth seemed bemused by the sight of Laura's daughter. Not that Rita was peculiar-looking—certainly no more peculiar-looking than most thirteen-year-old girls. But Laura suspected that he still hadn't come to terms with the fact that one of his contemporaries—one of his friends—could be the mother of a person, an adolescent-type person, who stood five feet four inches and wore metallic enamel on her fingernails.

Rita was undoubtedly equally bemused by Seth's presence. Laura rarely dated, even more rarely brought a man home to the apartment—and the men she introduced to Rita never wore white suits and red high-tops. Indeed, none of them looked even remotely as hip as Seth. Rita sized him up again and then glanced at Courtney. The two girls giggled.

"I guess I'd better go," Courtney said, as usual much more diplomatic than Rita. She eyed Seth, then covered her mouth with her hand and giggled some more. "I'll see you, Rita," she said as she stood.

"Hang on, Courtney. Let me take you home," Laura offered. "It's awfully late."

"I could give her a ride home in the limo," Seth suggested.

Laura started to explain that since Courtney lived on the second floor of the building the only vehicle she needed to ride home in was the elevator, but before she could speak, the two girls were shrieking. "A limo? Ma-a! Does he have a limo?"

Laura rolled her eyes and grinned reproachfully at Seth. "Now see what you've done," she muttered.

"What's wrong with what I did?" Seth protested. "I gave you a ride home. Why can't I give your daughter's friend a ride home?"

"She lives in this building," Laura informed him.

But it was too late. The girls were clamoring to see the limousine. "Come on, Ma," Rita begged. "Just let us look at it. Come on! I've never seen one, except at Grampa's funeral, and that doesn't count because it was a funeral. Okay? Just one spin around the block, okay?"

Laura opened her mouth to respond, but closed it when she saw Rita and Courtney racing toward the door. She turned to Seth. "Oh, come on, *Ma*," he whispered, taking her hand and dragging her out of the apartment with the girls.

The truth was, Laura wasn't much good at pretending to be angry. And she really wasn't angry about taking the girls outside to look at the limousine, even at the ungodly hour of 1:20 a.m. Tomorrow was Saturday; they'd all sleep late. And while looking at a limo wasn't high on Laura's list of important things one ought to do during the course of one's life, she knew that Rita probably wouldn't have another opportunity to see a limo—or ride in one—until Laura's mother passed away. Or Laura herself. Such eventualities, Laura hoped, were far, far in Rita's future. Feeling rather generous, she decided to let Seth take Rita and Courtney for a ride in the car.

The driver set down his book and smiled stoically as the two giddy, overtired girls darted to the limo and shrieked some more. "Look, Rita, it's white!" Courtney observed. "This is one radical car."

"What's she talking about?" Seth asked Laura. "I always thought the most radical car you could own was a VW van with a peace sign painted on the roof."

"'Radical' means cool," Laura translated. "If they call something 'radical,' they mean it's far-out."

"Uh-huh," Seth grunted. "And I thought people talked funny in Hollywood." He chivalrously opened the passenger door, then lifted the jump seats up from the floor for the girls. "Hop into my chariot, lovely ladies," he said, gesturing them inside.

Rita and Courtney giggled again. "Wait till I tell my mother about this," Courtney squealed.

"Forget your mother," Rita contradicted her. "Wait till we tell Becky LoCaffio!"

"Yeah! Can we drive past Becky's building?" Courtney asked Seth.

"At this hour," Laura pointed out dryly, sliding along the seat to make room for Seth, "I doubt that Becky will be awake."

"Who cares? She's such a flaming slime," Rita said brightly. "Let's drive past her building, anyway. This car is great, Seth. What are you, a drug dealer or something?"

"No," Seth replied calmly. "I'm not a drug dealer. Does your mother usually hang out with drug dealers?"

Rita shrugged. "So how come you've got this car?"

"He rented it," Laura explained, then called to the driver to cruise slowly around the block.

Rita seemed much too excited to care whether they actually drove past Becky LoCaffio's building. "You rented it? Just for the party?" She knelt on the jump seat to face her mother. "I told you you should have worn something nicer."

"What's wrong with what your mother's wearing?" Seth defended Laura. "I think she looks wonderful."

"Yuck," Rita grumbled. "So, did you and my mom go out in college?"

"Go out? As in 'date'?" Seth appeared to find Rita's tactless questions refreshing. "No truth to the rumor. We were just friends."

"Yeah," Rita concurred. "Ma's told me she dated mostly weenies in college."

"Did you?" Seth asked, turning to Laura. "You dated Mark Hofkiss. He wasn't a weenie. At least, I don't think he was. What's a weenie, anyway?"

"Mark Hofkiss wasn't one," Laura agreed. "But we only went out a few times. Most of them were weenies, Seth. Rita's right about that."

Courtney had discovered the control buttons on the door and was systematically trying them all out. The glass panel slid up and down; reading lights flickered on and off; music filled the compartment and then stopped. Seth laughed, and so did Laura. It was fun taking the girls for a brief drive.

And driving in the limousine gave Laura a few more minutes with Seth. She was exhausted, but she wasn't ready to say goodbye to him yet. The understanding that he was going to be back in California Sunday night saddened Laura more than she might have expected. They had only just renewed their friendship, after all. They had only just found each other again. She didn't want to have to wait another fifteen years before she got to spend time with him again.

"On a bus," he was telling the girls, and Laura directed her attention to the conversation. "It was a bus to Washington, D.C., one of the buses Columbia chartered. Right, Laura?"

"You mean, when we met?"

Seth looped his arm around Laura's shoulders and turned back to the girls, who were listening attentively. "The Moratorium, November of 1969. We wound up sitting together even though we didn't know each other. The bus left the city at some ghastly hour, and by the time we hit Newark, your mother had fallen asleep on my shoulder. Do you believe it? Never saw me before, and she was already sleeping with me." He winked at Laura. "Am I shocking your daughter?"

Laura chuckled, unconcerned. "Rita is basically unshockable."

"So what was this Moratorium thing?" Rita wanted to know.

"What was this Moratorium *thing*?" Seth echoed, astounded. "This Moratorium *thing*, as you call it, was a march on Washington to end the war."

"The Vietnam War," Laura supplied, aware that the history curriculum of Rita's school wasn't all that it ought to be. "It was a huge march, with folks pouring in from all over the country. They had National Guardsmen standing on the roofs of all the federal buildings, armed with rifles. Remember?"

Seth nodded. "And it was freezing cold. And Peter, Paul and Mary sang 'Blowing in the Wind.' And we marched and sang and drank some wine that someone was passing around, and then we all piled onto the bus and traveled back to New York."

"And the war went on for another four-odd years," Laura concluded with a bittersweet smile.

"Well, at least we got a friendship out of it," Seth reflected, giving Laura a squeeze. "So when we found ourselves stuck in the same rhetorics class a few years later, we were naturals for working together on a class project."

"*The Dream*," Rita said with exaggerated boredom. "Ma told me all about that already. Ever since she got invited to that party it's all she's been talking about."

"Well," said Laura, justifying herself, "I was excited about getting to see my old friends. If you and Courtney didn't see each other for fifteen years you'd be excited about a reunion, too."

"That'll never happen," Courtney swore. "We're going to share an apartment when we finish high school. We already worked it all out."

This was news to Laura, but she let it pass without comment. By next week, she suspected, that plan would be supplanted by a new plan: Rita and Courtney running off together to join a circus. Or moving to Puerto Rico together to live with Courtney's grandmother. Or applying to attend M.I.T. together. Or opening a clothing store in the East Village and making lots of money together.

"So what's your thing, Seth?" Rita asked bluntly. "How come you've got the bucks for a car like this?"

"She means, what do you do for a living?" Laura helpfully interpreted her daughter's question. Then she smiled at Rita and Courtney. "You're going to love this, girls. He writes screenplays."

"What do you mean, screenplays?" Courtney asked.

"For movies," Seth explained. "I write scripts for movies."

The girls shared a glance, not certain how to react. "What movies?" Rita asked.

"I've written some of the *Ax Man* movies," Seth told her.

"*Ax Man*? You wrote *Ax Man*?" Courtney and Rita squealed in unison.

"Not the original, but three of the sequels."

"Oh." The girls lapsed into a worshipful silence. Then Courtney turned to Rita. "I like your mom's friend," she declared in a stage whisper that caused Seth and Laura to laugh.

"As you can see, I know the way to a girl's heart," Seth murmured to Laura. "All it takes is one white limo and one fictional psychotic killer armed with a hatchet."

"You sure do know all the right moves," Laura concurred with a chuckle.

The limousine had returned to Laura's building and coasted to a halt in front of the fire hydrant. "Show's over, girls," Seth said, swinging the door open and helping the passengers out.

"Thank you, Seth," Courtney said, then elbowed Rita, who vocalized her thanks, as well. If Courtney wanted to share an apartment with Rita, Laura decided, she would give the girls her blessing. Courtney was definitely a good influence on her daughter.

"The pleasure's all mine," Seth said grandly.

He rode with them to the second floor, waiting in the elevator with Rita while Laura walked Courtney to the Gonzalez apartment and saw her safely inside. "I don't know what your plans are," Laura remarked as they continued up to the fifth floor, "but you're more than welcome to spend the night here. The living room sofa isn't that uncomfortable—Rita sleeps on it all the time," she couldn't resist adding. Her joke earned her a withering look from Rita.

"I've got a room reserved at the Sheraton Center in Manhattan," said Seth.

Laura nodded. Given that he was used to traveling in limousines—or in Porsche 944's—he probably would prefer to stay at a fancy hotel rather than in her homey but distinctly unluxurious apartment. "Well," she said as they entered the oniony hallway that led to her apartment, "then I guess this is goodbye." She hoped she didn't sound too glum.

If she did sound glum, Seth looked even glummer. He gazed at Laura for a long time, memorizing her upturned face, the sensuous waves of her hair and her dark, resonant eyes. Then his face brightened. "Screw the Sheraton," he decided. "I'll stay here."

Laura tried not to look too pleased as she unlocked the apartment door and opened it. Seth hovered in the doorway, then said, "Let me run downstairs to get my bag—it's in the trunk of the limo."

"Okay. Just buzz from the lobby and I'll let you back inside," Laura told him. She and Rita stood in the doorway, watching as the elevator carried Seth away. Then Laura turned to Rita. "You've got all of thirteen seconds to get ready for bed, toots," she said as sternly as she could.

Rita ignored her. "Are you sure he's sleeping on the couch?"

"Positive. I have to disappoint you, Ms. Buttinsky, but Seth wasn't kidding when he said we were just friends."

"You ought to give that some thought, Ma," Rita advised her as she headed toward her bedroom. "He wrote *Ax Man* and he rides around in a limo. He's definitely not a weenie."

"No, he's definitely not." Laura had to agree.

"He's got nice eyes, too," Rita called over her shoulder before shutting herself into her bedroom.

He does have nice eyes, Laura mused silently as she gathered up the sticky spoons and the yogurt container and carried them into the kitchen. Seth had always had nice eyes, even after he'd pulled an all-nighter or indulged in the sort of excesses that had won him the nickname "Stoned." His eyes, no matter how bloodshot or bleary, were always dancing with laughter, always sparkling with a dazzling multitude of colors. Laura was infinitely glad he was going to stay for the night.

She was on her way to the linen closet to get a sheet and a pillow for him, when she heard the buzz of the intercom. After she pressed the button that unlocked the door to the building's lobby, she fixed up the couch for him. Like all her furniture, the couch was old and battered, but she knew it was comfortable. She herself slept on it whenever her mother came for a visit.

Seth rang the doorbell as Laura was tucking the blanket around the cushions. Straightening, she noticed the line of light beneath Rita's bedroom door flicker out. There was no reason to feel relieved that Rita was in bed for the night, other than ordinary maternal concern for a daughter who had stayed up way past her bedtime. Yet Laura did feel relieved. Nothing was going to happen between her and Seth. But she didn't want her daughter to witness that nothing.

She moved to the entry hall and opened the door for him. He lingered in the doorway for a minute, one hand clutching a lightweight garment bag and the other the doorjamb. "Excuse me, is this the Sheraton?" he asked.

"Flatbush Annex," Laura said, playing along. "Your room is all ready, sir."

"'Sir,'" he snorted as he entered the apartment. "That's almost as bad as 'Mr. Stone.'" He set his bag down in the center of the living room and inspected the couch. "Would I be out of line if I asked where you're sleeping tonight?" he inquired, grinning mischievously.

Laura shrugged, refusing to read anything serious into his question. "I guess that depends on your reason for asking."

His gaze roamed the room, examining the mismatched but clean furnishings and the numerous potted plants adorning the windowsill and the end tables. Then he focused on Laura and his smile expanded. "Hey, you lived on a commune, don't forget. A guy can't help but be curious."

Laura knew Seth well enough to recognize that he was teasing her. "Even during my communal youth I was never an advocate of free love."

"Okay. How much do you charge?"

Laura gave him a playful shove. "If I'd known you were going to act like this, Seth, I never would have invited you to stay."

He captured her hands and drew them to his sides. Then he wrapped his arms around her and planted a gentle kiss on her forehead. "I'll be a good boy," he promised. "But you can't blame me for thinking these past fifteen years have done you good, lady. Even just holding you feels great."

Holding Seth felt great, too. Laura tilted her head back to view him, then lightly touched her lips to his. It was an impulsive action; she intended it only as a way of sealing their restored friendship. Yet his eyes seemed suddenly to brighten, and his hands held her just a touch more firmly.

"Uh-oh," he said ominously, unable to suppress his smile as he gazed down at Laura. "Is passion about to rear its ugly head?"

His remark prompted her to laugh. "Let's be grown-ups, Seth," she began.

"That's exactly what we *were* being," he noted.

"Yes, well..." She drew in another deep breath. "You're going to sleep on the couch and I'm going to sleep in my bedroom, so whatever you've got in mind had better accommodate that fact."

"You're hard, woman," he complained, though he was grinning. "Were you always this sensible?"

"Always," she insisted.

He reflected for a moment, then nodded. "I guess you were. Okay. Take your hands off me, and I might just let you go to sleep."

Laura complied, but not before giving him a good-night hug. She crossed to the hall, then hesitated. "Listen, Seth—I don't know if you brought pajamas with you, but if you didn't...please be discreet. Rita's at a funny age."

"So am I," he countered. "Don't worry, Brodie. From here on in I'll be the epitome of good taste."

"That'll be the day, Ax Man," she scoffed before vanishing into her bedroom.

Chapter Three

Someone was watching him.

There was a time in Seth's life when he believed that being paranoid was as essential to his sense of self as knowing all the lyrics to Bob Dylan's "Positively Fourth Street" or all of Dennis Hopper's lines in *Easy Rider*. There was a time when paranoia was as faddish as bell-bottom blue jeans, as hip as granola, as ubiquitous as Boone's Farm Apple Wine. You were supposed to be paranoid; before lighting a joint, you were supposed to look over your shoulder, fully expecting to see a cop standing there spying on you. You were supposed to call the cop a pig and hate him, and presume that he hated you, too. In retrospect, Seth couldn't shake the notion that smoking grass had been pretty boring in and of itself and that the high had actually come from the special thrill of paranoia, the giddy understanding that one of "them" might be right behind you, just waiting to blow your head off if you smiled the wrong way.

Until Laura had reminded him, he had all but forgotten about the armed National Guardsmen who had been posted on the roofs of downtown Washington buildings during the Moratorium march, perfect symbols of the paranoia prevalent at that time. What Seth had remembered was the numbingly cold weather, the gray, threatening sky, the frizzy-haired, friendly Barnard girl who had sat next to him on the bus. He had remembered the walk, too, the mass of humanity surging along Constitution Avenue and assembling on the Mall in the shadow of the Washington Monument. He had remembered everyone stepping back to make way for a group from Vietnam Veterans against the War. One of their number wore opaque-lens spectacles that marked him as blind and rode in a wheelchair bedecked with black flags.

Those were days designed for paranoia. But today Seth rarely suffered from that sort of "us" versus "them" neurosis. Today he called cops "officers," or sometimes even "peace officers," and experienced a twinge of relief whenever he saw one late at night. Today he rarely felt as if he were being watched.

Yet he sensed that someone was watching him now. Not quite asleep and not quite awake, he lay prostrate on the couch in Laura's living room, trying to muster either the strength to wake up fully or else the nerve to go right on sleeping while the day passed around him. He could easily justify such laziness—no matter how late it was in Brooklyn, it was three hours earlier in California, and nobody could possibly expect his inner clock to have adjusted to Eastern time yet. He was entitled to sleep in.

Only he wasn't at the hotel, and he wasn't alone. He was in Laura's apartment, in her home. Being watched.

He had enjoyed a montage of dreams during the night, but he couldn't remember any of the dreams specifically. All he remembered was that every dream had been pleasant, relaxing, delightful. Images of the previous evening's party had intermingled with memories of his college days, of writing exuberant articles critiquing popular songs, films and television shows for *The Dream*. But the most pleasant, delightful part of last night had been spending time with Laura. And that hadn't been a dream at all.

Aging had definitely improved her. He liked the mature curves of her body—she really had been too skinny in college—and the generous fullness of her face. Her nose seemed less prominent now, and her eyes rounder and darker. No one would ever mistake her for a Hollywood starlet, but so what? Starlets were like potato chips—tasty, fine for snacking, but they left you hungry. Laura was substantial. She was solid and ripe. She was strong, independent, self-sufficient, giving. She was a real woman, a mother.

A mother... Oh, no. Where the hell was the blanket? Why didn't he feel its weight on him? Had he kicked it off in his sleep? He was always shoving off his blanket at home; he liked to feel the fresh night air on his skin, and he invariably woke up to discover the blanket crumpled up at the foot of the bed or heaped on the floor. No doubt the blanket Laura had given him was on the floor now, and Seth was sprawled out on the sofa in his birthday suit for all the world to view. *Please,* he prayed silently, *please, if I'm being watched, let it be by Laura, not by Rita.*

He cautiously opened one eye. All he could see was the faded brown brocade of the fabric covering the arm of the couch. Inhaling for courage, he opened the other eye, then lifted himself from the cushion and glanced over his shoulder.

Rita slouched in the arched opening connecting the living room to the hall. She wore a pair of balloon-legged jeans with a floral pattern on the denim, a T-shirt and an enormous lime-green knit vest with armholes that reached nearly to her waist. Her dark hair was brushed upward to resemble a spiked helmet, and large silver trapezoids hung from her ears. Her eyes resembled Laura's, Seth observed. They were large and dark, and they were riveted on him.

He cringed and turned his gaze to the carpet beside the couch. Uh-huh. There was the blanket.

"So, Rita," he said as calmly as he could, dangling his arm over the edge of the sofa in an attempt to snare the blanket without exposing himself. "Have you taken any anatomy courses in school yet?"

Rita giggled.

"If you haven't—" he caught the blanket with his fingers and hoisted it up over his body "—let me explain to you what it was you just saw." He gathered the blanket around himself before sitting. "What you just saw was a very embarrassed man."

"You've got a cute tush," Rita told him.

If he had been embarrassed to start with, Rita's comment increased the feeling tenfold. "What on earth would a nice young lady like you know about men's tushes?" he asked, deciding that his best tactic was to act indignant.

"I know some stuff," Rita declared slyly. "You think you're the only naked man who's ever been in our home?"

"I think..." Seth faltered. He supposed he ought to assume that Laura had men visiting her from time to time. But in all honesty, he would rather not know about the other men in her life. "I think," he resumed, "that I'm probably the only man stupid enough to let your mother's daughter see his tush."

Rita giggled again. "Here, I'll show you something," she said, bounding across the room to a cabinet that held a record player and a shelf of records. She flipped through the records until she found the album she was looking for. Sliding it from the shelf, she carried it to Seth and dropped onto the sofa next to him.

Refusing to let Rita realize how disconcerted he was by the situation, he tucked the blanket securely about his waist and offered a weak smile before accepting the album from her. He recognized it at once: it was the three-record *Woodstock* album, complete with a blurry photograph on the jacket of a man and a woman skinny-dipping in a muddy pool beneath the leafy bough of a tree. The man's rear end was only partially visible in the picture, but Seth imagined that to a thirteen-year-old girl, the murky photograph represented the ultimate in smut.

"So, speaking tush-wise, I compare favorably to this yo-yo?" he asked Rita.

"You're all right, Seth," Rita solemnly told him. "I think sleeping nude is radical, but Ma says I've got to wear pajamas till I'm sixteen."

"Your mother says that?" Seth let out a surprised laugh. He was having enough difficulty reconciling himself to the fact that Laura had a teenage daughter. But to learn that Laura laid down rules and regulations just like a normal parent seemed incredible. "Why sixteen? What's supposed to happen when you're sixteen?"

Rita shrugged. "I don't know. But I want a big party. One of my friends, her sister had a sweet-sixteen party at a restaurant, and everybody got all duded up, and they even had a deejay. That's the kind of party I want."

This from a child born on a commune, Seth mused wryly. He set the *Woodstock* record on the coffee table and tried to figure out how he could get himself to the bathroom without embarrassing himself further. "Where's your mother?" he asked.

"She went out to buy some breakfast for you. Did you go to Woodstock?"

"Sort of," he said, settling against the cushions and drawing the blanket up over his shoulders like an imitation Indian chief. He couldn't see any way of escaping to the bathroom before Laura got home. He would just have to chat with Rita until then and pretend he didn't feel like a first-class jerk.

"What do you mean, 'sort of'?"

"My friends and I got as far as Goshen before we gave up. Everyone thinks of Woodstock as the ultimate concert—

which it was—and all those good vibes. But the *real* story of Woodstock is that it was the biggest traffic jam in the history of the world. They closed the New York Thruway, you know? We were all stuck on the road in the rain. Nobody could drive anywhere. So we strolled from car to car and rapped with the other kids." He gazed at the album and smiled in reminiscence. "There was a truck in the middle of the mess, a farm truck filled with peaches. I guess the guy was trying to get them to market, but he realized he wasn't going to reach his destination on time, so he just climbed onto the back of the truck and started handing out the peaches to anyone who wanted one. There must have been dozens of us, hundreds of us, stuck on Route 17 with nowhere to go and no way to get there, eating these delicious peaches that had just been washed by the rain."

Rita mulled over the scene he'd described and scowled. "Peaches?" she finally said.

He couldn't have expected her to understand. Even today, Seth had a special place in his heart for peaches. Everyone else might associate Woodstock with music, but Seth associated it with the sweetest, freshest, juiciest peaches he had ever eaten in his life.

"Ma didn't go to Woodstock," Rita told him. "She said it was too far away."

"She's originally from the Phillie area, isn't she?"

"King of Prussia. My grandmother lives there. Isn't that a dumb name for a town? King of Prussia. Tell me about where you live," Rita requested. "Do you know lots of stars?"

Seth chuckled and shook his head. "I'm a writer, not an actor. I work mostly in a secluded little office with a typewriter. Sometimes they'll drag me to the set when they need a scene rewritten—but, then, the actors who work in movies like *Victory of the Ninja Women* aren't exactly contenders for the Oscars."

"Ma won't let me see violent movies," Rita complained.

"I don't blame her." Seth grinned. "Maybe when you're sixteen, when she lets you sleep à la raw, she'll also let you go to the theater and watch all kinds of blood and gore. You've got a lot to look forward to, lovely Rita."

"Yuck!" Rita leaped from the couch and glowered at him. "Don't!"

"Don't what?" he asked, bewildered.

"Don't sing that song. Ma named me after it and it makes me sick!"

"What song?" Seth puzzled over what he'd said, then nodded. " 'Lovely Rita, Meter Maid.' "

Even though he hadn't sung it, Rita pressed her hands to her ears and groaned. "Yuck. Meter maid. I mean, is it sick? My mother named me after a *meter maid*."

"She named you after a song," Seth corrected her. "A terrific song, too. A Beatles song." He began to sing the refrain.

"Yuck!" Rita wrinkled her nose and stormed out of the room.

Whatever works, Seth pondered, standing and wrapping the blanket toga-style around his body. If he had known that a classic Beatles song was his ticket to the bathroom, he would have started singing much sooner.

He crossed to his garment bag, which he'd left open on an easy chair, and pulled out some clean underwear, a pair of jeans and a white cotton sweater with a series of red-and-black concentric circles decorating the front like a bull's eye-target. He often wore the sweater when he visited New York City, joking that he wanted to help the muggers and snipers out by offering them a clear target. Lifting his clothing, he headed toward the hall. The sound of a key in the front door lock caused him to halt, and he turned in time to see Laura enter the apartment, carrying a white paper bag.

"Good morning, lazybones!" she greeted him.

Seth momentarily forgot his awkward encounter with Rita. All he was aware of was an unexpected rush of joy at being in Laura's presence. She looked refreshed from her outing, her cheeks pink and her eyes sparkling, her smile contagious, her windblown hair tumbling in dense, dark curls past her shoulders. She wore a pair of brown corduroy slacks, and Seth found himself admiring the feminine spread of her hips, an asset the skirt she'd worn to the party had downplayed. Seth liked a solid bottom on a woman, and he considered Laura's weight gain, minimal though it appeared to be, a definite improvement over her boyish figure in college.

If he'd considered it, he might have been astonished by the fact that he was thinking of Laura in sexual terms. Yet from what he could see, Laura appeared to be a remarkably sexy woman. If you wanted to talk about cute tushes...

His mouth shaped a grim line as he recalled his recent humiliation beneath Rita's inquisitive eyes. Exhaling, he greeted Laura with the bad news. "I've traumatized your daughter."

Laura's smile waned. "What do you mean, you 'traumatized' her?" she asked warily as she carried the bag into the kitchen and set it on a counter.

"Well...I have this habit," he explained. "You know how some people are so selfish in bed, they hog the blanket and wrap themselves up in it like a mummy and leave their lovers freezing to death?"

Laura eyed him quizzically. "Is that a rhetorical question, Seth?"

He smiled nervously. "The point is, Laura I'm *not* one of those people. I'm kind of the opposite—"

"You aren't selfish in bed?" Laura smiled wickedly. "Sounds interesting, Seth. I'm all ears."

He drew in a deep breath, trying to ignore her teasing and the uncomfortably arousing effect it had on him. "I'm so unselfish," he continued, "that I do the opposite with the blanket. I *don't* wrap myself up in it like a mummy. And... well... I guess I unwittingly gave Rita an up-close-and-personal demonstration of my utter selflessness...."

Laura rolled her eyes. "You flashed her? Wonderful," she grunted. "What did she say?"

"Do you want to know the truth?" Seth smiled modestly. "She said I had a 'cute tush.' Look, Laura, if the kid needs years and years of therapy to work it out, I'd be more than willing to foot the bills..."

But Laura was laughing too hard to hear him. "'A cute tush'? Is that what she said? Oh, she's something, all right." "Yeah," Seth agreed. "Just like her mother."

"Well, go get dressed before you do any more damage," Laura ordered him, sniffling away her laughter. Seth nodded grumpily and pivoted on his bare foot. Before he could escape, Laura pulled a spatula from a wall rack and used it to lift the corner of the blanket. "Rita's right. It *is* cute," she asserted before dissolving in fresh laughter.

Seth tried to appear annoyed, but he really wasn't. It was unfortunate that Rita had happened upon him that morning, but Laura... if she thought his rear end was cute, that was quite all right with him.

LAURA HAD BOUGHT THE BAGELS for Seth and Rita, and she didn't eat any herself. She had slept late, after all, and she had a one o'clock engagement for lunch with Julianne and Kimberly. Walking to the bakery on Flatbush Avenue just to buy fresh bagels hadn't been necessary; she could as easily have made toast for Seth, or served him cereal. But she had wanted to get something special for him; she had wanted to put forth a little extra effort for her old friend.

Laura knew that Rita didn't care one way or the other about having fresh bagels for breakfast. She and Courtney were planning to spend the afternoon at the Kings Plaza shopping mall, where they would alternately stuff their faces with pizza and ice cream and bemoan their imaginary blubber; the only foods Rita showed much enthusiasm for were foods that Laura urged her not to eat. As long as Laura had brought home bagels and not chocolate-covered doughnuts, Rita wasn't disposed to appreciate her mother's hike to the bakery.

But Seth did seem to appreciate it. He ate two entire bagels and part of a third, slathering them with cream cheese and describing the rarity of good New York-style bagels in Southern California. "There's one deli in downtown L.A.," he told them, "with genuine bagels, pickles, pastrami, lox...astronomical prices, but desperate ex-New Yorkers will pay almost anything for a taste of home," he explained. "Trouble is, it's a long drive from Topanga Canyon to downtown L.A. If I happen to be in the neighborhood, I'll stock up. But on a weekend morning, given a choice between fighting the traffic and rolling over and going back to sleep, I inevitably roll over."

Seth had appreciated the bagels, and Laura had wanted to do something he'd appreciate. She had also wanted to leave the apartment for a few minutes, to breathe in the crisp spring air, to clear her head and think things through.

She was reasonably sure that Seth wasn't angry at her for stranding him on the couch last night. He hadn't accepted her invitation to stay at her apartment because he expected anything to happen between them. When she'd kissed him good-night, she herself hadn't expected that the kiss would be taken as anything other than a gesture of friendship. And his suggestive questions about where Laura would be sleeping while he was on the couch—she was sure he had only been kidding.

She liked Seth, not just the Seth she'd known fifteen years ago, but the Seth he was today. She liked him a lot more than she liked most of the men she met. But he would be in town only for the weekend, and even if she found a way to visit him in California, that would be at most another week they might spend together. And then what? A transcontinental love affair was hardly what Laura was looking for.

Not that sleeping with Seth while he was in town would constitute a love affair. At issue was a few hours of pleasure, if anything, a few hours of closeness. Not a full-fledged capital *R* relationship. Hadn't Seth made that comment about free love?

Laura had never been an advocate of free love, even though she'd lived on a commune. What she had liked about the commune was its ethic: sharing, openness, a commitment to others. All the adult members had contributed what they could to the community: cooking, keeping the main house functioning, growing vegetables in the garden, or taking a job "outside," in the nearby town of Ithaca, to bring money into their closed community. Laura had found work transcribing tapes and proofreading manuscripts for a professor of sociology at Cornell University, but she'd quit the job just before Rita was born, choosing to remain full-time at the commune, where she could attend to her new daughter.

She had loved the flexibility and fluidity of the place. She'd loved the hard work, the rugged life, the bucolic environment, the philosophy of giving of oneself for the betterment of the larger family. She'd loved some of the people, too. But as far as free love went...no. Her relationship with Neil had been exclusive. It had also been unfortunately public, even before Laura had become pregnant. Everyone had known almost from the start that she and Neil were lovers; everyone had known when they were fighting, when they were getting along, even when they were anxious for privacy. "Leave Neil and Laura alone," someone would announce at dinnertime. "They want to be alone." Their attempts to find solitude became, ironically, a group concern. And then, of course, when Laura became pregnant, her pregnancy became another group concern. Rita became the group's baby.

After Neil left, Laura wasn't about to become involved with another man on the commune. To her, the only free love worth pursuing was a love that was free from outside interference.

She had no idea what Seth expected of her now—other than what he'd told her just before she left for Julianne's apartment. "I'm going to try to pick up some tickets to a show for tonight, Laura. So if you haven't already got plans for this evening, don't make any."

"I'll erase everything on my calendar," she had said, kissing his cheek on her way out the door.

She climbed the stairs leading from the subway station up into the glaring afternoon sunshine. Julianne's apartment was situated in a fairly new building in the East Seventies. If Laura hadn't already known that the residence was in the high-rent district, the doorman's uniform, a navy double-breasted coat trimmed with gold braid, would have proved it.

Shrugging the strap of her purse higher on her shoulder, Laura entered the swanky foyer and gave the doorman Julianne's name. He lifted the telephone receiver from an intercom console, announced Laura's arrival and then indicated with a nod that Laura was cleared to go upstairs.

What do magazine editors earn? Laura wondered as the mirror-and-chrome elevator car whisked her up to the seventeenth floor. Not that she cared about the exact figure, but... She couldn't shake off her memory of the dingy basement office in which *The Dream* had been born and from which it had been disseminated. Comparing that tomblike cubicle, with its grilled windows and continually buzzing fluorescent lighting, to Julianne's elegant apartment building—or to the equally elegant suite of offices where *Dream*'s birthday party had been held—pointed up to Laura how many times the earth had circled the sun since *The Dream* had first been hatched and how far it had carried her and her friends.

Julianne had her door open by the time Laura stepped out of the elevator. Seeing Julianne's wonderfully familiar face made Laura forget all about her affluent surroundings. She broke into a glowing smile and hurried down the hall.

"Come on in," Julianne greeted Laura, ushering her into the living room. Its decor communicated impeccable taste. The furnishings were understated, the colors—primarily beige and blue—muted, every oak tabletop polished to a high gloss. A vase holding six white tulips stood at the center of the elliptical coffee table. More than anything else in the room, the tulips appealed to Laura. Tulips seemed so like Julianne—tall and graceful, straightforward in their beauty, nothing showy or gaudy about them.

"This is fantastic," Laura said, turning to Julianne. Dressed in a neatly tailored shirt and pleated gray slacks, she looked as tasteful as her living room, her appearance polished and understated. "I feel like such a grown-up, having lunch with you and Kim." Laura was used to brown-bagging her lunches during the week and on the weekends either skipping lunch or grabbing a snack while she caught up on her reading or did her shopping. To attend a luncheon in such a fancy apartment, with only adult women present, was a rare treat.

Julianne laughed. "*I* feel like a baby. This morning Kim and I baked chocolate chip cookies and we fought over who would get to lick the bowl."

"Chocolate chip cookies." Laura sighed. Feeling the need to set a healthy example for Rita, she generally restricted her baking to such wholesome treats as whole-grain bread and carrot cake. But she couldn't deny that she had a soft spot in her heart for homemade cookies, especially chocolate chip ones. "Where is Kim, anyway? Shut up in the bedroom with the bowl?"

As if in answer, the bathroom door swung open and Kimberly emerged. Although she was smiling, her eyes were red rimmed and devoid of makeup, and her lush golden-blond hair was mussed. "Hi, Laura," she said, gliding into the living room. "Here I am, sans the bowl."

"You've been crying," Laura guessed, taken aback by Kimberly's dismal appearance. She realized at once that her comment wasn't exactly tactful, and she tried to soften it with a joke. "Did the cookie batter taste that bad?"

Kimberly smiled feebly and shrugged. "I cry a lot these days," she admitted. "Come on, let's eat. Let's drink, too. Julianne has wine, and I could surely use some." Slipping her arm around Laura's shoulders, Kimberly led her into the compact modern kitchen. "Julianne has everything, Laura. It's amazing. Do you know what she's got? Cloth table mats with matching linen napkins and napkin rings. Straight out of the pages of *Good Housekeeping*."

"Do you read *Good Housekeeping*?" Laura asked Julianne, who had slipped past them to pull an ironstone bowl containing a spinach salad from the refrigerator.

"Got to," Julianne admitted. "I've got to keep up with the competition."

"*Dream* isn't anything like *Good Housekeeping*," Laura argued. "I have yet to read a single article about how to set a table in your magazine."

"There's one in the upcoming July issue," Julianne warned her with a chuckle. "Not exactly about how to set a table, but it's an article on how our eating habits reflect our prejudices. Interesting piece. I'm betting on lots of mail in reaction to it." She pulled another bowl from the refrigerator, this one filled with crabmeat salad. She carried the two bowls from the kitchen to the dining table in one corner of the living room.

Laura sighed again. Crabmeat salad. Matching table mats and napkins. "Don't you have matching napkins, too?" she asked Kimberly. "I always thought you were the matching-napkins type."

"I was, once upon a time," Kimberly said. Her eyes seemed to water, and she averted her face, concentrating on peeling the lead from the top of a bottle of imported white wine.

"And then what happened?" Laura asked, figuring that there was no need for tact when someone you cared about was on the verge of weeping.

"It's a long story," Kimberly groaned dramatically.

"It's a short story, Kim," Julianne chided her in a matter-of-fact tone. "She's getting a divorce."

"Oh," said Laura. She touched Kimberly's shoulder. "I'm sorry."

"Thanks for being supportive," Kimberly said, forcing another crooked smile.

Laura laughed. "I'm not being supportive. All I said was I'm sorry. If you want to know the truth, I hate the word 'supportive.'"

"And you call yourself a social worker," Kimberly sniffed. "What's wrong with supportive?"

"It sounds so trendy." Laura followed Kimberly to the table, where each of the matching blue place mats was set with a beige ironstone plate and a large crystal goblet. She watched for a moment as Kimberly poured the wine, but was distracted by a framed photograph now standing on the window ledge by the table. She had noticed the photo at the party last night, but hadn't had a chance to examine it closely. Moving closer, she reached for it and picked it up.

"This is a scream, Julianne. I can't believe you unearthed this for the party."

Julianne joined Laura and gazed at the picture. "I didn't dig it up. I keep it hanging over my desk in my office all the time."

"Why?" Laura asked with a laugh. The photo's six subjects looked barely out of puberty—which, Laura supposed, was what they were. Julianne seemed impossibly fresh scrubbed, the epitome of a wholesome midwestern girl, despite her waist-length hair and the stencil adorning her T-shirt: a clenched fist enclosed within a "Woman" symbol. Kimberly's hair, too, was long, lusciously wavy, and her blue work shirt appeared recently pressed. The guys all looked much scruffier, as did Laura. In fact, she looked rather like a scarecrow, quite bony, her face slightly drawn and surrounded by a thundercloud of bushy curls. "If I were you, Julianne, I'd burn this thing. And the negative, too."

"Nonsense," Julianne said, indicating with a wave of her hand where Laura was to sit at the table. "I think it's important to remember one's origins."

"If you buy Darwin, our origins are the apes. There are certain things I'd just as soon not remember," Laura maintained, though she was still laughing. She set down the photograph and took her seat. When Kimberly and Julianne were also seated, Laura lifted her goblet. "Let's drink a toast to Kim's newfound freedom."

"Hear, hear," Julianne chimed in.

Kimberly grinned pathetically, but she raised her glass and clinked it against the others. "I don't feel particularly free," she declared as the bowls of salad were passed around. "I don't know how you handled the split with your daughter's father, Laura, but things have got to be a whole lot easier when you circumvent the law. I mean, it's mortifying to have to reveal all your heartache to an utter stranger who's billing you by the hour." She speared a chunk of crabmeat with her fork and smiled bravely. "Let's not talk about me," she decided. "I'm too depressing. Let's talk about the men."

"What about them?" Julianne asked.

Kimberly's large hazel eyes glittered impishly. "What do you think was the best thing about Seth last night?"

Laura permitted herself a private smile. The best thing about Seth had been giving him a friendly kiss, holding him, feeling his arms around her. But she wasn't about to tell that to Kimberly and Julianne. Nor was she going to admit that another very nice thing about him was his rear end—the truth was, she hadn't gotten to see how nice it was until that morning, and the question Kimberly had posed referred specifically to the previous night.

"His red high-tops," she answered.

Julianne contemplated Laura's reply and nodded. "Yes. They added a great deal of style to his ensemble. In fact, they added a great deal of style to the party."

Kimberly nodded, too. "And what do you think was the worst thing about Seth? What's the worst thing the past fifteen years have done to him?"

"He writes trash," Laura said, not even having to think.

"How do you know it's trash?" Julianne asked. "Have you seen the *Ax Man* movies? According to *Dream*'s film critic, there's a certain *film noir* quality about them."

"Spare me," Laura grunted. "They're trash because Seth told me they're trash, and he wouldn't lie about it." She sipped her wine, then lowered her glass and shook her head. "Remember those impassioned critiques he used to write for the newspaper? Analyzing the political implications of every movie, every song? Remember that in-depth piece he wrote on *All in the Family* as a barometer of American culture? And now he's writing film scripts about psychopaths with hatchets."

"And making a bundle," Kimberly mused.

"So what? Is making money that important?" Laura challenged her. Then she bit her lip. Here she was, sitting at a beautiful dining table, eating crabmeat and sipping an expensive wine. Here she was, having lunch with a successful magazine editor and a senator's speech writer, each of them wearing upward of one hundred dollars' worth of clothing.

It was all very impressive, just as impressive as riding in Seth's rented limousine had been. But while Laura could enjoy such things, and could admire them, and could even wonder, every now and then, whether her life might be improved if it had a few material niceties in it, being in possession of abundant wealth wasn't vital to her.

She had no right to judge Seth, but she was disappointed that he was writing trash. He had been a fine writer in his youth, full of passions and ideals. Surely he oughtn't to have abandoned those passions and ideals for the mere rewards of money. He was too decent a person to have sold out so totally.

The possibility that he had was disheartening, and she distracted herself by asking, "What do you think was the best thing about Andrew last night?"

"His chin," Julianne said quickly.

"Do you like his chin?" Kimberly debated her. "I thought it jutted too much."

"I liked his eyeglasses," Laura remarked. "I thought they made him look very intellectual."

"He doesn't need eyeglasses to make him look intellectual," Kimberly argued, her tone laced with sarcasm. "I bet he looks intellectual even when he's going to the bathroom."

Laura sipped her wine. Kimberly and Andrew had always been antagonists, even when they'd been collaborating on *The Dream*. Andrew *had* been an intellectual, and he had always been putting Kimberly down for not being intellectual enough. Kimberly was smart, but she wasn't given to pondering the universe or wearing her knowledge on her sleeve. She had always been bouncy, full of constructive energy, cheering on the newspaper staff as fervently as she had once cheered her high school's football team to victory. She could even turn a discussion about their reunion into a game: what's the best thing, what's the worst thing. Laura found Kimberly's spirit endearing.

She gauged Kimberly's acidic tone when talking about Andrew and asked, "What do you think was the worst thing about him?"

"His control," Kimberly said.

"What control?"

"He holds everything back," Kimberly explained. "He always did. He still does. He's an emotional miser. Don't you think so, Julianne?"

"He's reserved," Julianne allowed.

"He's a widower," Laura announced.

Julianne and Kimberly turned to her, aghast. "Where did you hear that?" Julianne asked.

"Seth told me. Andrew got married and then his wife died. Seth said it slipped out, and Andrew didn't want to talk about it."

"Oh, Lord," Julianne said with a deep sigh. "That's terrible."

"I'd rather be a widow than a divorcee," Kimberly commented thoughtfully. "Not that I wish Todd would die, although sometimes... No, as vile a creature as he is, I truly don't wish he would die. But Andrew...he'll never hate the woman he lost. He can go on loving her forever and remember his marriage as something beautiful. I mean, I feel sorry for Andrew, but—"

"But you feel sorrier for yourself," Julianne concluded. "Drink some more wine, Kim. I like you better when you're drunk than when you're maudlin."

"If you insist," Kimberly complied, polishing off the wine in her goblet and refilling it. She eyed Laura, and they both giggled. Julianne was a born boss. She was forever telling people what to do, and she was invariably right. It was no wonder she'd become *The Dream's* editor in chief by acclamation.

"How about Troy? What's the best thing about him?" Laura asked.

"He's gorgeous," Kimberly said at once. "Don't you think so?"

"He always was a knockout," Laura concurred. "I never knew what bedroom eyes were until I met him."

"What do you think, Julianne?" Kimberly asked. "Is he still gorgeous?"

"Yes," said Julianne, sipping her wine. "Still gorgeous."

"And what's the worst thing about him?"

Julianne's gaze moved from Kimberly to Laura and then past them to one of the bookshelves built into a wall of her living room. She rose from the table and pulled a notebook-sized paperback from one of the shelves. "Do you want to know the worst thing about Troy?" she asked the others. "It's right here."

She handed the book to Laura, and Kimberly slid her chair closer so she could see the book, as well. It was entitled *Maritime*, and it was a collection of stark black-and-white photographs, mostly of fishermen, laborers, impoverished children and weary women, and a few of landscapes. Each picture was striking, unsentimental but moving. The portraits in particular captured frozen moments of unvoiced pain, deprivation, yearning.

"This is his book," Laura murmured. "The small-press book Kim was talking about last night."

Julianne nodded. "He took most of the photos on Cape Breton Island."

"It's wonderful," Laura exclaimed, poring over the photographs. "How can you say this is the worst thing about him?"

"It's the worst thing about him because—" Julianne inhaled. Laura could tell she was bristling with emotion, which was unusual for someone as self-possessed as Julianne. "A man who can take photographs like that is supporting himself by snapping pictures of wedding parties."

"All right." Kimberly shrugged. "Seth writes *Ax Man* movies. Troy takes pictures of brides. Welcome to the real world."

"At least Seth is making a fortune writing *Ax Man* movies. And apparently enjoying it," Julianne pointed out. "Troy doesn't enjoy taking pictures of brides, and all he's making is a living. He could make a living doing photojournalism if he wanted. Not putting out small-press books like this one, granted. But I bet *Dream* could pay him more for doing magazine photos than he's making in his studio in Canada."

"So offer him a job," Laura suggested.

Julianne pressed her lips together, then took the book and set it aside. "He wouldn't accept it," she said quietly. "I know he wouldn't. He has too much pride."

Laura wanted to question Julianne further, but she didn't dare. With Kimberly she could be tactless, but not with Julianne. She detected pain in Julianne's lucid blue eyes, pain and conflict, something that demanded respect, that begged for distance. If Julianne wanted to talk about it, she would. And if she didn't, Laura would never ask.

Fortunately Kimberly decided that she wanted to talk about her divorce, after all, so Laura asked her about that, instead. They emptied the bottle of wine into their glasses, and Julianne's eyes came into focus again as she gave Kimberly plenty of her typically clearheaded advice. Julianne spoke in defense of lawyers, and Laura spoke in defense of

Kimberly's inner strength and her emotional resources. It was marvelous talking with women about something real, not about shopping and not about Rita, but about how to steer through life and avoid the shoals.

She didn't want to leave, but at four o'clock, after promising to call both Julianne and Kimberly soon, Laura made her departure. She felt as if she had just found two long-lost sisters; she swore to herself that she would never lose them again.

And in the meantime, she was about to spend an evening with another long-lost friend. But not a brother. After kissing Seth last night, however briefly, however casually, she would never be able to think of him as a brother.

After kissing him, she would definitely never want to.

Chapter Four

"Okay, they can close the show now," Laura joked as she and Seth emerged from the theater into the chilly night. "I've finally seen it. They don't have to keep it running anymore."

Turning up the collar of his white suit jacket, which he'd worn over his bull's-eye sweater, Seth laughed and steered Laura through the throng of theater goers crowding Shubert Alley. "You think the only reason *A Chorus Line* is still running is that they didn't want to close it until you'd had a chance to see it?"

"Of course," Laura answered with a straight face. "I'm sure the producers got together and said, 'Say, if we can keep Laura Brodie away from our play for ten years or so, we might just wind up with a hit on our hands.'"

"The fact that it's a good play has nothing to do with it, I suppose," said Seth.

"It *is* a good play," Laura readily agreed, no longer joking. "Thank you for taking me to see it, Seth. I really enjoyed it."

"I figured, since we've already seen the longest running off-off-Broadway show together, we ought to see the longest running Broadway show together, too."

"We weren't exactly 'together' when we saw *The Fantasticks*," Laura recalled.

"Sure we were."

"I was with Mark Hofkiss," she corrected him, "and you were with... Meryl Banks, wasn't it?"

"You've got a good memory," Seth praised her.

"So do you." Until Seth had mentioned it, Laura had all but forgotten about the double date they'd gone on in college. They had decided to see *The Fantasticks*, in part because the tickets were cheap, in part because the musical had been written by two Columbia alumni, but mostly because the minuscule theater where the show was being staged was located in Greenwich Village, the Mecca of New York hippies.

The four of them had taken the subway down to West Fourth Street one afternoon after their final classes of the day. They'd sauntered around Washington Square, which at that time had been appealingly rundown, a point of convergence for panhandlers, N.Y.U. students, elderly men in cardigans playing chess, self-defined *artistes*, free-lance vendors of tooled leather belts, silver jewelry and marijuana and folk singers strumming guitars and vying to become the next Bob Dylan or Joan Baez or Richie Havens. Seth and Laura and their dates had journeyed from the carnivallike atmosphere of the park to MacDougall Street, where they'd browsed in the head shops and bookstores and poster emporiums, and from there they'd gone to dinner at an amazingly inexpensive Italian restaurant. Then they'd seen *The Fantasticks*, splurged on ice-cream cones afterward and, at midnight, taken the subway back to the Columbia campus on the opposite end of Manhattan, singing "Try To Remember" and arguing over the lyrics. In those days one could still ride on the subway at midnight—even sing on the subway, if one felt like it—without fearing for one's life.

That outing seemed much further in Laura's past than sixteen years ago. She had been a different person then, practically a child. She'd been so eager for experience that she rarely allowed herself the luxury of reflecting, of pausing to digest what it was she was experiencing. Now she was older, more mature, less interested in accumulating new experiences than in savoring whatever was occurring in the present. In the theater tonight, she had been acutely aware of everything: the solid, enveloping darkness before the curtain rose, the distinctively musty aroma of the air, the muted tapping sounds the dancers' feet made on the stage, the glittering row of top hats in the final, gloriously strutting song. The fuzzy texture of Seth's sweater against her fingers as she slipped her hand around his elbow on the armrest between their seats. The lingering scent of his shampoo. The sharp angle of his jaw in profile as he watched the performers dance.

"Wanna go out for a drink or something?" he asked as they ambled toward Broadway, hand in hand.

"Not really," Laura replied. She wasn't sure what would happen when she and Seth got to her apartment, but her uncertainty wasn't much of a reason to delay their getting there. She felt comfortable enough with Seth to want to remain sober, no matter how their night would progress.

At the corner of Broadway, Seth scouted for a cab. "No limo tonight, love," he said apologetically as the cab he signaled sped past them, its Off Duty light glowing. "We're going to have to rough it."

Laura chuckled. "Taking a cab is hardly what I'd call roughing it."

Seth eyed her with spurious annoyance. "That's easy for you to say. *I'm* the one standing in the middle of the road waving my hands like a maniac," he pointed out before spotting another cab and trying to flag it down. It, too, cruised past Seth without slowing. "What is this?" he muttered. "Do I have bad breath?"

"Be patient," Laura chided him affectionately. "Sooner or later we'll get a cab."

"Later," Seth griped. "Sooner is already out of the question."

After several traffic-light changes, an on-duty taxi coasted to a halt in front of Seth. He had to leap backward onto the curb to avoid having his toes crushed under the car's wheels, and Laura smiled as she glimpsed his bright red sneakers. His sputtering curses concerning the driver's homicidal bent only caused Laura's smile to widen.

He was still grumbling when they climbed into the back seat, but as soon as Laura guided his arm around her shoulders and snuggled against him, he softened. "Ocean Avenue in Brooklyn," he called to the driver. Then he settled back in the seat and entangled his fingers in Laura's thick, flowing mane. "It's all right if we go straight to your place?" he half asked.

"Why wouldn't it be all right?"

She felt his fingers digging through the mass of her hair in search of the back of her neck. He found it and gently stroked the warm skin. "Because...maybe this is an off-the-wall idea, Brodie, but..."

"But...?"

"The God's honest truth is, the minute we get there, I'm going to want to do something very carnal with you."

"Carnal, huh." She laughed quietly. For some reason, the idea didn't seem particularly off the wall to her. Impractical, impulsive, imprudent, maybe, but not outlandish. "I hate to break the news to you, Seth," she warned him, "but the minute we get to my place, we're probably going to have to make small talk with Rita."

"We can give her a quarter and send her to the movies."

"If anyone should know how much movies cost these days it's you," Laura reproached him.

Seth touched his lips to the crown of Laura's head. "Okay, pal. Give it to me straight. What's the best strategy for getting the mother of a teenage girl into bed?"

"I'm not sure," Laura played along. "But I've got to tell you, Seth, exposing your naked body to the teenage girl doesn't win you points with her mother."

"Would it help if I told you you're beautiful?"

He sounded so sincere that Laura chose to believe that he wasn't simply feeding her a line. But, then, Seth would never feed her lines. They had known each other too long, too well. "Telling me I'm beautiful definitely wins you points," she granted.

"Yeah? How many?" His thumb located her earlobe and traced its curve, causing Laura to sigh. "Look, I'm trying to be reasonable," he defended himself in a hushed voice. "I've been thinking about you all day, Laura, thinking about you and getting turned on."

"That's very intriguing," Laura said, unsure of how to react. At least her words were honest. She *was* intrigued. She was intrigued by the constant shimmer in his eyes, by the sensation of his thumb stroking the skin behind her ear, by his nearness, his bluntness.

"What are you going to do about it?" he asked, his question less a challenge than an expression of genuine curiosity.

She contemplated the situation. She hadn't been seriously involved with a man since moving to Brooklyn over three years ago, and she might have explained her interest in Seth as nothing more than the arousal of a lonely woman in the presence of an attractive man. Except that she wasn't lonely; she had enough opportunities to date, and the lack of a serious relationship in her life was Laura's choice.

Besides, she wasn't simply responding to an attractive man. She was responding to Seth, her friend, her old, trusted buddy. "I'm not sure," she finally answered.

He kissed her brow again. "If you're planning to say no to me, the least you can do is tell me whether you're saying no because of Rita or because of me."

"I don't know what I'm planning," Laura confessed. "In all honesty, Seth, I don't think I'm planning at all."

"In that case, let me do the planning," he offered, cupping his free hand beneath her chin and angling her face to his. His mouth covered hers, and his tongue gently coaxed her lips apart.

Laura twisted on the seat to face him and slid her fingers upward to caress his cheek. His skin was slightly scratchy; he hadn't shaved since late that morning, and a hint of his beard had broken through. She molded her palm to the bristly surface and deepened the kiss.

Their tongues moved slowly, one against the other, in a sensuous exploration. As arousing as it was to kiss Seth, she was equally aroused by what he had just told her. She was aroused by his forthright expression of desire for her: *I've been thinking about you all day and getting turned on.* There was nothing subtle in Seth's statement, nothing sneaky about it. And if anything could turn Laura on more than a kiss like the one she was sharing with him right now, it was directness and honesty.

His hand tensed at the back of her head for a moment, then relaxed. He drew his mouth from hers, grazing her cheek and then her temple with his lips. "God, this is fun," he said, slightly out of breath. "I haven't necked in the back seat of a car since I was a kid. I forgot how much fun it could be."

"Maybe when you return to California you can get back into the habit of it," Laura proposed.

Seth shook his head. "Porsche 944's are pretty underendowed in the back-seat department. And anyway," he added, brushing his lips against her temple again, "it wouldn't be much fun if you weren't there." His mouth found hers and lingered, his tongue darting inside only long enough to tease hers. Then he tucked her head into the hollow of his neck and wrapped his arms snugly around her.

His comment had struck a nerve. Once more she was forced to acknowledge the fact that he would be leaving for home the following day and she would be staying in Brooklyn, and that whatever was occurring between them now would be finite, its conclusion already written. She didn't want to have a one-night stand with Seth. She didn't want to be a one-night stand for him.

But she didn't want to let go of him, either. She wanted to remain cuddled close to him, breathing in his clean, masculine fragrance, tasting the underside of his chin with her lips. She wanted him to keep holding her. She wanted to pull off his garish sweater, his gaudy sneakers, to touch the lean contours of the chest she'd barely glimpsed behind the shield of his blanket that morning and—sure, why not?—to get a closer look at his cute tush.

Amazing as it seemed, she wanted Seth as much as he wanted her.

"Let's go home," she murmured, closing her eyes and hugging him tightly.

He glanced out the window, then shouted to the driver, "Step on it!" Bowing his head to Laura's ear, he whispered, "I've always wanted to say that to a taxi driver."

"This has been quite a weekend for you," Laura mused. "First you got to say 'I just flew in from the coast,' and now this. I bet you're just dying to order the driver, 'Follow that car!' "

"You've got me down pretty well," Seth conceded with a laugh. His fingers slipped inside her collar to stroke the skin of her shoulder. "Give me half a chance, lady, and I could probably fall in love with you."

"I doubt that," Laura said, only partly in jest. Seth was much too carefree to fall in love with someone who lived a continent away from him. Long-distance love was complicated, difficult. If Seth were truly looking for complicated, difficult challenges in his life, he wouldn't be writing *Ax Man* movies for the fun of it. He wouldn't be frittering his professional energy on trash and his emotional energy on seven hundred starlets.

Unnerved by the direction her thoughts had taken, she inched away from him and sat upright. Seth didn't comment on her movement. Undoubtedly he interpreted it as her way of composing herself for their arrival at her home, where her daughter was waiting. The cab had reached her block, and Seth indicated the building to the driver.

After paying the fare, he escorted Laura into the building. "Maybe we can give Rita a quarter and send her downstairs to her friend's apartment," he suggested.

"Maybe we can behave responsibly," Laura retorted. She bit her lip, trying to smother her apprehension. Rita wasn't Laura's primary concern. What was gnawing at her was the understanding that, even if Seth didn't give her half a chance, she could probably fall in love with him. And she honestly didn't think that was a good idea. She simply didn't believe there was much promise in pursuing a deep relationship with Seth.

When they entered the apartment, they found Rita watching television, two incriminating candy wrappers lying on the coffee table. Seeing her mother, Rita sprang off the couch and crumpled the wrappers into a ball. "You're home early," she announced with a sheepish grin as she scampered into the kitchen to toss the evidence into the trash can.

Laura smiled in resignation. "Stuff your mouth with junk, Rita, if that's what you want to do. But don't blame me if you turn into a blimp."

Rita spun from the trash can and shrugged. "See, Courtney bought a ten-pack at Kings Plaza, but she didn't want to bring the whole package home because then her brother would eat them and he's got zits," she explained vaguely. Then she turned to Seth. "So," she said brightly, "how was the show?"

"Terrific," he reported.

"What was it about?"

Laura rummaged in her handbag for her *Playbill* and handed it to Rita. "It's about a bunch of struggling dancers auditioning for parts in a musical," she told her daughter.

"And then what happens?" Rita asked.

"Some of them get parts and some of them don't."

Rita issued an exaggerated yawn. "Sounds exciting," she said sarcastically.

"It was," Seth claimed, helping Laura off with her jacket and then removing his blazer. "The auditioners each do a song or a dance and they get you involved in their lives, and then you start rooting for them, hoping for them. It's heartbreaking when some of them don't get cast in the show."

Rita eyed him dubiously. "Don't lose sleep over it, Seth. They already *are* in the show."

"She tends to operate on a very literal level at times," Laura said, explaining her daughter. "Well, Ms. Candy Bar, speaking of losing sleep, it's eleven thirty. Your pillow awaits."

"So does yours, Ma," Rita said, shooting Seth another knowing look before confronting her mother. "Be careful, all right? You're too old to have any more kids."

Laura faked an openhanded swat at Rita's backside, and Rita danced out of reach. Giggling, she scurried down the hall to her bedroom and shut herself inside.

Her arms folded across her chest, Laura glowered for a moment at her daughter's closed door, then permitted herself a reluctant chuckle. "Too old to have kids, huh," she muttered. "Somebody ought to explain the facts of life to her."

"Yeah, like her mother," Seth suggested before succumbing to laughter. He planted his hands on Laura's shoulders and rotated her to face him. "If you ask me, she's got the facts pretty well sorted out. Let's be careful, okay?"

"Seth..." Taking a deep breath, Laura averted her gaze. She wished he weren't looking at her so seductively. She wished his eyes weren't quite so radiant, his smile quite so sexy. She wished his hair weren't glittering with golden highlights below the circular ceiling light. She wished his hands didn't feel so strong and confident on her. "Seth, can we—can we just talk?"

He appeared surprised, but not particularly upset. "We can do whatever you want, Laura," he said earnestly.

"You—you wouldn't be bummed out if we didn't go any further than that?"

His eyebrows quirked upward as he considered his response. "Other than the fact that I'll probably wind up walking bowlegged and talking in a funny, squeaky voice for the rest of my life, why should I be bummed out?"

"Oh, Seth." Laura grinned wistfully. It was more than his eyes, his smile, his hair and his hands on her that made her want him. It was his ability to find comedy in what surely had to be a frustrating situation. "I don't want to turn you into a soprano," she swore, arching her arms around his waist. "Let's... let's just talk for a while and see what happens."

"Okay by me," he agreed in a piping falsetto, causing her to laugh. In his normal voice he continued, "Let's talk dirty. I've got a way with words—maybe I'll get you in the mood."

"I'm already in the mood," Laura confessed, unwilling to be dishonest with Seth when he was accepting her decision with such civility.

"Good," he murmured. "Let's go talk on your bed."

"With our clothing on," she insisted. She knew that allowing Seth onto her bed was foolhardy, but she was unable to resist his mischievous humor.

He took her hand, and she led him into her bedroom. Like the living room, it was furnished with mismatched pieces, cast-offs, she'd accumulated over the years. But the double bed was made with fresh linen and the patchwork quilt covering it was a source of great pride to Laura. She herself had sewn it when she was living on the commune.

Seth kicked off his sneakers and dove onto the mattress as she turned the lamp on the night table to its brightest setting. He extended his arms to her, and she lowered herself onto the bed next to him, stretching out on her side and propping her head in her hand. "Go ahead, talk dirty," she dared him, grinning.

"Soot," he complied good-naturedly. "Cigarette butts. Sweat stains. Axle grease."

"Boy, am I ever in the mood!" Laura hooted.

"All right, I'll talk clean, then," he decided. He scooped a thick lock of her hair off the pillow and toyed with it, tracing the convoluted whirls and coils of the waves with his index finger. "I didn't come to New York looking for a roll in the hay, you know," he said solemnly.

"I know," Laura assured him.

"And I sure didn't come to New York figuring I'd make a pass at one of the old gang. I mean, talk about your far-fetched ideas!" He snorted and shook his head. "I'm a big boy. I've got a good life in L.A. Nothing for the record books, but I'm content. I don't have to prove anything. My idea of fun and games is the Mets versus the Dodgers. I'm not on the make. Lying in bed with you—even with all my clothes on—is not what I expected to happen this weekend. But I'm not telling you anything you don't already know."

How like Seth not to drown her in sentimental claptrap. She smiled tenderly, touched by his candor. "Who do you root for, the Dodgers or the Mets?" she asked.

He chuckled. "Maybe it's all your fault, Laura. I mean, why do you have to look so great? Why couldn't you have gotten all fat and wrinkled or something?"

"I *have* gotten fat," she argued.

"What you've gotten are breasts, which I don't think you had fifteen years ago."

"I did so!"

"Not that I ever noticed." Letting her hair fall back to the pillow, he ran his hand lightly over the full swell of her bosom.

Laura allowed herself to enjoy his provocative exploration for only a moment before covering his hand with hers and lifting it to her lips. She kissed his fingertips, then pinned his hand safely beneath hers on the pillow between them. "Let's talk about *A Chorus Line*," she said.

If Seth was nonplussed by her choice of topic, he hid it well. "Okay, let's talk about it," he said. "You go first."

Laura studied his hand. Next to his long, graceful fingers, her own hand looked short and stubby. She had stopped trying to cultivate well-shaped nails when she moved to the commune, where her manicures were constantly being destroyed by gardening, sweeping the kitchen and typing notes for the Cornell University professor on her sticky manual typewriter. But now, lying beside Seth, she wished her hands were prettier. His starlets in California probably had beautiful hands.

She didn't want to think about his other women or his West Coast life. What she wanted was to remind herself why she wasn't at that very moment making love with Seth. "You know that song from the show, 'What I Did For Love'? I've heard it a million times on the radio, and I always assumed that it was a love song, something a woman is singing about a man. I never knew until tonight that it was about a woman's decision to become a Broadway dancer."

"There's women's lib for you," Seth scoffed. "Nowadays a woman can belt out a love song about her career that's just as schmaltzy as any of the love songs women used to sing about their men."

"That song could have been sung by a man," Laura declared. "What it's about is having so much faith in your talent and your dreams that you never take the easy way out. You just keep pursuing your goal." She twined her fingers through Seth's, seeking the strength to continue. She had no right to say what she was about to say; she had no right to sit in judgment of him and of the choices he'd made. But he deserved to know why she was backing off from him, when she desired him as much as he desired her. "Seth." She took a deep breath, then addressed his hand. "You have so much talent, such a good mind, so many things to say to the world. Why are you writing trash?"

"Uh-oh," Seth intoned. His eyes were sparkling, though, and despite the absence of a smile, his cheeks were marked with dimples. "Am I about to get chewed out?"

"No," Laura swore. Then she smiled sheepishly. "Maybe," she admitted. "It really—Seth, it bothers me that you're writing scripts about a madman who hacks nude baby-sitters and camp counselors into little pieces, when you could be writing scripts that have some value."

"My scripts have value," Seth maintained amiably. "If they didn't have value, do you think I'd own a Topanga Canyon house and a Porsche 944 right now?"

"That's just it," said Laura. "They've got a monetary value, period. And you've got a fancy house and a fancy car. Is owning a house and a car so important to you?"

Seth chuckled. "If you ever saw the dive I was living in when I first moved to L.A., you would never have asked that question. We're talking 'Hotel California,' Laura.

Sleazeball City. And as far as a car, well, there's no such animal as the D train out there. If you don't own a car you've got three choices—walk, hitch, or don't go. I tried to make do with a bicycle, but the bad news was, it *did* rain in Southern California, and it always rained when I was riding from here to there with a script under my arm. So yes, I'm into good housing and an enclosed vehicle."

"That's fine, Seth," she said, smiling gently. "I don't want you getting pneumonia. But is it really necessary to sell your talent short in order to keep from getting rained on?"

"Sell my talent short?" He rolled his eyes. "Laura, let me explain to you the facts of life in Hollywood. For every five hundred or so screenplays that get written, maybe one gets bought. For every fifty or so that get bought, maybe one gets into production. For every twenty that get into production, maybe one makes it into distribution. For me to write a screenplay that actually survives all the way to distribution is a small miracle. Believe me, I'm not selling my talent short."

"If you've got enough talent to be able to write a screenplay that survives," Laura asserted, "then couldn't you put that talent to work writing screenplays that can make the world a better place?"

"Spare me, Brodie," Seth grunted. "We can't all be social workers, you know."

"You don't have to be a social worker to do good," Laura countered, her eyes aglow as she considered Seth's powerful situation. She was excited by the possibilities of what Seth could accomplish if he put his mind—and his writing gifts—to the task. "You're in a position to do a whole lot more good than most social workers. Think of it, Seth. I meet with only twenty-five clients a week. Your screenplays can reach thousands and thousands of people in a single day!"

"They can't if they aren't produced," Seth reminded her.

Laura eased onto her back and studied the ceiling. She was vexed by what Seth was saying, even though she knew it was probably true. That he had achieved so much in such a tough field was cause for congratulations, not criticism.

Yet she couldn't help being critical. Once again she reminded herself that it wasn't fair of her to judge Seth—and certainly not to judge him against the standards they'd lived by fifteen years ago. Ideals often had to give way to reality; that was a simple fact of growing up. Laura herself would rather be living in a rural environment than in overcrowded Brooklyn, but she had a daughter to support, and New York City paid its social workers much more than most rural counties did. So Laura worked for the city.

But Seth did have choices. He was an artist, abundantly talented, and his only dependent was his pet dog. Perhaps he needed a car, but he didn't need a Porsche. Perhaps he needed a house, but he didn't need an eight-room palace perched on a hillside in an affluent suburb of Los Angeles. Given his unique skill at molding words and enunciating ideas, shouldn't he be putting himself at the service of those less fortunate? Laura could help only a few single mothers, but Seth...he was blessed with the ability to move others through his words.

And what had he done with his ability? Zilch.

"Laura." He peered down at her, obviously aware of her disapproval. His jaw moved as he contemplated his words, and the corners of his mouth twitched upward. "Have you ever seen any of my movies?"

"I—" Laura pressed her lips together. Lord, how presumptuous she was! "No," she confessed. "I never have."

"No big deal," he reassured her. "They aren't made with audiences like you in mind. But...you know, I'm not as much of a sellout as you seem to think I am. I do sneak little messages into my movies sometimes."

"You do?" She gazed up at him hopefully.

"Sure. Take *Victory of the Ninja Women*, for instance. You wouldn't believe the hoops I had to jump through to get that flick made. Seems Ninjas are supposed to be pure macho. Oh, an occasional Ninja woman is all right, sure. Let her kick her feet a bit, throw a saber once or twice and screw around with the hero—and then make sure she gets killed so the hero can be hell-bent on revenge. But to have an entire squad of female Ninjas running around beating the living daylights out of all those bad guys—well, you would have thought I was trying to pitch the studio on Betty Friedan's life story, the way they were carrying on."

"If you could sell them on female Ninjas, I bet you could sell them on Betty Friedan's life story, too," Laura posed.

"Uh-huh. With Jane Fonda playing the lead. Give me a break, will you?" His patience was beginning to wear thin, and his dimples vanished. "You wanna know the truth, pal? If I were dirt poor—and I'm speaking from experience, because I *was* dirt poor when I was first getting started—if I were dirt poor, the last thing I'd want to see, if I got up a few bucks and decided to blow them on a movie, is some film about people who are dirt poor. Right? What movies did people go to see during the depression? Busby Berkeley. Fred Astaire and Ginger Rogers. Screwball comedies."

"*The Grapes of Wrath*," said Laura.

"All right. One *Grapes of Wrath* versus hundreds of screwball comedies. People go to the movies because they want to escape. They don't want to be harangued."

"And you give them what they want, Seth. You give the people what they want, and in return you get a hotshot sports car."

"Damn it, Laura—" He sat up and stared at the scratched chest of drawers that stood against the far wall. He bent his knees to his chest, rested his forearms across them and simmered.

Laura had never seen Seth angry before. Oh, sure, he'd been angry about the big issues back in their past, angry about the war, censorship, the first tiny hints of the Watergate scandal that were leaking out even before Nixon's reelection. But she had never seen him angry with a person before, and she felt extremely guilty.

Maybe she'd been too hard on him. Maybe she'd been too hard on him because if she hadn't been hard on him, she would have fallen in love with him.

She sat up, too, and cautiously touched his arm. "I'm sorry, Seth."

"Don't be," he said curtly.

"I'm in no position to pass judgment on you." She ran her fingers up to his shoulder and squeezed it. "Do you hate me?"

He twisted to look at her. A crooked smile flickered across his lips. "If I *did* hate you, Brodie, it would be because we're sitting here fully clothed instead of having the time of our lives. But, no, I don't hate you." He turned fully to her and kissed her lips lightly. "If anyone is in a position to pass judgment on me, lady, it's you. You haven't sold out, Laura. You're still trying to save the world. And I love you for it. I mean that." He kissed her again, another light kiss, more friendly than passionate. Then he reached behind her and clicked off the lamp. "Let's catch some *z*'s, okay?"

He lay back down and pulled Laura into his arms. She cushioned her head with his shoulder and closed her eyes. She was glad that he would be spending the night in her bed, even if they had all their clothing on.

Especially if they had all their clothing on. She wasn't feeling particularly romantic anymore, but she didn't want Seth to leave her. She wanted the reassurance of his arms around her, the warmth of his lanky body next to hers. With their clothing on, they could lie together as friends, bound by trust rather than lust. And that was what she wanted right now—Seth's trust, his friendship.

HE COULD PRETEND that the problem was the time zones. It was only ten-thirty Pacific time, and he rarely crashed that early. He could pretend that his inner clock was skewed, that his nervous system was keyed to to the wrong longitude.

Or he could pretend that Laura's mere presence was keeping him awake. Not that she snored, not that her head was too heavy on his arm, not that he found the pressure of her knees against his particularly annoying. Nor was it that her closeness was causing him to suffer the agonies of unfulfilled passion. She looked utterly beautiful to him, her long, dark lashes visible against her cheeks even in the room's shadows, her mouth unmoving, her hair tumbling wildly about her face and shoulders, but lying beside her while she slept and not making love to her wasn't truly going to render him bowlegged for the rest of his life.

He could pretend a lot of things, but the truth was, he was awake because Laura was right. He had sold out.

A sellout. When Seth was younger, labeling someone a sellout was just about the worst thing you could call him, worse than an SOB, a fascist pig, a hawk, a brownnose. You weren't supposed to trust anyone over thirty because, chances were, people over thirty were sellouts.

Take a bow, Seth, he muttered silently. *This one's for you.*

It wasn't as if he had abandoned his principles. It wasn't as if he no longer cared about the needy, nuclear proliferation, racism, the greenhouse effect... But honest to God, nobody wanted to see movies about that sort of stuff. Sure, once in a while you could get something like *The China Syndrome* made, or *Roots*, or *Apocalypse Now*. But it wasn't as if every producer in town were currently ready to do armed battle over the rights to *The Mother Theresa Story*.

Seth had done his best. He had honestly given it the old college try. In one of the file cabinets in his office he had a drawer filled with his early efforts: one screenplay about a racial incident in a supposedly enlightened town, another about a small village that discovers its water supply tainted with carcinogens and another one about ethnic clashes among inner-city gangs. Seth had ultimately cannibalized that one for *Barrio Warlords*, but the original offered some keen insights into racial and cultural conflicts.

The first writing job he had landed when he arrived in Los Angeles was pure hack: contributing to the joke-filled scripts of a syndicated game show. The job paid dreadfully, and eventually Seth obtained a better job cranking out dialogue for a soap opera. But from the start, even before he'd snared the game-show position, he had labored at odd hours, on weekends and late into the night on noble, important screenplays, scripts that would undoubtedly bring tears to Laura's eyes. He had pedaled around town on his bicycle, conniving his way into the offices of agents and producers, cajoling receptionists, begging anyone and everyone to read his noble, important scripts.

"You've got a genuine sensitivity, kid," they used to say, "but I'm overbooked at the moment." Or "Interesting, but it doesn't work for me," or "Racial themes are out this year." An agent named Melinda Greiss, a blunt, gum-chewing woman working out of a downtown skyscraper, read all of Seth's scripts and invited him to her office for a chat. "Okay," she said. "If you're willing to write violence I'll represent you."

At the time Seth had been chagrined. Four years later, when the soap opera ceased production and he was down to his last dollar, he decided he was ready to write violence. Melinda Greiss signed him on.

It hadn't been an easy decision. Seth had been far from overjoyed by the first assignment she obtained for him—an anonymous rewrite on a made-for-television script about a Ph.D. candidate in archaeology who has to support her child by working nights as a topless dancer in a go-go bar. Real high art, Seth recalled with a snort. But the bottom line was the bottom line—he had gotten paid for the job, paid enough to be able to buy a used but reliable Volkswagen Beetle.

Then Melinda scored him another anonymous rewrite job, and that one enabled Seth to pay back some of the money he owed his parents. He actually got a screen credit on his third job, paid back the rest of his debt to his folks and moved to a safer neighborhood. He began to live like a human being, eating real food, wearing real clothes. It was fun.

And it was still fun today. *Ax Man* movies were a kick to write not because Seth loved blood and gore, but because he enjoyed knowing that he was reaching millions of people with his words, entertaining them, distracting them from their own miseries for ninety minutes on a Friday night. And he derived private pleasure from sneaking in his little messages: the speech he gave the psychologist in *Final Cut* about how greed is the root of all evil and the subplot in *Return of Ax Man* about the herbicide being used on poison ivy that caused a skin rash identical to the rash caused by the poison ivy itself. And the feminist slant of *Ninja Women*. *Coed Summer* had no little messages to redeem it, but who needed messages in a movie costarring those two delectable actresses with the matching Kewpie-doll smiles....

Sellout, he berated himself.

What the hell. If the past fifteen years had a lesson to teach, it was that no one individual could save the world. You did what you could, sure, but the truth was, no matter what sort of scripts Seth wrote, he couldn't stop the earth from turning. He couldn't stop world leaders from making fools of themselves. He couldn't stop anyone from falling in love with the wrong person or falling out of love with the right person. No matter what Seth wrote, crazed street thugs would still prey on elderly widows. Crazed parents would still abuse their children. Crazed assassins would still shoot heads of state.

But at least it was possible that, for a short time, in a darkened theater, with a tub of popcorn in your lap and a friend by your side, you could forget about all the real crazies and lose yourself in the travails of a beautiful psychologist doing battle with a fictitious murderer. You could, for a few minutes, put out of your mind all the horrors of the world, all the horrors of your own life.

Maybe Seth had sold out. But maybe, just maybe, he was doing what he could to help others. People needed more than peace, love and freedom to keep them going day to day. They needed laughs, phony scares, visceral thrills, a chance to escape every once and a while.

That was what Seth contributed to the world: a chance to escape. And damn it, that was important, too.

Chapter Five

"Let's be real, Zeke," Seth argued. "The grenade blew off his arm, so now he needs an artificial limb. We're agreed on that. But this isn't the *Six Million Dollar Man* we're making here—it's *Ax Man*. Sure, he can wield an ax with an artificial arm, but firing bullets out of a bionic index finger? No way, José."

Smiling smugly, Zeke rubbed his scented black cigarette out in the ashtray Seth kept on hand for him. He was seated in the leather La-Z-Boy in Seth's in-home office, his legs crossed at the ankles, the sleeves of his patterned silk shirt rolled up to his elbows, his silver hair so smoothly combed it almost looked like tempered metal. "Imagination, Seth," he said calmly. "Think big."

"I can think big," Seth maintained. "But let's be real. Let's talk motivation. Granted, the technician who designs the limb is under pressure—"

"Pressure?" Zeke laughed at Seth's understatement. "Ax Man has all but destroyed the lab. He's wrought havoc. He has the technician's scantily clad assistant under his thumb, so to speak, and—"

"Ax Man doesn't *have* a thumb at this point," Seth grumbled. "Sure, he can pressure the technician to make him a limb. But a limb that fires bullets is way out of line, Zeke. I stand by my original proposal—that the technician manages to build a blade into the side of the hand so that whenever Ax Man karates somebody he cuts the guy to ribbons. But no shooting fingers, Zeke. It destroys the entire concept."

"You're going to instruct me on concept? Who's directing this mother, anyway?"

Seth ground his teeth and turned back to the electric typewriter on his desk. "All I'm saying is, motivation, Zeke. Where's the technician's motivation? Building a prosthesis that can fire bullets is above and beyond."

"You're saying motivation. *I'm* saying imagination. Let's not be so psychologically constrained, chump. We need the bullets for the big climactic scene. That's a beautiful scene you wrote, Seth, that gorgeous shoot-out at the little suburban house, with the inferno at the end. Where did you come up with that image, anyway?"

"Patty Hearst," Seth told him. "Remember when Cincque's house was surrounded by feds and blasted to hell? Talk about special effects—and that was for real, man, right there on the six o'clock news." Closing his eyes, he indulged in a memory of the spectacular public shoot-out at the modest house where the kidnapped heiress had been held for a while. He had seen the replay numerous times on various news reports, and he'd considered that shoot-out almost obscene. Indeed, it was just the sort of imagery that made the *Ax Man* movies what they were.

Opening his eyes again, he was confronted by the sight of his director seated too comfortably in Seth's favorite chair, and he added, "Cincque didn't have any ammo popping out of his fingertips, Zeke. What he had—if I can refresh your memory—was a good old gun. Why can't we give Ax Man a gun and leave it at that?"

"There's no imagination in a gun," Zeke disputed him placidly. "Humor me, Seth. I promise you, however you write it, I can make it work."

Staring at the typewriter, Seth grinned reluctantly. After having composed so many film scripts, he ought to have been used to writing scenes to order.

And out of chronological order. Zeke had already begun secondary shooting on *Ax Man Cuts Both Ways*—sex scenes, mostly. Sex scenes could always be spliced in, no matter what plot finally emerged from Seth's typewriter. Whatever motivation the sex scenes needed was more than amply supplied by the very appearance of the actresses Zeke had already hired for the film. Darla Dupree, for instance, with her big eyes and her cute little button nose and her 38-C bra size.... The way she looked in a bikini was all the motivation anyone could ask for in a sex scene.

"All right," he capitulated with a sigh. Why should he care? Given the fee plus points he had coming to him on this picture, he ought to be a professional and write whatever idiotic crap his director requested of him. "You want bullets in his finger? You've got bullets in his finger. But give me a chance to build up to it. Maybe Ax Man can torture the scantily clad assistant first."

"Torture?" Zeke echoed, intrigued. "What kind of torture can he do? He hasn't got an arm yet, don't forget."

"Try this on for size," Seth suggested, his thoughts taking a new tack. "Ax Man barges into the lab and finds the technician and the assistant in flagrante delicto."

"All she's got on under her lab coat is some filmy underwear," Zeke chimed in, eagerly adopting the spirit of Seth's idea.

"Whatever," Seth said with a shrug. "The technician is in love with the assistant. The assistant is married to the technician's boss. The technician will do *anything* to keep her old man from finding out that he's been diddling her."

"Perfect," Zeke agreed, chuckling with satisfaction. "Good old-fashioned blackmail, with as much kink as possible thrown in. There's your motivation."

"I'll have the scene in your hands by tomorrow morning," Seth promised.

"Beautiful." Zeke stacked his papers into a tidy pile and kicked down the footrest of the chair. "Meanwhile we'll sub these pages for the original scenes twenty-four through twenty-seven. This is good stuff, Seth. You're a genius."

"I wouldn't go that far," Seth said with false modesty. He supposed that anyone who could come up with a decent justification for Ax Man's ability to fire bullets out of his finger probably possessed some sort of grotesque genius.

He escorted Zeke through the rambling ranch house to the front door. As soon as he opened it, Barney bounded inside from the yard, panting and drooling. Zeke leaped out of the huge dalmatian's path and fastidiously dusted his designer jeans. "God, I hate that creature," he grumbled.

"And he hates you, too," Seth countered cheerfully. He curled his fingers around Barney's collar to keep the dog from attempting to hug Zeke. They remained in the open doorway as Zeke left the house, climbed into his fire-engine-red Lotus and peeled down the driveway. "What a jerk," Seth whispered to Barney as they watched the dust settle along the driveway in the sports car's wake. "Bullets out of an artificial finger. The guy's got oatmeal for brains." Barney expressed his agreement with a gleeful bark.

After shutting the door, Seth shambled back to his office with Barney doing his darnedest to get underfoot. In the office the dog circled the earthen-hued Navaho rug several times before curling up on it and settling down for a nap. Seth dropped onto the swivel chair by the desk, glared at his typewriter and switched it off with an impatient grunt.

He wasn't in the mood to write the revised scene. He had to get it done by tomorrow, and he would, even if it meant pulling an all-nighter. Given his habit of procrastinating, a habit that harkened back to his college days, Seth was no stranger to all-nighters. He was too old to forgo sleep as often as he did in his youth, but if he had to, he could do it. As always, he'd get his scene written by deadline.

But right now he didn't feel like tackling it. Shoving aside his folder of notes, he lifted the oversize paperback book he'd been examining when Zeke had arrived an hour ago. Seth had found the book that morning at his favorite new-and-used bookstore. It was a collection of photographs of Nova Scotia, its people and scenery. *Maritime*, it was called.

Seth opened the book for the fourth time that day, and for the fourth time that day, he wondered. If Troy Bennett could produce stuff as exciting as this, why the hell was he wasting his time taking wedding pictures?

Seth pored over each of the book's photographs, dazzled by Troy's mastery of natural light, his ability to convey texture and celebrate nuance. How in God's name could Troy work with prissy little brides and panic-stricken grooms, when he was capable of magic like the photos in *Maritime*?

His gaze lingered on a photograph of a young boy standing beside a grizzled fisherman who was repairing a net. The fisherman sat hunched over his work, evidently oblivious of the photographer, but the child stared directly at the camera, his eyes large and haunting, curiously accusing. He was too young ever to have seen any of Seth's movies, but even if the boy had been older, Seth would have hoped that he didn't blow the contents of his piggy bank on trashy films. It wasn't for kids like him that Seth was writing.

Nor was it for the girls Laura worked with, girls barely a few years older than Rita, already on welfare, already saddled with babies, oppressed beyond belief. What little money they had ought to be earmarked for food, rent, diapers—and books. Not cinematic junk.

Who was Seth kidding? The only people his scripts were designed to reach were people who had the wherewithal to find healthier ways to escape. Why lose yourself in an *Ax*

Man movie when you could lose yourself in a five-mile jog or a Dickens novel?

And, more important, why should Seth be wasting his time and exhausting his creative energy trying to find a rationale for the firepower of Ax Man's mechanical arm, when he could be writing something that would touch pregnant inner-city teenagers and lonely yearning youngsters in Nova Scotia?

It wasn't as if Laura had suffused him with guilt. It wasn't as if she didn't understand the need people felt to escape. She was as in need of escaping every now and then as any of the people who flocked to Seth's movies.

In a way, Seth realized, the weekend he and Laura had spent together was an escape for both of them. He knew she didn't often get to attend Broadway shows. Nor, he imagined, did she make a habit of visiting Prospect Park with Rita. When Seth had suggested that the three of them take a trip to the park on Sunday morning, Laura had welcomed the idea with genuine excitement.

Prospect Park was only a dozen blocks from her apartment. A sprawling oasis in the heart of Brooklyn, it rivaled Central Park as a respite from the city's overcrowded neighborhoods. At ten o'clock on Sunday morning the park was relatively empty.

Initially Rita had balked at riding on the carousel. "I'm too old," she'd complained. "What if someone from school sees me or something?"

"If someone from school sees you, they'll be jealous," Seth had predicted. "Look how old your mother is. If she can ride on a merry-go-round, so can you. Right, Brodie?"

Laura had pretended to be insulted by Seth's crack about her age, but she had happily climbed onto the ride and selected a black pony with a white mane and gilt saddle to sit on. Seth had chosen the horse beside hers, and Rita had reluctantly climbed on board, as well, making a great show of being blasé about the ride and deliberately choosing a horse several rows ahead of her mother's and Seth's so she could act as if she didn't know who they were.

That had been fine with Seth. He had wanted to concentrate fully on Laura, watching as she clasped the brass pole with her small, graceful hand, watching as her thick, dark hair streamed back from her face. Watching her face, illuminated with pleasure as her pony carried her away.

Lord, but she was beautiful. She had seemed so peaceful, relaxing in the rhythm of the ride, giggling at Seth's antics as he kicked his sneaker heels into his horse's rump and chided it for its leisurely gait, shrieking when he leaned far out over the side of the platform in search of a gold ring. If he had won one, he would have made her wear it.

She had looked equally beautiful when they'd abandoned the carousel for the zoo. Seth's behavior around animals was to get down to their level, to scratch his armpits in front of the gorilla cage, to roar and strut for the lions and caw nasally for the tropical birds, to clap his hands for the sea lions. Whether or not he was communicating with the beasts, he believed that it was a sign of respect to meet them on their own ground.

Despite her disdainful expression, Rita had clearly been amused by Seth's mimicry. Laura, however, had dealt with the animals quite differently. Instead of roaring and prowling in tandem with the lion, she had leaned over the railing and cooed to it, humming a lullaby, soothing it with her sweet song. At the elephant cage she had insisted on buying a bag of peanuts and feeding the lumbering gray animals. At the monkey house she had asked each of the monkeys if it knew where Curious George might be. When she, Rita and Seth finally left the zoo, she had sighed wistfully and remarked that she wished the animals didn't have to live in cages.

How like her, Seth mused. How like her to empathize with animals, to overflow with love for them. How like her to try to reach every creature, human or otherwise, with her kindness. It had been agony leaving her after they had gotten back to her apartment. It had been a kind of torture saying good-bye and summoning a cab to take him to the airport. He'd spent the entire flight back to Los Angeles staring blankly out the window and hearing her soft, mellifluous voice crooning "Hush, Little Baby" to the lion.

She needed escape just like anyone else. But even in escape she never lost track of who she was. She would never find movies like Seth's a valid way of escaping. And while he didn't think she would begrudge other people the escape Seth's films offered, he knew she believed that Seth himself was capable of something more. Even scratching your arm pits and screeching with the apes was a superior way of escaping when compared to watching gory flicks.

Setting down the book, he lifted the receiver of his desk phone and began to dial Laura's number. Halfway through he hung up. He had already called her twice in the four days since he'd left Brooklyn. The first time it had been after ten o'clock in New York and he'd awakened her. She had been too drowsy to talk coherently, so he'd made the call brief, promising that he would phone again soon. The second time he had called earlier in the evening, and Rita had informed him that her mother was out leading a weekly group therapy session for pregnant high school students. Seth had had a pleasant chat with Rita, but chatting pleasantly with Rita hadn't been his purpose in calling.

If he called now, he might or might not reach Laura. And if he did reach her, he wouldn't know what to say, other than that he hadn't stopped thinking about her since he'd left New York the previous Sunday. He hadn't stopped thinking about her dark, shimmering eyes and the captivating lushness of her hair, about the way her breath had caught in her throat when he'd stroked her breast. More than once since returning to California he had found himself puzzling over whether he was angrier about her indictment of his work or about her refusal to make love with him.

These were not the sort of subjects he wished to discuss with Rita while her mother was leading some after-hours group therapy session.

He flipped back and forth through his phone book until he located the business card Troy had given him at the *Dream* party. It was a plain white rectangle with Troy's name and the address and telephone number of his studio printed in block letters, and along the bottom *Portraits, Parties, Passports*. Passports, Seth mused with a snort of disgust. The genius responsible for a book like *Maritime* was doing passport photos. All was not right with the world.

He dialed the number, listened to the electronic clicks as the long-distance call was connected and then heard a woman's voice recite crisply, "Bennett-Chartier Photography Studio, can I help you?"

Belatedly Seth checked his wristwatch. Quarter to four—that made it quarter to seven in Montreal. Photographers must work at odd hours, like scriptwriters. "Is Troy Bennett in?" he asked.

"Who's calling?"

"Seth Stone."

"Well, he's just on his way out," the woman reported. "Let me see if I can catch him."

Seth started to protest that his call wasn't that important, but before he could get very far, he realized that she had put him on hold. Within ten seconds Troy was on the line. "Stoned? Is it you?"

"Last time I looked it was," Seth joked. "I need a passport. Do you do U.S. passports, or only Canadian ones?"

"Hey, as long as you aren't calling me on a wedding. I'm booked up to here with those jobbers."

Troy didn't sound as if he were on his way out, but Seth courteously said, "Listen, if you can't talk now, I can try you some other time. Your secretary just told me you were about to take off."

"I'm always about to take off," Troy said wryly. "It's the story of my life."

"Do you want me to call back later?"

"Nah. It's just some retirement party I'm supposed to shoot. The guy's worked at the firm for forty-one years. He can wait a few more minutes before scoring his gold wristwatch." He paused for a moment, then said, "So? To what do I owe the honor?"

"Well..." Seth fingered the book on the desk. "I was at a bookstore this morning, and while I was scrounging around, I found a big paperback on a back shelf. It was a little dusty, but none the worse for wear. A terrific book, if you want to know the truth. Maybe you've heard of it. It's called *Maritime*."

After a brief silence Troy said, "Dusty, huh?"

"The thing's dated 1982," Seth noted, opening the book to the copyright page. "And what the hell is Voyager Press? I never heard of it before."

"It's a small, independent press run by a guy named Peter Dubin. He publishes a lot of poetry, monographs, stuff like that. He doesn't do much photography because it costs too much to print. I guess I lucked out—he decided to do a limited run of my C.B.I. photos."

"C.B.I.?"

"Cape Breton Island," said Troy.

"Yeah, well, I'd say *I'm* the one who lucked out, getting my hands on a book like this," Seth claimed as he thumbed through the book's pages. "These photos are strong, Troy, really excellent work. Right now you'd never guess what I'm supposed to be doing, but instead, here I am, staring at this picture of a little kid and an old man fixing a net."

"All right, I'll never guess," Troy said with a laugh. "What are you supposed to be doing?"

"I'm supposed to be writing a scene that explains how the resurrected Ax Man manages to get an artificial arm that can fire bullets out of its index finger."

"Its index finger?" Troy guffawed. "Why the index finger? Why not get gross, Seth, and have him fire out of his middle finger? Or better yet, skip the euphemistic fingers altogether and have him fire out of his—"

"Whoa!" Seth cut him off before joining him in laughter. "And I thought *I* was perverted!"

"Face it, Stoned, what are guns?" Troy contended. "Phallic symbols, am I right? Why not extend the metaphor to its ultimate expression?"

"Sick," Seth groaned. "You're sick, Troy. Why are you wasting your life up there in Moose City? With a brain like yours you could make it big in Hollywood."

"Is that a compliment?"

Seth chuckled. "No, Troy, it's not. Forget I ever said it." His gaze fell once more to the photograph of the fisherman and the boy, and his laughter faded. "Look, I don't want to keep you from your work—"

"No problem, Seth," Troy assured him. "It's not like I can't wait to take pictures of a bunch of drunks making long-winded speeches about what a swell ol' guy the guest of honor is."

Seth digested Troy's remark. "Why do you do it?" he asked. "I mean, why aren't you out on Cape Breton Island, doing photographic essays about grizzled fishermen and little kids? The photos in *Maritime* are so good, Troy. Why aren't you doing more stuff like that?"

"In ten words or less?" Troy shot back. "Because I'm old and I've got rent to pay. Do you know how much I earned making *Maritime*?"

"A few hundred dollars?" Seth guessed. He had no idea of what small press publications brought in.

"Try nothing," Troy told him. "Actually, if you count travel expenses, I lost money on it. What Pete paid me barely covered the cost of the film and chemicals. Fun is fun, Seth, but you can't eat fun."

"Laura thinks I've sold out," Seth confessed.

"Laura?" Troy hesitated, trying to follow Seth's apparent change of topic. "Laura Brodie?"

"I spent a lot of time with her last weekend. We took in a show together, I met her kid, the whole trip. And we talked, Troy. It was so good talking to her." He sighed. "Saturday night she lit into me for not doing something worthwhile with my life. I gave her the same story you just gave me, about how I like to eat food on a regular basis, and she made me feel as if I'd sold out."

"What does she understand about eating food?" Troy posed. "She lived on a commune for years. She probably learned how to thrive on twigs and pebbles."

"Come on, Troy, I'm being serious. Have we sold out? Does taking pictures of a drunken guy getting a gold watch mean you've sold out? Does writing *Ax Man* movies mean I've sold out?"

Troy laughed. "You've sold out for a much better price, if that signifies anything."

"It doesn't," Seth said. "The bottom line is, Laura *hasn't* sold out."

"Laura doesn't have to," Troy opined. "She's an earth mother. A nurturer. Everything she does is at one with the universe." He ruminated for a minute. "Remember when we used to have our staff meetings at *The Dream* and she would always arrive downstairs in the office with a huge bag of Good Shepherd Granola and a stack of paper cups? And she'd divvy up the granola among all of us and make sure everyone got the same number of raisins."

Seth chuckled at the memory. "That was Laura, all right," he agreed.

"The issue," Troy went on, "was never, where did Laura get all that Good Shepherd Granola and how did she pay for it? You know the kind of person Laura is. If someone were walking down the street pushing a wheelbarrow filled with Good Shepherd Granola and he saw her he would say, 'She can do more good with this than I can,' and he'd give it to her. That's the way she is. Some women have a baby out of wedlock and their lives fall apart. Laura has a baby out of wedlock and she's so together she winds up making it her job to pick up the lives of all the other unwed mothers and put them back together, too. Don't compare us to her," he concluded. "She's in a class by herself."

"Maybe," Seth allowed. He agreed with Troy's assessment of Laura. But to agree too wholeheartedly would mean to accept that Seth and Troy were in a much lower class, beyond redemption. If someone with a wheelbarrow full of granola saw both Seth and Laura, he would undoubtedly give it to Laura. But at the very least, Seth wanted to believe that if *he* were the one with the wheelbarrow, he'd have the decency to give it to someone like her.

"My secretary just appeared in the doorway and did a pantomime involving her wristwatch, a steering wheel and a strangulation," Troy said. "I think she's trying to tell me that if I don't get it together and leave for the retirement party I'm dead."

"Right." Seth closed the book of photographs and sat up straighter. "It was good talking to you, Troy."

"Take my advice," Troy said by way of parting. "Have Ax Man fire bullets through his fly. Make a statement with it."

"I'm not sure I want to know exactly what statement that makes," Seth remarked with a smile. "Take it easy, Troy."

"You, too, Stoned."

Seth hung up the phone. He swiveled from the desk when he heard Barney making a whimpering noise. The dog stood, marched in a wide oval and curled up on the rug again, facing the opposite direction. Then he closed his eyes, yawned and fell back to sleep. A sentimental warmth filled Seth as he gazed at his beloved dog.

His lips shaping a pensive smile, he turned back to his telephone and dialed Laura's number. He heard a busy signal and hung up. Then he inhaled deeply, clicked on his typewriter and typed:

> *INT. LAB. MLS—camera tracks slowly through the room. Off-camera sound of grunts and pants—a man and a woman engaged in torrid lovemaking. Camera tracks to door, stops. Door opens silently. Enter Ax Man.*

"WHAT DO YOU MEAN, a story about me?" Laura tucked the telephone receiver more securely between her chin and shoulder and wrestled with the silverware drawer. The drawers in her kitchen were constructed of thick wood, with several drippy layers of paint slathered on. On damp days the drawers always stuck. "It's bad enough that, thanks to you, I'm going to be on that *Evening Potpourri* show. I don't think I can handle any more fame at the moment."

"*Evening Potpourri* is just a PR thing for the magazine," Julianne explained calmly. "Kim told me to milk the birthday for as much publicity as I could, and given that she's got a background in public relations, I urged my publisher to heed her advice."

"Exploiting your old friends in the process," Laura muttered, though she was laughing. With a final, vicious jerk, she succeeded in wrenching the drawer open. She sagged against the counter to catch her breath. "All right. Explain this brainstorm of yours to me."

"What I have in mind is an article about the people you work with—teenagers who are unwed mothers. Not a dry, statistical piece, not a tear-stained heart-warmer. Just a day-in-the-life sort of story with you as the focal point and a few of your clients as the spin-offs. I have a wonderful reporter in mind for the article, and we'll illustrate it with a few photographs, if we can get permission from your clients." Julianne sounded utterly sure of herself, the epitome of a confident, successful editor in chief. But that was the way Julianne was—always on top of things, always in possession of herself. Laura would be willing to bet good money that the drawers in Julianne's well-appointed kitchen never got stuck.

Her proposal interested Laura, not because she wanted to be the subject of a magazine essay that would be read nationally, but because she wanted to see the issue of teenage pregnancy discussed dispassionately in the media, as often as possible, until ways were found to solve the problem. Most of the time stories on unwed mothers dealt with the matter in a sensational way. But if anyone could produce the right sort of essay, presenting the subject in a thoughtful and comprehensive manner, it was Julianne.

"Some of my clients treasure their privacy," Laura warned her, handing Rita some forks and pointing her in the direction of the table. "I can't make any promises on their behalf."

"We could change names, of course," Julianne assured her. "And we wouldn't photograph anyone indiscriminately. We're not out to pillory these girls—or their boyfriends, for that matter. We just want our readers to know what it's like trying to make it as a fifteen-year-old single mother. Social issues are a mainstay of *Dream*."

"I know. I'm a regular reader," Laura reminded Julianne, her gaze following Rita as she haphazardly set the table.

"Then it's all right with you if I pass your name along to the reporter?" Julianne asked.

"Sure. Let me give you my work number." Laura recited the phone number for Julianne, then called to Rita, "Not the steak knives. We're having cheese-and-spinach loaf." Rita curled her lip and put the serrated knives back into the silverware tray. "Sorry," Laura apologized into the telephone. "As usual, I'm doing fourteen things at once."

"I'm so impressed by how you manage," Julianne said genuinely. "A career and a daughter. *Dream* has done the subject of Superwomen to death, but if we ever decide to do another story on women juggling careers and families, I'll be sure to put your name on the list."

Laura laughed incredulously. The last word she'd used to describe herself was "super." "Frankly, Julianne, I'm amazed that you wouldn't rather do an article on Kim. She's right there, in the heart of the nation's power structure—"

"The powerful have plenty of journals singing their praises. I'd rather run stories about the powerless. Teenage motherhood is just the sort of thing I like."

"Napkins," Laura reminded Rita, then apologized again to Julianne. "I'd better get off. I've got to teach my Superdaughter how to juggle the table settings."

"All right, I'll let you go," Julianne said. "We'll talk soon. And thanks, Laura. It's so great to be working with you again."

"It's so great to be *talking* with you again," Laura replied. "And working, too. If I've got to have my life bluepenciled and God isn't available, I would be honored to have you edit me, Julianne. I'll talk to you later."

After setting the receiver in place on the kitchen's wall phone, she pulled the casserole dish out of the oven and carried it to the table. She had prepared it the previous evening and baked it halfway, so it only needed fifteen minutes in the oven that night. One didn't have to be a Superwoman to have learned how to get dinner on the table within thirty minutes of one's arrival home from work.

She carried the salad bowl to the table, paused and then went back to the refrigerator to pour herself a glass of white wine. She wasn't a big drinker, but until Julianne's call, Laura's day had been reasonably lousy. She deserved a glass of wine.

Rita flopped onto her chair, and despite the face she'd made when Laura had told her what was for dinner, she spooned an enormous portion of the spinach and cheese concoction onto her plate. "What was that all about?" she asked, nodding toward the telephone.

"My old friend Julianne wants to do a magazine article about me."

"How come? Because you're friends with a famous movie writer?"

Laura smiled wanly. Rita somehow found a way to introduce Seth into every conversation they had. Laura was glad that Rita liked Seth, but she couldn't shake the suspicion that what Rita liked best about him were the most inconsequential aspects of his character: that he had access to limousines, that he favored chic attire, that what he wrote could only be considered the cinematic equivalent of Snickers bars.

Furthermore, Rita's constant mention of Seth made Laura fearful that her daughter might be expecting too much of his friendship with Laura. He had spent a couple of days at their apartment and he had telephoned a couple of times, but Rita kept behaving as if she expected a world-class love affair to blossom between her mother and Seth.

If a world-class love affair had been fated to blossom between them, Laura believed, it would have blossomed when Seth was in her bed. But there hadn't been any blossoms that night. Only some good, solid commonsensical friend-to-friend talk. For which Laura had to take the blame—or the credit.

"The article is going to be about teenage mothers," Laura told her daughter. "How was school today?"

"The usual. Do you think Seth is going to call tonight?"

"I don't want to talk about him," Laura said, a touch too sharply. She sighed, then managed a contrite smile. "I'm sorry, Rita, but I'd really much rather hear about your day in school."

"You wanna know the truth?" Rita took a swig of milk, then lowered her glass. "It stank. I got a ninety-three on my algebra test."

"A ninety-three?" Laura's face lit up with maternal pride. "Rita, that's wonderful! Thank goodness you didn't inherit my math ability. Or should I say, my math *in*ability."

Rita shrugged, feigning nonchalance about her grade. But Laura knew her daughter too well to be taken in by Rita's attitude. Laura recognized the glimmer of satisfaction in Rita's dark eyes. "Yeah, well, the test was easy. I don't know why everybody else did so bad on it."

"They did badly because it *wasn't* easy," Laura praised her. "And you did well because you're brilliant." Rita snorted bashfully, but again Laura had no trouble discerning her daughter's pleasure at her high grade. "So," she inquired, "what's so stinky about being a budding Einstein?"

"That wasn't the stinky part. What stinks is, Becky LoCaffio's getting cable. Everybody's getting it, Ma. I'm the only kid in the whole school who doesn't get MTV."

"We've already discussed this," Laura said wearily. "The cable subscription is much too expensive. And anyway, Courtney lets you watch at her house."

"Yeah, except now it's baseball season and her brother wants to watch baseball all the time. We can't even watch *The Monkees*."

"*The Monkees*?" Laura's fork clattered to her plate and her eyebrows shot up. "As in, 'Hey—hey, we're the Monkees'?" she asked, singing a few bars of the old television show's theme song.

"See, if we got cable here," Rita pressed on, "Courtney could watch *The Monkees* with me up here, and her brother could watch his dumb ball games at their place. I honestly don't think it's fair that I should always have to watch TV at the Gonzalezes'," she concluded piously.

"You don't always have to watch TV at the Gonzalezes'," Laura pointed out. "You could do other things there—read books, play cards, help Courtney's mother with the dishes...."

Rita rolled her eyes disdainfully.

"*The Monkees*, huh," Laura reflected, smiling nostalgically. "I used to watch that show all the time."

"It's a radical show," Rita declared. "They're so cute. All that mod clothing and stuff, the funny bell-bottoms and paisley shirts. And the music is neat, too. Which Monkee was your favorite?"

"The blond one," Laura answered at once. "I think his name was Peter something—or—other."

"Tork," Rita informed her. "Peter Tork. He's the weenie of the band, Ma. I think Mickey Dolenz is much cuter."

"I guess my taste always ran to weenies," Laura said with a whimsical shrug. She had been a big fan of *The Monkees* during its first run on network television, back when she wasn't much older than Rita was now. The fact that the show was currently being rebroadcast on cable television was almost reason enough to subscribe to a cable service.

"I guess if your taste runs to weenies, you aren't going to get together with Seth, huh," Rita predicted. "He isn't a weenie."

"He's blond," Laura noted, not bothering to resist Rita's reintroduction of Seth into the conversation. "His hair is about the same color as Peter Tork's. And when I first knew Seth it was as long as Peter Tork's. Even longer. He used to wear it down past his shoulders. Sometimes he'd even fasten it in a ponytail."

"Those were weird times," Rita remarked philosophically.

"I suppose they were."

"But Peter Tork's hair is kind of nice. I bet Seth looked cute with long hair."

"He did," Laura confirmed.

"He still looks cute," said Rita. "If I were you—"

"You aren't me," Laura cut her off, deciding that the discussion had gone on long enough. "Finish your supper."

HE CALLED an hour later. Rita was in the living room, doing her homework to the raucous accompaniment of the television. Laura had refilled her glass with wine and was lounging on her bed, reading the *New York Times* and getting depressed about all the bad news that filled its pages. The ringing of the telephone came as a relief to Laura; she was more than ready to toss aside the newspaper and pretend for a few minutes that the world wasn't falling apart.

"Hello?"

"Hi, Laura, it's me," Seth said.

A warm smile brightened her face at the familiar sound of his voice. She still hadn't forgiven herself for having not been at home the last time he had called, and for having been grouchy and muddled the time before. She still hadn't forgiven herself for having come down on him so hard the Saturday night they'd spent together.

She hadn't forgiven herself, but obviously Seth had forgiven her. If he hadn't, he wouldn't keep calling her.

"Hello, Seth," she greeted him. "How are you?"

"Other than going through a minor life crisis, I'm fine," he reported. "How are you?"

Her own dreary mood went forgotten as a wave of concern washed over her. "Minor life crisis?" she asked.

"Yeah. The way I figure it, my only chance of survival is if you come out to California and visit me."

He sounded on the verge of laughter, and Laura's panic abated. "What kind of life crisis?" she asked politely.

"Just the usual. I've got a scene due tomorrow and I don't feel like writing it. It's an incredibly dumb scene, complete with sex, violence and crude dialogue. I wrote about four lines, and I'm already sick of it."

"Oh, that sounds really major to me," Laura commented with pretended dismay.

"Remember when we were working on *The Dream,* and I used to get blocked while I was trying to write my 'Kulchah Column'? How did I handle it?"

"You ordered a pizza and stuffed your face," Laura reminisced with a grin.

"As I recall, I started by listening to Grateful Dead music in order to mellow out," Seth asserted. "Then I'd telephone you, and you'd suggest a new slant for the column. You'd share your insights with me. You've got a whole lot of insight, Laura. It's no wonder you're such a good social worker."

"I'm not," she argued, her smile fading. "I'm pretty ordinary as social workers go." She reached for her glass of wine and took a sip to silence herself. She didn't want to bore Seth with her travails at work. She didn't want to burden him. "Julianne wants to run a story in the magazine on the girls I work with. I doubt she'd want to do a story about me if I wasn't representative."

"A story about you in *Dream*?" Seth exclaimed, ignoring Laura's modest explanation for Julianne's interest in her as the subject of an article. "Wow, that's fantastic."

"I don't know..." She sighed.

"What don't you know?" he asked gently.

She meditated for a moment. Perhaps it was just the raw, drizzly weather that had gotten her down, or mere exhaustion. She didn't want to whine to Seth.

Yet he had asked. He wouldn't have asked if he wasn't willing to listen. And if he was willing to listen, the least she could do was talk. "Seth, one of my clients is pregnant again. I went to her apartment today, and there she was, with her baby on her hip and this stupid smirk plastered across her face. She's sixteen years old, Seth, and I've been working with her for months, trying to teach her about birth control, about responsibility. And what was her excuse for her current predicament? 'My boyfriend called on me,' she said, 'and he's got this way about him and I just can't say no.'" Laura shuddered. "A guy's got a way about him, and all the months I've been knocking myself out trying to counsel some common sense into this girl—it all goes right down the tubes. I think I'm in the wrong line of work, Seth."

She hadn't intended to go into all that with Seth, and her spate of words surprised her. She was in the habit of keeping her frustrations to herself. She had seen too many of the single mothers who were her clients take their frustrations out on their children, or else rely too much on their children for emotional support because no one else was around to talk to.

Laura did her best to avoid unloading her tensions on Rita. She had become so adept at it that she rarely shared her professional problems with anyone. When Julianne had called earlier that evening, it hadn't even occurred to Laura to mention her irritation about Sandra Miller's new pregnancy.

Yet she *had* mentioned it to Seth. More than mentioned it—she had released her exasperation in an uncontrolled spurt. She took a moment to assess what she'd done, and discovered that sharing her frustration with Seth was far more therapeutic than consuming a glass and a half of wine. For the first time since she'd left Sandra Miller's apartment in Bedford-Stuyvesant, Laura felt genuinely relaxed. Even a supposedly good social worker like her needed to unload every now and then.

Apparently Seth found nothing remarkable about Laura's having poured out her anger to him. "Don't be so hard on her," he said placatingly. "Accidents happen. Maybe the girl just lost track or something—"

"It wasn't an accident," Laura informed Seth, not bothering to question whether he was in any way qualified to discuss a client with her. She felt such relief in simply talking about the girl with another intelligent adult. "She said her boyfriend likes what he calls 'pure sex,' and he's got this way about him, so she took a chance. And now another baby's going to be born into that mess. On days like this, Seth, I wonder why I bother at all."

Her statement obviously took him aback. He didn't speak right away, and when he did, he sounded solemn. "You bother, Laura, because you care."

"Do I really?" She fingered her wineglass, then set it down without drinking.

"Of course you do. You've had a rough day, that's all. Maybe you need a break."

"What did you have in mind, Dr. Stone?"

"I already told you what I had in mind. Come to California. Play with Barney. I read somewhere once that petting dogs is supposed to lower your blood pressure."

"My blood pressure is normal," Laura said, laughing.

"Mine always spikes when I have to write sex and violence on a deadline," Seth revealed. "Why don't you come out here and watch *me* pet Barney?"

"Oh, Seth." She sighed again. The idea of flying out to California, even if only to watch Seth pet his dog, was so tempting that she had to smother the urge to say yes at once. "When?" she said, instead. "When should I come?"

"Now. This minute. This very instant," Seth answered exuberantly. "The second I hang up the phone, I want you to walk through my front door."

"Barring the impossible, that won't happen," Laura warned him.

"Then when can you come?" he asked. When she hesitated, he said, "The airfare is my treat, by the way."

"Seth—"

"That isn't open to discussion," he silenced her. "I've got money. I'll pay."

"You really want to see me, don't you?" Laura murmured, appreciating the unspoken compliment in his offer.

"No," he responded sarcastically. "I always pay the airfare for someone I don't want to see. Of course I want to see you. When can you get here?"

"Well..." She closed her eyes and let her head settle comfortably into the pillow. She wanted to see Seth, too. Not only for romantic reasons, but because for the first time in aeons, she had found someone she could confide in, someone she could complain to. She had spent so much of her life taking care of others, helping others to work out their problems, that she had neglected her own desire to be taken care of. If anyone could take care of her, it was Seth.

She could talk to him. She could share her difficulties with him.

"Tomorrow?" he suggested.

"I work for a bureaucracy," she reminded him. "Finagling some vacation time isn't as easy as all that."

"What vacation time? Trade with someone and forget the bureaucracy. Rules were made to be broken."

She grinned. She could probably negotiate something with a couple of the other case workers in her department. They could cover for her for a week, and she could cover for them sometime down the road. "What about Rita?" she asked.

"Bring her along."

"No," Laura said firmly. If this trip was going to be a genuine break for her, then it ought to be a break from the pressures of motherhood as well as the pressures of work. She wanted time alone with Seth, without having to worry about entertaining Rita or making sure that Seth was always fully clothed in Rita's presence. "I'll talk to Courtney's mother and see if Rita can stay with them for a few days. Rita's got school, after all."

"Okay. Terrific. The minute you've got it all worked out, Laura, let me know and I'll arrange for a ticket for you."

"Are you sure you want to pay for it?" she asked. She didn't doubt his generosity, but she didn't believe that she was truly going to be visiting him, either.

"Is Columbia the gem of the ocean? I'm rich, lovely Laura. I'll pay for the ticket, and then you can come here and scold me for being so extravagant. Doesn't that sound like fun?"

"Tons of fun, Seth. I'll give you a call after I rearrange my entire life."

"I'll be waiting with bated breath," he promised before hanging up.

Laura lowered the receiver and stared at the telephone. Her gaze wandered to her wineglass, and she lifted it in the phone's direction, offering a silent toast to Seth before she sipped. Once her wine was gone, she would worry about rearranging her life, working out the many details that would make her trip to California possible. Glenda Gonzalez would probably agree to let Rita stay with Courtney for the week. And Laura would do whatever was necessary to wrangle some time off from work. If she couldn't trade around with her colleagues for some leave time, she would tell her supervisor that she was suffering from a temporary case of burnout. Given how furious Laura had been with Sandra Miller that day, such a diagnosis wouldn't be much of an exaggeration.

The pieces would fall into place. If they didn't, Laura would force them into place. She wanted to see Seth, and she would see him. No matter what.

Chapter Six

She ought to have felt free. An entire week away from home stretched ahead, as clear as the cloudless sky surrounding the airplane. An entire week during which Laura wouldn't have to hear the words "weenie" or "everybody else does." A week away from Rita, and a week away from Sandra Miller and all Laura's other clients, those troubled, thoughtless girls who claimed with astounding certainty that they had heard from a reliable source that you couldn't get pregnant if, one, you had your period, or two, you went on top, or three, you took an aspirin immediately afterward.

Laura ought to have felt free, but she didn't. As she was learning, cloudless skies didn't guarantee a smooth flight. The wide-bodied jet kept bucking and trembling as it hit invisible pockets of turbulence, and each jolt caused Laura's stomach to lurch up toward her throat. She wasn't the most seasoned of air travelers.

She probably should have taken an inner seat and slept throughout the trip. But she had requested a window seat, and, turbulence notwithstanding, she couldn't fight the compulsion to stare out the window at the miniature world below, the green-and-brown checkerboard of farmland, the hairbreadth threads of rivers, the dense, shadowy blur of a forest. She wasn't sentimental enough to romanticize the glorious vista. She knew that some, if not most, of those impressive checkerboard farms were owned by families teetering on the brink of financial collapse and that somewhere, in the back seat of a car parked beside one of those meandering silver threads of water, a seventeen-year-old boy was busy convincing his sixteen-year-old girlfriend that if she went on top she wouldn't get pregnant.

It wasn't that Laura was a pessimist. She had enormous faith in the human race, in the capacity of ordinary people to conduct their lives with decency and love. All they needed was knowledge, sensitivity to others and a willingness to accept responsibility—precisely the characteristics she sought to instill in her clients. Social work wasn't for cynics.

Yet she was glad to get away from her job for a few days. Maybe she *was* burning out just a little bit; maybe she was getting old, her supply of patience running dangerously low.

The hell with her job. What she was getting away from wasn't nearly as important as what she was traveling toward. She was excited about seeing Seth.

Excited, and a touch anxious. She tried to convince herself that her primary reason for seeing him was that he was a friend, but she knew better. She knew that she was seeing him because his eyes were hypnotic and his smile was irresistible, because, even though they'd done little but talk the night they'd spent in her bed, she was overwhelmingly attracted to him.

And that was what made her nervous. As she'd recognized when he was in Brooklyn, it would be quite easy for her to fall in love with him. Not only because of his eyes and his smile, not only because of his lean, sexy body, but because he had the sensitivity to comprehend how desperately she needed a break from her daily worries—and because he had the strength to demand that she take that break. He had the perception to understand that she needed a good dose of playtime to regain her perspective on things.

She could fall in love with him, but she questioned whether she should. Deep in her heart, she questioned whether he could truly return her love. That doubt, as much as the plane's bumps and jumps, contributed heavily to her queasiness.

A steward came to remove Laura's lunch tray. All Laura had consumed was a glass of milk and a few bites of something called a "nature treat," which seemed to be little more than a glorified candy bar with some rolled oats mixed in with the sugar and chocolate. The rest of the meal had looked too unappetizing to taste. She was happy to have the fresh-scrubbed young man take the food away.

As soon as the steward left, Laura turned her attention to the window again. The rolling hills that marked the beginning of the continent's incline to the Rockies reminded her of the hills near Ithaca, where the commune had been located.

She had learned about the place from a college friend in the fall of her senior year. After graduation, Laura and her friend had traveled up to Ithaca to visit the commune. Her friend had left after a couple of weeks, but Laura had remained.

It wasn't merely the warmth and generosity of the commune's residents that had persuaded Laura to stay, or the charmingly decrepit farmhouse, or the barn that a few of the men had skillfully converted into additional living quarters, or the flourishing garden, or the rustic beauty of the region. Nor was it Neil, although the attraction he and Laura felt for each other had been instant and intense. All those things contributed to her decision to join the commune, but the main reason she chose to live there was theoretical. She loved the idea of it.

She loved learning how to cook dinner for twenty hungry people and how to put up homemade preserves. She loved walking into the bustling kitchen shortly after sunrise each day and hearing three different people shout "Good morning!" She loved pitching in, doing chores, stacking split logs in the shed for the winter, hiking five miles with a bucket to pick wild blueberries and then hiking five miles back to the farmhouse with her harvest. She loved the two young children who lived on the commune with their parents. She loved the camaraderie, the sense of family. As an only child, and one who, like so many of her generation, had rebelled against her parents' traditional views, Laura had been delighted to adopt the communal family as her own.

It seemed only natural that she would want a child, to extend her sense of family even further. When she broached the subject with Neil, he greeted it with enthusiasm. She hadn't expected to conceive so quickly, but when she did, she was secretly pleased by her fertility. Being pregnant made her feel wholesome, womanly, rich in mysterious ways.

She took the job assisting the sociology professor at Cornell because she figured she'd need some extra money for the baby, and Neil kept his job at a food co-op because it provided medical insurance. Laura gave birth to Rita at the farmhouse, with only Neil and a midwife in attendance, which was exactly as Laura had wanted it.

She was shocked that Neil decided to leave the commune when Rita was less than six months old. Other commune residents had moved away and were replaced by newcomers, and each departure had disturbed Laura to a certain extent. But she had been positive that Neil would want to stay, even if he fell out of love with Laura. She had assumed that he would want to be near his daughter.

As he had explained it, the last person he wanted to be near was Rita. He hadn't fallen out of love with Laura; he honestly didn't want to leave her. But being a father wasn't at all what he had expected. It was too much work, with too little immediate return. He felt trapped.

"You aren't trapped," Laura had told him. She wouldn't ask him to stay if he wanted to go. The last thing she would ever want to do was trap a man. "There's the door," she had said, dry eyed and resolved. "It's unlocked."

And he'd left.

Perhaps it was then that Laura had first learned to keep her feelings to herself. Neil's abrupt departure became the major focus of Laura's communal family. They fretted over her and Rita—in part because they were genuinely worried about how she would manage, but mostly because Neil's abandonment of his daughter was the most exciting thing to occur at the generally uneventful commune for some time. Laura soon came to realize that, in the guise of concern, her companions were simply gossips, delighting in a scandal. So she kept her mouth shut, shaped into a passive smile. The commune was based on shared possessions, but Laura's feelings belonged to herself.

"There's the Grand Canyon," the elderly man beside Laura announced, nudging her ribs and then reaching across her body to point out the sight.

She blinked herself back into the present and gazed down through the window. A few tufted clouds momentarily obscured her view, and then she saw what appeared to be a wrinkled brown gash in the earth. "This is the first time I've ever seen it," she confessed, thrilled by the sight, even though it was too remote to be breathtaking.

"First time? You ought to get a look at it up close," the man advised her. "Take one of the burros down. It makes you feel insignificant, I'll tell you."

"I'm not sure I want to feel insignificant," Laura said with a laugh.

She chatted with the man for the remainder of the flight, delighted to be distracted from thoughts of her past, as well as from thoughts of her immediate future. She didn't know what was going to happen when she saw Seth. But everytime she allowed herself to think that her time with him would proceed smoothly, the plane hit another pocket of turbulence and reminded her that a rough ride was sometimes impossible to foresee.

The bumpiness of the flight ended once they passed over the Santa Ana Mountains and entered a new weather system. But if Laura had hoped to relax and feel her stomach settle back into its proper place for the final stretch of the journey, she was disappointed. The gentleman beside her regaled her with detailed accounts of the last few times he'd flown to California. "Last year, for instance, we were coming in to San Jose, and they had seventy-mile-an-hour wind shears. Although I hear it's worse taking off in a wind shear than landing in one. Still, I'll tell you, it wasn't much fun. Or the time a few months ago, I was on a jet landing at San Francisco and it nearly missed the runway and dropped into the Bay. Swooped up at the last minute and circled again. What a scare. You could practically feel the water splashing against the underside of the plane."

Laura swallowed and eyed the discomfort bag in the seat pocket in front of her. Forget about her immediate future. If by some miracle she survived the flight to California, what did she have to look forward to but a return flight to New York? Maybe she would cash in her return ticket and take a train back. Or maybe she wouldn't go back at all. Maybe she'd stay with Seth forever. That was a surprisingly consoling thought.

"You look a little peaked" were Seth's first words when, twenty minutes later, after the plane had made a perfectly safe, ordinary landing, Laura staggered off the craft and into the terminal. Seth was standing just beyond the security gates, waving frantically. She stumbled into his arms and issued a shaky sigh. "What happened?" he asked. "Was it a bad flight?"

"I'm alive, so I guess it couldn't have been all that bad," she conceded, smiling sheepishly and tilting her head back to see Seth. He happened to look wonderful, his hazel eyes radiant, his pale hair windblown and glistening with golden streaks, his dimples cutting deep lines into his sun-bronzed cheeks. But even if he had looked horrendous, Laura would have considered him the most wonderful sight in the world—infinitely more inspiring than the Grand Canyon from eighty thousand feet.

He appraised her thoughtfully, then frowned. "Then what's wrong? You're as white as a sheet, and you look as if you tried to eat your lower lip for lunch."

She laughed. "There was this man sitting next to me, Seth..." Her laughter increased as she realized how absurd her fear had been. "He looked like someone's grandfather, so sweet and Santa Clausy. In fact, he probably *is* someone's grandfather. Anyway, he spent the last hour of the flight telling me about every near miss in history. There he is," she said, angling her head toward the cherubic-faced man in the crowd swarming from her plane's gate.

"Sadist," Seth muttered under his breath. Laura's laughter increased, dispelling the last of her anxiety. "You've got to watch out for those Santa Claus look-alikes," Seth confided, slipping his arm around her waist and ushering her down the corridor to the baggage claim area. "Never trust anyone who looks sweet."

"Maybe I shouldn't trust you," Laura mused.

"Me? I don't look sweet." Seth twisted around to face her and bared his teeth menacingly. He emitted a growl from the back of his throat, then winked. "See? I'm trustworthy."

"Very, I'm sure," Laura played along.

He planted an affectionate kiss on her cheek. "Maybe *I* shouldn't trust *you*," he remarked. "Other than looking a little green, you're a sight for sore eyes."

"You mean, looking at me makes your eyes sore?" she teased.

"I mean, lovely Laura, that looking at you makes my eyes very, very happy." He kissed her again. "If your flight was all that scary, I don't suppose you'll want me to show off my Porsche on the winding back roads." He scanned the bags as they slid down the chute to the carousel. "Which one's yours?"

Laura spotted her battered suitcase and reached for it. Seth chivalrously lifted it from the carousel, then took her hand and led her out of the terminal. The sun was high and hot above them, and she realized that late March in Los Angeles was a drastically different season from late March in Brooklyn. "I'm overdressed," she murmured.

Seth surveyed her outfit: a pair of evenly faded jeans, a long-sleeved blouse, a lightweight Windbreaker, socks and loafers. He was also wearing jeans, but his Hawaiian-print shirt had short sleeves, and he didn't have a jacket. Instead of his red high-tops, he was wearing water buffalo sandals. Laura tried to remember the last time she'd seen someone wearing sandals like his. In college, she recalled. On Seth's feet.

"Sure you're overdressed," he ribbed her. "All of us oddballs in Southern California are really closet nudists."

His car, which was parked in a short-term lot, was black, streamlined and low to the ground. "This is it, huh," she said, wondering exactly how impressed she was supposed to be.

"This is my baby, all right," Seth announced with the sort of pride Laura felt ought to be reserved for one's offspring. "I'd let you take it for a spin yourself, but you look like you're about to pass out, and frankly, I don't want you keeling over when you're at the wheel."

"You're all heart, Seth," Laura muttered. "I just know it's my well-being, and not your car, that you're thinking of."

He chuckled and unlocked the passenger-side door for her. "Well, it's too late to rent a limo. Rumor has it that all the limos in L.A. County are currently in the shop, being tuned up for the Academy Awards next week. So you're stuck with good ol' Chauffeur Stoned."

The Academy Awards. She really was in Lotusland. She waited until Seth had tossed her suitcase into the back seat and taken the wheel before asking, with as much nonchalance as she could muster, "Are you going to attend the awards?"

He tossed back his head and guffawed. "Me? Mr. Counterculture?" He twisted the ignition key, and the engine emitted a surprisingly quiet hum. "If you want to know the truth," he admitted, steering carefully through the crowded lot, "I did try to go once, the first year I was out here. I had this brainstorm that I would write a daring exposé about it and sell it to some muckraking magazine."

"What happened?"

Seth braked at the exit gate to pay the attendant the parking fee. "What happened? I found out that getting a ticket to the awards isn't exactly like getting a ticket to a Rolling Stones concert. Everybody and his second cousin tries to palm himself off as a journalist in order to get within ten feet of the Dorothy Chandler Pavilion. In addition to regular press credentials—which I didn't have at the time—I think you've got to submit a urine sample and three character witnesses." He pocketed his change, rolled up his window and hit the air-condition button on his dashboard as he pulled away from the gate.

"I bet you get an engraved invitation to the awards ceremony now," Laura noted. "Surely the author of *Ax Man* movies must be a revered member of the Hollywood community."

"Revered?" He shrugged again. "I get an invitation because I'm a member of the Screen Writers' Guild. But if I decided to go, I'd have to fork over some ridiculous premium for tickets for myself and a date, and then I'd have to rent a monkey suit, pay some jacked-up parking cost—or rent a limo—and run the gantlet of all those screaming meemies who hang out in front of the theater, looking for stars. And then, to add insult to injury, I'd have to sit still for three-plus hours while the director of the best animated short subject wipes the tears from his eyes and thanks his wet nurse for making it all possible. Thanks, but I can think of better ways to spend a Monday evening."

Laura grinned. It was reassuring to hear Seth talk like this. The film industry may have made him richer, but deep in his heart he was still irreverent and antiestablishment, still able to view the monuments of contemporary culture with a jaundiced eye.

He manipulated the gear stick deftly as the car cruised away from the airport, and once the traffic began to thin, he fidgeted with the stereo console. An old Jefferson Airplane tape began to play. "I like your car," Laura said. "It has good taste in music."

He smiled and released the gear stick to squeeze Laura's hand. "I'm glad you could work things out and come, Laura," he told her earnestly. "I've missed you. And if anyone could use a good California suntan, it's you."

"The only reason I look so pale is that I'm still recovering from the flight," she reminded him, but her matching smile communicated that she was as glad as he was that she had come.

He steered onto the Pacific Coast Highway. It wasn't nearly as dramatic as she'd expected, but when she commented on that, Seth informed her that the spectacular scenery—the cliff-hugging hairpin turns—were located farther north, outside the city. Laura didn't really need any cliff-hugging hairpin turns after her bumpy plane trip, and she was content simply to view the pounding gray ocean that stretched toward the horizon to the west.

Just outside the city, Seth steered away from the water, taking a road that surely rivaled the coast highway. Low, dusty shrubs and dwarfed trees lined the road, and here and there she spotted a house clinging to the steep slopes. The houses seemed, for the most part, to be camouflaged by their surroundings.

It was a vastly different environment from the lush greenery of the East, but Laura found the tan, brown and olive-drab hues of the landscape strangely appealing. Before long, she was bravely peering down the slopes, enjoying the roller-coaster ruggedness of the terrain.

Eventually Seth turned off the road onto a driveway of packed dirt and loose gravel. The driveway they were on wove between dense clusters of red-barked bushes, which Seth identified as manzanita, before ending in front of a flat-roofed structure of fieldstone, wood and glass. "Be it ever so humble," he announced before shutting off the engine and swinging his door open.

A large, gangly dalmatian sprang out of nowhere and hurled itself at Seth, who miraculously remained upright under the animal's weight. "Barney!" Seth gave the dog a vigorous scratching behind its ears, then shoved it off himself and led it around the car to meet Laura. "Barney, this is Laura," he said, opening her door for her. "Take it from me, she smells good. So I'll thank you not to sniff her in unseemly parts of her anatomy."

"I know how to handle dogs," Laura assured Seth, extending her hand to Barney. He investigated it with his nose, then lifted his head so she could stroke him under his chin. He barked his approval.

"Phew!" Seth exhaled with exaggerated relief. "If he didn't like you, I'd have to put you on the next plane back to New York." He reached into the back seat to get Laura's bag, then escorted her into the house.

It hadn't appeared that big from the outside, but the interior spaciousness delighted her. Granted, she was used to cramped quarters—apartments in Brooklyn, and in Buffalo before that, and the low-ceilinged attic room she'd shared with Rita at the farmhouse on the commune. She waltzed through the vast living room, with its floor-to-ceiling windows on two walls, a cut-stone fireplace on a third wall and polished wood floors decorated with rust-and-gray woven rugs. "I love it," she said.

Seth seemed extraordinarily pleased. "Do you? I fixed it up myself."

"You've got the heart of an artist," she praised him, admiring the plump beige sofa and matching chairs, the teak tables, the abstract soapstone sculpture on a shelf built into one wall. The living room opened onto a dining room, which looked out on the overgrown backyard. Outcroppings of rock and tangled underbrush extended beyond the railed wooden deck to a cluster of trees that climbed the hill behind the house. "This is beautiful!" she exclaimed.

Seth smiled modestly. "Some people don't like it," he said. "It's practically a desert here, so brown and dusty. A lot of easterners find they can't adjust to life without crabgrass."

"I don't know about crabgrass, but I'd take this over concrete any day," she said, thinking not of the East Coast suburbs but of her densely built community of Flatbush. She wandered ahead of Seth into the kitchen. It was messier than the other rooms, with a dirty pot soaking in the sink and a stack of newspapers cluttering one counter, but Laura found it an infinite improvement over her own kitchen with its sticky drawers and archaic appliances. She crossed to the microwave oven, opened it and peered inside. "Fancy gear you've got here, Seth. Do you know how to use it?"

"Do I look like I'm starving?" he countered, attempting unsuccessfully to puff out his flat stomach. Laura burst into laughter, and Seth joined her. "All right, I haven't exactly mastered beef Wellington. But I do know how to make a baked potato in seven minutes flat."

"The rich are different from you and me," Laura quoted. "They don't have to wait a whole hour when they're in the mood for a potato."

"Money does have its compensations," Seth agreed, deadpan. He peeked into the sink, wrinkled his nose at the sudsy pot and headed out of the kitchen and down a back hall, with Laura following him.

The room they entered was clearly his office. A professional L-shaped desk stood in one corner by the broad window, a Selectric typewriter set up on the shorter surface and a thick black loose-leaf binder open on the longer surface, next to the telephone and an answering machine. Wall shelves held books and a number of other black binders, each spine labeled with a typewritten title. One wall was devoted to file cabinets. A leather reclining chair occupied a corner. Another beautiful handwoven rug covered the floor.

"So, this is where all that microwave money gets made," said Laura, drifting to one of the shelves and reading the titles on the binders: *Coed Summer*, *Barrio Warlords*, *Rich Intimacies*.

"This is where it happens," Seth confirmed, crossing to his desk and switching on his answering machine. "Let me scope my messages, and then we'll continue with the grand tour."

Nodding vaguely, Laura pulled one of the bound manuscripts from the shelf and opened it. The pages were nearly indecipherable to her, their contents typed in small clustered paragraphs with varying margins, bordered by numbers and unfamiliar abbreviations: "L.S." "C.U." "F/X." She slid the binder back into place on the shelf.

"Seth? Melinda," a voice said from the answering machine. "An update on that check New World still owes you. They assured me that it's in the mail. Ha, ha, if you catch my drift. I'll be in touch."

"That's my agent," Seth informed Laura as the tape whirled.

After a few clicks another woman's voice came on, this one soft and alluring: "Seth? It's me, Darla Dupree. I hate to bother you about this, but I'm having a real problem. It's this stuff about taking off my swimsuit before I go into the Jacuzzi. You know what I'm talking about, right? I mean, I'm still not clear on why I don't keep my swimsuit on. Zeke and I have been fighting about it, but you know him. Can you help me out maybe? I'll love you forever."

"A good friend of yours, I take it," Laura muttered wryly.

Seth offered a feeble smile and shut off the machine. "An actress," he said.

"One of your seven hundred starlets?"

Seth's smile widened. "Do I detect a smidgen of jealousy, lovely Laura?"

"Of course not," she retorted, irked that she might have sounded jealous. Whether or not Seth's lady friends went into Jacuzzis while wearing their swimsuits ought to have been of little concern to Laura.

That it evidently did concern her seemed to amuse Seth. He allowed her to stew for a moment before explaining, "She's starring in *Ax Man Cuts Both Ways*, and she's questioning her motivation for stripping in the Jacuzzi scene."

Laura forced a brittle smile. The truth was, she *was* jealous. She was jealous of Seth's glamorous life, his lovely home—and the existence of other women in his life. Even if the woman on the answering machine's tape was only a professional acquaintance of Seth's, Laura was jealous of her. She had never been a jealous person, and the realization that she was suffering from such uncharacteristic envy disconcerted her. Too rattled to speak, she pivoted and walked back into the hallway.

Seth picked up her suitcase on his way out of the office. They strolled down the hall to another open door, and he gestured her into the room. "This is the guest bedroom," he said as Laura took in the neatly made double bed and the clear-topped chest of drawers. She moved to the window and gazed out at a dark-leafed orange tree growing by the side of the house. Seth's silence prompted her to turn back to him. He stood hesitantly near the door, her suitcase still in his hand. "Do...uh...do you want me to leave this in here?" he asked, lifting the bag toward her.

He didn't exactly look awkward, but the question obviously made him feel a bit uncomfortable. Laura wasn't entirely sure what answer he expected—or wanted. If he had hoped for her to stay in his bed, wouldn't he have mentioned that when he had invited her? Yet if he didn't want her in his bed, he would have just dropped her suitcase and said, "This room's yours."

Apparently he hadn't made up his mind about where he wanted Laura to spend the night, so he was allowing her to make up his mind for him. She was touched, but like him a bit uncomfortable. Things would have been much simpler if they had worked the sleeping arrangements out beforehand.

On the other hand, there was that velvet-voiced woman on the answering machine, perhaps one of seven hundred. "I'll stay here," Laura decided. Better safe than sorry, she added silently, though she didn't want to think about why she might have been sorry if she had chosen to stay in Seth's room, instead.

He smiled enigmatically. "Okay," he said, setting down the suitcase by the bed. He studied her for a minute, and his smile grew gentle. "Would you like to sack out for a while? You really look bushed."

"That bad, huh." Laura glimpsed herself in the mirror above the bureau. Her hair was mussed, but given its curly, unpruned state, that wasn't worth mentioning. She did appear wan, but compared to Seth's burnished California complexion, any New Yorker would look wan. However, her flight hadn't been the most rejuvenating of experiences. Maybe a nap would do her some good. "What are you going to do while I rest?"

"Rewrite the Jacuzzi scene," he told her.

"Then I'll sleep for hours," she promised. "I don't want to interfere with your work."

He opened his mouth, then shut it. "Bathroom's across the hall," he told her as he backed out of the room. "There are fresh towels on the rack, so help yourself." Before Laura could say anything, he was gone.

YOU DO WANT TO INTERFERE with my work, Seth silently accused her. He stood in the doorway to his office, staring down the hall, imagining Laura opening her suitcase, brushing her hair, stretching out on the bed and closing her eyes. He was so happy she had come, so happy she was here with him, and yet...

Much as he wanted to, he couldn't blame Darla Dupree's poorly timed message for his uneasiness. It was his own fault for having turned on the answering machine while Laura was in the office. As soon as he'd heard Darla purring petulantly about having to strip off her clothes, he could almost feel condemnation oozing out of Laura.

Well, sure, *Cuts Both Ways* was a stupid flick. He wouldn't argue the point. But that didn't give Laura the right to be so damned sanctimonious about it. If it weren't for a fictional madman armed with a hatchet, who would have paid for Laura's airfare out West, anyway?

He stalked across the room to the desk and sank into his swivel chair. After leafing through the manuscript in front of him until he found the Jacuzzi scene, he rested his chin in his hands and perused what he'd written. "Ugh," he grunted softly.

Laura hadn't been sanctimonious. She hadn't been so terribly critical. It was Seth's own doubts about what he was doing that made him defensive around her.

He used to enjoy doing this sort of thing, didn't he? He used to enjoy concocting foolish plots, with all the flesh and gore a director like Zeke could dream of. Seth even used to enjoy rewriting scenes to satisfy the actors and actresses. He enjoyed satisfying them with his writing, just as he enjoyed the knowledge that what he wrote would ultimately satisfy an audience.

But he didn't want to be doing it now. He wanted to march into the guest room, shake Laura's shoulders and say, "You're right. Tell me what to do with my life, and I'll do it."

He wanted more than that. He wanted to march into the guest room, fling himself onto the bed and make love to Laura. He wanted to pull off her clothing and kiss her softly curved body from tip to toe, to bury his soul within her.

He wanted her. But like a first-class idiot, he had offered her the guest room. And she'd accepted the offer, damn it. When they were giving out the awards for the Academy of Twinkies, they'd have to save a special statuette for her. And one for him, too.

What was wrong with them? They were two mature, responsible adults. Seth hadn't imagined the magnetic pull they'd felt for each other in New York, or in the airport just hours ago, the moment they'd seen each other. Yet here they were, tiptoeing around each other like a couple of smitten kids.

They were adults, and more important, they were friends. They were supposed to be honest with each other.

Maybe Laura honestly *didn't* want him the way he wanted her. Maybe it wasn't his occupation that turned her off so much as his doubts and confusion. Maybe she had simply expected him to take charge, to make demands and determine the course of their relationship.

Seth wasn't particularly macho, and he preferred women who met him halfway. That was the problem, though. Laura hadn't met him halfway. She'd chosen the guest room.

All he needed now was a wacky character with an ax to chop down the wall separating Laura's room from his. All he needed was the nerve to chop down the intangible but definite wall separating Laura from him.

Chapter Seven

Laura woke up, disoriented and vaguely expectant. A muted gray light seeped through the thin drapes drawn shut across the open window. The semisheer fabric billowed inward on a gentle breeze that carried a tangy, unfamiliar fragrance into the room.

She sat, adjusting the shoulder straps of her nightgown, and gazed around her. She felt supremely well rested, which wasn't much of a surprise, given how much sleep she'd gotten the previous evening.

That evening was something of a muddle. She remembered stretching out on the bed in the afternoon for what she had thought would be a brief snooze. Then Seth had awakened her for dinner. They'd sat in the glass-wrapped breakfast area of the kitchen, looking out on the descending night, eating the broiled chicken and salad Seth had prepared and sharing a bottle of wine. Laura was pretty sure she hadn't drunk much wine—as groggy as she was, she probably shouldn't have had any—and shortly thereafter she'd stumbled back to bed for the night.

Maybe Seth could handle jet lag, but Laura obviously couldn't.

She groped on the night table for her wristwatch and read that it was seven-fifteen. Kicking off the lightweight blanket, she padded barefoot to the window to open the drapes.

The sky outside the window was an incandescent grayish pink, a faint, predawn hue. She wondered why the sun hadn't risen yet, and then recalled that Seth's house was set within a canyon whose walls undoubtedly blocked the early rays. The orange tree beside the house was covered with delicate buds; it was their delightful perfume that Laura smelled.

She had no idea what time Seth had finally retired for the night, and she didn't want to disturb him if he was sleeping in. Silently she made her way down the hall to the kitchen, where a quick search located an open can of coffee and filters for his coffee maker. She set a pot to brewing, then wandered into the living room.

The openness of the space appealed to her. No curtains blocked the windows; given that the only building visible through the glass was Barney's doghouse, Seth didn't need curtains to ensure his privacy. She gazed out at the thick brush climbing the slope behind the house and smiled. *The rich are different,* she mused, reflecting on the fact that, in the eighteen years since she had left her parents' suburban home for college, she had never lived in a house all her own. There had been the noisy, active dormitory at Barnard and then the swarming farmhouse on the commune, the stuffy apartment near the SUNY-Buffalo campus when she was studying for her master's degree in social work and the slightly larger apartment she and Rita had moved to once she'd completed her graduate schooling and landed a decent-paying job, and then her current home in Brooklyn. She wasn't complaining; she knew all too well that in New York City, adequate housing—let alone an affordable two-bedroom apartment only a couple of blocks from the IND station—was nearly impossible to find.

Yet how nice it would be not to have to tiptoe around a house in fear of disturbing the people living in the apartment below. How nice not to have to smell a neighbor's onion-laden casseroles every time one opened the front door.

Money could be useful when it came to housing, she admitted. And certainly there was nothing ostentatious about Seth's house, no matter how many screenplays he had had to write to earn the down payment. Laura shouldn't brand him a traitor to the cause just because he happened to own a lovely home.

Roaming back to the kitchen, she shut off the coffee maker and searched the cabinets until she found a mug. The sound of approaching footsteps startled her, and she spun around to discover Seth entering the room. He had on a pair of baggy beige trousers and he was slinging on a bright red shirt. Laura glimpsed the lean, tan expanse of his hairless chest and turned away, inexplicably bashful. "Did I wake you?" she asked, busying herself with the coffee grounds. "I'm sorry."

"No apologies necessary." He raked his fingers through his sleep-tousled hair and grinned. "Early to bed and early to rise, makes a man healthy, et cetera."

"Are you wise?" Laura asked, turning back to him. He was buttoning his shirt, and she felt a strange mixture of relief and deflation that his torso was no longer in view.

He shrugged, then reached into the cabinet for another mug. "Two out of three ain't bad." He set his mug on the counter beside hers. "How'd you sleep?"

"Like the proverbial log. I'm sorry I was such a deadhead yesterday, Seth."

"No big deal. It takes most people a while to reset their inner clocks." Appropriating the role of host, he nudged her toward the table in the breakfast nook and filled the mugs. "I expect you to make up for it today. What can I get you for breakfast?"

"What have you got?"

"No fresh bagels, alas." He swung open the refrigerator door and related its contents to her. "Eggs, bran muffins, pita bread, Famous Amos cookies, and I think I've got some cereal somewhere."

"Bran muffins sound delicious," she said. Seth pulled a box of muffins and a tub of whipped butter from the refrigerator and carried them to the table.

"So what's on the itinerary for today?" she asked, watching while he distributed plates, knives and napkins. She liked being waited on by him, and she didn't offer any assistance in getting breakfast onto the table.

"This morning, I've got to drop the scene I rewrote off at my director's house," he told her. "After that, whatever you want. Homes of the Stars, Mann's Chinese Theater, Sunset Strip, the La Brea Pits. I bet you want to see Watts, too."

"Why on earth would I want to see Watts?" Laura asked. "I didn't come all this way to look at slums. I see plenty enough of them at home."

"I meant Watts Towers." Seth bit into his muffin and smiled. "The towers are a must on the tour. Some crackpot Italian immigrant built them out of scrap... you'll see. The first time I saw them I freaked out."

"Then we'll go there."

Seth leaned back in his chair, extending his long legs beneath the table, and sipped his coffee. "On a totally unrelated subject, Laura, is that a nightgown you're wearing?"

She glanced down at herself. There was nothing even remotely suggestive about the loose-fitting cotton gown, but she felt her cheeks color, anyway. "It isn't a three-piece suit," she joked nervously.

"The reason I ask," Seth said, "is that I've heard complaints from a certain quarter that you won't allow Rita to sleep in the nude until she's sixteen."

Astonished that Seth would mention such a thing, she scowled. "Since when are you interested in Rita's nudity?" she asked hotly.

He laughed. "It isn't Rita I'm interested in—it's this whole 'I am the mother—I lay down the rules' trip. I can't believe that an over-the-hill flower child like you would really play the heavy with her."

Laura suffered a momentary defensiveness, but as she studied Seth across the table, taking note of his genial smile and sparkling eyes, she realized that he was asking only out of curiosity. Having never been a parent, he evidently wanted to know how Laura handled the job.

She took a leisurely drink of her coffee, using the time to gather her thoughts. When she lowered the mug, she found Seth still watching her, still brimming with curiosity. "I don't know that I'm playing the heavy," she began, then exhaled. "It's just that things are so different today than they were when we were young, Seth. Kids are pressured in a thousand different ways to be grown up, to be sexual. I see it constantly in my work, and it's awful. They never have a chance to be just plain kids." She ran her finger around the rim of her mug, meditating. "I don't know where Rita got the idea of sleeping nude, but I suspect she read about one of her idols, a rock star or something, sleeping in the raw and thought it was a neat idea."

"It is a neat idea," Seth observed.

"For an adult, sure. But she's not an adult. She wants to wear cosmetics, spike-heeled shoes, musk colognes. She dreams about dating a boy who shaves, a boy who drives—in other words, a boy who's a lot older than her. Most thirteen-year-old girls do, so it's not like she's weird. But I'm her mother, and it's up to me to counter all the pressure she gets from other sources. I don't see any good in her growing up too fast."

"So you don't let her drink or do drugs, either," Seth surmised.

"I certainly don't." Laura exhaled again. "Maybe she does those things behind my back. I don't know. I can only hope. It's scary being a mother. I'm so crazy about Rita. I worry about whether I can protect her from all the danger in the world—and then I worry that I'm overprotective. It sounds so trite to say that I only want what's best for her, but it's the truth."

Seth contemplated what she'd said, and his smile grew tentative. "When I was growing up, my parents had a list of laws a mile long. I used to swear that if I ever became a parent, I'd never hand down so many rules and regs to my kids."

"So did I," Laura admitted with a laugh. "It's different once you're a parent yourself, though. After I had Rita, I felt much closer to my own mother. I could empathize with what she'd gone through raising me. I could understand it."

"Were your parents upset that you didn't marry Rita's dad?"

Laura rolled her eyes as she reminisced. "'Upset' is an understatement. They were apoplectic. They were furious that I was living on the commune, and then that I had Rita. But...wounds heal. Love conquers. My father passed away a few years ago, but we were very close again by the time he died. My mother and I are still close now."

"I'd probably be closer with my folks if I had a kid," Seth confessed. "Both my brothers have families. My mother never passes up an opportunity to lecture me on the virtues of settling down. One of her pet questions is, 'When are you going to settle down?' As if I were bouncing off the ceiling or something."

"When *are* you going to settle down?" Laura asked.

Seth comprehended that she was teasing him, and he responded in kind. "After I've run out of starlets."

"We're talking decades, huh."

"At the minimum." He pushed his chair away from the table and stood. "Let's shake a leg. Zeke is probably panting to get his hands on the new Jacuzzi scene." He carried the dirty dishes to the sink, then lifted the dog's water dish from the corner of the floor and filled it with fresh water. "Barney gets room service," he explained before heading for the back door off the kitchen.

"And I don't?" Laura griped.

Seth winked. "You aren't a dog, Laura," he murmured with a seductive grin before striding outside in the direction of the doghouse.

His smile unnerved Laura, and as soon as she reached the guest bathroom she gave her reflection a careful examination in the full-length mirror attached to the door. By no stretch of the imagination could her nightgown be considered sexy. The lacy trim around the neckline gave it an almost girlish appearance. Seth's insinuations were definitely uncalled for.

No, they weren't, she refuted herself as she stripped and stepped into the shower. That she hadn't made love with him in New York, that she had asked to stay in the guest room—none of it did anything to dispel the sexual undercurrent that passed between her and Seth. Even if he hadn't been aware of her reaction to the sight of his bare chest, *she* was acutely aware of it. She was aware of his every graceful movement, his every sly smile, the untamed glint in his eyes. Why else would she have been jealous of a mere voice on an answering machine?

She showered quickly, wrapped a towel around herself and hurried across the hall to her room, shutting herself inside. Confronted by the sight of the broad bed in which she'd spent the night alone, she was again forced to acknowledge the attraction she felt toward him. She knew that all she had to do was quirk her finger and he would be tearing off his clothes, happy to satisfy her every urge.

Every urge but one. As long as he was still writing tripe, she feared that she might never be able to give herself completely to him. She feared that possibility, and so, she suspected, did Seth.

She dressed in a cotton skirt with a calico print and a gauzy white blouse, fastened her silver hoop earrings to her ears and made a futile attempt to brush out the tangles in her hair. When she emerged from the bedroom, she spotted Seth standing by the desk in his office, gathering a stack of papers into a folder. He turned from his desk to greet her, and she saw that he was wearing sunglasses. With regular lenses, not mirrors. "All set?"

"All set."

They left the house and climbed into the Porsche. The sun had risen high enough to cast long, mysterious shadows through the canyon, but the morning was brisk. Laura wondered where the famed Los Angeles smog was, but she said nothing, appreciating the clean, dry aroma of the air.

"Zeke is a first-class jerk," Seth warned her as he navigated the winding roads. "He's directing the picture. His favorite word is 'beautiful.' Everything is beautiful with him—my ideas, my writing, my typewriter ribbons. Don't let him get to you."

"If he tells me I'm beautiful, I'll thumb my nose at him," Laura promised.

"If he tells you you're beautiful, it'll be the first time I've ever heard him say something sensible," Seth countered, downshifting around a sharp curve in the road. "He lives in Beverly Hills. Or should I say, *beautiful* Beverly Hills."

All Laura knew about Beverly Hills was what she had seen on television, most particularly what she'd seen as a child watching *The Beverly Hillbillies*. " 'Swimming pools, movie stars,' " she intoned, quoting from the series' theme song.

"Something like that," Seth concurred with a chuckle.

Laura didn't notice any swimming pools as they entered the exclusive enclave nestled within Los Angeles and cruised down a broad boulevard lined with towering palm trees. She assumed that the swimming pools were behind the houses, out of view. The houses themselves were predominantly white stucco, with red Spanish tile roofs. They were unabashedly huge, oppressively opulent. She much preferred Seth's community to the neatly manicured lawns and massive homes past which they were driving now.

"Where are all the people?" she asked. It suddenly occurred to her why the neighborhood looked so stark. Not a pedestrian was in sight.

"There they are," Seth said, pointing to a slow-moving bus with huge tinted windows. "Taking the tour, looking for stars. Hello!" he hollered, waving wildly at the tourists in the bus. "Go ahead, Laura, wave at them. They'll think you're famous."

Laughing, Laura complied.

Seth steered onto a circular driveway in front of one of the Spanish-style houses, coasting to a halt by the oak double doors. "This shouldn't take long," he predicted as he gathered up his file and swung his legs out of the car. Laura got out, too, and accompanied him to the front door.

A young woman uniformed in a black dress and white pinafore answered their knock. "Yes?" she said automatically, then smiled at Seth in recognition. "Ah, Señor Stone," she welcomed him with a heavy Spanish accent. "You are expected."

"Pretentious, huh?" Seth whispered as he followed Laura and the maid into a tiled foyer that was easily as large as Laura's entire apartment.

A silver-haired gentleman in a silk bathrobe appeared from a broad hallway, a long black cigarette in one hand, a cup of coffee in the other. "Hello," he hailed them, smiling broadly. "Early for you, Seth, isn't it? And who is this beautiful lady?"

Seth gave Laura a subtle poke in the ribs, and she stifled the reflex to giggle at Zeke's choice of adjective. "Laura, meet Zeke Montgomery, Ax Man's alter ego. Zeke, an old friend of mine, Laura Brodie."

"Old? I'd hardly call her 'old,'" Zeke gushed, handing his cup to the maid and taking Laura's hand. "It's a pleasure, Laura. Can I get you something?"

She considered his question cryptic, but thought it best not to ask for clarification. "No, thank you," she said.

"You've caught me with my croissants down, I'm afraid," he apologized, gesturing at his robe. "But we're scheduled to shoot the Jacuzzi scene in an hour, so I'm glad you got here when you did." He released Laura's hand to accept the folder from Seth. He thumbed through the pages without reading them. "Did you come up with a solution for Miss Prissy?" he asked Seth.

"Yeah," Seth replied. "I have her spot Lance through the window, do a fantasy trip and pull off her bikini while she's spying on him. It's pretty steamy, Zeke, but the motivation is there."

"Beautiful." Zeke took the folder back from Seth. "As long as we get her down to the bare essentials. Motivation," he huffed, shooting a glance at Laura, as if he expected to find an ally in her. "These prima donnas take one acting class, and they think they've got to play every role as if it were written by Chekhov."

"Well." Seth took Laura's hand and angled his head toward the door. "I've got to take Laura around to see the sights. This is her first time in our part of the world, so..."

"Don't let me keep you," Zeke said graciously, indicating with a flick of his hand that the maid should escort them out. "I'll be in touch if I need more from you, Seth. But this will probably do the trick with Darla. It sounds beautiful. Thanks for smoothing the waters—if such a phrase is applicable in the context of a Jacuzzi." He laughed hard at his own joke, and Laura was exceedingly happy to be ushered out of the house.

"Yuck," she groaned once the oak double doors were shut behind them. "What a sleaze."

"It's mostly affectation," Seth said, defending the director. "The guy comes on pretty strong, but he does good work. Always gets his pictures in on time and underbudget, which goes a long way in the business." He opened the car door for Laura, then jogged around to take the wheel. "Onward," he said, igniting the engine. "You haven't lived until you've seen Rodeo Drive."

"What's Rodeo Drive?" Laura asked.

"It's something you haven't lived until you've seen."

He turned down another boulevard lined with palm trees. Or maybe it was the same one they'd driven on before—Laura couldn't tell. "It certainly is white here," she mumbled.

"Are we speaking architecturally or racially?"

"Both, I imagine."

Seth chuckled, then turned another corner. "This is Rodeo Drive. The most expensive shops in the world. I'm amazed they don't make you pay to drive on the street."

Laura stared out the window at the exclusive shops and boutiques. Rolls Royces and Jaguars were parked along the curb, and the pedestrians—at last Laura saw people actually walking on the sidewalks—were to a person tall, thin and gorgeous. She ought to have been put off by the sight, but she was too amused by the glitter and affluence on display. "Hey!" She sat taller and stared at an extraordinarily blond woman entering a jewelry store. "Wasn't that that actress—you know, the blond one?"

"What blond one? They're all blond ones," Seth quipped.

"The one from *Charlie's Angels.*"

Seth gave her a mocking look. "Don't tell me you're a *Charlie's Angels* fan!"

"Oops!" Laura laughed. "My dirty secret is out. I'm not a big fan of cop shows, but give me a cop show where three women get to do all the derring-do, and I'm a sucker for it."

"Laura, there are dimensions to you that I've never even suspected."

"Enough!" she protested, sitting back in her seat and succumbing to more laughter. "Okay. I've seen Rodeo Drive. Now I've lived."

Seth accelerated. "Next stop, Watts. From the sublime to the ridiculous, or vice-versa."

Watts was nothing like the slums Laura was used to back East. Although the houses were small and rundown, they *were* houses, complete with yards, grass and fences. Compared to the dreary tenements crowding the poor neighborhoods of most eastern cities, Watts struck Laura as a reasonably cheerful place.

Right in the midst of the neighborhood stood the towers, a pocket park decorated with bizarre sculptures and spires composed of refuse: broken bottles, scraps of metal, seashells, a society's discards welded together with cement and shaped into benches, bridges and soaring cone-shaped towers. "Incredible," Laura murmured in awe as she and Seth wandered through the tiny park and examined the colorful structures.

"See?" Seth ducked under a graceful span, pulling Laura behind him into one of the open towers. "Great works of art can be created from trash."

Laura understood Seth's unspoken message—that he, too, might be creating artistic screenplays even though they were trashy. But she derived another message from the magnificent towers and from the explanatory pamphlet she had obtained at the entrance gate to the park. "The man who built all this may have been a crackpot, Seth, but what a dreamer! He spent the better part of his life turning his dream into a reality. It wasn't practical. It wasn't reasonable—it was probably dangerous. But he didn't give up. He held on to his dream and made it come true. That's what makes this place so wonderful, Seth."

Seth studied her, his eyes hidden behind his sunglasses, his expression inscrutable. But she knew her comment had struck home. "The guy had a dream, sure," he granted. "He also had talent. . . ."

"So do you."

Seth turned away, then craned his neck to view the looming peak of the tower in which they were standing. The multicolored concrete girders climbing to the sky dwarfed him, giving him an almost slight appearance.

Laura had intended her statement as a compliment, but she knew he hadn't taken it as one. She moved closer to him and wrapped her arms around his waist, hugging him from behind. "Poor Seth," she whispered. "This'll teach you to invite your conscience for a visit."

He rotated within her arms to face her. "Is that what you are? My conscience?"

"I'm your friend," she swore. "Is it the same thing?"

"Damned close," he admitted. He struggled with his thoughts for a moment, then said, "It isn't like I never tried, you know. I've got a drawerful of Watts Towers in my office at home, but nobody wanted them. Maybe I haven't got the kind of talent it takes."

"Or maybe the people who didn't want them were nobodies, just as you said."

He laughed wistfully. "How can you be good and bad for my ego at the same time?"

"I'm your friend," Laura repeated.

"Yeah." He gazed past her for a long, silent minute, then brightened. "Let's go step on some stars," he suggested.

"Stepping on stars," Laura quickly learned, meant walking on Hollywood Boulevard and literally stepping on the star-shaped implants paved into the sidewalk to honor Hollywood's luminaries. Seth took this part of the tour to heart, bowing to the stars that bore the names of performers he admired and stomping on those he abhorred. "This guy was an A-1 fink during the blacklisting," Seth muttered, scuffing his sandal across one star. "Now this one's politically sound," he went on, carefully skirting another star rather than treading on it.

"Isn't one of these drugstores where that actress was discovered?" Laura asked.

"Lana Turner? You're thinking of Schwab's," Seth informed her. "How come you want to see that? Would you like to perch on one of the stools and wait for a talent scout to discover you?"

"I doubt I'd make much of an impression," Laura conceded with a laugh.

"Don't belittle yourself. You're going to be on TV tonight."

"Tonight?"

"Tonight's the night *Evening Potpourri* is broadcasting the piece on the *Dream* party," he reminded her.

Laura smacked her forehead lightly with her hand, as if to jar her memory. "Is that tonight? Oh, Seth—make sure I call Rita so she won't forget to turn it on."

He checked his wristwatch. "It'll be on back East three hours ahead of us. We'll give her a call around three."

They stopped for lunch in Malibu at a restaurant built on the end of a pier. Through the broad windows Laura could watch the beachcombers and sun worshippers gathering on the clean white sand. It took some effort to remember that April hadn't yet begun. Yet watching the golden-skinned bodies of the frolickers on the beach caused her a twinge of envy. She'd spent enough of her life in northern New York State to have been disabused of the notion that blizzards were pretty. To live in Southern California, where it was balmy all year, where one could cruise along winding canyon roads and step on stars whenever the urge struck, might not be such a terrible thing.

As soon as they were seated, Seth spotted a waitress delivering to an adjacent table two festive-looking drinks embellished with tiny paper parasols. When the waitress approached him and Laura, he asked, "What's that drink they're having?"

"Piña coladas," the waitress informed him.

Seth turned to Laura. "You want one?"

She shook her head. "I don't think so."

"How about a strawberry daiquiri?" He peered up at the waitress. "Does a daiquiri come with an umbrella?"

"Sure, if you want one."

Seth glanced at Laura, who shook her head again. "I really don't want a drink," she declined. "It's too early for me. You can have a daiquiri yourself, if you want an umbrella."

"I'm not in a daiquiri mood," he complained. "Maybe a beer. What beers have you got?" he asked the waitress. She proceeded to rattle off a few brands, and Seth cut her off as soon as she mentioned Dos Equis. "I'll have one of those," he requested. "With an umbrella."

Suppressing a grin, the waitress departed. She returned shortly, carrying a brown beer bottle with a pink paper parasol protruding from its open neck, and a chilled glass mug. "Perfect!" Seth crowed.

"What's it perfect for?" Laura asked, amused.

Seth pulled the parasol from the bottle and took a swig of beer. Then he stood, circled the table to Laura's chair and planted the toothpick-thin stem of the parasol in the dense curls at the top of her head.

"Seth!" she protested, twisting beneath his hands. "What are you doing?"

"Experimenting," he answered blithely. "You've got the thickest hair I've ever seen. I want to see if it's thick enough to support an umbrella." He arranged her hair around the umbrella, then stepped back to appraise the effect. "Magnificent, Laura," he decided, resuming his seat. "Now you're set for all kinds of weather."

"Even if 'it never rains in Southern California,'" she joked, groping through her hair for the parasol and untangling it. She extended the parasol to him. "Here, you wear it."

"I haven't got enough hair."

"I noticed," she chided. "You ought to grow it back."

"Do you think so?" He ran his fingers through his cropped hair and shrugged. Then he pushed the parasol back to her. "It's for you," he insisted. "I get the beer and you get the frills."

Grinning, she wedged the parasol behind her ear, balancing the delicate pink rice-paper circle against her hair. "There. Doesn't that look better?"

Seth squinted thoughtfully. Then he smiled. "Actually, it looks gorgeous. Did I tell you I've got a thing about umbrellas? Remind me to show you my Mickey Mouse umbrellas when we get home."

"I'd love to see them," Laura confirmed. "Do you wear them in your hair?"

"One behind each ear," he explained, shaping his hands into circles and lifting them above his temples like Mouseketeer ears. Then he whistled the Mickey Mouse Club song. Convulsed in laughter, Laura had a hard time concentrating on the menu's listings when the waitress returned for their orders.

After lunch, Seth drove her to the area of Sunset Boulevard known as Sunset Strip. Dingy rock clubs and nightclubs bordered the curving sidewalks, which teemed with street life. "You want to see the grimy underbelly of the city?" Seth goaded her. "There are probably more hookers here per square foot than in all of Times Square."

"They look so young," Laura murmured sadly as Seth pointed out a couple of skinny girls loitering on a corner.

"They *are* young," Seth confirmed. "Runaways, mostly. Prepubescent waifs with stars in their eyes."

"What's being done for them?" Laura asked.

He shot her a wry look. "Uh—oh. I smell the blood of a social worker."

Laura refused to let him rile her. "It's pathetic, little children selling themselves that way. Somebody ought to help them."

"I don't mean to sound hard-hearted, Laura," Seth debated her, "but not all of us are geared to saving the unfortunates of the world."

"I wasn't talking about you," Laura said. "I was only speaking generally. Look at them." She spotted another girl, wearing fishnet stockings and gobs of makeup on her eyes, leaning against the outer wall of a record shop, her gaze following a pair of strutting T-shirted men as they walked past her. Her heart brimming with pity, Laura turned from the dismal sight and rummaged through the collection of tapes in the glove compartment. She found "Sergeant Pepper" and shoved it into the cassette deck. The familiar rock music, and especially "Lovely Rita, Meter Maid," quickly restored her spirits.

It was nearly four by the time they reached Seth's house, and he ordered Laura to telephone her daughter at once so Rita wouldn't miss the seven o'clock broadcast of *Evening*

Potpourri. Laura made herself comfortable in his office at his desk while he lounged on the reclining chair, and dialed the Gonzalez number. A girl's voice sounded through the wire. "Hello?"

"Courtney?" Laura guessed.

"This is," Courtney replied, using one of the baffling telephone locutions Rita and her friends had recently adopted.

"Hi, Courtney, it's Rita's mother. Is she there?"

"Oh, yeah. Sure. Hey, Rita?" She hollered so loudly Laura had to pull the receiver away from her ear. "It's your mom!"

Laura heard some muffled shrieks and laughter, and then her daughter's voice. "Ma? Is that you? Are you in California?"

"Of course I'm in California," Laura said with a laugh.

"Wow! Hey, Courtney, she's in California!" Rita announced to her friend. More shrieks and laughter ensued.

"Rita." Laura demanded her daughter's attention. "You can talk to Courtney when it's not costing a fortune a minute, okay? How have you been?"

"Fine, Ma. We gave each other pedicures today. You won't recognize my feet when you get home."

Laura suppressed a grimace. "Have you been good to Courtney's mother? No misbehaving?"

"Ma-a," Rita groaned.

"All right. I don't want to talk long, because at seven o'clock you're supposed to watch *Evening Potpourri*. Tonight's the night I'm going to be on."

"Wow! Okay, Ma. Is Seth going to be on, too?"

"Yes, Seth's going to be on."

"All right! How's it going with you two, anyway? Kissie-kissie?"

"None of your business, Ms. Buttinsky," Laura retorted, though she was smiling.

"Yeah, well, you know what they say. If you can't be good, be careful," Rita advised her mother. "Becky LoCaffio said if you get pregnant when you're too old, you can have a baby with three eyes or something."

"I don't even want to know why you and Becky LoCaffio happened to be discussing such a topic," Laura muttered. "But rest assured, Rita, I have no intention of giving birth to any three-eyed babies in the near future."

"That's a real relief, Ma, you know? Hey, Courtney, turn on *Evening Potpourri*! My ma's gonna be on! And Seth, too! Tell your brother he can stuff the Mets up his zit nose!"

Laura didn't bother to suppress her grimace this time; the imagery was simply too gross. "It's been charming talking to you," she grumbled once she was sure she had Rita's attention again.

"You, too, Ma. I helped Mrs. Gonzalez with the dishes this evening, okay?"

"Good for you."

"And tomorrow Courtney and I are gonna tweeze our eyebrows. I better go and watch the tube. I don't want to miss Seth."

"I'm sure you don't. Take care, honey. I miss you."

"I miss you, too. Bye!" The line went dead, and Laura hung up.

"So?" Seth called over from the chair. "How's Rita doing?"

"I'm not going to recognize her feet when I get home," Laura reported, then laughed. "She's doing fine. She can't wait to see you on TV."

Seth appeared surprised. "She can't wait to see *me*?"

"I think she has a crush on you, Seth."

"She does?" A pleased smile lit his face. "My very first groupie!"

"I highly doubt that," Laura scoffed, then bit her lip. Had she sounded too sharp, too jealous? Hoping to make amends, she stood and crossed to the door. "I tell you what. Why don't I cook you dinner tonight? I'm psyched to try out that microwave oven of yours."

SETH FINISHED ADJUSTING his VCR to tape the show and joined Laura on the couch in his basement den. He had watched *Evening Potpourri*, a video magazine, only a few times before, mostly by accident while he was running through the buttons on his cable box. But this was one show he intended to tape. For posterity, he contemplated with a self-deprecating laugh. For the same posterity as the file cabinets full of chest-thumping screenplays that no producer worth his salt would spit on.

He was in a reflective mood, thanks to the excellent Bordeaux he and Laura had shared over dinner and were finishing off now as they waited for the show to begin. Thanks, also, to the tour they'd taken of the city, to the pitiful sight of those underage prostitutes lining Sunset Strip like malnourished cattle at an auction. Thanks to what Laura had said about those girls and what she'd said about the crazed sculptor who had dreamed up Watts Towers.

Did she honestly expect Seth to write a script about teenage runaways? He could think of few themes more depressing—and besides, that particular sordid subject had been done to death in made-for-TV movies. If Seth were ever to write something Laura would approve of, it wouldn't be about prostitution. He'd never even talked to a prostitute. He couldn't imagine what went on in their minds.

There had been a time when he believed he *could* imagine what went on in the minds of ethnic street gangs, suburban racists, crass industrial polluters. He had been in his twenties then, full of hubris, ready to take on the world with his pen. But he knew that if he ever bothered to reread the scripts he'd written then, he'd be embarrassed by them. When you were young and foolish, you believed you could write about anything. He wanted to think he knew better now.

The television show's theme music began, and Laura tapped her wineglass to his. "Here's to the boob tube's latest stars," she joked. "I usually don't drink much, Seth, but I can't help thinking I ought to be drunk to watch this."

"Then go to it," he encouraged her, taking a sip of his own wine. He looped his arm around her shoulders and turned to the television. "He-e-ere's Connie," he boomed in a fair Ed McMahon imitation as Connie Simmons, the reporter who had attended the *Dream* party, appeared on the screen, positioned in front of the birthday cake.

"Oh, no! There's that photograph, in the background!" Laura hooted, pointing at the black-and-white photo of the six of them, young and grungy, hoisting Julianne into the air in front of the building where the basement office of *The Dream* had been located.

"'Enterprising students,'" Seth groaned, latching on to a phrase the reporter used in her introduction. "Was that what we were?"

"'Foolhardy' would be more like it," Laura commented. "Julianne looks fantastic, doesn't she?" For now Julianne was standing beside Connie, talking about *Dream*'s origins.

"Julianne's got class," Seth remarked.

"And it helps being tall. Tall people always look better on TV. You're going to look great, Seth."

His image appeared on the screen to prove Laura's claim. Posing in his mirror sunglasses, the collar of his white blazer turned up and his smile inexplicably wicked, Seth chatted amiably with the reporter. "That's right, screenplays," he told her. "One thing about *The Dream*—working on it taught me how to type."

Laura exploded in laughter. "Type? That's what you told her?"

"I can't deny that I said it," Seth confessed, waving toward the screen. "You just saw for yourself."

The next person Connie Simmons interviewed was Andrew. "I think it's fair to say that we're all essentially the same people we were back then," he declared. "The outer trappings may have changed, but I think we're all still dedicated, hard-working and idealistic. One learns to accommodate reality, but that doesn't mean one has to rearrange his soul."

"Once a professor, always a professor," Seth critiqued Andrew. "Leave it to Dr. Collins to make the rest of us sound like pea-brains."

"Here comes Kim," Laura said, silencing Seth. "Oh, God, she looks even better than Julianne."

"Kim has a habit of looking better than everyone," Seth pointed out. Laura nodded and leaned forward to listen.

"Journalism, public relations, speech writing. It's all connected," Kim was saying in her languorous Southern drawl. "If it weren't for my work on *The Dream*, I doubt I would have had the career I've had. It's all been one form or another of communication."

"Platitudes," Seth snorted.

"Shut up, pea-brain," Laura scolded him. "Let's watch Troy."

"Now there's a guy with guts. I thought I was dressed like a maniac, but look at him. Blue jeans and boots. *That's* class."

The reporter had just asked Troy about his decision to live in Canada. He seemed uneasy, shifting slightly and clutching a cup of punch in one hand and a lit cigarette in the other. "A lot of people moved to Canada in the late sixties and early seventies," he mumbled. "For a lot of different reasons. I'd rather not talk about it."

Seth sat up straighter. "I thought for sure they'd edit that out," he said. "I mean, he answered more discreetly than I would have, but still—it's not like he's recanting, saying he's sorry he dodged the draft."

"Maybe he isn't sorry," Laura posed.

"I'm sure he isn't. But that's not fashionable these days. It's in to be patriotic, you know."

"Maybe he's a patriotic Canadian," said Laura. Before Seth could respond, Laura appeared on the screen. She let out a pained cry. "I look like a blimp!"

"You look gorgeous," Seth consoled her, squeezing her shoulder. "Buck up, Goodyear."

Laura socked him in the arm, then turned back to the screen. She had been so nervous during her interview with Connie Simmons that she couldn't even remember what she had said, and she listened to the broadcast with curiosity. "I was never a great writer," she addressed the microphone. "But I always felt very strongly about my subjects. I think that's what social work is all about—making a profession out of feeling strongly about your subjects."

"Ugh. How pompous," she moaned.

"No, it's not," Seth said. He meant it, too. Laura had always felt strongly about things, and she still did. If any of them had managed to avoid 'rearranging their souls,' to borrow Andrew's phrase, it was Laura. Seth wondered whether she had even bothered to learn how to accommodate reality.

The show broke for a commercial, and Seth switched off his VCR with the remote control. He turned to Laura, who was staring at the television, her elbows on her knees and her head propped in her hands. "Would you like me to replay it?" he asked.

"Maybe later," she said pensively.

He tried to interpret her poignant smile, and the strange glow in her large, dark eyes. She didn't seem to be enjoying her TV stardom in the least. "You looked nothing like a blimp," he said, hoping to cheer her up. "You looked great."

"Don't humor me, Seth. I looked fat."

"You looked beautiful," he contradicted her, totally earnest. "You *look* beautiful. You were too skinny in college. Now you look..." Thinking about her having chosen his guest room to sleep in, he drifted off.

"I look what?" she pressed him.

His eyes pored over her. He wondered whether his longing was apparent. He hoped it wasn't. She obviously was too troubled by what they'd just viewed on TV to be receptive to the ideas simmering inside Seth. "What's really bothering you?" he asked. "It isn't just the way you looked on the show, is it?"

Maybe she *had* sensed his longing. Her dark gaze held his for a long moment, then shifted away. "Seth...I enjoyed using your microwave," she confessed.

Taken aback by her non sequitur, he scowled. "What does cooking have to do with anything?"

"Don't you see?" She sighed. "I have this image of myself—we all do. You're the fun-loving rascal. I'm the purist. When I lived on the commune, I learned to bake bread in a wood-burning oven. I rejected things like microwaves and Porsches. And...and now I feel like a hypocrite, because I really like those things. I like your car. And your oven. Maybe I'd even like your movies, if I ever saw one."

"I'm corrupting you," he apologized, though he was secretly pleased. If Laura could actually like such symbols of financial success, then maybe she didn't disapprove of him as much as he feared.

"No, Seth. You aren't corrupting me. You're just making me face certain things about myself."

He arched his arm around her and cushioned her head against his shoulder. "All you have to face is the fact that you're human. You're allowed to like cars and appliances—and even bad movies, if they're fun. It isn't a crime."

"What if I get spoiled? What if I never want to go back to the life I used to live?"

Actually, Seth found that possibility immensely appealing, but he treated Laura's question with the solemnity it deserved. "None of us can go back, Laura. We can only go forward."

"I know." She nestled deeper into his shoulder and captured his hand in hers. "Growing up is hard, isn't it," she mused philosophically.

"To paraphrase George Bernard Shaw, it's preferable to the alternative." He kissed her brow. "Growing up isn't so hard when you're in the company of friends."

"One friend in particular," she murmured, tightening her hold on his hand. She didn't say anything more.

Chapter Eight

"Anything else I can get you?" the clerk asked.

Seth surveyed the assorted items he had deposited on the counter: a yet-to-be-assembled kite shaped like a butterfly with rainbow-striped wings, a board game called Organized Crime, a Velcro dart board that you were supposed to throw Velcro balls at—things had changed a lot since the time Seth had purchased his Spiro Agnew dart board.

"That'll be all," Seth told the clerk. Reaching into the hip pocket of his jeans for his wallet, he spotted a glass fishbowl filled with old-fashioned metal kazoos. "Wait!" He halted the clerk before the young man could hit the Total button on the cash register. "I'll take two kazoos, too." He crossed to the fishbowl and pulled out a yellow one and a blue one. He tried them both out, testing their timbre as he carried them to the counter for the clerk to ring up. "Hmm," he grunted, handing the blue one to the clerk. "This one needs to be tuned."

The clerk laughed and punched a few more buttons on his cash register. "That'll be forty-three ninety-five."

"Ouch," Seth yelped, though he handed over his credit card without hesitation. "Why can't I ever walk into this store without spending a fortune?"

"Some people leave here without parting with a dime," the clerk told him. "I guess you're just one of the weak-willed ones."

Seth grinned at the clerk's good-natured reproach. After signing the receipt, he pocketed his wallet, gathered the bulging bag into his arms and left the toy store.

The afternoon was balmy and breezy. If tomorrow turned out to be like today, he and Laura would be able to take the kite down to a beach and fly it. He doubted that she would be interested in trying it out today. The way things were going, he'd be lucky if he could get her out of the La-Z-Boy for dinner.

The way things were going... He issued a silent curse and started up the Porsche. The way things *weren't* going was the way he had hoped they would go. He wasn't sure what he had expected from Laura's visit, but having her beg him to let her read some of his old film scripts wasn't it. They had argued about it throughout their late-morning breakfast, Seth assuring her that the scripts were boring and pedantic, Laura insisting that she wanted to read them, anyway. He had given in, dug the old scripts out of his file cabinet and left her ensconced in the recliner with the damned things heaped on her lap.

All right. She'd read them; she'd see for herself that Seth wasn't cut out for writing that kind of stuff. She would get off his case, play Organized Crime with him, or Velcro darts, and tomorrow they'd fly a kite. He hadn't invited her to California to give him a hard time.

"Liar," he muttered aloud. He had brought her to California for just that reason. He had invited her because he was drifting, his mooring all but lost, and he wanted her to drag him back to shore. If she had to give him a hard time to do it, those were the breaks.

The hitch was that she was drifting, too.

At a red light, he glanced to his left and stared at a café on the corner. It was a classic California fern bar—lots of glass, natural wood and hanging plants. He had been there several times on dates. The bartender on the premises happened to make one of the better strawberry daiquiris in this part of the universe.

There was a pay telephone at the rear of the café, next to the rest rooms. Seth could park, hop inside, give Troy a ring and ask his old buddy for advice.

Except what sort of advice would Troy give him? He would probably lecture Seth on phallic symbols and gun control and then admit that he was in as much of a bind as Seth was. Troy hadn't figured out how to construct a solid life for himself. And he'd never indicated that he was much of an expert when it came to matters of the heart. How could he possibly help Seth?

Better to drive straight home, Seth resolved as the light turned green and he gunned the Porsche's engine. Better to go home, where he would undoubtedly find Laura making a bonfire with his old scripts.

He steered away from the coast and into the hills, playing the gear stick with as much virtuosic flair as Rampal his flute. Perhaps tomorrow Seth would let Laura take a turn behind the wheel. She had already admitted that she liked his car. For someone who relied on the New York City subway system as her main mode of transportation, piloting a Porsche ought to be a real thrill.

He was surprised when Barney didn't come bounding through the brush in welcome at the sound of the car's tires crunching up the driveway. Shrugging, Seth braked, shut off the engine and rummaged through his parcel until he located the yellow kazoo. Wedging it between his teeth, he locked the car and entered the house. Inside the door, he paused and listened. Not a sound, neither Barney nor Laura.

He proceeded down the hall to his office and stopped at the open doorway. Barney was fast asleep on the rug beside the recliner, where Laura was still seated. She might have been asleep, as well; she sat motionless, her head at a funny angle against the leather upholstery, her gaze fastened to the window. The stack of scripts lay unopened on her knees.

He took a deep breath, then let loose with a fanfare through the kazoo: "Tootle-di-TOO, di-TOO!"

Laura and Barney jumped in unison. The dog peered up at Seth, whimpered drowsily and dropped his head to his paws, closing his eyes once more. He was used to Seth's grand entrances.

Laura, however, needed a little more time to recover. "Good God," she gasped, settling back into the chair and laughing. "You scared me. What is that thing?"

"A kazoo," he told her, marching into the room. "I got one for you, too, so we can do duets." He dumped the bag on his desk and groped inside it for the blue kazoo, which he presented to Laura.

She studied it intently, then put it in her mouth and blew on it. No sound emerged.

"You've got to vocalize into it," he instructed her, then lifted his own kazoo to his lips and hummed a few bars of "Lovely Rita, Meter Maid."

"Oh." She tried again, singing this time, and the kazoo emitted a nasal, cartoony melody. "Aha!" she exclaimed, clearly delighted. She hummed a little more into the kazoo and smiled at the sound. "I've always wanted to learn how to play a musical instrument."

Seth leaned against his desk and watched her expectantly. He didn't know what he was waiting for—some sort of transformation, a glimmer of prideful joy at her mastery of the kazoo? Her mood did seem to change, but not in a way he could have foreseen. She lowered the kazoo and turned her attention to the binders on her lap. Her eyes became strangely distant, an intriguing glow emanating from their profoundly dark irises. When she lifted her gaze to him, she was smiling tenuously. "Can we talk?" she asked solemnly.

Uh-oh. The boom was about to fall, and he braced himself by slumping into his swivel chair, removing his sunglasses and folding his hands docilely in his lap. "Shoot."

"These are wonderful. Especially the one about the black family in the white middle-class neighborhood," she said, tapping the top binder. "*Good Fences*. It's fantastic, Seth. There's so much of you in it."

"There is?" he joked, finding her reaction a bit extreme. "Where? I'm not black, and I'm not a closet racist."

"Yes, but the way you tell the story, Seth. It's so—so passionate."

"Passionate? There isn't a single nude scene in it."

"Seth, I'm being serious." She kicked down the footrest and stood, then glided across the room to him. "Seth, it's a beautiful story—they all are. I'm not using that word the way your director does. I mean, they're *beautiful*. I'm very grateful you shared them with me."

She was so earnest he couldn't make any more jokes. Her eyes still glowing, she slid her hands beneath his arms and urged him out of his chair. Then she gave him a warm hug.

His arms reflexively circled her, returning her embrace. "If everybody responded to my work the way you do, I'd be a very happy man," he murmured.

"If everybody had the chance to see a film like *Good Fences*," she claimed, her voice slightly muffled by the fabric of his shirt, "they'd respond the way I'm responding. Oh, Seth, reading it...it was like finding you again, finding the Seth I know and love. You just can't keep ignoring what's inside you."

"I don't ignore it," he contradicted quietly, running his hands soothingly up and down her back. "What's inside me is all this kazoo music just dying to get out."

"Seth." She drew back an inch, then cupped her hands around his cheeks so he was forced to look at her. "There's more in you than kazoo music, and you know it. There's kazoo music, and there are symphonies. You can do it all, Seth. You're wonderful."

She had never looked lovelier to him than she did then, her entire face radiating her certainty, her faith in him. Impulsively he bowed to kiss her, and she didn't stop him.

IF HE HADN'T KISSED HER, she would have kissed him. She had spent the past few hours reading his scripts, devouring them, falling in love with Seth.

Was it because he feared rejection that he had kept his finest work hidden in a bottom drawer of his file cabinet? Was it because he preferred to remain detached from his professional endeavors, putting as little of himself as possible into them, taking his money and running? Or was it because he honestly hadn't realized how superb his early scripts were?

More than just the screenplays themselves had transported Laura. She was overwhelmed by the discovery that Seth was everything she had always believed him to be, everything she had hoped. The writing had been rough in spots, some scenes too obvious, others too muddy. But the sentiments in them moved her deeply. Seth's soul was in those scripts, and seeing into his soul, experiencing the sheer goodness of it, exhilarated Laura.

Her mouth moved with his, her hunger growing as he pulled her more firmly to himself. "You know what we're doing, don't you?" he whispered when he finally slid his mouth from hers. His breath was uneven, his body obviously aroused.

She nodded.

"We don't have to if you don't want to."

"I want to," she said steadily. "Do you really think I came all this way just to sleep in your guest room?"

His mouth opened and then shut as he worked through his thoughts. "As a matter of fact, yeah, I was beginning to think that."

"Well, why didn't you say something, you ninny?" she scolded him. "Why did you take me to the guest room if you didn't want me to sleep there?"

"Because...because we're friends, Laura," he said soberly. "Because friends owe each other the right to make choices."

"All right, then," she whispered, pressing her lips to the warm hollow of his neck. "I'm making my choice."

He slid his hand beneath her chin and lifted her face to his, then peered into her eyes, as if to seek confirmation in their glittering depths. Apparently he found what he was looking for. A shy, enchantingly dimpled smile danced across his lips, and he clasped Laura's hand in his own and led her out of the office.

His bedroom was at the end of the hall. Like the other rooms, it was large and airy, the open windows allowing a gentle, fragrant breeze inside. He walked with Laura as far as the bed, then turned her to face him and kissed her brow. "Do you mind if I lay down a couple of ground rules first?"

Ground rules? She smiled nervously. If Seth was about to recite a few kinky preferences, she would be appalled, to say the least. "What sort of rules?" she asked.

"Once we hit the bed, I don't want you harassing me about my work."

"Why on earth do you think I'd do that?"

"You did it when I was on your bed," he reminded her, grinning. "It was a real turnoff. And frankly—" he brushed her lips with a light kiss "—I would like to remain as turned on as I am right now."

"I'll do my best on that score," Laura promised, mirroring his grin. "What's the next rule?"

"That we be careful. Out of respect for Rita, of course."

"Of course," Laura agreed. "I'd hate to have a three-eyed baby at this stage of my life."

"What?"

"Don't ask," Laura said with a laugh as she headed for the door. "I'll be right back."

She raced down the hall to the guest bedroom, trying to ignore the acceleration of her pulse, the heated expectation drumming through her body. She had anticipated this moment with Seth enough to have brought along her diaphragm, yet she had packed it inside an inner pocket of her suitcase, as if she were hedging her bets, unsure of whether she would actually use it.

As soon as she was ready she returned to his bedroom. He had already removed his shirt and shoes, but at her entrance he stopped undressing to give her his full attention. "Come here, lovely Laura," he murmured, extending his arms to her. She happily obeyed. He kissed her soundly, then smiled. "Do you believe in love at four thousand five hundred seventy-first sight?" he asked.

She trailed her fingers across the well-toned muscles of his chest. "As a matter of fact, I do," she admitted.

"Glad to hear it." He tugged her blouse free of her jeans and unbuttoned it. He seemed shocked to discover that she was naked beneath her blouse, but his surprise quickly dissolved into pleasure as he cupped his hands under the round, heavy swells of her breasts. "Flower child," he murmured.

"Hmm?"

"You aren't wearing a bra."

"Does that make me a flower child?" she questioned him, laughing. "I've never worn a bra. I guess you didn't notice that the first four thousand five hundred however many times you looked at me."

"For at least the first three thousand of those times, you didn't need one," he recalled. "You were pretty flat-chested in college."

"Do you think I need one now?"

"No," he said decisively, then chuckled. "Especially not right this minute." He bent to kiss the warm crevice between her breasts.

His kiss ignited them both, and within an instant, it seemed, they had disposed of the rest of their clothing and tumbled onto the bed. Laura had never been particularly taken by bulging muscles on a man, and she found Seth's lean, lanky build incredibly attractive. She wanted to touch him everywhere, to stroke his streamlined muscles and hard flesh. Her hands moved insatiably across his body, savoring its sleek, firm lines.

He reciprocated, his fingers roaming over her breasts, along her slender waist, around the feminine softness of her bottom and thighs. "Did I happen to mention that I find you beautiful?" he asked, reaching as far as the crease behind one knee and tickling it.

She moaned softly, bending her leg around his hand to hold it in place. "I don't remember. You might mention it again."

"You're beautiful," he obliged, the words drifting across her skin on a gust of breath as he slid his lips down her throat to her collarbone.

"So are you," she complimented him. Her voice dissolved into another moan as his mouth ventured lower, skirting the full flesh of her breast before centering on her nipple.

"We're all beautiful people out here," he joked.

"No..." She drew in an erratic breath as her entire nervous system responded to the assault of his tongue. "You're different, Seth. Don't lump yourself with all the others. You're unique." His mouth roved to the other breast, and she twisted to accommodate him. Her hand rounded the broad ridge of his shoulder and stroked his back. "You have a gorgeous body."

He lifted his head to gaze down at her. "Do you think so?"

"I wouldn't have said it if I didn't."

He nodded, acknowledging that, whatever else Laura was, she was always brutally honest. "According to the statistics, I'm supposed to be past my prime," he pointed out, grinning wickedly.

"You've always been one to flout tradition," she parried. "I bet you aren't past your prime at all."

"An interesting bet," he mused, rising beside her and pressing his lips to hers. He nibbled tenderly at her lower lip, and his hand rose from the back of her leg to tangle in the mound of hair between her thighs. "A very interesting bet, but I don't think I'm going to take you up on it," he whispered.

"Please don't," she breathed, moving urgently against his hand. What little patience she had burned away beneath his provocative caresses, and she drew him onto her, demanding him.

He bound himself to her, then paused to catch his breath. His eyes bore down into hers, and she basked in their luminescence, their glittering array of color. She studied the dimples lining his cheeks, the brilliance of his smile, the tightness in his jaw as he struggled for control. "I was thinking—" he began, and then his voice broke off as his tension increased perceptibly.

"About what?"

He issued a shaky laugh. "About flying a kite with you."

"A kite?" she asked, bewildered.

"This afternoon." He inhaled sharply as his body reacted to the involuntary rocking motion of her hips. "I bought a kite, and I thought we'd..." He groaned, nearly surrendering. Shoring up his willpower, he inhaled again and continued. "I thought we'd fly it down on the beach this afternoon."

"Is that what you'd rather be doing right now?" Laura asked with a teasing smile.

His body answered for him, surging within her, succumbing to the longing that encompassed them both. He enveloped her, filled her, simultaneously giving and taking, following and leading.

She closed her eyes as waves of delight spread through her, fluid and honey sweet, buoying her, carrying her to the edge of sensation and then beyond. For an immeasurable moment, she lost all consciousness of where she was, who she was, and then Seth drew her back to reality with the wrenching force of his own release.

A low, helpless groan rose from his throat as he sank onto her. Her hands floated consolingly up his back and into the silky blond hair at the nape of his neck. His lips brushed her temple and he exhaled. "It was better than I expected," he whispered.

"Oh?" She drew back so she could view him. His face reflected exhaustion and utter contentment. "What did you expect?"

"Something wonderful," he answered. "But nothing *this* wonderful. I didn't know...I didn't think it was possible...."

His extravagant words elated her. She, too, hadn't known that it was possible to love someone so fully. She had loved Neil, but that had been so long ago, and she'd been so young. It was nothing like what she felt now, lying in Seth's arms, gazing up into his shimmering eyes and reading in them his resplendent satisfaction.

Then she noticed a change in his expression, a faltering, a flicker of doubt. "What, Seth?" she asked anxiously. "What's wrong?"

Brushing her hair back from her cheek, he wrestled with a pensive smile, then forced out the words. "I'm not—Laura, I don't know whether you were making love with the guy who wrote *Good Fences* or with *me*, the guy who wrote *Ax Man Cuts Both Ways*."

He looked so somber, so unnecessarily insecure, that Laura felt the need to make light of his remark. "You wrote *Ax Man Cuts Both Ways*?" she gasped with pretended horror. "I must be in the wrong bed!"

His smile widened only the slightest bit. "That's what I'm wondering," he confessed.

His worry was so genuine that she couldn't make any more jokes about it. It pained her to think that she could have undermined his confidence in himself.

Yet hadn't she? Wasn't that just like her, coming on so positively, behaving holier-than-thou, impugning his work while availing herself of the fruits of his labor, his oven, his car, the airline ticket that had brought her to him? She had been a hypocrite, afraid to admit that she loved him until she had read his old scripts and found in them the justification for her love.

She suddenly felt awful. She eased out from under him and rolled onto her side, staring at the window, abashed. "Why do you put up with me, Seth?" she groaned. "I'm so insufferably—"

"Braless," he completed. "I'm a sucker for jiggling jugs."

She shrieked at his deliberately crass phrase and tried to punch him. He easily caught her hand and pinned her to the bed below him. Staring up into his humor-filled eyes, she surrendered with a reluctant laugh. "You're disgusting, Stoned."

"And you love it," he goaded her.

"I wouldn't go that far." She attempted to look disappointed in him. "It's no wonder you write junk like *Coed Summer*. 'Jiggling jugs,'" she sniffed.

He scowled. She could sense his subtle withdrawal from her, and she wished she could retract what she'd said, specifically the word "junk." She had only been ribbing him, after all.

But she couldn't blame him for taking such teasing to heart. Most of the time, when she was criticizing his work, she wasn't ribbing him at all. "Am I harassing you?" she asked timidly.

"You're walking a fine line, Brodie."

She would salvage the moment. She had to. She loved Seth, and she had to restore his confidence. Managing a natural-looking smile, she swung off the bed.

"Hey—I didn't mean—"

"I'll be right back," she promised him, scampering out of the room. She dashed down the hall to his office, lifted *Good Fences* from the pile she'd left on the recliner and hastened back to his bedroom. She tossed the script onto the bed and climbed on beside Seth. "Read it," she ordered him.

"This minute?"

"Yes."

He sat and eyed her dubiously. "You sure you wouldn't rather fly a kite on the beach?"

"Read it, Stoned," she said sternly, placing the binder on his knees and opening it to the first page for him.

"Is there going to be a surprise quiz when I'm done?" he asked. At her glower, he smiled meekly and lowered his eyes to the script.

Laura curled up on the mattress, rested her head on Seth's shoulder and watched while he read. She wasn't bored; in fact, she could think of nothing she would rather be doing.

Even if Seth were sleeping she would enjoy lying beside him, admiring his physique, contemplating the shadowed contours of his smooth chest, the sinewy shape of his calves, the play of dusk's half-light through his hair.

But more engrossing to her than the sight of his naked body was his studious composure as he read. From his rapt expression, she could tell that he hadn't looked at *Good Fences* for a long time, maybe not since some myopic producer had rejected it a decade ago. Every now and then his eyebrows would arch in amazement at a perfectly constructed speech, a turn of phrase, a vivid image. Every now and then he'd gnaw on his lower lip or wrinkle his nose in disgust. But his attention never flagged. He perused the script without a break, without a quibble.

It took him much less time to read it than it had taken Laura. When he was done, he folded the binder shut and set the manuscript on the night table. Then he turned to her and found her still watching him. He laughed. "If you thought that was fun, perhaps I can arrange for you to watch some paint dry tomorrow."

"Quit stalling," she chided him. "Tell me what you thought."

"You can see for yourself," he said wryly. "The thing moved me to tears."

If she'd had infinite faith in him before, she entertained a sliver of doubt now. "You don't think it's beautiful?"

"I think . . ." He reflected for a minute. "I think it's well done for what it is."

"And what is it?"

"An uncommercial property."

"What's uncommercial about it?" she persisted. "Explain it to me, Seth. I don't know much about the film business."

He rolled his eyes. "That's obvious," he muttered. "All right. It doesn't have any nude scenes, for one thing," he said, echoing his earlier comment about it. "Nowadays, if you can't score an R-rating, it's the kiss of death. There's no sex in this script, and no violence—"

"No violence?" she exclaimed. "What about the emotional violence the family endures? The cruel rejections, the phoniness of the supposedly liberal neighbors? What about the bigotry the kid experiences in school? That scene where he tries out for the basketball team and he isn't good, and his classmates taunt him and say all those horrible things to him, calling him 'Globetrotter' and all that? Seth, that's an incredibly violent scene!"

"Maybe to you and me and the three other people in the world who like subtlety," Seth maintained. "But let's be real, Laura. I couldn't sell this thing if there were a famine in L.A. and I stuffed slabs of steak between the pages."

She eyed the binder then Seth. "What would you have to do to it to make it sellable?" she asked.

He snorted. "Shred it, for starters."

She ignored his sarcastic assessment. "You'd have to rewrite it, sure. It's got some rough spots—even I could see that. But you're pretty much done with that *Ax Man* script, and I'm sure that's going to pay you enough to keep the Porsche in gasoline for a while. Why don't you fix up *Good Fences* and see what you can do with it? "Ten years is a long time—you said it yourself. Maybe things have changed since then. Maybe, now that you've built yourself a reputation, someone will be willing to take a chance on it."

"You think so, huh," he muttered.

Laura sensed that he was half-convinced. "I think so," she maintained.

Seth stared at her for a long while, as if absorbing her certainty. A tentative smile cracked his face. "It does have some good things going for it," he admitted.

Laura felt a thrill of triumph ripple through her, as arousing as anything she'd felt while they were making love.

And indeed, this was a kind of lovemaking, too. Making Seth confront himself and his talent, making him recognize his abilities, restoring his faith . . . they were as valid, as vital to her love for him, as anything else they might share. She wrapped her arms around him and gave him an exuberant kiss.

"Go to it, comrade," she exhorted him. "Save the world."

Chapter Nine

"I had an abortion."

Laura flinched. She stared at Sandra Miller, who was seated on the other side of the desk in the cramped cubicle that served as Laura's office. Sandra's baby was balanced precariously on her knee, leaning toward the desk and trying to swipe Laura's stapler. Sandra smiled anxiously. She looked far younger than her sixteen years, and for a brief moment Laura wanted to cry.

She didn't, however. To do so would be unprofessional. Not that Laura felt that one had to adhere strictly to the codes of professional behavior in every instance, but today, also seated in the crowded cubicle was Susan Trevor, the reporter Julianne had sent to write an essay on a day in the life of a typical New York City social worker and her clients. Laura had to maintain a calm facade in the presence of the scribbling journalist.

"I get it," she said to Sandra, forcing a smile. "It's April Fool's Day."

"Huh?" Sandra appeared befuddled. "Is it?"

Laura sighed, accepting the fact that Sandra's announcement hadn't been a joke. "Would you like to talk about what happened?" she asked.

"I don't know." Sandra shrugged, hoisting her baby higher on her lap. "You were on your vacation, see, and you know. Dennis came to call on me, and he has this way about him, and he says, 'Get an abortion.' So I did it."

"It was your boyfriend's idea, then?" Laura confirmed, jotting a note into the file folder spread open before her on the desk.

"Yeah. I guess he was right. I mean, what am I gonna do with two of his babies when I can't even get him to help me out with one? So I did it."

"How do you feel?" Laura asked.

"You mean, like how do I *feel*?" Sandra shrugged again. "Okay, I guess. It didn't hurt too much or nothing. I mean, it hurt a little, you know? But it's all over now. The doctor, The doctor, he said I was okay."

Laura lowered her gaze to the folder. "Why didn't you tell Mrs. Sprinks?" she asked, naming the social worker who had covered for her while she was away. "She didn't leave me any information about this."

"I don't know. I figured, who is she? Just some strange lady. I wasn't gonna talk to her about it." Sandra angled her head slightly as she measured Laura's reaction. "I thought you'd be glad, Miss Brodie. I mean, like you said, I got to take responsibility and all. I thought the new baby, well, it would mean a bigger check from the welfare, but Dennis, I thought he was talking sense."

"You thought he was talking sense when he insisted on 'pure' sex," Laura snapped, then took a deep breath to compose herself. "We discussed the idea of an abortion the last time I saw you, Sandra," she reminded the girl. "You were dead set against it."

"Well, you don't know Dennis. You don't know how he can be. I mean, he started talking sense," Sandra said, justifying herself. "I thought you'd be glad."

"What would make me glad," Laura said grittily, "is if you would start taking responsibility for yourself, Sandra. You've got to stop doing everything Dennis tells you to do. You've got to think for yourself. Having an abortion is a very big decision, and one you'll be living with for the rest of your life. All I can say is, I hope you made the right choice." She suppressed the urge to shudder, and offered a limp smile. "Did you write up your budget for this week?"

Sandra handed over the budget she had prepared. Many of Laura's clients had little notion of how to run a household, let alone run one on the skimpy allowance welfare provided. One of Laura's duties was to help them organize their finances. This was an area in which she frequently had major disagreements with her clients; she found it difficult to understand why they would rather spend their meager funds on cosmetics and record albums than on rent and utilities.

Sandra was fairly disciplined when it came to budgeting, though, and as Laura reviewed the figures in front of her, she let her mind drift. She suffered a transient pang of guilt for having been in California when Sandra obviously would have benefited from having Laura to talk to. But she didn't dwell on it. She had earned the time away from work. She simply wasn't going to shoulder Sandra's traumas.

Still, a vague anxiety continued to eat at her, even after she'd finished her session with Sandra and updated the file. It saddened her to think that her client was raising one child and aborting another when she ought to be attending high school, giggling, getting crushes on boys, watching MTV. She ought to be living a life like Rita's.

If Seth were around, he would tell Laura to stop worrying about trying to save the world—and he would probably be right. She couldn't help all the people all the time. Maybe it was enough to know that she did help Sandra some of the time, that Sandra's life was better for having known Laura.

But Sandra alone wasn't the cause of Laura's uneasiness. Nor was it the presence of Susan, who seemed like an intelligent, pleasant young woman. What was bothering Laura was the understanding that she didn't want to be sitting in her office in downtown Brooklyn, helping Sandra, at all. She wanted to be back in California.

She missed the summery weather, the fresh, dry air, the tangy desert aromas of Topanga Canyon. She missed the sight of people lolling on the beach in bathing suits at the end of March. She missed the statuesque palm trees of Beverly Hills and the luxury cars on Rodeo Drive, the restaurants with their strange sandwiches concocted out of mashed avocado, alfalfa sprouts and cream cheese on seven-grain bread. She missed sprinting with Barney up and down the driveway and test-driving the powerful Porsche.

She missed Seth.

She was a fool to have fallen in love with him, knowing that at the end of the week she would have to return to New York. Friendship could endure over three thousand miles, just as it could endure over fifteen years. But love...

"I'm sorry," Susan was saying, and Laura dragged her attention back to the journalist. Sandra had just left the office, and Susan apparently felt free to express her opinion. "I have to agree with your client. Why wouldn't you be delighted that she's had an abortion? It's one less unwanted child in the world, right?"

Laura shoved her chair back from the desk and stood to return the file to its drawer. "My personal views on abortion don't belong in your article," she claimed. "Abortion is a fact of life for my clients, and that's how I deal with it. I suppose it's good when a client has an abortion for the right reasons, just as it's good when a client decides to keep her baby for the right reasons. But the truth is, clients who do things for the right reasons are few and far between in this office."

"What would you do if Rita got pregnant?" Susan asked. She had spent the entire day with Laura, and over lunch she had gathered some personal information about her subject, including the fact that Laura had a daughter. "Off the record, of course."

"Off the record? I'd kill her," Laura declared, then laughed. Susan laughed, too. "No, I wouldn't kill her," Laura said unnecessarily. "I would hope that she had become pregnant by choice, that she wanted the baby, and that she was ready, willing and able to be a good mother to it." She pulled her purse from the bottom drawer of her desk, then locked the desk for the night. "Rita's a good girl. Then again, so is Sandra Miller. She's just confused."

"Rita or Sandra?" Susan asked.

Laura grinned sadly. "Both, I suppose."

"Aren't we all?" Susan mused. She slid her camera onto her shoulder by its strap and accompanied Laura out of the office. "Is it all right if I come again tomorrow? I feel as though I've barely scratched the surface today."

"Sure. Tomorrow I'll be making house calls, so wear good walking shoes. I usually see Sandra at her place, but she had insisted on making this extra appointment. Now I know why."

A brisk gust of wind tugged at Laura's corduroy blazer as she left the building, and she turned up her collar against the early evening chill. If she were in California, she wouldn't be wearing the blazer at all, or stockings. She loathed stockings.

When Susan offered her a lift home in her car, Laura gratefully accepted. At the moment she probably would have loathed the subway, too.

"Ms. Robinson told me you were in Los Angeles last week," Susan mentioned as she maneuvered through the dense traffic.

"That's right," Laura said. She had told Julianne she was going to be visiting Seth when Julianne had called her to set things up with the reporter.

"I love Southern California," Susan confessed. "I know New Yorkers aren't supposed to admit to that. I laughed through *Annie Hall*, but even so, Woody Allen was kind of unfair to that part of the country, don't you think?"

"Yes," Laura concurred. "I had never been there before, but I liked it." She wondered whether she would have liked it as much if she hadn't been with Seth, then decided that was irrelevant. Seth and Southern California were incontrovertibly linked in her mind.

"My roommate in college came from Santa Cruz," Susan went on. "I visited her family out there a couple of times. It's a gorgeous part of the state, not far from Big Sur. Did you get that far north?"

"No."

"You ought to see it next time you go to California," Susan suggested.

If there is a next time, Laura responded silently, then remonstrated with herself for thinking so negatively. Why wouldn't there be a next time?

Because Seth hadn't called her since she'd left three days ago, that was why. Because, although she and Seth had had a wonderful time together, he had his own life out there, a very different life from Laura's. He had his career and his seven hundred starlets—a bevy of beautiful, compliant women who had no reason to harass him about his work. Surely he didn't want to have his conscience, in the person of Laura, harping on him at close range.

Her visit had entailed more than harping, of course. It had entailed some splendid times. One day they had driven, with Laura at the wheel, to a town called Solvang, the location of a restaurant reputed to have the best split-pea soup in the world. Not that Laura was wild about split-pea soup, but Seth had insisted that she consume a bowl of the stuff. Actually, she suspected that he had only been looking for an excuse to allow her to navigate his sports car on empty, out-of-the-way roads. The drive, she had to admit, had been far more exciting than the soup.

Another morning, they'd played catch with a football in Seth's driveway. Barney had romped back and forth between them, slobbering all over them and the ball. Keyed up by the game, Barney had then taken it upon himself to gallop into the underbrush surrounding Seth's house, sending Seth and Laura on a wild chase and giving Laura the opportunity to explore the region's flora in greater detail than she might have liked—particularly the shrubs that featured thorns. After their hectic chase, it had taken Seth nearly an hour to pull all the twigs and seeds from Laura's hair. "Just like those orangutans at the Prospect Park Zoo," he had observed, peppering his meticulous grooming of her hair with screeches and mugging and scratching beneath his arms. He'd completed his interpretation of orangutan behavior by pretending to discover in Laura's snarled tresses an array of insects, which he popped into his mouth, just as the orangutans had done when they'd groomed each other at the zoo. "Mmm! Lip-smacking good!" he'd squawked as Laura erupted in laughter. "Love them beetles!"

Yet another day, they'd taken the kite he had bought down to the beach and lofted it. Its rainbow-hued butterfly wings had cut daringly across the sun, and she and Seth had raced the length of the beach again and again, until they were both winded. Then they'd collapsed on the sand, and

Laura had griped about how the passage of years had destroyed her stamina. Seth had boasted that his stamina was as strong as ever, and had attempted to prove his claim by rolling onto her and showering her face with kisses. If it hadn't been for the few other beachcombers present, Laura was certain that he would have made love to her right there, beneath the warm California sky.

But Seth didn't really need Laura. He could play ball with Barney whether or not Laura was with him. He could take drives, eat pea soup and fly kites. He could have a healthy sex life without her, she was certain.

If he truly felt strongly about her, he would have called by now. He had called her often before she went to California; his failure to contact her since her departure vexed her. She supposed she could call him, but Seth knew as well as she did that long-distance phone calls were an extravagance she would have difficulty accommodating. When he drove her to the airport to catch her flight back East, he had promised he would spare her the expense of telephoning him. "'Don't call us. We'll call you,'" he had quoted with a grin.

So why hadn't he called?

"That's my place, right by the fire hydrant," she said, pointing her building out to Susan. "I really appreciate the lift."

"No problem," Susan assured her. "Would you like me to pick you up tomorrow morning?"

Laura shook her head as she opened the passenger door. "I know I'm out of your way, and you'll have enough trouble fighting the rush-hour traffic. I'll meet you at my office."

"Okay. See you then," Susan said, pulling away from the curb once Laura had shut the door.

Rita was seated on a kitchen counter, her legs hanging over the side and the telephone receiver pinned to her ear, when Laura entered the apartment. "No!" she was squealing into the phone. "Is he really? I'll die!"

Laura waved and hung her jacket in the coat closet. Not wishing to interrupt her daughter's conversation, she attempted to communicate in sign language that Rita shouldn't be sitting on the counter.

Rita deliberately ignored her, hooking one bare, gaudily pedicured foot under the other thigh and clutching the receiver. "Like, how fat are we talking? *Fat* fat? Or just a little chubby-cheeks fat?"

Laura lifted Rita's dangling leg to get to the silverware drawer. As usual, it was stuck. Rita squirmed, trying to give her mother some room to yank the drawer.

"A lardo, huh," Rita said glumly. She pulled on one of her brassy hexagonal earrings and sighed. "Maybe I should forget about him. You know who's really cute? This guy Jim Morrison. He's this awesome fox who used to sing with that old band the Doors. Only he's dead... Who said that? Becky LoCaffio? She's a slime. Oh, yuck. Guess what?" Rita reported into the phone. "My ma just pulled this thing out of the fridge for dinner. It's got lentils in it." She covered the mouthpiece with her hand and said to Laura, "Courtney says lentils are gross."

"Then tell Courtney she isn't invited for dinner tonight," Laura replied, sliding the casserole dish into the oven to heat and then preparing a salad.

Back into the phone, Rita said, "I better get off. Ma is making one of her healthy meals. I might just gag. Later, Courtney." She hung up the telephone, jumped off the counter and pouted. "You know what she told me? She said they had this special on MTV with the Monkees, and Mickey Dolenz is fat."

"We can't all age gracefully," Laura said, nostalgically recalling the slender figure she had boasted in her youth.

"Yeah, so I was thinking. You know Jim Morrison from the Doors?"

"He's dead," Laura remarked. "It's better to be fat than dead, don't you think?"

"Becky LoCaffio said maybe he isn't dead," Rita told her, sliding two paper napkins from their package and carrying them to the table. "She said some people think he's just pretending to be dead and he's actually living in France or something. But she's an idiot. You can't believe half of what she says. So how was work today?"

"All right," Laura said laconically. She didn't want to trouble Rita by telling her how upset she was about Sandra Miller.

"How did it go with the reporter?"

"It went well. Susan's a nice woman."

"Did you tell her about Seth?"

"Of course not." Laura wrenched a chunk of lettuce from the head and tore it with near violence into the salad bowl. It was hard enough trying not to think about him without having Rita mentioning his name every chance she got.

"I bet she'd be impressed. I bet she'd write something in her article about how you spent a week with a guy who writes movies."

"That's not what the article is going to be about, Rita." Laura sighed, then managed a smile. "How was school?"

"The usual. Do you think Seth will call tonight?"

"Not if you keep tying up the phone," Laura pointed out.

"I won't, I promise." She pulled two plates from an upper cabinet and set them on the table. "I hope he calls."

"So do I," Laura said before she could stop herself. Her eyes met Rita's for a brief instant, and then she averted her gaze. She could hide her frustration about her work from her daughter, but not everything.

Rita approached her mother from behind and gave her a bracing hug. "You'll see, Ma. He'll call. He's a good guy."

"I love you, Rita," Laura whispered, feeling her eyes grow moist. Sometimes Rita drove Laura insane, but...if only every mother were blessed with a daughter like her, Laura knew the world wouldn't be in such dire need of saving.

"IN TOWN? Now?"

"For a few more hours," said Andrew. "I was here to take care of some business, and I finished earlier than I expected. I thought maybe we could meet for lunch before I have to catch the red-eye back to Boston. Although I imagine it's kind of late for lunch by now..."

"That's okay," Seth assured him, clicking off his typewriter. "I haven't eaten. Where are you?"

"At the Best Western in West Hollywood. Do you know where that is?"

"It's only minutes away," said Seth.

"How many minutes?"

Seth laughed. Leave it to Andrew to demand a precise answer. "Beats me. If I don't show in a half-hour, give up."

"One half-hour," Andrew repeated. "Should we synchronize our watches?"

"Skip the watches. Count seconds, Andrew—one-Mississippi, two-Mississippi, up to eighteen hundred. By the time you're done, I'll be there."

He dropped the receiver back into its cradle, surveyed the mess of papers on his desk and the half-completed page rolled into his typewriter and shook his head. Andrew's call, as unexpected as it was, couldn't have come at a better time. Seth needed to get out for a while.

Standing, he shook his head again, trying to clear the fog from his brain. What time was it? What day? He definitely had to take a break.

He was out the front door before he realized that he didn't have on any shoes. And he wouldn't have realized that if Barney hadn't bounded gleefully through the shrubs and drooled all over his bare feet. "Sorry, pal," he muttered, retreating from Barney's exuberant greeting and sending him back into the yard with a friendly whack on the rump. Seth hadn't been giving Barney the usual amount of attention, and while Barney had been reasonably good-natured about having to fend for himself, he wasn't going to put up with such neglect forever. "Be grateful I'm still feeding you," Seth called after his dog, who had vanished around the side of the house. More than once since Laura had left, Seth had forgotten to feed himself.

He hurried back indoors to get his sandals from the bedroom closet and caught a glimpse of himself in the mirror above his bureau. He hadn't shaved since Laura left, either, and a thickening blond stubble decorated his jaw. What the hell, Seth consoled himself as he bolted from the house again. Andrew was an erstwhile beard man himself; he wouldn't object to Seth's ungroomed appearance.

Where had the time gone to? Where had Seth been? The hot wind rushing through the Porsche's open windows as he cruised along the twisting back roads reminded him that the world beyond his office still existed. He viewed the scenery with an alien fascination, as if it were something he'd never seen before.

The world still existed, filled with people. People like Darla Dupree, Zeke Montgomery and all the other clowns stupid enough to think that movies like *Ax Man Cuts Both Ways* mattered. People like Andrew, one of those lucky few who had their feet on the ground and their heads screwed on straight. People like Laura, who might not have her feet on the ground or her head screwed on straight, but who had heart and soul.

He would have to talk to her and tell her what he was doing. She would be so proud of him, so pleased. He had tried to call her once and gotten a busy signal, which he had decided to blame on Rita. Wasn't it true that teenage girls were always yakking on the telephone? A few other times, when his energy had petered out for the day and he'd put the typewriter to bed, Seth had considered phoning Laura, until he'd remembered the time. Lately he was working so obsessively that he often wasn't ready to call it quits until after midnight—much too late to call anyone, even without the three-hour time difference.

But he would call her soon. Now that Andrew had lured him away from his office for a couple of hours, perhaps Seth wouldn't be quite so compulsive about what he was doing. He wouldn't keep waiting until midnight before he withdrew enough from his work to think about Laura.

He arrived at the motel in under twenty minutes; even if he'd been living a hermit's existence for the past three days, he hadn't yet forgotten how to pilot his sports car like a pro. After parking, he jogged across the asphalt lot and into the impersonal lobby. He headed straight for the desk. "I'm supposed to meet someone who's staying here—Andrew Collins. *Dr.* Andrew Collins," he added because he liked the sound of it. He wondered whether Andrew was into his Ph.D. enough to register at a motel with his full title.

"Collins," the clerk echoed, scanning the register. He nodded, lifted his desk phone and rang Andrew's room. "There's a gentleman here to see you, Mr.—uh—Dr. Collins." Seth grinned.

The clerk had barely hung up, when Andrew strode into the lobby. Clad in pressed khaki slacks and a crisp cotton shirt, he looked appropriately collegiate as he crossed the room to Seth. "Seth! You're early. I was only up to fourteen-hundred-Mississippi."

Seth gripped his friend's hand in a robust soul shake. "Hey, man, it's really you! Why didn't you let me know you were going to be in town?"

"I would have, Seth," Andrew explained contritely. "But it was all planned at the last minute, and I'm out here for a ridiculously short time. I arrived yesterday afternoon, met a contact for dinner, met someone else this morning and I'm supposed to be back at the airport in two hours."

"I'm so glad you could squeeze me in," Seth mumbled with phony obsequiousness. "Two hours, huh. I don't know the hot spots in West Hollywood, but there's probably a McDonald's or something we could go to."

"The restaurant here isn't too bad," Andrew noted, pointing to the coffee shop off the lobby. "It isn't great, but in the interest of saving time..."

Seth eyed the glass-fronted eatery and shrugged. "I can tell just by looking at it that it must have gotten a three-star rating from Michelin. Have they got a liquor license?"

"Yes."

"My kind of place," Seth said agreeably, following Andrew into the restaurant.

They ordered hamburgers and Dos Equis beers. Waiting for his beer to arrive, Seth rubbed his jaw and smiled at the scratchy sound his beard made against the calloused surface of his thumb. He had made a serious effort to grow a beard once, in high school, but he had decided that the scraggly growth simply didn't suit him. Some guys looked good in beards, but Seth wasn't among them.

Andrew had looked good in his beard, but he looked better without it. He looked squarer, perhaps, more conservative, but, then, that could also be attributed to his neat attire and his shorter hair. Andrew was beginning to go gray, just a few strands at the temples, but enough to give him a nearly venerable appearance.

"So, tell me, Dr. Collins, what brings you to this part of the country?"

"What is this *Dr.* Collins stuff?" Andrew shot back. "You make me feel like I ought to be wearing a stethoscope around my neck."

"I'm impressed by you, that's all," said Seth. "You're a hotshot Amherst professor who covers six thousand miles in two days on business."

"You must travel a lot of miles on business, too," Andrew guessed.

Seth shook his head. "Not really. Occasionally I'll get shipped to some location for rewrites—if it's out of the state, it's usually Mexico, where production costs are cheaper. When I fly East it's almost always for pleasure." He thought for a moment of Laura, and of how much he'd like to fly East for the pleasure of being with her again. As soon as he was done, he promised himself. As soon as he had something he would be proud to show her.

The waitress arrived with their beers, and Seth lifted his mug in Andrew's direction. "A toast. Here's to your making more business trips to California."

"I sincerely hope not!" Andrew sipped from his mug, then smiled. "Not business trips, I mean. This sort of thing is exhausting. I had to cancel a bunch of classes to do it, and I've spent more time speaking Spanish in the past twenty-four hours than I did in four years of Spanish classes at Columbia."

"Hey, come on!" Seth protested. "I know some people think Southern California is like a foreign nation, but we do speak English here, most of us."

"Not the people I was meeting with."

"Chicanos?" Seth asked.

Andrew shook his head. "Salvadorans. I'm doing some research on El Salvador, and I was put in touch with a few refugees living here."

"Research, huh," Seth mused. The waitress delivered their hamburgers, and he reached for the bottle of ketchup on the table. "Are you going to write another book?"

"Maybe," Andrew replied noncommittally.

"If you do, tell me. I'll make sure all my friends buy a copy."

"If you made your friends read the books I write, I highly doubt that they'd be your friends for long," Andrew maintained with a modest smile. "I'm not looking to make the *New York Times* Best Seller list with my publications. Just trying to get tenure. Publish or perish, and all that."

"Tell me, Andrew," Seth ventured, genuinely curious. "When you're writing these publish-or-perish books, do you toe the line? Do you try to be objective, or do you push your own opinions?"

Andrew mulled over Seth's question. "I think . . . what I probably do is push my own opinions under the guise of objectivity," he conceded. "Of course, I'd like to think that my opinions are sound, based on an objective analysis of a given situation. But we all come from where we come from, Seth. I can't deny that I've got my biases."

"Same biases you had in '72?" Seth asked. "What's going on in El Salvador, anyway? I have trouble keeping up with all the global crises."

"It's depressing how many there are." Andrew chuckled. "In '72, I was much more concerned with Southeast Asia than with Central America. But my biases are probably the same. I still have a soft spot in my heart for such concepts as 'One man, One Vote'—although I suppose it ought to be 'One Person, One Vote.' Better yet, 'Power to the People.'"

"Once a fist-waving revolutionary, always a fist-waving revolutionary," Seth concluded. Regardless of his preppy clothes and his posh college affiliation, regardless of his eagerness to win tenure, Andrew obviously hadn't sold out. Seth wanted to believe that he remained as true to his principles as Andrew had. Today he had good cause to think he had.

Andrew seemed able to detect Seth's rejuvenated sense of himself. "Tell me what you've been up to," he demanded. "You're looking great."

"I am?" Seth guffawed. "I look like Rip Van Winkle." He took a hungry bite of his burger and tried to recall the last time he'd eaten. A stale cruller at his desk that morning, that was it. And coffee. Lots of coffee. He felt as if he'd been drinking coffee nonstop for three days.

"Are you working on a new film?" Andrew asked.

"Yeah." Seth took another bite, chewed and reconsidered his answer. "Not a new one, really. It's an old script I'm tearing apart and rewriting. I've got to tell you, Andrew, it's one of the most thrilling things I've ever done."

"Really? Another *Ax Man* opus?"

"No. I just finished one of those. This is different." He wondered whether his excitement about his reworking of *Good Fences* was apparent to Andrew, and then realized that it must be. Why else would Andrew have told him he was looking great? "This one's important, Andrew," he went on, energized by the mere thought of the excellent work he'd accomplished in the past few days. "It's about racism in the eighties. No barking dogs, no George Wallace barring the schoolhouse door. It's a human story, Andrew. Subtle. One of the subtlest things I've every written."

"You're really involved in it," Andrew stated.

"Involved in it? I'm drowning in it, man, and having the time of my life." He couldn't stifle his enthusiasm. "I've never felt so good about anything I've written before. I tell you, if this ever makes it to the screen—"

"If?" Andrew pounced on the word. "I thought you had the Midas touch out here in Hollywood, Seth. Don't tell me there's a chance this masterpiece *won't* make it to the screen."

"There is," Seth acknowledged. "And you know something? I don't care. I'm writing the damned thing, anyway. It's that important to me."

Andrew leaned back in his chair. The overhead light glanced off the lenses of his glasses, temporarily making his eyes invisible to Seth. He smiled enigmatically. "Who else is it important to?"

"Laura," Seth said automatically, then frowned. "How'd you guess?"

"It wasn't very hard." Andrew's smile expanded. "You look like someone in the throes of terminal passion, Seth. Possibly you're just feeling passionate about your current project, but I've known you a long time. I figured it was just as possible that someone special had inspired you to new heights." He took a sip of his beer. "Tell me about her, Seth. Tell me about this Laura. Is she one of your Hollywood nymphets?"

"Laura?" Seth almost choked on his sandwich. "No, yo-yo, it's *Laura*. Laura Brodie." As if there were no other Lauras in the world.

"Laura Brodie?" Now it was Andrew's turn to choke on his food. "From school?"

"Of course from school. She's turned me upside down—or maybe I should say, right side up. She's done wonders for me, Andrew. Made me rethink things, made me repent my sordid past. Gave me the courage to thumb my nose at psychopaths and Ninjas." He reached for his mug, fingered its smooth glass handle, ruminated. "It was great seeing everyone last month, Andrew. You and Troy and the ladies...."

Andrew nodded in agreement. "I've spent a lot of time worrying about Troy," he revealed. "It was reassuring to learn that he's made a fine go of it in Montreal. It's one thing to move away from home, but quite another to move to an entirely different country, a different culture. I'm glad he came to the party. I really wanted to see him. And Julianne, too. She's such a fine woman."

"And Kimberly," Seth added. "I didn't know thirty-five-year-old women could look that cute."

"Cute," Andrew snorted disdainfully. "Yes, she did look cute."

"Hey, I know you and she were never bosom buddies, Andrew, but give it a rest, man. Kim's done spectacularly with her life. She's tooling around in the halls of power, rubbing elbows with senators, and nary a hair out of place."

Andrew shrugged. "She was always good about maintaining appearances."

"It's more than appearances, and you know it."

Andrew pondered Seth's assertion, then relented with a shrug. "Okay. I'll admit she's doing better than I might have given her credit for."

"And looking better than any woman has a right to."

"If you're so madly in love with Laura, why are you so hung up on Kimberly's looks?" Andrew challenged Seth.

He grinned, unperturbed. "Kim's cute. Laura's beautiful," he distinguished. The mere mention of her name caused an infatuated smile to illuminate his face. "She believes in me, Andrew. She believes in my ability to write good things. I didn't believe in myself, but then she came and turned me around."

"Turned you right side up," Andrew corrected.

"That, too."

"Well, good for you. And good for her." He reflected for a minute, then grinned slyly. "Does this mean you're giving up on all the nymphets?"

"It might," Seth confessed, mirroring Andrew's smile. "Darla Dupree, queen of schlock, asked me out for last night, and I turned her down. Tell me what it means when you'd rather be shut up in your office, reworking a screenplay, than messing around with the likes of Darla Dupree."

"It means, you should have sent her over to the West Hollywood Best Western," Andrew scolded him. "I would have appreciated the company."

"I would have done just that," Seth insisted, "if I'd known you were in the neighborhood. Nah," he contradicted himself. "Darla isn't your type. A mental midget, if you'll forgive me for sounding like an intellectual snob. Darla has a lot going for her, but brains isn't it. You always were a brain man, Andrew."

"True enough." He checked his wristwatch and grimaced. "Much as I hate to eat and run... I do have a plane to catch."

"You old jet-setter, you," Seth taunted him. He groped for his wallet. "Let me cover this, okay? I feel bad that you didn't let me play host while you were in town."

"I'd rather put it on the motel bill," Andrew said, refusing Seth's offer. "This whole trip is being paid for by the organization that's funding my research."

"Generous organization," Seth observed. He himself had traveled on plenty of open-ended expense accounts, but he had always assumed that things were different in academia, where money was tight and every dime had to be accounted for.

"I'm not complaining," Andrew said. "They treat me well. May they only grease the wheels of the tenure machine. I'd feel a lot more secure about flaunting my oh-so-objective opinions if I knew I could count on having a job after I shot off my mouth."

"Job security isn't everything," Seth argued. For the first time since he'd begun making money as a script writer, he was laboring on a screenplay that came with no contract, no guarantees, no assurances. After sweating blood over it for weeks, he might have nothing more to show for it than a bouquet of "thanks, but no thanks" notes from every producer in town. He might never receive a cent in return for his efforts.

But he didn't care. More was at stake than money, and if he could earn Laura's respect, he would consider himself paid in full. If he could earn Laura's respect...and his own...

Even before finishing the script, he'd already rediscovered his self-respect. And for that he had to thank Laura.

Chapter Ten

The jolting ring of a telephone in the middle of the night was certain to frighten anyone, and Laura was no exception. She had been awakened by telephone calls numerous times before, but that was because she often collapsed into bed before ten o'clock, a habit Rita considered embarrassing, if not worse. But the last time someone had called Laura after midnight, it had been her mother, telling Laura that her father was dead. At times like that she thought wistfully of her life on the commune, where there were no phones bearing such mournful messages.

Her eyes struggled to make out the hands on the alarm clock by her bed: 2:30. The phone rang again, its shrill peal screeching along her nerve endings and causing her to shiver with dread. She sat up, gulped in a deep breath and reached for the phone. "Hello?" she whispered.

"Laura? Did I wake you up?"

Seth. A million emotions flooded her—relief and rage predominant among them. "What do you think?" she retorted. "Do you have any idea what time it is?"

"I know, I know," he mumbled, sounding not at all contrite. "It isn't exactly early here, either. But I've been snowed under, and it's all your fault, and I love you for it."

"What?"

"Listen," he said offensively exuberant. "I've been working on *Good Fences*. Do you remember it? About the racial problems in the middle-class town. I tore the thing to shreds, and I'm piecing it back together again. In the draft you read, Laura, I don't know if you remember it, but it had 'novice' written all over it. So what I did was, I cut down to the bare bones and figured out what it was I had here, and now I'm rebuilding the entire thing. For instance—" Through the wire she heard paper rustling "—in this new version, the basketball scene, remember, where Joshua tries out for the school team and all...I've moved that until later in the script, so it occurs closer to the climax. It gives the story a better shape. At least, I hope it does. And the block association scene, what I did there was—"

"Seth." Her joy at hearing from him gave way to anger. "Do you honestly think I want to be analyzing your script at two-thirty in the morning?"

"Umm..." He measured her tone. "I guess not, huh."

"A very good guess, Seth."

"Well, I'm sorry I didn't call you earlier, Laura, but I was on a roll here, really smoking on this thing. I'm excited about it, and I thought you would be, too."

"I would be, at a reasonable hour."

"Do you want me to call you back?" he asked, belatedly considerate.

"What for?" she grumbled. "I'm already awake." Her anger slowly dissipated, leaving room for joy to return. "What did you do with the block association scene?"

Seth laughed. "It's all your fault for living so far away, Laura," he complained. "If you were here, we could be discussing this like normal human beings."

"Well, I'm not there," Laura pointed out, wondering whether that fact disturbed Seth as much as it did her.

"Yeah. So why don't you come back?"

She smiled hesitantly. Did he want her to come back only because he needed her reliable criticism on his screenplay? Or for some other reason, some better reason? "You know, Seth, you could have called me sooner," she chided him. "You told me not to call you."

"I miss you," he said, ignoring her comment. "Why don't you come back?"

"I miss you, too," she confessed.

"Then it's settled. I'll arrange a ticket for you—"

"Seth, nothing's settled," she cut him off. "I can't keep doing disappearing acts at work. In fact, I shouldn't have done the last one. One of my clients was in big trouble and I wasn't there for her."

"Trouble? How big?"

Laura exhaled. She had gone to Sandra's apartment for her regular weekly visit that afternoon and found Sandra wallowing in despair. Dennis had said he was only joking, she told Laura between sobs, and he no longer wanted to have anything to do with a woman who would get rid of his child the way she had. Laura had tried to console Sandra with the observation that Dennis wasn't much of a caring father for the child she had already borne him, and suggested that he had merely been looking for an excuse to break off his relationship with Sandra. Privately Laura thought that Sandra would be much better off without Dennis in her life, but she knew she wouldn't be able to convince her heartbroken client of that.

It was too late at night for her to go into the whole sad story with Seth. Laura was too tired. If only he were with her, if only they could discuss it, as he said, like normal human beings....

Once more she was forced to acknowledge the futility of maintaining a relationship with him over such a long distance. He might think she could drop everything on a whim and fly out to see him again, but she couldn't.

"Earth to Laura, are you there?"

"I'm here," she answered. "Seth, it's just....my client is going through a rough time, and I feel so helpless about it."

This time the silence was on Seth's end. Finally he spoke, his voice steady and calm. "You stay there. I'll come."

"What?"

"All I need to know is, have you got a typewriter?"

"No," she said. "I used to have one, my old college portable. But it broke during the move to Buffalo. I never bothered to get a new one."

"It doesn't matter. I'll bring mine. I'll be in Brooklyn tomorrow. Or if not tomorrow, the next day. I'll see what I can arrange, plane-wise and Barney-wise."

"Could you really come so soon?" she asked.

"Is the Pope Catholic? I'm going crazy here without you."

She felt her heart race at his implication. He *did* miss her, as much as she missed him. Yet, after so many days of hearing nothing from him... "You should have called, Seth. When I didn't hear from you, I thought—" She broke off.

"You thought what?"

"That maybe you didn't want to talk to me, or something," she mumbled.

He could easily interpret what she was saying. "You thought I didn't care? You thought I don't love you? Brodie, what's wrong with you? You're always so sure of yourself."

"No, I'm not," she admitted. It took enormous courage to reveal her intimate doubts, but she loved Seth too much to keep her insecurities hidden from him.

"Okay. Watch my lips. I love you."

This time her heart seemed to stop beating altogether. She simply sat, dazed, dizzy with joy.

"What happened?" he questioned her silence. "Did I put you back to sleep?"

"No." She inhaled, coming back to life. "No, Seth. But I couldn't watch your lips."

"You'll be able to soon enough," he promised. "Only if you're close enough to see them, they won't be doing much talking. I'll see you a.s.a.p., Laura."

I love you, too, she mouthed, not daring to speak the words aloud. It was still possible that Seth wanted to see her only to garner criticism on his revised manuscript. That he could hop on an airplane and fly across the country at a moment's notice indicated that he was rich, not necessarily that he missed her as much as she missed him. Even his confession of love couldn't put her doubts fully to rest. "What about *Ax Man Cuts Both Ways*?" she asked him.

"What about it? Shooting starts next week, and I'm sure as hell not going to rewrite any more Jacuzzi scenes if I can help it. If it's all right with you, I'll give Zeke your number so he can reach me if there's an emergency on the set. Or maybe I'll give him the number for Dial-A-Prayer. It would serve him right if he couldn't reach me."

"Give him my number if you want," Laura said. "I don't mind."

"And I'm not going to sleep on the living room sofa, by the way," Seth said before hanging up.

"Of course not," Laura addressed the dead air on the telephone. Sleeping with Seth had been one of the nicest aspects of her stay in California, much nicer than driving the Porsche or flying a kite on the beach. Much, much nicer than learning how to play a kazoo.

SHE LEFT WORK shortly after six the following afternoon. Some days went that way, each client demanding extra time, paperwork piling up and staff meetings dragging on. Just before she'd been about to depart from her office, Susan had arrived to hand-deliver a draft of the article she'd written for *Dream*. "Why don't you read it through and give me your comments?" she had offered. "I know you and Ms. Robinson are good friends. She'd shoot me if I didn't give you first edit on it."

"She wouldn't shoot anybody," Laura had refuted Susan. "She's a pacifist." Secretly Laura suspected that Susan was presenting her with the article not because she feared for her life, but simply because she was a thoughtful person. "I'll call you as soon as I've read it," Laura promised.

Tucking the folder beneath her blazer to protect it from the evening drizzle, she jogged around the corner from the subway station and down the street to her building. In the lobby she pulled out the folder and checked to make sure the pages inside it hadn't gotten too soggy, then continued to the elevator and upstairs. Laura judged from the smell in the corridor that Mrs. Cobb in 5-D was cooking something with enough chili powder in it to ignite a forest fire. Wrinkling her nose at the aroma, Laura unlocked her own door.

She heard Rita chattering energetically and wondered whether she would once again find her daughter lounging on the kitchen counter with the telephone receiver growing out of her ear as she bemoaned the blight old age had cast upon yet another over-the-hill rock star. But her voice was coming from a different direction, and when Laura reached the arched doorway to the living room, she discovered Rita and Seth seated on the sofa, so engrossed in their conversation they weren't even aware of Laura's arrival.

"You're here," she announced in astonishment. Although Seth had mentioned that he might get to New York by that night, Laura hadn't actually believed that he would. Didn't long trips take time to plan? Didn't airlines like to wait until one's check cleared before issuing a ticket? Didn't dogs have to be delivered to kennels or willing neighbors?

Whatever magic Seth had performed to get himself to Laura's apartment in less than twenty-hours didn't matter. All that mattered was that he had done it.

He was dressed in one of his bizarre outfits—a cotton shirt of forest green, a vest the same screaming red color as his sneakers and a pair of pleated gray slacks. But Laura didn't care what he was wearing; no one had ever looked so wonderful to her. He sprang off the couch and strode across the room to welcome her with a lusty hug. "Cool it," she whispered jerking her head in Rita's direction.

"It's okay, Ma," Rita calmly assured her mother. "I'm on to the whole thing. He put his suitcase in your bedroom."

"You're presumptuous," Laura chided Seth.

"She's savvy," he countered, poking his thumb in Rita's direction.

"I'm cool," Rita declared, rising to her feet, as well. "You know what else he brought? His typewriter. *The* typewriter. The one he writes his movies on."

"It was all I could do to keep her from kissing it," Seth confided to Laura. "It's about time you got home, pal. Your daughter is famished. Another ten minutes, and I was going to take her out for a hot fudge sundae."

"You hear that, Ma? A hot fudge sundae," Rita chorused. "We can go out for pizza first, and then ice cream after," she resolved, dashing out of the living room to get her slicker.

"Hello," Seth murmured once he and Laura were alone. He kissed her gently, and her mouth instantly softened beneath his. He slid his tongue enticingly along her lower lip, then pulled back and smiled.

"How did you get here so soon?" she asked.

"Are you complaining?"

"No."

His smile expanded. "Where there's a will, et cetera," he said about his seeming wizardry. Laura felt a flush of pleasure wash through her. Seth wouldn't have had such a strong will to see her if he didn't truly love her.

"Hey, you guys!" Rita hollered from the doorway. "Enough kissie-kissie. I'm gonna die here."

"Sure, lardo," Laura teased, separating from Seth and leading him from the room.

The pizza place was crowded, with throbbing rock music pouring down on them from ceiling speakers. It gave Laura a mild headache, and she thought the pizza was much too spicy and greasy, but Rita didn't seem to mind in the least. Her only complaint was that no one she knew from school happened to enter the place. "I'd just love for someone to see me here with Seth," she declared. "You know Tara Drake, she once met Weird Al Yankovich by accident, like two years ago, and she still hasn't shut up about it."

"And you haven't shut up about Seth," Laura reminded her.

"Yes, I have," Rita defended herself piously as she pulled another gooey wedge of pizza from the round tin pan at the center of the table. "I'm eating, aren't I? I never talk with food in my mouth."

After dinner they headed down the street to an ice-cream parlor. Seth and Rita ordered hot fudge sundaes, and Laura a dish of sherbet, which she had trouble finishing. Yet seeing how much fun Rita was having with Seth and he with her was more satisfying to Laura than even the most sinfully caloric dessert. The sherbet was extraneous as far as she was concerned. The happiness she felt having Seth with her was more than sweet enough.

Rita begged to watch television once they got home, but deciding that she'd been lenient enough for one evening, Laura chose to be a mother and ordered Rita to do her homework at her desk. "I've got to do some work, too," she informed Seth, gathering up the folder Susan had given her. "I promised I'd read this right away."

"What is it?" he asked, taking the folder from her and leafing through the pages.

"It's the article about me that Julianne is going to run in *Dream*. The reporter wants my opinion of it before she submits it."

"It must do your ego good to know your opinion is in such demand by us lowly scribes," Seth teased her. "I'll let you read her masterpiece tonight, as long as you promise to read mine tomorrow."

"Heavens, so many masterpieces all at one time," Laura clucked, kicking off her shoes and dropping onto the sofa. Seth turned on the television to a baseball game and settled on the faded upholstery beside her.

While he watched the game, she read. The article was indisputably well written, accurate, moving but... Why didn't she like it? Why didn't it thrill her? Why did such a clear, literate depiction of her work leave her feeling so discomfited?

"Well?" Seth asked, noticing that she had stopped reading. "Today *Dream*, tomorrow *Donahue*?"

"I don't think so," she said, attempting to smile. She tossed the folder onto the table and sighed. "She makes me look... I don't know."

"Like an angel?" Seth guessed.

"Like a social worker," Laura corrected him. "A good social worker."

"Which you are."

"Oh, Seth..." She sighed again. "I *want* to save the world. But as hard as I try, I just can't seem to do it. Lately I've been feeling as if maybe the world doesn't want me saving it. I feel like I can't give my clients the help they need. And if I can't, what's the use?"

Seth scrutinized her downcast expression, then gingerly brushed his index finger along her cheek to her chin and cupped his hand beneath it. He lifted her face to his. "How long have you been like this?"

"Like what? Burned out?"

He kissed her brow. "Everybody burns out sometimes. I imagine that for someone doing the kind of work you do, burnout must be a common occurrence. It's nothing to feel hopeless about."

"I don't feel hopeless, Seth."

"Guilty?" he suggested. "Guilty that you haven't saved the world?"

"Maybe," she admitted.

"Forget the world," he whispered. "If you've saved one or two people, you're doing more than your share. And trust me, Laura, you *have* saved one or two. I'm speaking from personal experience." He kissed her forehead again, then slid his lips down her nose to her mouth. His kiss momentarily deepened, and then he twisted toward the doorway. "When is Rita's bedtime?"

Laura glanced past Seth at Rita's closed door. The dark crack under it indicated that Rita had retired for the night. She turned back to Seth. "I think the coast is clear," she murmured.

They tiptoed out of the living room. Laura thought it was an odd role reversal, a mother sneaking around with her boyfriend behind her daughter's back. But no matter how cool Rita claimed to be, thirteen years old was an awkward age for any girl, let alone a girl whose single mother was entertaining a lover in their home. Laura preferred to be discreet.

As soon as they had shut themselves inside the master bedroom, Seth attacked the buttons of Laura's blouse. "God, but you're sexy," he murmured as he slid the blouse off her shoulders. He skimmed his hands over the firm swells of her breasts, then let his fingers fall to the waistband of her skirt.

Her lips shaped a giddy smile. "Nobody's ever told me I was sexy before," she admitted.

"You've been hanging out with the wrong people," Seth asserted, then contradicted himself. "No, you've been hanging out with the right people. I'd just as soon no one else caught on to how sexy you are. Truth is—" he slid her skirt over her hips, then eased down her panty hose. "—I want you all to myself."

They quickly finished undressing and stretched out on the bed. Seth kissed her slowly and thoroughly, his tongue playing over hers, teasing and taking. His hands moved over the ripe curves and indentations of her body, and she was instantly engulfed in the luxuriant sensations she had known the last time they were together, the spreading warmth, the stunning surges of longing. She had experienced such intense pleasure only once before in her life, with Neil. Yet making love with him had been very different. It had been more physical, somehow, more imperative. With Seth she was loving a friend. With Seth there was understanding, trust, comfort.

She touched him as he touched her, with quiet assurance, understated power. She felt his desire rising within him, expanding through him, paralleling her own desire. She relished the tensing of his lean muscles along his back and across his abdomen, the uneven tempo of his breathing, the urgent pressure of his thigh wedged between hers, his hips surging against hers.

He didn't have to tell her that he found her sexy; it was obvious in his movements, in the tender assault of his fingers and lips. He didn't have to apologize for wanting her all to himself; she was completely, willingly his.

"I really did miss you," she whispered, trailing her fingers along the flat expanse of his stomach.

"You don't have to miss me now," he swore, closing his teeth gingerly about her earlobe. "I'm here."

She sighed, an inchoate sound of agreement.

His hand drew a long, unbroken line from the nape of her neck forward, along her collarbone, down between her breasts, across the pliant flesh of her abdomen and through the curling tendrils of hair below. He found her damp and eager, and her body tensed at his welcome touch. She didn't need to speak for him to know everything she could possibly tell him at that moment. Words weren't necessary to communicate her every secret, her every pulsing want. Her body revealed what Seth already knew.

Their bodies merged, moved together, found each other. Passion wove a timeless web around them, trapping them in its rapturous spell and then propelling them up the steep path to its peak. Laura arrived, Seth right behind her, their souls suddenly free to unite for a fleeting, exquisite instant.

Spent, Seth rested wearily upon her, his body heavy as it unwound. His hands rose to her hair, and he tangled his fingers deep into the soft curls. He grew still, and for a minute Laura suspected that he had fallen asleep.

He dispelled that thought by speaking. "You're a wonderful mother, too."

Surprised that he would refer to Rita at such a moment, she opened her eyes and slid out from under him. He opened his eyes, as well, their luminous blend of green and gray complementing his radiant smile. "Oh? What makes you say that?"

"I like Rita. She's turned out nicely."

"Thank you."

His lips flexed as he pondered his words. "I probably have no right to ask, Laura, and you're going to think I'm unforgivably possessive, to say nothing of nosy, but..." He drifted off uncertainly.

"But...?"

"Tell me about her father," he requested. "I want to know."

Laura lapsed into silence. She didn't find Seth's question unreasonable. If he loved her as much as she loved him, then he did have a right to ask. She simply wasn't sure of how to answer. "What do you want to know?"

"What was he like?"

"He was pretty quiet," she recalled. "The strong, silent type—only he wasn't terribly strong, as it turned out. He came from West Virginia and he had a wonderful mountain drawl. He had majored in literature in college, and he read a lot. He was a big Hermann Hesse fan."

"He sounds like a weenie," Seth remarked.

Laura smiled reflectively. "He wasn't. He was very good-looking. Just look at Rita—whatever doesn't resemble me, she got from him."

"Did you love him?" Seth asked tentatively.

"Of course I loved him. Do you think I would have had a baby with him if I didn't?"

"Do I think you would have had a baby with someone who walked out on you?" Seth countered, apparently trying not to appear too condemning.

"I wasn't expecting him to walk out on me," Laura replied. If Seth didn't approve of what she had done, that was his business. Laura had never felt the need to justify her past to anyone, and she wasn't about to now. "If you want to know the truth, I don't think Neil expected to walk out, either. But he was afraid of responsibility. He liked the idea of having a baby more than the reality of it."

"What made you so responsible?" Seth asked, sounding genuinely fascinated. "How come you didn't want to walk away from it all yourself?"

"I loved the reality of it," Laura told him simply. "I loved being a mother. I loved Rita."

"But it must have been tough at times."

"It was," she admitted. "But I don't believe in walking away from tough situations. I believe that if you live with your choices, if you commit yourself to them, you'll be all the better for it. And I believe that when someone needs you—the way Rita needs me—you...you have to be there."

"Of course," he whispered. He leaned forward and kissed her lightly. "Of course that's what you believe."

IF WAKING UP TO DISCOVER YOURSELF fully exposed to a thirteen-year-old girl was humiliating, even worse would be to face that thirteen-year-old girl after having made love to her mother the night before. Seth gratefully took Laura up on her suggestion that he roll over and go back to sleep when she and Rita awoke early the next morning.

He rolled over, but he didn't go back to sleep. It was difficult to sleep through a noisy altercation between mother and daughter over Rita's insistence that she wear mascara to school. Without mascara, according to Rita, a girl could just about die. Laura's assertion that the cosmetic caused eye infections struck Seth as a creative approach to the problem, but, then, thirteen-year-old girls probably didn't care as strongly about eye infections as about fitting in with their peers.

He didn't know much about teenage girls, but he was willing to learn. He had grown up the youngest of three boys, so he'd never had the opportunity to deal with young girls close up. When he himself was thirteen, he had considered females an alien breed. As he recollected, they were by and large vapid; the most pressing issue in their lives was what they were going to do with themselves now that Ringo Starr was married. They danced with each other at parties and they wore funny-looking stockings with patterns woven into them. On occasion, he had been obliged to kiss a few of them, since when the girls weren't dancing with each other at parties they were organizing rounds of Spin-the-Bottle and Post Office. "Special delivery from Nancy Shea to Seth Stone!" someone would squeal, and he'd be dragged into a closet where Nancy was waiting, reeking of some cloying perfume, and they'd push their mouths together amid the winter coats and think they were very mature.

For all Seth knew, Rita might also play Post Office at parties. But he doubted it. She *was* savvy. She was smart. He had almost been glad that Laura got home late from work the previous day, because it had given him the opportunity to talk to Rita. She had asked him his educated opinion of the music of the Monkees and Wang Chung, but she had also asked him his educated opinion of the Middle East. Admittedly their discussion hadn't been scholarly, but at least she knew about the world. "I read that in Iran the women have to wear masks," she'd declared. "I mean yuck! Like, how is a guy ever gonna ask you out if you're wearing some dumb mask, you know?"

He remained in bed until he heard the front door close, signaling that Rita had left for school and Laura for work.

Then he rose, donned the jeans he'd brought with him and stumbled out of the room.

The coffee in the pot was still hot, and Laura had left open a cabinet door to reveal boxes of shredded wheat and Grape Nuts. "Figures," he sniffed disdainfully, swinging the cabinet shut. He wasn't a big cereal fan, but when he did eat cereal, he liked it sweet. Frosted Flakes, Sugar Smacks, Fruit Loops—Laura would probably string him up if she ever found out that he ate such stuff. Then again, Rita would probably cheer for him. She had wolfed down that hot fudge sundae like a pro last night.

Perhaps he was being too optimistic, but he was fairly certain that Rita liked him. He wasn't exactly clear about why winning her affection was so important to him, but he definitely knew that it was.

He gulped down some coffee and orange juice, took a shower, got dressed and lugged his typewriter, his script and a ream of clean typing paper to the kitchen table. Until he'd walked into Laura's apartment, he hadn't been able to get his mind off *Good Fences*—even during his flight to New York he'd reread several scenes and slashed them up with a pen. He had never worried so much about any of his other screenplays, but this one... He wanted it to be perfect. Every word, every camera angle, every punctuation mark, utterly perfect.

Undaunted by jet lag, he plunged into his work. The constant purr of the typewriter's motor energized him; the concave plastic surfaces of the keys inspired him. That he was in an unfamiliar environment, without his trusty thesaurus, without his supply of red rubber bands, which he liked to shoot across his office when he was blocked, didn't faze him in the least. He had his characters, his situation and plot. He had his ideas and he had confidence. He didn't need anything else.

Hunger forced him to take a break after a few hours. Rummaging in Laura's refrigerator, he found a casserole dish containing some leftover lentil stew. He scooped some into a bowl and ate it cold. It couldn't compete with pizza, he decided, but for healthy slop it wasn't half bad.

Rita arrived home from school at three-thirty, and she nearly pounced on the typed pages stacked beside the typewriter. "Oh, Seth, what's this?" she bellowed. "I told Courtney you were actually going to write something at our house, and she almost didn't believe me. But look at all this! You wrote this *here*! In *my* kitchen! What is it? Is it about Ax Man?"

"No, Rita," he said, slumping in his chair and rolling his head from side to side to loosen the muscles of his neck. "This one's going to be a *good* script."

"Yeah?" She abandoned the pages to open the refrigerator door, poured herself a glass of milk, then shut the door. "You know who you ought to cast in it? Emilio Estevez. He's *fine*, Seth. I saw him in this movie, *The Breakfast Club*. It was an R movie, but Courtney's family gets cable and we saw it on TV."

"He's white," Seth pointed out. "This film is about a black kid, not a white one."

"Todd Bridges," Rita recommended. "From *Different Strokes*. He's a fox, too."

Seth considered her suggestion and smiled. "That's an interesting idea," he agreed. "You've got the makings of a casting director, Rita."

"Yeah? No kidding?" Rita danced in a circle around the table. "Maybe that's what Courtney and I will do. We were gonna open a boutique in the East Village, but I hear the rents are awesomely high there."

"If you became a casting director for the movies, you'd have to move to Los Angeles," Seth noted.

Rita stopped moving and stared at him. Her eyes were uncannily dark and piercing, adorned with lashes so thick that mascara wasn't necessary. Whatever she might have inherited from her father didn't include her eyes. They were identical to Laura's.

As he met her penetrating gaze, he contemplated what he'd just said. Rita would have to move to Los Angeles. With Laura. Of course.

Evidently Rita also understood the full implications of what he had suggested. She folded her slender body onto a chair facing him, raked her short hair with her fingers and studied him quizzically. "Let's talk, Seth," she said.

"About what?"

"What's going on with you and Ma? You want her to move in with you, or what?"

He tossed the question back to her. "How would you feel about that?"

"If she moved in with you, where would I live?"

"With us," he insisted. "I've got a big house. There's a bedroom in it for you. And I've got a dog. A dalmatian. Do you like dogs?"

"They're okay," Rita said with a shrug. "I'd rather have a car."

"I've got one of those, too," Seth told her. "A Porsche. You're too young to drive it now, Rita, but when you get older, I'll teach you how."

"Yeah?" She mulled over his offer. "What about Courtney?"

"I'll teach her, too, if she wants me to."

"No, I mean, what about her? She's my best friend. If I lived with you, Seth, I'd never get to see her."

"Of course you would. You could come back east to visit her. And she could come out to California to visit us there."

"On an airplane?"

"Flying beats walking."

Rita drank her milk and meditated. "What does Ma have to say about all this?"

"I haven't discussed it with her yet," Seth admitted. He hadn't even thought about it until ten minutes ago. Yet it was such a terrific idea, such an obvious one, that he was amazed he hadn't come up with it sooner.

Rita swung her feet back and forth as she considered Seth's words. "Ma is kind of weird, Seth, you know? She might not go for it. I mean, like, you'd lay it out for her, tell her about all the neat people who live in Los Angeles. You'd explain the whole thing to her, and you know what she'd do? She'd say something like, 'I can't leave my clients.' "

"Do you think she'd say that?" Seth asked, mildly alarmed. He had known Laura longer than Rita had, but Rita knew her better. And what Seth knew about Laura led him to believe that Rita might just be correct. Laura was attached to her work. She cared about her clients; she fretted over them. She felt guilty when one of them went through a rough time while she was out of town.

"You know my mother," Rita snorted. "El Weenie Supremo. She would probably worry about California being too cool. Look at the way she dresses, right? Move her out there, where everybody is rad, and she might just hate it."

"Not everybody is rad out there," Seth cautioned Rita, wondering whether she, and not her mother, might have difficulty adjusting to the West Coast. "Some people are neat and some are dorks. What's wrong with the way your mother dresses, anyway?"

Rita glared at him in horror. "You think she dresses right? I think she looks like an A-1 flame. To say nothing of her hair...."

"I think your mother is beautiful," Seth argued. "I love her hair."

"She's old," Rita grunted.

"Are you trying to talk me out of this plan?" Seth challenged her. "Or are you on my side?"

"I'm on your side, Seth," Rita said quickly.

"Okay, then. Leave everything to me."

Easier said than done, he ruminated as Rita grinned and bounced out of the kitchen. He turned back to his typewriter, but for the first time in days he couldn't even bring himself to read what he had just written, let alone write anything more. He couldn't concentrate on *Good Fences* when he had just decided that he wanted to live with Laura.

Maybe he hadn't just decided it. Pondering the idea, he couldn't shake the comprehension that he had known all along that he wanted to live with her. He loved her. He desired her. And he needed her—a whole hell of a lot more than any of her clients did.

He grew restless waiting for her to come home from work. He prowled the kitchen, the hall, the bathroom. He gave his reflection a harsh assessment in the mirror above the sink. He had shaved that morning after his shower, but perhaps he ought to shave again. Perhaps he ought to shower again. At the very least, he ought to tuck in his shirt.

He had never asked a woman to live with him before, and he tried to figure out how nervous he should be. What had it been like the first time he'd asked a girl out on a date? Well, he and Nancy Shea had already been kissing in closets for two years before they'd gone on an official date, so naturally Seth had been relaxed about it.

Why shouldn't he be relaxed this time, then? He had known Laura for over fifteen years. They were friends. The worst that would happen was that she'd say no. Which would be pretty bad, but he'd cross that bridge when he got to it.

Much to Seth's relief, she arrived home at five, clutching her mail. "Look what I got—a letter from Kim!" she announced, waving the pink envelope beneath Seth's nose. Then she ripped it open.

"Belmont?" Seth was strangely relieved by the delay. He was too edgy to jump right into the issue of Laura's moving in with him. "What does she have to say for herself?"

Laura pored over the neat script and frowned. Then she sighed. "Poor Kim. She's been working with a lawyer, finalizing the details of her divorce."

"Her divorce?" Cripes. Nothing like a divorce to put a hex on talk about living together. "How come she's getting a divorce?" he asked.

"Obviously because her marriage is a failure." Laura set down the letter and sighed again.

"I always thought she was a 'happily ever after' type," Seth mused.

"We all think we are, don't we?" Laura reread the letter, then folded it and inserted it in the tattered envelope. "She sounds as if she's holding up, under the circumstances. But it's a lousy break. You think you can trust your heart, and then reality intrudes and things go wrong. I feel so bad for her, Seth."

Cripes was right. This was definitely not the appropriate introduction to the subject he wished to talk over with Laura. "I feel bad for her, too," he noted, trying to remain optimistic. "But things don't always have to go rotten. Sometimes they can work out okay."

"You're right," Laura agreed, brightening. She gave him a hearty hug. "Lord, it's good having you here, Seth. You know how to cheer me up. So, how was your day?"

He felt his gut tighten into a knot, but he resolutely ignored the sensation. *Relax,* he admonished himself. *She's a friend.* "Let me help you with your jacket," he offered, sliding her blazer off her shoulders with uncharacteristic chivalry.

"What's the matter?" Laura asked suspiciously. "What did you break?"

Abruptly Rita bolted out of her bedroom and shouted, "Hi, Ma. What's for dinner?"

Seth laughed and eyed Rita. "Go back to your room and starve for a while," he ordered her. "Your mother and I have to talk."

"Huh?" Then Rita remembered what she and Seth had discussed earlier, and she grinned slyly. "Oh, yeah. *That.*" She spun around and darted back into her room, slamming her door shut behind her.

"Why do I have a sinking feeling in the pit of my stomach?" Laura asked skeptically, stepping out of her shoes and shoving up the sleeves of her sweater. "What have you two been cooking up?"

"Nothing fattening," Seth said to put her at ease. Stupid, really. It didn't even put *him* at ease.

She studied his face, absorbing his anxious expression, trying to interpret it and gradually coming to look pretty anxious herself. "Well?" she prodded him.

"How would you like to move to California?" There. He'd said it.

"California?" Laura echoed. "What's in California?"

"*I'm* in California, you twit."

"You mean, you want me to live with you?"

This wasn't going quite as well as he might have hoped. Why did Laura look so startled? Why didn't it seem as obviously right to her as it did to him? "I want you and Rita both to live with me. Rita loves the idea. She wants me to teach her how to drive the Porsche."

"You asked Rita before you asked me?" Laura asked, stunned. "Why?"

"I thought Rita was going to be the tough one to convince. I was sure you'd be easy." He reached for her hands, gathered them in his, lifted them to his lips. "I want you with me. We can make it work. I need you with me, not three thousand miles away. I know it's a big question, Laura, but things don't have to go rotten between us the way they did for Kim." No, too negative. He drew in a deep breath, then squeezed her hands. "I want you with me. You're good for me. Okay?"

She lowered her eyes to her hands clasped within his. He wished he could read her mind, wished he could guess at her reaction. "I'm good for you," she echoed uncertainly. "Like cod liver oil."

"Like sunshine," he corrected her. "Like a light through the shadows. You're helping me to find my way, and I need that."

She appeared curiously pained by his words. She broke from him and turned away, her eyes averted. "You want me with you to help you with your work," she summarized in a constrained voice.

"Of course I do. You've done wonders for me, professional-wise."

She shook her head. "That's not enough, Seth."

He gazed at her, at the resplendent fall of her hair down her back, at the way each hand gripped the opposite elbow, as if she were hugging herself, holding herself in. Did she think her assistance in steering him straight was the only reason he wanted her?

He reached for her shoulders and rotated her face to him. "I love you, Laura," he swore. "Is that enough?"

Her eyes lit up as they met his. "More than enough," she whispered.

"Are you sure? Would you like me to serenade you with something romantic? 'You Are the Sunshine of My Life' or something?"

"Wait a minute and I'll get my kazoo," Laura joked, but she didn't move from him. Instead she curled her fingers around his neck and pulled him closer. "I can think of a lot of practical reasons we ought to take the time to analyze this fully," she admitted. "But right now, Seth, I don't want to be practical. I just want to say yes." She rose to kiss him. "All right?"

He smiled. He was definitely relaxed, now, relaxed and elated both. "You *are* easy, aren't you."

"Easy, maybe. But don't forget, I don't believe in free love."

"That's all right," Seth reminded her, wrapping his arms around her in an exuberant hug. "I'm rich, pal. I can afford you."

Chapter Eleven

The practical considerations came later. One was her job. As burned out as she might be, she wasn't sure she was ready to give up on her career and turn her back on her clients.

Rita was another consideration. Although she was unrestrained in her excitement about the notion of moving to California, Laura worried whether Rita would truly like the place—or the move itself, a move away from her friends, her school and her community. Rita had had a rather unsettled childhood, and Laura wanted to provide her daughter with as much stability as possible. California was awfully different from Brooklyn. And if things between Seth and Laura didn't work out, if, after moving in with him, Laura and Rita had to move out...

That was the biggest consideration, of course: things between Seth and Laura. She loved him, and she was fairly secure in his love for her. Still, neither of them had even breathed a hint of "forever after" or "till death do us part." Not that Laura was obsessed by the legalities of the situation—although they, too, were a legitimate practical concern, if Laura lost the medical coverage and pension that came with her job. She recognized the possibility that her relationship with Seth might not work out, might not last. And then where would she and Rita be? Legal, sanctified marriages frequently didn't work out, either, but at least a married woman had some protection, some recourse.

In her youth Laura had never worried about such issues. She decided she wanted to live on a commune, and so she did. She decided she wanted a baby, and she had one. She didn't lose sleep over her finances; she wasn't wealthy, but she and her daughter never went hungry. She had faith that things would work out. Somehow they always did.

She was no longer young enough to rely on faith alone. Or maybe it had nothing to do with her age; maybe it was a matter of responsibility. If Rita were an independent adult, Laura wouldn't think twice about taking her chances with Seth, hoping for the best and trusting in love and luck. But Rita wasn't an independent adult. She depended on her mother to plan ahead, to steer a straight course for their tiny family. It would be unfair for Laura to take chances when Rita's future hung in the balance.

So, after the euphoria of Seth's invitation wore off, Laura proposed that she and Seth take things slowly. Rita's spring vacation from school was approaching. Laura would pull as many strings as necessary to obtain a few days off from work coinciding with Rita's holiday, and they would travel west then and try out the arrangement.

"You're so damned sensible, Laura," Seth griped, but he agreed to her plan, on the condition that she would let him stay with her in Brooklyn until she and Rita could accompany him back to California. Laura found nothing objectionable about that. On a practical level, that would give Rita more time to get used to the idea of her mother and Seth as a couple, and . . .

The hell with all the practical considerations. Laura wanted him to stay because she loved him.

"IT'S GREAT!" Rita shrieked, leaping out of the car. She had already expressed the same opinion of the taxi drive to JFK Airport, the airplane flight and the drive from Los Angeles International Airport to Topanga Canyon. Flying was great. The Porsche was great, even though the back seat was barely large enough for her to fit in. The hot, dry weather of Southern California was great. And now, Seth's house was great.

"You guys are probably wasted," Seth noted, unloading their luggage and his own from the car as Laura joined her daughter outside the car. "Why don't I get you settled, and then I'll scoot down to the Morgans' house for Barney and my mail."

"I want to go, too," Rita declared. "Who's Barney?"

"My dog." Seth unlocked the front door to the house, and Rita ran inside. "Oh, Ma, look at this living room!" she hollered, racing the length of it. "Isn't it great?"

"A vocabulary of one word," Laura muttered. With Seth beside her, instead of a genial-looking old man full of horror stories about airplane disasters, she had survived this flight to California better than her last one. But she still felt a touch queasy and worn out.

Seth appraised her and then her energetic daughter. "I tell you what," he suggested. "You go lie down for a while, and I'll take Rita with me. We've got to buy some groceries, too. Whatever I've got here has probably gone bad by now."

Laura was too exhausted to argue. She gratefully accepted Seth's offer and staggered through the house to his bedroom to sack out.

Barney's rambunctious barking roused her from her nap a couple of hours later. Dragging out of the bed, she stumbled to the bathroom and splashed some cold water on her face to revive herself. Then she followed the sound of Seth's and Rita's voices down the hall to the kitchen, where she discovered them unloading groceries from paper bags.

"Now that we've bought all this food," Seth said, stacking cans of dog food in one of the cabinets, "I think we ought to go out for dinner. Rita needs to taste real Mexican food. Remember that ace joint I took you to?" he asked Laura. "I figure I can stop off at Melinda's house on the way," he continued. "I want to drop *Good Fences* off for her to read."

He had already filled Laura in a bit about his agent, the woman who had told Seth when he was just starting out that she would gladly represent him if he would write violence for her. Laura wondered whether Melinda would care for Seth's new script, in which there was no overt violence at all, and no sex.

Whatever the woman's taste, whatever her sense of commercial viability, she had made plenty of money from Seth's screenplays. Laura believed that, having sold so much of his bad writing, Melinda owed it to Seth to sell something good.

For it was good. No question about it. Laura had read the revised version and been enthralled by the alterations Seth had made on the earlier draft. If she had liked *Good Fences* the first time she'd read it, she liked it even more now, in its new and improved version. It was so strong, so vital—she couldn't believe that anyone wouldn't be taken with it.

Not surprisingly, Rita was captivated by Melinda's Malibu beach house, which stood on stilts above the surging ocean. She was equally captivated by Melinda, a bleached-blond, middle-aged woman who chewed gum, called Rita "honey" and promised Seth that she would read his script overnight. "You really think this is special, huh?" she said, popping her gum in her molars. "And not a single decap in it?"

"Not a one," Seth told her. "Brace yourself."

"What's a decap?" Rita asked once they were in the car again and on the way to the Mexican restaurant.

"A decapitation," Seth replied. "Each of my *Ax Man* flicks had at least one decap in it. *Victory of the Ninjas* had two. I've developed a reputation in the industry as being one of the best decap writers around."

"What a laurel," Laura muttered, grimacing.

"At least I've got a head to wear it on," Seth joked.

"I think it's great that you're the best," Rita claimed. "Mrs. Tashki, she's my home-ec teacher at school, she's always saying, 'Find out what it is that you do well and be the best you can be at it.' If Seth does decapitations well, I think it's great that he's the best."

You think everything Seth does is great, Laura mused silently. She was thrilled that Rita adored Seth, but...Laura wanted Rita to like him not because he was the best decap writer in the business, but because he was talented and sensitive; not because he had a gorgeous house, but because he rained affection on his pet dog. Not because he owned a snazzy sports car, but because he was magnanimous enough to let his loved ones drive it. Not because he had made a mint writing trashy scripts, but because he possessed the wisdom and the vision to write a script like *Good Fences*.

Witnessing their playful banter over dinner, however, Laura cautioned herself that she ought to be thankful Rita liked Seth at all, even if her reasons weren't those Laura would have preferred. Things could be worse.

After dinner they returned to Seth's house and descended to the family room to watch television. "Wow!" Rita exclaimed, spotting the VCR on the lower shelf of the television cart. "You've got one of those!"

"I've got one of those," Seth confirmed, crossing the room to turn on the set.

"Do you rent dirty movies?" Rita asked.

Seth laughed. "I *write* dirty movies," he reminded her. "The last thing I want to do at the end of a day toiling in the trenches is watch a movie just like the one I've just been writing. However..." He switched on the VCR and rummaged through his modest collection of video cassettes. "Here's an oldie but a goodie." He inserted the cassette and returned to the sofa, taking a seat next to Laura.

Rita appeared disappointed that she wasn't going to get to view something X-rated, but her disappointment waned as soon as the screen lit up with the introductory titles for *Evening Potpourri*. "You taped this?" She crossed her legs on the sofa cushions and leaned forward. "The show you and Ma were on?"

"Do we have to watch this?" Laura protested, although she already knew the answer. Seth was lounging next to her with his arm around her shoulders and his feet kicked up on the coffee table. He showed no interest whatsoever in turning off the tape.

Within a minute Julianne appeared on the screen, describing *The Dream* with utter poise. Then Seth appeared, and Rita whistled and clapped. "You were a scream on this show, Seth," she recalled. "Most men wouldn't have the guts to admit they knew how to type. Don't you think Seth is liberated, Ma?"

"If he weren't liberated, do you think we'd be here now?" Laura responded, complimenting Seth. "After all, this is the man who wrote the most feminist Ninja movie in creation."

"This guy was boring," Rita remarked as Andrew appeared on the show. "He reminds me of a social studies teacher."

"He *is* a social studies teacher—of sorts," Seth told her.

Rita sniffed. "Which one is she?" she asked her mother as the camera focused on Kimberly. "That other lady, she looked kinda stuffy, but this one, Courtney and I both thought she was beautiful."

"She is," Laura said.

"Like, she ought to be in the movies or something—oh, yeah, here comes the fox." Rita sighed as Troy came into close-up. "He's so fine. He ought to get together with the blond lady. They'd look so good together."

Seth apparently found such a pairing absurd, and he guffawed. "Kim is a purebred Southern belle," he explained to Rita. "Troy is an inner-city outlaw."

"They always got along pretty well," Laura remembered. "Troy seemed to like Kim more than Andrew ever did."

"That's because Troy is mellow," Seth opined. "Ah, now here comes the star."

Laura cringed, bracing herself for her own appearance on the screen. As with the last time she had watched the show, she thought she looked obese and sounded like a prig. She shot a surreptitious glance at Rita, curious about her daughter's reaction.

"You did good, Ma," Rita said simply as soon as Laura's turn had ended.

Laura turned to Rita, astounded. "Do you really think so?"

"Sure I do," Rita replied, inspecting her polished fingernails. "You didn't do anything embarrassing."

Coming from Rita, Laura considered such a comment the highest praise. She impulsively leaned toward her daughter and kissed her brow. Rita recoiled with a bashful snort. Kissing one's daughter, Laura acknowledged—now *that* was embarrassing!

Rita's energy began to wind down at around nine-thirty, and once Seth reminded her of the fact that it was after midnight in New York, she didn't balk at Laura's command that she go to bed. As soon as Rita was settled in the spare bedroom, Laura and Seth retired to his room, undressed and climbed into bed.

"Seth," Laura murmured, cuddling against his warm body and savoring the familiar strength of his arms around her.

"Mmm."

"Seth, we've got to talk."

"Shoot."

She ran her finger in an abstract pattern across his chest as she collected her thoughts. She replayed in her mind Rita's excitement about Seth's house, his car, his agent, his VCR. The words came easily to her. "You live a very different life from what we're used to."

He pulled back to look at her. "Meaning...?"

"Well, it's all so—so comfortable and—"

"You mean because I'm rich? You mean because I can afford things?" He sounded somewhat rankled. "Come on, Laura. Adjusting to a nicer life is a lot easier than adjusting to a harder one. You've already admitted that you like the microwave, pal, so you can't deny it now."

"I won't deny it," she conceded. "But, Seth...you like all these things, too. And if Rita and I move here, well..." She took a deep breath, then went on. "I can't expect you to support us. That's asking too much of you."

He relaxed beside her and stroked his hands consolingly through her hair. "It's not asking too much of me," he assured her. "Do you think I was kidding when I said I could afford you? Money isn't a problem. You know that."

She nodded. Seth's hand felt so good against her cheek, so comforting, his fingers moving gracefully along the curve of her face. She wished she could just close her eyes and will away her uneasiness.

But she couldn't. "If it isn't money," Seth pressed her, "What is it?"

She took another deep breath. "If I'm going to stay here, Seth, what am I supposed to do about my job?"

"Your job?" A short laugh escaped him. "Quit," he said succinctly.

Quit? Just like that? Walk away from her clients? How could she do something so irresponsible? How could she strand all those hapless young girls?

He seemed able to sense her unspoken thoughts. "You need a break, Laura. You're burned out. You know that as well as I do. You can't do those poor kids much good when they're driving you up the wall."

"Driving me up the wall? Seth, I care about them!"

"Of course you do. But then one gets pregnant, and you get exasperated. You feel as if she's failed you, and then you feel as if you've failed her. It's crazy. And when things get that crazy, it's time to back off for a while." His fingers raveled deep in her hair, and his smile grew distant. "Let me tell you a story about a lady named Shirley Stone."

"A relative of yours?" Laura asked, settling against the pillow and smiling expectantly.

"My mother. A far-out lady, as mothers go. I like ol' Shirley, Laura. She was a very good mother to her three sons, but you know what happened? She burned out."

"What do you mean?" Laura asked, fascinated. "What happened to her?"

"Three sons was what happened to her. Back in those days, when you and I were growing up, mothers were never supposed to burn out. They did, of course, but if they did, they weren't supposed to let on about it. Instead they got frustrated. They took their frustrations out on their kids or their husband. They ate too much, drank too much. You name it. Right?"

Laura nodded. She knew enough women of her mother's generation who had been afflicted that way. They had loved their children and they had cared for them, but they hadn't derived the satisfaction they'd needed from the job. "What did your mother do?" she asked.

"One day she said, 'That's it, guys. I've had it. I need a break.' And she up and left."

"She left!" Laura didn't bother to conceal her shock. "She walked out on her family?"

Seth chuckled. "Nothing that dramatic, Laura. What she did was she got a job."

"A job?" Laura had been expecting a more profound revelation than that. "Lots of women got jobs back then."

"For the money, mostly. Few of them were willing to admit that they got jobs because they were burned out as full-time mothers. But one thing about my mother, she never played games. She said, 'I need a break, and I'm taking one.'" He curled a strand of Laura's hair around his finger as he reminisced. "She got a job as a secretary. My father was horrified, naturally. First of all, what little Mom was earning threw us into a higher tax bracket, so her income was basically a wash. But worse than that, if Mom worked, people might think Dad wasn't earning enough on his own. I mean, Scandal City! Alan Stone isn't earning enough! The guy's manhood was on the line!"

"And?" Laura prompted him. She could easily understand why Seth was such a successful writer. He had her hanging on his every word, dying to hear how his parents had resolved their crisis.

"And Mom refused to back down. After a few weeks Dad got off her case, because the job—the break from being a homemaker—had so refreshed her that she was like a new person. Suddenly she was charming with me and my brothers. Suddenly she wasn't a shrew anymore. She lost ten pounds and looked terrific. Dad started whistling and smiling right around bedtime. Taking a break from being a wife and mother made her a better wife and mother."

Laura waited for Seth to say more, but he presented her only with a smug grin. She had expected some earth-shattering revelation, and she felt deflated by his story's humdrum conclusion. "That's all very interesting," she said dryly.

Seth leaned toward her and kissed the tip of her nose. "Don't you get it, Laura? Nobody's saying you ought to stop being a social worker. What I'm saying is, if you quit for a while, you'll be a much better one when you decide to return to work sometime down the road. Take a break. You need it."

Her lips spread in a wide grin. Yes, the story Seth had just shared with her was humdrum, but its moral was significant. Laura would be a better social worker if she allowed herself the chance to get away from it, to cleanse herself of all the frustration she had been feeling lately in her job.

But still, to allow Seth to support her and Rita... "Are you sure I wouldn't be taking advantage of you, sponging off you like that?"

"I wish you *would* take advantage of me," he asserted. "I want you to, Laura. Let me spend my money on something more worthwhile than a Porsche, okay? Let me spend it on you and Rita. And every night, you can give your thanks to your buddy Ax Man for making it all possible."

"I didn't know this sort of thing was done nowadays," she mused, amazed by the appeal of Seth's suggestion. "Women have fought so long to take their place in the work force. And here I'll be, living off you. What will I do with myself, Seth? Cook and clean the house?"

"Cooking's fun in a microwave," he pointed out. "And forget about cleaning. I hire a housekeeping service to do that for me."

"I've got to do something," Laura protested. She had never not worked in her life. The mere idea of doing nothing exhilarated her, but it also daunted her. Without a job, without a routine, without taking care of everything and everyone that needed taking care of, how would she survive?

"You can relax," Seth proposed. "You can take it easy. Do you know how to take it easy, Laura?"

She laughed. "I'm not sure. I may be too old to learn."

"Consider it your new challenge in life."

"I've never minded a challenge," she said with a chuckle before rising to kiss him.

Chapter Twelve

"You're up early," Seth said, entering the kitchen.

Laura was seated at the table in the breakfast area, sipping a cup of coffee and reading the morning newspaper. A corn muffin, sliced and buttered, lay on a plate at her elbow. She glanced at the wall clock and smiled. "It's eleven o'clock in New York," she explained.

"Then how come Rita isn't awake?"

"Rita needs an alarm clock and a cattle prod to get her out of bed," Laura informed him. "Thank you for buying muffins. I read the ingredients on that box of cereal you bought and almost threw up."

"It's terrific stuff," Seth argued, filling a bowl with Sugar Pops. "Nothing can beat it when you've got the munchies." He filled a cup with coffee for himself and joined her at the table. "My appointment with Melinda is at nine-thirty. You can let Rita sleep late if you want. She might wake up by the time I get home, and then we can all do something together."

"Actually, what I was thinking was we'd drive into town with you," Laura suggested. "While you're seeing your agent, I can show Rita the Sidewalk of the Stars or something. If that's all right with you."

Seth smiled. He loved the way Laura looked, her hair more disheveled than usual, her eyes uncommonly bright. He loved the way she looked and even more, he loved her idea. He was delighted that she took enough of an interest in Los Angeles to want to play the tour guide for her daughter. "It's fine with me. You can drop me off and take the car, if you want."

"You don't mind?"

"Not at all. I'd just as soon have you both out of my hair for an hour."

Laura seemed startled by his statement. "Are you sick of us already?"

"No, of course not." He took a long drink of the coffee, ignoring its scalding temperature. He wanted to remain calm; he didn't want Laura to notice how tense he was. But he should have known better. Laura was too attuned to him not to be aware that he was on edge. "All right," he admitted without prompting. "I'm nervous, that's all."

"Nervous? About what?"

"About seeing Melinda."

Again his words startled Laura. She reached across the table and covered his hand with hers, giving it a comforting squeeze. "She's your agent. She's been working with you for years. Why on earth should you be nervous about seeing her?"

"She's going to hate *Good Fences*," he predicted, trying to smother the urge to shudder. "I just know she is."

"She's going to love it," Laura refuted him, her tone low but reassuringly firm. "It's such a fine screenplay, Seth. She can't help but love it."

"You aren't the most objective person in the world," he pointed out, dismissing her flattery.

"Like hell I'm not. *Good Fences* is the best thing you've ever written. If Melinda doesn't like it, then get yourself a new agent."

"Easier said than done," Seth muttered. But he took heart in Laura's confident words. Her abiding faith in him was almost enough.

Almost. It was more than meeting with Melinda that had him panicked.

He respected Laura's opinion as much as he respected Melinda's, but Melinda was a professional. She wasn't in love with him. She didn't have to deal with Seth's soul; she dealt with reality, with the marketplace, with his output, his product. Not with his intentions, but with his words.

For the past few weeks, Seth had put all thoughts of reality and the marketplace aside. He had essentially forgotten that he was a professional. He had written not from his head but from his heart... and he'd written for Laura's heart, as well. He had written a screenplay he knew Laura would approve of. He had written it because he had wanted to live up to her concept of who he was.

Yet if her objectivity was questionable—and it was—then his own was even more questionable. Melinda knew what Seth's career was about. If she liked the script—and God, how he hoped she would!—then he had nothing to worry about. But if she didn't like it, he would have to respect her opinion. He would have to accept that he'd blown it. He would have to acknowledge that he'd aimed too high and fallen short, that he had limits.

And if he acknowledged that and accepted it, then he might lose Laura.

He took another long drink of his coffee, then dug into his cereal. What the hell. Either Melinda would approve of the manuscript or she wouldn't. Eating himself up about it wasn't going to change a thing.

Checking the clock again, Laura folded the newspaper and stood, announcing that if she and Rita were going to drive Seth to his appointment, she would have to get her daughter's rear in gear. She bounded out of the kitchen, and Seth watched her, wishing he were as cheerful as she was.

Laura could afford to be cheerful; she was ignorant of the film business, of the severe difficulty of getting something like *Good Fences* produced. Ignorance *was* bliss, he mused morosely, setting down his spoon. Even his favorite cereal didn't taste good that morning.

Laura had such an abundance of faith. If only Seth had half as much faith, he would rest assured that Laura would love him no matter what. He would understand that she would love him even if his magnificent opus was found to be little more than cow droppings in Melinda's esteem.

But his faith was a shaky thing. He remembered with acute clarity the first time Laura had revealed her love for him: it was right after she'd read the original version of *Good Fences*. Laura hadn't been able to love him, himself, alone. She had loved him not for who he was, but for who she wanted to believe he was. If the real world came crashing down on him with the news that all Seth was, and all he would ever be, was a skilled, successful hack, would Laura still be able to love him?

He doubted it.

He thought about what they had discussed last night in bed. For Laura, taking a break from saving the world was just that: a break. She would use her sabbatical to restore herself, to spend time with Rita, to plant a garden, or learn how to bake bread in his oven, or read. And then, in a few years—Seth was certain of it—she would be ready to save the world again. If not as a social worker, she would do it some other way. Laura had too much goodness inside her to keep it all for herself and Rita and Seth. She would want to share it with others. That was the way she was.

But Seth...for him, writing *Good Fences* had been the break. Now that his soul was restored, would he find himself with no alternative but to return to writing junk? He still wasn't totally convinced that writing junk was such a terrible thing. Yet Laura believed that it was.

He would be happy to spend the rest of his life with Laura, even if she never returned to any sort of professional work. And he would be happy to spend the rest of his life with her if she *did* return to work. But if he couldn't sell *Good Fences*, and if he never returned to *his* professional work—writing commercial film scripts—he wouldn't be able to support Laura and Rita forever. And if he *did* resume that sort of writing, he would lose Laura. She would walk. Not because he was a sellout, but because he wasn't as brilliant and talented as she wanted him to be.

He heard Rita's plaintive whine from the spare bedroom, then Laura's voice announcing that if Rita wanted to see Sunset Strip she'd have to shake a leg. "Sunset Strip?" Rita chirped, abruptly awake and elated. "No kidding?"

A half-hour later, all three of them were in the Porsche, weaving through the canyon toward the congested Coast Highway. "This," Seth quipped, trying not to let his anxiety get the better of him as his car's overpowered engine moaned in the bumper-to-bumper traffic, "is what we call life in the fast lane."

"Isn't it great that you can wear Hawaiian print shirts to work?" Rita babbled. "Remember, Seth—tell Melinda, 'Todd Bridges. He's your man.'"

"Whatever you say, Rita," Seth mumbled, wondering whether she, too, would lose interest in him if Melinda deemed *Good Fences* a first-class flop. Probably not, he resolved. As long as he wrote a part for Todd Bridges in his next *Ax Man* feature, he'd have Rita's undying adulation.

After forty-five sweaty minutes, he steered the car to a halt in front of an imposing black-paned skyscraper in the center of Los Angeles's business district. "This here's the place," he said, taking a deep breath for courage. He handed his keys to Laura and swung open the door. "Meet me here in two hours. It won't take any longer than that. Wish me luck."

"You don't need any luck," Laura bolstered him.

Right, he muttered to himself as he watched her assume the driver's seat and restart the engine. He remained outside on the paved plaza until the car vanished into the flow of traffic, and for a brief, excruciating moment, he imagined that she had actually driven out of his life.

He couldn't bear to lose Laura—and he couldn't bear the thought that his future with her might very well be resting on what Melinda had to say about his script. Praying with all his heart that Melinda would greet him with a bottle of Mumm's and a slap on the back, he steeled his shoulders and valiantly approached the building.

"A HALF-HOUR ISN'T long enough," Rita complained as Laura prodded her out of the Tower Records shop on Sunset Boulevard. "I could have spent all day in there."

"You could spend all day staring at a single record album," Laura commented. "But I promised we'd meet Seth at his agent's office building in twenty minutes. We're running late."

"I thought you were going to take me to see some of the other sights," Rita sulked, folding herself into the passenger seat of the Porsche.

"And I thought that spending a half-hour in one of the world's largest record stores would satisfy you for the time being. Didn't you think that life-size poster of Sting was cute?"

Rita gaped at her mother. "You like Sting?"

"I think he's sexy," Laura admitted.

"He looks a little like Seth, the way he wears his hair. And the color, too," Rita observed. "He's a fox."

"Who? Sting or Seth?"

"Both," said Rita. Laura nodded in enthusiastic agreement.

As the car neared the building that housed Melinda's office, Laura spotted Seth loitering in the sprawling plaza in front of the building—it was hard to miss him when he was wearing such a brightly colored shirt. She downshifted, taking pride in her smooth manipulation of the gear stick, and cruised to a stop at the curb. He loped across the plaza to the car, and she and Rita climbed out, rearranging themselves so Seth could drive.

He smiled and kissed Laura's cheek as he took the key from her. "Well?" she asked expectantly as he fastened his seat belt and revved the engine.

"Let's drive a little," he said.

His reticence troubled Laura, but she didn't probe. She was by nature a patient person. She would wait until Seth was ready to give her a full report on his meeting with Melinda.

He drove onto the Coast Highway, but didn't take the turnoff at Topanga Canyon. Instead he continued north on the road bordering the twisting coastline, past sun-glazed beaches and dramatic houses, farther and farther from the heart of the city. After making one or two observations about the spellbinding scenery—and the good-looking guys on the beach—Rita subsided in the back seat, also respecting Seth's brooding silence.

Eventually he pulled off the road at a stretch of sand far enough from the city to be sparsely populated. An elderly man with a long-handled metal detector paced the beach, searching for hidden treasures. Two handsome women in daring maillots lay supine on beach towels, baking their skin, oblivious of the treasure seeker as well as the three people in the sleek black Porsche that had just parked in the graveled lot beside the sand.

Seth opened his door, and Laura took that as a signal to open hers, as well. Rita practically pushed her out of the car, shoving the back of Laura's seat forward and leaping out. "Oh, wow!" she shrieked. "This is beautiful!"

"Yes, it is," Laura agreed, inhaling the briny ocean scent and smiling.

"Go ahead, Rita," Seth urged her. "Go stick your big toe in the Pacific."

Rita needed no more encouragement. She yanked off her shoes and darted across the sand to the water's edge.

Seth took Laura's hand and guided her onto the beach at a leisurely gait. He was breathing deeply, too, filling his lungs with the clean, refreshing shore fragrance.

"Melinda hated it," Laura guessed. Even her patience couldn't last forever.

Seth shot Laura a quick look, then turned to gaze at the curling gray-green surf. "Yeah. She hated it."

Laura studied his harsh, angular profile. She knew he must be heartbroken. He had put so much of himself into the script. If his agent hated it, Seth would undoubtedly take such a rejection personally. "I'm so sorry, Seth," she murmured.

"That's the breaks, pal," he said stoically.

"Why did she hate it?" Laura asked. "What did she say?"

He shrugged. "I was in with her for a long time, Laura. We walked through my career, practically through my entire life." He turned to Laura, his eyes tinged with a sadness that nearly broke her heart. "The script is too quiet, she said. Too tame, too understated. Themes with a capital T aren't enough to carry the day. The bottom line is, I just don't have it."

Laura refused to succumb to his pessimism. "You don't have what, Seth?"

"I don't have..." He groaned. "I don't have the talent for it. What I can do, I do well. But what I *can't* do is write a human interest script that anyone in his right mind would be willing to produce. *Good Fences* is too soppy, she said. Too milky. It just won't make it."

"That's her opinion," Laura emphasized.

"Her opinion is worth a hell of a lot," Seth countered. "She's smart, Laura, and knowledgeable. Don't belittle her opinion just because you don't happen to agree with it. Melinda got me started, gave me guidance, helped me to find my talent and develop it. She isn't an idiot."

"She isn't infallible," Laura argued. "Just because she thinks—"

"She *knows*, Laura. All she did was put into words what I already guessed. I'm not—" He stared past Laura at the smooth seam of the horizon and exhaled. "I'm not good enough. I'm not good enough to pull off a script like *Good Fences*, and I'm not good enough for you."

His voice cracked slightly on those final few words, and Laura felt something crack inside herself, as well. "For me? What do I have to do with it?"

"You? I wrote the damned script for you!" His temper flared for a moment, but he resolutely swallowed his anger and returned his aching gaze to the horizon. "I wrote it because you asked me to. You pushed me into it, Laura. You tested me."

"Tested you?" She felt as if the sand were slipping beneath her feet, as if the world were no longer able to support her. How could Seth have thought such a thing? How could he have imagined that she was testing him?

She had urged him to write the script because she loved him. She loved him, and she thought he would enjoy writing something he could believe in. That was all.

She tried to ignore the irrational fear that clutched at her. "Seth," she said, daring to touch his arm. Her fingers curled about the muscle, and she took strength from the solid feel of him. "You don't honestly think I was testing you, do you?"

He twisted his head to peer down at her. "I wrote that script because I wanted it to be good for you, Laura."

"And I wanted it to be good for you," she countered. "I wanted you to write it because I knew you'd make something wonderful out of it."

He sighed, his gaze drifting downward, studying the ripples in the sand at their feet. "I didn't make something wonderful out of it. I flopped. You had faith in me, Laura, and I failed."

"I still have faith in you," she insisted. "And you didn't fail. Melinda might think you did, but that's only her opinion. Not yours, and not mine. Maybe..." She took a deep breath. Once again she was going to make a suggestion, based in total ignorance, about Seth's career. But she wasn't really ignorant. About the movie business, maybe, but not about Seth. "Maybe it's time to find another agent."

"Another agent?" he exclaimed, evidently astonished by Laura's naïveté. "You mean, quit Melinda? After all she's done for me?"

"You don't have to quit her if you want to keep writing the stuff you've been writing all along," Laura said, making a distinction. "That's what she wants. It's easier for her to sell trash than to sell something worthwhile."

"Perhaps writing trash is all I can do," he said grimly. "Perhaps you're giving me more credit than I deserve. Wake up and smell it, Laura. Be real. I'm not cut out for saving the world. I am what I am, and all that."

How could he be so negative? How could someone who had written something as lovely as *Good Fences*, someone with a brain like Seth's and a heart like his not know who he was? "Seth," she said steadily, "you are a brilliant, immensely talented man. I don't give a damn what your agent thinks of one script. *I* know it's the best thing you've ever created. And you know it, too. If she doesn't know it, then it's her misfortune."

He studied her quizzically, as if he weren't sure what she was saying. She wondered at his puzzlement. What could be more obvious? Seth *was* brilliant and talented. After all this time he ought to be aware of that.

"Bypass her," she recommended, desperate to make Seth understand. "Bypass Melinda. You must know people in the industry. An independent producer, maybe. Some rich eccentric looking for an unusual project to invest in. Invest your own money. If I had money, I'd invest in *Good Fences*. Someone somewhere must have enough taste to take a chance on it."

"Just because you like challenges doesn't mean everybody does," Seth pointed out.

"I don't care about everybody," Laura maintained. "I care about you. Your stupid agent likes scripts with blood and guts in them, but she hasn't got the good sense to realize that what you showed her is full of *your* blood, *your* guts. You can't turn your back on it now."

She detected the merest glimmer of a smile on his lips. "Would you like me to find you a windmill to fence while you're at it?" he offered.

"I've already found one," she answered calmly.

"Laura." He twisted back to face the water. Rita had rolled up the hems of her jeans and was wading in the foam. He watched her for a moment. "She's probably dreaming about becoming a surfer," he observed.

"Yes," Laura agreed. "Rita has dreams, and she doesn't quit on them. That's one reason I love her."

"Why do you love me?" he asked solemnly.

"Because you're you," she replied. "Because you've got dreams, too, and because you've shared them with me. *Good Fences* is one of your dreams, Seth. Don't quit on it."

His hand tightened on hers. "You'd love me even if I were a failure, wouldn't you," he half asked.

"As long as you were a noble failure," Laura swore. "As long as you didn't give up. But, then, as long as you didn't give up, you couldn't possibly be a failure."

He pulled her toward him and wrapped his arms around her. "And why do I love you?" he whispered.

"I don't know," she answered tentatively. "You think I'm pushy, testing you, that I forced you to do something you didn't want to do." She shivered as the truth of her words sank in. If Seth honestly believed such things of her, how could he ever love her?

"I'll tell you why I love you," he said, bowing to kiss her brow. "Not just because you've got dreams, but because you knock yourself out trying to make them come true." He smiled. "You didn't force me to do anything I didn't really want to do, Brodie. If you think I'm that easy to push around, think again."

"You're not easy to push around?" she asked, permitting herself a slight smile.

"Try me and find out," he dared her.

"Hmm," she mused, her smile expanding and growing mischievous. "That's a challenge I can't refuse."

He studied her face, and his lips slowly spread into a grin. "Does that mean you're going to stick around?"

"Of course I am. I want to master that fancy oven of yours."

"Now the truth comes out," he grumbled playfully. "You love me for my microwave."

She shook her head. "Your Porsche, Stoned," she corrected him.

"I knew it!" he crowed, lifting her off the sand and exuberantly swinging her in a circle. "I knew you'd come to love that car of mine."

"More than life itself, Seth," she deadpanned.

Seth began to laugh, although he didn't lower Laura back to her feet. Clinging to him, her arms tight around his neck, she laughed, too. The sweet harmony of their laughter lifted on the wind and mingled with the muffled roar of the surf pounding the earth.

And they discovered, much to their utter pleasure, that it was possible to laugh and kiss at the same time.

"Kimberly, this is Andrew Collins."

Andrew Collins. She had no idea why he, of all people, would be calling her. They hadn't been friends in college, merely fellow toilers on their newspaper. Andrew had never been particularly fond of her; he had never made any pretense of his lack of respect for her. She hadn't respected him much, either.

He had been condescending, arrogant, an egghead. He used to call her "cheerleader", pronouncing the word as if it were the highest insult. Yet she couldn't deny a perverse joy in hearing from him now. He was a man who had never made a pass at her, who never would. He was a man whom she could invite into her house for coffee knowing that he would never misinterpret her intentions.

Her large blue eyes flickered to Whitney, who was leaning against the counter and watching her with fascination. *Why not*? she contemplated mischievously. *Anything that will turn Whitney off...* "Andrew!" she exclaimed into the telephone. "Andrew, darling!"

COMMITMENTS

BY

JUDITH ARNOLD

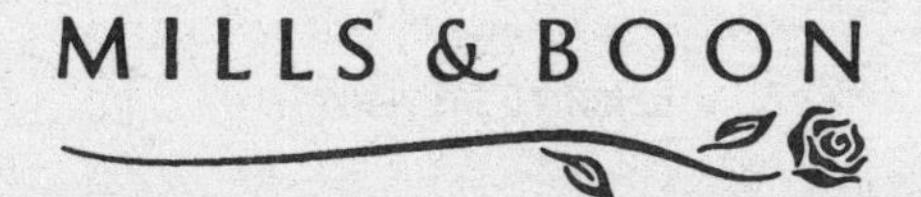

MILLS & BOON LIMITED
ETON HOUSE, 18-24 PARADISE ROAD
RICHMOND, SURREY TW9 1SR

Published in Great Britain in 1994 by Mills & Boon Limited, Eton House, 18-24 Paradise Road, Richmond, Surrey TW9 1SR

ISBN 0 263 78906 3

87-9406

Made and printed in Great Britain

Foreword

Commitments are hard to keep. Sometimes they're even harder to break.

The six characters who form the nucleus of these three books—Laura, Seth, Kimberly, Andrew, Julianne and Troy—all entered adulthood at the end of the 1960s, a time when people committed themselves less to their own fulfillment than to ideals, principles, the larger world. In college they chose to illustrate their commitment to peace and justice and their respect for humanity by publishing an underground newspaper, *The Dream.*

Eventually the sixties generation grew up. Once Laura, Kimberly, Julianne, Seth, Andrew and Troy were no longer protected by the ivy-covered walls of the university, they ventured into the real world and made new commitments: to careers, to children, to lovers.

In *Promises*, the first book of the trilogy, Seth and Laura were able, through their love, to rediscover and satisfy the promises of their youth. *Commitments* focuses on two young people who have, if anything, surpassed their early promise and who have not forgotten the priorities of their youth.

Kimberly Belmont has forged a successful career as a speech writer for a United States senator. Andrew Collins has earned a Ph.D. in political economics and joined the faculty of Amherst College. For both Kimberly and Andrew, the commitment they made to their professions has paid off. One reason they were able to make that commitment to their work is that in an equally important commitment—marriage—both of them saw their hopes and expectations shattered.

Loving another person can be difficult under the best of circumstances. For Kimberly and Andrew, it is almost impossible—not only because of their past heartbreaks, but because, when they were classmates at Columbia, they despised each other. For them to give their love the chance it deserves entails more than simply committing themselves to their relationship. They must first break the commitment they have to their memories—memories of each other and of the pain they've endured.

Breaking such commitments, they learn, can be as hard as making new ones.

Romance, no matter what one's age, no matter what generation one is part of, involves knowing when to commit oneself, and how and to whom. It also involves promises—making them and having the courage to live up to them. Ultimately romance involves dreams: the strength and imagination to dream of peace, contentment, perfection, love...the strength and imagination to chase those dreams, even knowing that they are often unattainable.

In *Dreams*, the final book of the trilogy, Julianne and Troy—and all their fellow "dreamers"—will discover whether it is possible to make dreams—even those seemingly unattainable ones—come true.

Chapter One

Dating, Kimberly mused, was a lot like riding a bicycle. Once you mastered the motions they were with you for life.

The last time Kimberly had ridden a bicycle had been about three years ago, with her niece Mary Catherine. M.C. had just received a new bike for her birthday, and Kimberly had used the child's old bike, a squeaky thing with a white wicker basket hanging off the handlebars and pink paint flaking from the frame. Touring the suburban Augusta neighborhood where Kimberly's sister and brother-in-law lived, Kimberly and M.C. had coasted past the large brick houses with their expansive, well-cultivated yards, inhaling the sweet spring fragrance of the blooming magnolias, the dogwood and fresh-cut grass. Although she hadn't been on a bike in ages before that afternoon, Kimberly had had little difficulty remembering the rhythm, the flow and balance of riding.

The last time Kimberly had been on a date was over fifteen years ago. But tonight, as she left the pricey French restaurant with Whitney Brannigan for a leisurely walk back to her Georgetown apartment, she reflected on the fact that she hadn't forgotten the rhythm, flow, or balance of this particular exercise, either. She had remembered when to smile at Whitney, how to smile, when to ask him the right questions, how to react to his answers. Her date with him hadn't been nearly as much fun as pedaling around town with M.C. But as Kimberly assessed her dinner outing with Whitney, she congratulated herself on having avoided falling, wobbling, crashing.

Whitney was a suitable partner for her first date in eons. He was handsome in the right way, with the sort of crisp, clean-cut looks that had always appealed to her, even during her flirtation with hippiedom in college. Whitney was two years her senior, well educated, ruthless enough professionally to be interesting, and, as her mother would put it, "as bright as a Christmas tree light." If Kimberly ever quoted her mother's pet phrase to him, he would cringe, but she thought the comparison appropriate. He reminded her of a pointy green bulb flashing on and off, reflecting off the surrounding tinsel.

She had known Whitney for four years, ever since she had joined Senator Milford's staff as a speech writer. Within a month of her arrival on Capitol Hill, Whitney had asked her out for a date. That she was married at the time hadn't fazed him in the least. "Your old man doesn't have to know," he had coolly pointed out, as if leaving Todd in ignorance would have made Whitney's proposition morally valid.

Tonight such moral questions weren't at issue. That very morning, Kimberly had gotten to work late, having first stopped at her attorney's office on her way to the senator's suite in the Hart Building. The lawyer had handed her the folded decree and shaken her hand. "That's it, Ms. Belmont," he had announced robustly. "It's all behind you now, all history. You're free and clear."

She didn't want to be free and clear. She didn't want to be divorced. But she was now in possession of a neatly typed and signed document that declared her free and clear. Unattached. Single. Alone.

She'd never before been so completely, officially, legally alone in her life.

"Didn't Henry Kissinger use to live on this block?" Whitney inquired as they strolled along one of the brick sidewalks lined with beautifully restored town houses, many of which dated back to colonial times. The street was paved with worn cobblestones, and no longer functional trolley tracks lay imbedded in the surface. The streetlights were designed to resemble antique gas lamps. Grasping for positive aspects in her current situation, Kimberly meditated on the pleasure she took in living in Georgetown. Todd had never liked that quaint community of Washington, D.C. He needed space, he insisted, the sort of space that came with a house on the outskirts of the city.

"Goodie for Henry Kissinger," Kimberly said, her tone a touch too biting. A proper lady wasn't supposed to be sarcastic on a date. But thirty-five-year-old divorcées didn't have to be all that proper, she decided.

Besides, she knew that her escort wasn't a big Kissinger fan. A foreign policy specialist on the senator's staff, Whitney tended to view the world from a slightly left-of-center perspective, just as their boss, the senator, did. In her college days, Kimberly would have considered an old-fashioned liberal like Senator Milford faintly reactionary. But times had changed, the center had shifted, and now men and women like the senator were the standard-bearers for the New Left. "Neoliberalism," a columnist had recently coined the political shading. As a political functionary, Kimberly believed it was her duty to keep up with the terminology.

"So Todd has decided to stay on in your old house?" Whitney asked.

"I thought we weren't going to discuss my divorce," Kimberly chastised him. *My divorce.* The words tasted acidic to her, but she supposed she'd have to get used to them.

"You laid down some pretty stringent rules, Kim," Whitney teased her, combing a flopping lock of dark brown hair back from his high brow and winking roguishly. "No shop talk tonight, and no divorce talk."

"I think we did just fine, considering," she said, matching his light tone. Indeed, Whitney had chattered up a veritable storm over dinner. He had described the renovated condominium he had bought in Alexandria, and the vacation trip he'd taken in March to Club Med on Eleuthera Island, and the vicissitudes of finding time for racquetball. One of the most important dating skills Kimberly's mother had drilled into her was to get one's companion to talk about himself. "Men love to talk about themselves," Mrs. Belmont had instructed her daughter years and years ago. "Feed them the right questions, dear, and they will go on forever."

At times Whitney had definitely seemed to go on forever, but that was all right with Kimberly. She preferred listening to him talk about himself to having to talk about herself. What would she have said about her current life? *I'm free and clear. Lucky me.*

"So you're going to remain in Georgetown?" Whitney asked.

"I've been living here for a year," she pointed out. "Why should I move?"

"It's an expensive area."

"I get by," she assured him. In order to stay on in their house in Chevy Chase, Todd had had to buy out her share of the place, and she'd invested the money in a nontaxable bond fund that helped to cover her costs. She hated having to think about such things as investments and taxes; the subject of family finance had always been Todd's responsibility when they were married. Part of being free and clear, she had learned since their separation, entailed taking care of one's own money. Which was definitely *not* the sort of thing a proper lady was supposed to do. But again, "proper" didn't seem a particularly applicable adjective for Kimberly at the moment.

In truth, she had never been especially proper. Not even in her youth, when she was still in the thrall of her distant but infinitely respectable father and her imperious mother, had she managed to live within the strict limits of ladylike propriety. Proper young ladies of the South were supposed to attend schools like Sweet Briar College, not Barnard. They were supposed to major in music or early childhood education, not political science. They were supposed to wear skirts, not jeans, and drink mint juleps, not Liebfraumilch. They were supposed to join sororities, admire men wearing uniforms and keep fluffy white stuffed kitten dolls on their French provincial bureaus.

They were not supposed to live in dormitories on the edge of Harlem, read the poetry of Langston Hughes, and view Eleanor Roosevelt and Gloria Steinem as appropriate role models. They were not supposed to listen to the Rolling Stones and rile their parents by singing "Let's Spend the Night Together" and "Sympathy for the Devil" at the breakfast table.

And, no matter how intelligent they were, they were supposed to strive to be ignorant about finances. They were supposed to giggle charmingly when the bills for their extravagant indulgences arrived in the mail, and their giggling charm was supposed to guarantee that their menfolk would willingly earn the money needed to pay for those indulgences.

No, Kimberly had never been proper, not that way. If her friends at college and later at work found her to be a bit more proper than they were used to, it was undoubtedly because their basis for comparison differed from Kimberly's. To her family she was a renegade, a black sheep, quite probably touched.

"This is my place," she said, turning up the walk that led to her apartment, a ground-floor walk-through of a brownstone across the street from the playing fields of a high school. The open expanse of grass facing the building gave her basement apartment a great deal of light, and she had private access to the tiny fenced-in yard behind the town house. Once she had come to terms with the reality that she was no longer living with Todd, she had grown to adore her apartment. "Would you like to come in for some coffee?" she asked Whitney.

He smiled with delight. "I was hoping you'd ask," he eagerly accepted.

She unlocked the front door, which was located underneath the concrete stairs leading up to the main door of the town house. As she understood it, the basement flat had been built several years back as an in-law apartment, but the landlord's mother-in-law had whimsically decided, after the construction had been completed, that she didn't want to live below her daughter's family. So they rented to Kimberly, instead.

She ushered Whitney through the entry hall and into the cozy living room. "I'm sure I have something harder than coffee, if you'd prefer a nightcap," she offered graciously.

He didn't answer immediately; he was too busy surveying the living room. An overstuffed sofa and matching easy chair, upholstered in a floral print, took up much of the room. Shelves neatly decorated with an assortment of books, a television, a stereo and a few strategically placed objets d'art lined another wall. The two windows overlooking the small front yard were covered with ornate wrought-iron grills.

After satisfying his curiosity, he turned to her, loosened his tie and unbuttoned the collar of his oxford shirt. "You've never invited me into your house before."

"We've never been on a date before," she reminded him.

"That wasn't my choice," he said, crossing to the counter that separated the dining area from the kitchen.

Kimberly smiled uneasily. She wished that Whitney hadn't loosened his tie. It made him appear too much at home, and she was far from ready for him to make himself at home in her apartment. This was their first date, after all, and the only reason she had invited him in was that they were adults and associates at work, and it seemed like a polite thing to do. "Coffee?" she asked, hoping that he would choose that over liquor.

He grinned and strode around the counter to join her in the kitchen. "Let me give you a hand," he suggested.

She laughed. "You needn't act as if I'm helpless," she chided him. "I can make a fine pot of coffee all by myself."

"Skip the coffee."

She shot him a suspicious glance. "Brandy?" she asked.

"Skip that, too." He curled his long fingers around her upper arms and drew her to him.

The warmth of his palms permeated the lightweight fabric of her sleeves, but paradoxically she shivered. "Don't be silly, Whitney," she said sharply, trying to shrug out of his grip. Calling a man silly was *not* a proper thing to do—one ought never to deflate a man's ego on a date—but she'd be damned if she'd let him kiss her just because he'd paid for dinner.

"I wasn't being silly," he said, obviously not at all deflated. "I was being romantic, which, under the circumstances, seems like a good way to end the evening."

"Oh, Whitney..." She watched as his mouth descended toward her from what seemed like an inordinate height. She stood only five feet four inches tall, and even though she generally wore high-heeled shoes, she was used to looking up to men physically. Whitney's superior height didn't alarm her. She deftly turned her head, and his lips landed on the soft golden tendrils covering her ear. "I hate to disillusion you, Whitney, but I think it would be a dreadful way to end the evening."

"I'm disillusioned," he said after spitting out her hair.

"Sorry." She occupied herself preparing a pot of coffee, even though she would rather he just leave. His silence provoked her to justify herself. "We work together, Whitney. We see each other every day. It would be a bit foolhardy to risk our working relationship, don't you think?" There, she commended herself. That wasn't nearly as ego-puncturing as calling him silly.

"Are you really sorry?" He pulled the glass decanter from the coffee maker out of her hands before she could fill it with water, and set it on the counter. Then he rotated her to face him once more. "I'm all in favor of being foolhardy, Kim."

He tried to kiss her again, and she slipped out of his embrace. "Please stop this, Whitney."

"Stop what?" He seemed slightly exasperated. "You're single now, Kim. Divorced. We aren't breaking any laws."

"I know that." She backed into the corner where the counter met the wall and watched him warily. That Whitney was good-looking was irrelevant. She had viewed his cleanly chiseled face and gazed into his limpid brown eyes countless times at work, and she had never felt the slightest pinch of desire for him. Their having just shared a nonbusiness dinner at an expensive restaurant didn't change anything. "I *am* sorry," she drawled. "But I'm asking you very nicely, friend to friend, colleague to colleague—please don't make a pass at me."

"And I'm asking you very nicely to stop being such a virginal prig," he countered as he approached her. His unwelcome nearness gave her the distinct impression that she was trapped. "It's 1987, Kim. When a woman invites a man into her home in 1987 she ought to know what to expect."

"Well, I don't," she defended herself. "I'm new at this, remember?"

"Fair enough. That's why I'm briefing you on it." He was practically upon her, and his hands alighted on her shoulders. "You're a beautiful woman. I'm a healthy man. We know each other and we like each other. So what's the hang-up?"

"The hang-up is, I asked if you wanted coffee, not if you wanted me." She didn't bother to conceal her anger. "If a woman can't invite a man into her home for a cup of coffee, period, then the world of 1987 is in pitiful shape."

"I won't argue about the shape of the world," Whitney allowed. "But it's the only world I've got, and this is how things are done in it. A man takes a woman out for dinner, and when she invites him back to her place afterward, he has every right to make assumptions."

"And she has every right to correct him if he's made the wrong ones," Kimberly asserted. She wasn't frightened by his proximity and his stubbornness. Only supremely annoyed. If he persisted in his muleheaded attempt to seduce her, she would become disgusted with him. And then, when they had to face each other the next day at work, she would be inclined to spit on him. Which would make going to work a difficult proposition. "Please, Whitney. Cool off. If you can't handle being invited into my apartment without attaching all sorts of innuendo to it, then I'll thank you to leave."

He engaged in an internal debate, apparently trying to come up with a new tactic. *Lord help us both,* Kimberly muttered under her breath, *but if he tries anything, anything at all, I'll slam the nearest skillet right into his skull.* Even proper Southern ladies—*especially* proper Southern ladies—knew how to protect themselves from wolves.

"Is it me?" Whitney asked, appearing absurdly innocent. "You don't like me?"

"I like you just fine," Kimberly retorted. "But I don't like your behavior at the moment."

He seemed totally unable to fathom the possibility that Kimberly could be rejecting him. "Your marriage fell apart a year ago. I can't believe you've been living a nun's life for a whole year. Is it someone else? You're seeing someone else, is that it?"

What she couldn't believe was how thickheaded he was behaving. She had always admired Whitney's intelligence, but right now he was acting like a genuine dolt.

Or maybe it was merely a matter of his being a man. Men were congenitally unable to accept that women could turn them down for the simple reason that they weren't interested in them sexually. They always had to grasp at far-fetched explanations.

Before she could come up with a diplomatic way of telling him that although there wasn't anybody else in her life she wasn't going to go to bed with him, the telephone rang. Smiling with unbridled relief, she eased away from the counter to reach for the receiver. "Hello?"

"Kimberly?" A vaguely familiar baritone crackled through the long-distance static on the wire. "Kimberly, this is Andrew Collins."

Andrew Collins. Her acquaintance from college, her co-worker on that old, radical student newspaper *The Dream*. Until she had seen him at the reunion Julianne had arranged for the staff, Kimberly hadn't thought about Andrew Collins for fifteen years. And although they'd made amiable chitchat at the reunion, she hadn't anticipated that she would ever think about him again.

She had no idea why he, of all people, would be calling her. They hadn't been friends in college, merely fellow toilers on their newspaper. Andrew had never been particularly fond of her; he had never made any pretense of his lack of respect for her. She hadn't respected him much, either.

He had been condescending, arrogant, an egghead. He used to call her "cheerleader," pronouncing the word as if it were the highest insult. Kimberly *had* been a cheerleader in high school, and she saw nothing wrong with that. That Andrew Collins did made her distrust him during the years they had known each other.

Yet she couldn't deny a perverse joy in hearing from him now. He was a man who had never made a pass at her, who never would. He was a man whom she could invite into her house for coffee knowing that he would never misinterpret her intentions. Even if her intentions were dishonorable, he would never presume to take advantage of her.

Her large blue eyes flickered to Whitney, who was leaning against the counter and watching her with fascination. *Why not?* she contemplated mischievously. *Anything that will turn the fool off....* "Andrew!" she exclaimed into the telephone. "Andrew, darling!"

DARLING?

A deep frown line dented Andrew's brow as he tried to analyze Kimberly's surprisingly affectionate greeting. By no stretch of the imagination could he and Kimberly consider their relationship one in which the word "darling" would be apt. He had phoned her because he was desperate, that was all.

It had been a long day, long and difficult. He was still reeling from it, still trying to make sense of how something that had seemed so right could have gone so terribly wrong.

Bob McIntyre had first connected him with John Wilding at the Latin American Research Council last autumn. "They're looking for an ambitious young researcher to fund," Bob had explained. "They need some data on the farm economy in El Salvador. The research that comes out of it could be infinitely helpful to you here. A few articles, maybe a book...I don't have to tell you that with your tenure decision coming up next year, another publication won't hurt you. L.A.R.C. has financial resources. They'll fund you generously. If you're interested in pursuing this, I'll put you in touch with Wilding."

Interested? Andrew had been ecstatic. Funding for extracurricular research was hard to come by in the academic world, particularly when one was a social scientist. The think tanks had their pets, and private industry supported its own economists, not assistant professors from private colleges. Andrew's specialty was the economy of Central America. Being offered nearly unlimited funding to delve into the agricultural economy of El Salvador was a gift of almost unseemly proportions.

More was at stake than simply research funding. Andrew had been teaching at Amherst College for five years, and he wanted to remain on the faculty, to get tenure, to feel secure. He wanted to know that something was his and that it wouldn't be taken away from him.

He had already published one book and numerous articles. His student evaluations were positive, and his colleagues in the department seemed to like him. With a powerful man like Bob McIntyre in his corner, tenure was almost guaranteed.

So he'd met with John Wilding. "L.A.R.C. is a private organization with some modest government backing," Wilding had explained. "Things are unstable in El Salvador, as well you know. We're trying to formulate an idea of how unstable. If you want to get some publications out of the research you do for us, I have no objections."

It had all sounded so reasonable, so pure, so believable. And Andrew was a man who needed to believe. The promise of a happily-ever-after future had already been snatched from him once. Like anyone whose faith had been severely shaken, he needed possibilities. He needed hope.

So he had accepted Wilding's offer of funding. He'd accepted L.A.R.C.'s bounty. He had traveled twice to El Salvador, driven through the rugged, revolution-torn interior to interview the sugar and coffee farmers and then conferred with agricultural experts in the government in San Salvador. He had flown to Los Angeles to meet several refugees. Then he'd compiled his data, interpolated it, put it all into a nice, neat package for the council. And patted himself on the back for a job well done.

But that morning, when he'd met with John Wilding to discuss his findings, everything had come crashing down upon him.

As soon as he had made some sense of what he was involved in, he had decided to call Kimberly. Not because he liked her, not because he admired her, but because she worked for a senator. He wasn't sure whether what Wilding was doing with L.A.R.C. was legal, whether the man had the blessings of the federal government. But if anyone was to investigate Wilding, it would have to be someone with access to government power, someone Andrew could trust. He prayed that Kimberly was that someone. She *had* to be—he had no one else to turn to.

Yet why on earth had she called him "darling"?

"Is this Kimberly Belmont?" he asked, wondering whether he had dialed the wrong number.

"Of course it is, Andrew," she replied in her unmistakable drawl. Her Southern accent wasn't overbearing, but it grated on Andrew. Southern accents made him think of such cultural icons as Scarlett O'Hara and Colonel Sanders. Southerners spoke too slowly; they made Andrew impatient.

"I got your telephone number from Julianne," he informed her, feeling that he had to justify his call. "I hope I'm not disturbing you—"

"Not at all."

"Well... there's something I want to talk to you about. Business," he felt obliged to add. "I think we ought to discuss it in person, if that's at all possible."

"Anything's possible, Andrew."

What was with her? Why did she sound so downright pleased to hear from him? "If it's all right with you," he proceeded, doing his best not to succumb to utter bewilderment, "I could fly down after my last class Friday morning. I could get to D.C. by mid-afternoon."

"That would be absolutely lovely," she purred, increasing his puzzlement. "Why don't you come straight to my office? It's in Senator Milford's suite, in the Hart Building."

"All right," he said, at a loss. "I'll met you there around three or so."

"Fine."

He hesitated. What else was he supposed to say? Should he be civil and ask how she was doing? Should he tell her he was looking forward to seeing her? That wouldn't be completely honest. The truth was, he wished he didn't have to see her. He wished he didn't have to travel to Washington and try to unravel the mess in which his career was currently tangled.

But he had to say something. "Thank you," he mumbled. "I appreciate this."

"It's my pleasure, Andrew," Kimberly responded before hanging up.

"What did she say?" Donna asked.

Andrew lowered the receiver and turned from his desk. Across the room, Donna was seated on the couch, her long, denim-clad legs crossed squaw-style beneath her, with the newspaper spread open to the crossword puzzle on her knees. She closed her pen with a quiet click and gazed inquisitively at Andrew.

For not the first time, he was struck by how much Donna resembled his wife. Marjorie, too, had been tall and slim, with short-cropped, dark hair, brown eyes that sloped down at the outer corners, a narrow, pointy nose and sharp chin. Like Marjorie, Donna gave off an aura of scholarly interest in the world. Which wasn't terribly surprising, Andrew acknowledged, since Donna was a doctoral candidate in psychology at the University of Massachusetts, just down the road from Amherst College. He often wondered whether he had taken up with her simply because she reminded him so much of Marjorie.

Becoming involved with someone because she brought to mind the woman he had loved and lost wasn't really a ghoulish thing, Andrew consoled himself. It was probably quite normal. The only problem was, he couldn't bring himself to love Donna. She *wasn't* Marjorie, and no matter how close she came, he would always be disappointed by her failure to replace his dead wife.

"I take it she's willing to see you?" Donna half asked, her curiosity brimming over.

"Yes. I'm going to Washington on Friday."

"You don't have to look so shaken about the whole thing," Donna scolded him breezily. "You said this woman is an old friend of yours. You've known her for fifteen years. You worked together on that newspaper of yours when you were undergraduates. Why shouldn't she help you out?"

"It's not seeing her that's bothering me," Andrew argued, then sighed and pulled off his eyeglasses. He rubbed the bridge of his nose with his thumb and forefinger and reflected on his edginess. The thought of seeing Kimberly did bother him, but he could think of no good reason it should.

Except that she'd called him "darling." Except that she'd claimed that it would be "lovely" to see him. Except that she'd said, "Anything's possible."

Why?

Although he had told Donna that Kimberly was an old friend of his, "friend" was hardly the word he would use to describe her. They were more like adversaries, antagonists. From the moment he'd laid eyes on her, she had rubbed him the wrong way.

Well, maybe not from that first moment. He recalled the first time he had seen her, when he and his buddy Troy Bennett had entered the classroom for the initial meeting of their advanced rhetoric class. Kimberly had been impossible to miss, with all that blond hair falling to her waist like a shimmering river of gold, and those enormous blue eyes, those delicate cheeks and perpetually pursed lips. "Who the hell is that?" Troy had whispered, nudging Andrew and pointing her out. "Somebody's date?"

It had been a joke among Columbia men at the time that there was no such thing as a pretty Barnard girl. That was an exaggeration, of course; there were as many attractive women at Barnard as at any other school. But for the most part, even those few who qualified as knockouts did their best to appear frumpy and studious. They thought they were being liberated. Evidently they wanted to attract the attentions of men with their brains, not their bodies. Barnard wasn't called "Barnyard" for nothing.

But Kimberly Belmont had done nothing to conceal her extraordinary beauty. Rather than wearing men's cut Levi's, she wore jeans that actually fit, that displayed her narrow waist and flaring hips. Occasionally she even wore eye makeup and a touch of lipstick. She smiled a lot.

How she wound up being close friends with such a bright, sensible woman as Julianne Robinson had always been a mystery to Andrew. But when, for a class project, Julianne and Kimberly, Seth Stone, Laura Brodie, Troy and Andrew decided to put together a newspaper, Andrew was forced to concede that Kimberly was truly a Barnard student—albeit an anomalous one.

She didn't seem serious enough to be a *real* student. She was always so damned chipper and ebullient. Rather than writing gritty articles for *The Dream*, she always wanted to write uplifting stories, essays not about the downtrodden residents of Morningside Heights but about the Korean immigrant who ran the produce market on Broadway. "A success story!" she would exclaim. "Let me write about someone who's made it. People want to read happy things, too, sometimes."

She reminded Andrew of those circular yellow smile faces that had been the rage at the time. Sunny, perky, superficial. She was awfully nice to look at, but you couldn't really talk to her without feeling you were stuck in the middle of a pep rally.

Now she worked as a speech writer for Howard Milford, a senator for whom Andrew harbored a modicum of respect. Not that he trusted politicians as a class, but Milford usually voted the right way on issues. If Milford trusted Kimberly enough to give her such an important position on his staff, Andrew figured she must have something going for her. Reputable senators didn't hire women as speech writers simply because they were gorgeous. Secretaries, perhaps, but not speech writers.

"Why don't we get some food?" Donna broke into his thoughts. "I'm ravenous."

He slipped his eyeglasses back up his nose and gazed at the woman across the living room. She wasn't really far away—the dimensions of his apartment, one of four in a converted old house, were tiny—but she seemed to be seated in another galaxy.

"I'm not very hungry," he said. "If you want, we can open a can of something."

Donna grinned and stretched, her oversize T-shirt draping loosely across her bony body. "Forget it, Andy. I just said I was ravenous. Take me to Friendly's for a tuna melt and an ice cream, and I might love you forever."

He forced a smile. "You're easy to please."

She stood and crossed the room. "I hate seeing you look so worried, Andy," she said, slinging her arms around his neck and planting a kiss on his forehead. "Personally, I think this whole thing is a tempest in a teapot."

"I wish you were right. But you're not," he contended. "Wilding is a dangerous man. And if I blow the whistle on him, I'm going to embarrass Bob McIntyre. And if I embarrass Bob McIntyre, I can kiss tenure goodbye. Q.E.D."

"If I were you," Donna remarked, "I'd pocket that whistle until after you've got tenure. Why make waves?"

She wasn't from a different galaxy, he realized, but rather from a different time zone. Donna was twenty-eight, and in many ways, being eight years younger than Andrew put her into an entirely different generation. She was a child of the seventies, not the sixties, a product of the "Me Generation." He had no doubt whatsoever that Donna would have done whatever it took to finish her Ph.D., land herself a dream job and keep it for as long as she wanted it. She knew how to be earnest without being committed, and that was probably a very healthy way to go about life these days.

But Andrew couldn't live like that.

He couldn't explain himself to Donna. She wouldn't understand. Andrew was a product of an older, more idealistic generation, and sometimes he acted reflexively. Sometimes, even though it risked his stable life, he felt compelled to take a stand.

"Friendly's," he said, hoisting himself to his feet. He ought to feed Donna, no matter how meager his own appetite was. He ought to feed her and bring her back to his place afterward and enjoy her company for a few hours. Whether Andrew could resolve his plight wasn't contingent on skipping meals or locking out his current girlfriend.

He pocketed his key, took her hand and accompanied her out of the apartment.

Chapter Two

Kimberly was on the telephone when Andrew reached the open door of her office. Without interrupting her phone conversation, she tossed him a quick smile and beckoned him inside with a wave. As soon as he had crossed the threshold, she held up her index finger to indicate that she would be off the phone in a minute. Then she angled her face away from Andrew and addressed her caller. "The Kiwanis may or may not be brighter than the Junior Achievers, Lee, but they *are* older. The senator is not going to give a speech written for high school students to a professional group like the Kiwanis. If you all can just cool your heels until next week, I will gladly juice up the Junior Achievers speech. But you'll simply have to give me a chance to dip into my book of anecdotes, Lee. We can't have the senator regaling a bunch of grown men with that shaggy-dog story about the time his father's car broke down on his way to the senior prom."

She listened for a moment, caught Andrew's eye and smiled helplessly. "No, he's not going to get into heavy issues," she said into the phone. "He'll be speaking after dinner. The fine gentlemen in the audience are all going to be soused. I'm sure the senator will want to avoid policy statements. That includes his views on trade tariffs."

Doing his best not to eavesdrop, Andrew tightened his grip on his battered leather briefcase and surveyed the small inner office. Kimberly's desk was impeccably tidy, her blotter clear and all loose papers stacked neatly in a wire tray occupying one corner. The perpendicular extension of the desk held a compact word processor. White file cabinets stood along a wall and an unabridged dictionary lay open on a polished oak book stand in one corner. Although the office lacked a window, it seemed uncommonly bright.

That might have been due less to the glaring overhead fixture than to Kimberly's radiant presence, he admitted. She had always had the ability to illuminate her surroundings. Andrew wasn't sure whether to attribute that ability to her lustrous blond hair, which was no less striking in its stylish chin-length shag than it had been back in college, when she'd worn it long and free-flowing, or to her beaming smile. Although her suit was a pale gray hue and her blouse a muted pink, her attire also seemed to add light to the room.

"Lee, we both know that this won't be the proper forum for enunciating policy positions. I assure you, the senator will agree with me on this. It's going to be a backslapping, I'm-one-of-the-guys speech, that's all."

Andrew shouldn't have been impressed by her end of the conversation. He should have assumed that a woman in Kimberly's position would have backbone and clout, would be able to argue decisively, would use phrases like "trade tariffs" and "enunciating policy positions." If the woman were as much of a ninny as she had so often seemed to him years ago, she wouldn't be the head speech writer for a senator.

Still, he found that listening to Kimberly haggle about an upcoming speech was something of a revelation. He had trouble reconciling his image of the delicate, nearly fragile-looking blond woman he had known in college with the high-powered, articulate professional now seated at the desk across the office from him. Seeing her in such a milieu and hearing her speak with such utter confidence was disorienting. Far from appearing delicate and fragile, she seemed dynamic to Andrew, almost nerve-wrackingly bright.

Perhaps she had more on the ball than he had ever given her credit for. He certainly hoped so. If she was going to help him, she would have to be more than a frivolous Southern belle.

"I'll have something for you next week, Lee," she said, signing off. "Stick with me on this. I know the senator will appreciate it." She hung up the phone and smiled again. "Hello, Andrew. I'm sorry I got tied up on the telephone. Please sit down."

Her greeting was only the slightest bit warmer than strictly businesslike, and Andrew was reassured by it. He hadn't yet recovered from their bizarre conversation two days ago, when she had called him "darling." But since her manner with him today was pleasantly aloof, he decided not to question her about her reasons for implying an intimacy between them the last time they had spoken.

"How was your trip down?" she asked politely.

He cautiously took a seat on the vinyl upholstered chair facing her desk and set his briefcase on the floor at his feet. Kimberly appeared so well groomed that he wished he had worn a tie. He had packed one, but he hadn't bothered to put it on when he'd stopped at the motel to check in on his way from the airport. At work he generally wore jeans or corduroys, and comfortable shirts with the collars left unbuttoned. Ties were reserved for cocktail parties and meetings with the dean of the college, not for hectic jaunts to Washington to confer with a former acquaintance.

At least his shirt was crisp, his blazer fairly new, his loafers recently polished. He was surprised to find himself so concerned about the impression he was making on Kimberly.

"The flight was okay," he answered her. "I've got to say, though, this Metro system of yours is absolutely mystifying. The train carried me from Crystal City to downtown Washington without any mishaps, but then when I got off, I couldn't get out of the station. Every time I inserted my fare card in the exit slot, the damned machine spit it back out at me. It took me a few minutes to realize that I had to pay an extra fare just to get through the gate and win my freedom."

"The Metro takes some getting used to," Kimberly agreed. "You're staying in Crystal City, then?"

"I've got a room at one of the motels there. They're cheaper than the hotels in the city."

Kimberly nodded. Andrew wondered whether she found their conversation as stilted as he did. "Would you like some coffee?" she offered.

Before he could answer, a fresh-faced young man tapped on Kimberly's open door and poked his head inside. "Ms. Belmont— Oh, excuse me," he said, belatedly noticing Andrew.

"That's all right, Barry," Kimberly assured him. "What can I do for you?"

Grinning meekly, the young man stepped inside the office. "I was just wondering if you've had a chance to look over my first draft for the 'Letter to the Constituents' flyer."

"I've gone through it," Kimberly said, lifting a stapled collection of pages from the top of her basket and extending it toward her associate. "You touch all the bases just fine, Barry, but as usual you've tended to be long-winded. Especially in the Social Security report. Cut it down and punch it up. You've got to keep it lively, or you'll bore the voters."

"Got it." Barry took the papers and headed for the door. "Thanks, Ms. Belmont. I'll get a new draft to you by Monday."

Kimberly watched his departure and turned back to Andrew. "My newest assistant," she explained. "He's very eager, but he has a lot to learn. I'm sorry for all these distractions," she apologized again.

Once more, Andrew reminded himself that he had no right to be surprised by her professional polish. If Kimberly was still a cheerleader, well, leading cheers for a United States senator was quite a different thing from leading cheers for a high school quarterback. "I'm sorry," he countered.

"What for?"

For misjudging you, he almost replied. *For thinking you were just another pretty face.* Although, damn, she was pretty. Andrew had always known that, but his awareness of her appearance seemed more acute today than it had ever been before.

"I seem to have barged in here when you're buried in work," he remembered to answer her. "If this is a bad time for you, Kimberly—"

She laughed. "There's no such thing as a good time around here," she informed him. "I'm always buried in work. Now...I was about to get you some coffee, wasn't I?"

"I'll pass, thanks," he declined with a shake of his head. He wanted to get on with it, to tell her what he had come to tell her and to see what she could do, then to leave and resume his normal life. "Let's get down to business."

She leaned back in her chair and folded her hands primly on her blotter. "I must say, Andrew, I can't wait to hear this business of yours. You surely were mysterious on the telephone the other night."

So were you, darling, Andrew responded silently. He was tempted to ask her about that "darling" comment, extremely tempted. Especially now, after he had seen her at work, asserting herself on the phone and then gently but firmly instructing an underling. Especially after admitting, for not the first time in his life, that he considered Kimberly almost irritatingly beautiful. Being called "darling" by someone like Kimberly could put any man's hormones into orbit, and even Andrew, who generally considered himself above such things, was no exception.

Business, he reproached himself. *Get on with it. Get it over with.* "I've been doing some research on the agricultural economy of El Salvador," he began.

Kimberly cut him off with a grin. "I'm afraid that's not the senator's area of expertise, Andrew. He's very involved in domestic farm policy, of course, but—"

"That's not why I'm here," Andrew said impatiently. Did she actually think he had come all the way to Washington for help on a term paper?

His sharp retort seemed to startle Kimberly. She took a moment to assess him, then composed herself and cued him with a nod to continue.

"The research was funded by an organization called the Latin American Research Council. L.A.R.C."

"I don't believe I've ever heard of it," she commented.

"It's a front for the C.I.A.," Andrew announced. At her blank stare, he added, "A phony cover."

"A proprietary," she said, using the correct term. "The C.I.A. frequently sets up proprietaries, fake outfits to disguise their work."

He gave her a hard look, trying to interpret her complacent expression. "Doesn't that bother you?"

She laughed. "Don't be so naive, Andrew," she reproached him. "The C.I.A. does a great deal of sensitive work. They have to operate sub rosa. Sometimes they're looking for particular information. They can't very well paint a billboard advertising for it."

He bristled at her patronizing tone. "Maybe you think the C.I.A. is swell, Kimberly," he muttered. "Maybe you think the secret war in Cambodia was terrific and Pinochet in Chile is one hell of a wonderful guy."

"That was a long time ago," Kimberly pointed out. "Whatever evils the C.I.A. may have perpetrated in the past, they do serve an important purpose. I suppose you think I'm a wild-eyed right-winger for saying such a thing, but—"

"No, I'll grant that the C.I.A. serves a purpose," Andrew conceded. He hadn't come to Washington to fight with Kimberly. And much as it rankled, he had to admit the nation wouldn't be able to function without the C.I.A. "The issue isn't the C.I.A. itself. It's L.A.R.C. Wednesday morning, I met with L.A.R.C.'s chief, a guy named John Wilding, and presented him with my findings. He said things that frightened me, Kimberly. He implied that he was going to do some pretty scary things with the data I gave him."

"Scary things?" Her vivid blue eyes grew wide. "What sort of things?"

"Economic sabotage. Things are unstable in El Salvador. The government is being attacked from the left and from the right. If the farm economy—shaky as it is—collapses, it would in all likelihood lead to a revolution. The only way to quash a revolution would be to install a strongman. I think that's what Wilding and his C.I.A. cronies are planning."

Kimberly tapped her fingertips together thoughtfully. Her nails were polished, Andrew noted, her hands tiny, her fingers slender and graceful. She appeared more concerned than alarmed by what he had told her. "What makes you believe this is what your Mr. Wilding is planning?" she asked.

"Things he said," Andrew replied vaguely. His answer obviously didn't satisfy Kimberly, and he mentally ran through his meeting with John Wilding again, searching for specifics. "The topics that interested him most in my report had to do with fertilizer shipments and marketing pipelines. Interfere with either of those, and you can easily destroy the farmers. Wilding wanted the names of all of my contacts down there, people who willingly spoke to me because I was an academic, but who told me in no uncertain terms that they didn't want to talk to government agents because they didn't trust them. I was sent to do research for the C.I.A. because the C.I.A. was being shut out."

"How do you know this Wilding person is really C.I.A.?"

"I don't know for sure. But he told me he was. After I handed over my report, of course."

"He *told* you?"

"He's strange, Kimberly. He seems like a man possessed." Andrew exhaled, wondering if he himself sounded like a man possessed. "I thought... since you work for a senator who happens to serve on the Intelligence Committee, maybe you could check out Wilding. And L.A.R.C. Find out what they're up to. Discreetly, if possible. Can you do that for me?"

She gazed at him for a long while, meditating. A knock on her open door jarred her, and she and Andrew turned to see a tall, dark-haired man enter. "Hi, Kim," he greeted her familiarly. "Are you busy right now?"

"You can see that I am, Whitney," she said, her tone distinctly chilly. Then she glanced at Andrew, and he detected an enigmatic glimmer in her eye. "But come right in," she welcomed the intruder, abruptly smiling, speaking in a sensuous drawl. She stood and glided around the desk to Andrew, urging him to his feet with her hand on his elbow. "I'd like for you to meet my very dear friend, Andrew Collins. I believe I've told you about him. Andrew, meet Whitney Brannigan."

The way she said "my very dear friend" reminded Andrew of the way she had said "darling" on the telephone a couple of days ago. He recognized that she had shifted gears on him; she was suddenly exuding honey. And her hand remained on his elbow, pinching him through the tweed of his blazer just hard enough for him to know that she wanted him to follow her lead.

"How do you do?" he said courteously, offering his hand to Whitney.

Whitney shook it, then sized him up with a speculative perusal. "So you're Andrew," he said. "Yes, Kim's told me about you. You're a lucky man."

Kimberly pinched Andrew's arm again. He almost yelped in pain, and he almost burst into laughter. He had no idea what charade she was involved in, but sure, he'd go along with it for a while, just out of curiosity. "Luck ebbs and flows, Whitney," he remarked philosophically. It seemed like a safe thing to say, and given that Andrew was in the dark, he figured it best not to commit himself further.

"As a matter of fact, Whitney," Kimberly interjected, "we could use your brains right now. Andrew has just been telling me a fascinating tale about a C.I.A. proprietary he's recently had dealings with. I think some delving is in order."

She turned to Andrew and presented him with a winning smile. Her eyes bore into him, sparkling with an odd blend of humor and supplication. He gave her a nearly imperceptible nod. Typical of Kimberly to be playing some silly game with men, although Andrew thought that a married woman ought to be above such nonsense. But he wouldn't give her away. Yet.

Whitney scrutinized Andrew again. Andrew tried to guess what the sharply dressed, undeniably handsome man was thinking. "Fill me in," Whitney requested.

Without a clear idea of what was going on between Whitney and Kimberly, Andrew wasn't certain what to say. Fortunately Kimberly bailed him out. "Andrew has been working with a gentleman named John Wilding. His proprietary is called the Latin American Resource Center."

"Research Council," Andrew corrected her.

"Andrew thinks the man wants to sabotage the farm economy of El Salvador," she explained.

"Whoa!" Whitney staggered backward. "That's a pretty serious charge."

"Andrew is a brilliant man," Kimberly cooed, tightening her grip on his elbow and batting her eyes up at him coquettishly. Andrew willfully looked past her, hoping to convey that he didn't exactly approve of whatever it was she was doing. Her smile tensing slightly, she turned back to Whitney. "I'm sure he wouldn't make such a charge without having adequate justification. Could you run this John Wilding through your contacts and see what you come up with?" She spun back to Andrew again. "Whitney is one of the senator's foreign policy experts," she revealed. "He knows a lot of people who know a lot of things."

"Okay," Andrew mumbled, still at sea. He decided that, even more than her mysterious game with Whitney, he didn't like her surprisingly strong hand on him. He didn't like the faint, intoxicating scent of her perfume, the bewitching curve of her lower lip as she smiled at him. She was definitely prettier than any woman had a right to be.

"John Wilding. Latin American Research Council," Whitney recited. "It's Friday afternoon, so I don't know how far I'm going to get with this."

"Do the best you can," Kimberly requested, turning her dazzling smile to Whitney once more.

"Don't I always?" He pivoted and left the office.

As soon as he was gone, Kimberly released Andrew, and he took a safe step back from her. "What the hell was that all about?" he inquired.

She shrugged negligently. "Whitney has been courting me—in a rather obnoxious way, I'm afraid. I had to find a way to call him off, and I had to be diplomatic about it since we work together. So I told him you were my beau. I hope you don't mind."

"Don't mind?" Andrew exclaimed, astounded. "What about your husband, for crying out loud? Why don't you just tell the guy you're married?"

"I'm not," she said bluntly. She averted her eyes, but not before Andrew caught a glimpse of keen pain in them. "I've just been divorced."

"Oh." It took a minute to sink in. Kimberly, the gorgeous coed betrothed to her hometown boyfriend, wearing that ridiculous one-and-a-half carat diamond ring on her finger throughout her senior year, hurrying back to Georgia to marry her sweetheart before the ink had a chance to dry on her diploma. Divorced. "I'm sorry," he said automatically.

"Don't worry about it." She shrugged again. "It happens to the best of people."

Maybe it happened to the best of people, but why to Kimberly? What man in his right mind would let a woman as enchanting as she was get away?

Now *that* was a peculiar thought. Kimberly might be enchanting, but Andrew had always been immune to her spell in the past. Why should he question her husband's sanity in ending his marriage to her? If, in fact, her husband had ended it. For all Andrew knew, Kimberly might have been the one to do the walking. She had said she had *been* divorced, not that she *was* divorced, which implied that her husband had divorced her. But that was probably just some quaint Southern way of talking.

Yet the sadness lingered in her eyes, casting them in shadow, causing Andrew to brim with heartfelt sympathy for her. Whatever his history with her, he could understand her pain, because he had endured a similar pain himself. "I really am sorry," he said, quietly this time, fervently.

She lifted her gaze to him. Evidently she comprehended how sincere he was. "Thank you, Andrew."

He wished he could put his arm around her, hold her, comfort her. She looked so forlorn, and so far away from him. Yet he and Kimberly had never been particularly close, and there was no way he could offer her more than the most basic condolences.

So he shoved his hands into his pockets and smiled. "Can I ask you a personal question?"

She managed a smile. "Be my guest."

"The other night when you called me 'darling,' what was that all about? Did that have something to do with the guy who was just in here?"

"You are brilliant," she praised him, smiling. "Whitney was at my house at the time. It was our first—and I daresay our last—date. He was all over me. The man was like Silly Putty, Andrew, twisting and gooey and oozing every which way. And then you called, and I was able to slip out of his clutches. Saved by the bell, wasn't I?"

"Your first date and he was all over you," Andrew mused. "He did seem to have 'fast track' written across his forehead."

Kimberly chuckled. "Dating rituals have apparently changed during the years I was married. I remember a time when a decent man didn't kiss you until the third date."

"You're that old, huh?" Andrew teased her.

"I suppose I am. But you've been playing this game yourself, Andrew. Do you wait until the third date before you come on like gangbusters?"

"I—" He closed his mouth and frowned. How did Kimberly know about Marjorie? He hadn't mentioned that he was widowed to any of the women at the *Dream* reunion six weeks ago. And then he recalled that he hadn't mentioned to any of the women that he had been married, either. Kimberly probably assumed that he was still a bachelor. "I'm a decent man," he assured her with a whimsical smile. "I always wait until the third date."

"And then you come on like gangbusters?"

"I'd like to think I'm a little more subtle than that."

"You probably are," Kimberly agreed. "We've had our differences, Andrew, and I know you don't think very highly of me, but I've always considered you a decent man."

He wasn't sure whether he ought to be complimented or chagrined by her statement. At least two thirds of it was uncomfortably true. He hoped the last third was true, as well. He wanted Kimberly to consider him a decent man.

A sudden awkwardness enveloped him. Kimberly no longer looked depressed. She was gazing at him with an unnerving steadiness. In all the time they had known each other, she had never spoken so directly to him before, and he had never reacted with such overwhelming interest to how she thought of him.

He pointedly reminded himself that, for all the grit she'd displayed in her behavior with her colleagues, she had been playing a rather juvenile game with him and Whitney. She was still cutesy Kimberly, the coquettish Georgia peach.

"Let me give you my number at the motel," he suggested, digging in an inner pocket of his blazer for the card he'd picked up at the check-in desk. "You can call me when you've got the dirt on John Wilding."

She grinned. "You can wait here if you'd like."

"But you're busy."

"I worked late three nights out of the last four. I'm entitled to visit with an old college chum this afternoon." She gestured toward the vinyl chair, then moved around the desk to resume her seat.

Against his better judgment, Andrew sat. He didn't know what to say to Kimberly, how to make small talk with her. All he knew was that her smile was holding him in place, exerting a power over him that he was unable to combat.

"How have you been?" she asked.

"Didn't we have this conversation at Julianne's party?" he countered.

Her smile expanded. "I was busy catching up with all the others there. Now it's our turn. By the way—" her eyes began to sparkle "—did you hear about Seth and Laura?"

"You mean that Stoned has gone bonkers over her?"

"They're going to get married," Kimberly told him. "Julianne called me a couple of days ago to tell me the news. Isn't it exciting?"

"Yes," Andrew said genuinely. He liked both Laura and Seth a great deal, and he was very happy for them. "I didn't know they'd taken it as far as marriage. But the last time I saw Seth, he told me Laura had turned his life around. Married, huh." He ruminated on the idea, then laughed. "Stoned is actually going to take on Laura's teenage daughter?"

"Apparently they get along well," Kimberly said. "According to Julianne, they're all planning to live in Brooklyn until the school term ends, and then Laura and Rita are going to move to California with Seth. I've tried to call Laura a few times, but her line is always tied up. She must be busy making plans. Lord, it's all so romantic." Kimberly sighed.

"Do you think marriage is romantic?" Andrew questioned her. "Aren't divorcées supposed to be jaded?"

Her smile waned. "I hope I never become jaded," she declared earnestly. "That's one thing that scares me. I don't want to turn bitter and nasty."

"I can't imagine you bitter and nasty," Andrew assured her. People who put one in mind of circular yellow smiling faces couldn't change their personalities overnight.

"So," Kimberly persevered, "how have you been?"

"Fine," he answered. "I've been fine. Until Wednesday, when I found out I was unwittingly working for the C.I.A."

She settled back in her swivel chair, smiling cryptically, looking oddly amused by Andrew's predicament. She lifted a fountain pen from her blotter, tapped it absently against her desk, then set it down. Her smile widened, revealing a straight row of small, pearly teeth. "How did you hook up with John Wilding, anyway?"

"It isn't funny," Andrew grumbled, irked by her good-humored attitude.

She laughed. "Oh, yes, Andrew, it is. I always think of you as so solemn, so dedicated and principled. You're nobody's fool. How in the world did you let some C.I.A. operative pull the wool over your eyes?"

"I didn't—" Andrew drew in a sharp breath and mulled over his response. The truth was, Kimberly had interpreted the situation precisely. Andrew had let someone pull the wool over his eyes. Willingly. "One of the people I work with in the economics department at Amherst made the introduction. He's a highly esteemed man, a full professor, and the fact that he recommended me to Wilding was a real vote of confidence. It implied that he was ready to champion me for tenure next year, and so...so I didn't ask the questions I should have."

"What are you going to do if all your suspicions are borne out, if you find out that John Wilding is a nut? Won't it mortify this full professor if you make an issue out of it?"

"It may well cost me tenure," Andrew admitted grimly. "And that's not a happy thought."

Whitney appeared at the doorway, empty-handed. "You know what they ought to do?" he announced grandly, marching into the office. "They ought to shut down the government at noon on Friday. You can't find out nothin', nohow, at this time of the week."

"Nothing at all?" Kimberly asked, disappointed.

"Well...all right, I found out a little. Wilding is employed by the C.I.A. His present field is Central America. He's been with the agency for twelve years. Nobody knows anything about the Latin American Research Council, but that's just safe talk."

"And? What's your educated opinion, Whitney?" Kimberly pressed him.

His gaze traveled from her to Andrew and back again. "I think we may be on to something here. It's worth digging further. If it's as juicy as your very dear friend Andrew suspects, we could get a lot of mileage out of it for the senator. So sure, I'm willing to stick with it for a while."

"How about tomorrow?" Kimberly asked. "Can you do anything with this over the weekend?"

"Better over the weekend than during the week. People talk more freely when they're at home than when they're in Langley, Virginia, being watched. I can call some people and see what we come up with. For the senator," he stressed, shooting Andrew a disgruntled look.

"Thank you," Andrew said dutifully. No matter how stupid Kimberly's act with Andrew was, he couldn't deny that he enjoyed being thought of, however mistakenly, as the "very dear friend" of a woman as enticing as she.

"This is all quite intriguing," Kimberly commented. "I can picture the senator giving a thundering oration on the subject of C.I.A. abuses—penned by me, of course."

"Of course," Whitney said dryly.

He remained hovering near the door, and Kimberly asked, "Was there something else? I forgot to ask you why you dropped in earlier."

Whitney's vision shuttled between her and Andrew again. "Just wanted to know whether you might be interested in dinner with me this evening," he said. "It's pretty clear that you aren't available."

"I'm afraid not," Kimberly said, sounding not at all regretful. "Andrew and I have already made plans."

Andrew grinned. "Yes, *darling*," he backed her up. "We've already made plans."

"PIZZA?" ANDREW BLURTED OUT. "I never took you for a pizza type."

Kimberly smiled. "I'm almost afraid to ask what type you took me for. Not pig's knuckles and grits, I hope."

Andrew shook his head. "More the veal cordon bleu type."

"Ah, yes, I'm so terribly refined," she said with a self-deprecating sigh. They were ambling down Pennsylvania Avenue in the shadow of the Capitol Rotunda, heading toward a restaurant. The evening was balmy; Washington's infamous mugginess rarely settled in as early as mid-April. "I'm sure you must have seen me eating pizza at some of our staff meetings when we were working on *The Dream*."

"We usually ate granola at those meetings," Andrew recalled. "Laura always came armed with a sack of it."

"That's right. Granola." Kimberly grimaced. "Hippie fuel. I used to make my folks buy granola for me to eat when I was home on vacation, just to get their goat. I loathed the stuff. It seemed more suited to rodents than humans."

"Humans have a lot in common with rats," Andrew pointed out.

"That's a fact I'd rather not be reminded of." She veered toward the front door of an elegantly decorated eatery.

"Rest assured, Andrew, the pizza here is of gourmet quality. They even serve it on dishes with pedestals."

Twenty minutes later a waiter delivered a sizzling pie on a pedestaled silver cake tray, just as Kimberly had predicted. She and Andrew had already consumed some Chianti, and she was feeling mellow.

Much to her delight, she was enjoying Andrew's company. She hadn't known what to expect from his visit, either in the business that had brought him to town or in his presence itself. But his business was indeed fascinating. Washington thrived on scandals, and given the secretive nature of the C.I.A., she believed that it deserved to be tweaked and twitted whenever possible. The senator believed that, too, and Kimberly had little doubt that when she and Whitney informed him of their investigation of L.A.R.C., their boss would make hay of it.

Andrew's presence was also fascinating. Seated across the small linen-covered table from him, she studied him intently, comparing his current appearance with the way he had groomed himself in college. Back then his face had been half-hidden by a shrubby brown beard, and when she'd seen him at the reunion in early March, she had considered his now clean-shaven jaw too jutting. But it wasn't really. It was large and square, appealingly rugged.

She also preferred his aviator-shaped eyeglasses to the wire-rimmed spectacles he had favored in college. The thin tortoiseshell frames matched his pale brown eyes. She liked the barely discernible laugh lines fanning out from their corners. And she liked the casual neatness of his dark hair, which contained a few visible strands of premature silver at his temples. All in all, he was aging quite attractively.

Back in school she had thought of Andrew as somehow gnomelike, despite his taller-than-average height and well-proportioned physique. He had always looked as if he had just climbed out from the pages of a dusty tome. Or a hundred dusty tomes. He had generally conveyed an aura of learnedness. She hadn't been exaggerating to Whitney when she'd said that Andrew was brilliant.

In the past his brilliance used to turn her off. She had nothing against intellectuals, but she had resented Andrew's habit of hiding behind his erudition. The man had a brain, but she often doubted whether he had any spirit.

She was now conscious of cracks in his intellectual armor, however, and she was thrilled by the opportunity to peek behind his scholarly veneer. She was thrilled by the fact that high-and-mighty Andrew had come to her, of all people, for assistance.

More than his professional vulnerability was seeping through the cracks. Kimberly had learned about his wife's death from Laura, who had in turn learned about it from Seth after the reunion. Andrew didn't seem to want to discuss his wife's passing with Kimberly, and she was tactful enough not to probe. But knowing that he had suffered such a tragedy altered her perception of him. The lopsided twist of his smile no longer connoted cynicism and arrogance to her. It connoted unspoken sadness.

"I've got to hand it to you," he commented after swallowing the last of his pizza slice. "This is delicious. Much better than anything in Amherst."

"What's it like up there?" Kimberly asked. She might have asked such a question of Whitney in an effort to get him to talk about himself, as one was supposed to do on a date. But this dinner with Andrew didn't really constitute a date, and she asked out of genuine interest.

"It's beautiful, in an almost unreal way," he replied. "They could have filmed the Andy Hardy movies on Amherst's campus. Rolling lawns, rolling hills, towering trees, ivy-covered buildings. Endless blue skies. It smells good there, Kimberly. The air is so clean."

"What are your students like?" she asked before biting into her pizza.

"They're sharp. A bit spoiled, though. Most of them have never had to fight for anything, so they sometimes strike me as flabby."

"Physically or mentally?" she asked, then smiled. "When I think of Amherst I think of tall young men named 'Buckey' and 'Shep,' wearing rugby shirts and Topsider shoes."

Andrew guffawed. "I hate to break the news to you, Kimberly, but Amherst has been coed for years." He mused for a moment, then laughed again. "Admittedly, I've encountered a few female students who'd fit that description, right down to the names."

"Do you have a house there?"

"No. A small apartment," he told her.

"Big homes are such a bother, don't you think?" Kimberly remarked. "They're so much effort to keep clean."

He seemed on the verge of saying something, then changed his mind. Instead he nodded and refilled their goblets with wine from the straw-wrapped bottle.

She wondered what he had been about to say. Lord, but she wished he'd open up a bit more. "There was a time in my life," she ventured, deciding to introduce a more personal note to their conversation, "when I thought all I'd ever want in life was to keep a nice house for my husband. But that palls. Running a vacuum cleaner is hardly creative."

"Is that why you went to work for Senator Milford?" Andrew asked.

"The senator wasn't elected until 1976," she told him. "I took my first job about six months after I got married. Todd wasn't too pleased about having a working wife, but we had a mighty big mortgage to pay off."

"You worked in public relations or something, didn't you?" Andrew recollected. "I think you mentioned that at the reunion."

"Yes. I got a job with one of the big P.R. firms in town. Glorified lobbying, that's what it was. Writing position papers for clients. The National Retail Merchants' Association, the National Society of Undertakers, you name it. They all had legislative axes to grind, and my job was to sharpen those axes for them."

"Did you enjoy it?"

She sipped her wine and reminisced. "I enjoyed the writing aspect of it. Ever since working on *The Dream* I've enjoyed playing with words. But I didn't always enjoy the positions I had to present. I happen to believe that undertakers ought to be held more accountable than they are." She bit her lip, suddenly anxious. Wasn't it tasteless to talk about undertakers with a man whose wife had died? If this had been a real date, she would have watched her words more carefully.

Much to her relief, Andrew didn't seem particularly troubled by her remark. "So now that you work for Milford you spend all your time trying to blunt those axes."

"I do my best." She took another sip of wine, then helped herself to a second slice of pizza from the tray. "The senator stands for some very good things. I'm proud to be on his staff. I can't say that my former job ever gave me a feeling of pride."

Andrew had lifted his goblet, but at her confession he lowered it without drinking. "You amaze me, Kimberly," he said.

She laughed. "Do I?"

"You were right. What you said back in your office about how I don't think highly of you." He gazed steadily at her, his eyes large and uncharacteristically tender behind the lenses of his eyeglasses. "I'd like to put that in the past tense, if it's all right with you."

She was inordinately flattered by his request, although it was a backhanded compliment at best. "Dare I ask what's made you change your opinion?"

"Just about everything that's happened today. Everything except that stupid game you're playing with Whitney."

So much for feeling flattered, she thought. Once again Andrew was judging her, condescending to her. "It's not a stupid game," she protested. "The man seems to be unable to take no for an answer. I tried honesty with him. I tried firmness. But Whitney's such a boob. Nothing worked. I made a mistake in accepting an invitation to dinner with him, but I'm not going to let that one mistake destroy my working relationship with him. So I'll do what I have to do." She offered Andrew a frosty smile. "I appreciate your having backed me up at the office, but if you don't want to anymore, that's quite all right with me. I'll figure out something else."

"It's no skin off my nose," Andrew hastened to placate her. "All I meant was, it's kind of stupid."

"Whitney is kind of stupid," Kimberly snapped. "Sometimes you have to stoop to your opponent's level."

He shrugged. "Fair enough, Kimberly." He hesitated, then said, "He calls you 'Kim.'"

"Not because I invited him to," she noted. She had no objection to her closest friends calling her "Kim," but Whitney had chosen to refer to her by that nickname almost from the first. It annoyed her, but she'd given up on correcting him. "I've never heard anyone call you 'Andy,'" she remarked, turning the spotlight back on Andrew.

"A few people do," he conceded. "I'm not crazy about it, though."

"It makes you think of Andy Hardy," she joked.

"Andy Hardy, Andy Devine, Raggedy Andy."

"You can call me 'Kim,'" she said impulsively. She forgave him for having criticized her ploy with Whitney. He was right—it was stupid. But, as she'd told him, she had run out of reasonable approaches to discouraging Whitney's attentions.

And even though Andrew thought it was stupid, he was going along with it, which was awfully generous of him. She wasn't used to generosity from Andrew, and she treasured his willingness to do something so utterly stupid for her.

"All right," he agreed, smiling shyly. He tried out the name, appraising the way it sounded. "Kim. Have another slice, Kim." He lifted a slice of pizza from the pan.

She waved it away from her plate. "I'm afraid I've reached my limit, Andrew. You eat it."

"It's pretty filling," he admitted, though he took the slice for himself. "So, when are you going to tell Senator Milford about L.A.R.C.?"

"If we find something really exciting we'll call him. If not, I imagine it can wait until he gets back to town."

"He's not in Washington?" Andrew looked sorely disappointed.

"No, he's home," Kimberly answered. "He comes up for reelection next year, and he's been trying to spend as much of his time as possible on the stump." She measured Andrew's crestfallen look and grinned. "You were hoping to meet him, weren't you?"

"It would have been fun," he conceded. "I happen to like the guy's politics."

"Next time you come down I'll try to set up an appointment with him for you," she said without thinking. Andrew hadn't mentioned anything about planning to come to Washington a second time. Yet she hoped he would want to. She hoped that after all this time she and Andrew could become friends.

She watched him carefully, gauging his reaction to her suggestion. He nibbled his pizza thoughtfully, then smiled. "That would be great," he said.

His words were casual, almost offhanded, but Kimberly felt a thrill of joy at their underlying meaning. There would be a next time. She would see Andrew again after this weekend. He did want to be her friend.

She felt as if she'd just received an unexpected gift—from a man who was unused to giving. Unexpected and wonderful. A warm wave of gratitude washed through her.

She raised her glass in a silent toast to their newfound friendship, then drank.

Chapter Three

"Laura!" Kimberly set down the documents she had been perusing and gave her full attention to the telephone. "Laura, I have been trying to reach you all for days, but your line is always busy. Congratulations!"

"Oh, you've heard?"

"Julianne called me a few days ago to tell me. You and Seth—it's so romantic! I can't believe it."

"I'm not sure I believe it myself," Laura agreed with a laugh. "But it's true. We're doing it up right, complete with the legal piece of paper. My mother wants to make a big thing out of it—she's only got one daughter, and how often does one's daughter get married and all that."

"Really? A full-fledged wedding?"

"Well, it's not going to be anything that traditional if I have anything to say in the matter," Laura admitted, laughing again. "We're just going to have a party at her house. Don't worry, when we get it all worked out you'll receive an invitation. Engraved, if I know my mother."

"Has she met Seth?" Kimberly asked, eager for all the details. "Does she like him?"

"She adores him. I suspect she'd adore anyone who would do right by her daughter at this late stage. Don't forget, the poor woman has been a grandmother for thirteen years, without ever getting to host a wedding first. But Seth is adorable, even if I must say so myself." Her tone became serious. "How are you, Kim? How's it going?"

"It's going," Kimberly answered vaguely. She didn't want to burden her friend with her own story about the finalization of her divorce. The fact was, she didn't feel particularly sorry for herself that morning.

Instead she felt uncommonly cheerful. The only explanation she could come up with for her elevated spirits was that she had won Andrew's friendship. She never would have expected that Andrew's opinion of her could be so important to her, but now that it had changed for the better, she was immeasurably pleased.

Their dinner together the previous evening had gone delightfully. He had let her pick up the tab, and that, too, had delighted her. She had told him that since he was a visitor to her town, the least she could do was treat him to a meal, and he had accepted her generosity without a fuss. She wanted to believe that this was one more bit of proof that he was finally ready to view her as an equal.

Outside the restaurant she'd shown him where the nearest Metro station was, and then he had waited with her until she caught a bus to Georgetown, which wasn't served by the city's underground rail system. Before she had boarded the bus, he'd opened his briefcase and handed her a folder. "You might want to read this," he'd said almost diffidently. "I'd rather you didn't show it to anyone else, though. At least not yet. I'm still hoping to get a paper or two out of it."

She had waited until she arrived home before scanning the contents of the folder. It contained the information he'd gathered for L.A.R.C., neatly organized and typed. That he would share it with her was more evidence that he trusted her.

She wanted his trust. She desired it. She longed to seep beneath his armor, once and for all, and vanquish the pain she knew was lurking there. Perhaps it was an irrational longing, but throughout a surprisingly restless night, all she could think of was that she wanted to reach him, to touch him, to heal him.

She decided not to mention to Laura that Andrew was in Washington. Clearly he didn't want it made public that he was about to have a run-in with one of his superiors at Amherst College—to say nothing of the C.I.A.

"So what does Rita think of all this?" she asked Laura brightly.

"Of all what? Seth and me getting married?" Laura snorted. "Seth practically proposed to her before he proposed to me. She's ecstatic about it. But listen, Kim..." She trailed off for a moment, then continued. "The reason I'm calling is, I have to ask a big favor of you."

"Yes. I would love to be your maid of honor," Kimberly joked.

Laura guffawed. "Kim, you know me better than that. My mother wants to make a big thing of it, but we've vetoed the processional stuff. Rita said there was no way on earth she was going to be a flower girl—only she kept calling it a 'flower child.' The way she said it, I got the distinct impression that she considers flower children one step removed from slugs."

"All right," Kimberly said. "No maid of honor. What's the big favor, then?"

"Seth wants to take Rita to Washington for a couple of days. Partly it's because once we move out to California in June she might not have another opportunity to see the capital for a while. Partly it's because I've got a ton of work to do here, packing up and closing out my case load at work, and I want them both out of my way. But mostly it's because Seth thinks Rita ought to see where he and I met."

"You met at school," Kimberly argued, bewildered.

"We met on a chartered bus heading down to Washington to march against the war, back in November of '69," Laura corrected her. "Seth thinks Rita's life won't be complete until she marches the route with him. Anyway, they're going to be arriving in D.C. next Thursday evening for a long weekend."

"Does Rita have time off from school?"

"No. I'm letting her play hooky Friday. Seth insists that visiting Washington is going to be very educational. Hah," Laura grunted. "But I'm willing to pretend I believe him for the few days of peace their absence will give me. Kim, you wouldn't believe the madhouse it's been here—Seth's junk is all over the place, my mother's arriving today to shop for a dress for me.... She keeps talking about color schemes, Kim. Color schemes! For a backyard party! I told her that given that the lawn is green we ought to go with green, but she keeps saying lilac, yellow, fuchsia, mandarin orange..."

Dusty rose, Kimberly almost blurted out. That had been the color of her wedding. Her attendants—she'd had seven of them—had worn dusty-rose gowns, and she had carried a bouquet of dark pink roses and trailing ivy, and her dress had been inlaid with pink-hued cultured pearls, and they'd drunk pink champagne.... Her mother had done most of the planning, too. A full year of planning. The catered engagement party, the catered bridal shower, the wedding, the reception—everything, from the tablecloths and napkins to the ribbons on the favors, had been dusty rose. So much pink, so much money spent, and what did Kimberly have to show for it?

No. She wasn't going to think that way. Not today, not when, for the first time since she'd moved out of the house in Chevy Chase a year ago, she was feeling happy.

"Seth and Rita in D.C.," she said, directing her thoughts back to Laura. "What do you want me to do?"

"Say hello, keep an eye on them, whatever," Laura replied. "You don't have to put them up or anything. They've got a couple of rooms reserved at—" Kimberly heard Laura fumbling with some papers on her end of the line "—L'Enfant Plaza. But I just can't shake the notion that they're going to need some looking after. The two of them, alone together—it's the halt leading the blind. Or the crazy leading the insane. Can I have them call you when they get into town?"

"Of course. Better yet, have them stop by my office Friday morning. I'll take them out to lunch."

"You're wonderful, Kim," Laura gushed.

"I won't argue that," said Kimberly. "Is Seth around now? I'd like to give him my congratulations, too."

"I'm afraid he's out," Laura told her. "He went into Manhattan to meet some independent producer for brunch. He's trying to wrangle money for his new film. It's called *Good Fences*, and it's wonderful, Kim. It's the best thing he's ever written. Unfortunately he's having quite a time convincing investors of that. But you'll see him next week. If you want, you can congratulate him then."

"Fair enough. Laura, I'm just so happy for the both of you. I mean that."

"Thank you, Kim," Laura said, sounding oddly shy. "I'm almost sorry I'm going to be moving so far away now that we've found each other again."

"We won't lose touch this time," Kimberly swore. "Take care, Laura. And stick to your guns. It's your wedding, not your mother's."

"Yeah. If only I can convince her of that," Laura grumbled before bidding Kimberly farewell.

Kimberly lowered the receiver and gazed at the papers spread across her bed. Weddings, she mused, were a much different matter than marriages. Weddings were celebrations, occasions of joy, color-coordinated. Marriages, on the other hand...well, they ought to be joyful celebrations, too, but when reality intruded, you never knew. Divorce might occur. Or death.

She banished that thought with a shake of her head. Andrew wasn't wallowing in grief, surrendering to morbid moods. In spite of his loss, he struck her as very in command of himself, very strong. He was doing just fine, teaching, writing, bucking for tenure. The papers she had read from his folder thus far indicated that he was a busy, productive man.

He wrote well. She found nothing pompous in his essays, nothing screaming of scholarship or academic credentials. But, then, he'd written well in college, too. She had always enjoyed reading his articles in *The Dream,* even though she'd never told him so. If she had, he probably would have been offended to think that some cheerleader with an inferior brain actually liked what he was writing.

She didn't have an inferior brain. And if Andrew hadn't figured that out by now, he wouldn't have entrusted her with his file—or with his professional future.

The telephone rang again. She had expected the last telephone call to be from Andrew, not Laura; perhaps this time he would be on the other end. She reflexively smoothed the satin lapels of her baby-blue bathrobe and tightened the knot of the sash, as if Andrew could see her through the telephone wire. Then she lifted the receiver. "Hello?"

"Kim? Whitney here."

She slumped against the pillow and prayed that he was calling her on business and not to find out if his presumed rival had departed, leaving Kimberly available for dinner that night. "Hello, Whitney," she said with forced politeness.

"Is Andrew there? I'd like to speak to him."

That brought her up sharply. Obviously Whitney had believed her little ruse about Andrew's being her "very dear friend." He'd believed it too well. She couldn't blame him for assuming that Andrew had spent the night at her place and not in a motel across the river. Hadn't that been exactly what she had wanted him to assume?

"He's out right now," she informed Whitney. "He—he went out for a walk." Did that sound as lame to Whitney as it did to her? Before he had a chance to question her further, she went on. "Perhaps I can help you. Have you found out anything about L.A.R.C.?"

"A few tidbits," Whitney remarked cryptically. "When is Andrew going to be back?"

"I honestly don't know," Kimberly mumbled. "Why don't you tell me all these tidbits you've found out, and I'll pass the word along."

"All I've got right now is that L.A.R.C. was set up to gather economic information on several Central American nations. It's Wilding's brain child. I'm meeting a guy for dinner who's worked with Wilding before. If I ply him with enough whiskey, I might pry some interesting stuff out of him. I'm planning to see somebody else this afternoon, and I'd like to get a little more background dope from Andrew before I go. Could you have him call me as soon as he gets back?"

"Of course," Kimberly promised. "Where can he reach you? Are you at home?"

"Yeah. You've got my number, right?"

Oh, have I ever, Kimberly muttered silently. "I'm sure it's in my book," she told him. "I'll have Andrew call you as soon as possible."

"Thanks. You know, Kim, I'm doing this for the senator," Whitney felt obliged to add. "I wouldn't kill a weekend just to satisfy your sweetheart."

"I understand that," she said, her voice cool and poised. "I'm sure my—my sweetheart understands that, too." She hoped she didn't sound as awkward as she felt using the word "sweetheart" in reference to Andrew.

"Have him get back to me," Whitney said, concluding the call.

She stared at the telephone on her night table and sighed. She truly didn't like getting herself so caught up in lies, but what alternative did she have? Whitney's closing remark was strangely reassuring to her. It implied that he was coming to terms with the fact that as far as he was concerned, she wasn't interested in pursuing a personal relationship.

Given that he was expecting Andrew to return his call, she didn't have time to waste either congratulating herself on her successful con or berating herself for her petty deception. She riffled through the folder on the bed until she found the card Andrew had given her with his hotel's number on it. She dialed and asked the desk clerk to connect her with Andrew's room.

He answered on the first ring. "Hello?"

"Andrew? It's me."

"Kim." Her nickname sounded so sweet when he uttered it. "Good morning."

"Good morning," she said, relishing the warmth of his tone. "Andrew, I just got off the phone with Whitney. He wants you to call him."

"Okay." Andrew waited, and when Kimberly remained silent, he said, "Why don't you give me his number?"

"Andrew." She drew in a deep breath, then proceeded. "He expected that you would be here at my apartment. I guess he figured that you had spent the night with me."

Andrew didn't speak immediately. "Oh?"

"I—I didn't correct him," she confessed. "I told him you were out taking a walk and that you'd call him when you got back."

Again Andrew was momentarily silent. "This is asinine," he muttered. "I can't stand this sort of game playing. It's really asinine, Kim."

At least he hadn't reverted to calling her "Kimberly." But she couldn't fail to detect his haughty attitude, his blatant disapproval of her. His attitude hurt her more than it should have, far more than it used to hurt her fifteen years ago. "Today you tell me you can't stand it. Yesterday you swore it was no skin off your nose," she asserted sharply. "I'm in a bind with Whitney. I'm sorry I thought I could count on you to help me out of it—"

"All right, all right," he cut her off with a resigned sigh. "'Oh, what tangled webs we weave—'"

"Now is not the time to discuss spiders," she interrupted him. "How soon can you get to Georgetown?"

"Why can't I call him from here?" Andrew asked. "I can tell him I'm calling from your place if he asks."

"And what if he wants to talk to me again?" she countered. "You can't very well say that I've gone out for a walk."

"Why not?" Andrew argued. "Maybe he'll think we both like to take walks by ourselves. Maybe he'll think we've got something bizarre going."

If that was what Whitney thought, he wouldn't be far from the mark, Kimberly acknowledged. "Just come here, Andrew," she commanded. "It would make life a whole lot easier."

"For you, maybe. All right, I'll come over," he acquiesced. "But I'm warning you, Kim, I've got work to do today, so you'd better let me do it while I'm there. How do I get to your place?"

She gave him the address. "The closest Metro stop is the one for George Washington University. It's rather a long walk from there, I'm afraid."

"Forget it. I'll take a cab," he said before hanging up.

A cab would take him much less time than the Metro and a major hike. If Andrew was willing to go to the extra expense of riding a cab to her home, then he was obviously willing to continue playing her game, even if he considered it asinine. No matter how condemning he had sounded on the phone, Andrew was still her friend. If he wasn't, he would have called a halt to the game right then and there.

Gratified, she sprang from the bed and hastened down the hall to the bathroom for a quick shower. Then she raced back to her room and donned a pair of snug-fitting white jeans and a pink knit jersey. She ran her brush through her hair a few times, fluffed it with her fingers and hurried to the kitchen to prepare a fresh pot of coffee. The least she could do when Andrew arrived was to offer him some refreshment.

By the time the coffee had run through the machine, he was knocking on her door. She fluffed her hair again, shaped her lips into a welcoming smile and offered a silent prayer that Andrew wouldn't use the word "asinine" in reference to her anymore that day.

She swung open the door and he stepped into the entry hall. He was dressed in brown corduroy slacks and a plaid shirt, and he carried his briefcase. His expression was inscrutable.

"Thank you for coming," she said.

"Uh-huh," he grumbled brusquely, marching past her and into the living room. "Where's the phone? Let's get this stupidity over with."

She pointed out the kitchen extension, a wall phone above the counter. Then she fetched her personal telephone book and opened it to Brannigan. She handed Andrew the receiver and began to dial for him.

"Where was I supposed to have been?" he questioned her.

"For a walk. Down Wisconsin Avenue, if he decides to ask. Tell him you went window-shopping or something."

"Window-shopping?" Andrew snorted. "The last thing I'd ever do in my life is go window-shopping."

"All right. Tell him..." She refrained from dialing the last digit as she scrambled for a better alibi. "Tell him you went out to buy some pastries."

"I don't like pastries," he objected, but she dialed the last number anyway.

"Swenson's," she whispered as he pressed the receiver to his ear. "For ice cream. Do you like ice cream?"

"At eleven o'clock in the morning?" he shot back before speaking into the phone. "Hello, Whitney, it's Andrew. Kim told me you wanted to talk to me."

His expression once again became unreadable to her. Hoping to ameliorate the situation, she filled a large porcelain mug with coffee and handed it to him. He took it with a slight nod.

"That's right," he said to Whitney. "Fertilizer shipments. They import it, mostly." Without looking at Kimberly, he lifted the mug to his mouth and sipped. "The address was Fairfax, Virginia. The few times I called him I got an answering machine. For all I know he may have been running the council out of his own home." He listened for a minute. "No, never heard of him.... No. Wilding never mentioned any other names. I assumed he was farming most of the work out to academics like me." He drank some more coffee, then tossed a skeptical smile Kimberly's way. "She's right here if you'd like to speak to her," he said. "No? Okay, then, Whitney. Keep in touch. And thanks." He handed the receiver back to Kimberly.

"I suppose you could have called from your hotel, after all," she murmured contritely as she set the receiver in its cradle.

Andrew shrugged. "He said he'd be calling back in a couple of hours. I seem to be stuck here."

She cringed at the word "stuck." She didn't like the idea that Andrew considered himself a prisoner in her home. "Well," she said crisply, refusing to let him know how much she appreciated his having come to her apartment. "You said you had some work to do. Make yourself comfortable."

He surveyed the living room, then carried his coffee to the dining table and took a seat. He pulled a sheaf of student papers and a pen from his briefcase and spread them on the table in front of himself. "What are you going to do?" he asked, less from courtesy than from curiosity.

"I've got to take some clothes to the dry cleaners," she told him. "And I'd like to finish looking through the file you gave me yesterday. I've been studying it, Andrew, and it's very interesting."

"Is it?" he asked dubiously. "Don't tell me you get off on peasant agronomy."

His withering tone caused her patience to fray. "I don't suppose you care one way or another what I get off on," she responded, keeping her voice level and detached. "I'll be back from the cleaners in a little while. Help yourself to more coffee if you want it."

With that she spun on her heel and stalked from the kitchen. Gathering up the suits she wanted cleaned and slinging the strap of her purse onto her shoulder, she left the apartment.

The late-morning air was balmy as she turned onto a side street and strode toward Wisconsin Avenue. She hoped that the mild spring weather and her brisk walk would calm her down. She didn't want to remain furious with Andrew for the rest of the day, particularly since it seemed that they were going to spend it "stuck" in each other's company, to use his unflattering term.

Yet how could she keep from being furious with him? Asinine, he had all but called her. The nerve of him!

She was going out of her way to help him, without complaint, without hesitation. Was it really demanding so very much that he pretend for a couple of days that he was her boyfriend? Was it really demanding so very much that he stop looking down his nose at her?

A couple of years ago she had read an article about an organization that was devoted to the problems of unusually good-looking people. According to the members, handsome men and pretty women had difficulty getting people to take them seriously, to associate with them as easily as they did with others. When Kimberly had read the story, she'd found the unspoken conceitedness of the club's members offensive.

She knew she was pretty, but her beauty had never worked against her. She had never had problems dealing with people because of her looks. Women like Julianne and Laura had accepted her for the human being she was. Men were frequently attracted to her, but she knew she wasn't irresistible to the opposite sex. She still remembered the adolescent heartache of having crushes on boys who wouldn't give her the time of day. She still remembered the many hours she'd spent staring at her reflection in the mirror as a teenager, comparing herself to Twiggy, feeling rejected and bemoaning her physical flaws.

But Andrew's rejection of her rankled more than anyone else's. She knew that he didn't fully accept her intelligence, and she couldn't shake the suspicion that his failure to respect her mind had something to do with her blond hair and blue eyes, her slender figure, her chipper disposition. In his snobbish view of things, a woman who had been on the cheerleading squad in high school couldn't compare to a woman who had been on the tennis team, or the yearbook staff, or the student council.

Andrew had viewed her as a lightweight even before he'd gotten to know her very well. And he still didn't know her very well. *Asinine,* she huffed.

Her visit to the dry cleaners didn't take long, and after she had dropped off her suits, she wasn't ready to return home yet. Instead she decided to take the walk Andrew was alleged to have taken.

She strolled down Wisconsin Avenue, browsing in the shop windows, contemplating which dresses she would buy if she could afford them. Getting used to living on a constrained budget had been difficult for her. Until her separation from Todd she had spent her entire life knowing that she could have anything she wanted—which was why it had been so much fun, back in her rebellious youth, to refuse the gifts her wealthy parents had wanted to lavish on her. All those lovely outfits her mother used to buy while Kimberly was away at school.... She'd come home for a vacation, find three or four new dresses spread across her canopied bed, and toss them onto the floor with vicious glee. Then she'd storm down the stairs, singing "Sympathy For The Devil" just for the thrill of watching her mother blanch.

At a *pâtisserie* she halted and studied the cakes and éclairs on display in the showcase. The hell with Andrew, she fumed. *She* liked pastries. She marched into the store, requested a box of six petits fours and refused herself the merest twinge of guilt when she handed the clerk a five-dollar bill.

Feeling rather pleased with herself, she strolled home, toting her purchase in a tissue-lined white box. If Andrew wanted to be so damned supercilious, she would take the box outside into the backyard with a glass of lemonade and a good book and eat all the petits fours herself.

When she entered her apartment, she found Andrew hunched over the table, immersed in his work. How intent he looked, peering through his eyeglasses, wielding his pen.

Like a gnome just climbed out of a tome, she reflected, then shook her head. Perhaps when he'd had his beard he had looked like a gnome, but not now, with his sharp, square jaw, with his thin lips fully visible, pressed together in a line of concentration, and his broad, strong shoulders stretching smooth the cotton of his shirt. He mumbled a greeting at her entrance, but he didn't glance up.

She set the box of petits fours on the counter and peeked at the paper he was marking with his pen. "'Bombastic, pleonastic, irrelevant bull,'" she read, struggling to decipher his nearly illegible scrawl. "Are you really going to write that on a student's paper?"

"I already did," he pointed out, permitting himself a slight grin.

"If you won't think I'm a bubble head for asking, what does 'pleonastic' mean?"

Although she had taken care to insult herself before Andrew could insult her, she knew that asking such a question put her at risk. Fortunately Andrew didn't leap at the opportunity she'd given him to belittle her. "It means redundant. The next time that assistant of yours hands you one of his wordy drafts for Senator Milford's 'Letter to the Constituents,' tell him it's pleonastic."

"I surely will," she concurred, her eyes shifting back to the paper Andrew was grading. "Bombastic and irrelevant, too? Won't your student be crushed?"

"I'm the one who ought to be crushed, having to read a paper like this. What's in the box?" he asked, his gaze drifting past her to the counter.

She chuckled. Old stick-in-the-mud egghead Andrew was conscious of the world outside his skull, after all. "Pastries," she drawled, her smile challenging him. "I'm sure you all don't want any." She opened the box with deliberate slowness, plucked one of the chocolate-covered cakes from the tissue lining and took a dainty bite.

Andrew watched her. He observed the graceful position of her hands as she held the petit four, the delicate tip of her tongue circling her lips, savoring the sweetness. Abruptly he laughed. "What is this, revenge?"

"You said you didn't like pastries," she said with feigned innocence. "I'm so sorry, Andrew. Did you want one?"

His laughter increased, and she was unable to keep herself from joining him. "It isn't as if I flee at the sight of them," he said, accepting the box from her and pulling out a petit four. "To tell you the truth, Kim, the breakfast I ate at the coffee shop in my motel was pretty awful. I'm starving."

"Would you like some lunch?" she asked.

He shook his head. "No. Just a pastry." He popped the whole petit four into his mouth.

"How about some more coffee?" she offered. Not waiting for an answer, she lifted the empty mug from the table and carried it into the kitchen to refill it.

Andrew continued to watch her, his smile relaxed and his eyes glowing with a gentle amber light. "What a well-bred lady you are," he commented. "Here I am, taking over your apartment, being rude, and you serve me coffee."

Kimberly returned his smile. "Maybe that's my revenge, Andrew," she hinted. "By being so utterly charming, I take all the wind out of your sails. You've simply got no choice but to be charming back."

"One thing I've never been is charming," Andrew declared.

Kimberly had to agree. But Andrew's shortcoming didn't bother her. Her experience with charming men had taught her that charm wasn't a particularly valuable asset in a man. Todd had been charming. He'd been ever so gracious as he told Kimberly, in no uncertain terms, that if she wanted to have children, she would have to quit her job and take full responsibility for rearing them, because he didn't have much faith in nursery schools or baby-sitters and he had no intention of being saddled with dirty diapers and formula bottles himself. He'd been ever so polite the first time he confessed that he was having an affair, ever so diplomatic as he told her, over a dignified snifter of cognac, that their marriage was obviously not working out as either of them had planned and so they might as well cut their losses.

She was glad Andrew wasn't charming that way. She appreciated his bluntness, even if he sometimes insulted her. She would rather know where she stood with a man than to have to interpret every nuance of his smile, every quirk of his eyebrow, in order to make sense of him.

"I should let you get back to work," she said, placing the steaming mug of coffee at his elbow. "If you'd like," she added, lifting the box and grinning mischievously, "I'll hide these loathsome pastries so you won't be tempted."

"Oh, you'd better," he played along. "I'm a fiend when it comes to loathsome pastries. That's why I hate them so much—I know how easily they could lead to my downfall."

Laughing, she put the box on the counter and departed for the bedroom. The papers she had been reading that morning lay scattered across the bed. She stacked them into a neat pile, kicked off her shoes and stretched out on the bed to resume reading.

An hour later the telephone rang. She had just reached the last page, and she let the phone ring twice more so she could finish the final paragraph. Then she answered.

"Kim? Whitney again. Is Andrew there? I'd like to speak to him."

She was relieved that Andrew was in fact at her apartment; it spared her the necessity of having to lie to Whitney again. But she couldn't deny being somewhat irked by Whitney's insistence on talking to Andrew rather than to her. After all, she was as much a part of the investigation as

Whitney was. Almost as much a part of it, anyway. He was doing the legwork, yes, but she had access to Andrew's papers. And to Andrew.

She didn't want to quarrel with Whitney over his attempt to shut her out of things, however. "Hang on," she said, then hollered through her open bedroom door. "Andrew? Whitney wants to talk to you."

"Okay, *darling*," Andrew shouted back before picking up the kitchen extension.

She stifled the urge to laugh. She also stifled the urge to listen in on their conversation. Resolutely she hung up the phone and waited.

Within a few minutes Andrew appeared at her bedroom door. "Well?" she asked.

He didn't speak immediately. Instead he took a moment to examine her bedroom—the heavy maple dresser with an embroidered linen runner decorating its buffed surface, the matching mirror above, the double bed with its pale blue comforter and dust ruffle, the framed Monet print of water lilies, hanging on the wall above it, and the "blue period" Picasso on the wall by the window overlooking the backyard. His gaze ultimately came to rest on Kimberly, who stared at him expectantly.

"He met with someone who worked with John Wilding several years ago at another proprietary, doing research in the Middle East," Andrew reported. "He said the man told him that Wilding had tried to take over the proprietary. He had some crackpot idea of fomenting unrest in Syria."

"What's so crackpot about that?" Kimberly asked. "I'm not crazy about Syria myself."

Andrew frowned. "For one thing, there's enough unrest in Syria without the C.I.A. adding its two cents. For another, it isn't supposed to be the C.I.A.'s job to overthrow unfriendly governments. Apparently the C.I.A. knows that, since they removed Wilding from the project and tied him to a desk for a while. L.A.R.C. is his first foray back into the real world."

"In other words, the man has a history of being naughty," Kimberly summed up.

"Something like that. Whitney told me he's going to spend the afternoon trying to track down the origins of L.A.R.C. Then he's supposed to meet someone for dinner, and if he gets home by a reasonable hour, he'll call again."

Kimberly allowed herself a minute to digest Andrew's announcement. If Whitney intended to telephone her house after dinner with an updated report, Andrew would have to remain with her through the evening.

She wondered what he thought of that. Did he feel "stuck," trapped by her "asinine" game? His eyes, partly obscured by his eyeglasses, refused to offer any answers. Neither did his mouth. He wasn't smiling, and he wasn't scowling.

"That's my folder," he said abruptly.

She was unnerved by his mildly accusatory tone of voice. "You gave it to me to read last night," she reminded him.

"Yes, but—" He smiled sheepishly. "I didn't know whether you'd bother to."

"I did bother," she informed him. "It's awfully interesting, Andrew. All these people you met and interviewed... How on earth did you find them?"

He shrugged. "It's called research, Kim. You do what you have to do to find out what you have to find out."

"I'm amazed that you got them all to open up so much to you," she remarked, then refuted herself. "No, I shouldn't be amazed. You always wrote wonderful interviews in *The Dream*, too. You obviously have a knack for this sort of thing."

"It isn't a knack," Andrew asserted modestly. "If you ask the right questions, most people are more than willing to talk about themselves."

Kimberly pondered his claim. She wanted Andrew to talk about himself. She wanted to know everything that was going on in that enormous, constantly toiling brain of his. If only she knew the right questions to ask....

"I have an idea," she said abruptly, gathering up the papers and stacking them neatly back inside the folder. "Whitney won't be calling back till this evening, you said. Let's take a drive."

Her suggestion obviously took Andrew by surprise. "A drive? Where?"

"To Fairfax." She stood and straightened her sweater. Then she crossed purposefully to her dresser to pick up her purse and keys. "Let's go look at John Wilding's house. You told Whitney he lived in Fairfax, right?"

Andrew's lips flexed as he mulled over her idea. "What's to be gained by looking at his house?"

Kimberly smiled. The most important thing to be gained, she comprehended, was that she and Andrew would be outdoors. If they spent all afternoon trapped together in the house, she would feel as much a prisoner as he would. And besides, she'd be damned if she was going to sit around doing nothing while Whitney knocked himself out learning everything there was to learn about L.A.R.C. She was tired of his refusal to include her in his investigation.

What was to be gained was that she and Andrew would be doing something together. How else would she learn the right questions to ask him?

"I'm curious," she remembered to reply. "I bet you are, too. It's a beautiful day. Let's go."

He didn't appear completely convinced, but she was already out the door of her bedroom, moving rapidly toward the front door and leaving him no choice but to follow. Reluctantly he did.

Chapter Four

"How can you afford a car like this on a civil servant's salary?" he asked.

Kimberly navigated her silver BMW through the narrow, congested Georgetown streets toward the Key Bridge. The car appeared fairly new, the plush floor mats spotless and the upholstery in showroom shape. Since Andrew hadn't gone car shopping in a decade, he didn't know much about current automobile prices. But he suspected that Kimberly's car must have cost a small fortune.

She smiled bitterly. "Todd and I bought it when we were still married," she explained, downshifting as they reached the bridge leading across the Potomac River into Virginia. "My lawyer recommended that I leave him this car and take the Mazda. He warned me that a car this expensive would foul up the accounting when we divided our assets. But we bought this car for me, and I insisted on keeping it."

"Any regrets?"

She shook her head, and her smile softened. "None at all," she swore.

The light breeze entering the car through the open sun roof ruffled her hair as she accelerated. Andrew might have expected a woman like Kimberly to own a fancy car, but he had never guessed that she would own a car with a stick shift. She had always struck him as the automatic transmission type. It seemed incongruous, a woman as delicately feminine as she was, tapping the clutch and dancing the stick through the gears with finesse. Incongruous, and oddly sexy.

He turned resolutely to the windshield, following the moderate weekend traffic with his gaze. Although he had always considered Kimberly pretty, he had never considered her sexy before.

Yes, he had. Yesterday, watching her while she fielded telephone calls and questions from underlings in her office, and later, when she skillfully ordered their pizza and then settled the check, he had found her sexy. In his mind, a woman's sex appeal related directly to her competence, her intelligence, her mastery of the world around her. By those standards, he was coming to realize, Kimberly was an undeniably sexy woman.

It was a discomfiting thought. If he had known that she would make such a disturbing impact on him, he wouldn't have come to Washington. The last thing he wanted was to find himself turned on by a pampered blond debutante, no matter how competent and intelligent she seemed.

"What's the address again?" she asked, cruising west on the highway.

Andrew shuffled through his folder until he found John Wilding's address. He read it to Kimberly. "How are we going to find his place?" he asked.

She shrugged. "When we get to Fairfax, we'll ask directions. It's a pretty small town."

"What if he's home?"

She shrugged again.

"Kim, he'll recognize me. We've met a few times. I can't very well march up to the front door and ring his bell." The more Andrew thought about it, the more he realized that this was a harebrained idea. He didn't know what had possessed him to let Kimberly talk him into driving to Wilding's house. She had seemed so excited when she'd suggested it, her face aglow, her eyes animated with sparks of light. He couldn't refuse a woman who looked as exuberant as she had.

But now, in the car, with time to reflect, he concluded that nothing productive would come out of their visit to Wilding's address. In all likelihood Wilding would be home. They would drive past his house—and if they were lucky, Wilding wouldn't happen to notice them—and then they'd drive back to Washington. Perhaps all Kimberly had wanted was an excuse to take her elegant car out for a spin on a sunny spring afternoon.

"If worse comes to worst and he is home," she opined, gunning the engine to pass a truck, "at least we'll see where he lives. We'll see if he's the sort to keep his lawn mowed. What do you think, Andrew? Is he a good-neighbor kind of man?"

"I wouldn't want him for one of my neighbors," Andrew grumbled.

Kimberly eased back into the right lane and then cast Andrew a probing glance. She remained silent for a minute, then took a deep breath and let up on the gas pedal. "What are the right questions, Andrew?"

"Hmm?" He scowled. "The right questions for what?"

"You told me before that most people like to talk about themselves if you ask the right questions. What are the right questions for you?"

He studied her face in profile. Her forehead was smooth, not a line marring the clear skin. Her tiny nose had a natural bob to it, and the skin beneath her chin cut a sleek line to her throat. He focused on her lips for a moment, then turned away. "I don't know, Kim," he said. "Ask and find out."

She lapsed into another brief silence, then said, "Tell me about your childhood."

That wasn't the question he expected. Actually, he hadn't known what to expect, but an inquisition on his childhood definitely wasn't it. He issued a short, surprised laugh, then said, "What about it?"

"Where are you from? Where did you grow up? I know so little about you, Andrew."

"I grew up in Canton, Ohio. My father owns an auto parts store. My mother is a housewife. I have two younger sisters."

She appeared astounded by his sudden outpouring. He wasn't sure why she should be; he hadn't told her anything notably intimate about himself. Yet he, too, was struck by the comprehension that in all the years they had known each other, Kimberly had never before asked him anything about his background.

"Was it a happy childhood?" she inquired.

"Happier than most, I imagine. We weren't rich, but we had everything we needed. My parents loved us. They raised us pretty well."

"Would you like to have children?"

Her innocent question caused a shard of pain to cut through him. Children. It had all started with Marjorie's pregnancy, their baby, the child they were never to have. Even though they had still been in graduate school, barely scraping by, Andrew and Marjorie had wanted that child more than anything. Compared to losing Marjorie, losing the baby had seemed almost tolerable. Almost. But not quite.

He turned away, wondering whether Kimberly had noticed his momentary anguish. His failure to answer prompted her to apologize. "I'm sorry, Andrew. I guess that wasn't the right question."

"It was a valid question," he assured her quietly, doing his best to recover. "Yes. I would like to have children someday."

She flashed a quick look his way, evidently trying to gauge the reason for his altered mood. Then she turned her attention back to the road. "So would I," she confessed. "I reckon I'm too old, though."

"You aren't that old."

"I'm old enough not to have known that nowadays men come on like gangbusters on the first date," she said with a wry chuckle.

"Women are having children later than they used to," he commented. "With all the tests they have, all the screening they can do, it's not such a dangerous risk."

Kimberly laughed incredulously. Andrew had only stated the truth, and he didn't understand her reaction. "I can't believe we're talking this way," she explained, swallowing a final laugh. "It's nice, Andrew. I miss having my old friends to talk to. I have friends, of course, but other than Julianne, I don't keep up with anyone who knew me back when. Remember how we all used to sit around rapping in the basement office of *The Dream*, back in school?"

Andrew smiled. "The staff meetings."

"There Julianne would be, at the head of the table, trying to maintain some sort of order," Kimberly reminisced. "She'd be discoursing on whether it was a mortal sin to accept advertisements from a conglomerate like A & P, and Troy would be spinning his lens cap on the table and muttering about how he was constitutionally unsuited to bureaucratic meetings, and Laura would be divvying up the granola...."

"Counting the raisins to make sure nobody got gypped," Andrew recalled.

"Right." Kimberly slowed down to read an exit sign, then sped up again, grinning as her memories took shape. "Then Seth would come barging in, always ten minutes late, wearing one of his weird T-shirts—"

"'Better Stoned Than Sorry,'" Andrew quoted. "That one was one of his favorites, wasn't it?"

"All his T-shirts were his favorites," Kimberly contended. "He had a slogan for every occasion. 'Better Living Through Chemistry,' 'Keep In Shape—Have Loose Joints,' 'I'd Rather Be Here Than In Vietnam.'"

"'Frankly, My Dear, I Do Give A Damn,'" Andrew recollected, relaxing, the last of his sorrow ebbing away. His gaze drifted for a minute, then sharpened on Kimberly. "You had a shirt that said, 'Smile—It Increases Your Face Power.'"

"I hardly ever wore T-shirts," Kimberly protested. "And certainly not with slogans. 'Smile—It Increases Your Face Power' was printed on a poster I brought to our office and hung on the wall."

"Wherever it was, the slogan was pretty damned corny," Andrew said.

Kimberly seemed temporarily riled by his provocative comment. Then she grinned placidly and remarked, "Maybe it was corny, but it was true. Smiling does wonderful things to the face."

Andrew wrestled with the temptation to argue, but he checked himself. He agreed with Kimberly; it was nice talking this way, nice sharing the memories with her. "What a cheerleader you are," he murmured. "That's what you and I used to talk about at those meetings, wasn't it."

Kimberly nodded. "Seth would race in and announce that he'd decided to write his next column on the moral bankruptcy of dancing to George Harrison's 'Bangladesh,' the tastelessness of dancing to a song about children starving. And I'd say, if George Harrison didn't want people dancing to it, he wouldn't have written such a catchy tune. And you'd squint through those granny glasses of yours and carp about how typical it was of a cheerleader to care more about the tune than the lyrics."

"I didn't squint," Andrew objected.

"Whenever you looked at me you did," she maintained somberly. "It was a squint of disapproval, Andrew, as if you couldn't bear to look directly at me."

"Oh, I could bear it," Andrew said good-naturedly. He stared across the seat at her. Looking directly at her was more than bearable. It was delightful. Her beauty was mesmerizing. He could stare at her for a long time and never feel the urge to squint. And he could have back in college, too. Did he really squint then? "Maybe I squinted because looking at you was like looking at the sun," he posed, conceding that her recollection was more accurate than his. "You were always so bright and glowing."

His compliment took her aback. "That bothered you, didn't it," she said, mildly accusing.

"Yes," he admitted. "Those were serious times, Kim. I couldn't understand how someone could be so cheerful when so many things were wrong with the world."

"I was no more cheerful than anyone else," Kimberly claimed.

"More optimistic, maybe?" he suggested. "More hopeful?"

"I don't know." She meditated for a moment, then sighed. "Maybe I was. It wasn't that I wasn't aware of what was going on in the world. It was just that...it was more fun to believe that everything would work out somehow, someday. It seemed healthier to believe that we'd all overcome and live happily ever after. The folly of youth," she concluded with a snort.

"That's one of the best things about youth," Andrew noted, not at all pleased by her self-derision. "You're right, it is more fun to believe everything will work out. It's unrealistic, but a lot more fun."

"Things didn't work out as well as I had thought they would," she mused wistfully.

"But you still had the courage to be hopeful back then," Andrew pointed out. "You were very brave, Kim. It was much easier to be a cynic, much safer. I think I envied your bravery."

She released the gear stick, reached for his hand and squeezed it. "I wasn't very brave," she disputed him. "I was just behaving the only way I knew how to behave. Ignorance is bliss, Andrew, and I was fairly ignorant."

"And you were blissful." He had been totally unprepared for her friendly hand clasp, but he was touched by it. He liked the feel of her hand in his, so small and dainty against his. He twined his fingers through hers to keep her from pulling away. "Life was strange then, Kim. I'm sorry I was such an ass around you."

"We were all asses back then," she remarked, veering onto a ramp. "Let's try this exit and see where it takes us."

They coasted to a quiet street. Andrew spotted a gas station up ahead, then turned to survey the street signs. "Slow down!" he shouted, reading a sign bearing the name of Wilding's street. "That's his address."

Kimberly braked and then turned right onto a residential road. "What number are we looking for?"

Andrew told her. As they glided past a block of modest but well-maintained houses, he began to grow apprehensive. Perhaps they were asses in their youth, but what he and Kimberly were doing now seemed far more foolish than anything they had done back then.

"That's his place," she announced, pulling up to the curb before a trim brick ranch house and halting. "It looks like no one's home."

"You can't tell that," Andrew muttered, slouching in his seat and peeking surreptitiously over the dashboard. "His garage is closed. His car could be in there."

Kimberly perused the house thoughtfully. "Why don't I ring the bell and find out?"

"What are you going to do if he is home?"

"I'll tell him...I'll tell him I'm from the League of Women Voters, doing a survey on who he's planning to vote for in the next presidential election."

"Kimberly, that's over a year away," Andrew reminded her. He found her stubbornness exasperating, but also rather appealing.

"I can still be doing a survey," she said resolutely, unbuckling her seat belt and swinging open her door.

He grabbed her arm to stop her. "If you're supposed to be doing a survey, you can't visit him empty-handed," he pointed out.

She hesitated, then eyed his briefcase, which stood on the floor between his legs. "Give me a piece of paper," she ordered.

He thumbed through the folder on his lap. He couldn't give her anything from that; Wilding might recognize the papers as photocopies of the documents Andrew had given him. Rummaging through his briefcase, he found a pen and a student paper and handed them to her. "Here," he grunted. "I'm sure most League of Women Voters people take surveys on the backs of essays on Soviet imperialism in the Western Hemisphere."

Smiling, Kimberly took the paper and pen and climbed out of the car.

Slouching lower, Andrew spied on Kimberly as she marched boldly up the walk to the front door. He was daunted by her fearlessness, unnerved by it. Never in his wildest dreams would he have imagined that Kimberly Belmont, the belle of Atlanta, was willing to meet a C.I.A. operative head-on.

Yet she didn't really seem aware of the danger in what she was doing. To her it was just another silly game. Andrew could imagine Kimberly the cheerleader taking a classmate up on a dare and stealing the ladies' room sign, or setting a thumbtack on a teacher's chair. Apparently she viewed this escapade as no more serious than that.

Sneaking a look out the side window, he watched her press the doorbell, wait, then press it again. Slowly he unwound from his cramped position. She smiled and waved him over.

Drawing in a deep breath, he pursed his lips and joined her on the front walk. As silly as her latest game was, he wasn't about to let her show him up at it. He could play it as well as she could.

"At least he mows his grass," she observed, sprinting across the lawn to a break in the decorative shrubs surrounding the house. "Let's look through a window."

"Kim—"

She ignored him, gripping the window frame and peering inside. "His living room," she announced. "Colonial-style furniture with plaid Herculon upholstery. Straight from Sears, if I'm not mistaken."

"And what does that tell you about him?" Andrew inquired indulgently.

"Well, if he's skimming, he isn't sinking the money into his house," she said, dusting off her hands and stalking around to the side of the house, Andrew at her heels. "Remember that other C.I.A. fellow... what's his name? The one who sold plastic explosives to Libya."

"Edwin Wilson," Andrew supplied. He had learned all he could about every other incident in recent history where C.I.A. agents had overstepped the law.

"That's the one. Didn't he own a showplace in horse country? That man made a fortune on his double-dealing."

"And now he's rotting in jail," Andrew remarked.

Kimberly tossed him a triumphant smile. "See? Things do work out sometimes. Boost me up, Andrew. This window's too high."

He glanced left and right, checking to see if anyone might be watching them. Then, drawing in another deep breath, he lifted Kimberly by her waist. She was unusually slim, and his long fingers splayed out over her sides. She was light, so slender and compact. The flesh of her belly was firm beneath his fingertips, the fabric of her sweater soft. Her cologne filled his nostrils.

He didn't want to be prowling about John Wilding's house. But for the chance to hold Kimberly, to take her in his arms and support her weight, the peril of being caught was almost worth it.

He brusquely shook his head clear of that notion. How on earth could he think that risking life and limb to find out God knows what—how could he think that was worth the opportunity to hold Kimberly? How, for that matter, could he have thought that she looked sexy driving a stick shift? What was wrong with him?

Nothing, he assured himself as Kimberly descended, her back sliding along his chest as she reached for the ground with her feet. Nothing was wrong with finding Kimberly gorgeous. Undoubtedly any normal man would enjoy holding a woman like her for a few minutes. There was nothing disreputable, nothing embarrassing about it.

"That was his bedroom," she whispered, turning to face Andrew as he loosened his hold on her. He let his hands linger on her hips, and she didn't object. Instead she leaned closer to him and giggled. "He has a water bed."

"He does?"

"A king-size one. Big enough for plenty of hanky-panky. Is he married?"

"I don't know," Andrew answered. "We never got that personal in our conversations."

"I bet he isn't," Kimberly guessed, slipping out of Andrew's arms and tiptoeing around to the backyard. "Most married women wouldn't put up with a king-size water bed."

"Some might," Andrew argued. Water beds weren't worth arguing about with Kimberly, but he felt a sudden need to put some distance between her and himself. "The world is filled with adventurous wives."

Kimberly shot him a disgruntled look. "Sure," she sniffed. "And it's filled with men who come on like gangbusters. A gas grill," she noticed, pointing to the grill on the patio. "How mundane."

"Admit it," Andrew teased her. "If you think a gas grill is mundane, you probably find water beds infinitely exotic."

"I assure you, I don't," she said piously. "I'd think water beds would make one seasick."

He couldn't keep from goading her. "Maybe you ought to try one out and see."

"Not in this lifetime," she declared with finality. "I may be a divorcée, but that doesn't mean I'm into water sports."

"But you've already proved that you're adventurous. We wouldn't be here if you weren't."

Kimberly pivoted to face him. His eyes wandered from her tousled hair, which had a few dead leaves from one of the shrubs tangled into it, to her graceful shoulders, her bosom, the tiny waist he had briefly clutched, the swell of her hips, her tapering legs. She *was* adventurous, and he would be willing to wager big money that she'd have the time of her life on a water bed.

He tore his eyes from her. This was not a productive line of thought. He wished they'd never come to Fairfax, not because of the inherent danger but because he honestly didn't like thinking erotic thoughts about Kimberly.

"His garbage pail!" she exclaimed, bringing his attention back to their present situation. She jogged across the patio to the aluminum trash can standing at the corner of the house. "Let's see what's inside it."

The entire masquerade had gone on long enough. Andrew was not about to paw through a week's worth of coffee grounds and banana peels just to satisfy Kimberly's whim. "Don't be absurd," he snapped.

"I wasn't being absurd," she protested, lifting the lid of the can and gazing in. "He smokes," she commented unnecessarily. The pail was brimming with dead cigarette butts.

"There you have it," Andrew muttered. "The secret to the man's behavior. He's a nicotine freak. Can we go now?"

Before Kimberly could reply, they heard the sound of an approaching car. Andrew grabbed the lid and set it noiselessly back onto the pail, then flattened himself to the brick wall and shifted his head a centimeter to gaze around the side. A black Cadillac had pulled up to the curb in front of Kimberly's BMW and sat idling. Two men were in the Cadillac's front seat, but Andrew couldn't decipher their faces.

"Is that him?" Kimberly hissed.

Andrew pressed her to the wall beside him, his arm pinning her against the bricks. The passenger door of the Cadillac opened, and although he couldn't see the man's face, he recognized Wilding's voice.

"Don't move," he whispered, nodding in answer to Kimberly's question. "Don't even breathe."

Wilding swung out of the car and shut the passenger door. He bent to address the driver through the open window. Andrew felt Kimberly's ribs moving against his arm, shifting slowly as she took a controlled breath, and he detected the faint flutter of her heart. It was all her fault that they were in such a dangerous position, but he wanted to protect her. He wanted to save her far more than he wanted to save himself.

They waited. The men talked for a few seconds longer, and then Wilding straightened. Andrew turned to Kimberly. "The hedge," he mouthed, tilting his head toward a hedge of yews separating Wilding's backyard from his next-door neighbor's.

Kimberly nodded slightly. Her lips were pressed together, clenched bloodlessly, but her eyes were twinkling.

Andrew twisted back to watch Wilding, who waved at his colleague and then rotated, starting toward the house across the front lawn. Andrew pressed his ear to the wall, listening for the vibration of the door opening. As soon as he heard it, he released Kimberly. They both dove for cover beneath the bushes, crawling through the dirt and emerging in the adjacent yard. "Run!" she panted, darting toward the street.

Andrew could have overtaken her easily, but he didn't. For some inexplicable reason he wanted to remain behind her, to be able to shove her out of harm's way if the need arose.

Gasping for breath, they glimpsed Wilding's house from behind the edge of the row of yews to ascertain that Wilding was safely inside. The black Cadillac was gone. They bolted for the BMW and collapsed inside. "Which way did he go?" Kimberly asked, fumbling with the key.

Andrew inserted it into the ignition for her, then fell back against the seat as the car peeled wildly away from the curb. "I think he turned left at the corner."

She didn't bother slowing down to take the turn, and Andrew was tossed against the door as the BMW skidded around the corner. Belatedly he groped for his seat belt. "There he is!" she shrieked energetically, spotting the black car just before it made another left turn.

"Slow down," Andrew cautioned her. "You don't want him to see us tailing him."

"All right, all right," Kimberly muttered, though she didn't ease her foot much on the accelerator pedal. She turned left, and they found the Cadillac waiting at a stop sign. "Diplomatic plate," she said. "Write it down—I'll be able to trace the number at work."

Andrew reached for his briefcase to get a pen, then froze. The student paper. Where was it? Still at Wilding's place? With Andrew's name incriminatingly typed in the upper right-hand margin? "Kim," he barked. "Where? Where's the paper?"

"What paper?" she asked innocently.

"The student paper, damn it! The essay I gave you!"

She turned to him, able to read the panic in his eyes. She let him fret for a second before presenting him with a smug grin. "Relax, Double-O Seven. It's in my back pocket."

He sank into the upholstery, then let loose with a laugh. "Good enough, Agent 99. Give me the pen."

She shifted to pull from her hip pocket the pen and the paper, which was wrinkled but intact. Andrew jotted down the Cadillac's license number, then surrendered to more laughter. "You're crazy, Kim," he declared. "Absolutely nuts."

She joined his laughter. "Not nuts enough to like water beds," she maintained.

He lifted his hand to her hair and pulled out two broken leaves. Cupping them in his palm, he displayed them for her. "I think you'll be thrown off the cheerleading squad for this."

"Their loss," she said, shrugging blithely.

Chapter Five

Pastel shades flattered her.

Andrew supposed that Kimberly would look good in anything she wore—army fatigues, a tuxedo, baggy chartreuse pajamas. But the soft hues of her clothing complemented her fair coloring in a magnificent way, highlighting her lucid blue eyes, giving her complexion a healthy glow.

At the moment she was attired in a peach-colored dress with long sleeves and a simple cut, snug at her slender waist and flaring down to the hem. The neckline wasn't daring, but it revealed her throat and her graceful collarbone. The only jewelry she wore was a pair of pearl studs in her earlobes and a narrow gold watch on her wrist. She looked exquisite.

Andrew tried to recall the last time he had been with a woman as beautiful as Kimberly, and all he could come up with was the hours he'd spent seated across the Formica-topped work table from Kimberly herself, in *The Dream*'s basement office fifteen years ago. She had often worn pastels then, too. But he couldn't remember her looking nearly as good as she looked now.

It was more than just the colors of her clothes that enhanced her appearance. It was their unobtrusive style and her meticulous grooming, her subtle use of cosmetics, her smooth hands, her understated perfume. She knew what to do with herself, how to make the most of nature's generous gifts.

Marjorie had been a slob. Andrew had loved her, so he hadn't cared much about the way the corduroy of her slacks was always eroded at the knees, the way her untucked shirt-tails always drooped below the ribbed edge of her sweaters, the way her sweaters themselves were always stretched out of shape and worn to near transparency at the elbows. Nor had he minded the fact that their compact apartment in the married students' housing at the University of Michigan was always a mess. Marjorie used to joke that she vacuumed once a year, whether or not the carpet needed it, and that allowing dust to accumulate on the tables ought to be accepted as a physics experiment, since dust was a product of meteors.

Andrew had straightened out the place as best he could, and he had always chosen to give her articles of clothing for Christmas and her birthday. Invariaoly, the first time she would wear some new sweater he'd given her, she would spill ketchup or grape juice on it.

They had argued about her slovenliness. But if Andrew had been able to view the future, if he had had any inkling of how little time together he and Marjorie were to be granted, he wouldn't have wasted so many precious minutes berating her for her carelessness and wishing she were neater. Bickering was a natural part of any intimate relationship, but if he had known how close he was to losing her, he never would have fought with her.

No, that wasn't true. Even after they *had* known that the end was upon them, they had fought. Living with Henry and Edith for that last year had been excruciatingly tough, and the chemotherapy had been wretched, leaving Marjorie exhausted and listless. But even as she and Andrew watched her life ebb away, they still quarreled over her habit of leaving books open on the floor, her failure to return record albums to their jackets when she was through listening to them and her refusal to hang her towel back on the rack when she was done with it. The things she had no control over—Andrew didn't mind any of that. He had lovingly changed the bed sheets daily and bathed her when she was too tired to bathe herself, clipped her toenails and held her head when nausea overcame her. He would gladly have done those things for her forever—if only he had been given the chance. He hadn't, though. Marjorie died, leaving him with little but his own insufferable tidiness.

Marjorie had been typical of the women Andrew had dated throughout his life: attractive, if not classically beautiful, and dazzlingly intelligent. He had never associated much with women like Kimberly.

He had liked the restaurant they'd gone to, an elegant establishment located inside the Georgetown Inn. He wondered if she had selected the place because it had pink napkins and pink flowers in the bud vases on the tables. Clad in her peach dress, surrounded by so much pink, she had appeared as gently tinted and delicate as the water lilies in the Monet print hanging above her bed in her apartment.

On their way back to Fairfax, she had driven Andrew to his motel so he could change his clothing. He had donned his tie, his tweed blazer and a pair of dark blue trousers. Although he'd brought the tie and the tailored slacks in the hope of wearing them when he met Senator Milford, he was just as happy to wear them for Kimberly.

"What was it like being a cheerleader?" he asked, genuinely interested. They had just left the restaurant, and he was in an expansive mood. He was trying to reconcile the image of a teenage Kimberly doing splits in the air with the reality of her dashing through the bushes at Wilding's house, scaling the walls, taking maniacal chances with her own life and Andrew's. Sometimes the two images coincided, and sometimes they seemed poles apart. An inveterate analyzer, Andrew needed to make sense of Kimberly. He needed to find a logical explanation for how the cheerleader had evolved into this astonishing woman by his side.

She peered up at him and smiled. "Do you want to know the truth?" she asked, leaning toward him conspiratorially. "I loved it."

"Did you really?"

"Oh, Andrew... I know you're going to think I'm a moron for saying so, but it was great. I loved everything about it—the short pleated skirts we wore, and the letter sweaters, and the saddle shoes, and riding in the team bus to the away games. I loved the megaphones and the pom-poms. Maybe I'm an egomaniac, but I loved the recognition, too. Being a cheerleader in my high school was a real coup. We were admired, we were envied.... We were popular."

"You probably would have been popular even if you hadn't been a cheerleader," he commented.

She shrugged, drawing to a stop at the corner as they waited for the light to change. "That's like saying I would have been popular if I'd been a poet, or a dog breeder. Maybe I would have been and maybe I wouldn't. The fact was, I *was* a cheerleader."

"In my high school," he recalled, "the cheerleaders were very aloof. And they always tended to be superstraight. There were three distinct cliques in the school: the jocks, the freaks and the hoods. Cheerleaders were female jocks."

"And you were a freak," Kimberly accurately guessed.

He chuckled and nodded. "I hung out with my classmates in the A-track, listened to The Doors, talked about drugs with aplomb. The jocks—cheerleaders included—tended to be Beach Boys fans and beer drinkers."

"Heavens!" Kimberly gasped in mock dismay. "In *my* high school, no proper young lady worth her salt would ever be caught drinking beer. We drank mint juleps and Southern Comfort. Beer was considered a man's beverage."

"I'm sorry I ordered the wine at dinner," Andrew teased her. "I didn't realize that my masculinity hung in the balance. I should have asked for a pitcher of whatever they had on tap."

"Frankly, I don't like beer much," Kimberly confessed. "I'm glad you ordered the wine." The light changed, and she started across the street, Andrew following. "It's such a lovely evening, I wish we could take a stroll to work down all that food. But we've got to get home. Whitney could be calling anytime now." Her gaze narrowed on Andrew and her smile faded. "Do you mind coming back to my apartment for a while? I know you think this is all silly, but I'm sure he's going to want to talk to you when he calls, and if you aren't there—"

"That's all right," he assured her. "I don't mind." He honestly didn't. His eyes glinted wickedly when he added, "Are you sure you trust me not to come on like gangbusters once I enter your apartment?"

Kimberly tossed back her head and laughed.

The night air was pleasantly cool. She slipped her hand through Andrew's elbow as they turned off Wisconsin Avenue and proceeded down a picturesque block of restored town houses. "This is such a delightful neighborhood," Andrew commented. "I almost feel as if I've stepped into another century. Look at these gas lamps." He paused beneath one of the decorative streetlights and gazed up at it.

Kimberly grinned. "The last time I walked down this block I was with Whitney," she told Andrew.

"And?" He noticed dimples forming at the corners of her mouth. "What's so funny?"

"Just how different you are from him," she explained. "You talk about the streetlights. He talked about whether Henry Kissinger had lived on this street."

Andrew mulled over what she'd said. He wondered what his having mentioned the streetlights indicated to her and why she was so amused. "So? Did Henry Kissinger live on this street?"

"I don't know," Kimberly answered as they resumed their stroll. "If he did, he never invited me to his house. I'm afraid he and I travel in different circles."

"I think you ought to get to know your neighbors better," Andrew chided her. "You ought to find out where they stand on the issues. Look at Wilding's neighborhood. Do you think his neighbors on that charming little block have any idea of what he's scheming?"

"Every neighborhood has its hidden snakes and flakes." She crossed the street with him. "Especially in the Washington area. Ignore these government types and they just might do something heinous, like creating a revolution in El Salvador."

"You never know," Andrew commented lightly.

"You still don't trust the government, Andrew, do you?" she half asked.

He weighed his answer. "I don't distrust it as much as I used to fifteen years ago," he conceded. "But I can't shake the notion that it tends to attract people who are hungry for power—exactly the sort of people I don't want representing me."

"Nonsense," she debated. "It attracts people who wish to serve their country. Most politicians take office because they think they can make the world a better place. Maybe you disagree with their positions, maybe you think they're going about it the wrong way. Maybe their definition of 'better' is different from yours. But their motives are usually pure."

"God, you're such an optimist," he observed with a smile. He found Kimberly's positive opinion of politicians sweet, even if he didn't quite agree with it. He envied her ability to approach the universe in such a positive manner. He had spent enough of his life being bitter, seeing the world as a bleak and hostile place. And it hadn't done him a lick of good. Kimberly's attitude didn't mark her as shallow, only as sensible.

They had reached her apartment. She unlocked the door and ushered Andrew inside. Once she shut and bolted the door, she preceded him into the living room and switched on a lamp.

"Do you think he's called yet?" Andrew asked.

Kimberly read her wristwatch and shrugged. "It's nine o'clock. If he missed us he'll call again." She crossed to the kitchen. "Would you like something to drink?"

Andrew removed his blazer and tugged his necktie loose. "What have you got?"

"Coffee, brandy, some orange liqueur..."

"No beer, huh," he joked.

Her eyes met his across the counter, and she smiled. "No beer. But being a Southerner, I do have bourbon."

"Wild Turkey?"

"Jack Daniel's."

"Sounds great."

He watched as she pulled a bottle of Jack Daniel's from one cabinet and two highball glasses from another. He was glad she was going to join him. "Ice?" she asked as she unscrewed the bottle top. "Or water?"

"I'll take it straight," he requested.

Her smile expanded. She poured two hefty portions of bourbon, left the bottle on the counter and carried the glasses into the living room. Andrew took his drink from her and sank onto the sofa. Kimberly stepped out of her shoes and curled up on the easy chair, tucking her stockinged feet beneath her. Then she took a sip. She held her glass like a lady, he observed, with her pinkie crooked into the air, but she drank her booze strong and neat, just like a man. He liked that.

Before tasting the bourbon, he glanced at the wall phone in the kitchen. He wanted to learn what Whitney had found out about L.A.R.C., but he almost wished they wouldn't be hearing from him for a while. Once they did, once Whitney called and made his report, Andrew would no longer have a good excuse to stay at Kimberly's apartment. And he wanted to stay. He wanted to enjoy a leisurely drink with a beautiful woman.

She must have noticed his gaze drifting to the telephone, because she asked, "Would you like to watch some television? Or I could turn on the stereo—"

"No, that's all right," he hastened to assure her. He didn't want her to feel obliged to entertain him. "Why don't we just talk?"

"Fine." She settled back in the overstuffed chair and took another bracing sip of bourbon. Her index finger traced the circular rim of her glass, but her eyes remained fixed on Andrew, their clear, shimmering blue reminding him of a still, deep pond in the Berkshires, mirroring the Massachusetts sky. She smiled tenuously. "Tell me about your wife," she said.

IT WAS A RISKY THING to ask. Kimberly recognized how risky it was when Andrew froze in his seat at the sound of the word "wife," his glass in midair, his eyes suddenly searing behind his eyeglasses, the muscles of his jaw stiffening. But she wasn't sorry she'd broached the subject. Maybe it was the wrong question, but she wouldn't take it back.

At his lengthening silence, she felt the need to justify herself. "I know she passed away, Andrew. Seth told Laura and she told me." When he still didn't speak, she added, "I was terribly sorry to hear about it."

He finally moved, lifting his glass to his lips and taking a long sip. But even the bourbon couldn't erase the aching pain in his eyes, the tension around his mouth and neck. She wished she had the nerve to march across the room to the couch and sit beside him, to wrap her arms around him in comfort. But she'd exhausted her supply of courage simply by giving voice to the question, and she remained where she was.

Not a word from him as he swallowed, lowered his glass to the coffee table in front of him and stared at her. "I tell you what," she offered, trying to placate him. She would do anything to ease his agony, anything to get him to open up to her again. Anything to see him bare the soul he had managed to hide from her for so long. "I'll fill you in on my sad marriage story first."

"Okay," he said softly.

Although she didn't particularly want to discuss her divorce, she intuited that Andrew's willingness to listen to her talk about it meant that eventually he would be willing to tell her his own sad story. "Divorce is such a common thing," she said, studying the dark amber fluid in her glass. "But you never think it's going to happen to you. I always figured that if you could survive the first couple of years of marriage, you were set for life. Or at least until the midlife crises struck. Todd and I aren't old enough to suffer midlife crises."

"So why did you split?" Andrew asked.

"Little things," she replied pensively. "Little things that added up to big things. He had affairs—"

"That's a pretty big thing, if you ask me," Andrew commented.

She lifted her gaze to him and smiled. He *was* a decent man. How many men in this day and age would consider extramarital affairs anything but trivial? "In the society I grew up in," she explained, "men always have affairs. A proper wife is supposed to look the other way. And I did—the first time."

"Why the hell did he want anyone else when he had you?"

Andrew's compliment warmed her deeply. Her eyes met his, and she was equally warmed by their tenderness, their steadiness on her. Telling Andrew about her divorce wasn't as difficult as she had expected, not when he seemed so sympathetic and caring. "What Todd had was a wife," she distinguished. "As soon as it's legal, it isn't so much fun anymore. I guess." Her smile grew bittersweet. "I probably would have continued to look the other way if it hadn't been for all the other little things. He had so many confusions about me, about what I should be doing and feeling. He resented the fact that I had a career, but then he liked the income I was bringing in. He didn't mind when I worked for the P.R. firm, but he hated my working for the senator. He considers my boss a closet pinko."

"Milford?" Andrew guffawed. "A Communist?"

She shrugged. "What can I say? The senator believes that prayer is a private matter. He believes that we ought to negotiate arms treaties with the Soviet Union. Very suspect behavior in the eyes of someone like Todd."

"Why did you marry him?" Andrew asked, leaning forward and resting his forearms on his spread knees. "Didn't you know all this about him before you tied the knot?"

She chuckled sadly. "I've known Todd ever since we were children. His parents and mine were good friends. But knowing someone a long time doesn't mean you know him well. We got along fine, we were attracted to each other, we came from similar backgrounds. Even though we dated other people before we got married, it was always a given that we'd get married eventually." She laughed again. "If he was scandalized that I went to Barnard College up north in Sin City, he was even more scandalized that I didn't go through all the premarriage rituals with him. I was never lavaliered—"

"What?"

"Lavaliered. That's when a fellow gives you a pendant with his fraternity letters on it, and he and his fraternity brothers stand under your window and serenade you. After that you get pinned. Then you get engaged. I can just imagine Todd and his brothers driving up to Harlem to serenade me!" She chuckled at the absurdity of the idea. "I think he believed that my time at Barnard was my last fling, that I was going to 'get it out of my system' before we got married. I'm not sure what 'it' was, but it was supposed to be behind me by the time I got married."

"Kim." Andrew shook his head incredulously. "It was 1972. I can't believe people were doing that sort of thing in 1972."

"They probably weren't in Canton, Ohio," she conceded. "And they certainly weren't doing it at Columbia. But life was different where I came from. This was how things were done."

"Especially if you were a cheerleader," he ribbed her.

She looked sharply at him, anxious to ascertain that he wasn't denigrating her again. When she had confessed, during their walk home from the restaurant, that she loved being a cheerleader, Andrew had appeared fascinated. She didn't want to think he had relapsed into his original view of her as an empty-headed goose.

But his smile was gentle, not mocking. It was an utterly beautiful, nonjudgmental smile. She nestled into the chair's cushions and continued her tale. "We had a big, grand wedding. Half of Augusta was invited. Everyone told us we made a perfect couple."

"Why didn't you have any children?"

She had already told Andrew that she wanted children, so his question was reasonable. "I don't think Todd cared to become a father," she admitted. "At first he protested that we needed my income to pay for our house—which we did, I'm afraid. It was a huge place, much larger than any childless couple requires. The fact that he loved it so much led me to assume he would want to have children eventually. So I waited. I paid my share of the mortgage. I closed my eyes to his affairs. And I waited some more. After I turned thirty I began to get nervous about it. Finally I called him to account, and he said the only way he'd have children with me was if I did it his way—I'd have to quit my job and stay at home with them."

"Is there anything so terrible about that?" Andrew asked. "I don't mean to sound sexist, Kim, but lots of women—even today—stay at home with their children. My mother did, and she found it very fulfilling."

"I love my work," Kimberly argued, then meditated on her insistence, in her marriage, of maintaining her career. She sighed. "Andrew, I would have quit my job to have children if I had thought for one minute that Todd was going to be a willing father. But he truly didn't want children. He only wanted to get me to quit the senator's staff. It was like a bargain he was cutting with me—he'd let me have my children if I'd stop working for a pinko." She drank her bourbon and sighed again. "That's not the right way to have children, as some sort of trade agreement, some sort of compromise. If both partners aren't ready to put their all into parenthood, it's not right."

Andrew pondered her statement and nodded.

"Why didn't you have children?" she countered, deciding that she'd talked long enough about her divorce. The subject no longer depressed her, but she found it tiresome. Now it was his turn to talk.

He lowered his gaze to his glass, examined it intently and drained it in one long gulp. "Is it all right if I help myself?" he asked, rising.

That he was trying to evade her question was obvious. She forgave him, but she wasn't about to let him off the hook. "Go right ahead," she said generously, angling her head toward the counter where the bottle stood. Then she took another sip from her own glass and handed it to him. He refilled his glass, added some bourbon to hers and delivered it to her on his way back to the couch.

He drank. She waited. He drank some more. "How strong is this?" he asked.

"The proof must be written on the bottle somewhere," she told him. "Do you want me to check?"

"No." He inspected his glass, took a parting sip and set it on the coffee table. "I just wish I was feeling it a little more, that's all." He settled back on the cushions and smiled sheepishly. "We've never gotten drunk together, Kim."

"Stoned, either."

His eyebrows arched in surprise. "Do you smoke grass?"

"No." She returned his smile. "I'm ashamed to admit I've never touched the stuff. But it would have been fun getting stoned with you."

"Do you think so?" He ruminated, then snorted. "I didn't smoke much in college. Every time I did I got gloomy and introspective."

Kimberly didn't bother to point out that even when he wasn't stoned, he'd had a tendency to be gloomy and introspective. Well, maybe not gloomy. But dreadfully solemn and somber, as if all those heavy thoughts of his allowed no room for laughter. What had he said earlier? Something about how those had been serious times. He hadn't needed marijuana; he'd been introspective enough without it.

He eyed his glass, then bravely refused to hide behind it any longer. He seemed able to sense that Kimberly was growing impatient, that he couldn't keep stalling. "We tried to have children," he said slowly, quietly, his gaze fastened to the wall behind Kimberly. "After a long time she conceived, but then she had a miscarriage. That's when they discovered she had some abnormal cells." He grimaced at the memory. "That's how they break the news to you: 'Abnormal cells.'"

"She had cancer?"

Andrew nodded, still unable to look directly at Kimberly. "Vaginal cancer, uterine cancer, ovarian cancer.... It had already metastasized. It's such an amazing vocabulary they have, Kim. A million words ending with the suffix *oma*. As soon as you hear something that ends in 'oma' you know you're in big trouble."

"How long had you been married?" she asked.

"When she was diagnosed? Almost four years."

"How did you meet her?"

A vague smile shaped his lips as he reminisced. "We met in graduate school. She was a grad student in the physics department. We got married about a year later."

"What was her name? What did she look like? Have you got a picture of her?" Kimberly couldn't keep the spate of questions from pouring out. As impossible as it seemed, Andrew was finally opening up to her. She felt an urgent need to learn everything at once, before he rethought things and clammed up again.

He laughed dryly. "She's dead, Kim. Why on earth would I be carrying around a picture of a dead woman?"

"I don't know," Kimberly defended herself. "I'm just trying to imagine her. I want to know about her."

He raised his glass and drank. "This *is* strong," he assessed the bourbon. "I think I'm beginning to feel it."

Kimberly smiled. In any other circumstance she would abhor the idea of having a drunk man in her home. But Andrew wasn't the sort to get obnoxious and don a lampshade. If the liquor helped him to talk, then she hoped he'd get plastered.

"What was her name?" she repeated.

"Marjorie."

"Was she pretty?"

"Sure. No." He exhaled, and his gaze alighted on Kimberly. "She wasn't pretty, not in the traditional sense. But she was beautiful."

"Of course she was beautiful. You loved her," Kimberly pointed out. One of her mother's many pet clichés was "Beauty is in the eye of the beholder." Like so many clichés, that one was absolutely true.

"I loved her," he confirmed, his tone husky with emotion.

Kimberly wondered whether he was going to cry. She almost wished that he would. If he did, she would definitely cross the room to him, definitely fold her arms around him. She would welcome his tears, welcome the intimacy they would represent.

Yet he seemed resolutely dry-eyed, and Kimberly remained in her chair. "Did she suffer long? I should think it would be terrible to see someone you love suffering," she mused.

"She died about a year and a half after she was diagnosed," he said. "It wasn't a whole year and a half of unremitting suffering, though. We had ups and downs, moments of hope, good days." He kicked off his loafers and propped his legs up on the coffee table, as if making himself more comfortable would enable the words to flow more easily. "As soon as we found out how sick she was, we left Ann Arbor and moved in with her parents in White Plains so we could be near Memorial Sloan-Kettering in Manhattan. It's one of the finest cancer treatment hospitals in the world. I wanted her to have the best care available."

"That's certainly understandable."

"Unfortunately living with Edith and Henry had its drawbacks."

"You didn't like your in-laws?"

"Oh, I loved them," he corrected her. "I still do. They're great people. But . . . you need privacy. You realize how little time you have left, and you want to run away and just be by yourselves as much as possible. We had enough coming down on us without having to prop up Edith and Henry all the time." He pulled off his eyeglasses and rubbed the pale red marks they left on the bridge of his nose. "Sometimes, when I wasn't able to fall asleep, I'd go downstairs to the kitchen for a glass of milk and find Henry there, also unable to sleep. And he'd say, 'She shouldn't have gone into physics. Maybe she was exposed to radioactivity in a lab, maybe her research was what made her sick.' And I'd think, her research was one of her great joys. How could this man say she would have been better off without it? How could he be so insensitive?"

"Insensitive?" Kimberly protested. "She was his daughter. He was grieving."

"I know that. I tried not to hold it against him. But it was hard, Kim. Very hard." He turned to the window and gazed out at the darkness. "They're good people, Edith and Henry. I keep in touch with them. I see them from time to time. In some ways they're easier to take than my own parents. After Marjorie died I spent some time back in Ohio, trying to unwind, trying to pull myself together. My parents wanted to baby me. My dad wanted to give me a job in his store so I wouldn't have to go back to Ann Arbor and relive all the memories while I finished my degree. They thought they could protect me from ever getting hurt again. They still want to protect me."

"That also seems like a natural response," Kimberly asserted. "You're their son and they love you."

"Maybe." His eyes drifted back to Kimberly. "When you're trying to come to grips with yourself, the last thing you want is to have everyone else crowding you, no matter how good their intentions are."

"Is that why you don't like to talk about it?" Kimberly asked.

"I'm talking about it now." He lifted his glass, then lowered it without drinking. "I talk about it with people I can trust not to crowd me, not to pity me, not to baby me. What happened with Marjorie is a part of my life, just like breaking my arm falling off a skateboard when I was eight was part of my life, and having the neighbors call the police one evening because I was playing 'The Soft Parade' too loud, and graduating from Columbia and from the University of Michigan. Those few people who can accept it, whom I can trust... I can talk about it to them."

She recognized that he had complimented her again, a much more significant compliment than any he had ever given her before. Yet she didn't bask in Andrew's flattery. He hadn't told her he trusted her as a means of softening her up. He had simply stated a fact.

"Do you date much now?" she asked.

"What constitutes 'much'?" he returned, smiling crookedly.

Kimberly grinned. "One of the things that frightens me about being divorced is that now I have to start all over again. Dating is fun when you're sixteen, Andrew, but not when you're thirty-five. I'm too old for it."

"You aren't so old," he said, for not the first time. "And you're gorgeous, Kim. If you wanted to go out on dates, I'm sure you could have men beating a path to your door. Look at Whitney."

"Ugh. Look at him," she grunted. Then her gaze met Andrew's, and they both laughed. "Did you find it hard, starting all over again? I reckon you didn't," she answered herself. "According to the latest statistics, the odds are slanted strongly in favor of men. Single women past thirty-five may as well forget about ever marrying again."

"You want to get married again?"

"Definitely. I want to have a child, Andrew. I already told you that. I suppose I could have one by myself if I had to—and oh, Lord, wouldn't that shock my family!" She laughed. "How about you? Will you get married again?"

"I hope so."

"Are you seeing anyone now? Anyone special?"

He accepted her question as she'd intended it—not nosy, not prying, only curious. "I've dated a few women since I moved to Amherst," he told her. "The woman I've been seeing lately is a grad student at U-Mass. She's got a job lined up for next September at Cal-State Fullerton if she wants it, and she says she does. So even if she doesn't finish her dissertation in time, she's going to be leaving for California in a couple of months." He shrugged. "Obviously this one isn't going to lead to marriage."

Kimberly tilted her glass against her lips and emptied it. "How do you meet women?" she asked. Before he could answer, she stood and walked to the counter. She hesitated, then brought her glass and the bottle to the coffee table and dropped onto the couch next to Andrew. She could no longer tolerate being seated so far away from him when she felt so close to him.

She poured some bourbon into her glass, then dribbled a bit more into his. "Are we going to get drunk together?" he asked, smiling whimsically, twisting on the cushion in order to face her.

She was pleased that he hadn't questioned her decision to change her seat. His smile and the way he'd angled his shoulders toward her, sliding one arm along the back of the sofa, indicated that he was delighted by her company. "I'm not drunk," she assured him. "Now tell me, how do you go about the dating business? Do people set you up? Or do you go to bars?" At his laugh she persisted. "I'm serious, Andrew. I'm such a novice at this. I've talked to Julianne about it—she's my closest single woman friend. But she doesn't date much at all. I don't think she really cares one way or another about getting married. Whenever I ask her for advice, she tells me to accentuate the positive and things will work out."

"Once you're ready to start dating you'll have your hands full," Andrew predicted. "When a woman is available she shows it. And when a woman as pretty as you are shows that she's available, she should have no trouble attracting men."

"You really think I'm pretty?" she asked. She wasn't fishing for more compliments from Andrew. But he had never before talked to her this way, and she couldn't help wondering whether he was only complimenting her to boost her ego.

"I think..." He brushed a stray lock of her hair from her cheek. "I think you're the prettiest woman I've ever known."

"You do?"

"Oh, come on, Kim. You don't need me to tell you what your mirror tells you. You're a beautiful woman."

"Do I look available?" she asked. The question surprised her; it struck her as incredibly forward. Yet an unfathomable compulsion to know precisely what Andrew thought of her forced the words out. "Right now? Do I look available?"

He gave her a long, thoughtful examination. She watched as his lips moved, shaping his words before he gave voice to them. He had lovely lips, she noticed. Strong and thin, expressive.

He didn't say anything for a moment. Instead he lifted his hand to her cheek again, tracing the arching bone that gave it its shape. "It was good today," he whispered.

"What?" Her voice sounded tremulous to her, curiously husky. She was conscious of the narrow distance between them. Andrew was close enough for her to smell his clean scent, his woodsy after-shave. He was close enough for her to feel the warmth of his body. "What was good?"

"Going to Wilding's house."

"Oh?"

"No," he contradicted himself. "Not going there. What was good was holding you. At his house, by the bedroom window." His hand dropped to his lap, and he abruptly glanced away, as if rattled by his confession.

Her heart seemed to stop beating for a moment. What now? What to do? His words elicited a powerful yearning inside her, yet the way he averted his eyes informed her that he didn't wish to follow through. Andrew was smart; he was wisely trying to douse whatever was heating up between them. He was backing off again, before it was too late, before Kimberly could reach his soul.

Unable to ignore her disappointment, she looked at her watch. It was nearly eleven-thirty.

Andrew wrapped his fingers around her lower arm and lifted her wrist so he could check her watch, as well. "He isn't going to call," he said. "Not this late."

He raised his eyes to her. Kimberly remembered that the only reason Andrew had come home with her was to abet her in her scheme to detour Whitney's attentions. She eased her wrist from his loose grip and said, as much to herself as to him, "You probably want to leave."

"No."

His gaze remained steadfast on her, searching. She ran her tongue over her lips, a nervous reflex. She didn't know what to say.

"I'll—I'll go if you want me to," he added.

"No." She wanted him to touch her hair again, and her face and her wrist. She wanted to feel his arms around her and his beautiful lips on her. She wanted to remain in the company of this fine, decent friend, this man who had survived a pain far worse than hers.

She didn't want him to leave.

Chapter Six

The luscious flavor of his kiss lingered on her lips as she led him down the hallway to her bedroom. She had never kissed a man wearing eyeglasses before. She had thought that Michael Caine looked cute when, as a teenager, she'd seen him in *Alfie*, but she hadn't fantasized about kissing him. And if she'd ever dated a nearsighted man, he must have been wearing contacts.

She wasn't sure what she had expected. Would the frames collide with her brow? Would she bang into them and bruise Andrew's nose? Would the lenses steam up?

None of those disasters had occurred, however. Obviously Andrew was accustomed to his eyeglasses, and he knew how to angle his face, how to tilt her chin with his thumb to avoid any interference when their mouths met. His kiss had been sublime, informing Kimberly that her decision to invite him to stay the night hadn't been a mistake.

As soon as she reached her bed, his hands fell to her shoulders and turned her to him. He bowed his head to kiss her again, and this kiss vanquished her memory of the previous one. His mouth tasted of bourbon and maleness, a heady combination, and his tongue moved sensuously against hers, alluringly. How had she ever thought that this sexy man was an egghead? How had she ever considered him an intellectual snob when he had such strong arms, such firm lips and such a lean, well-toned body?

She ran her fingers up his sides, feeling his ribs through the cotton of his shirt. The knowledge that he would shortly be removing that shirt and baring his chest to her caused a thick, warm longing to course through her. She couldn't recall ever responding so rapidly to Todd.

Kimberly had never made love with anyone but her husband. She had kept her inexperience a secret from everybody except Todd, because in the late sixties and early seventies, when she was coming of age, liberated women were supposed to be sexually adventurous, experimenting, sowing their wild oats with all the abandon of their male counterparts. Kimberly had remained a virgin by choice, but she hadn't discussed that choice with her friends in college. She had listened to their exploits and only smiled enigmatically when their attention turned to her. She hadn't wanted her classmates to think she was a prude or a weirdo.

Todd had been overjoyed by Kimberly's chastity—which, she acknowledged in retrospect, ought to have given her a fair idea of how strongly he adhered to the double standard. Even after she'd accepted his proposal, he had refused to sleep with her until they were married. "You've lasted this long, Kim, you may as well go for it," he'd explained, as time after time he warded off her sexual overtures and extricated himself from her embraces. That she was a mature twenty-one-year-old woman with healthy desires didn't matter to him. *He* wasn't a virgin, but he went on and on about what a thrill it would be for him to take a virgin to bed on his honeymoon.

Perhaps it had been a thrill for him. For Kimberly it had been agony. Nearly a full year had passed before she'd finally begun to enjoy sex. Privately she conceded that the problem was her lack of experience, but she had never dared discuss her theory with Todd. He probably would have considered her a wanton slut if she had.

Andrew's lips had moved to her temple, and all thoughts of Todd dissolved in the heat of her passion for the man with her now. His hands drifted across her back to the zipper of her dress and tugged it open. She shuddered slightly.

At her involuntary motion he pulled back. "Should we be doing this?" he asked in a low, hoarse voice.

She peered up at him. His eyes were clear and heartbreakingly gentle. "Are you having doubts, Andrew?" she returned, praying that he would answer in the negative.

"No," he murmured, answering her prayers. "All I meant was . . . you've had a lot to drink, Kim. I don't want to take advantage of you if you're—"

"Smashed?" She laughed. "Let me assure you, Andrew, mingled among all my slave-owning ancestors are a few moonshiners. I know how to hold my liquor. How about you?"

"My grandfather's brother was a bootlegger during Prohibition."

"Then you've got good genes," she concluded.

"How nice of you to notice." He slid the silk of her dress down her arms and over her hips, pulling her panty hose with it and letting the garments drop to the floor. Then he took a step back to study her in her lacy pink bra and matching panties. He took a deep breath and shook his head. "It doesn't seem possible that any woman could be as beautiful as you are," he muttered, sounding strangely disapproving.

"I'm sorry," she said reflexively.

"I'm not." He reached for his tie, but Kimberly pushed his hands away and undid the knot herself. Then she unbuttoned his shirt and shoved it off his shoulders. His torso was more muscular than she had expected. Gnomes who climbed out of tomes weren't supposed to boast such rugged physiques. But, then, her impression of Andrew as a bookworm had obviously been in error.

She combed her fingernails through the dark curls of hair adorning his chest, and he sucked in another sharp breath. Her tantalizing touch was apparently driving him to distraction, but, exercising great self-control, he withstood it without protest. When her hands dropped to his belt, however, he groaned and gathered her to himself for another devastating kiss.

Refusing to break from her, he helped her to remove the rest of his clothing. He set his eyeglasses on the night table, then lifted her onto the bed and dove on beside her. "Don't you want to take off my underthings?" she asked.

"Eventually." Lying on his side, he let his hands roam along the trim of her bra and then the lacy cups, teasing her nipples through the delicate fabric. He bent to kiss one swollen nipple, his warm breath seeping through the cloth.

Todd had never paid so much attention to her lingerie. But, then, she mused dreamily as Andrew shifted to kiss her other breast, Todd had never paid so much attention to her breasts, either. With him lovemaking had centered on one part of her anatomy to the exclusion of all else.

Andrew deliberately avoided that part of her anatomy, instead taking time to explore the arching wings of her collarbone, the smooth skin of her throat, the indentation of her navel, the sleek lines of her thighs. "You're so beautiful," he said with a sigh.

"How can you even see me with your glasses off?"

He gazed at her, and once again the steady, fire-tinged light of his eyes reached to her heart and melted it. "Kim, I could close my eyes and still see you," he swore. "If I closed my eyes right now, all I'd see would be you." He kissed her with exquisite tenderness, then wedged his hand beneath her to unfasten the clasp of her bra. As soon as it was off, he turned his attention to her panties, running his finger along the elastic that stretched taut between her hipbones, then venturing beneath it to trace the edge of her hair.

Andrew had always struck Kimberly as an impatient man, yet she was the one bristling with impatience now. Her hips moved reflexively, urgently, and he obeyed her unspoken demand by stripping the panties down her legs and tossing them away. Then he stroked back up her legs to touch her.

She was unprepared for the sudden spasm, the frantic clenching of her soul in response to his caress. She was embarrassed to be reacting so fiercely, so swiftly. Proper ladies weren't supposed to be overcome by sexual need so immediately. Truly proper ladies weren't supposed to be overcome at all, if Kimberly's mother was to be believed. Mrs. Belmont had hardly been a font of information for her inquisitive daughter, but what little she had taught Kimberly about her own body bore an unfortunate resemblance to the timeworn Victorian dictum about closing one's eyes and thinking of England.

Kimberly wasn't thinking of England at the moment, or even of the glory that was Dixie. She was thinking only of Andrew, of his hard, virile body next to hers, his uneven breath, his glittering eyes, the exotic strands of silver woven into his dark hair. She was thinking of the smooth contours of his back as she trailed her hands over its surface, and the unyielding curve of his buttocks, the flat stretch of his abdomen and the eager fullness of his erection as she daringly draped her hand around it. She was thinking of how much she wanted him, how anxious her body was for him, how miraculous it was that she could be falling in love with a man like Andrew Collins.

Her touch seemed to galvanize him. A low, broken sound emanated from deep within his chest as she tightened her grip. In a fluid motion, he rolled onto his back, drawing her over him, guiding her legs around him and arching up into her.

For a moment she was dazed, unable to move. She had never before made love in that position—Todd would never have allowed such a thing—and she wasn't sure what to do. Andrew showed her, clasping her hips with his hands and imparting his rhythm to her. As soon as she took over, his hands rose to her waist and he let her lead him.

She felt free, wildly free and powerful above him, her hair tumbling into her face and brushing lightly against his jaw, her body compelling his, inciting it. The unfamiliar freedom fed her arousal, gave her strength, drove her with undue speed to the crest of sensation. She felt the dark tremors building within her, spreading through her, conquering her as she conquered Andrew. She surrendered with a breathless gasp, then sank fully onto him in time to absorb his shattering climax.

She remained on top of him, utterly relaxed, too weary to consider moving from him. Her soft flesh molded to the hard angles of his body in a surprisingly comfortable way. She hoped he was comfortable, too, because she wanted to stay exactly where she was forever.

Andrew clearly wasn't as exhausted as Kimberly. His lips browsed along her hairline and his fingers roamed the length of her spine. He bent one of his legs between hers so he could rub her thigh with his knee.

His energy astounded her. Whenever she and Todd used to make love, he had always been completely wasted afterward, interested in nothing more than drawing up the covers and going to sleep. Yet Andrew seemed invigorated by what he and Kimberly had just shared. His leg rose higher, flexing against her, getting her excited all over again. Her helpless moan caused him to laugh.

She laughed, as well. "Could you have imagined fifteen years ago that we'd end up like this?"

"No." He lifted his head from the pillow to kiss the tip of her nose, then curled his arm around her and held her close. "We're different people now than we were then."

"No, we're not," she argued. "I haven't changed that much, and neither have you. We're both just a little more tolerant, that's all."

"Tolerant?" His laughter increased. "Is that why I'm here? Because you're tolerating me?"

You're here because I'm falling in love with you, Kimberly almost said. She gazed down at him, savoring his strong, handsome features. She could nearly detect an incipient dimple on one of his cheeks. One more reason to love him, she admitted. Smiling definitely increased his face power.

"Do you mind talking?" she asked. Todd had always become irritated when she tried to embark on a conversation with him after sex. But that was because her talking had disturbed his sleep. "Do you want me to shut up?"

"What for?" He kissed her again. "Now seems like as good a time as any to debate the function of the C.I.A. in a democratic society."

"Andrew..." He was laughing too hard to hear the warning in her voice. She didn't want him making fun of her when she was so captivated by him.

"No, come on," he insisted, belying his artificially sober expression by flexing his leg against her again. He seemed inordinately pleased by her ragged sigh, but he maintained a straight face when he said, "Take wiretapping, for instance. Illegal domestic surveillance. What's your opinion of that, Kim?"

"Stop it!" she protested, succumbing to a chuckle. She tried to punch his arm, but he held her too tightly, and she had no choice but to subside on top of him again. Her fingers drew a twisting line through the hair surrounding his flat, brown nipple, and this time the ragged sigh came from him. "I like your chest," she told him.

"I like yours, too. I bet I like yours more than you like mine."

"It's probably a toss-up," she said diplomatically. Her finger skimmed upward to his broad shoulder, and she cushioned her head against his chest, beneath his chin. "I've never done it this way before, on top," she confessed.

"Did you like it?"

"Very much," she answered truthfully. She kissed the hollow at the base of his neck. "Let's do it again."

He shifted his hips beneath her, analyzing his condition. "Give me a few more minutes," he requested good-naturedly.

Amazing. It really was amazing, talking with him this way, so easily, so naturally. Why couldn't it have ever been like this with Todd?

Because Todd wasn't Andrew, that was why. Because Andrew was unique, marvelous, an incredible human being.

She wondered whether it was right for her to be comparing Andrew to Todd, even if Andrew fared spectacularly in the comparison. She wondered whether he was comparing her to the other women he had known. "Do you think about your wife when you're making love?" she asked.

She felt his withdrawal subliminally. Yet he didn't curse, he didn't shove her away. His arms remained ringed around her. His chin remained still and rigid against her hair.

"I'm sorry," she whispered. "You don't have to answer that."

"I do sometimes," he admitted, his voice drifting down to her from above her head. "Think about her, I mean." His words came haltingly. "But not now. Not with you."

She didn't know if she was supposed to take that as a compliment, but she did. "I'm usually much more tactful," she said contritely. "I don't know what it is about you that makes me speak my mind this way—"

"We've always spoken our minds with each other, Kim," he pointed out.

That was true enough. In the past what had been on their minds were insults. They wouldn't feel the need to insult each other anymore. She was certain at last that Andrew no longer looked down on her, no longer viewed her as a dumb blonde, a pretty, trivial airhead. If he did, he wouldn't be lying with her now, holding her, loving her.

They had always spoken their minds and they always would. Kimberly would always be this honest with Andrew, this open to him. "I like you," she whispered. She had meant to say that she loved him, but "like" slipped out, instead. Yet that, too, was the truth. She genuinely liked him.

He seemed both touched and amused by her admission. "You have a funny way of showing it," he teased, before rising to kiss her. His mouth opened against hers, and the moment their tongues found each other his body tensed beneath her. "I think my few minutes are up," he declared as he pulled his lips from hers.

"So are you," she joked, rocking her hips to his.

With a deep groan he filled her again. And this time she allowed herself no thoughts of anything but him. No comparisons, no memories. Only Andrew, merging with her, fusing himself to her, accepting her body, her mind, her heart.

AT ONE TIME OR ANOTHER every heterosexual man must have dreamed of waking up beside a cheerleader.

A cheerleader, a prom queen, a debutante, a cool, blond goddess. A shiksa, as David Schiffman, Andrew's best friend in high school, used to call it. "Literally a shiksa is a gentile girl," he had defined the Yiddish term. "But spiritually she's the beautiful blond girl you can never have, the unobtainable."

Andrew wasn't Jewish, but he had understood what David had meant. The shiksa was the woman you dreamed about.

But dreams didn't come true. So when you woke up, you defended yourself against the dream. You viewed the shiksas from afar and invented justifications for your inability to capture them. You talked yourself out of wanting them. You decided that they were stupid, that they were shallow, that they weren't worth your time. You assured yourself that they were stuck-up, that they took men for granted, that the lady within your reach was actually the one worth having.

His vision took in the woman sleeping at his side. Sunlight filtered through the translucent curtains drawn shut across her window and imbued her hair with glints of gold. It fell in graceful waves against the creamy skin of her cheek. Her eyes were closed, and he saw that her eyelashes were uncommonly long. If she opened her eyes, Andrew knew that their clear irises would match the delicate blue of her bedspread.

Everything about her was too good to be true. Like a dream. Now he was awake, no longer dreaming. She *was* too good to be true, and he felt his defenses rising again.

He couldn't blame the bourbon, at least not for his own behavior last night. Maybe for hers. Maybe, despite her protestations, she'd been blitzed last night, and when she woke up she'd be full of regret, embarrassed and entertaining a whopping headache. But Andrew wasn't hung over, and if he wasn't hung over he couldn't have been drunk the night before.

Then what was he doing in Kimberly's bed? Besides, perhaps, indulging in a dream?

He was in her bed because she had been using him to detour the advances of another man. He was in her bed because she had been playing a foolish game and had gotten a little carried away with the spirit of it. He didn't feel exploited—he had enjoyed himself too greatly—but he wasn't going to be irrational about the situation now that dawn had broken and he'd returned to full consciousness.

All right. A dream. That was all it was. A delightful, breathtaking dream, evanescing in the glare of daylight. Kimberly was a fun person—by definition, all cheerleaders had to be fun—and he was fond of her, but he was too much of a realist to believe that what they had experienced last night could possibly be love. Because if it were, if he let himself love her, he would lose her. He knew it instinctively; he knew he was not designed for true love with gorgeous blond-goddess cheerleaders who represented the stuff of dreams. It simply wasn't in him, any more than it was in Kimberly to love a cynical four-eyed highbrow.

And he couldn't bear losing someone he loved, not again. The last time he'd had no control over what had happened. But this time he did have control. He could take emotional precautions.

She stirred beside him, and her eyes fluttered open. As soon as they came into focus on Andrew, she smiled. "Good morning," she murmured drowsily.

Even her voice, clogged with sleep, was too good to be true. It was as creamy as her complexion, as voluptuously feminine as her body. He steeled himself against it, then presented her with a remote smile. "Good morning, Kim."

"What time is it?"

"Time to get up," he answered, shoving back the covers and swinging his legs over the side of the bed.

She twisted to see the alarm clock on her night table. "Nine-thirty," she announced, pushing herself to sit. "Whitney might be calling soon."

Of course. Whitney. That was why Andrew was here.

He located his shorts and trousers on the floor, where they'd fallen the night before, and donned them. Then he slid his eyeglasses on and reached for his shirt. "Don't put your shirt on," Kimberly requested as he slung his arms through the sleeves. Her smile became flirtatious. "I want to be able to look at your chest."

"I'm not going topless unless you do," he challenged her. "Tit for tat—no pun intended."

"I'll bet," she snorted before conceding with a laugh. She glided across the room to her closet and pulled a baby-blue satin bathrobe from the hook on the back of the door. More blue, Andrew noted, exerting himself not to let the resonant color of her eyes disarm him. She slipped on the robe and secured it by tying the sash. But when Andrew started to close his shirt, her expression reflected such strong disappointment that he let his hands drop from the buttons. Let her feast her damned eyes on his chest if it meant so much to her, he allowed begrudgingly. Probably—if he couldn't blame it on the bourbon—the only reason she'd made love with him last night was that she admired his build.

He followed her out of the bedroom to the kitchen, where she occupied herself preparing coffee. "What would you like for breakfast?" she asked. "We've got some leftover petits fours."

"Ugh," Andrew grunted. "Too sweet." *Just like you,* he added internally. *Sweet and delicious and gone before the taste has faded.*

"How about English muffins, then?" she offered. "I've also got some grapefruit."

"Fine." He felt uncomfortably idle, standing to one side while she bustled around the kitchen. "Anything you want me to do?" he asked.

"Just sit," she said, beckoning toward the dining table.

He obeyed. He balanced one ankle across the other knee and jiggled his bare foot nervously. Was it his imagination, or were he and Kimberly acting as stilted as they had when he'd arrived at her office two days ago? Was she already suffering from remorse, wondering how in high hell she and Andrew had let down their guard so totally last night?

She sliced a grapefruit in two and carried the halves to the table. Setting one half in front of him, she leaned over and kissed the crown of his head. The gesture seemed natural, but he suspected that it was simply her way of putting them both at ease.

She returned to the kitchen and busied herself with the toaster. Neither of them spoke until their breakfast was on the table and Kimberly took a seat facing Andrew. She helped herself to a muffin half, buttered it and set down her knife. Before biting into the muffin she gave Andrew a critical glance. "Why do I have the distinct feeling that you're closing up on me?" she asked.

He chewed on his muffin, swallowed, then washed down the crumbs with a bracing gulp of coffee. "I'm not closing up on you," he countered.

"You're entertaining doubts about last night, is that it?"

He drummed his fingers against the table as he collected his thoughts. He couldn't read her expression—it seemed a bit accusing, a bit wounded, a bit . . . mocking, perhaps. He took another sip of coffee before responding to her charge. "We both had a lot to drink last night."

"We weren't drunk," she said forcefully.

"Look. Your divorce is very recent. You're lonely. You're on the rebound—"

"The rebound?" she exclaimed, her knife clattering against her plate. "Andrew, I was separated from Todd for an entire year before our divorce became final. And even before that Todd and I were hardly having a romantic relationship."

"Then you must be very lonely," he emphasized. "You don't have to apologize for it, Kim. It's a normal reaction to look to a friend for comfort and companionship—"

"What the hell do you think I am?" she erupted. "Comfort? Companionship? Do you honestly think I'm that superficial?"

"No, of course not," he hastened to assure her. Then he fell silent. He hadn't meant to offend her. His analysis of why Kimberly had invited him to spend the night with her was the only one that made sense to him. She had said she liked him, and he liked her, too. But beyond that, what existed between them? Other than the fact that they had attended college together, that they had both endured the demise of their marriages? Other than the fact that, for one crazy afternoon, they had playacted at being spies together?

The doorbell rang. Kimberly's obvious anger at Andrew redirected itself toward her caller. "God help me if Whitney had the gall to come here instead of phoning..." she muttered as she stood and marched into the entry hall.

Andrew pushed back his chair and watched her until she was out of sight. He listened to her unbolt the door and open it. Then he heard an unfamiliar woman's voice. "Hello, Kimberly. I hope you all don't mind a little surprise visit."

"Mother." Kimberly's tone was impressively calm. Indeed, she sounded much calmer than Andrew felt, lounging at Kimberly's table with his chest exposed while the mother of the woman he'd spent the night with barged into the apartment. He sprang to his feet in time to greet the two women as they entered the living room together.

If her mother was any indication, Kimberly was destined to age beautifully. Mrs. Belmont was strikingly handsome, petite like her daughter, with fair coloring. Her blond hair was carefully coiffed, pinned into a bouffant knot at the nape of her neck. She wore an expensive-looking tailored suit of white silk, with a violet blouse beneath and a string of pearls around her swanlike neck. She held a white envelope purse in her hand. Her eyes, the same vivid blue shade as Kimberly's, settled on Andrew and narrowed.

"Mother, this is Andrew Collins," Kimberly smoothly introduced them. "Andrew, my mother."

He extended his hand. "How do you do, Mrs. Belmont?" he mumbled politely.

Without bothering to shake his hand, she pivoted on the heels of her pumps to confront Kimberly. "What, may I ask, is the meaning of this?" Her drawl was much more pronounced than her daughter's.

Kimberly laughed. "For heaven's sake, Mother—if you don't know the meaning of this, then Father has my sympathy."

Mrs. Belmont's cheeks paled slightly at her daughter's impertinent remark. Her eyes sharpened on Andrew again, and he fumbled with the buttons on his shirt. "Need I remind you that your divorce—" she seemed to have difficulty shaping her lips around the word "—became final a mere five days ago."

"Oh? Who's counting?" Kimberly responded blithely. She strode into the kitchen and pulled a mug from a cabinet. "Have some coffee, Mother. You look as if you could use a cup. I haven't got any cream, so you'll have to make do with milk." Ignoring her mother's disdainful inspection of Andrew, she asked, "What brings you to town, anyway?"

"Your father's name has been bandied about in reference to a federal judgeship," Mrs. Belmont informed her, her gaze remaining on Andrew. "We flew up so that he could introduce himself to the right people. It's quite an honor, you know." Without comment she accepted the coffee Kimberly had fixed for her and sipped it. "What did you say your name was?" she asked Andrew.

"Andrew Collins."

"I see," Mrs. Belmont said, although Andrew could hardly guess precisely what it was she saw. Other than his chest, which was no longer in view as he finished closing his shirt and tucked the tails inside the waist of his slacks.

"Andrew is an old friend of mine," Kimberly elaborated.

"I should hope so," Mrs. Belmont sniffed. "How is Todd?"

"Beats me," Kimberly said with a flippancy Andrew suspected was reserved only for her mother. "Why don't you go drop in on him unannounced, too?"

"Kimberly." Mrs. Belmont gave her daughter a grave stare. "Need I remind you of your position?"

"My position, Mother, is that of a single woman. Surely a single woman is allowed to share breakfast with a gentleman in her home."

"A gentleman," Mrs. Belmont retorted, lowering her gaze to Andrew's bare feet, "wears shoes when he comes to call."

"Perhaps I ought to leave you two to talk alone," Andrew suggested discreetly, starting toward the bedroom.

Kimberly snagged his arm and held him in place beside her. "Don't be silly, Andrew," she remonstrated. "I'm sure that anything my mother has to say at this point will concern you. You may as well hang around and listen." She turned to her mother with a winsome smile. "Why don't you be courteous, Mother? Why don't you ask Andrew about himself? Ask him the right questions and he'll go on forever, isn't that so?"

Mrs. Belmont pursed her lips in disapproval. "Do you work for that senator of Kimberly's?" she inquired.

"No. I'm a college professor," he told her.

She sniffed again, as if college professors were the dregs of society. "Here at Georgetown?"

"At Amherst College," he replied.

"Amherst College. That's one of those northern schools, isn't it?"

"Yes, Mother. Like Barnard," Kimberly interjected.

"I wish I could say I was surprised. I suppose I am." Mrs. Belmont shook her head and sighed. "This all seems so tawdry." Her acute blue eyes flitted back and forth between Kimberly and Andrew. "How long has this been going on?"

"Breakfast? About twenty minutes," Kimberly replied. "We slept late," she added with the sole purpose of riling her mother.

Mrs. Belmont did her best to remain composed. "Does Todd know about it?"

"About what? That his former wife is an independent adult with her own life to lead? If he hasn't figured that out by now, more's the pity. Where's Father?" Kimberly inquired.

"He chose to stay at the hotel. Thank heavens for that. If he saw you behaving so brazenly, Kimberly—"

"Brazenly?" Rather than exploding with rage, as Andrew would have expected, she smiled demurely. "If I know Father, the sum total of his reaction would be to warn me that the people considering him for a judgeship had better not find out that his daughter had a man at her house at nine-thirty on a Sunday morning. Father always has his own best interests at heart." She released Andrew to cross the living room and drew the drapes open. "What a lovely day it's shaping up to be."

Her mother glowered at her. "Don't be sassy, Kimberly. It's disgraceful enough that you got a divorce, but now this...."

Kimberly turned to confront her mother. She easily met Mrs. Belmont's ferocious gaze. "What was disgraceful was that I married a man I was totally unsuited for," she said, her voice underlined with an uncharacteristic grittiness. "What was disgraceful was that I did the right thing, the proper thing. I followed your advice, Mother, and it was without a doubt the biggest mistake of my life. With your permission, I'd just as soon make my own mistakes from here on in."

"Well, you're certainly doing your best in that department," Mrs. Belmont muttered.

Andrew had been silent throughout their argument, but he had absorbed Kimberly's every word, her every motion, the defiant tilt of her chin and her proud bearing. As awkward as he felt, she appeared perfectly poised, completely unruffled. He was awed by her performance.

He couldn't stand by in silence while her mother reviled her so mercilessly. Even though Kimberly apparently didn't require Andrew's assistance in this showdown, he was a gentleman—bare feet notwithstanding—and he couldn't prevent himself from speaking up on her behalf. "Mrs. Belmont, Kimberly and I are good friends of long standing. We've known each other for years, and—"

"That's all right, Andrew," Kimberly said smoothly. "You aren't obliged to trot out my respectability for my mother. She should have given up on expecting me to behave properly by now."

"But there's nothing improper about—about—"

"About our having an affair, Andrew," she supplied for him. "You're absolutely right. Whether or not Mother agrees with us is beyond our control." She walked back to her mother and kissed her cheek. "I do love you, Mother, but you are truly being a pain right now. Why don't you go back to the hotel, and we'll meet for lunch."

Mrs. Belmont appeared nonplussed for a moment, unsure of whether to accept or reject her daughter's placating kiss. "Will he be joining us?" she asked tautly, shooting Andrew a hostile look.

He answered for himself. "No. I have to catch a plane back to Hartford."

"But it was so thoughtful of you to invite him," Kimberly cooed, deliberately misunderstanding her mother. "What hotel are you and Father staying at?"

"The Four Seasons," Mrs. Belmont answered limply. She apparently realized that she had been outmaneuvered by her daughter, and she conceded with as much grace as she could muster. "Come at one."

"I'll get there when I can," Kimberly remarked, clearly refusing to accede to even that most innocuous order. She took her mother's coffee mug, set it on the table and guided the older woman toward the front door. "So long, Mother."

Mrs. Belmont hesitated on the threshold. "Please don't let M.C. find out about this, Kimberly," she whispered, eyeing Andrew one last time. "She looks up to you so."

"I won't mention it unless it comes up" was all Kimberly would promise. "So long." She nudged her mother outside, kissed her cheek again and shut the door. Then she returned to the living room.

Andrew remained mute as he tried to unscramble his thoughts. He struggled to remember what he and Kimberly had been quarreling about before Mrs. Belmont's arrival, but he came up blank. All he could think of was how marvelously Kimberly had comported herself in what had to be considered a humiliating situation.

Did cheerleaders really possess such backbone? Had cutesy Kimberly really held her own against such a powerful adversary? It was one thing to take on a stranger like Wilding, but quite another to take on one's own mother. If anything about Kimberly commanded respect, it was her abundance of feistiness and courage.

"Who's M.C.?" he asked.

"My niece. She's eleven years old now. Much to my mother's horror, she's shown an interest in learning the facts of life." Kimberly moved past him to the kitchen to rinse her mother's mug in the sink.

He drifted to the counter and studied Kimberly. She seemed as collected with him as she'd been with her mother, as detached. Evidently she remembered their earlier argument better than he did. Or else she was angry with him for having been present in her apartment at the worst possible time. "I'm sorry," he said.

"About what?" Her voice was crisp and contained.

"About your having to go through that."

"Go through what? Andrew, I've been through far worse with my mother. There's nothing to be sorry about."

"You handled yourself splendidly," he noted, eager to make amends, although he still wasn't certain of why she was angry with him. "You were fantastic."

"Was I?" she asked frostily.

"Your mother seems like a tough cookie. You didn't let her rattle you. *I* was rattled, Kim, but you weren't."

"Goodie for me," she grumbled.

"I'm not kidding, Kim," he persisted. He had to make her see how dazzling she had been. "You've bowled me over. I thought you were spectacular yesterday, but today, after this... I never realized you had such guts."

"Yes, well, that's your problem, Andrew," she snapped, giving the clean mug a vicious shake before setting it in the drying rack. "You never realized a lot of things about me. You think I'm just a softheaded, softhearted twit, right? A cockeyed optimist, too brainless to comprehend the seriousness of the world."

"I didn't say—"

"You don't have to say it, Andrew," she cut him off. "You've always thought that of me. You've always looked down at me and judged me. Now you're doing it again."

She had a point. But he wouldn't let her astute observation derail him. "I'm judging you positively," he asserted.

"Spare me, Andrew. You're in no position to judge me at all. You think I'm just a poor, lonely divorcée looking for comfort. You think I'm the sort to kowtow to my mother. I'm sorry to disillusion you."

"I'm delighted to be disillusioned," he asserted, wishing that she'd recognize how sincere he was.

"Oh, you are not," she refuted him testily. "You like things neat and orderly, Andrew. You like to cling to your own narrow perception of things. I didn't put on that show with my mother to improve your opinion of me. I did it because that's the way I am with her. Always. With or without witnesses."

"Is there anything wrong with my being impressed by you?" he asked, bewildered.

"There's something wrong with my feeling that I have to prove myself to you, that you're so damned surprised whenever I do something that doesn't match with your condescending attitude toward me."

Her fury dumbfounded him. He grasped at a logical explanation for it. "Maybe you're still sore about your mother—"

"No. I'm sore about you," she corrected him in a clipped voice as she stormed past him to gather up the breakfast dishes. "Why don't you just leave?"

"Leave? Now?" A half-hour ago he was sure that the night he'd spent with Kimberly was some sort of accident, best forgotten. But now he was determined to prove to her—and himself—that it wasn't an accident, that whatever was irking her, they ought to work it out. Now it was his turn to prove himself to her. "You really want me to leave?"

"That's what I just said, isn't it?"

"What if Whitney calls?" he asked, desperate to find a way to stay with her.

"I'll give him your telephone number at the motel," she replied. "I'll tell him the truth. Far be it from me to want to make you put up any longer with my asinine games."

"Kimberly—"

He noticed tears taking shape along her eyelashes, but she didn't relent. "Go, Andrew. Please. Go be a stuffy intellectual at Amherst. Surely you don't need a dumb blonde in your life."

"You aren't a dumb blonde." He inhaled for strength and reached across the counter to grip her shoulder. He wanted to shake her until her teeth rattled if that was what it took to get her to see sense. But he didn't dare. Instead he softened his hold on her, massaging the flesh of her upper arm with his fingertips. "Listen to what I'm saying, Kim," he murmured. "I'm complimenting you."

She eyed him wearily. "You're squinting at me, Andrew."

He knew his eyes were wide open; she was speaking figuratively. And maybe she was right. Revering her for behaving in a manner he would take for granted with any other woman was condescending.

When he had awakened that morning, he had believed that the previous night had been a dream. Perhaps Kimberly believed the same thing. Perhaps, in the brutal light of day, she also viewed their night together as an aberration, a reckless episode, not a realistic beginning to anything significant. They were too different from each other, too poorly matched. They both ached for company, for intimacy, and while they had temporarily found those things in each other's arms, it wasn't fair for either of them to expect something lasting from it.

Of course he couldn't love her. He was already losing her—he had already lost her. She was once again the blond goddess, utterly beautiful, utterly baffling.

"All right," he acquiesced. "I'll leave."

Chapter Seven

"There's somebody downstairs to see you," Helen informed Kimberly through the intercom. "I just got a call from the guard at the Constitution Avenue entrance. He says some man down there wants to see you, but he can't get through the metal detector without setting off the alarm."

Some man wants to see you. Andrew, Kimberly instantly hoped, although she knew it couldn't be he. Wishful thinking. Just because she wanted to see him didn't mean he would ever want to see her again.

She had been too harsh with him last Sunday, dismissing him too quickly, too reflexively. Yet that had seemed the best way to protect herself at the time. She had loved a man once, and he had wounded her terribly. She wasn't going to let that happen again. Especially not with Andrew, someone who could wound her much worse. She knew intuitively that he could. Like a wild animal, when a man had been wounded himself he was more likely to wound others. And Andrew had suffered the worst of wounds.

She knew she would have to confront him sooner or later—sooner, she sternly reproached herself. Before leaving for his home state a couple of days ago, the senator had spent two hours in conference with Kimberly and Whitney so they could fill him in on everything they had learned about John Wilding and L.A.R.C. Discovering the driver of the black Cadillac had been easy enough. The diplomatic license plate had been issued to the Salvadoran Embassy. The driver, a garrulous secretary had informed Kimberly, had been a general in that country's army, a man who, according to the secretary, was at odds with the current government and aspired toward a leadership position himself. Just the sort of strongman someone like Wilding was looking for to squelch his manufactured revolution.

Officially the C.I.A. claimed to know nothing of Wilding's visit with the Salvadoran army officer. But individuals were willing to speak privately against Wilding. Nobody liked a megalomaniac, no matter how loudly he touted himself as a patriot with America's best interests at heart.

"I want to meet this nervy young Professor Collins," the senator had declared. "I want to know everything he has to tell us. If we're going to take on his case, we've got to do so armed with all the information he can give us."

"Kim will set it up," Whitney had assured the senator. "She and the nervy young professor are close."

About as close as San Salvador is to Washington, Kimberly muttered beneath her breath. Even announcing that Andrew wasn't at her apartment when Whitney had called Sunday morning hadn't dispelled his conviction that she and Andrew were "very dear friends." "I've got a racquetball game in fifteen minutes, so I'll just give you the scoop and you can pass it along to him when he gets back," Whitney had said before filling Kimberly in on his latest findings—that Wilding was a loner who operated L.A.R.C. by himself, boasting to a few associates that once El Salvador fell apart he would be its new hero, the only man with enough knowledge and foresight to put it back together again. Whitney had also learned that Andrew wasn't the sole academic L.A.R.C. had commissioned to do research for him. Andrew was the sole academic who had willingly stepped forward to expose Wilding, however.

Kimberly had derived a vague pleasure from knowing that morning that Whitney wasn't the only member of the senator's staff hot on Wilding's trail. Yet she wouldn't be able to find out about the black Cadillac until the following day, when she got to her office. So she had only thanked Whitney for the information. As soon as he had hung up, she had tried to reach Andrew at his hotel in Crystal City. But he'd already checked out, the desk clerk told her.

As gutsy as Andrew had considered her in her face-off with her mother, she hadn't yet found the courage to telephone him at Amherst. Instead she had taken the cowardly route and typed him a letter—a rather formal one—identifying the Salvadoran general for him and asking him if he would be so good as to return to Washington for a meeting with the senator. She had made no reference to the night she had spent with Andrew—or the morning after. What could she have written? "I thought I loved you, Andrew, but that's probably because I'm basically old-fashioned about sex, and I couldn't have allowed myself to sleep with you unless I was first convinced that I loved you. You are brilliant—I've always thought so—and I can't deny your contention that I'm lonely and on the rebound. It was easier for me to think that I loved you than to rationalize what happened between us the honest way."

She couldn't confess such things to him. She was having enough difficulty confessing them to herself. But for all of Andrew's annoying traits, for all his arrogance and eggheadedness, he was a remarkably perceptive man. The night they had spent together was unspeakably lovely, but how could that one night negate the fifteen years Andrew and Kimberly had known each other?

She couldn't truly be in love with him. It wasn't possible. It didn't make sense.

"Kimberly? Are you still there?" Helen's voice scratched through the intercom box.

"Oh," she said, snapping back into the present. "Sorry, Helen. Did the man downstairs give his name?"

"The guard said his name was Seth Stone. He's got a sweet young thing in tow, too. It sounds like major May-December stuff, given the way the guard was talking. Who is this guy, anyway?"

"Seth!" Kim had been so obsessed with thoughts of Andrew that she'd all but forgotten about Seth's scheduled visit to Washington with Laura's daughter. She laughed at the absurdity of Helen's remark about Seth's relationship with Rita. Like the secretary at the embassy, the senator's receptionist was a blabbermouth. "Please tell the guard I'll be right down," Kimberly requested.

She lifted her white blazer from the back of her chair and slipped it on over her flowered aqua-hued shirtwaist dress. Then she clicked off the word processor, grabbed her purse and left her office. Under other circumstances she would be delighted to see her old college friend, and she resolved to be cheerful with Seth even if he wound up making her think only of Andrew, that other friend from their college days.

Stepping from the elevator into the vaulted lobby of the modern Senate office building, she spotted a tall, lanky man in pleated gray trousers and a gaudy Hawaiian-print shirt, bickering with the uniformed guard by the door. Even if she hadn't recognized Seth, his bizarre mirror sunglasses, which he had worn when she'd seen him at Julianne's reunion over a month ago, would have given him away. Standing beside him was a slight teenage girl clad in an oversize white T-shirt, baggy knee-length shorts featuring a pattern as loud as that on Seth's shirt and leather sneakers. The girl's hair was dark and cropped short to expose her ears, which were adorned with dangling triangular earrings. She, too, sported a pair of mirror sunglasses.

Regardless of her troubling weekend with Andrew, Kimberly was thrilled to see Seth. She raced across the lobby.

"Seth!" she hollered in welcome. "What sort of trouble have you all gotten yourself into?"

He and the guard both turned to her. Seth appeared highly indignant, the guard cool and complacent. "Look at this," Seth complained, gesturing toward the table beside the metal detector. Across the top were strewn assorted metal objects: keys, coins, a nail clipper, a New York City subway token, a kazoo. "He's cleaned me out, Kim. I keep telling him, all I've got left metal-wise are my fillings and my fly. So what should I do, pull out my teeth or drop my drawers?"

The girl beside him giggled. "I think you should drop your drawers, Seth," she egged him on. "I think you've got a cute—"

"I know what you think, and keep your fresh mouth shut," he snarled at his companion, although he was laughing. "Help me out, Kim. Am I gonna wind up in jail or something?"

Kimberly's gaze traveled from Seth to the girl. "You must be Rita," she said warmly. "I'm Kimberly Belmont, your mother's friend."

"Yeah," Rita said, tucking her chin against her chest bashfully. "Hi."

Kimberly planted her hands on her hips, affecting a maternal pose. "What I'd like to know, young lady, is why you want Seth to drop his drawers. This doesn't seem at all appropriate for the daughter of the bride-to-be."

Rita shrugged and grinned mischievously. "Well, Seth, like, he isn't exactly inhibited, you know? Like the first time he stayed at our place, you know what he did?"

"She doesn't want to know," Seth muttered in warning. He turned helplessly to Kimberly. "Are you going to vouch for me, or are you going to stand there and watch me be utterly humiliated by this power-hungry Rambo clone?"

"Rambo clone?" Kimberly turned to the guard and guffawed. "William is very sweet," she objected. "And his gun is just for show. Isn't that right, William?"

The guard only smiled noncommittally.

"Sweet, huh." Seth sounded dubious. "If he's so sweet, how come he's hassling me about the fact that I don't wear pants with Talon zippers?"

"All right," she relented. "I'll vouch for you." She turned to the guard again. "Seth is a very strange man, William, but he's virtually harmless."

"Virtually?" the guard and Andrew echoed in unison.

"Seth isn't virtual," Rita piped up, comically misunderstanding the word. "He and Ma are kissie-kissie all the time, you know?"

"Speaking of kissers, you're going to get a pow in yours," Seth grumbled.

"Yeah?" Rita skipped through the metal detector and grinned defiantly. "Come and get me."

"Why don't we leave, instead?" Kimberly tactfully suggested. "I'm not planning to get any more work done this morning, anyway. If you'd like, I can show you all some of the sights."

Rita agreeably marched back through the metal detector as, mumbling beneath his breath, Seth gathered his belongings from the table and shoved them back into his pockets. "So help me, if I'm missing any money, I'm going to sue the federal government," he alerted the guard before accompanying Rita and Kimberly through the door and outside.

"What sights are we going to see?" Rita asked. "You know who I want to see? That senator, you know, the fox, from Massachusetts."

"Kennedy or Kerry?" Kimberly asked. "They're both foxes. So was Tsongas, for that matter. Massachusetts specializes in good-looking senators."

"She's neat, Seth," Rita appraised Kimberly. Addressing her directly, she added, "You were prettier on TV, though."

"Was I?" Kimberly frowned. "When did you ever see me on television?"

"*Evening Potpourri*," Seth reminded her, naming the television show all *The Dream*'s founders had appeared on at their reunion in March.

"Oh, Lord, yes," Kimberly recalled with a laugh. "How embarrassing that was. I sounded like a birdbrain."

"What's with you ladies?" Seth argued. "Laura thought she sounded bad, too. I thought you sounded great. We all sounded great. I sounded the best, of course...."

"Of course," Kimberly concurred somberly.

"And you sounded drawlingly Georgian, and Laura sounded like the bleeding heart she is, and Julianne sounded like an editor, and Troy sounded like a draft resister, and Andrew sounded like a pompous windbag."

Kimberly winced, then covered with a feeble smile. She would have to prepare herself for the likelihood that Seth would want to talk about their mutual friends from their college days. She would have to inure herself to any mention of Andrew. She didn't want to let on that merely hearing his name could put her nerves into a tailspin.

"So can we see this Kennedy dude?" Rita persevered. "I've ridden in a limousine twice, but I've never met a Kennedy."

"You've got to have something to look forward to in life," Seth dryly pointed out.

"I don't know if he's in town," Kimberly commented. "But if you'd like, I can get you passes into the Senate gallery for this afternoon—even though nothing much happens on a Friday afternoon. In the meantime, would you like to go to the Air and Space Museum? Or we could visit the I. M. Pei wing of the National Gallery. Or the First Ladies' gowns, if you'd rather. What have you seen so far?"

"The bar at L'Enfant Plaza," Seth grunted.

Kimberly eyed Rita, then clicked her tongue at Seth. "Have you been plying Rita with liquor?"

"Cokes. She downed three of them last night, chugalug, bottoms up like a regular sailor. She's got a crush on one of the mixologists."

"He was a bartender," Rita corrected Seth. Kimberly laughed.

"What we really want to see," Seth informed her, "is the route Laura and I marched in November of '69."

"That's what *you* want to see," Rita interjected, but she obediently followed Seth as he headed west toward the grass-covered Mall across the street from the Capitol.

"Where were you during the big march?" Seth asked Kimberly.

"Who remembers?" She frowned as she thought back to that period of her youth. "We were sophomores then, right? I was probably in the library, reading up on de Tocqueville."

"Who's that?" Rita asked. "Is he a fox, too?"

"Rita is demented," Seth confided to Kimberly, deliberately loud enough for Rita to hear him. "All she talks about is foxy guys."

"It happens to be a subject of great interest to many of us," Kimberly said, grinning at Rita. Then she slung her arm around Seth's waist and gave him a hug. "I was so pleased to hear about you and Laura, Seth. I think it's wonderful."

"I thought it was wonderful until I realized that Rita was part of the package," Seth groused, though he was clearly kidding. "Adolescent girls are absolute horror shows."

"Grown-up men are weird," Rita countered.

"And Seth is the weirdest of all," Kimberly confirmed. She shifted her hand to the crook of his elbow and peered up at him. "Your hair is getting long," she noted.

"Yeah. Laura likes it this way," he said, raking his hand through the shaggy dark blond locks. "She's reforming me, Kim. Turning me into a hippie again."

"You were supposed to reform her," Rita criticized him, glancing at Kimberly and then imitating her, slipping her hand through the bend of his other elbow. "You're falling down on the job, Seth."

"Go ahead, say it," he goaded her. "I'm a regular flame."

"What's a flame?" Kimberly asked.

"It's something like a slime, only less virtual," Seth replied. "Now that, if I'm not mistaken, is the National Archives," he said, pointing to a pillared building across the street. "As I recall, there was a street theater troupe with camouflage paint on their faces gathered there, doing t'ai chi. Do you know what t'ai chi is, Rita?"

"Uh-uh."

"It's an Eastern form of body movement," he told her. "Very spiritual. And here—" he indicated the stretch of roadway ahead of them "—is where we all stepped aside so a group from the Vietnam Veterans Against the War could parade through. One of them was blind, seated in a wheelchair with black flags attached to it."

"That sounds depressing," Kimberly reflected.

"It wasn't. It was incredibly moving."

"I think it sounds depressing, too," Rita sided with Kimberly. "How about let's go look at those dresses?"

"Listen up, Rita," Seth lectured her. "What we're doing here is more important than dresses. The Moratorium March is living, breathing history."

"Yeah," she scoffed sarcastically.

Seth ignored her. "Somewhere along here is the Department of Justice, isn't it?" he asked Kimberly. "We called it the Department of Injustice. There was a secondary demonstration there after the big one. That one was advertised as including gas."

"Gas?" Rita asked, her interest perking up. "Like, for cars?"

"Like tear gas," Andrew instructed her. "All along the route everyone kept saying, 'Hey, you gonna go to the demonstration at the Department of Injustice afterward? They're gonna be using gas at that one.'"

"Seth, that's sick," Kimberly protested. "Why would anyone knowingly go to a demonstration where tear gas was going to be used?"

Seth shrugged. "To be able to tell their grandchildren about it someday. 'I got gassed at the November Moratorium.' What do you think, Rita? Are you going to make your mother a grandma one of these days?"

"What for?" she responded. "I bet Ma didn't go to that demonstration, not if it had tear gas. She would never do anything that wasn't healthy."

"You're right," Seth agreed. "Neither of us went. We had to catch our bus back to Columbia. Now here—" he paused and gazed around him with a nostalgic smile "—this was the best part of the whole day. Out of the blue, all of a sudden, a whole bunch of us—total strangers—joined hands and started singing. 'Give Peace A Chance' and 'All You Need Is Love.' The classics. That was when I learned that Laura couldn't carry a tune."

"Yeah?" Rita surveyed their surroundings. "You were with my ma the whole time?"

"The whole time," Seth confirmed. "Maybe fate was trying to tell us that we were meant for each other."

"You sure took your time figuring it out," Rita carped. "If it wasn't for me, Ma still wouldn't have figured it out."

Seth turned sharply toward her. "What's that supposed to mean?"

"It means, if I hadn't pointed out to her that you were a pretty awesome dude, she probably wouldn't have noticed."

"You think I'm a pretty awesome dude, Rita?" Seth asked, obviously flattered.

"You're foxier than Kennedy," she praised him. "And that's saying a lot. How about these dresses, Kimberly? Are they radical or what?"

Kimberly floundered for a moment, puzzled by Rita's question. "They're fairly conservative, actually," she told the girl.

"'Radical' means cool," Seth translated. "Rita's taught me a whole lot about the English language. I tell you what, Rita—why don't you go look at the dresses, and Kim and I can hang out and talk like grown-ups?"

"You want to lose me? Sure, Seth," Rita complied. "I know how to make myself scarce."

"Not that I've noticed," he muttered as they approached the branch of the Smithsonian that contained the display of the First Ladies' gowns.

A long line of visitors snaked beyond the display and into the museum's entry. Rita darted to the line, and Seth and Kimberly shared a bench in the echoing foyer in full view of the original star-spangled banner. Seth pulled off his sunglasses, waved reassuringly at Rita and then turned his attention fully to Kimberly. "How are you doing, Kim?" he asked, taking her hand and giving it an affectionate squeeze. "Laura told me about your divorce. That's a tough one, pal. I'm really sorry."

"Thanks, but I'm fine," Kimberly said.

"So what comes next? Are you going to play the field for a while? Live the swinging singles life?"

Kimberly grinned. Seth had always shot straight from the hip. She should have expected such a grilling from him. "I don't know," she answered. "I may just join a nunnery. Swinging singly is surely much more your style than mine."

"Not anymore," Seth said, pretending to look dejected. "It's Monogamy City for me now. Time to climb off the old single swing. I bet my hair turns gray within six months of tying the knot."

Did marriage make men's hair turn gray? Kimberly wondered, picturing the silver strands that wove through Andrew's dark hair. He had been married, and now he was going gray.

Damn, but she couldn't let herself keep dwelling on thoughts of him. "I was married for fifteen years and it didn't change the color of my hair," she told Seth. "I suspect that if anything makes a person go gray, it's the ending of a marriage, not the starting of one."

"Well, look at the bright side," Seth consoled her. "At least you don't have to deal with in-laws anymore."

Kimberly had never had much trouble getting along with Todd's parents—certainly no more trouble than she had getting along with her own. Both her parents and Todd's were cut from the same pattern, after all. Wealthy, Southern, traditional. "Are you having a hard time dealing with Laura's mother?" she asked Seth.

He rolled his hazel eyes in dismay. "'A hard time' is putting it mildly."

"Laura said her mother adored you."

"She does. That's the problem. Before I even had a chance to say hello to the woman, she had me in a strangulating bear hug. She thinks I've rescued her old-maid daughter from a fate worse than death." He shook his head. "Rita adores me, too. It's freaky, being surrounded by so many adoring women."

"Oh? I should think you'd be used to that, after your swinging single days," Kimberly teased him.

"Correction—so many adoring women from the same family. We're talking three generations of Brodies."

"You love it," Kimberly guessed.

Andrew conceded with an enthusiastic nod. "I love it. Laura's done wonders for me, Kim. And I've done wonders for her, too."

"Oh? What wonders have you done for her, Seth?"

He smiled reflectively. "You know Laura—she's too generous for her own good. She's so busy taking care of humanity that she forgets to take care of herself. I've finally convinced her that it's okay to stop worrying about everyone else for a little while and to let someone else take care of her. Namely me."

"I'm almost afraid to ask how you're going to take care of her," Kimberly joked.

Seth accepted her teasing good-naturedly. "I'm making her quit her job. The lady's burned out and she needs a break. She needs to be pampered, to have some fun. Admit it, Kim, aren't I fun?"

"No argument there," Kimberly agreed.

"I don't know if Laura told you," he went on, "but we're planning a big bash to celebrate the wedding in May. We're going to invite the whole *Dream* gang. These reunions are far-out, Kim. If it weren't for the last reunion, Laura and I would have never gotten together. Who knows what great love affair will arise out of the next one?"

Not the Kimberly-Andrew love affair, she answered internally. As much as she'd been looking forward to attending Laura and Seth's wedding at Laura's mother's house, the notion now filled her with apprehension. If she went to their big bash, she would have to see Andrew.

She wanted to see him, but she was afraid to. If she saw him, he might be his usual cutting, condescending self, and she couldn't bear that thought. But if he wasn't, if he was instead gentle and vulnerable, as he had been on Saturday night, then she might once again believe that she loved him. And she couldn't bear that thought, either.

She was going to have to see him, whether or not she wanted to. He would have to come back to Washington to meet with the senator. Even if she managed to escape from the city limits on a last-minute vacation when Andrew came back to town, she couldn't avoid him forever. She knew he would want to attend Seth and Laura's wedding, just as she would want to.

She would be forced to see him, and he would be arrogant toward her. And she would loathe him.

"Seth," she murmured solemnly. "What do you think of me?"

Her question clearly surprised him. He smiled. "I think you're gorgeous. If I weren't so madly in love with Laura, I'd ask you to marry me."

"You're really psyched on getting married, aren't you?" she asked.

"What can I say?" He shrugged and offered an easy smile. "I'm just an old softie, a romantic fool. Everybody ought to be a romantic fool at least once in his life."

"No more than once," Kimberly mused. She'd been a romantic fool with Todd, and that had been quite enough. She simply wouldn't allow herself to be a romantic fool with Andrew, as well.

Rita emerged from the gown display looking dissatisfied. "Yuck," she announced. "Ugly, ugly, ugly. How come none of them wore minis?"

"They wore those dresses to inaugural balls, Rita," Kimberly explained, happy for the distraction Rita provided. "Formal dances."

"Yeah, but they're so ugly. If I were a First Lady, I'd want to wear something awesome."

"That's what we need," Seth decided, greeting Rita's comment with enthusiasm. "Someone awesome for president. A burned-out hippie. A Grateful Dead-head. Someone who, if the Soviets got restive, would say, 'Let's do a number and meditate.' And if the economy was in the pits, he'd say, 'Score me some blotter and we'll get some visions on it.' "

"Are you announcing your candidacy?" Kimberly teased him. "If you are, I'll be your speech writer."

"And then what would poor Senator Howie do?" Seth posed.

"Run the country while you were in never-never land," Kimberly answered.

"Yeah, well, I'm starving," Rita declared, twirling her sunglasses between her thumb and forefinger and eyeing the door. "Is there a McDonald's around here or something?"

"She's a real gourmet," Seth joked, rising from the bench. "Her favorite food is anything loaded with cholesterol."

"Zit fuel," Rita elaborated.

"You all are my guests for lunch," said Kimberly, trying not to grimace at Rita's terminology. "So you may as well take advantage of me and pick someplace expensive."

"She's neat, Seth," Rita decided before prancing out of the museum.

"PROFESSOR COLLINS?"

Andrew glanced up from his desk to see Chip Wilton peering around the edge of his office door. Tall, with fresh-scrubbed good looks, Chip was clad in a red Izod shirt, beige corduroys and deck shoes without socks. He appeared to be the embodiment of Kimberly's description of an Amherst College man—except for the fact that he wasn't wearing a rugby shirt. The balmy spring weather called for short sleeves.

"Come on in, Chip," Andrew said, beckoning him inside the small, tidy room. Office space was at a premium at the college, and Andrew had to make do with a room barely larger than a walk-in closet. Countless books crowded the metal shelves lining one wall, and Andrew's desk, typing table and swivel chair took up most of the floor space. He'd managed to cheer up the office with a few posters on the walls: one of Martin Luther King; one of F.D.R.; one, a relic of his college days, depicting an impressionistic tree silhouetted against a yellow background, its limbs covered with the words "War is unhealthy for children and other living things." The poster was admittedly corny, perhaps as corny as "Smile—it increases your face power." But Andrew had saved it all these years. It made him think of Troy Bennett, one of his closest friends in college, who had fled the country to avoid having to serve in what had arguably been the nation's most unhealthy war.

Andrew folded the letter he had been reading and out of some obsessive neatness inserted it back into the envelope. Then he smiled at Chip and nodded toward the folding metal chair across the desk from him. A junior economics major, Chip was one of Andrew's most promising students. Andrew would always be willing to make time for kids like Chip.

"I know this isn't your scheduled office hour," Chip apologized for his intrusion. "But I saw your door open, and—"

"No problem," Andrew assured Chip. He was relieved that Chip had interrupted him. Andrew honestly didn't want to be reading that particular letter right now. Leaning back in his chair, he gritted his teeth at the squeak the chair's hinge invariably produced and adjusted his eyeglasses. "What's on your mind?"

Chip's expression was earnest and mildly uneasy. He sat, balanced his spiral notebook on his knees and took a deep breath. "Well... I don't know if you remember, but we've talked once or twice about the possibility of my going to grad school for a doctorate after I finish up here...." He trailed off uncertainly.

"I do remember."

"Yes, well..." The boy smiled sheepishly. "I think I may be having a change of heart."

"That's allowed," Andrew remarked. "You don't have to go to grad school immediately after college. Sometimes it's a wise idea to take a year off and unwind."

"That wasn't what I was thinking," Chip continued. "The truth is, I think I want to go to business school, instead."

"Business school," Andrew said, exerting himself to sound noncommittal.

"I've been giving this a great deal of thought, Professor Collins," he continued. "I've talked at length with my friends about it—not just my friends here at Amherst, but a lot of my friends from home when I was there over spring break. Business school seems so much more sensible in this day and age—"

"This day and age," Andrew echoed scornfully. Why was it that the best and the brightest in "this day and age" all wanted to go to business school?

He knew too well the answer to that: they wanted the bucks. They wanted to go into investment banking and pocket millions. They wanted to wear Brooks Brothers suits, own VCRs and work in offices more elegant than Andrew's. Then, when they were thirty, they wanted to marry corporate lawyers, start families, name their children Melissa and Zachary. They wanted to become "involved" fathers—or mothers—and spend "quality time" with their children without missing a day's work or a day's pay. They wanted to commute to their Wall Street offices from Darien and Greenwich and spend their weekends at "the cot-tage" in East Hampton or on Martha's Vineyard, sailing "the boat," drinking Beefeater's martinis and vintage wines. They wanted to live the life Andrew and his compatriots used to thumb their noses at.

"Tell me, Chip," he proposed. "Do you think it's *sensible*, or do you think it's *practical*?"

"Both, I suppose," Chip acknowledged. "I love school and I love research, but where does it all lead?"

To this, Andrew almost replied. To a fulfilling, intellectually stimulating position at a low wage where one could help mold young minds, where one could think great thoughts. And, if one was lucky, where one could get tenure. "As you said, you love research," Andrew observed. "Business school offers few opportunities for research."

"Yes, but it offers a degree that's worth something on the market," Chip countered.

"Are you sure you aren't just succumbing to peer pressure?" Andrew asked, aware of the irony in his question. In his era, when the older generation worried about their offspring succumbing to peer pressure, they had in mind such evils as drug abuse and dropping out. Nowadays, when a youngster succumbed to peer pressure, chances were he'd wind up with a blond secretary and an office overlooking the Hudson River.

An image of Kimberly flitted across Andrew's mind. Not that she was a secretary, but she was blond, blond and beautiful, the sort of prize men who graduated from business schools tended to expect. Women like Kimberly weren't supposed to be included in the life of an assistant professor.

Don't even think about her, he chided himself, knowing that it was impossible not to think about her when her letter was lying right before him on his desk. Ever since pulling the envelope from his campus mailbox after his last class twenty minutes ago, he had been holed up in his office, reading it, reading it again, reliving every minute he'd spent with her.

"If you came here to receive my blessings," he said, abruptly remembering Chip in his office, "then you probably already know that you're going to be disappointed. I think you're an ideal candidate for an academic career—and I think you'd find it incredibly rewarding. But if you're looking to be *practical*, then go to business school."

"I plan to visit Harvard and Wharton this summer," Chip went on, brushing off Andrew's obvious condemnation of his choice. "Possibly Stanford, too. And I've heard a few good things about Northwestern's program. I was wondering if you had any other recommendations."

"Besides scrapping the idea? No," Andrew told him. "I know plenty about graduate programs, but not business schools. I've heard that as a rule, Harvard and Stanford B-School graduates are offered phenomenal starting salaries. If that's what you're interested in," he added pointedly.

Chip appeared slightly deflated. "You don't know anybody teaching at any of those schools, then? Anybody you could suggest that I should contact?"

"No," Andrew muttered wryly. "I don't travel in those circles."

"Well, I'll give it some more thought," Chip promised before standing. "I appreciate your opinions, Professor Collins—"

"No, you don't," Andrew mocked him with gentle resignation. "You wish I had said, 'Hey, that's swell, Chip. Business school! Go for it!'"

Chip smiled. "Yeah, I guess I was hoping you would."

"That's the way it goes, kid." He watched as Chip headed for the door, then called after him, "By the way, I haven't finished grading all the papers, but your paper on Cuba's economic dependency on the Soviet Union was outstanding."

"Thank you, Professor Collins," Chip said, his smile brightening as he sauntered out of the office.

"The kids today," Andrew mumbled under his breath. Not only did they all want to go to business school, but they all insisted on calling him "Professor Collins." When he had attended college, the students were far less respectful. They had called their favorite professors by their first names and their least favorites by their last names, without any title attached. The only exception Andrew could think of was that pompous poli-sci professor who had spent at least half the semester boasting about how he'd flunked all his students who had participated in the Columbia riots in 1968. As Andrew recalled, he and Troy had dubbed that teacher "Dr. Barfbag."

Left in solitude, Andrew couldn't keep himself from pulling out Kimberly's letter and reading it yet another time. "Dear Andrew, Would you please be so good as to return to Washington for a meeting with Senator Milford..."

The stuff she'd found out about the general intrigued him. The general's name was familiar to him. Several of the farmers he'd interviewed in El Salvador had mentioned him as the leader of one of the roving bands of army men who regularly terrorized the peasants. That Andrew and Kimberly had actually witnessed a meeting between the general and Wilding was exciting.

It was exciting to have made such a connection between the two. Even more exciting had been Andrew and Kimberly's trip to Fairfax, their snooping, their moments of fear, their exhilaration. Their touching. Andrew's hands around her waist, his arm across her chest, the pounding of her heart against his limb....

He cursed as a blaze of emotion seared through him. He wasn't used to feeling so strongly about anything anymore—or, more accurately, about *anybody*. His job, yes, he felt strongly about that. His job, his health and his politics. But not a person. Not a woman.

The emotion was hard to define, but he had pretty well narrowed it down to rage. Rage at Kimberly for shutting him out. Damn it, so he'd fumbled. So he'd expressed himself poorly. So, in the course of revising his view of her, he had let her see that his view had been in need of revision. Was that reason enough for her to show him the door?

Rage, yes. But even more than rage, guilt. Guilt at having fallen for her beauty, at having been sucked in by her undeniable charm. Guilt at having experienced with her a pleasure he'd never known with a woman before, not even with Marjorie.

He had spent the past five days trying to ignore the truth. But he was a scholar, inherently unable to turn his back on the facts. In this case, the fact was that not once in what he had considered a nearly perfect marriage had he ever felt anything quite as strong as what he'd felt in Kimberly's arms. They were such graceful arms, he reflected, her skin so soft, her hands so delicate, and her fingernails... Marjorie used to bite her fingernails down to the cuticle. But not Kimberly. Her fingernails were oval, smoothly filed. He still hadn't forgotten the sensation of them scraping tenderly across his skin.

Nor had he forgotten the smell of her, the delectable curves of her body, the golden silk of her hair dipping against his jaw. Or her almost superfluously feminine underwear. Underwear! Andrew had never been a fetishist, but Kimberly, in that dainty bra and panties...

Rage again. Rage that he could have been so receptive to her, only to have her turn her back on him. And guilt that he could have been so receptive to someone like her in the first place.

"Would you please be so good as to return to Washington for a meeting with Senator Milford," he read. Not for a meeting with her, not for the time they needed to work things out. Evidently she felt that nothing needed working out. The working out had already been accomplished as far as she was concerned. She had worked him out of her life.

"Hey, Andy—how about lunch?" Bob McIntyre called through the open door.

Andrew again folded the letter and stuffed it into the envelope. Then he lifted his gaze to the man filling the doorway. Bob was smaller than average in build—no more than five-seven, with a slim frame. Yet owing to his status in the department, he seemed to cut a powerful, looming figure.

"Hello, Bob," Andrew said smoothly, hoping that he had concealed the edginess he currently felt in his mentor's presence.

"Lunch?" Bob repeated.

He ought to accept Bob's invitation. He ought to be congenial and collegial, as one was supposed to be in order to win tenure. Yet he couldn't picture himself chatting amicably over a sandwich with the man who had hooked him up with the C.I.A., the man responsible for getting Andrew entangled with John Wilding and L.A.R.C.—and, indirectly, with Kimberly.

"Thanks, but I can't," he declined. "I've got some errands to run."

"You're a busy man," Bob joked. "I hear you were down in D.C. last weekend. More research for that El Salvador study?"

How did you guess? Andrew grunted silently. "Visiting a college friend," he said aloud. He wasn't ready to discuss the L.A.R.C. situation with Bob yet. He wasn't even certain precisely what the situation was. And he wouldn't learn what it was unless he would be so good as to return to Washington for a meeting with Senator Milford.

"Well, I won't keep you. Maybe we can have lunch next week." Bob smiled and vanished from the doorway.

Restless, Andrew gathered up Kimberly's letter and the student papers he still had to grade, slipped them inside his briefcase and left his office. He strolled across the campus, trying to let the warm April sun relax him, trying to appreciate the fragrance of sprouting grass and budding leaves and the uninterrupted blue of the Berkshire sky above him. He waved at students who shouted greetings his way and sidestepped a game of catch between two baseball-mitted students on the lawn.

Given the mild weather, Andrew had walked to the college that morning instead of driving his car. His apartment was slightly more than a mile away. Ordinarily he enjoyed his stroll home through the heart of Amherst's business district, which was adjacent to the campus. The town had evolved a great deal in the five years Andrew had lived there; new shops, restaurants, theaters and clubs were thriving, endowing the neighborhood with the same sort of liveliness Andrew had felt in Georgetown.

He didn't enjoy the stroll today, not only because it reminded him of Georgetown, but because, even if it hadn't reminded him of Georgetown, he was too immersed in thoughts of Kimberly to enjoy much of anything. He would have to go back to Washington—no question about that—but what would happen when he got there? Would the blond goddess snub him again? Would she perform her magic on him, make him feel irresistibly comfortable with her and able to confide in her and then accuse him of some hideous crime and boot him out?

Or would she once again be the woman he had known in college, pretty and bubbly, the ebullient cheerleader who thought Andrew was squinting at her?

He hadn't come to any resolutions by the time he had reached his place. He unlocked his apartment door, stared into the starkly neat living room, then tossed his briefcase inside and left the house again. His ten-year-old red Volvo was parked in the paved lot behind the house. He climbed in, started the engine and coasted down the driveway.

He wasn't sure where to go. He had never been one for cruising—driving aimlessly seemed wasteful to him, especially since he'd lived through two oil crises in the past decade and a half. He shifted into idle at the corner of his block and struggled to decide on a destination.

Donna's apartment. He hadn't seen Donna since his return from Washington, although he'd spoken with her once. She had been curious to hear what he'd learned about L.A.R.C., but Andrew hadn't wanted to see her until he came to terms with his feelings for Kimberly.

He still hadn't come to terms with them, but he couldn't put off seeing Donna indefinitely. He headed north toward the University of Massachusetts campus and reached Donna's apartment building before he had any concept of what he was doing there, what he would say to her or, for that matter, whether she was even at home.

She was, and through the intercom she sounded delighted by Andrew's unscheduled visit. "I'll buzz you in," she said. "Come on up."

He entered and climbed the stairs. The building was about twelve years old, brightly lit, with apartments much larger than Andrew's, at lower rents. However, he liked his own place better. It had more character. Also, ever since Marjorie had died, Andrew had preferred to live in a small place. At first he had felt as though large apartments emphasized his aloneness, making him too acutely conscious of Marjorie's absence. Now it was merely a habit. He was used to compact living.

Donna had her front door open for him when he arrived at her floor. He stepped inside, closed the door and searched the vacant living room. "Hello? Donna?"

"In here," she shouted from the bedroom.

He walked through the living room to the bedroom. Donna was seated crosslegged on the floor, dressed in a pair of old dungarees and a baggy sweatshirt, surrounded by cardboard cartons from the neighborhood supermarket. One of her bookcases was almost empty, its contents packed into two of the cartons. "What's going on?" he asked.

She smiled and shoved her hair back from her angular face. Then she got to her feet and surveyed the mess around her. "I decided to get a head start on packing. By the way, can I ask a big favor of you? What I was thinking was, I could pack up my books for the post office and leave them in your apartment. Then I could call you as soon as I find a place in Fullerton and you could address them and mail them to me. Would you mind doing that?"

"Not at all," he told her. As she picked her way across the room to him, he assessed her lanky body, her haphazard grooming, her puppy-dog appeal. He felt nothing resembling Kimberly's effect on him last weekend. No surge of longing, no aching desire either to make love to her or to bare his soul to her. No misery at the thought that he would be losing her to a teaching job in Fullerton. He felt friendly toward Donna, that was all. Friendly and safe. "I take it you've decided to accept the job at Cal-State," he remarked.

"Yeah. I got another rejection letter this week, from the University of Southern Mississippi. It seems that nobody but Cal-State Fullerton wants me A.B.D.," she explained, referring to her "all-but-dissertation" academic status. "Thanks, Andy. I know it's going to be a pain getting all these heavy cartons to the post office, but—"

"Don't pack them so full, and then they won't be so heavy," Andrew suggested.

Donna grinned at his pragmatic suggestion and kissed his cheek. "You're a sweetheart," she said before piling the empty cartons along one wall, out of the way. "So tell me, how did your visit to Washington go?"

"I'm not sure," he said. "I have to go back. Senator Milford wants to meet me." *There,* he added silently. *I've admitted it. I've said it out loud. I have to go back.*

"That must make you feel pretty important—a command performance for a U.S. senator." She resumed the chore of packing her books into cartons. "Your namesake Andy Warhol said everyone's supposed to be famous for fifteen minutes. Maybe meeting with a senator is going to be your big moment in the sun." She dusted her hands off on her thighs and lifted her gaze to him. Her smile was quizzical. "Why the long face? Don't you want your allotted fifteen minutes?"

Andrew shrugged. "If I'm going to fly all the way down to D.C., I'd better get more than fifteen minutes with the man." He managed a chuckle. "Actually, fame is the last thing I want out of this. I'd rather just keep the meeting as quiet as possible." He found a clear space on her desk and rested his hips against it, thinking that the room's clutter would be easier to take sitting down. "If I've got a long face, it's probably because one of my smartest students just told me he wants to go to business school."

"He sounds smart, all right," Donna commented. "Business school is the safest route to go these days."

Andrew contemplated her observation. He had always thought that winning tenure was the safest route. Tenure was safe—but winning tenure entailed minding one's own business and not ruffling the feathers of one's colleagues by meeting with senators in Washington.

It was too late for Andrew to opt for safety. He had already set things in motion. By returning to the capital to see Senator Milford, he was probably risking his career, his future, everything that still mattered to him.

Including Kimberly. She still mattered to him, even if only as a source of rage and guilt. By returning to the capital, he was probably risking his friendship with her—if it was a friendship. Whatever the hell it was, he was risking it.

On the other hand, if he didn't return to Washington, whatever he had with her was already doomed.

He had to go.

Chapter Eight

"So the phone rang—this was about nine-thirty, Saturday night—and it was Seth. He said, 'They're about to lock me up, Kim, but I demanded my one telephone call first. Do you know any good lawyers?' "

"Oh, no!" Julianne dissolved in laughter. She was laughing so hard she had to hold her cordial glass with both hands in order not to spill any of her crème de menthe. She fell back against the sofa cushions as her shoulders shook. "First the metal detector and now this! What was he arrested for?"

"He said they were charging him with drunk driving."

Julianne's laughter waned, and her clear blue eyes widened with dismay. "Drunk driving? With Rita in the car? Kim, that's serious."

"He was innocent," Kimberly defended Seth. She tucked her feet beneath her and nestled deeper into the plush upholstery of the sofa, twisting to face Julianne. They had already eaten dinner and were now relaxing in the comfortable living room of Julianne's Manhattan apartment, sipping after-dinner cordials and listening to a tape of Joni Mitchell songs. Although in her youth Kimberly had derived malicious pleasure from shocking her parents by serenading them with Rolling Stones rock and roll, she honestly preferred the gentler acoustic music of her era—Joni Mitchell, James Taylor, Simon and Garfunkel. Her parents probably would have approved of such musicians, so Kimberly had kept her taste a secret from them.

Julianne had an excellent collection of late-sixties folk music. She and Kimberly had dined to the accompaniment of Crosby, Stills and Nash. Once that tape had expended itself, Julianne had put on one of her Joni Mitchell tapes, and the singer's sweet, distilled soprano floated in the air around Julianne and Kimberly as they caught up on each other's lives. The senator, Whitney Brannigan and Lee Pappelli, the senator's chief aide, weren't due to arrive in New York City until the following morning for a meeting with the mayor and a scheduled speech before a convention of electronics manufacturers, but Kimberly had traveled up ahead of time in order to visit Julianne.

"Anyway," she related, "according to Seth, he had rented a car to take Rita to see Mount Vernon. On their way back to the city, they stopped for dinner at a place in Arlington that makes the best Peking Duck outside China. Then they drove back into Washington. He was cruising on a street in Southwest that has two lanes of traffic in each direction, with a dotted white line separating the lanes. A few cars were parked along the curb and they jutted out into the right lane. But he had to make a right turn to get back to L'Enfant Plaza. So he was weaving in and out of the right lane, sometimes straddling the dotted line, because of the parked cars. A policeman thought he was driving erratically and pulled him over."

"Didn't he explain what he was doing?" Julianne asked.

"You know Seth. His explanations usually require explanations." Kimberly took a sip of the sweet, minty liqueur in her glass and set it on the coffee table. She raked her hair back from her face with her fingers and chuckled.

"He told me the policeman asked him to touch his nose with his eyes closed, and he did that just fine. Then the policeman asked him to walk a straight line, heel to toe, and he passed that test, too. But *then* the policeman asked him to do a pirouette on his left foot and walk *backward*, heel to toe. At that point Seth said something like, 'Who the heck do you think I am, Mikhail Baryshnikov?' Only I don't think he used the word 'heck.'"

"I'm sure he didn't," Julianne concurred with a smile.

"So the policeman asked Seth if he'd been drinking, and Seth, true to form, said, 'All I've had is some Coke.' Not surprisingly, the policeman misunderstood him and decided to frisk him."

"Good Lord!" Julianne was overcome with fresh laughter. "Couldn't he have just taken a Breathalyzer test and gotten it over with?"

"He refused to. He said he wouldn't take one without a lawyer present. Naturally the cop ran him in."

"What did you do? Did you find a lawyer for him?"

"At nine-thirty on a Saturday night?" Kimberly snorted. "Washington may be overrun with lawyers, Julianne, but most of them have better things to do on Saturday night than bail out an obstreperous former hippie. I went down to the station house myself." She reached for her glass and took another sip. "What a scene! They had Seth locked into a holding cell with three dissolute street drunks who smelled like sewers, and Seth was attempting to teach them the words to 'Alice's Restaurant' while he accompanied them on his kazoo. It was an absolute scream."

"I wish I could have seen it," Julianne said wistfully. "I wish Laura could have seen it. Maybe she'd rethink her decision to marry him."

"I bet it would only have made her love him more," Kimberly argued, eliciting a nod of agreement from Julianne. "I found Rita perched on the desk of the night sergeant, wearing her mirror sunglasses and describing how cute Seth's backside is."

"What?"

"You didn't hear about that?" Kimberly grinned. "It seems that the first time Seth stayed the night at Laura's apartment, before they were a couple, he slept on the living room couch. In the buff. His blanket fell off, and guess who found him sprawled out in all his glory the following morning?"

"You're kidding!" Julianne's guffaw temporarily drowned out the stereo. "That probably made Laura love him more, too. They're so much in love, Kimberly—it's incredible. You should see them together. They're so affectionate, so adoring, it's just marvelous. I wish they could have come to dinner tonight, too, but Laura was busy with a group therapy session she runs for pregnant high school students and Seth had a meeting with a couple of investors to pitch his new movie." She stretched her long legs, propping her feet up on the coffee table, and sighed. "Well? How did you spring Seth from the slammer?"

Kimberly shrugged. "He sprang himself. It was all an interesting adventure to him—something he can make use of the next time he writes a socially relevant screenplay. But by the time I showed up, the whole thing had pretty much played itself out. He blew into the balloon, passed with flying colors and thanked the police officers for an edifying experience."

"It sounds like his little sojourn to the capital was eventful, to say the least," Julianne concluded.

"I believe he had the time of his life. It doesn't take much to make good old Stoned happy—an hour in jail, a chance to holler 'Up against the wall!' and a stroll down memory lane." She glanced at the tall, conservatively attired woman sharing the sofa with her. "You didn't march in the November Moratorium, did you?"

Julianne shook her head. "I spent the day on a street corner on Upper Broadway, collecting signatures for an antiwar petition. How about you?"

Kimberly scowled. "I worked on a research paper about de Tocqueville. Aren't I a drip? Seth thinks I won't have anything to tell my grandchildren."

She sighed, suddenly pensive. She used to dream of telling her grandchildren juicy stories about her youth. But how would she ever have grandchildren if she didn't have a child?

She had become obsessed lately with thoughts of motherhood. Her longing to bear a child was nothing new; the problems with her marriage might not have come to a head if it hadn't been for her implacable desire for children. But ever since spending the previous weekend with Rita and Seth, viewing the relationship blossoming between the soon-to-be stepdaughter and stepfather and sensing the genuine affection that existed just beneath its playfully antagonistic veneer, Kimberly hadn't been able to get the notion of having a child out of her mind.

No, her obsession predated Rita's visit to Washington. It had arisen from her conversations with Andrew. When she wasn't busy fuming about his supercilious attitude—and even when she *was* fuming, sometimes—she meditated on the story he had told her about his wife's passing. It was tragic enough to lose one's wife at such a young age, but even more tragic was losing one's wife at a moment when all one's hopes and plans centered around conceiving a child. As irrational as it seemed, Kimberly imagined that hearing his wife's dire diagnosis wouldn't have been quite as painful for Andrew if it hadn't come as a result of the woman's miscarriage. In a sense he had suffered two losses at once.

She knew he had endured something terrible. She knew that he had been through hell...and she knew that, for a few brief hours, she had touched him, carried him away from his grief, enabled him to experience the rewards of opening himself up to joy again. Why couldn't he have admitted it? Why couldn't he have accepted that Kimberly was someone who could make him happy?

He couldn't admit it and he couldn't accept it because he still didn't think very highly of her. In his eyes she was still a brainless cheerleader. Nothing more.

She was tired of dwelling on thoughts of Andrew and the weekend they'd spent together. With a determined shrug she focused on Julianne. "How's work? How are things at *Dream*?"

"Hectic," Julianne reported, although her placid smile belied her claim. That was the way Julianne was—even-keeled, mellow, unflappable. Undoubtedly her life was as full of ups and downs as Kimberly's, but one would never guess by looking at her. "We've decided to devote a full edition of the magazine to the topic of changes in the American family. I told you about the article we have on Laura's work with unwed mothers, didn't I?"

Kimberly nodded.

"The article is terrific," Julianne continued. "Instead of running it right away, I thought it would be interesting to publish it with a few complementary pieces that are still in the works. One is an analysis of demographic trends, another one deals with current welfare policy, and then the story on Laura offers the human side of the issue. All we need now is some solid art. The reporter I assigned to Laura's story took scads of photos, but they aren't good enough. Susan's an excellent writer, but she's pretty much a hack when it comes to photography."

"Why didn't you assign someone else to do the photos?" Kimberly asked.

"Laura's suggestion. She was concerned about imposing on her clients with not one but two strangers in tow. So I let Susan do the photos. They're okay, but..." She wrinkled her nose. "They aren't great. I'm not sure what to do about it, though. Laura's going to be meeting with her teenage mothers for only a month and a half more before she moves out to California with Seth. If I want better art, I suppose I'll have to move quickly on it."

Kimberly eyed her friend speculatively. Julianne's calm attitude might reveal little to most people, but Kimberly had known her long enough to discern that something significant lay beneath Julianne's uncertainty about hiring another photographer. "Why haven't you moved on it yet?" she probed. "You must know enough talented photographers to fill a NYNEX telephone book. Why don't you just commission one and get on with it?"

Julianne eyed Kimberly and smiled hesitantly. "I already know the photographer I want for the job."

"Troy Bennett," Kimberly guessed, naming their college classmate, the man who had filled the pages of *The Dream* with his striking, powerful photographs. She knew as well as Julianne how superbly Troy would be able to capture on film the moods and feelings of struggling young mothers. His portraits expressed far more than merely a catalogue of a subject's physical characteristics. His pictures literally told stories.

"He's not available," Julianne said swiftly.

"Have you already asked him?" Kimberly leaned forward to keep the sofa cushions from swallowing her up. "I know he's got his photography studio up in Montreal, Julianne, but if you paid him enough, covered expenses and all, he might do it."

Julianne shook her head. "He wouldn't," she said laconically. Before Kimberly could question her further, Julianne smoothly redirected the conversation to Kimberly. "Once I finish this Broken Families in America issue, I'm going to expect a hot scoop for the magazine from you and Andrew on his involvement with the C.I.A. So don't you dare leak the story to anyone else." She took a sip of her cordial, then asked, "When is Andrew supposed to arrive in New York to meet with Senator Milford?"

"Tomorrow at three," Kimberly reported, hoping that her voice didn't betray her turbulent emotions when it came to Andrew. "The senator's spending the morning at Gracie Mansion, having lunch with the mayor there, and then he has a few hours free in the afternoon before he has to deliver his speech to the electronics folks. That's when Andrew's been sandwiched in."

"He must have been pleased that you could set up the meeting here in the city so he wouldn't have to travel all the way to Washington again."

"'Pleased' is an understatement," Kimberly muttered, her facade cracking. "I doubt he'll ever want to return to Washington."

"Why?"

Kimberly circled the rim of her glass with her finger as she ruminated. She usually had no difficulty confiding in Julianne; they had known each other since their sophomore year at Barnard, and unlike the other founders of *The Dream*, Kimberly and Julianne had maintained close contact in the fifteen years since they'd graduated from college. During the course of those years Kimberly had never hesitated to tell Julianne about anything that was bothering her, particularly in matters of the heart. Julianne had absorbed Kimberly's tirades about Todd, about the problems in their marriage and the hardships of her separation and divorce. Julianne was easy to talk to; she never stood in judgment of Kimberly, never lapsed into pity, but always offered sympathy and sound advice.

Yet telling Julianne about Andrew seemed risky. Julianne had seen for herself the tension and animosity that marked Kimberly's relationship with Andrew in college. If Kimberly revealed that Andrew had spent the night with her, Julianne might berate her for her lack of common sense. Worse yet, Julianne might laugh at her.

"I slept with him," Kimberly blurted out before she could stop herself.

Julianne choked on her drink. "You did what?"

Kimberly averted her gaze. "When Andrew was in Washington I slept with him."

Julianne took a moment to collect herself. She lowered her glass carefully to the table and turned her gaze to Kimberly. "And?" she said expectantly.

"And it was a mistake," Kimberly lamely summed up.

"Why?" Julianne pressed her. "Wasn't he good in bed?"

"Don't be crass," Kimberly scolded her.

Julianne smiled hesitantly. "I'm sorry, but you've taken me by surprise. I mean, you and Andrew Collins, archenemies... Why was it a mistake?"

"You just said it yourself, Julianne. We were archenemies."

"Are you still?"

Kimberly pondered the question. As angry as she was with Andrew, and as hurt, she couldn't consider him her enemy. "The whole thing was silly," she said, trying to justify what had occurred. "We'd both had a lot to drink and we were talking too much, and one thing led to another."

"Oh, come off it," Julianne scoffed. "You aren't the sort of person who drifts into something like that. Neither is he.

People don't wind up making love by accident—certainly not people like you and Andrew."

Kimberly conceded with a slight nod. "I think... I think it was more that I was feeling lonely, rebounding from the divorce, and he was there," she said, relying on his explanation for her behavior. "We had spent a lot of time together and we were getting along..."

"You were getting along, so just for the hell of it you made love. Come on, Kim!" Julianne's tone was laced with sarcasm. "You've got more control over yourself than that. If you slept with Andrew, it was because you wanted to sleep with him. With *him* in particular, not with anyone who just happened to be handy."

"I know," Kimberly admitted in a small voice. "And yes, he was good in bed. It was wonderful, Julianne, but... but I've never slept with anyone I didn't love before." She didn't bother to add that she'd never slept with anyone but her husband. Numbers didn't matter. All that mattered was that she had always believed that love and sex were irrevocably intertwined.

"Do you love Andrew?"

"No!" Kimberly said vehemently.

Julianne measured her heated denial and sighed. Then she reached across the sofa to pat Kimberly's arm reassuringly. "You aren't the first woman who's made love without being in love, Kim. You don't have to act as if it's the end of the world."

"Have you ever slept with someone you didn't love?" Kimberly shot back.

Julianne smiled. "It's your situation we're talking about, not mine. Do you feel guilty? Did you hurt Andrew's feelings?"

"I don't know. No," Kimberly decided. "He's much stronger than I am about these things. He's a man, after all."

"A man," Julianne repeated. "Not an ogre. He's a very sweet man, and he's not constructed of steel. If you're feeling bad because you might have hurt him, then you'll feel a lot better if you make up with him."

"It isn't that," Kimberly asserted. She closed her eyes and let Joni Mitchell's soothing music spill over her. The ballad was unfortunately melancholy and soulful, and it didn't improve her spirits. "He was the one who hurt me," she confessed. "The morning after he said things that implied... Julianne, he's never thought much of me. I'm sick of men treating me like I'm an idiot, like I haven't got a functioning mind. Todd always talked down to me, and Andrew does, too. I don't want to be insulted anymore. I don't want to be hurt."

"Nobody wants to be hurt," Julianne said quietly. "But it comes with the territory." She stood and crossed to the dining table, where she'd left the bottle of crème de menthe. "What are you going to say to Andrew when you see him tomorrow?" she asked.

"I'm going to say, 'Andrew, I'd like you to meet Senator Milford. Senator, this is Professor Andrew Collins.' Then I'm going to leave the room."

Julianne stared at her from across the room. She laughed. "That's about the worst strategy I've ever heard."

"What's wrong with it?"

"It's called running away, Kim. And if I know Andrew, he's not going to let you get away with it."

"Why not? He's got a girlfriend up in Amherst. Probably some whiz kid who loves discussing logarithms with him over dinner."

"He's an economist, not a mathematician," Julianne pointed out.

"All right. The gross national product."

"Are you jealous?"

"Of course I'm jealous," Kimberly retorted. "He respects her more than he respects me."

"How do you know that?" Julianne posed. When Kimberly failed to speak, she returned to the sofa and refilled their glasses. "I've always gotten along better with Andrew than you have," she observed. "I can't say I know him inside and out, but I honestly don't think he's the type to take advantage of a woman, especially a woman who's recovering from a painful divorce. Don't forget, he's a widower. He's endured his share of pain, too. Whatever happened when he was in Washington, whatever he did, I can't believe that he deliberately wanted to hurt you." She sipped from her replenished glass, then added, "Talk to him tomorrow, Kim. Work it out, or it's going to fester inside you forever."

"Why are you always so damned sensible?" Kimberly complained.

"Good midwestern breeding," Julianne joked. "All that manure-scented air I inhaled as a child. Drink up, Kim."

AT A QUARTER TO THREE, Lee rang Kimberly's room to announce that he and the senator had returned from their luncheon with the mayor. "Come on up," Lee requested. "The senator wants you to background him a little more on the professor. He gets so edgy when he has to face someone who's smarter than he is."

"Don't we all?" she grunted before hanging up. She ran her brush briskly through her hair, straightened the jacket of her cream-colored suit, adjusted the collar of her royal-blue blouse and left her room for the senator's suite.

Whitney was already in the sitting room with Lee and the senator when Kimberly entered. A fresh pot of coffee stood on a room-service tray and a side table held a few bottles of liquor. The senator had loosened his tie and removed his shoes. His dense gray hair was neatly combed, however, and he seemed refreshed.

"How did your meeting with the mayor go?" she asked politely.

"Not badly," he replied, helping himself to a cup of coffee. "The man tends to go on and on, and he's awfully full of himself. But, then, I suppose we politicians always are. I've looked over everything you and Whitney have ferreted out about this L.A.R.C. proprietary," the senator continued. "It's all very juicy, but let's face it. I can't make an issue out of a bunch of off-the-record innuendos. Does this friend of yours have the—" he checked himself before using one of his off-color phrases in Kimberly's presence "—brass to follow through if I start something with the committee?"

"Andrew is very brassy," Kimberly said emotionlessly. "You can see how far he wants to go with it when you meet him."

The hotel concierge telephoned to inform the senator that Professor Collins was in the lobby and had identified himself to the hotel guard's satisfaction. "Send him up," Lee said.

Kimberly paced nervously to the window and peered out at Central Park. A hard rain descended from the swollen gray clouds overhead. The expanse of grass and trees to the north of the hotel appeared blurred and soggy.

At the light rap on the door she jumped, then spun around in time to see Whitney answer. "Hi, there," he hailed Andrew familiarly. "How's life treating you at that bastion of intellectual excellence?"

Kimberly recognized that with his robust greeting, Whitney was merely trying to put both the senator and Andrew at ease. Yet Andrew didn't appear particularly relaxed. Dressed in a tweedy tan blazer, dark brown corduroy slacks, a white shirt and a brown tie, he clutched his leather briefcase and smiled woodenly as he stepped inside the room. His gaze moved from Whitney, whose hand he dutifully shook, to Lee, to the senator, and finally to Kimberly, where it lingered.

Perhaps she was imagining things, but his square jaw seemed to grow visibly stiffer as his eyes coursed over her. She prayed that he would smile and reveal that uncharacteristic dimple of his, but he didn't oblige. Instead he turned back to the senator, who was padding in his socks over the thick carpet toward him. "Andrew Collins? Thanks so much for coming all the way down from Massachusetts."

"Thank you for having me," Andrew responded, accepting the senator's beefy handshake. "It's an honor."

"An honor, is it?" The senator chuckled. "I like you already. Can I get you something to drink? I've got coffee and booze."

"Coffee, thank you," Andrew said, permitting himself the slightest hint of a smile at the senator's down-to-earth manner.

The senator looked to Lee, who looked to Kimberly. With an inaudible sigh she strode to the cart and fixed a cup of coffee for Andrew. She understood that fixing coffee was her responsibility because she had the least seniority of anyone in the room, but she bristled at the knowledge that Andrew would interpret her action as a sign of her feminine subservience.

She exerted herself to present Andrew with a smile as she handed him the cup. "I hope your drive down wasn't too tiring," she said coolly.

"The weather could have been better," he remarked, just as formally.

Stifling the urge to wince, she lowered her eyes to his hand as he took the cup. She suffered a fleeting memory of the way his fingers had felt on her body, so gentle in their caresses, and took an abrupt step back from him. "Perhaps you'd like to meet with the senator in private," she said, not only because she was eager to get away from Andrew but because she knew he was concerned about protecting his research from inquisitive eavesdroppers. "You'll be able to speak more freely with him if we all aren't around."

"Thank you," he murmured. She caught a glimpse of his dimple and felt her innards unclench slightly.

"Why don't we retire to my bedroom?" the senator suggested, leading the way to an inner door. As his suggestion registered, he issued a hearty laugh. "Don't worry, Andrew—you're perfectly safe with me. I'm a happily married man."

Grinning affably, Andrew followed the senator through the door. The door closed.

"Is it just me, or are things getting chilly in here?" Whitney asked Kimberly, shooting her a wily grin.

"It's just you," Kimberly said curtly. "I'll be down in my room if anybody needs me." She marched out of the suite and slammed the door shut behind her.

Locked inside her own room, she groaned. She tried to recall Julianne's counsel about talking to Andrew and getting her feelings off her chest. The recommendation had sounded so logical last night, but Kimberly knew it wouldn't be easy to talk to Andrew. Especially since she had no idea what she would say.

To distract herself, she slumped in the chair by the desk and leafed through her notes for the senator's speech. She didn't need to read the speech; she'd fussed with it all morning, and by now she practically had the thing memorized. She knew its cadences, its stresses. She knew exactly how the senator would sound when he spoke the words she'd written for him.

She wished she had a speech writer for herself, someone who could compose a magnificent oratory for her to deliver to Andrew. "I am distressed by the way things ended between us a week and a half ago. I am distressed by the way I feel about you. I am distressed by the way I seem not to know whether I am coming or going, whether we are friends or enemies, whether you love me or loathe me, desire me or despise me. I am distressed by the way you explain away my emotions." That sounded magnificent, full of rhythm and punch, the phrases carrying a music all their own. She knew the senator could make a speech like that soar. If only he could recite it on Kimberly's behalf....

She tried not to be so conscious of the passage of time, but each tick of her watch seemed to resonate inside her. One hour, an hour and a half, two. What on earth could Andrew be telling the senator for two hours?

Her room phone rang. Inhaling deeply, she walked to the night table and lifted the receiver. "Hello?"

"Kim? Whitney here. Lover boy is all done with the big man. He's on his way down to your room."

"Oh." She thought it rather presumptuous that Andrew would head directly for her room without first asking if he was welcome. Moreover, she wondered how he had learned her room number. From Whitney, probably. Andrew was apparently still playing Kimberly's game, permitting Whitney to think they were an item.

She thanked Whitney for the warning, hung up and threw back her shoulders. Trying to remember the speech she had mentally written for herself, she came up blank. A quick glance in her mirror informed her that her hair was mussed and her lipstick bitten off. But before she could repair her appearance, she heard Andrew's knock.

She glimpsed through the peephole to ascertain that it was he, then opened the door to admit him.

"Hello," he said.

She opened her mouth and then shut it. As if in a stupor, she watched him close the door behind him and set down his briefcase. Then he pulled off his eyeglasses and massaged his nose, a gesture of weariness. "Was it rough?" she asked, suddenly solicitous.

"Rough?" He smiled wryly. "No. Your boss is a nice guy."

"Then why do you look as if you just completed a marathon?" She mulled over what she'd said, then grinned. "I reckon two-plus hours is a long time to be shut up in a bedroom with another man."

Apparently hearing the word "bedroom" gave Andrew pause. He slipped his eyeglasses on and gazed around Kimberly's room, which was markedly smaller and less elegant than the senator's suite. His eyes came to rest on the double bed with its quilted brown cover, and one corner of his mouth skewed upward, shaping something that was a cross between a smile and a grimace. "Kimberly—"

"He wants you to testify, doesn't he?" she said briskly, trying to ignore the disappointment she felt at hearing Andrew use her full name. "Whitney's told me that the senator has discussed setting up hearings on the issue, and the senator's also made some mention of the idea to me. He wants you to testify before the Intelligence Committee. Right?"

Andrew didn't answer. He only stared at Kimberly, his expression unreadable, his eyes half-hidden behind the glare the bedside lamp created on the lenses of his glasses. His lips softened, and then he looked toward the bed again. "How are you?" he asked.

Despite the fact that he was standing only inches from the bed, he hardly sounded passionate. Rather, his tone was polite and reserved. She didn't want courtesy from him, but that seemed to be the level on which he intended to deal with her. "Are you going to testify?" she asked, bypassing his innocuous question. Maybe she should have taken him up on his gambit, answering him in a way that would introduce a more intimate note into their conversation. But as soon as she spoke, she realized that the opportunity for personal dialogue was gone.

"I don't know," Andrew replied.

"It's important," she stressed. "If you want to uncover this nefarious Wilding character—"

"Kim, I don't know," he replied tersely. "I have to give it some thought."

She sensed him sealing himself up, recoiling, retreating. She wouldn't allow him to slip away from her. Julianne was right; Kimberly and Andrew had to talk. Lifting her face to his, she suggested, "Let's have dinner together and discuss it. I'll put it on the senator's tab. The least he owes you is a good meal for having come all this way."

Andrew contemplated her invitation. "I've got to make a call first."

Kimberly pointed to the telephone and crossed the room to the window, affording him a measure of privacy. Still, she couldn't help but overhear his end of the call. He requested an outside line, dialed the numbers and waited. "Hello, Edith. It's Andrew," he said. "I've got to beg off for dinner tonight. I'll be eating in town.... No, thanks anyway. Maybe next time. Take care now." He hung up.

"You didn't have to break a date," she remarked, hoping she didn't sound querulous. She already knew that Andrew had a girlfriend, but she couldn't prevent herself from suffering a pang of jealousy at listening to his conversation with another woman.

"It wasn't a date," Andrew told her. "Edith is my mother-in-law." He checked himself. "My former mother-in-law," he clarified. "She and Marjorie's father live in White Plains. They invited me to stop at their place for dinner on the way back to Amherst. But we hadn't made a definite plan."

That Andrew felt he owed Kimberly such an extensive explanation placated her. She smiled weakly, gathered her purse from the bureau and preceded him from the room.

They rode the elevator downstairs in silence and strolled through the teeming lobby to the hotel's restaurant. Kimberly identified herself to the maître d', who promptly seated them at a cozy table against the wall. Within a minute a waiter approached, pencil at the ready, and asked if they wanted drinks.

"No," Kimberly said hurriedly. She wasn't going to let them use alcohol as an excuse for their behavior with each other this time.

Still without speaking, they buried themselves in their menus until the waiter returned to take their orders. Once he was gone they had no choice but to confront each other. "Why don't you want to testify before the committee?" she asked, figuring that the best way to begin was to concentrate on business.

Andrew pondered the question for a moment before answering. "You know I want to keep this thing as quiet as possible. It's endangering my status at Amherst. To go public in such a big way would be foolhardy—to say nothing of embarrassing."

"Embarrassing? What's embarrassing about it?"

"It's embarrassing that I got hoodwinked," he explained. "It's embarrassing for someone like me to find out I was working for the C.I.A. And I know it's going to embarrass Bob McIntyre—my mentor at Amherst. If there's any way I can spare him a major humiliation—"

"Andrew, testifying before the committee isn't like appearing on Johnny Carson. The whole matter can be handled discreetly."

He laughed caustically. "Tell me about it. I know what these Senate hearings are like. I watched nearly every minute of the Watergate hearings on television. I watched as James McCord and Alexander Butterworth entered living rooms all across the country. I watched John Dean become a celebrity simply by testifying. How could he not become a celebrity? The journalists outnumbered the participants by about ten to one. It was a circus, Kim."

"That was the Ethics Committee. And that was a very different situation. The Intelligence Committee never holds open hearings, Andrew. No journalists will be present."

He frowned, evidently unpersuaded.

Giving him time to reflect, she scanned the dining room. At the doorway, she spotted Lee and Whitney awaiting a table. Whitney caught her eye and inquired with a few gestures of his hand and some mouthed words whether he and Lee could join her and Andrew for dinner. She shook her head.

Andrew noticed her movement and glanced over his shoulder to see whom she was communicating with. "Lee and Whitney," she whispered. "I don't want them sitting with us."

Andrew smiled wryly. "Of course not. It's much more fun playing games with Whitney, isn't it."

Kimberly's anxiety boiled over into pure fury. "Will you shut up about that, Andrew? Will you just do me a favor and forget the whole thing? If you think that's all that's going on here, all we've got between us—"

"No," he said quickly. "No, I don't think that."

"Then what in high heaven do you think?"

He was spared from responding by the arrival of the waiter with their salads. Once they were alone again, Kimberly fixed Andrew with a brutal stare. He met it unflinchingly. "I think...I think you were a bit too rash with me the last time we were together."

"I surely was," she muttered, trying to dissipate her anger by stabbing a tomato wedge with her fork. "I was most definitely too rash with you. I should never have allowed you to stay—"

"That wasn't what I was talking about," Andrew corrected her, his voice low and intense. "You were rash when you threw me out the next morning."

"You deserved to be thrown out," she snapped. "Impugning me that way, claiming that I was some lonely lady who didn't know her own mind...."

"Ah, Kimberly." He sighed. "Kim. I've—" He mulled over his words, then boldly plowed ahead. "I've missed you."

She didn't dare to interpret his confession as a positive sign. "What did you miss about me? The fact that I crammed pastry down your throat?"

"Among other things." His eyes drifted past her, focusing on the wall. "I haven't stopped thinking about you since I left Washington, Kim. I honestly don't think we're right for each other. But...but the night we spent together felt right. It felt better than right—it felt good. I haven't felt that good in a long, long time." His words spent, he returned his gaze to her and smiled hesitantly.

His unexpected declaration stunned her. She set down her fork and studied him, searching his face for a clue to what she was supposed to think, what she was supposed to say. When Andrew opened his soul to her so completely, she knew she was correct to love him. When he let down his guard and allowed her to see the man he truly was, she had no choice but to let down her guard, as well.

"It did feel good," she whispered shyly.

"Then what went wrong?" he asked. "Why did we blow it the next morning?"

"You're so smart, you ought to know," she countered.

"I know...I know I insulted you. I didn't mean to, Kim, but whatever I said obviously rubbed you the wrong way."

"You said you didn't believe I could love you," she reminded him.

"Did I?"

"Not in so many words, but yes. That's what came across."

He lowered his eyes to his salad, fidgeted with his fork, then let his hand come to rest on the table. "It's the truth. I don't believe you love me."

"Why not?"

"Because..." He sighed again. "You're so beautiful, Kim, so—so precious. You're like a fragile piece of china, delicate and fine—"

She laughed nervously. It felt wonderful to laugh in Andrew's presence, so wonderful her nervousness vanished and her laughter became genuine. "Fragile? Oh, sure, I can break. But trust me, Andrew. I'm not some sort of object you ought to put on a shelf and stare at. I'm no more china than you're steel," she concluded, recalling what Julianne had said about Andrew the night before. "We're both just flesh and blood. And on those rare occasions when you deign to get off your high horse, yes, I sure as hell believe that I love you."

Her announcement startled them both. She hadn't intended to tell him she loved him, and he clearly hadn't expected to hear her express such a feeling. But now the words had been spoken, and they hung in the air between her and Andrew like a solid link, a tangible connection.

"Stay," she murmured, her eyes riveted to his, her hand reaching across the table to him. "Spend the night with me."

"I can't," he said. He didn't pull his hand from hers as her fingers curved gently around it, but his gaze broke away, dropping to his salad again, as if he could no longer bear to look directly at her.

How could he refuse her? How could he refuse them both? After she had publicly acknowledged her love for him, how could he turn away? "Why not?" she asked, her voice resonant with dismay.

"I have to teach a class tomorrow morning."

That was a feeble excuse, and they both knew it. "You could stay for a while, at least—"

"No, Kim. No. I can't."

"Why not?"

He willfully pulled his hand out from under hers and fumbled with his napkin. "You know what will happen if I testify before the committee, don't you?"

She scowled, nonplussed. Why had he decided to reintroduce that subject? "What will happen?" she pressed him, trying to stifle her impatience.

"I'll probably lose my job. The department will let me ride out the last year of my contract and then they'll drop me."

"Maybe they won't," Kimberly disputed him. "Maybe they'll admire your courage and—"

"That's not the way things work in academia," he cut her off. "They'll think I'm an upstart, rocking the boat, putting one of their esteemed colleagues into an untenable position. I'll lose my job," he said with finality. His gaze rose to hers again. "I've lost too much in my life already, Kim. I'm not a kid anymore. I'm too old to go through anything like that again."

She tried to discern the meaning beneath his words. "What does that have to do with us?" she asked softly.

His poignant smile contradicted the somber glow of his eyes as he stared at her. "I don't want to have to lose you, too."

"*Have* to lose me? What makes you so sure you'd lose me? I just told you I love you, Andrew." Saying it reinforced her certainty that she did.

He warred with his thoughts for several minutes, then relented. "I'm not sure. I just don't know."

"Then take a chance," she implored him. "Take a chance and find out."

His smile grew warmer, and she noticed his delectable dimple taking shape at the corner of his mouth.

Chapter Nine

The waiter tactfully refrained from commenting when Kimberly refused their dinner order and signed the check. She figured that if she and Andrew were hungry later they could always order room service. She thought briefly about the waste of the dinner they had canceled, the millions of starving people in the world, and the danger of running up an extravagant bill when one was a public servant. Then she blithely shrugged off those considerations. She doubted that the senator would care, but if he did, she would reimburse his travel fund.

She didn't want to worry about such practical matters. Nor did she want to worry about Andrew's uncertainty regarding her. He had never been reckless, even in their college days, when recklessness was considered the height of fashion. He had always been a cautious man, analyzing every detail to death. That he was reluctant to accept what was obviously developing between him and Kimberly wasn't surprising.

She forgave him his apprehension; as he had said, he'd lost enough in his life. But so had she. And she was sure of her love for him, positive of it. She knew that in time he would be sure of it, too.

Their ride upstairs was as silent as the trip downstairs had been, but the only tension between them now was the electric anticipation of what lay ahead once they reached her room. Her pulse accelerated as she unlocked her door. Before she could close it, Andrew gave her an adorable smile and slung the Do Not Disturb sign over the outer doorknob. "I've always wanted to do that," he confessed.

"Do what?"

"Use a Do Not Disturb sign—for something besides sleeping." He wrapped his arms around her and kissed her brow. "Would I be shattering your illusions if I told you I've never made love in a hotel room before?"

Kimberly laughed airily. She wondered what Andrew would think if he learned about her own inexperience. Hotel rooms were the least of it.

Her laughter ebbed as he fingered the top button of her blouse and eased it through the slit in the cloth. His hands moved efficiently down the front of her blouse, unbuttoning it and tugging it free of the waistband of her skirt. "Is making love in a hotel room one of your fantasies?" she asked, loosening his tie.

He abandoned her blouse to remove his jacket and open his shirt. His smile faded as she reached out to stroke his bare skin. "When I fantasize, Kim, it's about beautiful blond women with dazzling blue eyes."

"And razor-sharp minds?" she inquired, only half joking.

"Minds like yours," he whispered before covering her mouth with his.

His kiss seemed to last an eternity. As her tongue danced with his, her entire body responded, her fingers fisting against the soft wisps of hair covering his chest, her scalp tingling, her hips growing heavy with yearning. The only thing that made ending the kiss endurable for her was the understanding that there would be more to come.

It took them little time to finish undressing. They tumbled onto the bed, their lips fusing again, their fingers interlocked as Andrew's naked body pressed along hers. She wanted to touch him, to stroke the smooth skin of his back and sides, to strum across the surface of his chest again, but his firm clasp wouldn't allow any exploration. She comprehended that he was deliberately pinning her hands to the mattress in order to prolong their lovemaking, and she knew that she would ultimately thank him for setting a leisurely pace. But her frustration was almost palpable, her desire for him a swelling ache deep inside her.

"Underwear, too," he mumbled, lifting his face and gasping for breath. "I've fantasized about your underwear."

"You have?" she exclaimed. "You like ladies' underwear?"

"Not underwear in the general sense," he explained before bowing to graze her throat. "Only yours, Kim. It's so pretty."

"You seemed in an awfully big hurry to tear it off me just now," she playfully reminded him.

"Maybe I ought to put it on you again," he mused.

"Don't you dare."

As if there were any question that he would want her dressed at that moment. His mouth had already shifted downward to taste her breast, and her voice disintegrated into a sigh of pleasure as his lips tightened around her nipple and sucked. At last he released her hands, and she curled her fingers helplessly into his thick dark hair, holding his head to her. Her toes slid along the hard muscle of his calf and he groaned.

"You," he whispered hoarsely, nibbling a meandering path down to her stomach. "The hell with your underwear. I fantasize about you." His lips drifted lower, skirting the golden thatch of hair to browse along the skin of her inner thigh, then rising again and finding her.

A momentary panic seized Kimberly. Once more Andrew was introducing her to something new; once more her ignorance abashed her. And once more the sensations he aroused within her vanquished her panic and her bashfulness, leaving in their wake a maelstrom of thundering emotion.

She heard an unfamiliar sound tearing from her throat as he cupped his hands beneath her hips and deepened his kiss. A distant moan of passion, of glorious torment as her body slipped away from her, submitting fully to the force of his tender assault. She soared to a crest, swept up in a throbbing current, losing consciousness of who she was, where she was, everything she had ever known before.

When Andrew rose onto her she clung to his sturdy shoulders, struggling to regain her bearings. But before her mind could clarify itself, he was in her, filling her, giving her no respite from the storm. Her body moved with his, enveloping him, carrying him with her this time. They reached the peak together, surrendered, hurled themselves into ecstasy.

For a long time afterward, the only reality Kimberly was aware of was Andrew's motionless weight upon her, his chest crushing down on hers with his every ragged breath, his head sharing her pillow, his lips brushing her earlobe. Eventually he raised himself and peered down at her. His thumb glided across her cheek, capturing a tear. Until that moment Kimberly hadn't realized that she was crying.

"Are you all right?" he asked, his voice a husky rumble.

She nodded, then lifted away from the pillow to kiss him. Her arms snaked around his neck and pulled him back down to her. "You're wonderful, Andrew," she whispered.

"I think you deserve at least half the credit."

"No." Her arms tightened on him. "It's all your doing. I'm sure of that."

She couldn't see his face, but she could sense his pleasure. She hadn't spoken to boost his ego, but simply because what she'd said was the truth. He was wonderful.

Closing her eyes, she twirled her fingers through his hair and reminisced about the long, desolate stretch of days between their last meeting and now, when her only contact with him had been a brief, awkward telephone call during which Kimberly had informed him that the senator would be willing to meet with him during an upcoming trip to New York. She had arranged to have Helen, the senator's receptionist, call Andrew to finalize the appointment.

One cold, strained telephone call. And days of recriminations, days of anguish and anger. Why couldn't it have been this way, instead? Why couldn't they have stayed this close, sharing themselves this intimately even when four hundred miles stood between them? "I've missed you, too," she revealed, massaging the muscles at the base of his neck.

"It was nice of Milford to provide us with this little love nest halfway between D.C. and Massachusetts," he teased. "How did you talk him into it?"

She snorted. "I didn't talk him into reserving me a room with this in mind," she pointed out. "He's giving another series of speeches in Chicago tomorrow, and he brought some of us along with him so we could fly from New York together. It made more sense than flying back to Washington and taking off from there. Not that I'm complaining, as things worked out."

Andrew nipped her shoulder before pulling away and rolling onto his side. His gaze ran the length of her body and then lifted to her face. "Have you lost weight?" he asked.

She let out a startled laugh. The fact was, her appetite had been markedly smaller than normal lately, a direct result of her emotional turmoil. But the two pounds she'd lost were hardly noticeable. "How can you tell? You're not even wearing your eyeglasses."

He smiled enigmatically. "I memorized you last time. I memorized the way you looked, the way you felt...."

She was inordinately flattered by his words. "Should I gain the weight back?" she asked. "Do I look better this way or that way?"

"Both," he answered tactfully. "You weren't overweight before. You aren't underweight now. Either way you're perfect."

"How do you think I'd look if I were pregnant?" she asked whimsically.

Andrew was obviously startled. His eyebrows dipped in a frown of consternation as he scrutinized her. "What are you getting at?"

"What do you think I'm getting at?" she returned, shifting onto her side to face him and grinning at his bewildered expression. "Pregnant. With my stomach popped out and funny blue veins rippling up my legs." His stunned silence prompted her to continue. "Why do you look so shocked, Andrew? We talked about this when you were in Washington, remember? You assured me that I wasn't too old to have a baby."

He took his time digesting her words. Finally he spoke. "Um—can we back up a few steps here?" He inhaled steadily, then added, "I thought we were speaking hypothetically then."

"I wasn't," Kimberly maintained. "I want a child so badly, Andrew. I'm supposed to be among the first generation of Superwomen, having it all. And that's what I want."

"Kimberly." His tone was stern and somewhat tense. "Couldn't we have discussed this first?"

Suddenly the reason for his stricken appearance dawned on her. She burst into laughter. "Oh, Andrew, do you think—do you think I tricked you into something just now? Do you think I schemed to seduce you in order to get pregnant? Oh, my!"

Her thrilling giggles thawed him, and he settled against the pillow again. "Okay," he murmured sheepishly. "I admit I should have taken a little more responsibility here and made sure you were using something. When I'm with you, I guess I get carried away. I didn't think to ask."

"There's nothing to ask," Kimberly assured him. "If I'm pregnant now, there's a big drug company we'll have to sue." She leaned forward to kiss him. "I don't know if you heard, but Seth was in Washington last week with Laura's daughter. She's turned out so well, Andrew. She's kind of weird, but she's thirteen, after all, and you have to expect some weirdness at that age. But she's a terrific kid. I would have loved to spend some more time with her than I did. Laura's done a magnificent job raising her. All by herself, too. I'm envious."

"You could have a child by yourself," Andrew noted. "Isn't that all the rage among Superwomen these days?"

"Oh, I couldn't," Kimberly disagreed. "I'm not nearly as strong as Laura is. And don't forget, when she had Rita, she was living on a commune, with lots of adults for help and companionship and no full-time job outside the home. Besides—" she grinned mischievously "—can you imagine what my mother would say if I became pregnant out of wedlock? The poor woman still hasn't come to terms with the fact that I could have a strange man in my apartment at nine-thirty in the morning."

"Barefoot, too," Andrew recalled with a tenuous smile.

Kimberly sighed wistfully. "I've always been a closet square, Andrew. I'm afraid I'm just old-fashioned enough to think I ought to get married before I become a mother."

He brushed a wavy strand of hair back from her face, then let his hand drift to her shoulder and down her graceful arm to clasp her hand. "Is this a proposal?"

She tried to interpret his cryptic smile and the solemn amber radiance of his eyes. His question hadn't been asked in rancor or revulsion. She recognized that she could hardly ask Andrew to marry her when he wasn't even ready to admit that he loved her, but the fact that he wasn't running for his life at the mere idea heartened her immensely. "It's a thought," she said.

He slid his hand to the center of her back and pulled her closer to himself. His mouth met hers, and he kissed her profoundly. As if by instinct, her legs tangled with his and her arms drew him onto her again, and every thought burned away in the immediacy of her passion for Andrew.

THE WINDSHIELD WIPERS swept rhythmically across his vision, clicking in a counterpoint to the progressive rock music blaring from his radio. A four-hour drive through a downpour late at night wasn't Andrew's notion of a good time. But he didn't complain. It was a small price to pay for the evening he had spent with Kimberly.

He felt invigorated, almost hyperactive. Sex had a way of keying up his nervous system, fueling his soul. There had been times, after making love with Marjorie, when he had been tempted to abandon her and take a five-mile jog to unwind.

He didn't want to jog right now; driving would suffice. And he certainly didn't want to think about Marjorie. He wanted to think only of the breathtaking blond woman he had kissed goodbye less than thirty minutes ago, the alluring woman he had left standing in her pale blue bathrobe, pushing the room-service cart out into the hallway and then watching until Andrew disappeared into the elevator. He wanted to think only of Kimberly.

Yet as soon as a memory of Marjorie flitted across his mind, he couldn't fight off the inevitable wave of emotion that crashed over him. Tonight the wave carried not grief, as it often did, but guilt, the same guilt that had been plaguing him ever since the last time he had been with Kimberly. The same guilt and the same fear.

He had nothing to feel guilty about, he lectured himself. If Marjorie could speak to him from beyond the grave, she would probably tell him to go for it, to chase Kimberly and enjoy her and put the past behind him.

However, she would undoubtedly question Andrew's taste. *Her? You want a pretty little snippet like her? All that pale hair and those big kootchie-kootchie eyes? Well, whatever turns you on, lover....*

Guilt was supposed to have been one of those emotions that was trashed back in the late sixties. It had been reserved for the adults of an earlier time, people who had spent the best years of their lives polluting the environment and supporting the arms race. But not for young folks like Andrew, who were determined to live by their principles and who held fast to their inalienable right to pursue happiness—even if principles and happiness sometimes lay at cross-purposes.

He had no reason to feel guilty about wanting Kimberly. But the fear...the fear that he might lose her was harder to vanquish. He could pursue Kimberly and he could enjoy her, but could he really keep her? Could a four-eyed high-brow like him truly possess the love of a woman as ravishing as Kimberly? Regardless of her profession of love for him and her oblique introduction of the subject of marriage, Andrew couldn't shake off the doubt that gnawed at him.

He knew that she hadn't yet recovered completely from the heartache of her divorce. But in time she would. And when she did, hundreds of far more suitable men would be pounding on her door. Classically handsome, cultured, rich men. She could find among them one with good genes—not merely a bootlegger among his ancestors, but also twenty-twenty vision and nary a trace of gray hair—and she could mate with him and have herself the child she longed for, a child as beautiful and well-bred as she herself was.

Andrew wouldn't deny that a strong bond existed between Kimberly and him. He wouldn't deny that he was very close to falling in love with Kimberly—if he hadn't already fallen. And he couldn't stand the possibility of again losing someone he loved. Kimberly had told him to take a chance and he wanted to. But he was scared.

If only things were different, if only Kimberly weren't quite so irresistible, if only they lived closer to each other so they could take this thing one step at a time....

He cursed. "If only" was a habit he thought he had broken long ago. He had resorted to the phrase too many times after Marjorie had become sick. If only she hadn't had the miscarriage, if only they hadn't tried to conceive, if only he hadn't married her, if only he hadn't met her in the first place. If only he were an ostrich with his head in the sand.

It was pointless to torture oneself with "if onlys." What happened happened. Marjorie died. Andrew finished his Ph.D. and landed a position at Amherst. Kimberly entered his heart. What happened between Kimberly and him from here on in was still within his control.

What happened with his job, too. Protecting himself emotionally was one thing; protecting himself professionally was another.

What should he do about Senator Milford's request that he testify before the Intelligence Committee? Kimberly had probably been correct when she'd assured him that the hearing would be closed and that Andrew's face wouldn't be splashed across every television screen in the country simply because he had gone public with the information that a lunatic in the C.I.A. wanted to destroy the economy of El Salvador. But still, the entire nation didn't have to know about it to put an end to Andrew's career at Amherst. Only Bob McIntyre and his cronies in the economics department had to know. If Andrew testified, there was no way he could keep it a secret from them.

Senator Milford had seemed like a good man. He had quickly put Andrew at ease with his relaxed demeanor. Seated cross-legged on his bed, he had loosened Andrew up by chatting at length about his dealings with the C.I.A., sounding not like a politician polishing his image but like a human being with a genuine concern for the way the government functioned.

If Kimberly's mother had met Milford, she wouldn't have considered him a gentleman. Not only because of his liberal bent, but because he hadn't been wearing shoes.

Damn. Andrew probably should have kept his mouth shut about the whole L.A.R.C. affair. He probably should have handed his notes to John Wilding, published a few papers and put the entire episode behind him.

"Coward," he muttered aloud, succumbing to a surge of self-contempt. At a younger age he wouldn't have been so careful. He would have met Wilding head-on, with fists raised. He would have issued a score of papers, not on the agronomy of El Salvador but on the dangerous excesses of a certain C.I.A. operative. If he lost his job in the process, he would have issued a score more papers on Amherst's capitulation to government pressure. He would have moved into a cheap efficiency apartment somewhere and survived on canned sardines—he'd been a graduate student, he knew how to live on next to nothing. Maybe he would have founded another underground newspaper.

Not that such a venture would succeed as it had fifteen years ago. College students nowadays dreamed of going to business school, not of overthrowing the power structure and shaping a more equitable society. Julianne had known full well what she was doing when she turned *The Dream* into a slick-format monthly magazine featuring articles with mass appeal.

The rain began to let up. "Here's a golden oldie," the late-night deejay babbled on the car radio, introducing the Rolling Stones classic, "You Can't Always Get What You Want."

"If that's a golden oldie, so am I," Andrew mused. He recalled the morning, several years back, when he had discovered a few strands of silver infiltrating his beard and had been forced to contend with the reality that he was aging. Three days later—three silver beard hairs later—he'd shaved his chin smooth. Without the beard he looked noticeably younger, but he still carried within himself the knowledge that he was growing old, that his body was giving him away. In time the hair on his head had begun to turn silver, as well. By now he ought to be used to the fact that he wasn't a kid anymore.

How odd that the Rolling Stones song, which had been written the year Andrew graduated from high school, was so much more pertinent today. In his youth he had been convinced that one *could* always get what one wanted. He had long since been disabused of that idea.

By the time he arrived at his home around one o'clock, the rain had ended. The night air was heavy with the fragrance of spring and wetness as he parked behind the massive brick house and strolled around to the front door to let himself inside. Before unlocking the door, he emptied his mailbox, one of four fastened to the wall alongside the door.

A gas bill, an advertisement for computer software and a stiff cream-colored envelope with his address handwritten across it. He refrained from opening it until he was inside his apartment and the door was bolted behind him. Then he dropped his briefcase beside his desk and slid his finger beneath the envelope flap.

Laura Brodie
and
Seth Stone
cordially invite you to share
in the celebration of their marriage
Sunday, the Seventeenth of May
Nineteen Hundred and Eighty-Seven
Two O'Clock p.m.
at the home of Arlene Brodie
King of Prussia, Pennsylvania

Enclosed in the fold of the invitation was an R.S.V.P. card and a map and printed directions to Arlene Brodie's house.

Andrew reread the invitation and smiled. Laura and Stoned. They were really going to do it.

He carried the invitation to the sofa and sank onto it. Marriage. He wondered whether Laura and Seth comprehended the amount of courage one needed to get married, to survive a marriage. When Andrew had married Marjorie, he had had no idea whatsoever. He'd had no inkling of how his commitment to Marjorie would sap his reserves of strength, of how enormous a price love could exact. With good fortune, neither Laura nor Seth would ever have to pay that price, but still...anything was possible. When love was involved, when one was committed, one couldn't conveniently walk away from the hardships.

Setting the invitation on the cushion next to him, he reached over the arm of the sofa to the neat stack of magazines on the end table and located the April edition of *Dream*. Julianne had dedicated her "Editor's Page" to the magazine's fifteenth anniversary. In her essay, she had written a history of the magazine's founding and evolution and a succinct description of what each of the founders was doing currently. The piece was illustrated with an amusing photograph of the six of them as undergraduates, clowning around on the Columbia campus in front of the building that had contained *The Dream*'s office.

Andrew had noticed the photo on display during the reunion Julianne had orchestrated in honor of the magazine's fifteenth birthday. He had laughed at it then, joking with the others about how vastly they'd all changed. Fifteen years of barbers and beauticians had altered them at least as much fifteen years of "real life."

He studied the photograph on the magazine page intently. Maybe they hadn't changed that much. Seth, although shorn of his wild sand-colored mane, was still the sort to wear bizarre T-shirts and wave his hand in a V-for-Victory salute, as he was doing in the picture. Laura appeared to have added a few pounds to her scrawny frame since college—a definite improvement, Andrew allowed—but she seemed at peace with herself in the photograph, her

Mona Lisa smile hinting at inner contentment. They made a good couple, he decided. They would be happy together.

His gaze shifted to Kimberly. In the photo she had waist-length hair that was pinned back from her face with barrettes. She looked like a professional model—too short, perhaps, but no less beautiful. Her lips curved in a radiant smile. Because her hands were hidden, Kimberly's engagement ring was invisible. But Andrew knew she had been wearing it that day. She had always worn it. He doubted that she had recognized at that time what her marriage would do to her, what misery she would experience because of it. Like Andrew, she had entered into it in ignorance.

He continued to stare at her face, comparing it to that of the mature woman he had left in New York City. She was just as lovely today, just as radiant, just as hopeful—hoping for a child now, if not for true love.

His forehead ached from his rigid expression, and he folded the magazine shut. Then he felt his brow and the bridge of his nose relax. He had been squinting at her, he realized.

He wanted Kimberly, wanted her immeasurably. If he were careless, if he let himself, he would undoubtedly grow to need her. But that wouldn't have to happen if he protected himself.

He would never stop wanting her. But he could keep himself from needing her.

Mick Jagger knew what he was talking about. You couldn't always get what you wanted, but if you tried sometimes... if you tried very hard, sometimes, if luck was with you, you just might get what you needed.

"ANY QUESTIONS?"

The hour was nearly up, and he scanned the class of attentive, bright-faced youngsters, waiting. He had just delivered one of his favorite lectures, concerning the repercussions of colonization on the impoverished nations of the Caribbean Basin. As he had outlined it, the stranglehold the Duvaliers, *père* and *fils*, had maintained on the downtrodden population of Haiti, rendering it the poorest nation in the hemisphere, wouldn't have been possible if the country hadn't been browbeaten by centuries of economic exploitation by Western powers.

A hand shot up and he smiled. "Duff?"

The young man grinned sheepishly. "I was wondering if you could talk a little about the final exam, Professor Collins," he requested.

"The final exam?" Andrew exclaimed, closing his folder of notes. "That's over a month away."

"I know," Duff conceded. "But, well, could you at least tell us what form it's going to take? What material is going to be on it? How heavily is it going to count in our final grades? I'm sure I'm not the only person here who wants to know." This assertion was greeted by a great deal of head bobbing from his classmates. Even Chip Wilton, who was seated in the front row, nodded vigorously.

Andrew groaned inwardly. His students were far too obsessed with grades. They were intelligent, they worked hard, but Andrew rarely sensed that their primary motive was the simple lust for knowledge.

In his own day grades hadn't mattered to him and his friends nearly as much. Of course, he himself had never had to worry about his grades; he could have coasted through college without exerting himself and managed to graduate with a respectable record. That he had exerted himself had resulted in his election to Phi Beta Kappa and the inclusion of summa cum laude on his diploma, but such honors hadn't been paramount in his decision to make the most of his college years. He had wanted to know things, to gather information, to deepen his perspective. He had wanted to leave Columbia a wiser man than he had been when he'd entered. He had known he was about to be thrust into a harsh world, and he had wanted to confront it armed with every intellectual weapon at his command.

To his current students the most important weapon was a high grade-point average. Such a weapon would unlock the doors to professional schools, to corporate offices. Heaven forbid that they should bother to learn anything that wasn't necessary for making a fat income once they left the ivory tower.

"I'm not going to discuss the final," he said resolutely. "It's much too premature."

"But you know what's going to be on it," Duff persisted.

Andrew chuckled sardonically. "Of course I do. I'm the teacher, remember?"

A few of the students joined his laughter. As the minute hand on the large wall clock swept across the twelve, they gathered their notebooks and rose from their desks, chattering softly among themselves. Andrew slipped his folder into his briefcase and watched his pupils file out of the classroom. When the last pair had departed, he switched off the light and exited.

He spotted Bob McIntyre at the end of the hallway, approaching. "Andy!" the wiry, energetic man shouted, increasing his pace. "Wait up."

Andrew complied. As the older man neared him, Andrew concentrated his vision on Bob's curly salt-and-pepper hair to avoid having to meet his colleague's gaze directly.

"How about lunch?" Bob asked. "I feel as though we haven't talked in ages."

"Well..." Andrew made a big show of checking his wristwatch, even though he knew it was noon. "I've got a few things to take care of—"

"Take care of them later," Bob insisted cheerfully. "It's time to take care of your stomach now."

Andrew relented with a sigh. He couldn't keep avoiding Bob indefinitely. Managing a faint smile, he accompanied Bob down the corridor to the stairs.

"If I didn't know better," Bob babbled, "I'd suspect that you've been trying to keep your distance from me lately. What's got you so tied up these days?"

"Things," Andrew answered with a vague shrug.

"Research things?" Bob pressed him. "Or something better? You know, my wife still wants to introduce you to that divorced cousin of hers. You ought to thank me for sparing you from a fate worse than death."

"Many thanks," Andrew obliged. "I don't need any matchmakers in my life at the moment."

"Glad to hear that." Bob's eyes coursed over Andrew. "Stay a bachelor much longer, pal, and we're going to be seeing you walking around in mismatched socks."

"I've always been very precise about my socks, Bob," Andrew claimed, figuring that he ought to maintain a spritely attitude with the man whose company he had come to dread.

"Let's eat off campus," Bob suggested as they emerged from the building into the noontime sun. "I've had enough of dealing with these jackass undergraduates for a while."

"So have I," Andrew concurred. "They're already pestering me about the final exam. Is it just my imagination, Bob, or do they get worse every year?"

"They get worse every year," Bob confirmed, ambling across the grass with Andrew. "If the seventies was the 'Me Decade,' the eighties must be the 'Brownnose Decade.'"

They headed for a chic eatery a few blocks north of the campus. Andrew liked the place; its glass walls lent it the atmosphere of a greenhouse and its food was fresh and reasonably priced. Although the restaurant was crowded, he and Bob didn't have to wait long for a table.

Once they had ordered, Bob embarked on a long-winded discourse about a reputed shake-up in the dean's office. Andrew did his best to remain calm. He used to enjoy listening to Bob explain the ins and outs of the college's bureaucracy. If they could spend their entire meal conversing on such safe topics, Andrew would be supremely pleased.

However, the arrival of their sandwiches dashed that hope. "So," Bob said before treating his hamburger to a blizzard of salt. "How's that El Salvador project coming along? When am I going to see your byline in some journals?"

Andrew squeezed a lemon wedge into his iced tea and stirred the drink, playing for time. He thought about his students, that meek, frightened herd dedicated to the proposition that security was all that counted in life. He thought, too, about Donna, whose preparations for her move to Fullerton were in high gear and who rambled constantly about how she was going to finish her dissertation, get tenure and live happily ever after in California. He thought, as well, about Seth and Laura, about their bravery in following their hearts, about how different they were from his students and Donna.

And he thought about Kimberly. He thought about the crystalline light of her eyes as she had gazed across a table at him in the Essex House's restaurant and said, "Take a chance."

She had been talking about something else at the time. She had issued her challenge in the context of their relationship. And Andrew still hadn't decided whether to accept the challenge.

But there was a limit to how many risks Andrew could shrink from. His soul was one thing. His integrity was quite another.

"When you put me in touch with the Latin-American Research Council," he began, resolving to confront Bob, "what did you know about it?"

Bob smiled quizzically. "What do you mean?"

"I mean," Andrew said emphatically, "did you know it was a proprietary of the C.I.A.?"

Bob hesitated before biting into his hamburger. Then he took a robust mouthful, chewed, swallowed and shrugged. "So?"

"So? Why didn't you tell me you were hooking me up with a C.I.A. agent?"

"I didn't know," Bob declared. "I may have had my suspicions, Andy, but who am I to lead you by the nose? You've got a good head on your shoulders. I figured you could handle whatever you had to handle."

"I *can* handle it," Andrew stressed. "But it would have been nice of you to share your suspicions with me. I might not have participated in anything with Wilding if I'd known."

"Wilding's a reasonable man," said Bob. "I've worked with him before."

"You have?" Andrew gaped at Bob. He hoped he didn't look as accusing as he felt.

Bob ate some more, then shrugged again. "A few years ago I worked up some projections he wanted on Syria's oil exports."

Andrew swore beneath his breath. The information Whitney had accumulated on John Wilding's activities in the Middle East—his plan to undermine Syria single-handedly—reverberated inside Andrew's skull. "Honest to God, Bob! Didn't it occur to you that if Wilding was acting within the limits of the law, he could have found out everything he wanted to know about Syria's future oil exports through legitimate C.I.A. channels? He didn't have to hire an academic to make projections for him. The C.I.A. has more than enough analysts on the payroll."

Bob appeared unperturbed. "I've already told you, I don't know whether the man's affiliated with the C.I.A. I didn't know then and I don't know now."

"I do know," Andrew muttered. "I went to the effort of investigating Wilding."

"Well." Bob dabbed his lips with his napkin, then leaned back in his chair and took a languorous sip of his lemonade. "All right, Andy. You went to the effort of investigating. I'm sure that if the C.I.A. actually told you Wilding was working for them, that's what they want you to believe."

"If he isn't working for the C.I.A., then it's even worse," Andrew argued. "The guy's a one-man army out to overthrow foreign governments."

Bob scoffed. "You've got a vivid imagination. Maybe you've been reading too many spy thrillers."

"I haven't read a spy thriller since high school," Andrew informed him dryly. "And my imagination isn't working overtime. Wilding himself told me he was working for the C.I.A."

"For what that's worth," Bob grunted.

"I didn't know whether to take him at face value, either," Andrew admitted. "So I dug deeper. I've got a contact in Congress, Bob. An aide to a senator on the Intelligence Committee. They found out that under the cover of the C.I.A., Wilding is trying to wreak economic havoc in El Salvador. That's what he tried to do with oil exports in

Syria, and now he's trying to do it again. It isn't right, Bob. You know it and I know it. This thing isn't right."

For the first time since the subject arose, Bob looked disturbed. He sat up straighter and eyed Andrew with piercing curiosity. "An aide to a senator?"

"I've been asked to testify before the committee," Andrew announced.

"Testify? About this?" Bob fidgeted with his straw wrapper, rolled it into a ball and tossed it into the ashtray. "What the hell is there to testify about?"

"Whether the C.I.A. condones this sort of surreptitious intervention in other countries."

"Now, Andrew," Bob said, abruptly conciliatory. "What's the good of testifying? Do you realize the damage you could do?"

"To whom?" Andrew shot back. "To me? Or to you?"

"To Amherst," Bob explained. "The school has a reputation to protect, for crying out loud. Do you think we're the only two college teachers who have ever done research for the C.I.A.? More faculty members at more universities than you can count are involved in this sort of activity. It isn't a sin. It does bring about negative publicity, however. The students get all riled up. The administration finds itself with egg on its face. And what for? Grandstanding about the situation doesn't help anybody."

Andrew contemplated Bob's argument. It probably wouldn't be such a terrible thing to rile up Amherst's student body, he mused. They were too complacent; a rowdy uprising would probably do his students a world of good.

On the other hand, would testifying before Senator Milford's committee change anything? Perhaps the C.I.A. would fire Wilding, but then what? Would they stop recruiting academic professionals for research? Would they stop disguising their activities behind proprietaries? Of course not.

As if he could sense that Andrew was wavering, Bob pressed his case. "Look, Andy. What exactly do you want? The same thing I want. To work at Amherst, a school where we're left alone, where we're given a great deal of freedom to teach the way we see fit, and the chance to work with gifted young minds. We sure as hell aren't here for the money—you don't need me to tell you that our salaries are barely adequate. We're here for the intellectual stimulation and the freedom. So what's to be gained by humiliating the college?

"If Wilding is as dangerous as you seem to think he is, then it's the C.I.A's responsibility to take care of him, not yours, not mine. And, for that matter, not the Senate's. I'll grant that I didn't inquire as deeply as you did about Wilding's intentions. But so what? I gave him solid data. I earned the stipend he gave me. And I've got a clear conscience. You should have a clear conscience, too." He paused to catch his breath, then smiled, evidently certain that he had persuaded Andrew to see things his way. For added effect, he queried, "If a man buys a screwdriver and uses it to break into someone's house, is it the hardware store's fault?"

Andrew pondered Bob's analogy. "Is it the gun store owner's fault that people buy pistols from him and use them to shoot other people? Is the brokerage house implicated when one of its executives is charged with insider trading? Albert Einstein had enough dignity to be horrified when the results of his genius helped others to build an atom bomb."

"I hardly think you and I are in the same class as Albert Einstein," Bob remarked.

Andrew shook his head. "You know what they used to say when I was in school? 'If you aren't part of the solution, you're part of the problem.'"

"They also used to say, 'Never trust anybody over thirty.' You're over thirty, Andrew. It's time to grow up."

Andrew didn't need Bob to remind him of his age. But perhaps he did need Bob to remind him of what was at stake. If Andrew testified before the Intelligence Committee, Bob wouldn't be the only one embarrassed. The news that two of Amherst's esteemed faculty members had, however guilelessly, collaborated with the C.I.A. would tarnish the college in the public eye. If that happened, Andrew's tenure decision would no longer rest with Bob McIntyre or with the economics department. The highest levels of the school's administration would want a troublemaker like Andrew out.

"Don't do anything precipitous," Bob counseled Andrew. "Take your time. Think things through. I'm sorry I put you in touch with Wilding. I thought you'd benefit from the association. I thought you'd be flattered."

"I was," Andrew acknowledged.

"Then think about it," Bob concluded before signaling the waitress for the check.

Andrew would indeed think about it. After parting ways with Bob and returning to his office cubicle, he slumped in his desk chair, removed his eyeglasses and rested his head in his hands. Bob had made some valid points. To spill the beans before a Senate committee might help to purge Andrew of his resentment and anger, but would it really change anything? Senator Milford already had enough information to demand that the C.I.A. get rid of Wilding and keep a tighter rein on its other operatives. It wasn't necessary for Andrew to beat his breast in public.

He'd done enough. He owed it to Amherst to keep quiet from here on in. Bob's final words implied everything Andrew needed to know about what would happen to him if he didn't keep quiet.

There was a limit to how many chances a person could take. Andrew couldn't risk everything—his career *and* his emotions—at the same time. Opening his heart to love again was dangerous enough. He didn't have to imperil himself professionally, too.

He wanted his job. He wanted peace in his life, and security and continuity. The days when a person could score points toward salvation by lambasting the C.I.A. were long gone.

It was definitely time to grow up.

Chapter Ten

Kimberly's rented Buick swallowed up the miles of the Massachusetts Turnpike. Andrew had told her that the drive from Boston would take her about two hours, but she didn't mind. The weather was mild, the trees lining the highway lush with foliage. The cartoonish Pilgrim's hat that appeared on all the road signs, symbolizing the turnpike, appealed to her.

She and Andrew had spoken three times in the week since she'd seen him in New York—once when she'd called to say hello from Chicago, once when he had called her after she had returned to Washington and then again the next day, when she had found out that she was going to be traveling to Massachusetts. "The senator's got to be in Boston Thursday to confer with the head of the American Society for the Prevention of Cruelty to Animals over some pending legislation," she had informed Andrew excitedly, "and I've talked him into letting me hitch a ride. Exactly how far is Amherst from Boston?"

"Too far for me to meet you there," Andrew had answered. "I've got classes to teach."

"I was thinking, maybe I could stick around at the A.S.P.C.A. long enough for the senator to think I've earned my keep, and then bolt and visit you. I'd love to see Amherst. I'd love to see you, too."

"I'd love to have you," he swore. "If you don't mind driving all that way, and sitting through my afternoon class..."

"I think I could stomach it," she joked. "Expect me around two-thirty."

Reviewing their conversation in her mind as she drove, she decided that Andrew had sounded delighted by her impulsive plan. She comprehended that he still wasn't ready to make a commitment to her. But as long as he wasn't backing off from her, she was hardly about to complain.

She had on a pair of crisp white slacks and a yellow knit jersey; a dress and a pair of shorts were packed in the overnight bag she had stowed on the back seat. She wished she could have made a long weekend of her visit and returned to Washington on Sunday. But a surprise party had been scheduled for the following night in honor of one of the senator's long-time aides, who was retiring. Kimberly couldn't miss it.

Maybe she could talk Andrew into returning to Washington with her. Falling in love with someone who lived so far away from her was inconvenient, to say the least.

The traffic jam caused by a jackknifed truck just outside Boston slowed her pace, as did a bottleneck in Worcester. It took her close to fifteen minutes to find a parking space near the college—Andrew had warned her that her car would be ticketed if she parked in one of the campus lots without an appropriate sticker. Yet even as she raced across the campus to his office, she had a chance to glimpse the lovely scenery. Amherst was as different from Columbia as the bucolic Berkshires were from gritty Harlem. The clean, well-maintained grounds, with their towering trees, manicured lawns and stately buildings, could definitely serve as the setting for an Andy Hardy movie.

She was panting slightly when she reached his office. "Am I late for your class?" she asked as he swung open the door in response to her knock.

He smiled, a warm, dimpled smile that would have made her breathless even if she hadn't just run half a mile at breakneck speed. "I wish all my students were as concerned about getting to my classes on time," he remarked, drawing her into his arms and kicking the door shut behind them.

His kiss was slow and sweet. She sighed happily, then pulled back to view him. "Why don't your eyeglasses ever steam up when we kiss?" she asked.

"Believe me, it's not because you aren't a very steamy lady," he complimented her in a hoarse voice. Then he cleared his throat and turned toward his desk. "However, since you mentioned it, we are running late. Did you bring any paper with you to take notes on? I intend to quiz you after class."

She laughed, watching as he slipped a folder into his briefcase. "I shall inscribe your every word on my heart," she promised melodramatically. As soon as he joined her at the door, she smoothed out the collar of his oxford shirt. "It won't do, Professor, to arrive at class looking like you've just checked out of an orgy."

"I'm always rumpled," Andrew told her. "It's the official professorial style. My students wouldn't take me seriously if my shirts were ironed." He clearly enjoyed the sensation of her cool, slender fingers against his neck, but after a moment he pulled her hands from him and opened the door. "We'd better get moving—the class meets in another building."

Again Kimberly found herself dashing across the campus. Andrew seemed to have forgotten that she was a good eight inches shorter than he. She had a difficult time keeping up with his brisk, loose-limbed gait.

The classroom he led her to was already nearly filled with attentive young men and women when Kimberly and Andrew entered. He nodded her toward a vacant desk at the rear of the room, and she felt the curious stares of his students following her as she took her seat. In answer to their unspoken questions he announced, "A friend of mine is visiting today. Kimberly Belmont is the head speech writer for Senator Howard Milford. If you'd like, I'll try to end a little early so you can ask her some questions."

Kimberly's jaw dropped in astonishment. How dare Andrew put her on the spot like that? Her chagrin gradually dissipated as she took note of the excitement his announcement had generated. Of course college students would love to question a senator's speech writer. In their place she'd be agog, too, just as eager as they were to learn what life was like in the corridors of government power.

She settled back in her seat, feeling her cheeks cool as the students directed their attention back to Andrew. He opened his folder of notes and proceeded to lecture on sugar price supports and their effect on the economies of foreign countries. She would never have imagined that so much could be said on such an esoteric subject. More than that, she never would have imagined that she would be so interested in it. Perhaps it was just Andrew's riveting presentation that made the subject seem fascinating. Losing track of time, she absorbed his talk, accumulating all sorts of intriguing information about the international value of empty calories.

When Andrew concluded his lecture, his eyes met hers and he grinned. Then he addressed his students. "All right, boys and girls. I think I'll turn the class over to Ms. Belmont now, and she can fill you in on the inside story of how sugar tariffs are enacted."

Kimberly's cheeks colored slightly as en masse the students twisted in their seats to gawk at her. Andrew beckoned her to the front of the room, and forcing a modest smile, she inhaled and strolled forward to stand at the chipped wooden lectern. He moved out of her way, taking his place by the window and lounging against the sill.

"I'm afraid I'm more used to writing speeches than giving them," she began apologetically. "And as far as sugar tariffs go, all I can tell you is that they're generally introduced into law by senators from the South, not by my boss."

A hand shot up, and before she could acknowledge the student, he spoke. "How did you get your job?" he asked.

Kimberly ought to have expected such a question, not only because her job conveyed a certain glamour but because students of the eighties were allegedly obsessed with the mechanics of obtaining equally glamorous jobs once they finished their schooling. "I began my career with a public relations firm in Washington," she related. "A few years ago, Senator Milford received an information packet I had prepared on behalf of a client. The senator was impressed with what I'd put together, and he offered me a position as a speech writer on his staff."

"What about connections?" another student called out. "Don't you have to know the right people if you want to wind up in a prestigious job like yours?"

Kimberly shook her head. "There's something to be said for networking, but that's not the way I got my job."

"She got it through talent and hard work," Andrew piped up on her behalf. "I know all of you have read every best-selling book ever written on the subject of how to become president of the corporate world in five years or less, and those books always exhort you to use your connections and grease palms. But believe it or not, a lot of people wind up in high places through something as basic as ability."

"Thank you, Andrew," she said, tossing him a smile. Obviously Andrew had finally come to terms with the fact that Kimberly was not a mental midget.

"Do you ever get a chance to influence legislation?" a young woman seated at the back of the room called out.

Kimberly contemplated the question. "I can't say that I have a direct influence," she admitted. "But sometimes I'm lucky enough to introduce new issues to the senator," she added, thinking about the Intelligence Committee hearings the senator planned to set up as a result of Andrew's experience with the C.I.A. "You've got to remember, our form of government doesn't follow straight lines and clear paths. It's hard to say specifically where one person's influence ends and the next person's begins."

"Forgive me for being forward," a fellow seated a few feet from her spoke up, "but you're an attractive woman. Isn't it true that a lot of congressmen set up little love nests for their pretty female employees?"

Kimberly fought valiantly against the surge of anger that threatened her in response to the boy's offensive question. Stifling the impulse to tell the leering young fellow that she would never forgive him, she said calmly, "I don't suppose you'd have asked that if I worked for a woman senator. Frankly, I don't believe it deserves an answer."

The class fell silent for a moment; apparently nobody wanted to risk raising her hackles again. Finally, a young woman broke the stillness. "First, Ms. Belmont, I'd like to thank you for putting creeps like him in his place." This comment brought cheers from the other women in the room, as well as a few of the men. "I'm a theater major," the student went on, "and I'm curious—as a speech writer, would it help to have experience in the theater?"

Kimberly laughed. "I reckon it wouldn't hurt. Most politicians are indeed actors, aren't they?"

Her audience broke into laughter again, evidence that the mood of the class was once again upbeat, and Andrew took that as his cue to relieve Kimberly. He crossed to the lectern and announced to the students, "We've run out of time for today, gang, so let Ms. Belmont off the hook. Remember to read the assigned articles on G.A.T.T. for next Tuesday. They're on reserve at the library." With that he dropped his folder into his briefcase, a sign that the class was dismissed.

"Why did you do that to me?" Kimberly muttered beneath her breath once the last few students had departed from the room.

"Do what?" Andrew asked ingenuously.

"Put me on display that way."

"I knew the kids would be interested in what you do," he justified himself.

"Yes, but you could have given me some warning," she reproached him. "You didn't have to spring it on me by surprise."

Andrew took his time clasping his briefcase shut. Then he turned fully to her. "You're right, Kim. I could have warned you," he granted. "But... I guess I was curious to see how well you would think on your feet."

"Damn it, Andrew!" She suffered another surge of anger, not the standard annoyance she had felt earlier at his student's patently sexist insinuation, but a deep, personal anger at the realization that Andrew had been testing her. "I don't have to prove anything to you. It ought to be obvious by now that if I couldn't think on my feet I wouldn't be where I was today."

"I know," he murmured contritely. "You're right, Kim. I just..." He cupped his hands about her upper arms and gave her a crooked smile. "I'm still a bit amazed by you. I'm still coming to terms with the fact that I was very mistaken about you fifteen years ago. It's such a kick for me to see how spectacular you can be in situations like this." He kissed her forehead tenderly. "I'm sorry."

As irked as she was, his candor touched her. She slung her arms around his waist and gave him a hug. "It's about time you started getting used to who I am," she complained.

"I know, Kim." He slid his hands to the nape of her neck, and his lips grazed her hair. "I love you."

Her heart froze in her chest for a moment, and the air seemed to grow still around her. Had he actually said what she thought? Had he really spoken those three magic words? She tried to fight off her disbelief, tried to bring her crazed nerves under control. "What?" she mumbled into his chest.

"You heard me."

"You mean, you love me because I held my own at that impromptu news conference you just threw for me?" she pressed him.

He drew back to gaze at her. "I mean that I love you because you can hold your own with me. When I'm a jerk you call me on it. You're honest, and true to yourself." He touched his lips to hers. "That's why." He kissed her lips once more, then grinned. "At the risk of igniting your wrath again, I kind of like that kid's idea about love nests. If you're interested, I've got a tiny apartment about a mile from here in dire need of some feathering."

"Andrew Collins, you're very fresh," she scolded him, but she was too thrilled to mean it.

He slipped his hand around hers and escorted her from the room. "I made dinner reservations for seven o'clock. That gives us plenty of time."

As if dinner mattered, Kimberly mused silently. The last time she'd been with Andrew, they'd made do without a fancy meal at a restaurant. And this time would be better. This time Andrew was finally ready to acknowledge that he loved her.

As they left the building, he informed her that he had left his car home and walked to campus that morning, which meant that they could drive to his house together. Trying to remember where she had parked her car, she made a wrong turn at the town green, then backtracked and located the rented Buick on the next block. A strange blend of anxiety and euphoria rendered her too jittery to drive, and she handed Andrew the keys and asked that he drive them home.

The broad brick colonial he took her to was set back from the street and surrounded by a lush, recently mowed lawn, with a blossoming apple tree and a thriving red maple standing on either side of the front walk. Andrew steered up a paved driveway that led to a small lot at the rear of the house. He lifted Kimberly's suitcase from the back seat, took her hand again and ushered her around the building to the front door. Not bothering to check his mailbox, he escorted her inside.

He had already mentioned that his apartment was small, and he hadn't exaggerated. She didn't mind its size, though. She liked Andrew's neatness, the array of books lining every inch of shelf space, the orderliness of his desk and the homely warmth of his other furnishings. Andrew was a man who didn't exert himself to make his living quarters decorator perfect, and Kimberly considered that a refreshing change from the rigidly impeccable taste of the people she had grown up with, people who were far too compulsive about appearances.

She followed Andrew down a short hall, which contained a closet and a bathroom, and into his bedroom. It, too, was clean and orderly, the furniture not distinctive but sturdy and serviceable. The open window admitted a cool breeze into the room, causing the curtains to flutter.

"I love you, too," Kimberly whispered, curling her arms around him and holding him close.

"I know. You've already told me."

"Does it bother you to hear it more than once?"

"Not from you," Andrew assured her. "Please feel free to say it as often as you wish."

If she had wanted to say it again, she wouldn't have been able to. Andrew's penetrating kiss swamped her, rendering her certain that she would be hard-pressed to utter a coherent sentence, let alone the most important sentence in the world. So she told him without words that she loved him, gripping his broad back and parrying the daring lunges of his tongue. By the time he broke from her, she doubted that he needed any further proof, verbal or otherwise, of her love for him.

It took them little time to undress and fall together onto the bed. Andrew's mouth conquered hers with another devastating kiss. Then he let his head drop to the pillow to catch his breath, as his fingers spun lazily through her hair. The pause gave her an opportunity to recover, to savor all over again what he had told her. "I don't mind hearing it more than once, either," she prompted him.

He grinned. "I love you," he obeyed. Then his smile grew wistful. "I'm sure you've noticed by now, Kim, but I'm not a very romantic person."

"What's your idea of a romantic person?" she asked, raising herself up on her elbow and peering down at him.

The movement of the drapes created faint, dancing shadows across the dynamic features of his face—his brow and jaw, his sharp nose, his surprisingly sensuous mouth, his eyes even clearer and more penetrating without his eyeglasses than with them. He shrugged. "Someone who doesn't have difficulty saying 'I love you,'" he replied. "Someone who sends you long-stemmed roses and gives you perfume on your birthday—"

"Flowers and perfume are meaningless," she assured him. "I was married to one of those romantic types, Andrew, and I don't recommend it."

"What's your idea of a romantic person, then?"

She kissed his jutting chin, then settled on the mattress beside him. "A man who waits until he's absolutely sure before he uses the word 'love.' A man wise enough to make certain he knows his own mind before he shoots off his mouth."

Andrew mulled over her definition, and his smile faded. "There can be such a thing as too much wisdom," he muttered, a subtle self-criticism. "The last time I saw you, Kim... I wanted to tell you how I felt. But then, after I left..." He faltered, focusing on a memory. "I felt so guilty."

"Guilty?" she exclaimed, startled by his admission. "Why?" At his prolonged silence, she shored up her courage and asked, "Because of your wife?"

"Partly."

Kimberly wasn't terribly surprised by that. Given how much he had loved his wife, it must have been hard for him to admit that he could find himself in love with another woman. Irrational though it was, he might have felt disloyal to his wife, his first love. "I wish you had told me," she murmured. "We should talk about these things, Andrew. We shouldn't keep them from each other."

"I wasn't deliberately keeping anything from you, Kim," he swore. "It wasn't thoughts of Marjorie that had me so confused. It was more..." He reflected, collecting his thoughts, and then sighed. "It was more that I felt as if I had no right to want you as much as I do."

She recalled the astonishment she had experienced every other time she and Andrew had talked this freely with each other. By now, especially since he had told her he loved her, she ought to have grown accustomed to his willingness to open up to her. Yet his statement still came as a revelation. "Love has nothing to do with rights, Andrew."

"Now that's a romantic thought," he teased her. Then he grew solemn again. "I do want you, Kim. Very much. And I don't want to lose you."

"You won't," she swore before bending to kiss him.

He pulled her onto himself, his hands skimming down her back and his legs sandwiching hers. His arousal was as immediate as hers, as intense and consuming. She rocked her body against his, fully aware of the blissful torment she was causing him with her motions. His helpless moan as her teeth nipped his lower lip only fed her desire even more.

His fingers rounded her bottom to stroke her thighs. They parted and he arched up into her. His forceful thrusts sent shock waves through her flesh, inundating her with glorious sensations, rapidly driving her and him both to their moment of consummate satisfaction.

Whenever they had made love in the past, Andrew had always proceeded much more slowly, with great tenderness and patience. But this time, such preliminaries had been all but superfluous. This time, he had given Kimberly more than his lovemaking; he had given her his love. The single word, spoken in his rumbling baritone, was like an aphrodisiac. She didn't need anything else.

"You're incredible," he groaned, refusing to let her slide from him as his body softened beneath her. His arms bound her to him, holding her comfortably in place. "The most incredible woman in the world."

"Why, you romantic old fool," she joked before nuzzling the warm crook of his neck.

"I'm serious," he insisted. "You do things to me..."

"Andrew." She lifted her face from his shoulder and met his shimmering gaze. "I think—I think you ought to know something about me."

Her solemn expression seemed to unnerve him. He gave her an inquisitive scrutiny, then sank deeper into the pillow and smiled. "Forget about suing the big drug company," he declared. "Maybe it's a blessing in disguise."

There was nothing facetious in his tone. Nor was there a hint of dismay as he gave voice to his erroneous deduction that Kimberly was pregnant. One more sign that he loved her, she thought with a contented sigh. "No, it's nothing like that," she reassured him, gingerly pushing a dark lock of hair back from his brow. "It's—I'm kind of embarrassed to admit it, Andrew, but—well, I'm not very experienced."

"Experienced at what?"

"At *this*, you fool," she said, punching his shoulder playfully. "At sex."

He pondered her confession, then grinned wickedly. "Well, sweetheart, you've sure got good instincts."

She leaned back to punch him again, but he trapped her wrist in his strong fingers and pulled her down to him again. "Don't make fun of me, Andrew," she said. "I thought you ought to know this about me. I was a virgin when I got married."

"The last of a dying breed," he quipped.

"Andrew!" She laughed in spite of herself. "I just told you something very important about myself."

"You obviously think it's more important than I do," he countered, embracing her more snugly. "You were with your husband for, what, fourteen years? I'd hardly call that inexperience."

"It was," she insisted. Then she reconsidered. "I take back what I said. It isn't sex I'm inexperienced in. It's making love. You're the one who does incredible things, Andrew."

"I've got good instincts," he remarked.

"Andrew. I'm trying to compliment you, and—"

"And I'm very, very complimented," he whispered, at last accepting her words as she intended them. "The truth is, Kim, it's all a matter of inspiration. And you, lovely woman, are inspiring beyond description." His lips met hers, and his body, decisively putting an end to the conversation.

"HOW WAS BOSTON?" he asked.

They were seated at a table in the Lord Jeffrey Amherst, a charming inn not far from the campus. The dining room's decor was colonial, with dark, heavy furnishings, thick rugs, and waiters garbed in costumes that suggested the historical period of the town's founding. Kimberly had donned her dress for their dinner out, and Andrew was wearing a tie and a tailored jacket. He looked dashingly handsome, not the least bit rumpled.

She sipped her wine and shrugged. "I can't say that I saw much of the city," she allowed. "We arrived at around nine-thirty, went straight to the A.S.P.C.A. headquarters, took a tour of the facilities and talked shop."

"What kind of shop?" Andrew inquired. "Or is that privileged information?"

"It has to do with a bill regulating research using animals," she told him.

Andrew scowled, obviously disgruntled. "Don't tell me Milford is going to capitulate to those idiots."

"What idiots?"

"The idiots who want to stop all medical research that requires testing on live animals." He shook his head scornfully. "Don't these people realize that without animal tests, doctors are never going to be able to conquer certain diseases?"

Like cancer, Kimberly mutely supplied. Given that Andrew had lost his wife to cancer, it was no surprise that he supported all attempts to discover a cure for the disease. A great deal of medical research using animals was performed in pursuit of that elusive cure. "The senator doesn't want to put a stop to all animal tests," she explained. "However, there are a few research centers performing horrible, pointless tests and treating their animals inhumanely. If those researchers aren't controlled, Congress won't have to outlaw animal tests—the public outcry will put a stop to the research. The purpose of the new regulations is to end the inhumane testing in order to restore public confidence in the field of animal testing as a whole."

Mollified, Andrew subsided in his chair. A waiter brought them their salads and a basket of warm popovers. Andrew passed the basket to Kimberly, then helped himself to one of the popovers. He broke it open, releasing a puff of steam, and spread some butter onto its eggy crust. "I guess I shouldn't have used the word 'idiots,'" he conceded. "But I have no patience for people who want to curtail research efforts. I'm a professor, after all. Research is what I do. You can't learn anything by sitting back and waiting for knowledge to drop into your lap. It just doesn't work that way."

"I know that," Kimberly agreed. "On the other hand, if you were doing your research on—on El Salvador, for instance, and a source didn't want to tell you what he knew, you wouldn't resort to torturing him, would you? There's a right way and a wrong way to gather information."

Andrew fell silent. He bit into his popover, swallowed, reached for his goblet and took a long drink of wine. His eyes shifted from Kimberly to focus on the enormous brick fireplace built into the wall across the dining room from their table.

Kimberly recognized that Andrew was applying what she'd said about animal testing to his entanglement with John Wilding and L.A.R.C. She'd deliberately referred to El Salvador in the hope that he'd make that connection. What John Wilding had done, in the name of research, was to try to gather information the wrong way, by misrepresenting himself to Andrew. What the agent was planning to do with that information was far worse than the way he'd obtained the information, of course. But surely, after having been misled by Wilding, Andrew had to acknowledge that research wasn't always performed in the purest and most noble fashion.

She and Andrew hadn't discussed the problem of his unintentional involvement with the C.I.A. since they'd seen each other in New York. She had avoided broaching the subject during their telephone conversations, figuring that he needed the freedom to reach a decision, without any interference from her, about testifying before the senator's committee. There was no reason for her to try to pressure him into testifying; if he gave the idea the careful consideration he gave to most things, he would have no choice but to conclude that testifying was the right thing to do.

Nine days had passed since he had met the senator in New York. Andrew had had enough time to think about the issue. And since it was hanging between him and Kimberly now, she decided to question him about his plans. "Have you made up your mind whether to honor the senator's request that you appear before the Intelligence Committee?"

Andrew meditated for a moment, running his fingers along the rim of his goblet. "Exactly what does he expect to accomplish by holding a hearing?"

"It won't be a hearing," Kimberly clarified. "It will be a closed session. And what he hopes to accomplish is to find out exactly what Wilding was up to, whether there are other operatives like him engaged in efforts to undermine foreign governments and whether the C.I.A. officially condones such activities."

Andrew digested her answer. "Does Milford really need me there to accomplish that?"

"You're a first-hand witness, Andrew. Nobody else has had the courage to come forward and speak out against Wilding. Of course he needs you."

"Kimberly." Andrew paused, then took a bracing gulp of wine. "If I thought he couldn't do it without me, I would testify. But... Look. I'm an economist. I've done a cost-benefit analysis on the situation, and I can't help but think that the cost of my testifying is far greater than the benefit Milford would accrue from it."

"It isn't just for the senator's benefit," Kimberly argued. "It's for the benefit of the country. Ideally, it's for the benefit of the C.I.A., too. They're just like the medical researchers, Andrew. A few bad apples can destroy their public support and prevent them from doing the work they've got to do. If the Intelligence Committee can root out the troublemakers, everyone will benefit."

Andrew whispered an oath. He seemed exasperated, although Kimberly couldn't guess why. "All right," he muttered. "I had the courage to come forward and speak out. I gave your boss everything I had on Wilding. Everything. Even the data I was going to use for my articles. He can share them with his damned committee if that's what he wants. But he doesn't need me there in person."

"If he didn't need you there, he wouldn't have asked you to do it," Kimberly pointed out, refusing to allow Andrew's foul temper to discourage her. "When you decided to share your data with the senator, you made a commitment to him. Now you've got to follow through on it." Afraid that she was coming across as too preachy, she softened her tone before adding, "He understands that it's a hardship for you to appear, but—"

"A hardship?" Andrew snorted. "It's my job, Kim. Not his. *Mine.*"

"Andrew," she cajoled, "I really think you're blowing things out of proportion when you say you think your job is at risk because of this."

His frown intensified. "If that's what you think, then you're wrong. I've already discussed the matter with Bob McIntyre."

"Who?"

"Bob McIntyre. My alleged mentor. The generous full professor who did me a whopping big favor by putting me in touch with Wilding in the first place."

"You did? You spoke with him?" Despite Andrew's obvious anger, she considered his having confronted his mentor a hopeful sign. Surely facing the man who had such a large say in Andrew's professional future must have been more difficult than facing a session of a Senate committee would be. If Andrew had survived that, he could survive anything. "What happened?" she questioned him.

The waiter arrived with their entrées, and Andrew waited until he and Kimberly were alone again before replying. "He let me know that if I testified, it would count in a big way against me because it would reflect badly on the college."

"He's crazy," Kimberly asserted. "I think it would reflect much more badly on the college if you *didn't* testify."

"Not that you're particularly impartial about whether I testify," Andrew grumbled. "If I do, it will make your boss look good, and it's your job to make him look good. But that's beside the point." He cut off her protest before it could take shape. "If I testify, people are going to learn that Amherst College faculty members do research for the C.I.A. That's not the sort of news university administrations want to publicize. It taints their image as objective bastions of truth with a capital *T*. If I testify about L.A.R.C., it's going to hurt Amherst's image."

"Poor, poor Amherst," Kimberly cooed sarcastically. "We don't want to hurt its pretty little image now, do we."

"I don't care about Amherst's image. I care about my job," Andrew claimed. "I've worked too hard to get this far. It's difficult enough completing a Ph.D. under the best of circumstances, but I earned mine under the worst of circumstances. It's difficult enough getting any teaching job at all, but I busted my butt, and I managed to land an excellent teaching job."

"Sure, it's an excellent teaching job," she agreed. "But what are you committed to, your job or the truth? I thought professors were dedicated to seeking the truth."

"I sought the truth," Andrew maintained. "And I found it and I passed it along to your boss. But I'm not going to be forced out of my job, Kim. My work is all I have."

"You have me," she reminded him in a low voice.

He fell back in his seat and angled his head, appraising her in a new light. A cryptic smile crossed his lips. "Am I supposed to sacrifice my job to make your boss look good simply because I love you?" he posed. "That sounds like blackmail to me."

"It isn't just my boss," she shot back, stung by his accusation. "It's a matter of principle, Andrew. If you aren't willing to put your job on the line, then you're a coward."

"Don't hand me that crap," he retorted caustically. "If anyone should understand what it means to be committed to one's work it's you. You told me yourself that one of the reasons your marriage broke up was that you didn't want to give up your job."

That was true enough. But at that time her job was all she'd had. Her marriage had been loveless by then. Her career had been her entire life.

And teaching was Andrew's entire life. Not Kimberly, not the love he had so recently admitted to. Only teaching.

Her soul grew brittle inside her, then cracked, then splintered into a million pieces. Perhaps Andrew loved her, but not enough. Not as much as she loved him. Not enough to believe that he needed nothing else.

She gazed forlornly at the plate in front of her, the thick pink slab of roast beef, the baby peas, stuffed potato and parsley garnish. "I'm not hungry," she whispered.

Andrew groped for her hand and covered it with his. "I'm sorry if you're disappointed, Kim, but—"

"Disappointed?" Her head jerked up and she stared at him. She couldn't very well tell him that he had just shattered her heart. She had too much pride to say that. "Yes, I'm disappointed," she conceded bitterly. "I thought you had more guts than you've just shown me."

He appeared wounded, but he refrained from responding until he had composed himself. "I'm not a kid anymore," he said quietly. "It's easy enough to be gutsy when you're a kid. It's easy enough to stick your neck out when you're young, when you believe you're invincible. But I'm not that young. I want to remain in one piece."

"That's your choice," she said coolly. "Let's go."

Another dinner uneaten, Kimberly mused miserably as Andrew settled the bill. They left the restaurant wrapped in a silence so icy that even the balmy, starlit night couldn't thaw it. When Andrew unlocked the passenger door of his Volvo for her, she slumped on the seat and stared straight ahead, stubbornly refusing to look at him. He closed the door behind her, stalked around the car to the driver's side and climbed in. He inserted the key in the ignition, then hesitated and turned to her. "How bad is this thing, Kim?" he asked, slipping his hand beneath her chin and urging her around to face him. "Do you hate me?"

"No," she said with a sigh. "I don't hate you, Andrew. I just—" She felt tears accumulating along the fringe of her lashes and batted her eyes. She didn't hate Andrew, but she wasn't sure she loved him, either. When she had fallen in love with him, she had done so with the conviction that he was the strongest, bravest man she had ever known. He had been strong enough to overcome a crushing grief, strong enough to fight for what he had, strong enough to devote his life to seeking the truth and righting wrongs. Strong enough to return her love.

He was only human, however. His strength had limits. She wished those limits had revealed themselves in some other way, in some other context. But they hadn't. He had fallen short of her ideals exactly where she had expected him to be strongest. In his principles. In his morality. He was opting for safety over righteousness, and she questioned whether her feelings for him could recover from the shock.

Aware that he was waiting for her to speak, she fought against the waver in her voice and said, "I think I ought to go back to Washington tonight." She clung to the logistics, afraid to verbalize her despair. "I can drive back to Boston and catch the next shuttle flight down. I think they run pretty late into the night."

Andrew assessed her decision and exhaled. His hand fell from her face and he turned resolutely toward the steering wheel. His lips set in a grim line, he drove through downtown Amherst to his home.

Neither of them spoke as she packed her overnight bag. Andrew merely watched her from the doorway as she moved about his bedroom, gathering the slacks and shirt she'd worn for her drive to Amherst and tossing them into the small suitcase, rummaging through her purse for her car keys. His eyes were partially obscured by his eyeglasses, but his lips remained clamped shut, as if to keep his thoughts from slipping out.

At last she was ready to go. When she approached him, he caught her in his arms. "I do love you, Kim," he murmured.

Standing so close to him, she could see the sadness glimmering in his honey-brown eyes. She willfully averted her gaze. It hurt too much to look at him directly.

"You're only saying that to get me to stay," she charged.

He held her for a split second longer, then let his hands fall to his sides. "There's no way I can get you to stay if you want to go," he said in resignation. He stepped out of her path. "Goodbye, Kim."

"Goodbye," she mouthed, too disconsolate to speak the words aloud.

Later, when she was able to sort out her thoughts and regain control over her nerves, she would be able to convince herself that she was doing the right thing by leaving. Later—much later—when she had the chance to reflect objectively on what had happened, she would console herself with the fact that she couldn't possibly love a man who wasn't as committed to love and honor as she herself was, a man who had made the choice Andrew had.

And then, perhaps, she would be able to live with her own choice—leaving him.

Chapter Eleven

"Weddings depress me," said Troy.

Andrew carried two fresh bottles of beer outside to the small front porch. He handed one to Troy, then dropped onto the concrete step beside him and stared out at the silver semicircle of moon hanging just above the horizon in the sky. The night air held a slight chill, and when Andrew had gone into his apartment for the beers, he'd pulled on a plaid wool jacket over his cotton shirt. Troy was wearing a denim dungaree jacket with the collar turned up and heavy leather boots. But Andrew didn't suggest that they head indoors to warm up. He wanted to sit outside on the porch with Troy for a while longer, to gaze across the trimmed front lawn and listen to the shrill song of the crickets.

The rasp of a match scraping against flint caused him to turn to his friend. He watched as Troy lit a cigarette, shook the match dead and dropped it into the empty beer bottle at his feet. "You smoke too much," Andrew remarked.

"What else is new?" Troy dragged on his cigarette, exhaled, then sighed. "Don't get me wrong," he said, reverting to his initial comment. "I'm not saying the thought of Laura and Seth getting married is depressing. I like them both. I wish them the best. I'm sure their wedding is going to be a gas, and I'm honored that they want me to do the photos for them. But most of the weddings I go to are real bummers."

"In what way?" Andrew asked.

Troy shoved a shock of wavy black hair back from his brow, tipped the bottle Andrew had given him against his mouth and swallowed a long draught of beer. Then he lowered the bottle and shrugged. "Any time I've got to wear my tuxedo it's a bummer," he clarified. "Did you know I own a tuxedo? Me, Troy Bennett, the owner of a tux. With three—count 'em, three—ruffled white dress shirts to match."

"It's a requirement of your job to own a tux," Andrew pointed out rationally.

"Don't remind me," Troy snorted. "At least I don't have to wear the tux for Laura and Seth. They'd probably kick me off the premises if I did."

Andrew chuckled in agreement.

"But my tux isn't the depressing part. It's the groom's tux. His tux and the bride's fancy gown and the whole scene. The bride and the groom always come into my studio sometime before the wedding to meet me and write up an order. They look so normal then, you know? They're usually wearing jeans, or maybe some nice clothes from work if they come in on their lunch hour. But they look like real people. Then I arrive at the church or the hall where they're having the wedding, and the bride and groom look so—so artificial. The bride can't move in her dress, and she's got makeup slathered all over her face, and her hair is all done up and sprayed to the consistency of plaster of paris. And the groom is in his tux, looking queasy, maybe a little hung over from his bachelor party. They don't look anything like the human beings I met earlier at the studio. It's the most important day of their lives, and they look like aliens from another planet."

"It's called rituals, Troy," Andrew noted. "A wedding is a ritual, and certain customs must be observed."

"Right." Troy laughed sardonically. "One ritual is the dehumanization of the bride and groom. Another is the champagne toast—they always serve that sweet, cloying champagne that tastes like soda pop—and another is the cutting of the cake, during which I'm supposed to take pictures while man and wife smear each other's faces with whipped-cream frosting. And then there's the bride dancing with her father-in-law and the groom dancing with his mother-in-law—the groom is probably never going to have a civil conversation with his mother-in-law for the rest of his life, but there they are, waltzing around the dance floor while the band plays 'Sunrise, Sunset' from *Fiddler on the Roof*. They're supposed to look like they're enjoying themselves, and I'm supposed to immortalize this precious moment on film." He laughed again and shook his head.

"You're a misanthrope," Andrew chided him. "The only reason you don't like photographing weddings is that you'd rather be photographing fishermen in Nova Scotia." He sipped his beer, savoring its cold, sour foam on his tongue. "How come you didn't find a job in journalism when you went to Montreal? You would have liked that much better."

"I'm sure I would have," Troy concurred. "I applied for work at a few newspapers, but they were sensitive about hiring expatriates from the States, taking valuable jobs away from Canadians. Those of us who were able to make a go of it up there did it by starting our own businesses." He smoked for a while, then angled his head toward Andrew. "How about you? Do weddings depress you?"

"Not as a rule," Andrew replied. "Certainly not when the featured players are people I care a lot for, like Laura and Seth."

"It doesn't bother you, going to weddings? I mean, given what happened to your marriage and all...."

Andrew watched the glowing orange coal of Troy's cigarette as it arced through the darkness. He offered a bittersweet smile. "You would have hated my wedding, Troy. It was as typical as any. A service at church, then dinner at a banquet hall. I even wore a tux."

"Rented, I bet," Troy guessed. "At least you didn't have to go out and buy three ruffled shirts." He dropped his cigarette carefully into the neck of his empty bottle, and it emitted a tiny hiss as the hot ashes hit the residue of beer at the bottom. "Do you think Seth'll be wearing a tux?"

"Not if his life depended on it," Andrew answered. "He'll probably be wearing something outrageous."

"Maybe they'll have a granola wedding cake," Troy commented. "I admit I'm looking forward to the affair. It'll be good to see everybody again, even if it's for something as depressing as a wedding."

Andrew's expression became pinched and he turned away. It would be good seeing Seth and Laura and Julianne, just as it was good seeing Troy now. He was glad he had been able to talk Troy into coming to Massachusetts the night preceding the wedding so they could visit a bit beforehand and then drive down to Pennsylvania together for the ceremony.

However, it wouldn't be good seeing Kimberly. Andrew imagined that having to see her tomorrow at the wedding would be something akin to torture.

"What?" Troy probed, easily discerning his friend's altered mood.

"Nothing," Andrew fibbed.

Troy assessed him for a moment. "I'm sorry I made you dredge up memories of your wedding. You should have just told me to shut up."

"It has nothing to do with that," Andrew claimed, inadvertently admitting that there was an "it," a specific something that was troubling him.

"What does it have to do with?" Troy pressed him.

Andrew took another drink of his beer. He almost wished he smoked; if ever he could use a rush of nicotine, it was now. "Kim," he finally admitted, trying not to choke when he gave voice to her name.

"Kim Belmont?" Troy scowled in bewilderment. "The cheerleader? What about her?"

"She isn't a cheerleader," Andrew retorted, then took a deep breath and focused on the luminous half-moon until his temper subsided.

If he had learned anything in the past few weeks, it was that Kimberly was smarter, deeper and much more complicated than the word "cheerleader" connoted. She *was* a cheerleader—not a vacuous little girl waving pom-poms and doing splits in midair, but someone who exerted herself to inspire others to do their best, to do what was best for them. Her cheers didn't rhyme, they lacked tune and tempo, but she was a cheerleader nonetheless.

Except that Andrew had turned a deaf ear to her exuberant cheers. Except that he had chosen sanity over valor. He had let her down, disappointed her—and he had lost her. And it hurt like the devil.

In the more than two weeks since he had last seen her, he had frequently found himself questioning his decision not to appear before the Intelligence Committee. He still wasn't sure whether Kimberly had only been pretending to love him in order to get him to testify, thereby promoting her boss's career. But Andrew had met Senator Milford, and he didn't think the man was that conniving. In Andrew's heart, he didn't believe that Kimberly could be that conniving, either.

If he had believed that, he wouldn't feel so disconsolate about losing her.

Losing Marjorie had also hurt him terribly, but that loss had been an act of fate, beyond his control. Losing Kimberly had been an act of will. He had to take full responsibility for it. The knowledge that he had saved his career in the process offered meager solace.

"All right," Troy said, apparently growing impatient with Andrew's extended silence. "She's not a cheerleader. Why are you so broken up about her?"

Andrew opened his mouth to protest that he wasn't broken up, then shut it again. Who was he kidding? He was devastated about what had happened between Kimberly and him. And he wasn't going to win points for stoicism. Denying the truth didn't automatically make it untrue.

"It's a long story," he began hesitantly.

"I've got time."

Andrew drained his bottle and set it between his feet on the bottom step. "I love her," he revealed.

"Kimberly?" Troy exclaimed. "Are we talking about the same person? Southern belle Belmont?"

"That's the one," Andrew confirmed glumly.

"How the hell did you fall in love with her? I'll grant you, Andrew, she's a knockout. But you and she detested each other in college."

"We've—we've gotten to know each other since then," Andrew explained. He gave Troy a sketchy description of his involvement with the C.I.A., his decision to turn to Kimberly for help, the time they'd spent together in Washington and the relationship that had blossomed between them and flourished—until he'd stupidly spoiled everything. "It took me so long to come to terms with the fact that I loved her," he groaned. "I swore to myself, after Marjorie died, that I'd never let myself go through this sort of thing again,

I'd never lose a woman I loved that much." He cursed softly.

"Andrew, if she loves you, too, then she'll want to make up with you. She's probably hurting as much as you are," Troy observed with supreme sensibility.

Andrew shook his head dubiously. "She loved me when she thought I was some sort of spiritually chaste knight," he argued. "Once she realized that I wasn't as full of noble principles as she expected me to be, she fell out of love with me. If she's hurt, it's only because I let her down."

"That's life," Troy maintained. "People let each other down sometimes."

"Tell me about it," Andrew muttered. He watched as Troy groped in the breast pocket of his jacket for his cigarettes and matches. "Is it different in Canada? Are the women easier to deal with up there?"

Troy chuckled. "Womanhood is a biological condition, not a nationalistic one." His grin contained an undefined sadness. "You aren't the only man who's loved and lost, Andrew. It happens to the best of us."

"Yeah, but I'm two for two," Andrew grumbled. "And this time I should have known better. I should have done things differently. What happened was my own fault."

"So what do you want, a medal? We do what we have to do," Troy said pointedly. "Sometimes the decision hurts, but you weigh your choices and do the best you can, and you hope you haven't blown it. And if, years later, you realize that you have..." He lit his cigarette and shook the match slowly to extinguish it. "If you realize that you did blow it, then you just have to learn to live with your mistake. There's no going back, Andrew. You learn to live with it."

Andrew surmised that Troy was speaking from personal experience. But he didn't want to hear about Troy's heartbreak any more than he wanted to relive his own. Tomorrow they would be attending a wedding. It would be in poor taste, to say the least, if they arrived at Laura's mother's house morose and bitter, not ready to celebrate Laura and Seth's love, but, eager instead, to consign all love affairs to the trash heap.

Andrew turned to gaze at the moon again, wondering whether Kimberly was as anxious about having to see him as he was about having to see her, wondering whether, as Troy had suggested, she loved him enough to want to make up with him. Wondering whether she loved him enough to accept him for what he was, not for what she desired him to be.

"We've got a long drive ahead of us," Troy remarked, extinguishing his cigarette in the empty beer bottle. "And I've got a sleeping bag to unroll on top of that couch of yours. What do you say we hit the hay?"

"Sure."

They collected their bottles, entered the house and shut the door behind them.

"I'VE KNOWN LAURA since she was a little girl, and I join with you, her family and friends, in deriving pleasure from this very special occasion, this day of immeasurable happiness for her and Seth," said the short, balding man who stood before Laura and Seth at one end of the rolling backyard. Julianne had already informed Andrew that the municipal judge performing the wedding ceremony had gone to high school with Laura's father and had remained a friend of the family even after Laura's father had passed away. Andrew liked that. He thought it appropriate that when people got married, the person who joined them as husband and wife was someone with a strong personal connection to the couple.

He liked the judge, and the spacious backyard of Arlene Brodie's suburban brick house, with its hedge of redolent lilacs and its circular tulip and daffodil beds carved into the carpet of grass. He liked Arlene Brodie, a matronly woman in her early sixties with a stylish mane of dark curls and a face as open and smiling as her daughter's. She was seated in the front row of folding chairs, beaming at Laura and Seth. Laura's daughter, Rita, wore a hot-pink minidress, and she, too, smiled broadly while she stood proudly behind her mother as the judge continued his affectionate speech.

The widest smiles belonged to Laura and Seth themselves. Laura looked utterly wonderful in a lacy white peasant dress that fell to midcalf, a pair of white sandals and a laurel of daisies crowning her thick, loose hair. She held a bouquet bursting with daisies, ivy and baby's breath. True to form, Seth wore nothing as typical as a tuxedo. He had on his white linen suit, a navy blue shirt, a bright red bowtie and his red high-top sneakers. A crimson carnation adorned his lapel.

Andrew wished he could concentrate fully on the wedding ceremony. But he was painfully distracted by the petite blond woman who sat on the chair next to his, wearing a silk dress the same baby-blue color as her eyes and a delicate perfume that wafted into his nostrils every time he inhaled. Julianne sat on Kimberly's other side, and Troy was kneeling in front of the assembly, taking pictures.

Andrew and Troy had arrived at the Brodie house early, since Troy had wanted to take some prenuptial photos. "None of the standard wooden-Indian poses, please," he ordered Seth and Laura, nudging them toward the lilacs and snapping the shutter of his camera before they could settle into position in front of the backdrop of lavender blossoms. "Come on, Seth, pick her up and throw her around. Let's capture the true you on film."

"If he throws me around, I'll kick him," Laura warned before succumbing to laughter.

"Sounds like a match made in heaven. I don't suppose it occurred to you, Seth, that the groom is supposed to visit a barber before his big day."

"If I'd gone to a barber," Seth complained, raking his shaggy dirty-blond hair out of his eyes, "Laura would have called the whole thing off. She intends to turn me into a hippie."

"And you intend to turn me into a Hollywood wife," she countered, disheveling his hair in time for Troy to snap the photo. "Don't forget to take some pictures of Rita, too. And my mother. Okay?"

"Hostess!" Troy obliged, jogging across the lawn to commandeer Arlene Brodie, who was conferring with the hired bartender as he set up his wares on a portable table. "I've got a negative here that has 'Mrs. Brodie' written all over it."

Laura's mother laughed. "If it's got writing on it, Troy, it's going to make a lousy picture."

"The real question, Mrs. Brodie," Troy said as he snapped a candid shot of her beside the bartender, "is, if I take enough pictures of you standing here, will people think you're a lush years from now when they're flipping through the pages of the wedding album?"

Arlene Brodie dissolved in more laughter. Obviously she was quite taken with Troy's unorthodox approach to his assignment.

Andrew remained out of the way during the pre-wedding bustle, keeping himself occupied by helping the caterer set up the rented chairs and chatting with Laura and Seth when they weren't being dragged off by Arlene, Rita, the judge or

Troy to attend to business. At one point, when Troy shepherded the three Brodie women into the house for what he promised would be some "feminist shots," Andrew and Seth took a leisurely stroll along the perimeter of the yard. "How are you doing?" Andrew asked.

Seth dug his hands into the pockets of his loose-fitting trousers and grinned. "Hanging in there," he replied. "I still haven't recovered from Laura's ban on sunglasses at this gig, but...as she likes to remind me, being in love means being willing to compromise. On the trivia, of course. We don't have to compromise on the big stuff, thank God. We're already in complete agreement on that."

"She's looking terrific," Andrew commented, casting a glance toward the house, into which Laura had disappeared. "So are you. Even if you do seem a bit more flamboyant than normal," he added, eyeing Seth's appealingly bizarre outfit.

"Yeah. You look more like a groom than I do," Seth observed, studying Andrew's conservatively styled blue suit—the only suit he owned—and striped necktie.

"Are you scared?"

Seth's dancing hazel eyes met Andrew's, and he shrugged. "I gather that I'm *supposed* to be scared," he confessed. "But I'm not. I'm really sure of what Laura and I are doing, Andrew. If you think about it objectively, this doesn't look like the easiest marriage in the world. I've got a teenage stepdaughter to cope with. And I'm uprooting her and Laura and taking them to California, far from Arlene—the only family Laura's got. My parents are happy I'm getting married, but they think maybe I've bitten off more than I can chew, marrying a woman with a kid."

"What do you think?" Andrew asked.

Seth shrugged again. "I think you've got to follow your heart and go for it," he said. "The bottom line is, I love

Laura. And she loves me. We're good for each other. Laura needs me as much as I need her. She tells me to grow my hair and not to wear sunglasses at weddings, and I teach her how to play the kazoo and how to get the most out of a Porsche. Obviously we're made for each other." He smiled gently. "Maybe we're taking a chance here, but if you can't take a chance on the woman you love, then what's the point of anything?"

He resumed his leisurely pace, Andrew falling into step beside him. "We love each other, Andrew," he continued. "We can handle the glitches. It really isn't much of a risk when you've got love on your side. There are my folks," he said, gesturing toward a man and a woman who had emerged from the house and waved to him. "Ten dollars says my mother's going to sob so loudly during the ceremony she'll drown out the judge." Sure enough, as Seth loped across the lawn to greet his parents, his mother pulled a handkerchief from her purse and dabbed at her glistening eyes.

More guests appeared: Seth's brothers and their wives and children; other relatives; a couple of Laura's colleagues from work; a girl who was apparently a close friend of Rita's, given their boisterous embrace when they saw each other; the girl's parents and brother. Andrew wandered around the side of the house in time to see a familiar BMW pull up to the curb. He smothered the urge to flee and stood bravely on the slate walk as Julianne and Kimberly climbed out of the car.

"Andrew!" Julianne hailed him, striding up the walk and giving him a warm hug. "How are you?"

"Fine, Julianne, and you?" he said reflexively. His eyes, however, fastened themselves to Kimberly, who seemed to be taking more time locking up her car than any reasonably dextrous person required.

"Kim is just as nervous as you are," Julianne whispered before sweeping into the house in search of Troy, Laura and Seth.

Andrew suspected that Julianne's ulterior motive in going inside was to leave Andrew and Kimberly alone to confront each other. He wondered when Kimberly had confided to Julianne about him, and what she had said.

Kimberly slipped her car keys into her purse, straightened up and threw back her shoulders. Her eyes were wide with an emotion he could define as either panic or hauteur. The high midday sun glanced off her hair, causing it to shimmer about her face like a golden halo.

Not a halo, Andrew silently corrected himself as she approached him. She wasn't an angel. She was a woman. An important distinction, that.

"Hello," he said, swallowing the catch in his throat, pretending that he didn't find her so dazzlingly beautiful.

"Hello," she responded, sounding calmer than he felt.

"Nice weather they've got for the big day," Andrew remarked. Then he winced inwardly. The weather? Couldn't he do better than that?

"Yes, they're really lucky," Kimberly agreed. "According to Laura, she and her mother were arguing up to the last minute about whether to rent one of those massive outdoor tents. Laura insisted that if it rained a huge tent wasn't going to do much good, anyway, and they'd have to move everyone into the living room. But it's much nicer having the party outdoors, isn't it?"

"Much nicer, yes," Andrew mumbled, feeling as if he were withering inside. Without exchanging another word, he and Kimberly walked together to the backyard and conveniently lost each other in the crowd of guests.

Now, as Seth and Laura, flanked by one of Seth's brothers as best man and Rita as maid of honor, exchanged rings, Andrew reflected on what Seth had confessed to him before the wedding. If you had love on your side, what was the risk? Why not take chances?

Because, Andrew answered internally. Because if one did a cost-benefit on it, the costs would in all likelihood outweigh the benefits.

If Andrew tried to repair his relationship with Kimberly, it would probably cost him his job, the one thing that had kept him going during his darkest hours, the one thing he had always been sure he could count on.

It would cost him the fear he would have to live with forever, the fear of losing Kimberly, the fear that she didn't love him enough, the fear that she was so beautiful that as soon as the rest of the male half of the world discovered she was available, she would have an army of attentive gentlemen from which to choose a partner. The persistent fear that she was still on the rebound, that Andrew was only a temporary cure for her loneliness.

And what were the benefits? He could think of only one: Kimberly herself. Having her as long as he could, loving her for as long as he had her.

Damn. What was wrong with him? Why did he have to reduce everything to an economics equation? At the rate he was going, he might as well just pull out his calculator, punch a few buttons and trust to the microchip wizardry to tell him what to do.

Seth's words echoed inside Andrew: *You've got to follow your heart and go for it. If you can't take a chance on the woman you love, then what's the point of anything?*

"By the power vested in me by the state of Pennsylvania," the judge intoned, "I now pronounce you husband and wife. You may kiss the bride," he informed Seth.

"It's about time!" Seth hooted, to the great amusement of his audience. He slung his arms around Laura, hoisted her high into the air and planted a resounding kiss on her lips.

If you can't take a chance, then what's the point? The hell with cost-benefit analyses, Andrew reproached himself. *The bottom line is, you love her.*

The three-piece combo set up on the patio broke into a rendition of Mendelssohn's wedding recessional. Their faces radiant with joy and promise, Seth and Laura skipped up the improvised aisle between the rows of chairs. They didn't break stride until they reached the patio, where they began a comical waltz to the classical music.

Around Andrew people were rising to their feet, stretching their legs and chattering. Andrew stood, as well, and turned to Kimberly, who was inspecting the wrinkles in her dress, as if to avoid having to look at him. "Let's talk," he murmured.

SHE HAD KNOWN that this would be an awkward day for her, and she had tried to prepare herself for it. Last night at Julianne's apartment she had downed glass after glass of white wine, until her head was buzzing. But the wine hadn't helped any more than Julianne's logical advice.

"Kimberly," Julianne had said, effecting her stern, I-am-the-boss-and-I-know-these-things manner. "If you love Andrew, can't you love his flaws as well as his strengths? The man's been through hell once in his life. He doesn't want to go through hell again. He wants some stability, something he can rely on. He loves his job and he doesn't want to risk it. What more can you expect from him?" At Kimberly's obdurate silence, Julianne had added, "He isn't a paragon, Kim. He's a human being."

"He's a chicken," Kimberly had countered. "He's a spineless coward. He brought me the matches, the kindling, the lighter fluid—and then, when I was about to start a fire, he ran for cover. What kind of human being is that?"

"A normal one, if you ask me," Julianne had argued. "It took incredible guts just to bring you the matches and the rest of it. If he doesn't feel like getting burned in the conflagration, can you blame him?"

"When I first knew him back in school, he wouldn't have minded getting burned," Kimberly had muttered. "He was just as brave as the rest of us. When the president of Columbia refused him an interview, Andrew hounded the man mercilessly until he got the story he wanted. When Troy was applying for his conscientious objector status, Andrew was the first to volunteer as a character witness at Troy's draft board hearing."

"And when he knew you in school, he thought you were a pretty pom-pom girl," Julianne had reminded her.

"Maybe he still thinks I am," Kimberly had mumbled sadly.

"I'm sure he doesn't," Julianne had refuted her. "He's a smart, perceptive guy. Fifteen years is a long time, Kim, and you've both been through a lot. Neither of you is the same person you were back then. Certainly Andrew is aware of that."

"I don't know." Kimberly had drained her glass and sighed. "What if he isn't?"

"He wouldn't be in love with you if he didn't recognize you for who you really are," Julianne had rationally pointed out. "He isn't blind. If you think he is . . . maybe it's your own insecurity that's eating you up." As Julianne's insightful words sank in, her eyes had met Kimberly's. "What's really bothering you, Kim? Are you upset because Andrew doesn't want to testify before your boss's committee, or are you upset because Andrew is refusing to do something *you've* asked him to do? Is it Senator Milford's hearing you're thinking of or your own ego?"

She'd had a valid point, one that Kimberly hadn't stopped meditating on. As soon as she'd seen Andrew, the notion had come into full focus. The Intelligence Committee hearing was important, but it couldn't be important enough to make her feel as despairing as she did about Andrew.

Maybe Julianne was right. Maybe Kimberly was ascribing personal motives to Andrew's decision, taking his rejection of her invitation to testify as a rejection of herself.

He said he wanted to talk. She wanted to talk, too. He looked miserable, and she loved him too much to allow herself to be the cause of his misery.

But the band was playing a soupy version of "Something in the Way She Moves," and before Kimberly could react to Andrew's suggestion, a strapping young man in a navy blazer and gray slacks gripped her hand and announced, "I'm Seth's cousin Larry and Seth says you're single. Care to dance?" Without giving her a chance to refuse, he dragged her to the patio.

She tossed Andrew a helpless smile, and he shrugged. Twisting her head in order to see him as Larry twirled her around the patio, she noticed Andrew guiding Julianne to the patio to join the dancers. He held Julianne a discreet distance from himself, and they talked and smiled as they danced. Kimberly tried to guess what they might be discussing. Was Julianne doling out some more of her commonsense advice to him?

The song wasn't that long, but it seemed to last forever. As soon as the band reached the final chord, Kimberly extricated herself from Larry's embrace, mumbled a hasty thank-you and wove among the dancers to Andrew. "All right," she said, gazing up into his gentle eyes and refusing herself the chance to evade him anymore. "Let's talk."

Andrew opened his mouth to speak. From the corner of her eye, Kimberly spotted another young man approaching her. *How many cousins does Seth have?* she wondered irritably. Slipping her hand through the bend of Andrew's elbow, she briskly urged him in the direction of the house before anyone else could waylay them—and before she lost her nerve.

They passed a linen-covered buffet table arrayed with hors d'oeuvres, chafing dishes and plates and entered the house through the back door. Inside the kitchen, a squad of uniformed waiters supplied by the caterer were swarming about, removing cookie sheets of canapés from the oven and loading doily-lined trays with stuffed mushrooms and pigs-in-blankets. Kimberly and Andrew exited the kitchen to find the living room also teeming with guests. Hoping that Mrs. Brodie wouldn't mind, Kimberly led Andrew toward the stairs leading to the second floor.

The upstairs hall was empty, and they stepped through an open doorway, entering a tidy guest bedroom. Kimberly smiled edgily and lowered herself onto the bed. Andrew sat beside her, but he made no move to put his arm around her or take her hand. That struck her as a bad sign—or else an extremely good sign. He was serious about talking, and he wasn't going to let their strong physical bond get in the way of their dialogue.

He didn't speak for several minutes. His gaze wandered from the open window to the bulletin board to his spread knees. "I've missed you," he finally said.

"I've missed you, too."

"Kimberly...Kim." He took a deep breath, then lifted his face to hers. His expression was inscrutable. "The last time we were together—"

"I'm sorry," she said in a timorous voice. Then the words tumbled out. "I shouldn't have run away from you, Andrew. That's what I did—I ran away. Just like the first time in Washington. I ran then and I ran again in Amherst. I was so busy thinking you were a coward, Andrew, but *I* was the coward, racing off like that. I should have given you a chance—"

"A chance to do what? To be more cowardly than you were?" He pulled off his eyeglasses, rubbed the bridge of his nose, then slipped the glasses back on and turned fully to her. "I've given a great deal of thought to my job, Kim. My work means a lot to me, you know that. But other things mean more to me than my work. They *have* to mean more. I haven't stopped thinking about this since we last saw each other, and I haven't stopped thinking about us. I'll—I'll testify for you."

"No," she said quickly.

He appeared startled. "What do you mean, no? Don't you want me to?"

Julianne's words resounded inside her skull, their truth overpowering her. "I don't want you to testify for *me*, Andrew. I want you to do it for *you*, because you yourself think it's the right thing to do—or else don't do it at all."

He gazed at her for a long moment, clearly puzzled. "Run that one by me again," he requested.

She smiled shyly, then busied herself smoothing out her skirt again. "I was wrong, Andrew, the way I tried to coerce you into doing it, as if you'd be doing it as a favor to me. If you testify, it has to be because you're committed to the idea of testifying. Not to satisfy me, but because you believe that some larger good will come from it." She sighed, then dared to meet his gaze. "I know how much your job means to you, Andrew. I don't want you to lose it."

"I don't want to lose it, either," he admitted. He rose from the bed and paced aimlessly. When he reached the window, he glanced out at the revelers in the yard below.

Then he turned back to Kimberly. "Do you know what my students dream of? They dream of going to business school. They dream of getting M.B.A.'s and earning lots of money and spending the rest of their lives in safety and security."

"There's nothing wrong with safety and security," Kimberly noted.

"Within reason, perhaps." He leaned against the windowsill, his eyes unwavering on her. "There's something wrong with safety and security when you make all your decisions with those questionable motives in mind. I . . ." He paused, mulling over his words, his angular jaw flexing as he gave shape to his thoughts. Then he continued. "I want safety and security. I want safety and security in my career, and I want them in my relationship with a woman. But I can't have them. Not without sacrificing something even more important."

She was unnerved by his having diverted the conversation to the personal issues that remained unresolved between them. She had thought that they were discussing his decision to testify, not his feelings for her.

But she wouldn't retreat from the emotional minefield into which Andrew had led them. If he was brave enough to introduce the subject, she would just as bravely meet him on that dangerous turf. "What is that important thing?"

"Love," he answered simply. "Love isn't always safe, Kim. It isn't always secure. But having it—even with all the risks . . . I'm beginning to think that maybe it's better to accept those risks than to avoid love altogether."

She wanted to rise from the bed, cross to him, fling her arms around him and hug him close. She wanted to tell him all over again, as often as he wanted to hear it, that she loved him.

But she didn't. He hadn't yet mentioned his love for her or hers for him. He was still speaking in generalities, and she thought it best to hold back. "Don't you think it's possible that love can sometimes be secure and safe?" she asked.

He shook his head solemnly. "No. And you don't believe it can, either, Kim. You know as well as I do that no matter how much you love a person, things don't necessarily work out. The man you loved and married wasn't the person you thought he was. The woman I loved and married died. There's no such thing as certainty."

"You're still a cynic," she chastised him, strangely deflated by his assertion. He claimed that he thought love might be worth the risks. So why couldn't he take an optimistic view of things? Why couldn't he also think that sometimes those risks were negligible?

"I'm a realist," he refuted her. Then his mouth softened, shaping a tenuous smile. "Okay, maybe there's a little bit of optimism inside me, too. Because every time I try to sort out my feelings, Kim, the realist in me says I should forget about everything between us, I should grab my tenure and live out a pleasant, trouble-free life in Amherst, teaching my students and taking home my pay.... And then that god-awful optimist in me tells me that I'd rather have you."

"Andrew—"

"He tells me that I should shore up my courage and face Milford's damned committee and get everyone into a lather at Amherst. He tells me that I should do what's right rather than what's safe, no matter what the cost. He tells me that if I don't do what's right, I'll wind up like my students—defeated by petty comforts and complacency."

"Why doesn't that optimist tell you that testifying before the senator's committee won't cost you your job?"

"Oh, he does," Andrew scoffed. "I tell him to shut up."

"He seems like a pretty talkative guy."

"Is he ever. Bombastic, pleonastic, irrelevant. . . ." Andrew chuckled. "Once I took the muzzle off him—or maybe it was you who took the muzzle off him, Kim—I can't seem to get him to quiet down."

"Don't even try." At last she yielded to the urge to close the distance between her and Andrew. Hoisting herself off the bed, she marched across the room, placed her hands on his shoulders and rose on tiptoe to kiss him. "It's that bombastic, pleonastic, irrelevant optimist inside you that makes me love you so much."

Andrew's arms drew her to him, and he returned her kiss. His embrace loosened, but he didn't release her. "When I was talking to Seth just before the wedding, I asked him if he was scared. He told me he was too sure of what he and Laura were doing to be scared." His lips touched the smooth skin of her forehead and he sighed. "I wish I were as sure."

"You'll never lose me, Andrew."

"That's a promise you can't make," he said.

She knew he was speaking from his own mournful experience. Yet she wouldn't concede, not even to the capriciousness of fate. "As long as I've got any power over things, I can promise it. We love each other. That's all we have to be sure of."

"Right," he muttered doubtfully. He stroked his fingers through her silky hair and scowled. "I live in Massachusetts—and even if I lose my job, I've got one more year on my contract. You live in Washington, except when you're flying around the country with Milford. You aren't about to quit your job. So how does this thing work out?"

"Maybe—" she grinned impishly "—maybe your getting fired from Amherst would be the best solution."

"Of course," he grunted sarcastically. "Then I'll be an unemployed wretch. Or, if I'm lucky, I'll be able to snag a part-time job, teaching nights at a community college in some rural county thousands of miles from the nearest airport. Any other brainstorms?"

"Someone with a razor-sharp mind like mine always has brainstorms," Kimberly declared. "Here's one. Stop worrying about what you have no control over. That includes what Amherst decides to do to you, and it includes what Mother Nature decides to do to both of us. We'll get by, Andrew. We'll work it out. We'll be together when we can, and when we can't... we'll be together in spirit."

"What a cheerleader you are," he commented, smiling reluctantly. "You almost make it sound easy."

"It won't be easy, Andrew. But it can be done."

"How about when you get pregnant?"

Unsure that she had heard him correctly, she stared up at him, trying to make sense of his enigmatic smile. His eyes remained steadfast on her, his mouth still curved in that lopsided grin she adored. "Are you serious?" she questioned him.

"As serious as you are," he replied. "You're not the only one who wants a child, Kim."

"Then we'll work it out," she said with conviction.

It definitely wouldn't be easy. She knew that. But if Andrew wanted a child as much as she did—if he wanted one *half* as much—they would find a way to do it. He could arrange his teaching schedule to concentrate all his classes on Tuesdays, Wednesdays and Thursdays. Or she could reduce her work load on the Senate staff. Barry, the newcomer on the senator's speech-writing staff, was speedily learning the ropes. He could take over some of her responsibilities. Or she could take a maternity leave. Somehow, with two geniuses like Andrew and her working on it, they would come up with a solution.

The combo's music drifted up and through the open bedroom window. The band was playing Billy Joel's "Just the Way You Are." Kimberly imagined that the song had become a kind of anthem for weddings; it had been played at every wedding she'd attended in the past ten years. With good reason, too.

Andrew would never be as optimistic as she was—it simply wasn't in him. But, try as he did to ignore it, there had always been a streak of optimism in him. She didn't need more than that. She would be the cheerleader of their partnership and Andrew the practical one, the sensible one, insisting that he wasn't romantic when Kimberly knew that he was in fact the most romantic man she had ever met. He had his flaws, but as Julianne had pointed out, Kimberly had to love his flaws as well as his strengths. He was a human being.

She did love him, just the way he was.

"If you don't ask me to dance," she remarked, flashing him a flirtatious smile, "another one of Seth's cousins is going to beat you to the punch."

Andrew mirrored her smile, exhibiting that marvelously understated dimple of his. He slid his right arm around her waist and folded his left hand over hers. "You know," he commented, gliding about the cozy bedroom, "for a well-bred Southern lady, you're pretty forward, inviting a fellow to dance."

"It must be the corrupting influence of all those damn-Yankee college friends of mine," she drawled. "Mother warned me I'd find myself in a fix if I went to Barnard, that heathen 'naw-thren' school."

"What's Mother going to say when you tell her a heathen northern man plans to marry you and get you pregnant?"

Kimberly laughed. "She'll probably lecture you about the etiquette of wearing socks on Sunday morning."

"She and I are going to have some wonderful fights over the next thirty or forty years," Andrew predicted, pulling Kimberly closer and kissing her temple.

She nestled her head into the warm shadow of his neck and sighed happily. *Over the next thirty or forty years.* That was the optimist in Andrew speaking, the courageous, principled, optimistic man she knew he was, at long last ready to commit himself to the future, to welcome it with hope and love.

Temptation

MILLS & BOON
Temptation
WEDDING BELL BLUES
MADELINE HARPER

MILLS & BOON

Damn the woman, but she was right

He was stagnating professionally; he ought to be jumping for joy that she'd come to him with such a stimulating assignment. If she were telling the truth, if he could believe her, then her personal feelings for him—whatever they might be—had nothing to do with her offer.

But what about his personal feelings? How could he possibly work for her without reliving in his mind everything that had transpired between them? If, for some reason, she did try to start up with him again, he would have a difficult time resisting her.

He didn't want to fall in love with Julianne Robinson. He wasn't right for her. He'd broken her heart once, wilfully, consciously. She deserved someone better…

DREAMS

BY

JUDITH ARNOLD

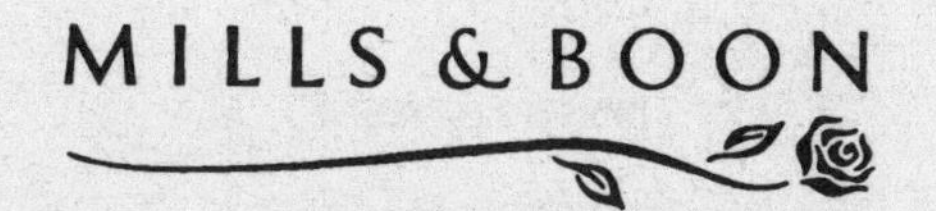

MILLS & BOON LIMITED
ETON HOUSE, 18-24 PARADISE ROAD
RICHMOND, SURREY TW9 1SR

All the characters in this book have no existence outside the imagination of the Author, and have no relation whatsoever to anyone bearing the same name or names. They are not even distantly inspired by any individual known or unknown to the Author, and all the incidents are pure invention.

Published in Great Britain in 1994 by Mills & Boon Limited, Eton House, 18-24 Paradise Road, Richmond, Surrey TW9 1SR

ISBN 0 263 78907 1

87-9406

Made and printed in Great Britain

Foreword

Writers are thieves.

We steal constantly from friends, neighbors, from acquaintances and total strangers. We steal from the six o'clock news, from street scenes viewed through our windows, from the personal ads in the alternative newspapers. We steal during vacation trips and during jaunts to the local supermarket. Nothing that passes before us is safe from our greed for ideas.

The only thing that redeems writers is that when we steal, we do our best to give back what we've taken. If we've done our job well, what we've taken is usually in better condition when we return it.

Dreams is the final book of the trilogy. I've stolen a great deal from the world to create *Promises*, *Commitments* and *Dreams*. None of the characters in the three novels is based literally on anyone I know, and, with a few exceptions, the incidents in the novels are pure fabrication. However, I am indebted to many people for having left the raw material of their lives lying around in places where I could help myself to what I needed.

I've stolen enormously from my own college friends, and as they read these novels, they will undoubtedly find familiar items woven into the stories. One of them will recognize Kimberly's Georgetown apartment and silver BMW as her own; another may identify with the generosity of spirit that, as with Laura, led my friend to a career in social work. Some of my women friends will understand the struggle that Julianne faced in pursuing a successful career at the expense of a social life. Many of my male friends from school attended Amherst College, so they will appreciate the fact that Andrew teaches there. All my friends were shaped by the politics of our day, so they will accept the power that world events play in my characters' lives. I hope the old gang hasn't forgotten about the time we all hiked to the top of Mount Everett. It is no coincidence that I've sent my characters on a similar outing. Such adventures are the cement of long-standing friendships.

I've stolen, as well, from Debra Matteucci, the editor of this trilogy. She was the one who pointed out to me the romance of my age and who encouraged me to share that romance with my readers.

Finally I've stolen from my husband. Like Seth, he is a "wild and crazy guy," a Grateful Dead fan who has never lost his boyish enthusiasm for life. Like Andrew, he is an intellectual, always hungering to learn more. Like Troy, he had a low number in the draft lottery, and the threat of serving in a war he didn't believe in hung over him throughout his college years. In a more general sense, I've stolen time from my husband, the time and concentration I needed to write these books.

I'm not asking my friends and loved ones for forgiveness. As Troy realizes in *Dreams*, nobody is going to forgive you. All we can do is learn to forgive ourselves and hope that the ends justify the means.

In writing these three books, I have done my best to keep faith: the faith that I've created something moving and worthy with all the goods I've stolen, and the faith that when my readers reach the final page of this final book, they will feel I've given back something of value.

One

Another wedding. Another paycheck.

Troy unlocked the front door of his photography studio, ignoring the cheerful tinkle of the attached bell, and entered the dark reception area. After closing the door behind him, he crossed to Stacy's desk and clicked on the small lamp there. He set his camera bag down on the blotter and emptied the labeled canisters of used film from the pockets of his tuxedo jacket. Sighing, he tugged his bow tie loose and removed the top stud of his dress shirt, then pulled his cigarettes from an inner pocket of his jacket and lit one. He collapsed onto Stacy's swivel chair and exhaled a thick stream of smoke into the air.

He was tired.

Although it was nearly midnight, the reception had still been in full swing when he'd left the hall. It didn't matter, though; he'd gotten all the photos he'd been hired to get: the sweet soft-focus shot of the bride gazing dreamily into the dressing room mirror as her maid of honor adjusted her veil, the cloyingly cute shot of the bride's father smirking and pointing an accusing finger at the groom, the obligatory shots of the tables, of the cake, of this one dancing with that one, of the best man making the toast.

Exiting the party before the last guest staggered home wasn't a crime. Troy had done his job.

As it was, he had left in the nick of time. Just before he'd reached the double doors leading out into the foyer, one of the bride's uncles had appropriated the band's microphone and begun a whiskey-sour rendition of "The More I See You," woefully out of tune. A soused bridesmaid had chased Troy into the parking lot and pressed a cocktail napkin into his hand. In his car Troy had looked at the napkin and discovered her name and telephone number scribbled across it, along with the words "any time." She had been making eyes at him throughout the entire wedding. He hadn't wanted to stick around and find out if she would catch the bouquet.

Maybe Andrew was right. Maybe Troy was turning into a misanthrope. Weddings were the most remunerative jobs for his photography studio business, and he ought to view them with more respect. Yet it was because he'd photographed so many weddings that he'd become cynical about them. To him a wedding no longer represented the start of a marriage, the forging of a lifetime commitment between two lovers. It represented anywhere from six hundred to twelve hundred dollars, depending on the order.

A mere week ago Troy had attended the wedding of his college friends Seth Stone and Laura Brodie. It had been the first wedding he'd gone to in ages that had actually meant something other than money to him. Not only because the party had been decorous—no obnoxious uncles stealing the microphone, no inebriated bridesmaids throwing themselves at Troy—but because he cared a great deal for Seth and Laura. They weren't kids—already in their mid-thirties, they'd both been around the block enough times to know what marriage meant, what they wanted *their* marriage to mean. That was the way a wedding was supposed to be.

He smoked, leaning back in the chair, running his fingers through the thick black waves that crowned his head. The groom at the wedding Troy had just left had looked as if he'd visited the barber that very morning. The skin behind his ears had a raw pink appearance, and beneath the evenly trimmed hair the nape of his neck had been shaved. Troy's hair was shorter now than it had been in college, but not by much. None of his clients ever complained about his unfashionable mane, however. Troy supposed that his formal attire was enough to appease them. If, with his shaggy mop of hair and his scruffy mustache, he looked like a hippie from the neck up, at least he looked like a proper professional from the neck down.

Stubbing out his cigarette, he turned on the answering machine next to Stacy's blotter. Much of Troy's work was done on weekends, but there was no need for his secretary to spend all day Saturday in the studio. Usually she dropped by for a few hours in the morning and then switched on the answering machine and disappeared.

The first few messages were typical business calls: queries about when an order would be ready, about the studio's rates, about when one could set up an appointment for a passport photo. Troy listened to them with half his mind, while the other half lingered on a memory of the wedding he'd been to a week ago.

Seth and Laura. Good people, and obviously in love. And then there had been Andrew Collins and Kimberly Belmont, two other friends from Troy's college years, two other compatriots on *The Dream*, the underground newspaper the group of them had founded their senior year at Columbia. Andrew and Kimberly—also obviously in love. Troy had been shocked by that bit of news. In college Andrew and Kim hadn't gotten along well, and in the intervening years their lives had taken widely differing paths. When Andrew had declared to Troy the night before the wedding that he loved Kimberly, Troy had almost choked on his beer. But when he had seen them together at the wedding, it had been apparent that Kimberly loved Andrew, too.

Love was a weird thing, Troy surmised. Six friends, six colleagues, lost to one another for fifteen years, and suddenly there were Seth and Laura tying the knot and Andrew and Kimberly all but making love with each other on the dance floor...and Julianne. Julianne and Troy. The two who, if history had allowed them, might have been an old married couple by now. And instead...instead there was nothing, nothing at all, between them.

On the answering machine tape, a woman was prattling about how she wanted Troy to photograph her children. They were gorgeous, she claimed, and she saw a future for them in advertisements, and she needed some glossies for their portfolios. Troy yawned and glanced at his wristwatch.

The voice of the doting mother was followed by a click, and then another voice, soft and steady, a voice that had always reminded Troy of the bell-like purity produced by tapping one's fingernail against crystal. "Troy, it's Julianne. I need you—"

He bolted upright. He almost forgot to listen to the rest of her sentence: "To take pictures for the magazine. I'm desperate for some good artwork to accompany a story we're running on unwed mothers. I don't know anyone who could do a better job than you. Please call me back as soon as you can."

I need you. Her voice resounded inside his skull. *It's Julianne. I need you.*

With a shaky hand he shut off the answering machine. Then he groped for another cigarette and lit it. He'd have to quit smoking one of these days. But after hearing a message like that, Troy knew that tonight definitely wasn't the time to break the habit.

He shouldn't have gone to Seth and Laura's wedding. He knew that Julianne would be there; he knew he'd have to see her; he knew they'd be surrounded by all that abounding love. He knew it would be difficult. But nothing could have kept him away from the wedding of such good friends. Especially since Laura had begged him to do the photos for her and Seth. She'd even wanted to pay Troy, but he wouldn't hear of that.

No, he couldn't have missed the wedding. But he could have missed the reunion, back in March, the fifteenth-anniversary celebration of Julianne's magazine. She had invited all the founders of *The Dream* to New York City for the bash, and Troy had seriously considered avoiding it. Even after he'd reached New York, even after he'd arrived at the Shelton Building, where the party was held, he'd had his doubts. Some misinformed notion had compelled him to believe that finally, after fifteen years, he could face Julianne and put their past to rest. He'd been wrong.

I need you.

She'd spoken those same words the night he'd left. He had thought, at the time, that the hard part would be leaving his country. That *had* been hard—no question about it. It had been the hardest thing he'd ever done—with one exception: saying goodbye to Julianne.

Once he turned the answering machine off, the studio fell silent. Little automobile traffic passed on the road outside the studio at this hour, and in late May, both the building's heating system and the air conditioner were left off. The only sounds in the room were Troy's breathing, his heartbeat, the whisper of smoke passing from his lips.

It hadn't been love at first sight. Julianne wasn't the sort of woman who could cause a hormone imbalance in a man at her first encounter with him. She was attractive, sure, her features pleasantly symmetrical, her eyes a pretty blue color and her smile warm and inviting. But for the first few weeks she and Troy had been classmates in the advanced rhetorics course, he had hardly noticed her. To him, she was simply that tall, alert girl who sat at the rear of the room and didn't speak up often—but when she did, she always had something valid and perceptive to say. When the class had been divided into teams of two for one of the first assignments, which involved writing about a single subject from various rhetorical stances, Troy had been surprised that Julianne had picked him, along with Seth, Kimberly, Laura and Andrew—the student with whom she had been linked by the professor—to pool their resources and write a mock newspaper.

The whole thing had been her brainchild. She'd conceived the idea, organized her troops, chosen their subject: an unremarkable block of brownstones in Morningside Heights. She had even come up with the newspaper's name, *The Dream*. That she would ultimately become the editor in chief was a foregone conclusion. Troy's impression of her during the first week of their newspaper's existence was that she was immensely intelligent and extraordinarily in control of things.

Once their newspaper caught on and they decided to continue publishing it, Troy's initial impression of Julianne evolved. Yes, she was intelligent and in control, but she was more than that. She saw angles to stories that nobody else noticed. She mediated staff squabbles and negotiated truces. She was principled. She held convictions, but she wasn't blind or single-minded about them. She was truly an unusual person in that era of freewheeling rowdies and drugged-out zombies.

And she was pure. Troy's consciousness of that purity, that clarity of soul that matched her clarity of vision, came gradually. He was intrigued by everything he learned about her: that she knew how to make fruit preserves; that she could guess, at a single glance, how many words an essay contained; that although she was still an undergraduate at Barnard, she was auditing courses in the Graduate School of Journalism; that she had mastered every knot necessary to earn a Boy Scout merit badge; that she was born and bred in Iowa. Iowa! All Troy knew about Iowa was that corn and soybeans came from there, and maybe pigs. He hadn't known that *people* came from Iowa, too.

Having grown up in a down-at-the-heels blue-collar neighborhood in Detroit, where his decision to attend college—an Ivy League college, at that—on a scholarship was viewed as an aberration, Troy had considered Iowa another universe. He'd considered Julianne Robinson an alien. A mystifying, infinitely fascinating alien.

She was thinner today than she'd been then. Her facial features now had an alluring angularity to them, the sort of delicacy Troy would love to capture on film. She currently wore her hair in a sleek pageboy that fell to her shoulders. She dressed well, too, in stylish but unsuggestive outfits that befitted her position as the editor of a nationally distributed magazine. She had fantastic legs, long and slim and well shaped.

Before the reunion last March, Troy had never even seen her in a dress. The first time he'd viewed her legs, she had been wearing red-and-white striped knee socks.

Remembering, he groaned. Fifteen years. He should have gotten over it by now.

But he hadn't. The memories had lain dormant all that time, but they'd never been vanquished. The moment he'd seen her at the reunion, those memories had bubbled to the surface again, as vivid as if everything had happened a day ago. And tonight, her voice on his answering machine awakened them yet again.

She'd been asleep when he found her. It was the end of March, the night of an out-like-a-lamb day. Troy had shot a roll of film with a bunch of pictures for the newspaper and a few personal photos just for the staff. They'd been outdoors, cavorting in the unexpectedly balmy afternoon, and he had balanced the camera on a bench, set the timer and taken some shots of the six of them clowning around. Julianne told him that she would be in *The Dream*'s basement office that evening, doing layout, and that as soon as Troy had the film developed he should bring his proofs over so they could pick out some photos for the stories she was planning to run that week.

He'd had to wait for hours to get a crack at the darkroom. He was lucky the photographers for the college's official newspaper allowed him access to their darkroom when they weren't using it, but that evening they were. Troy had waited and waited. Finally, shortly after the bell tower of the Riverside Church had chimed midnight, he emerged from the darkroom with his sheet of proofs.

He didn't expect that Julianne would still be in *The Dream*'s office so late, but he decided to detour to that building, just in case. Although the building was kept locked at night, Julianne had wrangled keys for the staff so they could work at all hours. Troy let himself inside, descended the stairs and noticed, through the frosted-glass window on the upper half of the office door, that the light inside was still on.

He entered and found Julianne seated at the long Formica-topped worktable, the layout pages spread before her, her arms crossed on the table, shaping a pillow for her head. Her long, brown hair draped her shoulders and gleamed beneath the buzzing fluorescent ceiling light. She was sound asleep.

She looked awfully uncomfortable, with half her body heaped onto the table and her booted feet curled around the legs of her chair. Troy put down his proofs and surveyed the office. He spotted the inspiration couch and smiled.

The inspiration couch was a seedy, sagging, legless sofa Seth had discovered on a sidewalk off campus, abandoned by someone with the expectation that a crew from the sanitation department would remove it. Neighborhood residents were always dumping old pieces of furniture onto the streets at night, and Seth was always scouting the pickings, searching for useful items. His dormitory room was adorned by, among other things, a chipped nursery lamp shaped like a merry-go-round, a cracked oval mirror and a moth-eaten rug, all scavenged from the streets of Harlem in the dead of night. When he'd happened upon the sofa a week earlier, he had enlisted the aid of Troy and Andrew to haul it to their office. "Every writer needs a couch to lie on for inspiration," he'd explained as they had jammed the unwieldy object into a corner of the cramped room.

"Yes, and for sacking out," Laura had teased Seth, although she had generously provided a gauzy Indian-print coverlet to hide the faded upholstery.

Troy's eyes shifted from the inspiration couch back to Julianne. He could probably get her to the couch without waking her up.

She was heavy. As tall and solidly built as she was, this came as no surprise. One of the photos he'd taken that afternoon depicted Laura and Kimberly looking on while he, Seth and Andrew held Julianne across their knees. With her weight distributed among three guys she hadn't seemed heavy at all. For Troy to lift her all by himself, however, was another matter.

But he was tall and solidly built himself, and he managed to cradle her in his strong arms. He liked the weight of her legs as they bent over his forearm and the serene expression on her face as her head nestled naturally against his shoulder. He carried her past the worktable, then lowered her onto the cushions. She sighed, but her eyes didn't open.

Straightening, he appraised her long body. She still looked uncomfortable.

He crossed to the light switch and shut it off, leaving the room bathed in the diffuse glow entering from the hall through the frosted glass window in the door. Then he returned to the couch. Her boots, he decided. He would remove her boots, and then she'd be able to get a good night's sleep.

Julianne always wore tooled Western boots, with thick soles. Ignorant as he was about Iowa, Troy had once asked her, much to her amusement, whether there were lots of cowboys in her state.

He'd never touched her before, not really. Just the usual playful shoving, nudging, pats on the back for a job well done, that sort of thing. Lifting her leg and gripping the heel of her boot, he felt a strange surge of undefinable emotion. It resembled friendship and something more: concern. A desire to give her ease, an irrational longing to make this night the most restful one of her life.

The boot didn't slide off. He rolled up the leg of her jeans to her knee and pushed down on the curved upper edge of the boot. Then he wiggled the heel. The boot loosened, and he pulled it off her foot. The sight of that garishly striped knee sock caused him to laugh out loud.

"Troy?" Her usually clear voice was thick and groggy.

Abashed, he glanced at her face. "Go back to sleep," he whispered, then turned away and tackled the other boot.

"What are you doing?"

"Taking off your boots. Go back to sleep." But as he freed her other foot, his hand remained on her ankle, on her instep, massaging the muscles at the base of her calf through the colorful knit fabric of her socks.

It was crazy, touching her leg that way. Yet he found himself unable to let go.

"Troy." She sounded completely awake. Her hushed tone wasn't a result of sleepiness.

He lowered her foot onto the cushion, then turned to face her. She was watching him, her eyes steady, piercing through the shadows. Her hair was disheveled, her lips parted, her sleepy gaze aglow with yearning. Maybe not, maybe he was just imagining it, but she looked—God help him—more beautiful than any woman had ever looked to him before.

He dropped to his knees on the floor beside the sofa. His fingers drifted up her sock to the denim bunched about her knee. He smoothed the fabric down her leg, then let his hand glide back up, tracing the double stitching of the inseam. She said nothing, even as his hand rose above her knee, along her thigh. She watched him, her eyes glittering, her breath shortening as his fingers reached the thick nub where the two inseams met.

She didn't stop him. Instead she extended her arms, gathering him to herself, pulling him up onto the couch with her. When they kissed, Troy understood that he hadn't imagined her yearning at all. It was as real as she herself was, as real as her silky hair and her powerful embrace, as real as her lips, her tongue, her taste. As real as her firm, strong body beneath him, her hands gripping his back, the soft, clean skin of her throat as his mouth grazed it, her quiet moan of pleasure....

A scorching sensation in his fingers brought him back to the present. His cigarette had burned down to the filter, leaving a column of gray ash dangling precariously over the desk. Troy jammed out the cigarette in the ashtray, then shoved himself brusquely from the desk and stood. He left the studio, slamming the door behind him, and stalked to his car, knowing too well that as exhausted as he was, sleep would elude him tonight.

"YOU'VE GOT A CALL FROM TROY BENNETT."

Julianne's fingers grew chilly as she held the telephone receiver to her ear. She had known he would be likely to return her call, and she'd done her best to prepare for it. Yet hearing her secretary announce that he was actually on the line caused a jolt of panic to shoot through her.

Julianne Robinson wasn't the sort of woman easily given to panic. As a rule she exuded confidence and poise. In her thirty-six years of living, only one person had ever been able to shatter her self-control.

And now he was on the line.

She probably shouldn't have telephoned him. But when she'd stopped by her office on Saturday, the emptiness of the suite of rooms that housed *Dream* magazine's headquarters had given her the rare opportunity to act stupidly. Nobody had been around to question what she was doing, to badger her with long-winded explanations about why a deadline was about to be missed or why an advertiser was going to be late with a payment. Nobody had been around to toss her those awe-filled looks of respect she frequently received, those stares of admiration she always felt obliged to live up to.

She had come to the office to give Susan Trevor's photographs one final appraisal. Susan had done a superlative job writing the article on unwed teenage mothers, but as a photographer she simply wasn't up to snuff. The magazine's art director had agreed with Julianne about that. They had delayed making a decision long enough. Julianne had to hire someone else.

She had pulled out the list of free-lance photographers her art director had provided for her and skimmed the names. Any one of them would do an adequate job, but Julianne wanted something better than adequate. The issue on "Broken Families in America" was going to be special, and the article on unwed mothers was going to be the most special feature. Julianne wanted the best photographer she knew to do the artwork for it.

The best photographer she knew was Troy Bennett.

More than her concern for her magazine had driven her to call Troy. She was worried about him. He wasn't simply an outstanding photojournalist; he was an outstanding photojournalist who was frittering away his talent taking pictures of weddings up in Montreal. The last two times she had seen him, at the reunion and then at Laura and Seth's wedding, she had been acutely aware of his dissatisfaction with his current work. He didn't belong in fancy reception halls taking posed portraits. He belonged on the streets, taking *real* pictures.

The last two times she'd seen Troy had informed her of something else: she and Troy could work together. Julianne couldn't deny that they had a history, but when she'd been with him, she had been able to match his cool reserve with her own polite composure. They had even managed to dance together at Laura and Seth's wedding. The band had been playing "Till There Was You," and Laura's mother had ordered Troy to put down his camera for a few minutes and enjoy himself. He had obediently approached Julianne and asked her to dance.

Placing his hand on the small of her back, folding his other hand around hers, he had spun her around the crowded patio. They'd chatted pleasantly about how lovely the wedding was, how happy they were for Seth and Laura, how pretty Laura's daughter looked. Julianne had said something about the weather and Troy had commented that this was the best wedding he'd been to in a long time.

Neither of them had alluded to the time they'd danced together in college, shut inside his cluttered room with his inexpensive stereo blasting The Who. Julianne barefoot, clapping her hands above her head, Troy gripping her hips and swiveling them, urging them to his, smiling with a sensuality that Julianne had always found devastating. If Troy had remembered that night, if he had remembered what had happened once the record ended and they'd found themselves on his bed, moving to a very different dance, a very different rhythm, he had tactfully refrained from talking about it. So had Julianne.

If they could dance discreetly at a wedding, then surely they could work together.

"Thanks, Brenda," she mumbled to her secretary. "Put him through."

She willfully refused to pick up her pen as she waited for her secretary to connect the call. If she lifted her pen, she would fidget with it, and fidgeting would only make her more nervous than she already was. Taking a deep breath, she spun her chair away from her desk. Her vision snagged on the framed photograph Troy had taken of her and the rest of *The Dream*'s staff frolicking on the lawn outside the building that housed their office. The picture reminded her of everything she'd rather forget, and she rotated back to her desk.

"Hello, Julianne." Troy's husky baritone cut through the long-distance static on the line.

"Hello, Troy," she said casually. *There,* she congratulated herself. *That wasn't so difficult.*

"I got your message on my machine last Saturday."

"I'm sorry I called you on a weekend. I know your work must make for strange hours, but I took a chance." Julianne didn't bother to add that as soon as she'd heard his secretary's taped voice on the machine she had nearly lost her nerve and hung up. It was only the display of Susan Trevor's mediocre photographs on her desk, reminding her that she was making a necessary business call, that had given her the courage to leave her message.

"That's what I've got an answering machine for," he said.

"Well, I'm calling for a professional reason," she announced. Her voice emerged crisply and evenly, reassuring her that she hadn't acted stupidly at all when she'd phoned Troy on Saturday. "We're running an issue on 'Broken Families in America,' and I'm in dire need of some good photographs."

"Unwed mothers," Troy supplied. Had Julianne mentioned that in her message? She couldn't recall exactly what she'd said.

"That's right."

"Julianne." He sighed. "I don't do that sort of thing anymore."

"But you *could*," she pointed out. "You could do it so well, Troy. It's right up your alley, and—"

"My alley these days is Bennett-Chartier Studio," he reminded her.

She measured his tone, trying to guess his mood. When they had known each other in school, Troy had always been easy to read. When he was happy, his smile used to all but explode from his face. When he was angry, his mustache used to bristle as his upper lip grew tense, and his dark eyes glowed like burning coals. When he was troubled, which was more and more frequently the case as their graduation date approached, his temper would grow short and the muscles in his shoulders would bunch into knots. And when he was aroused... Julianne had never had any difficulty understanding him then.

When she saw him recently, she easily comprehended that his work didn't fulfill him. But he was containing himself in this conversation, revealing nothing. Julianne had to reach him somehow. She simply had to, for his own sake as well as for the magazine's. "Don't you think it's time to walk out of that alley, Troy?" she suggested. "I know you don't get off on taking wedding pictures."

"Oh?" he asked calmly. "How do you know that, Julianne?"

"It's obvious," she answered, mimicking his impassive delivery. "You're too good for that kind of hack work. You know you are."

She had hoped her remark would rile him, but it didn't. He only chuckled. "Did you call me just to compliment me, Julie?"

Julie. He was the only man who had ever called her "Julie," the only man she'd ever allowed to use that nickname. She didn't care for it, except when it came from Troy. He sounded so sexy when he said it.

She steeled herself with a shrug and brushed a stray lock of hair back from her cheek. "I called you," she explained, "because I want to hire you to do some free-lance work for the magazine. That's all."

"Julianne." He sounded as if his patience was beginning to wear thin. "You know I'm not in the market for free-lance work."

"Even if you'd be doing it for Laura Brodie?" she asked.

"Laura?" He seemed startled, and mildly interested. "What does Laura have to do with it?"

"The article is about her. It's about the girls she's been counseling. It's a wonderful article, Troy—and it's about the wonderful work Laura has been doing with teenage mothers. It needs the kind of photographs only you can take."

"Other people can take good photographs," Troy argued. "I read your magazine. You've got some decent people working for you."

"But Laura's clients won't trust just anyone to invade their homes and take pictures of them. It's got to be someone Laura can present to them as trustworthy. You and she have known each other a long time, Troy. She'd feel comfortable with you, and she'd be able to convey that comfort to her clients." When he didn't respond, she added, "You can see what I'm up against, Troy. I can't just impose a stranger on these girls. Laura would never stand for it."

"I'd be a stranger to them," he noted.

Was he actually considering her offer? Permitting herself a shred of optimism, she pressed her case. "You wouldn't be a stranger to Laura. She trusts you."

He didn't speak.

"I can pay you a generous fee, plus expenses—"

"Money isn't the problem," he cut her off.

Of course it wasn't. But Julianne wasn't certain what the problem was. Was it that he felt totally committed to his studio in Canada? Or was it that he simply didn't want to work with her? "Please, Troy. You could do such a terrific job with this."

He exhaled. Closing her eyes, she tried to picture his face: his high, fierce brow, his sultry dark eyes, his prominent nose, his fringe of mustache, his dynamic chin. Did he look angry now? Pleased? Troubled? It agonized her not to know.

"When do you need the pictures?"

She hadn't realized that she'd been holding her breath. Hearing his words, she felt her lungs deflate, expelling along with the air all her tension. He was going to do it. He was going to take the pictures for her magazine. "As soon as possible," she told him. "Laura's going to be moving to California with Seth at the end of June—to say nothing of the deadline we're facing here at *Dream*. This coming weekend is the Memorial Day holiday, but the following week—"

"No," he said abruptly. "No, I can't."

"If the timing is no good, Troy, I'll reschedule—"

"No, Julianne." He sounded resigned, infinitely weary. "I can't do it. It has nothing to do with the timing or with the money. I just can't do it."

She didn't need him to spell it out: he didn't want to work with her.

Yet it seemed so pointless for him to deny himself the chance to do something he'd really enjoy, as well as to supply her magazine with the photos it needed. More than pointless, it seemed juvenile. She and Troy were mature. They could handle a professional arrangement. They'd lived their own separate lives for fifteen years, and they'd survived.

If she gave vent to her frustration, though, Troy would never agree to take the assignment. So she checked herself before speaking and shunted away her exasperation. "Maybe you can't say yes now, Troy, but please don't say absolutely no. Think about it for a few days. Will you do that much for me?"

As soon as the last sentence slipped out, she bit her lip. She shouldn't have permitted a personal element to enter their conversation. She shouldn't have asked him to do anything for *her*. It was for himself and for the magazine that he ought to reconsider her offer.

He sounded vexed when he finally responded. "I'll think about it, sure. I'll think about it for as long as you want, Julianne. And then I'll say absolutely no. Do you understand?"

"You're making a mistake, Troy," she warned him.

He issued a bitter laugh. "If I am, it won't be the first time," he muttered. His tone was strangely gentle when he added, "I appreciate your thinking of me, Julianne. I mean it. I'm flattered. But... I just can't. Okay?"

There was nothing more to discuss. Yet Julianne refused to accept defeat. "I'll be in touch," she said before hanging up.

She stared for a minute at the telephone, then shuddered. Standing, she straightened out the blazer of her suit and crossed to Susan Trevor's photos, which rested in a stack on the teak conference table occupying one-half of her spacious office. She spread the photographs out before her, studied them and shuddered again. They weren't good enough.

She had to think like an editor, not like a woman who had once been in love. The magazine needed artwork, and she couldn't put off getting the job accomplished while she tried to save Troy's soul. If he didn't want to take advantage of the opportunity she'd given him, then that was that. Her primary concern had to be getting the magazine out, getting the pictures taken.

She would go through her list of free-lancers, telephone them in alphabetical order until she found one available for a rush job, and then contact Laura and set up a meeting. If the chemistry was right, she'd send the free-lancer off with Laura to snap photos in Brooklyn. And if the chemistry was wrong, she'd call the next free-lancer, set up another meeting and . . .

Shaking her head, she turned from the table to gaze out the window of her corner office in the Shelton Building, one of the monolithic skyscrapers lining the Avenue of the Americas in midtown Manhattan. Below her the avenue teemed with cars and buses. To her north she could see a line of people snaking out from the box-office window of Radio City Music Hall, waiting to purchase tickets for the upcoming show. The morning sun cast long shadows across the street.

What was Montreal like, she wondered. Did Troy like it there? Did he feel at home? Did he have many friends, many lovers? Had he truly put his past behind him? Was he content?

She hadn't achieved her eminent position by backing off from challenges. She knew Troy wasn't content. And she wasn't going to hire anyone else for the job until she'd given him a little more time to think through what she was offering him.

Two

"You were good, Nathaniel."

Julianne's brother shifted his eyes from the windshield of their father's rugged Jeep to glimpse her. Then his attention returned to the empty county road, which cut a straight swath through the flat, verdant farmland from their tiny hometown of Meade to Davenport, eighty miles to the south. They had just left the well-tended cemetery behind the Congregational Church, where the town held its annual Memorial Day celebration. In honor of the occasion, many of the grave sites had been bedecked with small American flags.

This year Nathaniel Robinson had been invited to give a speech. It was a tradition in Meade for a town native who was a veteran to make a brief Memorial Day eulogy at the cemetery at sunrise. Dr. Robinson's son had been one of the ten Meade boys who had served in Vietnam, one of the seven who had made it back alive, one of the three who had come home to Meade for the holiday.

Nathaniel's speech had been brief but eloquent. Julianne was proud of him. She was proud of his success as a stock analyst in Chicago, proud of his clean-cut good looks, proud of his loving marriage and the two beautiful children it had produced. Proud of his commitment to his principles, even if they sometimes diverged drastically from hers.

Their relationship had endured a turbulent period when Nathaniel had decided to enlist in the army. Julianne had been sixteen at the time, but even at that tender age she'd already been militantly opposed to the war in Southeast Asia. When her older brother chose to defer attending college in order to serve in Vietnam, she had been crushed. "One of two things will happen," she had predicted morosely. "Either you'll have to kill someone, or someone will have to kill you. It's wrong, Nathaniel. All wars are wrong, and this one is very wrong. You mustn't go."

But he'd gone. Julianne's parents had raised their son and daughter to be independent, thoughtful, idealistic. Nathaniel and Julianne had been taught to act on their convictions, to be true to themselves. Nathaniel had believed that the United States belonged in Vietnam, fighting the Communist insurgency. He'd acted on that belief and joined the army.

Thank God he had come back. Julianne had never wanted to find out whether he'd killed anyone. She was only too grateful that her brother was home again in one piece. Whatever their differences of opinion, however strongly they disagreed on their country's foreign policy, Julianne was elated that her brother had survived.

Nathaniel grinned and rolled down his window, letting a warm breeze enter the Jeep. "You think I was good, huh?"

"The best Memorial Day speaker I can remember," Julianne praised him. She was glad he hadn't chosen to wear his old uniform—the previous year's speaker, a World War Two veteran, had gotten himself up in full battle regalia, complete with an array of medals above his breast pocket. To Julianne, Memorial Day was a time for mourning the loss of life, not for celebrating the supposed glory that led to that loss. She considered Nathaniel's somber gray suit and striped necktie far more appropriate attire for the ceremony.

He had loosened his tie for the drive to Davenport. Julianne was still wearing the demure shirtwaist dress of pale blue linen that she'd worn to the cemetery service. They'd barely had time to stop back at the house to pick up her suitcase before she'd had to leave for the airport. Nathaniel had sworn that he didn't mind driving her there, even though he'd have to make the trip again that evening with his family for their flight home to Chicago. The Robinson house had been bustling with friends and relatives since Friday night, and Nathaniel had insisted that he wanted to spend a little time alone with his baby sister.

"I especially liked what you said about how wars aren't just fought on battlefields, but also in the hearts of the soldiers and their loved ones at home," Julianne continued. "And about how no war is ever over until the human beings involved have ended the war in their hearts."

Nathaniel shrugged modestly. "It's the truth, Julianne." He eyed her speculatively. "How have you been, anyway? You've seemed on edge all weekend."

Shaping a faint smile, she stared out the window at the budding green acreage bordering the road. She *had* been on edge all weekend, not because of anything to do with her family but because of what she faced once she left Iowa. Her ultimate destination was not New York City but Montreal. She was going to visit Troy.

He wasn't expecting her. She had seen no point in warning him that she was coming—she entertained the vague hope that her surprise arrival at his studio would work in her favor. If his studio was even open when she got to Montreal. She didn't know whether Canada celebrated

Memorial Day, or, if the country did, whether Troy's studio would be open for business despite the holiday. Nor did she know his home address, although she suspected that she could find it easily enough once she reached Montreal. All she knew was that she had to see him, had to talk to him again, had to convince him to take pictures for her magazine.

"So?" Nathaniel prodded her. "What's going on?"

"Nothing," she answered evasively. "Just some hassles at work."

"All you've talked about all weekend was work," Nathaniel gently reproached her. "I know the magazine is a big part of your life, Julianne, but it can't be your entire life."

"Why not?"

Nathaniel chuckled. "If it is, that's reason enough for you to be on edge." He shot her another quick look. "Come on, Julianne, it's me. Tell me what's going on. Is some guy giving you a hard time?"

Julianne forced herself to join his laughter. "No, Nathaniel," she replied, aware that that wasn't a totally honest answer. "Even if some guy was giving me a hard time, I hardly think you're in a position to do anything about it."

"You mean, the way I did something about...what was that twerp's name? Dave Clay, wasn't it?"

This time Julianne's laughter was genuine. Dave Clay had been a boyfriend of hers in high school. On their fourth date he and Julianne had engaged in a tussle over her virtue in the back of his pickup. When Julianne had reported the incident to her protective older brother, he had stormed to Dave's house and given Dave a black eye.

She tried to imagine what Nathaniel would do if he ever met Troy. Just as Julianne avoided questioning her brother about his experiences in Vietnam, so she avoided questioning him about his feelings toward draft dodgers. All she had ever told Nathaniel about Troy was that he was someone she'd known in college, that they'd broken up and that she had recovered. There was no need for Nathaniel to blacken Troy's eye, she had assured her brother.

"When did the war end for you, Nathaniel?" she asked, abruptly reverting to their earlier subject.

Nathaniel fell silent, ruminating as he drove. Finally he spoke, his voice subdued. "The day they unveiled the Vietnam Memorial in Washington."

She hadn't expected such a specific answer. That Nathaniel could remember the precise date indicated that even for someone who had had complete faith in what he had done, coming to terms with his participation in the war hadn't been a simple matter. "You and Beth went down to Washington for the unveiling, didn't you?" she recalled.

Nathaniel nodded. "I knew I had to be there. I had to see it with my own eyes, in person."

"How did it end the war for you?" she asked.

Again he lapsed into silence. His gaze grew distant, as if he were reliving that exact moment in time. "I was standing on the Mall, surrounded by all those other veterans and all those families who had lost their sons and husbands. People were cheering and people were weeping. It was terribly moving, Julianne." He paused, reflecting. "And suddenly I realized that I didn't have to defend myself anymore. I didn't have to justify my actions. I did what I did because I had to, because I love America and I respect what it stands for. My motives were pure and honorable. I fought because of what I believed in. And I didn't owe anyone any explanations."

She gave herself several minutes to digest his words. "It was terrible, though, wasn't it? The war, I mean," she clarified, hoping she didn't sound disapproving. She was asking because she needed to know, not because she wished to stand in judgment of Nathaniel.

He accepted her question without rancor. "Yes," he told her. "It was terrible."

"Did it bother you, killing people?"

Nathaniel shot her a curious look. "Why are we having this conversation?" he asked, bemused. "We've never talked about this stuff before."

"Then it's high time we did," Julianne countered. "You're my brother, and I love you. I want to know."

He slid his hands lower on the steering wheel, leaned back in his seat and sighed. "I'm not a beast, Julianne. Of course it bothered me. To tell the truth, I'm not sure I ever killed anyone over there. I probably did, but I never went out of my way to find out where the bullets were landing. What mattered to me wasn't whether I was killing them, but whether I could save myself and my buddies. It was less that we were fighting against *them* than that we were fighting for *us*. And for our country, for the values we believed in." He sighed again. "It's too bad things ended the way they did. We didn't lose because we were wrong. We lost because we fought poorly and because we didn't understand our enemy. Look at that country now. I haven't heard a peep from all you antiwar protestors about what's happened in Vietnam since the Americans pulled out. But I bet there are a whole lot of Vietnamese who wished we'd stayed there and stuck it out."

Julianne couldn't argue that. But just as Nathaniel refused to feel guilty for what he'd done, she refused to feel guilty for the fact that Vietnam was in worse shape today than it had been during the conflict. She had protested the war not because she revered the Communists but because she believed that killing was not the way to settle issues.

Did Troy feel guilty? Did he feel guilty for having fled his country rather than serving it?

Long after she'd kissed her brother goodbye, taken the commuter flight to Chicago and boarded the jet to Montreal, she was still pondering what Nathaniel had told her and trying to apply it to Troy.

He had made his choices, just as Nathaniel had. Troy had followed his beliefs, pursued his convictions...and he had claimed that in fleeing, he was serving his country, too. "How am I helping the United States if I let them draft me and ship me overseas?" he had explained. "I love this country, but I can't blindly support it when it's making a mistake. If a kid commits a murder, his mother can't just slap him on the back and say, 'It's all right, because I love you.' It *isn't* all right. And sometimes the mother has to walk away, to say no."

They had had this dialogue many times before, speaking theoretically. Troy had a single-digit draft number. He'd applied several times for conscientious objector status, written essays, collected character witnesses who would vouch for the immutability of his pacifistic views, met with his draft board, filed appeals. He'd pursued every legal avenue in his effort not to have to serve in a war he didn't believe in. He'd shared his feelings with Julianne, and she'd supported every step he'd taken.

But on that rainy night, the eve of the Fourth of July fifteen years ago, the discussion was no longer hypothetical. Troy had arrived at Julianne's walk-up flat two blocks from campus, where she'd moved after graduation with the intention of continuing *The Dream* over the summer. The cloudburst had glued his dense black hair to his forehead and cheeks, and his clothing was soaked.

As usual, Julianne was thrilled to see him. She had been fixing spaghetti for their dinner, with Joni Mitchell's

"Blue" album providing background music. "Dinner won't be ready for a while," she informed Troy. "Why don't you get undressed and dry off?"

"No," he said.

His unexpected refusal and the tautness of his voice compelled her to study him more closely. His eyes were ablaze, his lips tense, his fingers curling into fists. "What's wrong, Troy?" she asked, trying to conceal the dread that coursed through her, rasping along her nerves.

"I've decided to leave," he announced.

"Leave?" she echoed uncertainly. "Leave New York City?"

"Leave the United States." He yanked a soggy envelope from the hip pocket of his jeans and thrust it at her. She pulled out the letter, unfolded it and read that Troy's final appeal had been rejected. In light of his having completed college, the letter reported, his 2-S draft status was no longer operable. He would be required to report for induction in two weeks.

The record shut off, and the small efficiency apartment filled with the sounds of water boiling on the stove and rain thrashing the windows. "What do you mean, leave?" she asked.

Troy paced the room. Given its minuscule size, he quickly reached a wall, about-faced, paced, reached another wall. He couldn't seem to stand still. "I mean *leave*, Julie. I'm going to go to Canada."

"When?"

"Tonight."

Anxious for something to do, some way to counter the trembling that threatened to overcome her, she turned off the heat under the pot of water. Then she reread the letter he'd received from his draft board, smoothing out the creases, staring at the neatly typed print. "You can't go," she said.

"Why not?" Troy stalked to the window and gazed out at the downpour. "I can't stay, Julianne. If I stay, I'll get drafted."

"You've got other options," she murmured. "What about alternate service?"

"I volunteered for alternate service in every one of my applications," he reminded her. "They don't need any more hospital orderlies. They need cannon fodder in 'Nam. That's what they want me for, and I'm not going to do it."

"If you believe so strongly in this, you could express your opposition by going to jail," she suggested.

He spun around to confront her. "Jail? What the hell do you think this is about? It's about freedom, Julianne. *Freedom.* The freedom for me to make up my own mind about what my life means, and how I should live it. Going to jail means giving up my freedom. If I'm going to give up anyway, what's the difference whether I go to jail or to 'Nam?"

"In jail you wouldn't have to kill anybody."

"That's not the point," he argued. "The point is, I'm right about this. The draft board is wrong. The government is wrong. Nixon is wrong, and Johnson was wrong before him. The war is wrong. I'm not going to let them punish me for being right."

"Don't you think—" She was desperate to keep him from leaving. "Don't you think going into exile is a kind of punishment?"

"I'll be able to live in Canada," he claimed, his voice muted, his eyes lowered. "I'll be free there. Nobody's going to lock me up for listening to my heart."

Listening to his heart. His heart told him that he had to live his life in freedom. Julianne's heart told her that she loved Troy, that she couldn't bear the thought of losing him.

She knew he hadn't reached his decision frivolously. He had analyzed his situation and made up his mind. And yet...if he went to prison, she could visit him, wait for him, welcome him upon his release. If he went to Canada, there would be no release. He would never come back. He wouldn't be able to, not without risking arrest.

Nor could she follow him there. The United States was her home. She loved her country as much as Troy did. Maybe more.

"If a kid murders somebody," she commented quietly, "of course his mother can't slap him on the back and congratulate him. But she doesn't have to turn away from him, either. She can stand by him, not because she approves of what he did but because she loves him and cares about what's going to happen to him."

"If it meant giving up her freedom, then maybe she wouldn't stand by him." Troy had dropped onto the narrow bed that doubled as a couch in the multipurpose room. He rested his elbows on his spread knees and propped his head up in his hands. "I'm not happy about this, Julie," he whispered. "You know I'm not. But...it's my life we're talking about. My life."

Dinner went forgotten. Julianne crossed to the bed, sat beside him, wrapped her arms around him. They kissed; they held each other; they loved each other. And through it all a profound sadness enveloped them, hollow, resounding with loneliness. Afterward they lay together, listening to the rain, watching the light fade from the windows as night settled around them.

Troy sat up, and Julianne began to shiver. Without his body beside her, her bed would never be warm again. "Please, Troy—"

"Don't." He cut her off, aware that she would try once more to persuade him to stay. Aware that if she did, she might just succeed.

"I don't want you to go," she went on, despite his silencing look. She had nothing to lose by speaking; if she didn't speak, she would lose everything. "I need you."

He stared at the wall. She could see only his back, his broad shoulders, the thick black tangle of his hair. She watched the shifting of the muscles beneath his suntanned skin, the tension gathering at the base of his neck. She knew he was laboring to contain himself, to resist her.

He sat that way for a long time, then swung his legs off the bed and reached for his jeans. He dressed quickly and strode to the door. When his hand touched the doorknob, he halted. Turning, he gazed at Julianne, his dark eyes anguished, his face registering pain, regret... and resolution.

Without another word, he was gone.

THE JET TOUCHED DOWN with a gentle bump. Julianne gazed out the window at the tarmac as the plane taxied to the terminal. Then she remembered to reset her watch, twisting the hands ahead an hour.

The gesture struck her as symbolic. Meditating on the past wasn't going to be of any use in the present. She intended to approach Troy as a potential employer, not as a former lover. Her sole purpose in coming to Montreal was to get the best possible photographs for *Dream* and, in the process, give Troy the professional opportunity he deserved. That was all.

After fetching her suitcase from the baggage carousel, she left the terminal and summoned a cab. Groping through her purse, she found the business card Troy had given her at the reunion in March. She recited the address printed on it, then settled back against the worn upholstery and let the cab sweep her into the city.

Under other circumstances she might have been curious to explore Montreal. She'd never visited that cosmopolitan center of Quebec before, and it appeared to be a beautiful place. But she ignored the scenery blurring past the window, concentrating only on the task before her.

Troy's studio occupied the ground floor of a quaint building on a side street. Climbing out of the cab, she peered through the glassed front wall, which was decorated with the words "Bennett-Chartier Photography Studio—Weddings, Portraits, Passports" in gold-embossed letters, and noticed signs of human life inside. Satisfied that the studio was open, she paid the driver and sent him away.

Hoisting her suitcase and inhaling deeply, she marched to the door and opened it. A bell fastened to the upper hinge signaled her entrance with a cheerful jingle. The middle-aged woman seated behind a reception desk near the door glanced up and smiled.

Before addressing the woman, Julianne took a moment to survey the room. It was paneled in honey-colored wood, with a thick brown carpet covering the floor. Built-in shelves along one wall displayed a variety of framed photos, many of misty-eyed brides and grooms and a few featuring adults or children in carefully wrought poses. The bottom shelf held bound photograph albums in different styles. A hallway led from the reception area to more rooms at the back of the building. The sound of a child throwing a high-decibel tantrum filtered down the hall.

"Can I help you?" the receptionist asked.

Julianne set her suitcase on the floor and turned to the woman. "I'm here to see Troy Bennett. Is he in?"

"Your name, please?"

"Julianne Robinson."

The receptionist scrutinized the calendar on her desk. "You don't have an appointment, do you?"

"No," Julianne admitted, then plowed ahead, refusing to let her nervousness overcome her. "I'm here to discuss some business with him."

The woman glanced toward the hallway. She was met with a shrill, childish chorus of "I won't, I won't, I won't!" and then a woman's voice, issuing a babble of placating words.

Wincing, the receptionist turned back to Julianne and presented her with a polite smile. "Would you like to speak to Mr. Chartier, instead? He's available right now."

"No, thank you," Julianne insisted. "If Mr. Bennett is busy at the moment, I can wait."

The receptionist chuckled conspiratorially. "You can hear for yourself, he's got his hands full. Well, if you want to wait, have a seat." She waved toward a sofa upholstered in plaid wool across the room from her desk. A coffee table stood in front of the sofa, holding an open wedding album and a few photography magazines.

Julianne started toward the sofa, but stopped when she heard Troy's familiar voice rumbling down the hallway. "Listen, Mrs. Block. Either you calm them down right now, or we're calling a halt to it. I'm a photographer, not a child psychologist." He appeared in the hallway, glowering, and stormed toward the reception area, groping in his shirt pocket for a cigarette. He pulled one out, lit it and lifted his face. Noticing Julianne, he froze.

"This woman is here to see you, Troy," the receptionist informed him. "Business."

His eyes never leaving Julianne, he shook the match out slowly, then crossed to the receptionist's desk and dropped it into her ashtray. "Thank you, Stacy," he mumbled.

Julianne drank in his presence. His leonine hair was mussed, but his white oxford shirt was crisp and pressed and his jeans appeared fairly new. His towering height and firm physique sent a thrill of desire through her, just as they had the very first time she'd seen him. But desire wasn't an appropriate emotion for this occasion, and she willed her gaze back to his face. She was unnerved by the dark power of his eyes, the sensuous curve of his lips beneath his mustache as they clamped down on his cigarette. "Hello, Troy," she said, relieved by her calm tone.

He seemed momentarily at a loss. Then he smiled shyly. "What are you doing here?"

A smile. He wasn't angry—or if he was, he'd learned in the past fifteen years how to disguise his anger. Choosing to believe the first possibility, she returned his smile. "I came to see you," she answered.

"What, you just happened to be in the neighborhood?"

"I just happened to be in Iowa," she told him. "I detoured here on my way back to New York."

His lips flexed as he mulled over his thoughts. He took a long drag on his cigarette, then extinguished it in the ashtray. "Julianne—"

A plump young woman emerged into the hallway, her blouse half untucked from her slacks and her hair in a state of disarray. She was carrying a worn teddy bear of indeterminate color and a half-eaten candy bar, and she was smiling. "Mr. Bennett?" she called to Troy. "I think we're ready to go. I've got them sitting so nicely—they look gorgeous. You'd better come quickly, before they start acting up again."

He grimaced and started toward the hallway. "Can I watch?" Julianne asked.

He shot her a cryptic look. "Have you got a strong stomach?"

Chuckling, she followed him down the hall into his studio. The room was small but brightly lit, with two white umbrellas diffusing the light from the glaring lamps and directing it toward a wall draped in blue cloth. In front of the wall, two youngsters, a boy and a girl, approximately five and three years old, were seated on a rug, grinning sheepishly. The girl had a lollipop stuck in her hair and a smear of chocolate on her chin. The boy was picking his nose.

Muttering beneath his breath, Troy wiped the girl's chin with his thumb and plucked the lollipop from her head. After tossing the candy into a trash can, he crossed to his camera, which was fastened to a tripod between the white umbrellas. "Okay, gang," he grumbled. "Let's get to work, shall we?"

"Smile, Jason!" the mother coached her children, making the teddy bear dance in the air. "Smile, sweetheart! Show me all those pretty teeth of yours!"

The boy bared his teeth. The little girl screamed in fright from his grotesque expression, then bolted from the rug and hid behind his mother's knees.

Troy cursed. Straightening, he gave the mother a remonstrative look. "Mrs. Block..."

"Go back, Jessica," the mother urged the girl. "Go back and smile for Mr. Bennett. He's going to make you a star."

"I don't want to be a star!" the girl whined. "I wanna be a rock-and-roll singer!"

"It's the same thing," Mrs. Block assured her, shoving her toward the rug. "Now go be a darling and sit by Jason. Jason, stop squinting. Let Mr. Bennett see your gorgeous eyes."

Jason squinted, then stuck out his tongue. Jessica howled. Troy cursed again. And Julianne burst into laughter.

"IT ISN'T ALWAYS like this," Troy remarked as he rewound his film. The rambunctious Block family had finally departed from the studio, leaving in their wake a soothing tranquility. In spite of the prevailing chaos during most of the sitting, Troy had managed to shoot two whole rolls of film of the brats. He was a skilled professional. He could take pictures of anyone, any time, regardless of the circumstances—and do a proficient job of it. Troy was certain that amid all the mugging and acting out of the children, he'd gotten more than enough good photographs for Mrs. Block's portfolios.

Julianne stood by the door, watching as he collected and labeled his film canisters and then shut off the lamps. Her presence hadn't distracted him—as if a quiet, polite observer could have been a distraction in the tumultuous studio.

As polite and quiet as she had been, Julianne *could* have distracted him, he admitted. Throughout the shoot, he'd never lost his consciousness of her nearness, of her serenity and poise. But having her there hadn't affected his work.

Although he'd seen her twice in the past few months, he still hadn't grown accustomed to the elegant gauntness of her cheeks or the slender proportions of her tall body. Was this what fifteen years in New York City did to a woman? he wondered, not at all displeased. When he'd known her in college, he'd found her hearty build appealing because it had put him in mind of farmland, clean air, freshly grown food, wholesome living—the antithesis of his own youth in a polluted, overcrowded city neighborhood.

She'd been attractive then, but she was more attractive now. She still looked wholesome and healthy, but she had a polish about her, a veneer of sophistication, an aura of wisdom that came with age and experience. Her brown hair was still silky and shiny, but its neat pageboy cut enhanced her facial features as her lanky hippie hairdo in college never had. Her irises were just as clear and blue as they'd been then, but today she knew enough to wear a dress the same blue color, magnifying the crystalline beauty of her eyes. And her lips . . .

Hell, what was he thinking of? Julianne had told Stacy she had come to the studio to see Troy on business. Her staid professional attire attested to that fact. After fifteen long years, during which Julianne had had adequate time and opportunity to recover from their fling in college, she certainly wouldn't have come all this way just to torment Troy with her beauty.

If she'd been interested in reigniting an old, burned-out flame, he reasoned, she would have tried something at the reunion. Or at Laura and Seth's wedding a couple of weeks ago. She hadn't, though. That wasn't what she wanted Troy for. The only reason she looked so terrific to him was that she happened to be a terrific-looking woman.

"You've come to talk business," he said, seeking confirmation of that essential fact.

Julianne nodded. "I can wait, though. If you've got other appointments—"

"No, I'm all through for today." Troy checked his wristwatch: a quarter past six. He wasn't surprised to discover he'd spent well over two hours with the Block children. It had seemed more like well over two years. "You just got here from Iowa?"

She nodded again. "It's been a long day for me," she allowed.

A long day. And she'd traveled all the way from Iowa. The least he could do was offer her something to eat—a business dinner, he cautioned himself. "Are you hungry?" he asked. "We could go get some food or something." Not a particularly romantic invitation, but that was just as well.

"All right."

Crossing the hall to the darkroom, he glanced automatically at the light bulb above the door to see if Claude was inside. The bulb was off, indicating that the room was unoccupied. Troy went inside and left his film in the "to-be-developed" bin on the workbench. Then he rejoined Julianne in the hall, closing the door behind him.

Without speaking, he ushered her to the reception area. Claude was perched on the corner of Stacy's desk, conferring with her. A few inches shorter than Troy, Claude had unusually light blond hair and a ruddy complexion that gave his pale eyebrows and lashes an almost freakish appearance. Like Troy, he had on a cotton shirt and jeans.

At their entrance, Claude stood and presented Julianne with a curious smile. "Julianne, my partner, Claude Chartier," Troy introduced them. "Claude, Julianne Robinson. A—" He almost identified her as a college friend, then caught himself. "A magazine editor."

His smile expanding, Claude shook her hand. "What magazine?"

"*Dream*," she answered.

"No kidding? The glossy incarnation of that old college rag of Troy's? He's told me about it."

Troy had indeed told Claude about *The Dream*. But never about Julianne. She was a part of his past—one of many parts of his past—that he never discussed.

"We're going out for some food," Troy informed his colleagues, giving Stacy's calendar a quick perusal. His first appointment the following day, he noted, was an on-location shoot at a research center in need of illustrations for their annual report. He was expected at the center at 10:00 a.m. Since he'd be driving there straight from his apartment, he wouldn't have to get too early a start in the morning. That meant that he could relax with Julianne this evening, enjoy a leisurely dinner, maybe show her around the city....

What was wrong with him? She hadn't flown to Montreal to take a tour. For that matter, she probably hadn't flown to Montreal to enjoy a leisurely dinner with Troy. She'd come on business.

He knew what that business was, too. She was going to try to talk him into doing the photos for her magazine. Troy wasn't going to take the job, not even for Laura's sake. He didn't do that sort of work anymore, and even if he did, he wouldn't do it in the United States, for Julianne. That was all behind him, and he was going to have to turn her down.

Once he did, she undoubtedly wouldn't care to have him give her a tour of the city. She'd probably want to head straight for the airport and return to New York.

Troy's assumption that Julianne was planning to leave Montreal that night was derailed by the sight of her suitcase, which stood by the front door. Well, she'd just spent some time visiting her folks in Iowa, so of course she'd have a suitcase with her. But still...was she planning to stay in Montreal for a while? How long? Where?

He turned to her and found her chatting amiably with Claude. "I like your magazine," he was telling her. "I like the stances you take. 'Course, it isn't a big seller in Canada—you're really geared to a U.S. readership. But Troy passes along his copies when he's done with them, and I read them. I like your approach to issues—informative without being preachy."

"Thank you," she said, accepting Claude's praise with a modest smile. "I wish I could take full credit for the magazine, but I can't. I've got a talented staff working for me."

"You *can* take full credit for it," Troy corrected her. "*Dream* is your baby—you've made it what it is today. Is this bag yours?" he asked, moving to the suitcase.

Julianne's smile veered to Troy. He sensed nothing in it beyond her appreciation at being complimented on her professional skill. "Yes," she replied.

"Well." He picked up the suitcase and opened the door. "We're taking off, guys. I'll be in tomorrow afternoon after my morning shoot."

"See you then." Claude waved. "Nice meeting you, Julianne."

Troy led her outside and down the street to his car. He put the suitcase in the rear, locked the hatchback and then opened the passenger door for Julianne. Walking around to the driver's side, he considered the selection of a restaurant. He wasn't dressed nicely enough for any of the many swanky eateries in the city, but even if he was, he didn't want to take her anywhere swanky. Fancy tablecloths and candlelight would create the wrong atmosphere, would cause him to dwell on how lovely she looked, how captivating her eyes were, and her smile. He wanted to take her someplace where he'd be able to focus on business, where he'd find the strength to refuse her offer of free-lance work.

He drove to a steak joint not far from his studio.

"I like Claude," she commented as he steered through the traffic.

"He's a good man," Troy confirmed. "I couldn't ask for a better partner."

"He speaks like an American."

Troy shot her a perplexed look. "He *is* an American."

"I mean, someone from the States," she clarified. "With a name like Claude Chartier, I thought he might be a French-Canadian."

Troy chuckled. "With a name like Claude Chartier, he comes from St. Louis," he informed her. "He's an expatriate, just like me."

"A draft evader?" she asked.

Troy's smile waned. He knew that Julianne was asking only out of curiosity, but he didn't like the reminder of his past. He answered with a brusque nod.

"Is that just a coincidence?"

"No," he informed her. "We met shortly after I got here. There was a small community of expatriates—dodgers and AWOLs—and we banded together for support. Canada allowed us to come in, but it didn't exactly embrace us. So we stuck with our own, hung out at our own bars, found work for one another. Kept one another from getting homesick."

Julianne lapsed into thought. "It must have been hard for you," she observed softly. "Uprooting yourself and moving to a new country."

"It beat the alternative," he remarked with a shrug. Spotting the restaurant, he searched the street for a parking space. As soon as he'd shut off the engine, Julianne let herself out of the car. Troy wondered whether her action was a deliberate way of denying him the chance to be chivalrous. Then he reproached himself for reading so much into her every smile and gesture. Whether or not he opened her door for her didn't signify anything.

The restaurant boasted an informal decor—leatherette booths, mock-Tiffany lamps, laminated wood-topped tables and forties jazz pouring out of unobtrusive ceiling speakers. A hostess escorted them to an empty booth and left two menus. Once Troy was seated, he lit a cigarette. He was edgy; he had to do something with his hands.

"This is nice," Julianne observed, ignoring her menu and scanning the room, studying the colorful framed lithographs adorning the walls.

It wasn't the nicest restaurant in Montreal, Troy conceded silently, but it was nicer than any other restaurant he'd ever gone to with Julianne. They'd never dined out together in college, except for an occasional pizza or a hamburger at one of the neighborhood dives. They couldn't have afforded the extravagance of a night on the town—Troy was a scholarship student, and although Julianne was a doctor's daughter, general practitioners plying their trade in farming communities in Iowa didn't exactly rake in the dough.

But even if they could have afforded to patronize classy restaurants, they wouldn't have. Julianne had determined that she and Troy should keep their romance a secret because she was afraid of upsetting the balance of *The Dream*'s staff. As it was, Andrew and Kimberly were always bickering, threatening that tenuous balance. If word leaked out that the newspaper's editor in chief was having an affair with the staff photographer, their colleagues on the paper might have started treating them differently and the camaraderie that was so vital to the smooth functioning of the newspaper might have been ruined.

Troy had agreed with Julianne's reasoning and had maintained a discreet distance from her in public. Even after graduation, when Laura had left the city to live on a commune and Kimberly had returned to Georgia to get married, Troy and Julianne had continued to pretend that nothing more than a friendship existed between them. Andrew and Seth had sublet an apartment in the city that summer, staying in town to work on *The Dream*, and Troy had wanted to share with them the news that he and Julianne were a couple. He had grown tired of hiding the truth, restraining himself around her, and he didn't like keeping such an important fact from his two close friends. He had decided that he *would* tell them, as soon as his conscientious objector status was approved and he could commit himself to remaining in New York, maybe even moving in with Julianne, living with her, marrying her.... Whatever they did, he was going be open about it.

Instead he'd wound up leaving the city, leaving the country. Fifteen years had to elapse before Troy had the opportunity to treat Julianne to a real meal at a real restaurant.

This was a dangerous line of thought, he chastised himself. Judging from Julianne's inscrutable expression, it was not the line of thought she herself was pursuing. Smart of her, too. Nothing was to be gained by dredging up what had been between them, what hadn't been, what might have been. "Let's talk shop," he said abruptly, stubbing out his cigarette.

Julianne opened her mouth, then closed it as a waitress approached. She skimmed the menu and ordered a chef's salad. No wonder she had lost weight, Troy contemplated as he requested a steak. A salad was hardly enough of a meal to fill that long, slim body of hers.

She waited until the waitress had departed before picking up Troy's conversational gambit. "You know why I'm here," she said evenly. "I want you to do the photos for the story on Laura."

He nodded. "And you know I'm going to say no."

"Troy." She settled back against the banquette, assessing him. "I know a lot of photojournalists. None of them is right for this assignment. I want the best for my magazine."

He chuckled grimly. "I'm flattered, Julianne, but..." He reached for another cigarette, then changed his mind and let his hands fall to the table. "The answer's still no. I used to be a photojournalist, but I'm not anymore."

"I don't believe that."

"Believe it," he argued, wishing she weren't looking at him so steadily. Her eyes seemed to drill through him, searching for some inner truth that would contradict his words. "You've seen for yourself—I've got a business to run."

Julianne laughed. "What I've seen for myself is that your business involves taking portraits of precocious, crabby youngsters. Don't tell me you find that more rewarding than photojournalism."

"I—" He exhaled, then relented with a grin. "No, I don't find it more rewarding. But it pays the bills and puts gas in my car. This is my life now, Julianne. It's what I do. It's what I am."

"You could do so much more by working for *Dream*," Julianne maintained, firm without being pushy. "You could be so much more."

His first impulse was to take offense at her presumptuousness. But he couldn't. She had only stated a fact. He could be so much more—if conditions allowed it.

But they didn't. He was a businessman, a portrait taker, a Canadian. A man who had broken his nation's laws and fled for his life. "Why are you being so stubborn about this, Julie?" he asked gently. "I've said no every way I can."

Something flickered in her eyes when he called her "Julie." A memory, an instant of recognition, an acknowledgment that something more than business had once existed between them. Troy hadn't used her nickname on purpose. It had emerged naturally, the pet name used by an old lover.

She took a moment to compose herself. "I'm being stubborn about it," she said slowly, weighing each word before she uttered it, "because you owe it to yourself to accept this job. I'm not asking you to fold up your business and move back to the States. I'm just asking you to try your hand at one simple free-lance assignment."

"For your magazine?" he probed, aware that he was leading them into treacherous waters. "Or for you?"

"For you," she answered laconically.

The waitress arrived with their orders. Troy sliced into his steak, using the time to analyze his thoughts. Damn the woman, but she was right. He was stagnating professionally; he ought to be jumping for joy that she'd come to him with such a stimulating assignment. If she were telling the truth, if he could believe her, then her personal feelings for him—whatever they might be—had nothing to do with her offer.

But what about *his* personal feelings? How could he possibly work for her without reliving in his mind everything that had transpired between them? If, for some reason, she did try to start up with him again, he would have a difficult time resisting her.

He didn't want to fall in love with Julianne Robinson. He wasn't right for her. He'd broken her heart once, willfully, consciously. She deserved someone better, and if she hadn't found that someone by now, she ought to put forth some effort in finding a man worthy of her. She ought to spend less energy courting Troy for her magazine and more energy courting a selfless, law-abiding gentleman for herself, somebody who would never put his own needs ahead of hers.

Troy chewed his steak without tasting it. He drank some water, took another bite of meat, swallowed. Julianne hadn't touched her salad. She simply studied him, her eyes glowing enigmatically, her mouth curved in an unjustifiably confident smile, her graceful hands in repose on the table.

"I haven't done any photojournalistic work in ages," he pointed out, suddenly eager to shake her out of her complacency.

"What about *Maritime*?" she asked.

Maritime—the small-press book of photos Troy had taken in Nova Scotia six years ago. His old pal Peter Dubin had published the collection of photos and sold nearly a thousand copies of the book—a phenomenal sales record for a small-press book, but nothing overwhelming. The photos were good; Troy wouldn't deny that. The pictures he'd taken of the men, women and children of that bleak but breathtakingly beautiful province represented some of the best work Troy had ever done.

But *Maritime* was a fluke, a one-shot deal. It wasn't the substance of his career. He'd lost money on the project. And if it weren't for that damned book, Julianne would never have found Troy, tracked him down and invited him to her reunion over two months ago. If it weren't for *Maritime*, they wouldn't be having this conversation now.

"How did you ever find *Maritime*, anyway?" he asked.

"I like browsing in out-of-the-way bookstores," Julianne replied, lifting her fork. "If you want to know the truth, I've always made a point of checking through the books in the photography section. Not only because I'm on the lookout for new photographers for the magazine, but because..." She raised her eyes to Troy and smiled meekly. "I was looking for books by you. I never forgot how gifted you were, and I kept thinking, maybe, wherever you were, you would publish a book one day. And you did."

Her confession astounded him. He lowered his silverware and met her unwavering gaze. "You were looking for my stuff?" he asked with an amazed laugh. "All those years?"

"I knew your talent, Troy. I had faith in it. I was hoping someone else would have faith in it, too, and publish your work. And someone finally did."

"Why did you send the invitation through him?" Troy asked, referring to the reunion. "You sent it to Peter and asked him to forward it. Why?"

"I didn't know how else to reach you," Julianne explained, digging into her salad, appearing far more relaxed than Troy felt. "Right after you went to Canada, I wrote to you a few times. I sent the letters to your parents, but you never responded."

"I never got them," he informed her, smiling bitterly. "As far as my parents are concerned, I'm dead. They would never forward anything to me."

"They still haven't forgiven you for leaving the country?" she asked, her eyes shimmering with sympathy.

He shook his head. "They never will, Julie. That's the way it goes."

"Well, you aren't dead to me," she declared. Her tone was warm without being overly suggestive. "The only way you could be dead to me is if you keep burying yourself up here, taking pictures of snotty kids instead of doing the kind of work you do best. And I'm not going to let that happen, Troy. I'm simply not going to let it happen."

She had been obstinate back then, too, he recalled. Muleheaded, cocksure and always right. Here she was again, so many years later: obstinate, muleheaded, cocksure. And right.

Why fight it? He wanted the work, and he did do it well. "For Laura," he said quietly. "I'll do it for Laura."

Julianne smiled. Not a triumphant smile, not a gloating one, but a smile of sheer, unfettered delight.

Three

"What was in those letters, anyway?" Troy asked.

He had already settled the bill, but they were dawdling over their coffee. Julianne was feeling surprisingly mellow, considering where she was and whom she was with.

She'd been feeling mellow ever since Troy had agreed to do the photographs. Mellow, grateful and satisfied. When it came to her professional life, Julianne was usually successful, but she never took success for granted. In this instance, she'd suffered serious misgivings about whether she would accomplish her goal. Flying on a whim to Canada and barging in on Troy had been a questionable strategy, to say the least. It could have backfired horribly.

But it hadn't. With her success came the understanding that getting Troy to accept the assignment had truly been her only purpose in coming. As soon as he'd capitulated, she had felt her body unwind, her nervous system revert to its normal placidity, her anxiety dissipate. If she had honestly wanted anything more from Troy, anything personal, she would still be keyed up. The fact that she wasn't proved something important to her.

Troy, too, seemed to have relaxed. As soon as he'd made the commitment to work for her, his entire demeanor had softened. They'd managed to talk freely about a wide variety of things over dinner. Troy had described the restored architecture of Old Montreal's historical waterfront district, the city's renowned botanical gardens and some of the comical mishaps of his trip to Nova Scotia six years ago, when he'd taken the photos that had ultimately been published as *Maritime*. Julianne had regaled him with the intrigues of her office and updated him on Laura and Seth.

"Laura's made a weekend ritual of distributing her furniture to the needy," Julianne related. "She's got every table and chair earmarked for her clients. Her stuff is so old Seth thinks she should just dump it. But you know Laura. Whatever she owns, she wants to give away."

Julianne and Troy hadn't spoken this easily in fifteen years, and Julianne relished the comprehension that, finally, they could revive their friendship. One of the things she'd missed most about Troy was their ability to talk, to share everything with each other, from the most trivial concerns to the most complex. Their friendship had been at least as important as their passion, and if they could recapture that friendship, Julianne would be immensely pleased.

That Troy introduced the subject of the letters she had written to him took her slightly aback, however. Discussing those long-ago missives, with their outpourings of emotion, was far different from discussing the staff feuds she was forced to resolve in her job captaining *Dream*.

He was waiting patiently for an answer. "I don't remember," she said evasively, aware that that wasn't the truth. She didn't recall the specifics of what she'd written to him, but she remembered enough: she'd written that she missed him, that she loved him, that she wished he hadn't left New York, but instead had shown the fortitude to stay and fight for his freedom in the United States. She'd also written about *The Dream*, about how, with its increase in advertisements and its newly instituted cover price, it was finally beginning to show a profit, so she could afford to pay stipends to the entire staff. But most of the letters had been consumed by melancholy drivel about how sorely she wanted Troy to return to New York.

Perhaps it was just as well he'd never received the letters. They wouldn't have brought him home; they would only have made him feel worse than he already did about leaving.

"You never wrote to me, did you?" she asked.

"No," he admitted, smiling wistfully.

"Even if you'd gotten my letters, you wouldn't have written, would you?"

"No." He seemed on the verge of elaborating on his terse reply, but he didn't. Just that one biting word, telling Julianne what she had always assumed, even as she'd sent her letters off to him. She'd written them with the bitter understanding that she would never hear from him again. She hadn't known that her letters were destined never to reach him, but she hadn't been surprised by his lack of response.

Still, it should have been his prerogative and not his family's to destroy her letters. "I'm sorry your parents kept the letters from reaching you," she remarked. "They don't really think of you as dead, do they?"

Troy sipped his coffee, then lit a cigarette. His eyes seemed to lose their warmth as he reflected. "They really do," he insisted.

"Fifteen years is a long time, Troy. Have you tried to contact them recently?"

Smoking, he reminisced. "I went back to see them after the amnesty," he revealed. "I went back to Detroit."

"And?"

He didn't speak again until he'd finished his cigarette. He put it out, drank the rest of his coffee and sighed. "I rang the bell," he told her. "It was a warm day and the front door was open. This kid raced to the screen door, a little boy about three years old. I didn't know who he was. I thought maybe my folks had moved away and another family was living there." His gaze grew distant, focusing on a memory. "It turned out he was my nephew. My sister had gotten married a year after I left, and I didn't know anything about it. And there was this kid, my nephew, shouting for my parents to come to the door—only he called them 'Gramma' and 'Grampa.' I was sure I was at the wrong house, until they appeared."

He paused again, and his voice was underlined with pain when he continued. "My dad took one look at me and called me a name—a curse. Then he grabbed my nephew and hauled him away, as if he didn't even want the kid to see me. My mom stood there for a while, just staring at me, looking as if she hated me, as if she wanted to spit on me. I asked if I could come in, and she said no, I didn't belong there, I wasn't welcome, I should just leave them alone. I had humiliated the family, she said. I was a shame to them, an embarrassment, a criminal, and all they wanted was for me to go away and never darken their doorstep again."

"Oh, Troy." Julianne's heart brimmed with compassion for him. Her family was so different from his. No matter how fiercely she and Nathaniel had disagreed on issues, the enduring bond of love had always remained strong between them. She couldn't imagine anything any member of her family could possibly do that could create such an unbreachable rift among them.

Once again her mind replayed the final night she'd spent with Troy before he'd left for Canada. He had claimed that if a mother believed that her child had erred, she sometimes had to turn her back on her child. Obviously Troy's parents believed that, as well. But Julianne believed that no matter what sins a child might have committed, his mother owed him her love and forgiveness.

"Are you done?" he asked, his tone noticeably lighter as he nodded toward her coffee cup. "It's getting late."

She glimpsed at the remaining coffee in her cup and shrugged. Any more coffee, and she wouldn't be able to fall asleep. "I've got a reservation for tonight at the Queen Elizabeth Hotel," she informed him. "Will I be able to get a cab from here?"

"Don't be ridiculous," he scoffed, rising and assisting her out of the booth, his fingers curling casually about her wrist. He released her as soon as she stood, and she hastily shook off the notion that his touch had implied anything beyond courtesy. "I'll drive you there."

The night sky was dotted with stars as they left the restaurant. Streetlights and headlights cut through the darkness, creating a glittering panorama of bustling life in the dark city. Troy let Julianne into his car, then took the wheel and started the engine. "On a strictly practical subject, Julie, when do you need the photos?" he asked as he pulled away from the curb.

"The sooner the better."

"Hmm." He performed some mental calculations as he drove. "It's going to take some manipulation of my schedule and Claude's so he can cover for me. Even if I can complete the shoot in a couple of days, I've got to add in travel time and all."

"We'll accommodate your schedule," Julianne promised. Indeed she would put off publishing the "Broken Families in America" issue for years and years if that was what it took to get Troy's photographs included.

"I'll work out something with him and Stacy and give you a call," Troy resolved. "How much longer did you say Laura is going to be in New York?"

"Till the end of June, until the school term ends for Laura's daughter. If we can't get it worked out quickly, I'll fly Laura back to New York. But she'll be pretty ticked off if I've got to do that," Julianne added with a laugh. "She doesn't like airplanes. They make her queasy."

"I'll do the shoot before she leaves," Troy swore. "I don't want Laura getting queasy on my account."

The car had reached the Queen Elizabeth Hotel, a large, boxy building constructed of pale stone. The hotel appeared rather bland and staid, but the rates had been lower than those of the other hotels Julianne had investigated. While *Dream*'s travel fund was more than adequate, Julianne budgeted the money scrupulously, leaving the bulk of it for the jaunts her reporters made to cover stories.

Troy pulled up to the curb behind a line of taxis and shut off the engine. Then he turned to Julianne. The sparkling warmth returned to his eyes as they absorbed her face, and his lips curved in a tentative smile. He didn't speak, but only gazed at her, his expression unreadable.

"Thanks for dinner," she said. Trite, but safe.

"Thank *you*," he countered.

She laughed hesitantly. "You're welcome," she mumbled. "Why are you thanking me?"

"For the job," he answered. "For being so damned stubborn and talking me into it. I could get off on doing some real work, for a change." He twisted away, ruminating, his fingers tracing the arc of the steering wheel. "I'm a little nervous about it, though," he confessed.

"Don't be," she assured him. "Even if you haven't done this sort of work for a while, I'm sure your skill hasn't atrophied. You'll do an excellent job."

His face remained forward, displaying his rugged profile to Julianne. His smile faded as he thought. "That's not why I'm nervous," he said.

Julianne nodded. He didn't have to go into detail; she knew what was bothering him. But they'd just shared a pleasant dinner, and she was certain that they could share a pleasant working relationship, too. "That was a long time ago," she reminded him, her voice soft, slightly tremulous. "We're both mature adults. We can forget about what happened then."

"Can we?"

No. Julianne couldn't. Neither, she realized, could Troy. She lapsed into silence, staring at her hands folded in her lap, and futilely tried to pretend she could ignore her unresolved feelings for the man at her side.

She felt his index finger against her cheek, stroking a wisp of hair back from her face. Lifting her eyes, she met his smoldering gaze. She watched as he leaned over the gear stick, as his mouth neared hers, as his lips brushed tenderly over hers.

"I wasn't going to do this," he whispered, sounding as helpless as she felt.

"Do what?" she breathed.

He kissed her again, less gently this time. His mouth moved sensuously against hers, coaxing her lips apart. Julianne made a feeble attempt to resist him, but she couldn't resist him any more than she could resist the onslaught of aching need his kiss awakened inside her. His tongue made a daring foray into her mouth, driving past her teeth in search of its partner.

A sigh lodged in her throat as her tongue met the potent thrusts of his. She wasn't going to do this either...but she *was* doing it, kissing Troy, kissing him wildly, as if he were her sustenance, her reason for living. Her fingers groped through the thick black waves of his hair, holding his head, clinging to him. He had left her once, and for a crazed moment she vowed to herself that she would never, ever let him leave her again.

His hand alighted on her shoulder, his fingertips digging into the flesh beneath the dress. His other arm reached around, pulling her awkwardly to him, pressing her body to his. As her breasts collided with the wall of his chest, her nipples hardened in an instantaneous reaction. She had never forgotten the feel of his firm body, the unspeakable yearning he aroused within her. How could she have suggested they could forget?

Groaning, he abruptly broke away. He fell back into his own seat, wrestling with his ragged breath, staring at the windshield with glassy eyes. "So much for that," he muttered wryly.

Panting as well, Julianne moistened her lips, hoping to facilitate her speaking ability. Her tongue detected the lingering taste of his mouth on hers, and his subtle flavor caused a hot, sharp shiver to ripple through her. "So much for what?" she rasped.

"So much for thinking we can forget." His fingers curled into a fist, and he gently pounded the plastic circle of the steering wheel a few times. Gradually he regained control of his breathing. "I'm sorry, Julianne. I shouldn't have done that," he said contritely.

"Why not?" Hearing the question was oddly enlightening to her. *Why not?* They were mature adults, as she'd noted, and just because they had a past didn't mean they had to refuse themselves a present and a future. They were no longer two infatuated college kids experiencing the first heady thrill of passionate love. But why couldn't they experience something else, something new, something even more meaningful? It already existed—Troy's kiss and her response to it proved that something was alive, burning between them. It was theirs if they wanted it. *Why not?*

He gave her a sidelong glance, then exhaled. Then he fished in his pocket for a cigarette and lit it. By now Julianne couldn't help but understand what that meant: he was tense, uneasy, troubled. "You don't want me, Julie," he declared, his voice hoarse but certain. "If you do, you shouldn't. I'm not good for you. We both know that."

Her gaze followed the red coal of his cigarette as it traced the air. "I'm not sure I know that," she murmured.

"If you don't, then you're not as smart as I took you for," he retorted, his tension evolving into anger. "Look at me, Julie. I'm an outlaw, for crying out loud! I broke the law, I went into exile—and I walked out on you. I left you, Julie. I abandoned you."

"You had no choice."

"I had plenty of choices. You know that as well as I do—you did your damnedest to make sure I was aware of all the choices I had. But I left. That was the choice I made. I left. I committed a crime. And I hurt you. You deserve better than that."

"I'm a grown woman," she snapped in a flare of rage that would have been uncharacteristic of her in any other circumstance. "Don't you think I'm allowed to make my own choices, too?"

He eyed her skeptically. "You're a grown woman, yes," he said, his voice low and gruff. "You're a beautiful, accomplished, successful woman. Why haven't you hooked up with someone else by now?"

"I've been busy," she answered curtly.

His eyes narrowed on her, and then he turned back to the windshield. He swore beneath his breath. "Don't tell me you've been carrying a torch for me all these years. Please. Don't tell me that's what it is."

Julianne's silence was all the answer he required.

He cursed again. "I'm a runaway, damn it. A criminal."

She took a moment to collect herself. Troy might be the only person in the whole world who could demolish her self-control, but if ever she needed her wits about her, it was now. "You aren't a criminal anymore," she pointed out calmly. "When Carter was president, he granted amnesty to all the draft evaders and welcomed you back."

"That doesn't change what happened when I left," he argued. "That doesn't change what I did then."

"And what about now?" she pressed him. "Why haven't *you* hooked up with anybody else? Have you been carrying a torch, too?"

"No!"

His vehemence was as informative as Julianne's silence had been. Troy still wanted her. He still cared for her. She was sure of it.

But instead of being elated by that comprehension, she felt a strange despair. It wasn't enough that Troy still cared for her. He seemed resolute in his decision not to allow their feelings to develop. Julianne could forgive him for what he'd done fifteen years ago, but as long as he hadn't forgiven himself, he could never give his love free rein—and he could never accept the love Julianne had to give him.

"I guess we ought to call off the photo assignment," he said, still staring straight ahead.

"Of course not," Julianne insisted, doing her best to collect herself, to reveal nothing of her churning emotions. "I want you to do the pictures. And you've already said you would. I'm not going to let you back out on me."

He issued one final curse. But his mouth contradicted him, curving into a grudging smile. "You always were such a boss, Julie."

"Bossing people around is one of the things I do best," she agreed, pulling on the chrome lever that unlatched the door. "Could you get my suitcase for me?"

"Yes, boss." He swung out of the car and met her at the rear bumper.

She allowed him to carry the suitcase inside the hotel for her, and he loitered near the elevator while she checked in. Once she'd signed the registration card and accepted her room key, she joined him at the elevator. "Don't look so panicked," she joked, struggling to salvage their earlier congeniality. "I'm not going to invite you up."

"What a relief," Troy parried her, although he didn't appear relieved at all. He looked pensive, and more than a little dubious.

The elevator door slid open, but before she could step in, Troy touched her shoulder, holding her in place just inches from him. His eyes pored over her upturned face, searching, reflecting his inner confusion. He bowed, as if about to kiss her, then swiftly straightened and set her bag inside the car. "Maybe this whole thing's a big mistake, Julie," he whispered before nudging her into the elevator.

Before she could respond, the door slid shut.

"SENATOR HOWARD MILFORD'S OFFICE," the secretary recited.

"This is Julianne Robinson from *Dream* magazine," Julianne identified herself. "May I speak to Kimberly Belmont?"

"One minute, please."

Julianne heard a click through the receiver as she was put on hold, and then Kimberly's lilting drawl. "Julianne! Greetings and salutations! How are you?"

"Busy, as usual," she answered noncommittally. Even though she and Kimberly were good friends, Julianne wasn't about to tell Kimberly the truth: that her spirits were at a low ebb, her mood glum, her mind embattled. It simply wasn't her style to bare her soul to others. That Kimberly had turned to Julianne for comfort during the upheaval of her recent divorce didn't enable Julianne to reciprocate, seeking comfort from Kimberly. Kimberly was good at confiding in others; Julianne wasn't. "How are things with you?" she asked.

"Ditto," Kimberly gaily reported. "Andrew's spring term at Amherst ends this week, and then he's coming down to Washington. He's going to testify before the Intelligence Committee sometime next week. I've been just about running myself ragged, trying to organize everything here for the committee session, getting the senator's speeches ready and helping Lee to coordinate the witnesses. Wilding's supervisor at the Central Intelligence Agency is playing hard to get, but we're gambling that Andrew's testimony will mortify him enough to show his face in the hearing room."

"How is Andrew bearing up?" Julianne asked. She remembered how reluctant Andrew had been about testifying, given his justifiable fear that going public about his accidental involvement in a research project with a C.I.A. agent named John Wilding would jeopardize his faculty position at Amherst College. He had ultimately found the courage to testify, just as he'd found the courage to fall in love with Kimberly. But a person could be courageous and frightened at the same time, as Julianne knew from her own recent experience in Montreal. "Is he scared?"

"Not at all," Kimberly reported, bursting with pride. "Once he made up his mind to do it, he became very stoical about the whole thing. I was right about him, Julianne. He's got strong principles, and when push came to shove, he couldn't abandon them." She issued a lovesick sigh. "Oh, Julianne. He's so good, so decent. He's such a fine man."

"I'm glad you found that out in time," Julianne affectionately ribbed her. "What's on the agenda after Andrew makes his appearance before the committee? Are you two going to elope?"

"Something like that," Kimberly revealed with a gleeful laugh. "We're going to do it quickly and quietly—just have our blood tested and sign some papers, and that'll be that. We've both already been through big weddings, after all. We don't want to have to get involved with all that hoopla again."

"Have you set a date?"

"Not yet," Kimberly told her. "It all depends on when I can get a week off from work here. Maybe during the August congressional recess. We're planning to go to London for our honeymoon. I'm so excited, Julianne—I've been spending every spare minute shopping for sexy lingerie."

Julianne guffawed. "Honestly, Kim!"

"Would you believe old stick-in-the-mud Andrew Collins gets turned on by lacy underthings?" Kimberly sighed again. "I adore him, Julianne. I can't believe it's possible to be so happy."

If she had it in her, Julianne might have succumbed to jealousy. But she'd never been a jealous person, and she was too delighted by Kimberly's good fortune to envy it. Kimberly had endured enough misery in her failed first marriage. Andrew had endured even worse misery when his first wife had died. After what they'd been through, they deserved all the joy they had finally found with each other.

As for Julianne—well, she'd had her share of joy once, and if that was all fate would grant her, she wasn't going to spend the rest of her life feeling sorry for herself. If Troy was determined to deny them future joy, that was his choice—another bad choice on his part, but Julianne had already lived through one bad choice he'd made. She would live through this one, too.

"Listen, I hate to have to talk shop while you're dancing around on cloud nine, Kim, but has Dan Eisner contacted you yet?"

"No," Kimberly answered. "Should I be expecting to hear from him?"

"He wants to do an up-close-and-personal on Andrew—and on you and Milford, too," Julianne explained. Kimberly already knew Dan Eisner, *Dream*'s national affairs correspondent. He had used Kimberly as an inside source on numerous articles before. "I'm aware that Andrew wants to keep a low profile regarding his testimony, and I know we can't get an exclusive on what goes on in the hearing. All the newspapers are going to be covering it, and I'm sure Milford is going to milk it for all the publicity it's worth. But what I've asked Dan to do is a human interest piece, portraying Andrew's side of the story, some background on how he got tangled up with the C.I.A. and how a principled college professor deals with this sort of thing. Does that sound all right?"

"As far as I'm concerned, sure," Kimberly remarked. "I can't speak for Andrew, though."

"I think it could prove useful to him," Julianne pointed out. "If he can air his position, if we treat his story with care and compassion, it could help him out when Amherst decides what to do about him. I'd give him first edit on it, if that would make a difference."

"Well, I know Dan. I know he can present things fairly," Kimberly assured Julianne. "If Andrew has any doubts, I'll vouch for Dan. And for you. Andrew trusts you, Julianne. If the article puts his situation in the right perspective, he probably won't balk."

"I hope he won't," Julianne said. "I think we could run an excellent piece about him."

Kimberly laughed. "I don't know, Julianne. It seems to me you and your magazine are doing quite a job of exploiting all your college cronies. First you've got that feature on Laura and her social work, and now you're going to write up me and Andrew. Next thing I know you'll be running profiles on Seth Stone, the born-again social-issues screenwriter, and Troy Bennett, our man in Canada."

Julianne stifled the urge to wince. "I'd be delighted to do a story on Seth," she granted impassively. "As far as Troy goes, I'm already exploiting him. He's down in New York even as we speak, taking photos for the story on Laura."

"No kidding! You all went ahead and hired him, then?" Kimberly exclaimed. "That last time we talked about it you were dead certain he wouldn't do it."

"It took all my powers of persuasion," Julianne allowed. "And I think he's doing it under duress. But even under duress Troy is far superior to any other photographer I could get for the job."

"Good for you, then," Kimberly bolstered her. "Three cheers for your powers of persuasion."

"He thinks I'm bossy," Julianne informed Kimberly. "He thinks I railroaded him into it. But he'll do a good job. That's all that matters," she added, trying to convince herself.

Kimberly ended the call. "Gotta run. The senator needs some text for a speech he's giving at a union dinner tonight. My word processor beckons."

"Okay, Kim," Julianne concluded. "Give my best to Andrew. And expect that call from Dan Eisner."

"Will do. Take care, Julianne."

Hanging up the telephone, Julianne let out a long breath. She stood, stretched and crossed to the window.

The morning was sunny and warm, the sidewalk below her swarming with pedestrians. Right now, right this minute, Troy was somewhere in the city. Under duress.

Kimberly's joke notwithstanding, Julianne knew she wasn't truly exploiting him. The job she'd commissioned him for was just the break he needed. Troy Bennett wasn't cut out for studio work. He wasn't fulfilled by his current assignments. He was more than ready for a new challenge.

And that, ultimately, was why he'd accepted her offer of work, she sternly reminded herself. It was an exciting professional opportunity—period.

According to his brief telephone call last night, he'd arrived safely in town and was settled in at the Greenwich Village apartment of Peter Dubin. Although Julianne had insisted that her magazine would cover Troy's hotel costs, he had assured her he preferred staying with Peter. "I come to New York so rarely," he'd explained. "Spending time with Peter is a treat for me."

Spending time with Peter. Not with Julianne.

Damn him. That one succinct phone call had conveyed to Julianne that Troy intended to avoid her as much as possible while he was in the city. Today and tomorrow he'd be in Brooklyn, visiting Laura's clients and taking pictures of them. By Friday he'd be returning to Montreal. After that Julianne would probably never see him again.

Why was he being so intransigent about their relationship? Why was he being so adamant about denying the truth of that one searing kiss they'd indulged in outside her hotel? They could love each other. They did love each other. How dare he decide unilaterally that he was wrong for Julianne?

She had dated other men in the intervening years. Nice, intelligent, charming men, the sort of men Troy apparently believed Julianne ought to hook up with. She hadn't hooked up with any of them for a reason: none of them was Troy. None of them could supplant him in her soul. "Carrying a torch" for him was a banal way of putting it, and Julianne wasn't certain it was an accurate description of her feelings. She hadn't made a concerted effort to shut out other men. She'd only been candid about acknowledging that unless she met someone who could mean as much to her as Troy had, she would rather be alone.

She was sure Troy had known other women since leaving her. He was a healthy, attractive man; no way would he have spent the past fifteen years living a celibate life. She didn't care whom he'd been with, though, or how often or why. All that counted was now, the present, proving to him that their love was viable.

Who was she kidding? Troy knew everything she did about their feelings for each other, and he was dead set against pursuing a relationship with her. Julianne couldn't pursue it single-handedly. She ought to give up and write it off, as she had fifteen years ago.

Yet that seemed absurd, and unnecessary. It was almost as if Troy were punishing himself for what he had done so long ago.

Punishing himself. Julianne sank into a chair beside the conference table and shook her head in astonishment. What had he said? *I left, I committed a crime...and I hurt you. You deserve better.*

Punishing himself. Of course. That was what he was doing. He hadn't gone to prison, but he *had* broken the law, and he was punishing himself still. He'd gone into exile, not just in body but in spirit.

Her memory of his words in the car was overtaken by other words, spoken in another car, a battered Jeep cruising along a county route through the Iowa farmland. Her brother had said that it had taken him years to come to terms with what he'd done by serving in Vietnam. It had taken him years to end the war in his heart.

For Nathaniel, a man who hadn't broken any laws, making peace with himself had been incredibly difficult. For Troy, shedding his guilt and finding that inner peace might be impossible. And until he ended the war in his heart, he would never have room in it for love.

Four

"Troy! Hey, man, good to see you! Come on in."

"Hey, yourself, Seth." Troy stepped into the entry hall of Laura's apartment and returned Seth's vigorous soul handshake. Clad in bright green drawstring sweatpants and a T-shirt, his feet bare and his blond hair disheveled, Seth looked as if he'd just gotten out of bed. It was nine o'clock, though, so Troy didn't think he'd awakened his friend.

Besides, Laura was expecting him. He peered past Seth in search of her, but all he saw were packing cartons and clutter. Boxes and rolled-up posters had converted the hallway into an obstacle course, and Troy picked his way carefully through the debris to the living room, which was in a similar state of disarray.

"If you're looking for Laura, give up," Seth alerted Troy, aware of his quizzical gaze. "She had to leave early this morning." Seth's lean body moved with agility through the mess, and he pushed his straight, shaggy hair out of his eyes and smiled. "An emergency cropped up. One of her clients was arrested last night, and Laura was summoned to the police station at the crack of dawn. I tried to call you this morning at your friend's place to give you some warning, but you'd already left."

"Does that mean the shoot's postponed?" Troy asked, adjusting the strap of his camera bag against his shoulder and digesting Seth's announcement. If he didn't start the job today, it would wreak havoc with his schedule.

Seth shook his head. "As far as she's concerned, you're still on. She said to tell you she'd meet you at her office at ten. There's a limit to how long she can stomach hanging around a police station." A stubborn straw-colored lock drooped onto his forehead again, and he impatiently brushed it away. "So, can I get you some coffee or something?"

"Coffee sounds great," said Troy. He could definitely use some caffeine; it would help to get his eyes focused and his nervous system in gear. He hadn't slept well the night before. Peter's futon couch had been about as comfortable to lie on as petrified lumps of concrete.

He issued a silent reproach. He wasn't worried about fouling up his schedule, and he couldn't blame the previous night's insomnia on Peter's furniture. He had been unable to sleep because he was in New York City, working for Julianne. He was worried about his schedule because he wanted to complete the job as quickly as possible and get out of town. As excited as he was by the prospect of engaging in some serious photojournalistic work, he still questioned whether he'd done the right thing in accepting the assignment.

But it was too late to back out. He'd made a commitment to Julianne and her magazine. He'd just have to live with it.

Seth's effervescence helped boost Troy's spirits. He followed Seth into the tiny kitchen, where an already brewed pot of coffee awaited them. As Seth pulled two mugs from a cabinet, Troy scrutinized him. Seth's hair had been fairly shaggy at the wedding a couple of weeks ago, and from their college days Troy was used to seeing Seth hirsute. Even so, Troy had grown accustomed to being the longest-haired man in any gathering. He found Seth's ungroomed appearance unexpected, yet oddly comforting.

The T-shirt Seth was wearing bore an inscription in bold red letters: "I DO." "Where'd you get that shirt?" Troy asked.

Seth glanced down at his chest, as if he needed a reminder of what shirt he had on. He laughed. "Laura got it for me. What do you think, Troy? Is it me?"

Troy's gaze shifted from the shirt to the thick gold band ringing the third finger of Seth's left hand. "Yes, Seth," he allowed. "It's you."

"You don't think it's obscene?" Seth inquired, filling the mugs with coffee.

"I think *you're* obscene," Troy joked as he trailed Seth to the cozy dining table. Seth had to clear a stack of papers and his typewriter out of the way before they could sit. Troy placed his camera case in front of him on the table. "What are you working on?" he asked with a nod toward the typed papers.

"Just a proposal," Seth informed him, flopping onto one of the chairs and sipping his coffee. "They're planning another Ax Man sequel, and they've asked me to put together some ideas."

"You're still writing Ax Man flicks?" Troy asked, surprised. "At the wedding you said you were working on something socially significant."

"*Good Fences*," Seth said, naming the film. "I've been circulating that script for—it feels like forever. It's gotten a few nibbles, but no real bites yet. Meantime I've got a mortgage to pay, and two lovely ladies to support. So it's back to Schlock City for me." He drank some of his coffee and shook his head good-naturedly. "Teenage girls are expensive, Troy. In a single week, Rita can spend the equivalent of the gross national product of Swaziland on cosmetics alone."

"The gross national product of Swaziland can't be that high," Troy pointed out.

Seth shrugged. "She's a terrific kid," he conceded, smiling fondly. "Even if she ignores me whenever I tell her she'd look better without all that crap on her face. She says the only reason I don't like make-up is that Laura's been a bad influence on me."

Troy studied Seth, taking note of his relaxed attitude, his genuine smile and the unrestrained sparkle in his hazel eyes. "Laura's been a good influence on you," he said.

Seth nodded, unabashed. "The best, Troy, the best. Stick around long enough, pal, and I'll start waxing sentimental."

"Good God!" Troy protested with a laugh. "It's too early in the morning for that."

"So, how's it going?" Without waiting for an answer, Seth pulled the camera case toward himself, unzipped the main compartment and surveyed its contents: two cameras, a flashgun, a wide-angle lens and a telephoto lens. "What kind of camera is this?" he asked, pulling one out of the bag. "I thought you liked Nikons. Didn't you have a Nikon back in college?"

"How can you remember stuff from that long ago?" Troy asked with an amazed laugh, although he was forced to acknowledge that lately he himself was having a serious problem with remembering too much stuff from that long ago. "I bought that Nikon secondhand in high school, and it died a natural death right around the time I opened my studio. The one you're holding is a Hasselblad."

"Hasselblad," Seth echoed, pulling the camera closer and examining it. "Never heard of that make, but if it's your camera, it must be good." He popped off the lens cap and peeked through the viewfinder. He twisted the focus, pointed the lens at Troy and then lowered the camera. "So," he declared, "how's it going? Did you get to see Julianne last night?"

It was a reasonable question, and Troy cautioned himself not to overreact. As far as Seth knew, Julianne was merely another friend from Troy's past, someone he'd be likely to contact when he visited the city. "I talked to her on the phone," he answered in a controlled voice. "I was just with her last week, up in Montreal, so it isn't as if we haven't seen each other in ages."

"I guess you'll get together with her once you've done the photos," Seth predicted. "Then you and she can celebrate your return to the real world. It must be a trip for you, getting out of that passport studio of yours and doing something meaningful for a change."

"This, from the man who brought us Ax Man," Troy snorted.

Seth guffawed. "Give me a break! I've done my bit for humanity. You wouldn't believe how many dorks I've had to wine and dine, trying to sell them on *Good Fences*. It's hard work being noble. But I'm not complaining," he hastily added. "Taking dorks out to dinner sure beats having to bail out wayward young things at the police station."

"Laura must work with a pretty nasty group of kids," Troy said, wondering what sort of people he would be photographing.

"Most of them are cream puffs," Seth assured him. "From what I gather, the deal with this one was that the father of her kid was selling drugs out of her apartment—apparently, with the girl's blessings." He rolled his eyes.

"It's ridiculous what some folks will do for the people they love."

Troy took a long drink of coffee and sorted through his thoughts. He wasn't taking pictures for Julianne because he loved her, he sternly reminded himself. He *didn't* love her. Just because he'd kissed her, just because his resolve had been momentarily weakened by her attractiveness, just because he'd allowed himself that one little lapse.... None of it meant that he loved her. It meant only that he was a normal man with a long memory. And just because he'd let her hire him to take some photos didn't mean he loved her, either.

Still, he couldn't shake off the mild uneasiness Seth's comment had provoked. Troy had been nursing doubts about the job ever since he dropped Julianne off at the Queen Elizabeth Hotel. Maybe accepting the job had been ridiculous, even if love didn't enter into it.

Restless and not at all pleased with the path his thoughts had followed, he drained his mug and stood. "If I'm supposed to meet Laura at ten, I probably ought to hit the road," he remarked, returning his camera to the case and slinging the strap over his shoulder.

Seth stood, as well. "I guess you'd better." He carried the empty mugs to the sink, then accompanied Troy down the hall to the door, instructing him on how to reach Laura's office. "Listen, Troy, if you've got any free time after you're done—today or whenever—come on back and have some supper with us. Rita would love to meet you. She saw you on *Evening Potpourri*, and she thinks you're a fox."

"Me? A fox?" Troy chuckled in astonishment. "Maybe I ought to check her out."

"Forget it," Seth warned him. "She's jailbait." He grinned incredulously. "I can't believe what instant fatherhood is doing to me, Troy. I used to kid Laura about being an overprotective mom, and now I'm twice as bad when it comes to Rita. I'm always examining her eyes to see whether her pupils are dilated when she gets home from school, and I've been thinking about getting her a chastity belt for her next birthday."

"If that's what instant fatherhood does to people, remind me to watch my step around pretty single mothers," Troy said with a laugh. "Take it easy, Stoned. I'll see you."

"Catch you later," Seth responded before waving and closing the apartment door.

The morning air was warm, almost muggy. Leaving the building, Troy recognized he didn't need his dungaree jacket, but he left it on so he wouldn't have to carry it. Two spare rolls of film were buttoned inside one of the breast pockets and a pack of cigarettes inside the other. He stopped to light a cigarette, then strolled down the street, his sneakers adding a bounce to his stride.

Thinking only about his destination and his assignment alleviated the edginess he'd felt ever since he'd arrived in New York late yesterday afternoon. Seeing Seth wasn't ridiculous. Working with Laura wasn't ridiculous, either. If he could keep his perspective, if he could think of Julianne simply as the editor who was going to okay his paycheck, he wouldn't have to believe he'd accepted the job because he was in love. He wasn't, so worrying about the situation was useless.

Turning onto Church Avenue, he approached the subway station. He halted near the entrance to finish his cigarette before going inside. He viewed the tired black woman selling tokens through the glass window of her booth. Her eyes were puffy, her hair a lackluster gray, her mouth stained with a purplish lipstick. She'd make an interesting subject for a photograph, he realized. But he didn't have time to shoot her. Putting out his cigarette, he dug in the pocket of his jeans for a token and pushed through the turnstile.

As he descended to the underground platform, he tried to recall the last time he'd thought about shooting photos of random subjects on the street. His gaze wandered down the platform, observing the people lined up and waiting for the train: the yuppie woman in the prim gray suit, clutching a leather briefcase and staring straight ahead, doing her utmost to ignore the people standing just inches from her. The scrawny teenage boy cutting school for the day, his white high-top sneakers unlaced and his arm cradling an oversize boom box. The shabby old man with the baggy pants, cracked shoes and bloodshot eyes, singing a tuneless melody to himself. Each of them would make a good shot, Troy realized.

He hadn't viewed the world this way, as a real photographer, since...probably since *Maritime*—too many years ago. When he was working in Montreal, that was what it was—work. His camera signified business: weddings, annual reports, the conversion of Mrs. Block's sniveling brats into presentable commercial models. He no longer thought about taking pictures for the pure joy of it.

Today, however, he did. The job he'd be doing with Laura would provide him with a dose of creative adrenaline. Simply thinking about it made him want to shoot everything—the surreal metal girders and winking yellow lights lining the tunnel, the chipped signs and scuffed stairs, the unposed, unassuming human beings positioning themselves along the platform.

Before he could give in to the temptation, a train wheezed to a halt beside the platform, and Troy boarded. Just as well, he decided. He had to save his film for Laura's clients.

Seth's directions were easy to follow, and Troy had no trouble finding Laura's office. It was actually less an office than a cramped cubicle hemmed in by movable partitions, but Laura had brightened the space by lining the windowsill with plants. A framed photo of her daughter stood on a corner of the desk.

"Troy!" she greeted him warmly, rising from her chair and giving him an exuberant hug. "I'm sorry about the hassle this morning. It was such a madhouse."

"No problem," he assured her, returning her hug and then stepping back to look at her. Her frizzy brown hair was tied off her face with a colorful silk scarf, and her loose-fitting white blouse and swirling denim skirt appealed to Troy far more than the straitlaced suit worn by the businesswoman on the subway. "How's your jailbird?"

"Feeling terribly sorry for herself," Laura answered with a smile. "She'll survive. Maybe she'll even learn something from the experience. Shall we go?"

"Whenever you're ready," he said agreeably. He followed Laura through the maze of partitioned cubicles occupied by other caseworkers and out of the bustling room. Laura's skirt swayed gracefully around her calves as she walked, and her steps were light and energetic. "You don't seem terribly concerned," he observed.

"Concerned?" She grinned up at him. "About what?"

"About the kid in jail."

Laura laughed. "In two more weeks, she won't be my client anymore—she'll be Mary Sprinks's. Let Mary be concerned." She pressed the elevator button, then turned fully to Troy. Reading his bemused expression, she justified herself. "I can't save the girl's life for her, Troy. She's got to save her own life. One thing I have to thank Seth for is teaching me that I can't take responsibility for everyone. I do what I can, and that's that."

"That sounds like a very healthy approach," said Troy.

The elevator door slid open and they stepped inside. Laura heaved her canvas tote bag onto her shoulder and studied Troy, her dark eyes beaming with delight. "You're looking great," she critiqued him. "How have you been?"

"Good," he lied. Then he reconsidered and decided that right now it wasn't a lie at all. He *was* feeling good.

"How's Montreal?"

"Cooler than Brooklyn," he answered, tugging at his jacket and grinning. "You and Seth seem to be doing wonderfully."

"We are," she confirmed, the glow in her eyes intensifying. "No complaints so far. How are our wedding pictures coming, by the way?"

"I'll get them to you before you leave for California," Troy promised. "I was hoping to develop them before I got here, but work got backed up at the studio. I had to take care of a million things just to be able to come down here and do this shoot. But don't worry—you'll like them."

"If you took them, they'll be great," she praised Troy, exiting the elevator ahead of him on the ground floor. "Even if I must say so myself, that wedding was a fantastic party. I had the time of my life. I was so glad everybody could come." She let him hold the heavy glass door open for her, then started down the street. "The first girl we're going to visit is Sandra Miller," she said, concentrating on the job at hand. "I should warn you, Troy, she's been pretty depressed lately. So be as low-key as you can, all right?"

"Low-key is my favorite way of working." He was relieved to be talking about the day's assignment instead of Laura's wedding. He knew whom she was referring to when she'd said, "I was so glad *everyone* could come." Not her co-workers, not her daughter's best friend, but the old gang from *The Dream*—Andrew and Kimberly and Julianne. As good as Troy was feeling at the moment, he didn't want to get into a nostalgia fest with Laura. That would force him to stop thinking of Julianne as his employer.

Walking at a brisk pace, Laura continued to discuss the first client they would be meeting. "This is my regular weekly session with Sandra, so I'll be doing business as usual," she explained. "The more you stay in the background, the better. Please don't let on if you're shocked or anything."

"Why would I be shocked?" Troy asked. He considered himself basically unshockable.

Laura smiled sadly. "It's pretty shocking to see a little girl raising a baby," she said. "Even after all these years as a social worker, I'm still shocked by the sight of it."

Although he wasn't really shocked by Sandra Miller, once they arrived at the girl's grim, grungy efficiency apartment in a dreary walk-up, Troy appreciated Laura's having prepared him. Sandra looked much younger than he'd expected. She was thin and sallow complexioned, with big, entreating eyes that put him in mind of those sentimental paintings of waiflike children that had been popular years ago. Clad in worn jeans and a sagging T-shirt, her feet bare and her hair pinned with two bow-shaped pink barrettes, she appeared barely old enough to have entered puberty, let alone to have given birth to a child. But the baby scuttling around on the cold linoleum floor in his puffy diaper and undershirt was living proof that she was indeed a mother.

The apartment consisted of a single large, disorganized room, with a stove, refrigerator and sink lined up along one wall and the rest of the room taken up by a cot, a crib, empty diaper boxes, a scratched bureau and a card table and chairs. The room was brightened by the larger-than-life posters of Prince, Madonna and the stars of *Miami Vice* that Sandra had taped to the water-stained walls.

As soon as Troy entered the apartment behind Laura, Sandra gave him a sullen look of distrust. "Sandra, this is Troy Bennett," Laura calmly introduced them. "Remember, I mentioned last time that I might be bringing a photographer with me today. Troy, Sandra Miller."

Troy contemplated shaking the girl's hand, then thought better of it. He offered her a noncommittal nod and wandered into the room, taking care to avoid stepping on the baby, who had crawled over to him and was pulling on the hem of his jeans.

Sandra heaved the baby up into her arms and smoothed his undershirt over his round belly. "Yeah, okay," she mumbled, crossing to the card table and slumping onto a chair. Laura joined her there, and they began to talk.

Troy tuned out their conversation as his eyes skimmed the room. He crossed to the window, leaned against the sill, popped the lens cap off his camera and focused it on the girl hunching in her chair, her squirming baby perched on her knee. With the high-speed film he used and the slow shutter speed, he didn't need the flashgun. In assignments like this the constant burst of a flashgun would undoubtedly make Troy's subjects self-conscious. He preferred to remain as unobtrusive as possible.

Sandra quickly became so immersed in her discussion with Laura that she lost track of Troy. He snapped a few pictures from near the window, then drifted around the room and took another couple of shots, with the *Miami Vice* duo offering an ironic background image.

Laura and Sandra talked for nearly an hour. When Laura finally shoved her folder into her tote bag and stood,

Sandra seemed totally at ease. She glanced up at Troy and asked, "When are you going to take my picture?"

He smiled. "I've already taken plenty."

"You have?" She appeared astonished. Gnawing her lip, she shifted the baby's weight in her arms and appraised Troy. "Maybe you better take a couple more. This is my good side," she informed him, angling her head to one side and smiling.

Her smile made her look even younger, poignantly childlike. Troy quickly lifted his camera and snapped the shutter.

From Sandra's apartment they went to another. This client was as garrulous as Sandra had been reserved. "I wanna be a model," she told Troy, dumping her squawking baby into Laura's arms and striking a sassy pose, one hand behind her head and her hip thrust out. "I figure, okay, like, I can't model bathing suits on account of the stretch marks, but other stuff, you know? Soon as I lose the rest of this weight."

The girl's breasts were swollen with milk, and her middle was still thick from the recent birth of her child. But if she truly wanted to become a model, Troy mused, she would have to do more than lose weight; she'd have to grow at least three more inches. He didn't say anything to discourage her, however. A fifteen-year-old child-mother of the slums needed every dream she could hang on to. So Troy played up to her outgoing nature and recorded on film every showy pose she gave him. Then, after she settled on the bed with Laura to review her weekly budget and her relationship with her boyfriend and her mother, Troy took the pictures he wanted—natural, discreet, candid.

He shot more photos than he would ever need, but he was having too much fun to care. This wasn't like taking pictures of brides and grooms in wooden arrangements, or like taking pictures of a smug CEO in his high-backed leather chair behind his grand mahogany desk for a glossy annual report. This was the real thing, real people, the nitty-gritty. Troy was no longer Troy—he was simply an extension of his camera, a pair of astute eyes absorbing his environment, stealing moments and preserving them on film.

The third client Laura took him to lived with her mother—who seemed to be not much older than Troy and Laura—her grandmother, her aunt and a tribe of siblings and cousins. Troy took some photos of the girl and her baby, a few crowded group photos of the entire family and several casual shots of various family members swarming through the kitchen of the railroad flat, fixing lunch.

"I bet you're hungry," Laura said as they left the clamorous apartment and climbed down the stairs. "Watching all those peanut-butter sandwiches getting slapped together sure made me hungry. How about some lunch?"

"All right," Troy agreed. He was too exhilarated to think about anything as mundane as eating, but his watch informed him that it was nearly one o'clock—definitely time to become Troy again and nourish his body as well as he had nourished his soul all morning.

Laura escorted him to a rundown but reasonably clean diner. Once they were seated at a booth, Laura ordered a tuna salad and Troy a hamburger. The waitress brought them both coffee and departed.

Lounging against the vinyl upholstery, Troy studied the woman facing him and sighed contentedly. "This is great," he admitted.

"What's great?" Her eyes circled the diner and she laughed. "If this greasy spoon is your idea of great, I hate to think of what passes for a restaurant in Montreal."

"I didn't mean this place," he clarified. "I meant the work—my work. Shooting all those girls and their kids."

Laura laughed again. "You ought to watch your language, Troy," she chided him. "If anybody's eavesdropping, they'll think you're a mass murderer or something."

"They'd sure have a wrong number," he remarked with a chuckle. "Cameras are the only weapon I'll go near. I can't even handle water pistols."

"I know," she said, her smile growing gentle. She waited until the waitress had delivered their lunches and left, then leaned forward and perused Troy carefully. "How have you really been, Troy?" she asked. "Are you happy up there in Canada?"

He exhaled. He had always been closer to Seth than to Laura, even though Seth would never assault him with such intimate questions. Probably *because* Seth never would. That was the way guys were. They talked about Ax Man or females or cameras. Women—especially social workers and most especially women like Laura, who cared almost too much about the well-being of her friends—were the ones who pried.

He aimed a ketchup bottle at his hamburger patty and pounded on its bottom to loosen the sluggish sauce. Once his burger was blanketed, he set down the bottle and met Laura's inquisitive gaze. "Sure, I'm happy," he answered.

"I worry about you," she confessed.

"You worry about everyone."

She grinned, accepting his accurate appraisal of her. "Are you ever going to come home?"

"Where's home?" Troy countered, closing the bun around his burger and taking a bite.

Laura refrained from eating as her eyes narrowed on him. "If you don't know, then you're in worse shape than I feared."

He chewed, swallowed and lowered his sandwich. Although Laura's questions rankled, he knew she was speaking from an abiding affection for him. "I'm in fine shape," he said quietly. "All I meant when I said that was...places don't mean much to me. I don't believe in having an allegiance to an address. These days Montreal's home. Tomorrow maybe it'll be someplace else."

Laura poked the rounded scoop of tuna salad on her plate and assessed Troy's claim, evidently unpersuaded. "I hate to quote my mother-in-law of all people, but when are you going to settle down?"

"Seth's mother asks you that?"

"She used to ask Seth that," Laura explained.

"And what did he use to tell her?"

Laura grinned. "Don't be so evasive, Troy. You're what—thirty-seven? And just as handsome as ever. Don't they believe in marriage in Canada?"

"Last I heard," Troy answered, maintaining a humorous tone, "they didn't believe in marriage unless you happened to be in love."

"Then you're not seeing anybody?" Laura pressed him. "Not involved with anyone? I know, I know—you think I'm insufferably nosy," she apologized. "But I worry about you all alone up there in that cold place."

He laughed. "Believe it or not, Laura, I'm not the only person living in Montreal. There must be at least, oh, eight or nine of us homo sapiens types, and then a few huskies and beavers. If I'm not mistaken, the last census counted fifteen Canada geese, too."

"Only in the summer," Laura commented, joining his laughter. "In the winter they all fly down to Miami, don't they?"

"Mm-hmm. They all invested in condos down there," Troy quipped before sipping his coffee. "Don't worry about me, Laura. Weren't you just saying something about how people have to save their own lives?"

"And when are you going to save yours?" she inquired. She was still smiling, but her eyes bore down on him, dark and solemn.

Several answers sprang to mind. He could complain to her that she was preaching with all the fervor of the newly converted; after all, she'd been married barely a month, so she was in no position to lecture him on settling down. Or he could assure her that he wasn't in need of saving, that he was perfectly satisfied with his life as it was. Or he could tell her to mind her own business.

Or he could tell her the truth: that, while he might need saving, he wasn't going to save himself by "settling down," becoming involved with a woman and getting hitched. Loneliness wasn't his problem.

In fact, his problem—if he had one—was that he didn't allow himself the time to pursue his craft in the proper manner. Today that problem seemed far away, farther away than the few hundred miles separating Montreal from Brooklyn. His hand moved reflexively to the camera case resting on the banquette beside him, his fingers reading its familiar zippers and snaps. Today his camera meant more than business. It meant art, energy, truth.

Meeting Laura's unwavering stare, he smiled hesitantly. "I think I've already saved my life," he murmured.

The afternoon went much as the morning had: Laura conferring with a client in a gloomy apartment while Troy melted into the background and shot his film, then he and

Laura hiking to the next gloomy apartment, and then Laura conferring with another client and Troy snapping more pictures. By four-thirty, when they left the final client's flat, he had used up all the film.

"Have you got any plans for dinner?" Laura asked as they strolled back to her office. "We'd love to have you."

"Thanks, but I'll have to take a rain check," Troy declined. Actually, he didn't have any plans, but he was feeling restless again. Not nervous, as he'd felt that morning, but charged up, anxious to move, to walk, to view the world through a photographer's eyes. He simply couldn't imagine himself spending the evening with Laura and Seth, reminiscing about old times. "You're going to take me around again tomorrow, right?"

"Assuming I don't have to counsel any more girls in jail," Laura confirmed. "My apartment at nine?"

"I'll be there," Troy promised. He kissed her cheek in farewell, then parted ways with her at the subway station.

He got off the subway at the West Fourth Street station in Greenwich Village and walked to Peter's apartment. The Village had changed enormously in the years since Troy had lived in New York. Once a haven for hippies, runaways and middle-class kids rejecting their roots, it was presently yet another chic enclave in a city that had little room for the middle class. Last night, over a beer, Peter had detailed for Troy his current dilemma concerning the conversion of his modest one-bedroom apartment into a co-op. "Ownership is everything nowadays," Peter had lamented. "And the ticket is absurd. They want two hundred fifty thousand dollars for this place. Can you grok it? A quarter of a million."

Troy let himself into the apartment with the spare key Peter had lent him. He didn't expect Peter to be home—the bookstore he owned and ran stayed open until nine o'clock most nights to accommodate the New York University students. After shouting Peter's name and being met with silence, Troy moved directly to his suitcase, which lay open on the floor beside the futon couch where he'd spent the night, and deposited his used canisters of film in a side pocket. Then he switched cameras in his equipment bag and loaded a fresh roll of film. His gaze lingered for a moment on the couch, reminding him of the sleepless night he'd endured, and he brusquely stood and hurried out of the apartment.

He didn't want to think about Julianne, but he couldn't help himself. It was thanks to her that he'd just had one of the most satisfying days of his professional life. Even *Maritime* hadn't been this much fun. The trip to Nova Scotia had been intended as a vacation, not work. And it almost hadn't taken place at all. A week before he was set to leave, Ellen—the woman he'd planned to take with him—had decided she wanted to renegotiate her relationship with her previous boyfriend and she'd begged off on the trip. Troy had hardly been heartbroken; if he had been, he wouldn't have taken the trip without her.

Laura didn't have to worry about Troy's being lonely. There were more than enough women in Montreal, and he maintained a reasonably active social life. Ellen was representative of the women he dated—good-looking, flighty, here today and gone tomorrow. That was the only kind of companionship Troy was looking for. Involvement was the furthest thing from his mind. He'd been involved once, and he'd failed at it.

"Hell," he muttered, the guttural rumble of his voice echoing in the empty elevator. He *wasn't* carrying a torch for Julianne. He *didn't* want to get back together with her. He had deliberately chosen women like Ellen and Daphne and Paulette, because if he'd sought a woman like Julianne, a woman as true to herself and to love as it was possible to be, he would only have wound up breaking her heart the way he'd broken Julianne's. He simply wasn't good enough for that kind of woman.

That was why he had to stay away from Julianne. He'd told her in Montreal. He wasn't good enough.

Peter was posted behind the cashier's desk when Troy entered the bookstore. A genuine relic of the sixties, Peter still wore round, rimless eyeglasses, and his below-the-shoulder hair, although streaked with gray, was fastened into a ponytail with a rubber band. If Troy's clients considered his hair long, he mused, they ought to have a look at Peter. No man could ever pull off wearing both a tuxedo and a ponytail.

A few years older than Troy, Peter had managed a small bookstore near the Columbia campus while Troy was a student. They had become acquainted when Troy had arranged to distribute copies of *The Dream* at Peter's old store, and Peter had offered Troy a job there after graduation. Clerking at a bookstore hadn't been Troy's ultimate career goal, but the salary would have enabled him to continue taking photographs for *The Dream* until the newspaper started to show a profit. If he hadn't gone to Canada, instead, Troy would have enjoyed the job.

He and Peter had kept in sporadic touch over the years. Eventually Peter had bought a bookstore in the Village, and the income from his retail sales covered the costs of Voyager Press, the small-press publishing enterprise he ran from a room in the building's basement. Voyager published poetry, occasional political tracts, avant-garde short fiction and—rarely—collections of photographs like *Maritime*.

Ringing up a purchase, Peter spotted Troy loitering near the door and waved him over. As soon as he'd shut the cash register drawer, he adjusted his eyeglasses and leaned on the counter. "How'd it go today?" he asked.

"Good," Troy reported. Then he smiled. "Damned good, if you want to know the truth."

"Brace yourself for some more good news, then," Peter announced. "I've arranged for a darkroom for you here in town, if you want it."

Troy stopped himself before blurting out that he planned to develop the photos back in Canada. For some reason he was no longer so anxious to race out of town the minute he'd taken his final shot. "What darkroom?" he asked.

"A guy I know has a studio uptown on Madison. He said that if you wanted, you could borrow the facilities and run off your proofs before you leave."

"That's very generous of him," Troy allowed. Developing the proofs in town would save him time, and he knew that Julianne needed the photos as soon as possible. "I may take him up on the offer."

"No big deal either way," Peter assured him. "I told him you'd give him a buzz tomorrow night."

"Thanks, Peter, I will." A customer arrived at the counter with a stack of paperbacks, and Troy courteously stepped out of her way. "Did we have anything going for dinner tonight?" he asked as Peter rang up the woman's sale.

Peter shrugged. "I promised my old lady I'd bring her a pizza," he informed Troy. "Why don't you join us? Sarah likes you."

"I like Sarah, too," Troy granted. He'd met Peter's longtime girlfriend last March, when he'd been in town for the reunion and had crashed at Peter's place. "But I'll pass. I've got some things I want to do."

"Oh?" As Peter pressed the "Total" button, his sparse eyebrows arched above the lenses of his eyeglasses. "Anything more interesting than pizza?"

"I like Sarah enough not to let you renege on a promise to her," Troy reproached his friend. "Anyway, I think I could use some time alone."

"Suit yourself." Peter shrugged amiably. "You've got the key. I'll see you when I see you."

"Thanks," said Troy. "Have a good time with Sarah."

He left the store. The sidewalks were beginning to fill with the five o'clock crowd leaving work, and the uptown IRT was jammed. Troy didn't mind having to stand in the clogged subway car; he clasped an overhead strap with one hand to steady himself and kept the other closed protectively around his camera case. The train lurched and squeaked, taking on more passengers at each stop. Troy had to squint to read the station signs through the spray-painted windows. Another thing that had changed since he'd lived in Manhattan, he noted, were the subways. They'd never been so mottled with graffiti when he was at Columbia.

He got off at the 116th Street exit and climbed the stairs to the street. Things had changed here, too, but he was struck less by the changes than by the sameness: the teeming life of Upper Broadway, the honking car horns, the grocers and health food stores, record shops and head shops lining the sidewalks. The infectious rhythm of Salsa emerging from a stereo speaker balanced on an upper windowsill. The sooty cluster of statuesque buildings on the west side of Broadway—Barnard College. The grander but equally sooty buildings, caged inside imposing wrought iron and brick walls on the east side of Broadway—Columbia University.

He ducked underneath the striped awning of a used-clothing store and watched as three boys on the corner danced to the Salsa music. They couldn't have been older than twelve or so, and they were obviously showing off, daring one another with their acrobatic movements. Troy opened his camera case and pulled out his Leica. He adjusted the shutter speed to accommodate the early evening light, lifted the camera to his eye and clicked.

He took another picture of an obese woman staggering out of a Laundromat, lugging a heaping basket of clean laundry. And another of an exotic Indian woman in a sari examining tomatoes at the outdoor stand of a grocery. Another of a beautiful black woman in skintight pants and a tube top, leaning against a car and eyeing Troy in a subtle flirtation.

He thought of Julianne again, not in the context of sleeplessness, but rather, as the woman who had driven him to rediscover what made him happy. "You could do so much more," she had said. "You could be so much more."

He had rejected her offer, but she had been more stubborn than he. She had told him he'd be doing the work not for her or for her magazine, but for himself.

He wasn't good enough for her, but... she was so good for him. His delight at the photos he was taking mingled with a deep ache, a longing to be good enough, a wish that he could do something as important for her as what she'd done for him in coercing him to accomplish real work, to take real pictures.

Sighing, he fastened the lens cap on his camera and stalked down the street. He reached one of the entry gates leading into the Columbia campus. A uniformed guard halted him. "ID?" the guard requested.

Troy peered past the guard to view the brick courtyard beyond. The grass surrounding it was unusually lush, and the few trees punctuating the lawn were thick with foliage. Behind them he saw the building....

"ID," the guard said, a touch more firmly.

"Oh," Troy mumbled, turning to the guard. "I, uh, I'm an alumnus. Can I just go in for a minute?"

The guard eyed him skeptically. "Can you prove you're an alumnus?"

Troy dug his wallet out of his hip pocket and opened it. He still carried with him a few documents that had once been as much a part of his identity as his appearance and his name. They were no longer necessary, but they'd survived three wallet changes, and he couldn't imagine being without them: his draft card, his expired Michigan driver's license and his Columbia student ID card. He used to carry a photo of Julianne, too, a picture he had taken of her, but he'd discarded that years ago.

He pulled out the student ID card and presented it to the guard. The photo on the plastic-coated card showed a younger version of Troy, hairier, his laugh lines less pronounced, his mustache untrimmed. But the resemblance between the photo and the man facing the guard was unarguable. Grunting, the guard opened the gate for him. "Just a few minutes," he instructed Troy. "It isn't Homecoming Weekend."

Nodding his thanks, Troy entered the campus.

The bench, he noticed, jogging across the courtyard. The bench where he'd balanced his old Nikon, set the timer and taken a group photo of the staff of *The Dream* that splendidly balmy afternoon. Hours later, he had discovered a much more intense splendor in Julianne's arms, on the inspiration couch in the office. Hours later, his body had confirmed what his soul had already recognized: he loved Julianne.

Viewing the bench didn't upset him. Nor did viewing the building. He approached it, tried the main door and found it locked.

It didn't matter. He didn't have to go inside to see the cramped basement office where he'd learned that his amateur skill with a camera could be nurtured into a profession, where he'd put his passionate opinions about the Vietnam War into newsprint words, before he'd been forced to put them into action. The office where he'd found Julianne sleeping one night and pulled off her boots. He didn't have to see it to remember.

More than an old newspaper office was inside the building. Troy's youth was in there, his dreams, his innocence. Julianne hadn't been the first woman he'd ever had sex with, but she'd been the first woman he had ever loved. He'd been innocent about love, then, and hopeful about his future, about the outcome of his draft board hearing. He'd been young, fired up, headstrong.

Ever since the night he'd left the United States, he'd felt weary and old. But today, after the magnificent work he'd done, he felt inexplicably young again.

Five

"Any messages?"

Julianne's secretary glanced up from her desk and smiled. "Dan Eisner called from Washington," she informed Julianne, tearing a slip of paper from her pink message pad. "He said he's set up something for next week with—" she read from the paper "—Kimberly Belmont and Andrew Collins." She handed Julianne the note.

Julianne accepted it without reading it. "Thanks, Brenda. Anything else?"

The secretary shook her head. "They're waiting for you in the large conference room."

Attempting a smile, Julianne tucked the message into an outer pocket of her leather briefcase and marched down the hall leading to the conference room, where her editorial staff was gathered for their weekly Thursday afternoon meeting. Julianne was a few minutes late; she and her advertising manager had just taken a marketing executive from a pharmaceutical firm out for lunch, and the man had been talkative in the extreme. Pretending to appear interested in his long-winded description of his target market had driven Julianne to distraction, but attending such boring luncheons was one of the many obligations of her job. Since the man had indicated a clear interest in buying advertising space in *Dream*, she considered her time well spent.

Alone in the hallway, she paused to collect herself. She was pleased that Dan had been able to arrange an interview with Andrew and Kimberly. But that wasn't the message Julianne had been hoping for.

Not a word from Troy, not a telephone call, not even the most superficial communication of how his work for her was coming along. She knew that it was going well because Laura had called her last night and given her a full report. "We had a wonderful time, Julianne," Laura had told her. "Troy works so quietly, so subtly. Half the time my clients weren't even conscious of him in the room. I'm so glad you were able to get him for the job."

"I'm glad, too," Julianne had agreed, meaning it. She was glad she'd been able to hire someone of Troy's ability. She was positive that the photos he produced during his brief sojourn in New York were going to be perfect.

"We invited him to have dinner with us, but he couldn't make it," Laura had continued. "I guess he wants to spend some time with his friend, Peter. But it was wonderful seeing him. He seemed much happier than he did at the reunion, Julianne. I think this kind of work really appeals to him."

"I'm sure it does," Julianne had concurred.

So the work appealed to him. So he was happy. Why did Julianne have to learn that from Laura instead of from Troy? Why couldn't he put forth the merest effort to express his happiness to Julianne?

Entering the conference room, she managed another artificial smile. A chair at the head of the elongated cherrywood table was vacant, waiting for her; the other chairs were all occupied by her editorial staff. The features editor and the assignments editor were embroiled in a heated debate, and Julianne drove from her mind her disappointment about Troy's failure to contact her in order to give her complete attention to their quarrel.

"I don't care how good it is," Tom was saying. "Running a story castigating that bozo in the Christmas issue is in poor taste."

"Some people would say that running the story at all is in poor taste," Cynthia retorted. "But this guy isn't just a television evangelist. He's been skimming his collections, and the story lays it all out, with proof. All those pitiful believers in the hinterlands take the money they ought to be using to buy milk for their kids, and they mail it to him with the promise of eternal salvation, and he uses it to buy himself an ocean-going yacht. I say there's no better time to run the piece than at Christmas."

"It may be dated by then," Julianne pointed out, assuming her seat and filling the empty tumbler at her elbow with ice water from one of the strategically placed pitchers. She had already seen a first draft of the article in question. She knew that attacking a popular television evangelist in print was going to cause controversy, but the information the reporter had uncovered concerning the minister's extravagant life-style and the unexplained drain of money from his church missions warranted publishing. *Dream* magazine never retreated from controversial subjects. "We'll run the piece in September," she resolved. "By Christmastime maybe we'll be able to print a follow-up on the man's arrest and conviction."

"Dream on, Julianne," another editor interjected with a chuckle. The laughter that greeted his comment defused the spat, and Julianne wasted no time in introducing the first item on that week's agenda.

She didn't mind the fact that her editors often argued, as long as they did so at the closed editorial meetings and not in front of the staff reporters. Julianne ran *Dream* like a benevolent despot; each of the eight editors had one vote and the editor in chief had nine votes. Because disputes were aired freely, however, no one ever felt as though Julianne were ramming an arbitrary decision down his or her throat.

Resolving disagreements, like wooing potential advertisers, was a part of her job. Another part of her job was keeping her private dilemmas carefully hidden from her associates. As she conducted the editorial meeting, she remained outwardly as cool and poised as she always appeared. Nobody at the conference table could have guessed that the tall woman in the crisply tailored silk-blend suit had anything on her mind other than the business at hand.

Yet even as she outlined the themes of the upcoming issues, as she appraised the various articles under contract, as she filled in her colleagues on the up-close-and-personal story Dan Eisner was planning to write about the Senate Intelligence Committee hearings at which Andrew would be testifying, thoughts of Troy never abandoned her.

She tried to picture him wielding his camera in the squalid homes of Laura's clients. She tried to picture him freezing their images on film, his astute eyes stalking their prey and trapping it inside his camera. She recalled the intensity with which he used to work in their college days. Even when he was fooling around, taking goofy shots of inconsequential scenes, the moment he'd lift his camera to focus, his entire body would hum with concentration and purpose. The resulting pictures, like the whimsical school scene she had framed and hung in her office, stood as evidence of his mastery.

She understood that the same intensity that ruled his professional endeavors ruled his life. If, when he was working, he could tune out everything but the moment he wished to photograph, he could certainly tune out his feelings for Julianne.

She had no doubt that he harbored strong feelings for her. If he didn't, he would have called her by now. She had worked with plenty of free-lance photographers, and it was common practice for them to update the magazine on their progress with an assignment. Troy's deliberate avoidance of Julianne implied that he didn't view himself as just another of her free-lance photographers.

Once again she pondered the possibility that he was punishing himself. She had thought about that possibility all last night, as she'd picked at her stir-fried pork and vegetables, as she'd chatted on the phone with Laura, as she'd turned on an old James Taylor tape and thumbed through the most recent issues of *Time* and *U.S. News and World Report*, searching for a hint of how other magazines might be covering the Intelligence Committee hearings the following week. *Dream* wasn't a hard-news journal like *Time* and *U.S. News*, but Julianne's magazine frequently published stories on the same current events, approaching them from a human-interest standpoint. She was consoled by the thought that no matter how *Time* and *U.S. News* covered the hearings, her magazine was the one that would feature an exclusive interview with Andrew.

It wasn't consolation enough, however. What she really wanted, what she wished for, had nothing to do with the thrill of scooping the stalwart news glossies on their own turf.

She had no one but herself to blame for her dismal condition. She must have been kidding herself when she'd sworn that her only aims in hiring Troy were to boost his career and enhance her magazine. Or perhaps she hadn't been fooling herself—perhaps those *had* been her only aims, until she'd seen him. Until she'd kissed him.

It had taken her a long time to get over Troy, but she'd done it. After the first anniversary of his disappearance, thinking about him didn't hurt so terribly. After the third year, she stopped thinking about him on a regular basis. After the fifth, she began negotiations with the publishing firm that had expressed an interest in adding her publication—which had by then expanded into a regional biweekly—to the company's extensive holdings. The deal had taken nearly a year to complete, and once it had gone through, Julianne found herself with no time to think about anything other than the enormous task of converting *The Dream* into *Dream*, guiding her "baby" into adulthood. Among the things she had no time to think about was Troy's long-ago departure from New York.

If she hadn't decided to arrange the reunion of the paper's founders as part of *Dream*'s fifteenth birthday celebration, she might have spent the rest of her life devoted to her magazine, with scarcely a thought of Troy. But as soon as she'd broken the years of silence by asking him to come to the reunion, as soon as she'd seen him at the party...everything changed. She was no longer the person she had been for the past decade. Suddenly she found herself remembering, dreaming of what had been, of what could have been.

She didn't like the mooning, pining woman she was turning into. She preferred the way she used to be, firmly in control of her life. She didn't like lying awake in bed late into the night, staring at the darkness, wondering why Troy was refusing to be logical about their past and their present.

Maybe he *was* being logical and she was the irrational one. She didn't like that idea, either.

Well, Troy would soon disappear from her life again. He would finish taking his pictures that afternoon, spend the night carousing with Peter, if that was what he wanted to do, and leave for Montreal the following day. Then he would mail her the photos, and she'd mail him his payment, and she would be able to revert to her normal, temperate self.

Or so she hoped.

"JULIANNE? It's Troy."

The long-awaited telephone call came Friday morning. When her secretary had announced that Troy was on the line, Julianne's nervous system had erupted into a break dance of sickening proportions. She believed that it was too late for him to call now, too late for him to touch base with her, to update her on his progress. And if the only reason he was calling was to say goodbye, then he was being cruel.

"Hello," she said quietly. No matter how many back flips and head spins her nerves were executing, her voice floated calmly and smoothly through the air, into the mouthpiece and over the wire. He would never guess at her tumultuous emotional state from her even tone.

"If you want the photos pronto, I can have them for you by this afternoon," he informed her. "How's that for service?"

Although he was discussing business, he sounded unconscionably cheerful. "How can you have them ready so soon?" she asked. "I thought you'd have to develop them at your studio, and—"

"Peter arranged for me to borrow the darkroom of a friend of his," Troy related. "It's on Madison Avenue in the seventies. I've got it all afternoon if I want it." He paused, and when Julianne didn't speak, he asked, "Tell me, boss, do I want it?"

"Sure," she replied. "Madison in the seventies isn't far from my apartment. If you can have the photos done by late this afternoon, I'll pick them up on my way home from work." Only after she spoke did she realize that picking up the photos would undoubtedly mean having to see Troy. But she'd only have to see him for a minute, she rationalized. She could focus on their professional arrangement for that long, get the pictures and, if they met with her approval and the art director's, mail Troy a check from her office Monday morning. It would spare her a great deal of nail biting over deadlines if she obtained the photos today.

"Great," said Troy. He provided her with the address. "How does five o'clock sound?"

"Maybe a little earlier," she suggested. "The publishing world tends to close early on Fridays."

"A little earlier, then," he agreed. "I'll be there the entire afternoon, so come whenever you want. See you later." The line went dead.

Come whenever you want, Julianne repeated silently. *See you later.* What was wrong with him? Didn't he realize that her innards had been braiding into knots for three days, that the perpetually sane Julianne Robinson had been going mad knowing that he was in the city, a mere subway ride away from her, and that he was refusing to see her? *See you later.* As if she were nothing but a passing acquaintance, someone he saw all the time and never thought about.

Perhaps she had gone mad. Perhaps Troy did view her as nothing but a passing acquaintance. Perhaps he hadn't even kissed her in Montreal. Her overactive imagination might have invented the episode.

Glancing down at her clothing, she grimaced. Because it was Friday and because she didn't have a luncheon engagement, she had worn a fairly informal outfit—a short-sleeved blouse and a matching pleated skirt of turquoise cotton. She wished she had on one of her prim suits, the sort of attire that would command respect.

Don't think about it, she chastised herself. As if she could prevent herself from thinking about her impending meeting with Troy. The understanding that they would soon be in the same room, face to face, obsessed her throughout the day. When she wasn't fretting about her clothes, she was fretting about whether the past two nights of tossing and turning had left purple shadows under her eyes, or whether her fine brown hair was too flyaway because she'd shampooed it the previous night, or whether she had drunk too much coffee that morning, or too little. She labored over her work without giving it her full attention; she initialed memos without reading them, skimmed proposals without comprehending them, and all the while a corner of her mind was calculating whether she would have the time to stop off at her apartment and change into a more impressive ensemble before she met Troy at his friend's friend's darkroom.

At four o'clock, unable to sit still any longer, she locked up her office. Her secretary had already departed for the weekend, as had most of the other support staffers. Julianne stopped inside the ladies' room to survey her appearance before she left the building.

Judging by her reflection in the mirror above the sink counter, her hair wasn't at all flyaway. It dropped in a smooth, shiny curve past her chin to her shoulders. Her eyes weren't underlined by shadows. Her skirt and blouse looked pleasantly summery. She couldn't find any visible evidence of her panic.

Realizing that she looked presentable made her feel better. She touched up her lipstick, gave her hair an unnecessary brushing and strode from the powder room and out of the offices to summon an elevator.

She had spent the past several days eating herself up for no good reason. Troy's behavior in New York implied that, one kiss notwithstanding, her relationship with him was long dead, beyond mourning. Julianne was a strong, confident woman. She'd gotten over Troy once, and if she had let his presence in town the past few days rattle her more than it should have, well, she'd get over him again. Seeing him wasn't going to be such a dreadful thing, she reassured herself.

She decided to walk uptown. The afternoon was warm but not muggy, and although the sidewalks were crowded with pedestrians, she wove briskly among them, maintaining a vigorous pace. A faint but refreshing breeze, hinting at the cool evening ahead, slid along her bare arms and dusted the skin of her throat, exposed above the loose-fitting neckline of her blouse. In her comfortable stack-heeled leather sandals, she found the twenty-odd-block stroll to the darkroom relaxing rather than exhausting. By the time she had arrived at the address Troy had given her, she was feeling as peaceful and poised as she ought to have felt all week.

The darkroom was situated inside a studio on the second floor of the building, above an expensive children's clothing boutique. Julianne climbed the stairs to the second-floor landing, located the right door and knocked. An unfamiliar man with thick reddish brown hair and a budding potbelly cracked open the door. "Yeah?"

"I'm Julianne Robinson," Julianne identified herself, trying unsuccessfully to peek past the man into the room. "I'm supposed to meet Troy Bennett here."

"Right." The man swung the door wider to allow Julianne entrance. This studio was much grubbier than Troy's studio up in Montreal. Folding metal chairs stood around the circumference of the reception area, and the walls were decorated with randomly taped eight-by-ten glossies of young men and women who resembled professional models or actors. The absence of clients in the reception area implied that the studio had closed for the day.

The stocky man led Julianne out of the reception area and down a short, dimly lit hall to a door at its end. The red light bulb screwed into the wall above the door was glowing. Rapping the doorframe with his knuckles, the man shouted, "Troy? You've got company."

Julianne barely had a chance to steel herself before the red light bulb flickered off and the door opened to reveal Troy. The sleeves of his wrinkled yellow shirt were rolled up to his elbows, his collar button undone, and his jeans were faded to a pale blue. His dense black hair was a jumble of waves. His eyes focused on Julianne, and she immediately discerned the animated sparkle in their dark irises. He was grinning.

Laura had said that this assignment had made Troy happy, and Julianne hadn't doubted her friend. But Troy's smile went beyond merely happy. It was the sort of all-encompassing smile he used to give her back in college, the sort of smile that reflected itself in every part of him, from his dancing eyes and his floppy mustache to his easy posture and his graceful hands. "Hi," he said.

She tried to interpret his greeting. It included more than just the single word. His dazzling smile was also a part of it, and the angle of his head as he gazed at her, and the intriguing glitter of his eyes. His palpable joy unnerved Julianne, and she tried to figure out what lay behind it. The thrill of knowing that he was about to return to Montreal? Or simply the relief of having completed his assignment?

She gave herself an internal shake. She wasn't going to start eating herself up again, allowing her imagination to run away with her. Shoring back her shoulders, she met Troy's mesmerizing stare and asked, as emotionlessly as possible, "Are the photos ready?"

"Come and see for yourself," he answered, inviting her to join him inside the darkroom.

Ignoring the slight odor of chemicals in the small, shadowy room, Julianne moved directly to the drying paper rectangles clipped to a cord that had been strung from wall to wall above the sinks. Several of the sheets were imprinted with tiny rows of proofs, but a few of them contained already enlarged photographs.

Troy had chosen to use black-and-white film, and the prints were all the more striking due to the starkly contrasting shades outlining their images. She silently complimented his artistic taste in having chosen black and white.

She inched her way along the drying line and examined the enlargements. The first one depicted a slender young girl with limp hair and a bittersweet smile, her gaze lowered to the baby cradled in her arms. The background showed a poster of the stars of *Miami Vice* slouching against a black Ferrari. The juxtaposition of the forlorn girl and the glamorous television stars struck Julianne as almost painfully ironic. She caught her lower lip between her teeth and sighed.

Her gaze traveled to the next enlargement, this one a group photo of a family of women and children gathered around a teenage girl who sat in an overstuffed easy chair with her baby on her lap. The resemblance among the family members was disarming; their identical smiles as they stared in unison at the camera gave the picture an eerie quality.

Next to it hung another enlarged photo, this one of three wiry youngsters dancing on a street corner. "What's this?" she asked.

"I took that one for myself," he explained. "It came out good, didn't it?"

"Yes," she said, studying it intently. She tilted a sheet of proofs and inspected the reduced images on it. "They're all good. No, they aren't," she contradicted herself. "They're better than good, Troy. They're excellent. They're wonderful."

She turned to face him. He was leaning against the sturdy plywood table that held the enlarger, his arms folded across his chest, his eyes glued to her. He extended his hand and smiled cryptically. "Come here," he murmured.

The anxiety she thought she had conquered reared up again in full force. Swallowing, she took a step toward him. He curled his fingers gently around her hand and drew her to him, then slung his arm over her shoulders and gave her a light hug. "If anything in this room is wonderful, it's you," he said, his grin widening as he gazed toward the drying photos. "If anything was wonderful, it was doing this kind of work. You pushed me into it, Julianne. You goaded me. And doing it made me feel like a new man. I don't know how to thank you."

His hold on her implied friendliness, nothing more—or so she tried to convince herself. She had hoped to reawaken some excitement in him regarding his work, and she had obviously succeeded. She wasn't sure that was enough to satisfy her. But it would have to be. "Getting to run these photos in *Dream* is all the thanks I need," she assured him, pleased by her level tone.

"Maybe it's all the thanks you need," he mused, "but it isn't all the thanks I want to give you."

"Then say thank you, and we'll call it a day," she said, a touch sharply. If he was so full of gratitude, he could have called her sooner. He could have spared a few minutes for her during his stay in the city.

His arm tightened on her, and he turned her to face him. "Julie." His expression was earnest, his smile curiously tender. "Don't cut me off. Hear me out, all right?"

Her pale blue eyes locked onto his, and she nodded. "I'm listening."

He stared at her for a long moment, taking stock of her attitude. "You're angry with me, aren't you?"

"No," she fibbed. She lowered her gaze to his rugged jaw and exhaled. Lying didn't sit well with her, especially lying to a man with whom she had always been painfully honest. "Yes, I am angry with you, Troy. I'm angry that you've been avoiding me these past few days."

"Guilty as charged," he agreed contritely.

"There was no need to," she scolded him. "We are working together. We had legitimate business with each other. Why did you feel you had to stay away?"

"Because..." His fingers drifted along her throat to her chin and he urged her face back up to his. "Because I was afraid that if I saw you I'd fall in love with you again," he confessed, his voice soft and enticingly husky. "So I didn't see you. Instead I took pictures. And...the funny thing is, I've fallen in love with you anyway."

Julianne snorted in disbelief. Surely Troy was confusing gratitude with love. If he had truly fallen in love with her, he would have wanted to see her well before he was about to leave for Montreal.

"When you came to Canada," he continued, "and you more or less implied that we ought to try again, I said something about not being good enough for you. Remember?"

She nodded again. Every second of the evening she'd spent with him in Montreal was etched permanently into her memory.

"I wasn't good enough for you then," he explained. "A man who runs away and hides himself in a foreign country and does hack work isn't good enough for a woman like you. But these past few days, I haven't been hiding in Canada and doing hack work. I've been doing what I should be doing—and doing it well. I don't mean to sound conceited, but this stuff—" he gestured toward the photos on the line "—is great. It's what I was made to do. And when I do it...then I'm good, too. You forced me to be good enough for you, Julianne. Good enough to admit that we can try again."

She gave herself time to let his words register. Troy was giving voice to her hopes, her dreams, the emotions she'd tucked inside a secret part of her heart so many years ago, relegated to deep storage. At long last, Troy was ready to acknowledge what she'd always known. They loved each other; they could make it work again.

He was waiting for a response from her. When she remained silent, he took the initiative, bowing and touching his lips to hers. His kiss was tentative, questioning, and before she could soften to it he pulled back to assess her.

"Why did you wait so long to call me?" she whispered.

He meditated for a minute. "If the pictures came out badly, I would have known you were wrong about me—about us."

"But you called before you saw the pictures."

He conceded the point with an enigmatic smile. "Either way, I owed you the shots. If they were bad, you would have found that out today and hired someone else. But they weren't bad, Julianne. I looked at them and I knew. I knew you were right to have faith in me, even when I didn't have faith in myself. You were right. As always."

He bent to kiss her again. This time he held nothing back. His mouth moved powerfully over hers, his tongue probing, searching. Her head fell back, and he dug his fingers into her hair, holding her steady as the kiss deepened.

Julianne reached for his shoulders and clung to them as her body reeled from his sensuous assault. Her faith in Troy had been a precarious thing, but now that he shared it, she allowed it to flood through her. He had found himself again. He was ready to forgive himself. Of course she could forgive him.

By the time he broke from her, her breath was short and shallow, her eyes glazed. "What do we do now?" she asked shakily.

Her words faded into a soft moan as he grazed along her brow. "Love each other," he replied.

Within minutes they were at her apartment building. The photographs and proofs were neatly stacked into a folder inside Julianne's briefcase, and Troy clasped the strap of his camera case in one hand and Julianne's fingers in the other. Julianne barely gave the building's doorman a nod of greeting before sweeping inside with Troy. Not bothering to check her mailbox—unable to delay them for the time that would take—she hastened with him to the elevator and let it carry them upstairs.

He seemed in as much of a hurry as she was. If he was at all curious about her apartment, he didn't show it. His eyes were on her, only her, as she ushered him down the hall to her bedroom.

Once inside, Troy set down his camera case, gathered her into his arms and kissed her again. His mustache brushed softly against her upper lip, tickling it. It was a sensation she knew well, and her memory of the kisses he had given her so long ago mingled with the experience of this kiss. As transported as she was, however, she was conscious of the difference between then and now. The urgency she felt in his embrace wasn't like the eagerness of two youthful lovers reveling in a new discovery, but rather of two more mature, wiser adults keenly aware of how transient love could be.

His fingers roved up her back to her shoulders, around them and down the front of her blouse. She lowered her eyes to watch as he traced the round contours of her breasts through the cloth, and a slight shiver gripped her. "Julianne," he murmured hoarsely, allowing his hands to come to rest on her narrow waist. He kissed the crown of her head. "I never forgot. In all the years, I never forgot how it was between us."

He had sworn, when she'd seen him in Montreal, that he hadn't carried a torch for her. She granted that he had probably been speaking the truth, just as she herself believed she hadn't been carrying a torch for him. Whether they had deliberately held themselves back in other relationships wasn't the issue, though. What existed between them was a fact that couldn't be denied, no matter how hard they'd tried to find with others something to equal it.

"I never forgot, either," she breathed.

He molded his palms over her hips and drew her snugly to himself. As his mouth sought hers once more, she raised her hands to his shirt and pulled at the buttons. With the few men she'd been involved with since Troy, she had never behaved in such an aggressive manner. But Troy's chest, his body, his love, had once belonged to her, and she felt a proprietary right to reclaim what had been hers.

His shirt fell open and her hands slid beneath the cotton fabric. His skin was as warm as she remembered, his pectorals still shrouded by a heart-shaped cloud of black hair. Her fingertips combed through the curling tendrils to explore the solid wall of muscle beneath. Time hadn't taken any toll on his well-toned physique.

She touched her lips to the base of his neck and he groaned. Roused to action, he unfastened the tiny buttons decorating the front of her blouse and freed it from the waistband of her skirt. He slid the blouse down her arms, then reached behind her to unclasp her bra. Releasing her breasts from their lacy confinement and then enclosing them in his cupped hands, he groaned again. "You're so beautiful, Julie."

"I'm old," she argued. Unlike Troy's body, Julianne was convinced that hers had aged. Her breasts were smaller than they'd been in college, when she had weighed a good ten pounds more than she did now, but they were no longer as firm. Her skin didn't seem to cushion her skeleton as it once had, but instead revealed her ribs and her shoulders, giving her torso a bony look. The changes her body had undergone never used to bother her, but they did now, when Troy studied her with the knowledge of how she had looked fifteen years back.

"Older and better," he refuted her. He leaned forward and kissed the valley between her breasts. "You're more beautiful than ever."

"You wouldn't want to photograph me now," she contended. In college, Troy had often asked her to let him photograph her in the nude. She had been too shy to let him, even though she knew he was asking only as an artist, without any salacious notions about centerfold poses.

"I would," he insisted, lifting his head and nipping her shoulder. His hands found the zipper of her skirt and slid it open, allowing the turquoise material to drop at her feet. Then he tugged down her panties, letting them join the rest of her clothing on the carpeted floor. His hands spread over the taut curves of her bottom, and he and Julianne gasped simultaneously. "But not now," he whispered, guiding her back into the cradle of his hips, permitting her to feel his hardness through the denim of his jeans. "Not this minute."

She yanked off his shirt, and he helped her to remove his jeans. Then he lay down with her on the bed, enveloping her in his arms and legs, crushing her tall, slender body against his taller, broader one. Their lovemaking in the past had often been marked by a raging impatience, but Julianne felt more impatient now than she'd ever felt then. She had been waiting too long for this moment, and she didn't want to wait a second longer.

She would have to wait. If Troy was as impatient as she was, he was doing a superb job of controlling himself. Staring up into his dark, penetrating eyes, stroking her hands along the rugged surface of his back, Julianne recalled the first time they'd been together, lying on the threadbare couch in a corner of *The Dream*'s office, groping and clutching at each other with almost unseemly abandon. Everything had been so sudden then, so reckless and delirious, from the moment when they'd recognized their mutual desire to the moment, an embarrassingly few minutes later, when they'd consummated that desire.

More than Julianne's body had aged since then. She was an adult now, seasoned and rational. If Troy could contain himself, so could she.

"Do you still like this?" he asked, touching the tip of her earlobe and then the crevice behind it with his tongue.

She sighed. It would be hard to remain calm and adult-like if Troy kept reminding her, with his actions as well as his words, of the crazy young love they'd experienced before.

"You do, don't you," he acknowledged softly, leaning away to study her face. He absorbed her blissful expression and smiled hesitantly. "I've dreamed about this, Julianne. I'm embarrassed to admit how often I've dreamed about this."

"Don't be."

"I'm not embarrassed about dreaming," he explained, letting his hand glide around her breast, then rubbing her nipple gently with his thumb. She sighed again, scarcely able to listen to what he was saying. Yet she forced herself to pay attention; his words were as important as his movements. "It's just that... dreams aren't supposed to come true. And this one *is* coming true."

"It isn't a dream anymore."

"It feels like a dream," he swore, sliding lower on the mattress and replacing his fingers with his lips. He sucked tenderly on her breast, stroking her nipple with his tongue until she moaned helplessly. "It feels too good to be real," he insisted. His mustache brushed against her skin, and the contrast between that light, silky friction and the moist hunger of his mouth caused the muscles in her thighs to clench.

Holding Troy, sensing the sweet unfurling of her body as it opened to him, did feel too good to be real. But it was real. Both their dreams were coming true.

She strummed her fingertips down his ribs to his abdomen, then lower. As her hand closed around him he lurched and let out a rough breath. "Troy," she implored him, urging him higher, trying to pin him to herself. "Please..."

He struggled against her, against his instinctive response to the tentative motion of her fingers on him. "I haven't even touched you," he protested, easing her hand away.

"I'm ready—"

He cut off her words with a kiss, his tongue conquering her mouth, silencing her. His hand journeyed through the downy thatch of hair between her legs to caress her. If she had thought she was ready, he seemed determined to prove her wrong. His fingers danced over her, drawing her out, luring deeper, more overwhelming responses from her. Her body moved with his hand, her tension building, the aching pull of it tightening inside her until she could no longer stand it.

When she reached for him again, he yielded to her unspoken demand. His body settled onto hers and he joined himself fully to her. For a second he remained motionless, simply savoring the moment. Then he forged deeper. "Oh, God," he breathed. "You feel so good, Julie, so good...."

She closed her eyes, directing every bit of her consciousness down into her, into the place where their bodies had taken possession of each other. She concentrated on the luscious sensation of his exquisitely slow, forceful thrusts. Each time he withdrew, she felt an agonizing loss that was assuaged only when he plunged into her again, filling her, filling her with himself, with everything that had been missing from her life for so many years.

His ragged breath fell hot against her ear as his tempo increased. "Come with me, Julie," he whispered, his words as erotic as his movements. "Stay with me."

She opened her mouth to protest that she was way ahead of him, but the only sound to emerge was a breathless cry. Her hands fisted in the thick black waves of his hair and her hips arched from the bed to meet him in a final, consuming surge. And then she was gone, aware of nothing but the release rushing through her in pounding waves, fierce at her core and radiating throughout her body, lapping at her extremities.

Aware of nothing but her ecstasy...and of him, Troy, the man who had brought her there, who was rapidly following her over the brink of emotion, into heaven. A broken gasp tore from him and he subsided heavily on top of her, his chest pumping erratically against her breasts, his skin damp, his face buried in the crook of her neck. One of his hands moved languidly down her arm to capture its mate, and he wove his fingers securely through hers. Then he lifted her hand to his chin and turned his head. He pressed his mouth to her knuckles.

"This was better than the dream," he mumbled.

Unable to speak, she nodded.

"Don't move," he ordered her. Evidently, even the slight bobbing of her head was more than he could bear.

Opening her eyes, she fell still beneath him. His lips coursed over her knuckles again, and his breathing became more regular. Gradually he found the fortitude to ease himself off her, although he kept one leg slung across her knees, pressing her to the bed beside him. He propped his head up with his free hand and stared at her. His tenuous smile and his shimmering eyes enchanted her.

"Now," he murmured, sweeping her with his gaze, "now I'd like to photograph you."

"Not a chance," she refused him with a laugh. The intimacy of her feelings for Troy did not extend to his camera. His eyes saw more than enough without the aid of an external lens. His brain could record her more accurately than any light-sensitive paper.

"If I could see you like this, whenever I wanted to, I wouldn't need a picture," he remarked.

If I could see you... whenever I wanted... But he couldn't. Not if he left, not if he returned to Canada.

A chill rippled down her spine as she digested his words. No matter what they'd just shared, no matter how sublimely they had just loved each other, Troy intended to leave. She knew in her gut that he wouldn't stay. He had his business in Montreal, his residence, his freedom. The freedom that he had always considered more important than anything else, including Julianne.

Caught up in the rapture of loving him, she had forgotten everything: that his home wasn't with her. That he'd made his choice long ago. That he had left her once and that he would leave her again. How could she have lost her perspective? How could she have abdicated her powers of reason and logic?

Only Troy could do this to her. Only he could shatter her composure, render her incapable of thought, make her believe that dreams really could come true. Only he could scramble her mind with a set of magnificent photographs and a few demoralizing kisses.

She would have to recover her wits, and quickly. She wasn't going to allow herself to wind up bereft and grieving all over again.

Shaping a brittle smile, she edged away from him and sat up. "Would you like something to drink?" she asked, her voice muted.

He rolled onto his back and grinned up at her, apparently unaware of her altered mood. "No, but I'll take an ashtray, if that's all right with you."

"I think I've got one in the kitchen." She rose, hoping that the trembling in her legs wasn't visible to him, and crossed to her closet. After donning a flowing kimono of beige silk, she left the bedroom, tying the sash as she went.

In the kitchen she sagged against the counter and took a steadying breath. She didn't want Troy to see her falling apart. And she wasn't going to beg him to stay. She'd begged him once, and all she had accomplished was to feel even worse about his going. They had made love that time, too. They'd bound themselves to each other with the same wild passion they had shared just minutes ago in her bedroom—and his departure had hurt that much more because of it. She must have been insane to let herself become so vulnerable to him again.

Remonstrating with herself wasn't going to help her to survive another leave-taking, however. Gulping in a second bracing breath, she rummaged in her cabinets until she located the cut-crystal ashtray she kept for guests who smoked. She held it, ran her fingers over its beveled edges and stared at the rainbows it refracted from the ceiling light fixture. She searched its delicate prisms, seeking the strength and balance she would need to get through the rest of the evening.

Hearing Troy enter the room behind her, she realized that she must have been standing in the kitchen for a long time, long enough for him to have come after her. He had put on his jeans, and he carried a pack of cigarettes and a book of matches. "What's going on in here?" he asked before noticing the ashtray and lifting it from her hands.

"When are you going to quit smoking?" she asked brusquely.

He examined her for a minute, trying to interpret the cause of her testiness. He placed the ashtray carefully on the counter and put his cigarettes and matches down beside it. "How about now?" he offered in an ameliorating voice.

"Fine."

His hands alighted on her shoulders, and he turned her around so he could see her face. "What's the problem, Julianne?" he asked.

"You," she snapped, hating herself for her lack of control but unable to stop the tears from beading along her eyelashes, or the words from tumbling out. "You're the problem, damn you!"

Six

He had never seen her cry before.

Julianne simply wasn't the type. She was too strong, too unsentimental. Troy recalled how Laura's eyes used to become moist at the mere mention of some example of social injustice or human suffering—starving children, napalmed Vietnamese villages, whatever. And Kimberly...hum a few bars of "Yesterday" and she'd start to sniffle. Allude to a movie like *The Way We Were* and she'd reach for the nearest box of tissues. Show her a cute little puppy dog and she'd start blubbering.

Julianne hadn't been like that. Social injustice riled her to action, not to tears. Melodramatic movies made her introspective, but not depressed. Cute dogs inspired her to laugh. That was one of the things Troy had always admired about her: her stability, her lack of emotional excessiveness..

Yet here she was, standing less than two feet away from him, weeping. She had turned her back on him and covered her face with her hands, but he could see her shoulders heaving and shaking beneath the smooth fabric of her robe. He could hear her hushed, throaty sobs.

Bewildered, yet eager to offer comfort, he touched her shoulder. She eluded his hand and stalked out of the kitchen.

Respecting her obvious desire to be alone, Troy remained where he was. He comprehended that she didn't want him to witness her misery. But he wished with all his heart that once she pulled herself together, she would explain what the hell was bothering her.

He pulled a cigarette from the pack, lit it and tried to make sense of this sudden crisis. He had thought Julianne would be rejoicing right now, as he was—or as he had been, until the moment he'd followed her into the kitchen and found himself the object of her unbridled wrath. What had he done to upset her? Had he been mistaken in assuming that she was as delighted as he was by what had occurred in her bedroom?

It had been good between them. Better than good. It had been magnificent, awesome, unbelievably fantastic. And it had been what she wanted—what they both wanted. What they had both wanted for fifteen years, what they had both dreamed of. Not just the sex, but the love, the return of their trust, the joy of reviving the intimacy they had experienced years ago.

They had never stopped loving each other. Julianne seemed to have recognized that fact all along. Now, at last, Troy was ready to agree with her, to accept that his feelings for her hadn't been weakened by time, distance, or doubt about whether he'd done the right thing in leaving the country so long ago.

Julianne wasn't coy; she couldn't have changed her mind about Troy so soon. She had made it quite evident, when she'd visited him in Montreal, that she wanted him back. And now he was back. So what was the problem?

He waited until he was done with his cigarette before he left the kitchen. He discovered her seated on the sofa in her living room, her bare feet propped up on the coffee table and her head tilted back against the cushions, her eyes fixed on the ceiling. The upholstery of the sofa was the same muted beige as her robe. If he shot her right now in black and white and overexposed the film, all that would show up against the milky background would be her legs, her hands, her head and the triangle of skin revealed above the sloping flaps of the robe's neckline. The robe itself would blend into the couch and become invisible.

It would make a striking picture: detached but beautiful limbs, shapely flesh burnished by the sun. Incredibly sensual.

How could he think about how sexy she was when she was so distressed? His body still resonated with the sublime satisfaction of their lovemaking. But Julianne had clearly recovered from their interlude on her bed. Or else—even worse—her tears were a direct result of that interlude. Did she resent him for having made love to her? Was she angry with him for it? Had he totally misread the entire situation?

She had stopped crying. But she didn't turn at his entrance. She continued to stare at the ceiling.

"Do you need some more time alone?" he asked solicitously.

"No." At last she lowered her eyes, but she avoided looking directly at Troy. Instead she inspected the sash of her robe. She wove it in and out among the fingers of one hand, then unraveled it and wove it among the fingers of the other.

He sat a discreet distance from her on the couch and watched her. Her expression was blank; he couldn't tell a thing from it. "Care to fill me in?" he asked.

She shook her head slightly, then offered a crooked grin. "I'm sorry, Troy. My little tantrum was really uncalled for."

"Was it?" Now, of all times, he wished she wasn't so stable and reserved. He longed to help; he longed to resolve whatever was causing her such despair. He longed to be reassured that he hadn't made another big mistake regarding Julianne. "Why don't you tell me about it?"

"There's nothing to tell," she maintained, shifting on the couch and raising her eyes to him. Her smile was pensive, uncertain.

There was plenty to tell, and Troy wasn't going to allow her to keep him in the dark forever. "I thought...I thought you wanted this," he said, bracing himself for her response. If she told him that he was wrong, that she hadn't wanted this, he'd be devastated, humiliated, unable to trust himself ever again.

"I did," she confirmed quietly, her pale, dry eyes steadfast on him.

"Did I hurt you?" he questioned her anxiously. She had seemed so receptive to him, so aroused by his touch. He didn't think he was blind enough to have misinterpreted her physical response. But given her hysteria afterward, he no longer knew. "Did I—" His voice cracked, but he forced out the words. "Did I blow it in bed?"

"Of course not," she answered, then looked away. "Not in bed," she added, her voice barely a whisper.

Not in bed. But he'd blown it elsewhere; he'd hurt her.

He should have telephoned her before that afternoon. That must be what was troubling her. He should have been in touch sooner. It would have been the civilized thing to do. He should have called her, met her for dinner or a drink, discussed his work. He had hidden from her because he thought he had to, for both their sakes. Perhaps she was wounded by his decision to keep himself a safe distance from her while he was in New York.

If that was all it was, he was sure he could make her understand why he'd shied from her. "I told you, Julianne...I didn't want to see you until I was convinced that I was good enough for you."

"It isn't that," she corrected him. She began to play with the sash of her robe again, a sign of her nervousness. It anguished Troy to think he could make Julianne nervous.

"Then when? When did I blow it?"

"Fifteen years ago."

He exhaled and turned from her. Fifteen years ago. At least he hadn't blown what had happened fifteen minutes ago. Yet, as pleased as he was about that, he wanted only to enjoy the aftermath of it, to curl up with Julianne and kiss her and reassure himself that they were truly together again. He was in no mood to rehash the past with her.

Assessing her graceful posture, her firm expression, her constant gaze, he inferred that he had no choice but to get into the mood. They couldn't simply ignore the unpleasant aspects of their history, especially not since they had just rekindled the most glorious aspect of it.

He tried to swallow his dissatisfaction, but it wasn't easy. His hands curled reflexively into fists on his spread knees, and his feet itched to move. Standing, he strode into the kitchen to retrieve his cigarettes. He would quit smoking for Julianne—he would do just about anything for her—but not this minute. The situation was evidently more critical than he'd anticipated.

Returning to the couch, he sat, placed the ashtray on the coffee table, lit a cigarette and pondered her accusation. Fair enough. He'd blown it fifteen years ago. He'd broken her heart; he'd broken his own heart, as well. But he'd had no alternative at the time.

Going to jail might have sounded like a pragmatic solution to Julianne, but not to Troy. If he had gone to prison, she could have turned him into a cause célèbre, a martyr. She could have protested his incarceration on street corners, on soapboxes, on the editorial page of *The Dream*. She could have made a career of it, like Joan Baez, who wrote mournful ballads for her draft-evader husband and produced an album of songs dedicated to him—and who, if memory served Troy, divorced the sap shortly after he was released.

Perhaps Troy's imprisonment would have given Julianne a purpose in life. Meanwhile, *he* would have been the one behind bars, eating off tin plates and watching his days dissolve into dust.

If he'd had it to do all over again, Troy would probably have done exactly what he did. He would have felt just as ghastly about the choice he was forced to make, but he wouldn't have chosen differently.

Taking good pictures of Laura's clients was apparently not enough to redeem him in Julianne's eyes. Nothing he could do at this point would change what he'd done then. "All right." He steeled himself with a sigh. "I'm a criminal. No argument there—I broke the law. Even after all these years, if you can't accept it, I—I understand."

"That's not what bothers me," Julianne disputed him. "I don't care that you broke the law, Troy. Maybe it was a law that had to be broken."

"Then what?" he asked, his patience beginning to fray. If it wasn't that he'd refused to do the noble thing and go to jail for his beliefs, what else had he done back then that could be bothering Julianne so much?

"You left me," she said in a small voice.

He put out his cigarette and twisted back to her. She was staring out the window at the fading dusk, her hands folded loosely in her lap and her shoulders straight and proud. "What was I supposed to do?" he asked, equally softly. "Bring you along with me? You wouldn't have come."

"How do you know that?" she challenged him, refusing to look at him. "You never asked."

"I couldn't ask," he defended himself, his memory of the night he'd left vivid in his mind. There had been nothing he'd rather have done than drag Julianne along with him, but he'd smothered the temptation to ask her to accompany him. "I was heading for the unknown and I was breaking the law. I couldn't bring you into it. I didn't know what the consequences would be. I didn't know that a few years later a president was going to come along and grant me a pardon." At her obdurate silence, he stressed, "It was too dangerous, Julie."

"You could have let me decide that for myself," she retorted.

"And what would you have decided? Would you have come with me?"

She ruminated for a long minute. "No," she admitted, smiling wistfully. "Probably not."

He settled back into the plush cushions and groaned. More memories spun through him, unwelcome ones, and he closed his eyes, unable to resist them. "It wasn't like I was acting impulsively, without caring about the repercussions. Do you know when I first started thinking about moving to Canada?"

"When?"

"Years before I left. Years." Inhaling deeply, he reminisced. "I first conceived of the idea the night of the lottery. I watched it on the tube with some friends, in the dorm lounge. I had already applied for C.O. status when I registered for the draft. But then they had their lottery, and I watched, and they called my birthday. Lucky me, in the top ten."

"Did the actual number matter?" Julianne posed. "You could have been in the top fifty and still been up the creek. Or the top one hundred."

"It was symbolic," he explained. "When I heard my birthday called so early in the drawing... having that low a number was like not just being shipped overseas but being offered a spot on the front line. I thought I would go crazy, Julie. I thought—correctly, as it turned out—that my life would never be the same again. I left the lounge, went outside and told myself that, if worse came to worst and my C.O. application was rejected, I'd leave the country." He snorted bitterly. "Then I threw up."

"You did?" With his eyes shut, he couldn't see her, but her voice carried interest and compassion.

He nodded. "My mother used to joke that I had a cast-iron stomach. Nothing made me sick, she thought. I could eat anything. I could survive a flu epidemic without getting nauseous. I do have a strong stomach, Julianne, but a couple of things in this world have made me sick. Learning my draft number was one of them."

"What was the other?" she asked.

He hesitated before replying. What she was asking was something he preferred not to talk about. As close as they'd been in college, he hadn't discussed it with Julianne then. Did he really want to go into it now?

He had to. He owed her the truth. "Hunting," he told her.

"Hunting!" Her astonished exclamation provoked him to open his eyes. She was gaping at him. "When did you ever go hunting?"

He issued a grim chuckle. "When I was fourteen, with my father."

"You never told me that."

"I never told anyone."

"What happened?"

He closed his eyes again, letting the memory suffuse him. "It was supposed to be a surprise for my fourteenth birthday," he related. "I knew Dad had gone hunting a few times when I was a kid, but he never brought any game home with him, and I figured his hunting expeditions were just an excuse to go out into the woods for a few days with his buddies to drink and play poker. But when I turned fourteen, he borrowed a rifle and rented a cabin up in northern Minnesota. It was a long drive, and I started getting antsy in the car. But I kept telling myself, we'd only be drinking suds and talking, and the gun would stay in the back of the station wagon for the weekend." He fell silent.

"And?" Julianne prompted him.

"The first day he taught me how to use the gun, shooting at empty cans. It was scary, Julie. The rifle was so heavy, and when you shot it, the noise..." He shook his head, unable to find an adequate word to describe the fearsome report of gunfire. "But I was fourteen, and it was my father, and I did my best for him. I wanted him to love me, you know? I wanted him to think I was a man. That was what the whole thing was about." He grimaced. "Empty cans I could handle. But then the second day we hiked a trail. There was this rabbit..." His voice drifted off and he shuddered.

"Did you kill the rabbit?" Julianne asked.

"I—I didn't want to, Julie. I mean, it wasn't a particularly adorable rabbit or anything, just a scrawny jackrabbit. Kind of scruffy and ugly. But I didn't want to kill it.

So I deliberately aimed high." He laughed dolefully. "What a joke. I was a kid who'd been playing with cameras for years. I could aim a lens with radar precision. And there I was, pretending I couldn't sight a damned jackrabbit with a gun." His laughter faded. "My dad lit into me, started giving me all sorts of abuse. What was wrong with me, what kind of loser was I that I couldn't even nail a puny rabbit? He thought I was ready to become a man, but I was obviously a sissy, some kind of faggot for letting the rabbit get the best of me. So...I killed it. I killed it, Julie."

He felt her hand on his, reaching for him, giving him a comforting squeeze. Opening his eyes, he found her scrutinizing him, her face registering deep concern. "And you were sick to your stomach?"

He nodded. "Right there on the trail, next to the carcass. Hunting—I mean, I can understand someone shooting an animal for food. It's not something I would ever want to do, but I can understand it. But to shoot a living thing for the sport of it—to kill a rabbit because if you don't kill it, you aren't a real man..." He cursed softly. "You asked me up in Canada why my family hadn't forgiven me for leaving the States. It was a longer story than you knew, Julianne. Ever since I killed that rabbit and got sick over it, things have been bad between me and my father. He was a marine in World War Two, and that was the high point of his existence. After he came back, he got a job on the Ford assembly line, married his high school sweetheart, had a couple of kids and lived from one pink slip to the next. He's basically powerless in his life. Except that every now and then, he goes off to Minnesota and slaughters a rabbit." Troy wondered if Julianne could fathom what he was telling her. He wondered if a pure, sweet woman, a doctor's daughter from Iowa, could possibly comprehend what had driven Troy to take flight. "My father kills a rabbit and feels like a hero again," he explained. "And I can't be the heroic son he wanted."

"Troy." Her hand tightened on his fingers and her eyes bore down on him. "It wasn't your going to Canada that hurt me," she gently pointed out. "You can understand someone shooting an animal for food, even if you can't do that yourself. Well, I can understand someone leaving the country, even if that's not what I might have done in your position."

"But you haven't forgiven me, either," he asserted. Hearing himself say it caused a leaden sense of despair to gather in his abdomen.

"I forgive you for going," she swore. "I forgave you for that years ago—right after you left. Even before you left, when you told me you were going to go. But..." She took a deep breath. "It sounds selfish to admit it, Troy, but you hurt me. Losing you hurt me very badly."

"Is that what made you cry?" he asked. "Were you crying for then?"

"Yes. No." She averted her eyes. Her voice was surprisingly calm when she said, "I was crying for now, Troy. It was silly of me. I'm sorry."

"It wasn't silly," he objected, pushing himself upright. He still wasn't sure what Julianne had been crying about, but whatever it was, it couldn't have been silly. Julianne wouldn't know how to be silly even if she wanted to. "Why were you crying for now? I thought...I thought what happened just now was pretty spectacular."

"Yes." She seemed to struggle with herself for a minute, and then her placidity returned. "It was wonderful. And now you're going to leave."

"Leave?" His eyes hardened on her, and his bewilderment increased. "This minute? Is this your way of kicking me out?"

"Troy." She impaled him with her somber gaze. "You're going to go back to Montreal. We both know that."

He smothered the impulse to protest that she was wrong, that he would never leave her, not now, not after they had each other again. If he made such a statement, she wouldn't believe him. He had spent too much time recently trying to convince her that his home was in Canada, that his work and his citizenship were there, that he wasn't about to relinquish what he'd found in his adopted nation.

But what had he found in Canada, after all? A studio where he photographed whining children, a nondescript apartment, a social life of featherweight relationships. Nothing that could compare with what he had known with Julianne, nothing that could compare with what they'd just rediscovered with each other.

"Maybe..." He spoke slowly, considering each word before he uttered it. "Maybe I'm still not good enough for you. But I want to be, Julianne. Tell me how to go about it."

She released his hand and stood. Edgy, she prowled to the window and rested her forehead against the pane. She stared down at the cars scuttling along the street below and sighed. "I'm not a child anymore, Troy," she murmured, rotating and leaning against the sill, gazing across the room at him. "I'm not foolish enough to believe in the impossible. And I'm not a mother, either. I'm not going to mold you into what I want you to be. Things are the way they are. You've taken some good pictures for me, and I'm very grateful. But you've also got a return ticket to Montreal, and I'm sure you're planning to use it."

Her painstaking sensibility grated on him. Not twenty minutes ago, she had let down her guard and given in to her emotions. Her tears had communicated to him what her words were concealing—that she felt strongly, passionately, about what existed between the two of them.

Now she was withdrawing again, playing the role of the reasonable editor, the competent boss. And he was enraged. He felt the muscles knotting in his shoulders, and his hands fisted up again. "Don't be sure of anything, Julie," he snapped, hoisting himself to his feet and approaching her.

His anger provoked an equal measure of fury from her. She held her ground unflinchingly as he neared. "I'll tell you what I'm sure of, Troy," she muttered. "I'm sure of this—that when I wasn't busy loving you fifteen years ago I was busy hating you. Hating you for leaving me. I don't want to hate you anymore, Troy. I'm too old for that. So let's just be practical about the situation. You're in Canada. I'm here. We've both got our own lives to live."

"And I want you in mine," he demanded, gripping her shoulders to hold her in place—as if she had any intention of escaping him. "You've never not been in it, Julie. Screw the practicality stuff. We're in each other's lives, and we've always been, and that's the way things are."

His outburst shocked them both. They stared into each other's eyes, neither blinking, neither retreating. Troy's breath came hard and deep, and he realized that he wanted her again, more than before. Not to love her, but to prove something, to force her to admit the truth. For an immeasurable moment, he wrestled with the urge to crush her mouth beneath his, to wrap his arms around her and squeeze her until she relented, until she begged him to believe that she saw things as he did. Until her fine bones cracked within his embrace, if necessary.

The violent overtone of his desire frightened him. His hands softened on her, then dropped to his sides. Brutishness was no more his style than weeping was Julianne's. They'd both had their moments of insanity, but now it was time to compose themselves, to deal with things logically.

He couldn't force Julianne to believe that they belonged together. Certainly not, given that when she had entertained that belief once before, he had abandoned her. If he wanted her to believe him now, he would have to court her, woo her, persuade her.

The idea of courting her struck him as bizarre. He hadn't courted her the first time around—but nobody courted anybody back then. There were no elegant dates, no glamorous costumes and flirting games in that era. Liberated women would have been affronted by such old-fashioned rituals, and counterculture men would have been turned off by a woman who required them.

Troy didn't think Julianne was interested in being courted in a traditional way. But he had to prove something to her, and he had to do it in the proper fashion. "Okay," he said, pacing the living room, verbalizing his thoughts as he formulated them. "My stuff is at Peter's place, down in the Village. And I've got to call Claude and Stacy."

She frowned, perplexed. "And tell them what?"

"I don't know," he mumbled. He hadn't thought things through that far yet. "I've got a wedding to shoot tomorrow night. It's June—a big month for wedding gigs at Bennett-Chartier. Maybe Claude can find someone to cover for me. That gives us the weekend."

"The weekend," she echoed vaguely.

"All right, I'll have to go back eventually. To tie up loose ends, and—" He cursed, furious with his brain for not sorting itself out quickly enough. "The apartment's no problem, but the studio—that's going to take some serious working out, Julie. I can't just strand Claude. It may take some time—"

"I don't understand," she interrupted. "What are you planning, Troy?"

"To move back to New York," he explained. "To come back to you. You don't believe me, Julie, but I'm going to make it right between us. I *am* good enough for you—damned good enough. You may not know that yet, but you'll figure it out in time."

"Moving back to New York isn't going to make you a better person, Troy."

"I don't have to be a better person," he countered. "I just have to be good enough—and close enough to you that you'll notice. I'm not going to leave you this time. Even if you wanted me to leave, I wouldn't, just to spite you."

Julianne laughed. "Troy—"

"And let me tell you this, boss," he went on, "you're usually right. Almost always. It's one of your most intriguing characteristics and sometimes one of your most annoying. But every now and then you miss a call. And you've missed this one, lady. I'm not going to leave, even if you beg me."

"I won't beg," she promised.

"Fine. Then point me in the direction of your telephone. I've got some calls to make."

SHE WOULDN'T BEG. She'd begged for something only once in her life, even though doing so went against her grain. She'd been desperate at the time, unthinking, beside herself with grief when Troy had told her he was leaving.

She'd begged him not to go. And it hadn't done a bit of good.

She had begged, and she had dreamed. Even after he was gone, even after her letters to him went unanswered, even after her intellect warned her time after time that he would never come back, she had dreamed that he would. She wasn't about to make that mistake again, either.

Of course, dreams came true sometimes. But only when they were realistic to begin with, and only when one applied oneself to the task of making them come true. One of Julianne's dreams had been to keep her newspaper alive, to see it flourish. Hard work and single-mindedness had enabled that dream to come true. But to dream that she and Troy could actually have a future—no, she wasn't going to allow herself to indulge in that fantasy.

He had shut himself up inside her bedroom with the telephone. Julianne was curious about whom he might be calling, what arrangements he might be making. But she refused to eavesdrop on his conversations. Whatever he was planning was his own business.

Instead she stayed in the living room. She turned on her stereo and set the tape player in motion. The James Taylor tape she had been listening to a couple of nights ago was still on the reels, and she settled into the couch and let the sweet music wash over her. James Taylor sang of seeing sunny days that he thought would never end, and Julianne nodded unconsciously. She had seen days like that, too, in college, with Troy.

The sunny days had ended, though. They had ended with a cloudburst on the night before Independence Day. When the fourth of July had arrived, Julianne had remained alone, locked inside her apartment, listening to the distant rumbles and blasts of the fireworks extravaganza taking place south of her apartment, above the Hudson

River. She had watched the diffused flashes of light that entered through her window to strafe her walls, and wondered whether fireworks were anything like what soldiers experienced in battle. The flares and spraying sparks and muted thunderclaps had frightened her.

She didn't doubt that Troy meant what he said about forcing his way back into her life. She was inordinately flattered by the idea. When she had lain with him earlier, loving him and letting him love her, she had shared his certainty that they belonged together, that no hurdles were insurmountable in keeping them together. It had always been that way with them. Even after telling her that he was going to leave that horrible night fifteen years ago, Julianne had been positive that making love with him would change everything, would make him recognize that he had to stay.

He might believe, as she had then, that such miracles were possible. But she no longer believed in miracles. No matter how many telephone calls he made, no matter how many practical details he worked out, she didn't think he was going to remain in her life forever.

It was more than merely the practical details, however. It was more than the fact that he had a business in Montreal and no job in New York, more than the fact that he was a citizen of Canada and simply a visitor in the United States. The real obstacle was that Troy still hadn't ended the war in his heart.

He could love Julianne. She permitted herself the luxury of assuming that he did. But even at that, he wouldn't belong with her until he belonged to himself again.

Smoothing the silk of her kimono over her knees, she reflected on what he had told her about his father. The war for Troy hadn't begun in Vietnam; it had begun at least twenty-three years ago, on a hunting trip with his dad.

That he had evaded the draft was only the culmination of the war he'd been fighting with his father probably all his life.

Perhaps Troy's father didn't consider his son heroic, but Julianne thought Troy was the most heroic man she'd ever known. She had thought him heroic when he'd held fast to his principles regarding the draft, even though his decision had cost her dearly. Some men in Troy's position had faked medical problems; some had signed up with the National Guard or had imposed upon relatives or friends to pull strings and get them assigned to West Germany or Korea. Troy had refused those easy outs, and Julianne admired his courage.

But his heroism was more complex than that. He was heroic in standing up to his father—which in his case had undoubtedly been more difficult than standing up to the United States government. Julianne could think of few things more heroic than reacting with disgust to the sight of a murdered rabbit, even when one's manhood hung in the balance.

He hadn't told Julianne about the hunting incident before. Yet she had comprehended his inner strength right from the start. When she had first spotted him in their rhetorics class, she had found him strikingly handsome, and she'd been thrilled when Andrew Collins, the student with whom she'd been linked on the class assignment that led to the founding of *The Dream*, turned out to be a good friend of Troy's. "Sure, let's ask Troy to join us," Andrew had agreed. "He can take photographs for us. He's a whiz with a camera."

She would have leaped at any opportunity to work with that tall, gorgeous, charismatic man with the thick black hair, delectable mustache and dark, mesmerizing eyes. But Andrew had provided her with a perfect excuse to invite

Troy to hook up with them, and Troy's enthusiasm for her newspaper idea had convinced her that he deserved her attention.

She hadn't intended to fall in love with him. She had a crush on him—she suspected that the majority of the women in the class did—but she knew the difference between a crush and true love, and she wasn't going to let her attraction to Troy ruin their working relationship. That relationship evolved into friendship, but so did her relationships with Laura, Andrew and Seth, none of whom she had known before they'd become classmates in the rhetorics course. The friendship with Troy deepened further because they often wound up working alone in the office, going over proofs and arranging layouts long after the other staff members had retired for the night. During those late-evening sessions with Troy, Julianne had been keenly aware of his virile good looks, his emotional intensity, his ability to zero in on the moods of others, to capture on film his subjects' essences as well as their surfaces. She had been dazzled by his extravagant talent, and by his size. As tall as she was, she frequently intimidated men who were smaller. But she never intimidated Troy.

And then one night, he found her in the office and carried her to the couch. And loved her. Those magic eyes of his had seen her feelings, and he returned them. How could she have thought she could hide her heart from him? He was Troy, after all, a man endowed with astonishing perception. He must have known, even before she did, that she loved him.

"Hello."

The sound of his voice jolted her. Spinning around on the sofa cushions, she saw him entering the living room. He had put on his shirt, but it hung unbuttoned outside his jeans. His hair looked as if he had run his fingers endlessly through it. Julianne stifled the temptation to race to his side and run her fingers through it, as well. She wasn't going to let her passion for him cloud her objectivity.

He was neither smiling nor frowning. He crossed to the couch and slumped on it, fatigued. As well he had a right to be. It seemed as if they'd both been through an emotional earthquake in the past hour.

"Hello," she greeted him.

He arched his arm around her and pulled her against himself. His fingers toyed with the clipped ends of her hair and he sighed. "This isn't going to be easy," he conceded.

Nothing worthwhile ever is, she responded silently. Then she mulled over his statement. It was the sort of thing men were supposed to say just before they broke up with women. "What isn't going to be easy?" she asked hesitantly.

He exhaled, his fingers moving implacably through the silky fringe of her hair. "I couldn't find anyone to replace me at the wedding tomorrow night, so I'm going to have to go back to Montreal tomorrow," he explained. "I don't want to go, but I can't seem to get out of it."

"Then you'll go," she said, already resigned to reality. Troy had allowed himself to get carried away. Now, at last, he was compelled to recognize that leaving Canada wasn't going to be so simple.

"But I'll come back," Troy went on optimistically. "Claude and I have a lot of things to work out, but we'll work them out. Whatever it takes, Julie. I'm serious about this."

"Do you really want to turn your life upside-down just because we had a good time in bed?" she asked, testing him.

He shifted away and peered down at her. "That's not what this is about, and you know it," he said sternly.

"Well... it all seems a bit sudden," she said, justifying her skepticism.

"It isn't sudden," he argued, drawing her against his shoulder again. "I've never stopped wanting you. Never, Julie."

"Being with me is going to involve more than just me," Julianne pointed out. "Even if you can work everything out with Claude, what are you going to do for a living here? I'm sure the city has more than enough wedding photographers."

"I'm not going to do that anymore," he said. "Don't worry. It's all going to fall into place eventually. Coming back can't be as hard as leaving was."

"Still—"

"I also talked to Peter just now," he cut her off. "He promised he could find something for me to do in his bookstore while I circulate a portfolio with the newspapers and see what I can dig up in the way of work."

Toiling in a bookstore was hardly an improvement over taking bridal photographs. Julianne could recommend Troy to her associates at the city's other glossies—if she really wanted him to stay. In fact, if she wanted him to stay, she could offer him more work herself. "I've got another job for you, if you're interested," she said. Hearing her words convinced her that she did want him to stay.

"No," he refused, almost too rapidly. "This is my situation, Julianne. If I'm going to prove myself to you, I can't do it with handouts from you."

"Not even if you'd be doing it for Kimberly and Andrew?"

He pulled away from her again. "Now what?" he asked with an amazed laugh. "You used that routine on me to get me to take pictures for Laura."

"And it worked," Julianne said, smiling confidently. "We're going to run an article on Andrew's testimony before the Intelligence Committee. You could go down to Washington and do the art for it. *Dream* pays well, Troy, and you'd do a good job."

"Julianne..." He appraised her thoughtfully, an enigmatic grin tickling his lips. "I'm not going to let you turn me into a charity case."

"Of course not. I wouldn't like you if that's what you became. I'm offering this as an editor. Even if you were a total stranger, if you supplied me with the sort of quality photos you took for the story on Laura, I'd hire you for more work. This is a professional request, Troy, not a handout." At his lingering uncertainty, she added, "I'm offering you an assignment, not a place to stay. If you want this to be your own thing, then you'd better not expect to move in with me."

Again her words, spoken instinctively, indicated something important to her. There was nothing she would love more than to have Troy living with her. But, as he'd said, returning to the States wasn't going to be easy. It shouldn't be easy. If she made it too easy for him, she would never know how committed he was to staying. And he would never have the chance to figure out for himself whether he wanted to come back badly enough to overcome all the obstacles. He would never have the chance to reconcile himself to the changes he was demanding of himself.

Her statement appeared to surprise him, and he took several seconds to weigh it. "All right. I'll find someplace else to stay. But tonight, Julianne...I want to be with you tonight."

Nestling against him, she closed her eyes and mentally replayed the rapture they'd shared in her bedroom. No matter what happened—no matter if Troy never worked it all out, never managed to come home to her—she wanted his love again. "Yes," she agreed. "You'll stay here tonight."

Seven

"When I come back," said Troy, "I'm going to bring a suit with me. We're going to get all duded up, and I'm going to take you someplace nice for dinner."

He emptied the last of the sangria into their glasses, straining out the soggy rounds of orange and lemon with the wooden spoon, and set the drinks down on the table between them. Julianne leaned back in her chair and surveyed the dimly lit restaurant. Across the dining room, the wall was decorated with a broad mural depicting a sunset over the Sierra Madre. A straw sombrero was tacked to the wall above their table. Mariachi music, piped into the room through hidden speakers, added to the ambience. "This is someplace nice," she commented, debating with herself over whether her stomach could accommodate the half enchilada still sitting on her plate. The meal had been delicious, but she was stuffed. She left her fork on the edge of her plate and sipped her wine.

"I mean, someplace *nice*," he stressed, lighting a cigarette and pulling the plastic ashtray toward him. "Someplace with exorbitant prices and a dozen waiters per table."

Julianne laughed. This Mexican restaurant, which they'd discovered up the block from Peter Dubin's bookstore, appealed to her. She and Troy had taken the subway downtown to Greenwich Village, retrieved Troy's bag from Peter's apartment and then stopped at the bookstore to drop off the spare key Peter had lent Troy. Julianne had never met Peter before, but he'd seemed like a personable man, his outdated ponytail and Ben Franklin spectacles notwithstanding.

In the bookstore Troy had told Peter that he would be spending the night with Julianne, that he would be leaving for Montreal in the morning, but that he expected to be back in New York City soon. Peter had remarked that it was high time Troy returned to the city and repeated his offer of a job clerking at the store if Troy needed the work. "I've been holding the job open for you for fifteen years, chump," Peter had joked. "Don't worry about being overqualified for the position. I expect all my clerks to have an Ivy League diploma, at the very least."

Even if the actual job at the bookstore turned out to be tedious, Julianne imagined that Troy would enjoy working with his good friend—for a while, at least. But she questioned how long he would be able to tolerate such work. Finding employment as a photographer was going to be difficult. Julianne could think of numerous photo assignments for him at *Dream*, but if she kept tossing him free-lance assignments, he'd accuse her, rightly, of viewing him as a charity case. He had to find his own way, his own work—they both knew that. And until he did, it was going to be tough. She wondered whether he could take it, whether his desire to return to the States was strong enough to endure the hardships such a move would entail.

"Taking me to a restaurant with exorbitant prices and a dozen waiters per table sounds a bit extravagant," she noted, keeping her tone light.

"I'm a grown-up," he reminded her with a whimsical grin. "I know how to budget my money."

"What money?" she posed, laughing. "You're going to be an unemployed wretch—with the possible exception of one photo assignment down in Washington."

Troy shrugged nonchalantly. "When I went to Canada, I had four hundred dollars to my name and a few thousand in outstanding loans to Columbia. I made ends meet. I took whatever jobs I could find—mopping floors at a bar after hours, answering phones at a hotline for draft dodgers, you name it. I know how to work for a living, Julie." He shrugged again. "I've got a lot saved up. My business has done well, and I don't live high on the hog in Montreal. I'm not going to starve."

"There's a big difference between not starving and dining out at overpriced restaurants," Julianne pointed out.

"But you're probably used to that kind of establishment," he countered. "A beautiful woman like you, in a high-powered job, with a swanky yuppie apartment.... You probably go out to eat at elegant restaurants all the time."

His observation took Julianne aback. Was he jealous of her success, of her social life? Not that she had much of a social life, but Troy sounded as if he were in competition with some imagined rival for Julianne's attention. And his comment about her apartment—had he even noticed her home? He hadn't mentioned anything about it when they were there.

Of course he had noticed her home. Troy's eyes didn't miss anything. He had undoubtedly taken in every detail, every item that hinted at the sort of life Julianne lived. He must have absorbed her expensive, classically styled furniture, the original watercolors framed and hanging on the walls, the matched bed linen and spread, the Lenox vase filled with fresh tulips in the living room.

Like Troy, Julianne had come a long way in the fifteen years since they'd graduated from college. She had lost none of her devotion to political and social causes, but her taste had become refined. Her apartment reflected that taste, even though she gave little thought to how others might view it. She rarely entertained, and she'd never been a show-off. She'd decorated her home nicely for her own benefit.

"Most of the time," she informed Troy, "when I go to an elegant restaurant, it's because I'm wining and dining a prospective advertiser. And I'm the one picking up the tab."

Troy smiled and put out his cigarette. "What's the hot spot for that sort of activity? Elaine's, isn't that what it's called?"

"Elaine's is one of the restaurants people in publishing like to patronize," she allowed, surprised that Troy was aware of dining trends in the city. "The Four Seasons is also popular among publishing people. But I don't go to those restaurants for pleasure."

"Where do you go for pleasure?"

He didn't really sound competitive, she decided. Merely intrigued by Julianne's life in New York, and eager to learn more about it. She hesitantly returned his smile. "I don't eat out much."

"You don't *eat* much," Troy amended. "How much weight have you lost since college?"

"About ten pounds, I guess."

He appraised her, his smile growing cryptic. "Why? Did you go on a diet or something?"

In college she would have thought nothing about the personal nature of Troy's inquiry. They used to talk about everything, then—nearly everything. Troy had never told her about his hunting trip with his father, but he had told her about his overcrowded high school, the history teacher who had whetted Troy's interest in Columbia University, the other history teacher who had threatened Troy with expulsion after he wrote what the teacher considered an unforgivably unpatriotic essay on the war for the school newspaper. Troy had told her about the time he and a friend had hitchhiked to Ann Arbor to attend a rock concert without telling their folks and about the time a policeman had accosted him outside a supermarket, accused him of "smiling funny," and searched him for drugs. He had told her about his introduction to sex, when he was seventeen, under the tutelage of his older sister's best friend. He had told Julianne about how he'd gotten thrown off the varsity basketball team because he refused to cut his hair, about the camera his late grandfather had given him for his birthday when he was ten, about how that simple piece of equipment had given him an entirely new way of viewing the universe. He had told her, as they wolfed down slices of greasy takeout pizza in the basement office, that he had a cast-iron stomach.

He had asked Julianne as much as he told her: about what farms were like, and small-town living, and her family. He had asked her how a doctor made house calls when the patient lived thirty miles away, and how teenagers in such a remote, rural village knew about fashions and rock and roll, and whether Iowa was full of cowboys. His ignorance of life in the hinterlands had tickled Julianne, but she had never denied him the answers he craved.

If he had asked her, back in college, about her diet, she wouldn't have been startled. But his question implied something different now. A few hours ago they had made love for the first time in an eternity. Troy had made love to the same woman, but to a changed body. His question about her weight reminded her of their intimacy, an intimacy she wasn't yet certain that she trusted.

"I didn't go on a diet, no," she answered carefully. "I just... life got so busy, I simply don't have the time to eat three well-balanced meals every day."

"Don't get me wrong," he hastened to placate her. "You look wonderful, Julie. But you don't look like a midwestern farm girl anymore."

"I'm not a midwestern farm girl anymore," she said with a smile. "I guess you're right—I'm a young urban professional, with a yuppie apartment."

"Why hasn't anyone snatched you up?" he asked, fingering his wineglass and gazing steadily at her. "How did you happen to wind up free on a Friday night? Why isn't your calendar booked solid for months?"

He still didn't sound competitive, but Julianne took the time to analyze his words fully before she responded to them. He wasn't asking her if she were carrying a torch for him—they'd already had that conversation, and besides, Troy didn't sound angry or accusing, as he had then. Rather, he sounded puzzled more than anything else. His question contained a scarcely veiled compliment, but he wasn't asking it to flatter her, either. He was asking only because he was curious.

She sipped her wine, then smiled again. "Being a young urban professional isn't what the media make it out to be," she conceded. "I work very hard, and I treasure my privacy. I have so little time to myself."

"It never mattered much to you, being a social butterfly," he recollected, lifting his glass and draining it. "Not like Kimberly, for instance. You could tell she needed a man in her life, even in college. She really got off on having men pay attention to her. You never seemed to care, though."

"I did care," Julianne argued. "I'm not abnormal, Troy, I'm not asexual. But...I have too many demands on me, too many demands I make on myself. If I'm going to let a man make demands on me, too, he's got to be pretty special."

"Did I make demands on you?" he asked, running his fingers thoughtfully over his mustache, pondering her statement. "Do I? Is that what frightens you?"

"I'm not frightened," she said quickly, then emitted a nervous laugh. She didn't think she was frightened by the thought of having Troy back, but she was frightened by the possibility that once she made room for him in her life, once she acclimated herself to his presence, he would disappear, leaving a gaping hole in her existence, as he had the last time. All he was demanding of her was a space big enough for him to fit into her world. But in allowing him that space, she was making a major demand on herself: the demand that she cut away the scar tissue and open her heart again.

He seemed to be waiting for her to elaborate, and when she didn't, he gave a nearly imperceptible nod and turned to signal the waiter. Once he had settled the check, he dragged his suitcase out from under his chair and escorted Julianne out of the restaurant.

She had hoped that the meal would help them both to calm down and regain their bearings. It hadn't. She felt as if the earth were moving beneath her feet once more, as if the ground were cracking, breaking apart, leaving bottomless chasms into which she could fall. If only Troy had delivered his photos and vanished, she would have been able to resume the routines she knew.

But it was too late for that. Her nerves had been rent by his powerful lovemaking, and then again by his abrupt announcement that he planned to force his way back into her life, and again, over dinner, by his personal questions. She ought to brace herself for the aftershocks to come; she knew there would be more. She and Troy were returning to her home, to her bed. And tomorrow morning, he would depart with the promise of returning. And then...he might not live up to his promise. The aftershocks might be more violent than the initial tremor had been.

Yet, when his hand folded warm and strong around hers, when, just outside the subway station, he stole a brief kiss, she knew she couldn't run for cover. She could only ride out the earthquake and hope that she survived.

Within a half-hour they arrived back at her apartment. She barely had time to lock the door behind them before Troy tossed down his suitcase, gathered her into his arms and kissed her again. This time it wasn't a stolen kiss, light and surreptitious, but rather a kiss of possession, a kiss that branded her with his certainty. Even in college he had never kissed her with such confidence. Perhaps he had suspected then that the future would never be theirs. As he had told her earlier that evening, he had considered moving to Canada years before he'd met her. He must have known, even after falling in love with her, that they would be able to stay together only if his draft board ruled the right way on his application.

The realization that Troy had been aware of his imminent departure even when he was busy winning her heart caused Julianne to shrink back into self-protection. But his arms tightened around her and his lips rose to her brow, his mustache ruffling along her hairline, and she abandoned herself to the moment. No matter what happened tomorrow, or the day after, or for the rest of their lives, they had tonight. Julianne wouldn't waste it.

As soon as he discerned her yielding to him, he loosened his hold on her. In one swift motion, he hoisted her off her feet, cradling her in his arms. "Ten pounds, huh," he teased, kissing her nose and then heading for the bedroom. "It feels like you've lost more weight than that."

He had carried her this way only once before—the night they'd first discovered their love. "People weigh more when they're asleep," she told him, cuddling to his chest.

"That's a myth," he scoffed.

"A scientific fact," she argued playfully, twining her fingers through the hair at the nape of his neck. "They've done studies—"

"When I see one of those studies written up in your magazine, I'll believe it," he muttered, depositing her at the center of her bed. Kicking off his sneakers, he climbed on next to her. He kissed her throat, her chin, her lips. "Ah, Julie... I don't know how I ever found the strength to leave you." His voice was low and husky, as tender as the brush of his lips against her cheek. "I don't know how I'll find the strength to go tomorrow."

"Don't think about it." In a saner moment she might have been amazed to hear herself exhorting Troy to be as impractical, as irrational as she was. But she had relinquished her sanity for this one night of bliss. They could both worry all they wanted about tomorrow when tomorrow came—but not now.

He tugged her short-sleeved knit sweater up along her ribs and over her head. Then he did away with her bra, her cream-colored slacks, her shoes, her panties. As soon as she was naked, he stripped himself, his hands moving purposefully even as his breath grew short and uneven. When she slid her fingers around his waist to his back and pulled him onto her, he groaned. "Don't rush me this time," he implored her, his lips close to her ear.

He nipped the edge of the lobe with his teeth, and she moaned. "I—"

He smothered her protest by covering her mouth with his. His tongue tangled with hers, and his body moved provocatively on top of hers. His hands floated through her hair to frame her face, and his thumbs traced the sharp contours of her cheekbones and then her temples. He nudged her head deeper into the pillow and kissed the underside of her jaw.

She willed herself to remain patient. They had all night, all night for each other—and while that would seem an infinitesimally short time when they looked back on it, she wanted to savor each luscious moment as it blossomed. Her hands relaxed on his back, and her fingers followed a meandering path across his shoulders, appreciating their firm breadth, their hollows and ridges.

His mouth journeyed lower, nibbling her collarbones, her sternum, the warm rise of her breast. His teeth scraped gently over her nipple and she moaned. "You taste better than dinner," he whispered.

"Maybe I wouldn't taste as good as dinner at one of those dozen-waiter restaurants," she teased him, combing her fingers through his hair, holding his head to her.

"We'll have to try it and find out," he decided, turning his attention to her other breast, stroking it with his hand and then his tongue.

"Troy..." She sighed as her hips rose to him, as her hands ran the length of his spine to probe the hard muscles of his buttocks. He shivered in her embrace, then journeyed farther down her body, lapping her navel with his tongue. Her fingers tightened reflexively on him, pinching his shoulders. He groaned, then slid lower yet. A vague anxiety seized her as his mouth skirted the mound of hair in its path and brushed over her inner thigh. "Troy—what are you doing?"

He answered with his actions. His tongue ventured upward, sought her, found her. It caressed her, sending a hot spiral of sensation deep into her.

She moaned again, powerless against his erotic assault, powerless to do anything but respond. Her body grew taut as he drove her to a towering peak, his hands unrelenting on her hips, his body bowed between her knees. Unable to reach his head, she clawed the blanket, crying out at her approach, at her surrender. The tension culminated in a sudden explosion, sending a cascade of heart-stopping pulses down through her flesh, through her bones and nerves, through every synapse and cell.

Spent, she fell limp against the mattress and struggled for breath. Troy seemed to be as exhausted as Julianne. He rested his head against her belly and exhaled shakily.

"You never—" Her voice emerged as a soundless rasp, and she cleared her throat. "We've never done that before."

His fingers moved consolingly along her thighs, up over her hips to the flat stretch of her abdomen. "We've done it now," he mumbled, his voice as thick and hoarse as hers. He lifted his head, resting his chin on her diaphragm, and stared at her. His face rose and fell with her every hard-earned breath. His expression was unreadable. "Should I apologize?"

"No." She reached for him, and he let her guide him up alongside her. She brushed back his sweat-soaked hair and kissed him. "Whatever you do, don't apologize."

He smiled tentatively. "I wanted..." He wedged one arm beneath her, closed the other over her and pulled her snugly to himself. She could see nothing but his chest and the rugged arch of his shoulder. His words drifted down through her hair, faltering and broken. "I've wanted to do that—to make love to you that way.... Even then I wanted to. I wanted to make love to you every way there was. But...I was afraid I would botch it, I wouldn't know what I was doing and I would...I don't know, disgust you."

"No," she said again. Nothing Troy could ever have done would have disgusted her. Perhaps he had viewed her as a fairly inexperienced, straight-as-an-arrow farm girl—which, she had to admit, was pretty much what she'd been—but nothing, nothing they had ever shared in love could be disgusting.

Closing her eyes, she sorted through his halting words. He may have been afraid of not knowing what he was doing then, but he had obviously known what he was doing now. In fifteen years he had learned. From experience. With other women.

She sorted through her jangled emotions and was pleased to find that jealousy wasn't part of them. It would have been impossible for Troy not to have known other women in all the time he was away from Julianne, and it would have been totally unlike him not to have learned from them. His mind was like a camera, recording events, storing them, preserving them. Always absorbing, always learning, always imbedding every instant in his memory.

His experience in the intervening years had undoubtedly been far more extensive than hers. None of the few men she'd been with since Troy had taught her anything about love. Everything she knew about her body, she had learned during the few months she and Troy had been lovers.

He had taught her incomprehensible things. And she wanted to learn more. Easing out of his embrace, she rolled him onto his back and peered down into his shimmering eyes. "Let me," she breathed, allowing her hand to roam down his body. "Let me love you, too."

"No, Julianne—you don't have to—"

"Yes," she insisted, twisting away from his arresting grip and sliding down the bed. "I do have to." Closing her eyes, she touched her lips to him.

She lost track of time. Hours may have passed, minutes, a mere instant. But for that instant, he was totally in her thrall. He belonged to her. She controlled his movements, his reactions, the torturously sweet sensations storming through his body. Troy was hers, completely hers.

And when it was over, when she had conquered his soul as he had conquered hers, she understood that she was completely his, as well.

THE TELEPHONE RANG. Julianne ignored it. But it rang again, a summons from the world beyond Troy's arms, reminding her that, sooner or later, she would have to return to reality. At the third ring she stirred, and Troy relaxed his hold on her only enough to permit her to reach across his body for the phone on the night table. She picked up the receiver. "Hello?"

"Julianne? It's Kimberly," the caller identified herself. "I'm sorry to call you so late. Did I wake you?"

"No," Julianne assured her, her eyes drifting to the alarm clock beside the telephone. A little after ten o'clock. Late, but not too late for a call from a close friend.

"Are you sure? You sound sleepy."

"No, I'm up." Julianne swallowed, trying to banish the tremulousness in her voice. She tried as well not to let her tone reveal how soothing Troy's fingers felt as they wound through her hair, how unfathomably pleasurable she found the continued contact of his body beneath hers.

Kimberly didn't sound convinced. "Well, I'll make this quick. I'm coming to New York tomorrow. Kind of a spur of the moment thing. Andrew has to go to Westchester County in the afternoon, and I've decided he needs my company for moral support. We're flying up on the shuttle, and then he'll go on to White Plains by himself. I thought, if you all were free, I could visit you for the afternoon."

If Julianne were free. By tomorrow afternoon, Troy would be gone, and she would be freer than she wanted to be. She might be in the mood for nothing but wallowing in her solitude, praying for Troy's quick return or berating herself for her rashness in allowing herself to fall in love with him again.

But how often did Kimberly come to New York? And what was Julianne to gain by isolating herself once Troy had departed? Entertaining Kimberly seemed healthier than sitting alone in her apartment, listening to depressing music on her stereo and licking her wounds. "Tomorrow afternoon is fine," she told Kimberly.

"Great! I should be at your place by about one," Kimberly estimated. "If it's a nice day, maybe we can take a walk, go window shopping or something. Andrew will pick me up when he's done, and we can all go out for dinner. Depending on the time, of course."

"You're welcome to stay the night," Julianne offered.

"Thanks, but we can't. Lee and Whitney from the senator's office are planning to spend most of Sunday briefing Andrew for the committee hearing next week. Did I tell you we're all set with Dan Eisner, by the way?"

"I got a message to that effect from Dan," Julianne informed her.

"Well, I reckon we can talk about it tomorrow," said Kimberly. "Although I'd probably prefer not to talk about it at all. I just wish the whole thing were over already.... But don't let me keep you, Julianne. Go back to sleep. I'll see you tomorrow at one."

"I'll see you then," Julianne confirmed before saying goodbye and dropping the receiver into place.

Troy's hand swept upward through Julianne's hair, turning her face to his. His eyes were glazed but shimmering, his smile inscrutable. "Already making other dates?" he asked.

She grinned and kissed his cheek. "That was Kimberly," she said. "She's going to be in town for a few hours tomorrow afternoon."

Troy urged Julianne's head against his shoulder. His hand wove back into her hair, following a twisting route behind her ear to her neck, and he tucked one of his legs between her thighs. "You didn't tell her I was here," he remarked.

"No."

He measured her succinct comment, his fingers still twining through her hair, his arms circling her. "Did you ever tell her about us?" he asked.

"No."

He fell silent for a moment, meditating. "You and she were such good friends in school," he noted. "You're still good friends. Why didn't you tell her?"

Her lips moved against his chest as she spoke. "I'm not good at confiding in others. You're the only person I've ever been able to confide in that way. I'm a private person, Troy. You know that." She sighed. "Did you ever tell anyone?"

"No. But that was your idea, not mine. And I was planning to break the silence, except..."

"Except that you left," Julianne concluded the thought. Her voice contained not bitterness or even sadness, but simply acceptance of what had occurred. "There was no need to break the silence then, Troy. It was all over. There was nothing to tell."

"So you never discussed us? You never told anyone?"

She reflected. "Just my brother," she recalled.

"Your brother." Troy's hand stopped moving in her hair, and he shifted slightly. "The one who served in 'Nam," he said, remembering what Julianne had revealed about her family. He sounded uneasy when he asked, "Why did you tell him?"

She understood the cause of Troy's discomfort. In spite of the years they'd spent apart, she still knew him well. She knew that he was wondering whether she'd told Nathaniel about Troy, not because Troy had left her, but because of the reason he had left her. He was wondering whether she'd confided in her brother because her lover had left her as a result of his own refusal to serve in the war her brother had fought in.

"I told him," she explained, "because he came to New York for a job interview a couple of months after you left, and we spent a few days together, and he couldn't help but see I was down in the dumps. He asked why, and I told him that my boyfriend from college and I had broken up."

"You didn't tell him why we broke up?" Troy pressed her. "You didn't tell him that his damned war had broken us up?"

"It wasn't Nathaniel's war," Julianne defended her brother. "He went to Vietnam for the same reasons you went to Canada, Troy—because he believed it was the right thing to do. But he didn't start the war, and he certainly didn't end it. It wasn't *his*."

"If more guys like him had rejected the war instead of fighting it, maybe it would have ended sooner," Troy pointed out, his voice soft but impassioned. "If everyone had done what I did, there wouldn't have been a war."

"You aren't everyone," Julianne debated him. "My brother did what he felt he had to do, just like you. Don't blame him for having different opinions." She sighed. "Anyway, it wasn't the war that broke us up. It was your decision to go to Canada."

"If I hadn't gone to Canada, I would have gone to Saigon," Troy mused. "Or Khe-San, or Hue, or My-Lai. Or Hamburger Hill. The whole damned country was Hamburger Hill by then. I would have gone there and gotten my head blown off. That would have broken us up pretty permanently, Julie."

Julianne closed her eyes and fought back a lump of tears. She didn't want to argue about the war with Troy. Yet the mere possibility that he might have died in Vietnam, that he might not have been as lucky as Nathaniel, horrified her. Canada had kept Troy alive, had given him the opportunity to come back to her.

"You were ashamed of me," he guessed, his voice still low, still intense. "You were ashamed of what I did. That's why you didn't tell your brother the whole truth."

"No!" she protested. She lifted herself off Troy and sat, staring down into his face, easily reading his troubled expression. "I was never ashamed of you, Troy. In your own way, you were as brave as Nathaniel was. Maybe braver."

"Then why?" he demanded. "Why didn't you tell him everything about me?"

"Because there are some things I don't talk about," she rationalized. "If I were ashamed of anything, it was of being so mopey and gloomy when I saw him. I'm not a complainer. I don't like to weep about my problems to other people."

Troy's gaze softened, growing quizzical. He extended his hand to her and ran his index finger over the indentation beneath her lips and then down to her angular chin. "You're so afraid of letting anyone find out that you aren't superhuman, Julie," he said. "You're so afraid of letting anyone find out that you aren't indomitable, that you can get hurt just like any other person. You're so busy being strong, being a leader, taking care of business—you can't even tell a good pal like Kimberly that Julianne Robinson, mistress of all she surveys, has her moments of suffering."

His astute observation struck her with shocking force. Was that why she had never told Kimberly about her relationship with Troy? Was that why she had kept her pain hidden, even from her closest friend? She was so intent on maintaining her confident facade, presenting herself as poised and on top of things, that she was unable to allow anyone to discover her weakness.

Perhaps that was why she hadn't let the other staff members of *The Dream* learn about her affair with Troy when they were all in college and Julianne had wrongly believed that she and Troy were destined to stay together. She had told Troy she didn't want to upset the balance of the newspaper's staff, and that had been a valid concern. But it hadn't been the entire reason. She had also kept their affair a secret because she wanted to project herself as the ultimate editor in chief, totally impartial and above the fray, always objective and composed. She hadn't wanted her colleagues to learn that she could be as emotional as they, as swayed by love, as giddy and romantic and out of control.

Her epiphany stunned her. Unable to confront the accuracy of Troy's statement directly, she lowered her eyes to his chest. She studied the delectable swirls of dark hair, the taut nubs of his nipples, the frame of his ribs. She opened her mouth to speak, but she couldn't think of what to say.

Apparently aware of her reeling emotions, Troy cupped his hand under her chin and drew her face back to his. "It's all right, Julie," he murmured. "You cried in front of me today. That was a start." His thumb caressed her cheek. "You were beautiful when you cried."

She grinned feebly. "I'm sure I wasn't," she disputed him. "I'm sure my eyes became bloodshot, and my nose turned red, and my cheeks got all puffy and mottled—"

"And you were beautiful," he insisted.

"I was furious with you, Troy," she asserted. "I was crying because I despised you."

"That's all right, too," he claimed. "There were times..." He took a deep breath. "There were so many times, Julie, after I left, when I thought, Julianne can handle this better than I can. I was hurting, too, I was hurting so badly, but I kept thinking, Julianne is strong. She's recovered. She doesn't even miss me anymore. She's all over it, dating other men, doing her thing, being the boss. My leaving couldn't possibly have hurt her as much as it hurt me." He pulled her down to him and kissed her gently. "Maybe if I had gotten your letters, if I had found out that you were still thinking of me... I don't know. It probably wouldn't have changed anything, but... Seeing you cry before, Julianne—even if you were crying because you despised me—it was reassuring. And it was beautiful."

If he thought it was beautiful, she pondered, nestling against him and wishing that his body would impart its warmth to her, then would he break her heart in the hope of making her beautiful again? Too many men seemed to think that a woman's vulnerability was her best asset. They exploited that vulnerability; they measured their own power against it. Knowing that they could make a woman cry enhanced their opinion of themselves.

Troy wasn't like most men, though. He wouldn't deliberately make her cry, just as his flight to Canada fifteen years ago hadn't been a deliberate act to wound her. If Troy made her cry again, if he left and failed to return, it would only be because circumstances forbade a return, because his studio, his finances, his commitment to one country and his aversion to the other militated against a return. Once more, the circumstances would stand between them.

She would cross that bridge when she got to it. Tomorrow she would get to it, and she'd wait, watching the water below, gauging the currents. Then she'd steel herself, become the strong, indomitable leader she was supposed to be, and she'd cross.

"LET'S GO to Bergdorf Goodman's," Kimberly suggested as she and Julianne left the apartment for a stroll. The sun was high and hot above them as they headed west toward Fifth Avenue. Kimberly looked radiant in a chic jumpsuit of daffodil yellow, her golden hair bouncing in time with her sprightly step. "I've heard they redid the store. Not that I can afford anything they might have for sale in it, but I'm a glutton for punishment. I just love to be tempted."

Browsing at Bergdorf's sounded like a terrific idea to Julianne. The elegant department store, with its couturier boutiques and outlandishly priced merchandise, would offer her a distraction—and she needed to be distracted. She didn't want to think about Troy, about his farewell that morning, about his kiss goodbye, his vow to call her, his disappearance. Watching him walk out of her apartment had been too reminiscent of the last time, despite the fact that this time he'd left on a sunny morning instead of a rainy night. She didn't want to think about how long she'd have to wait before she heard from him again.

She and Kimberly reached the sidewalk bordering Central Park's eastern boundary and turned south. The sidewalk teemed with life: roller skaters and skateboarders, dog-walkers, picnickers and museum-goers, all basking in the gloriously balmy weather. Tucking her purse beneath her elbow, Julianne shoved her hands into the pockets of her pleated linen slacks and slowed her long-legged pace to accommodate that of her petite friend.

"So, what's Andrew doing in White Plains?" she asked, sidestepping a hot-dog vendor stationed near one of the gateways into the park.

Kimberly exhaled and shook her head. "He's visiting his in-laws. His first wife's parents," she clarified. "He was going to make the trip alone, but as the day approached, he began to get exceedingly nervous about it. So I thought it would help if I traveled at least part of the distance with him." She brushed a delicate wave of hair off her forehead and smiled pensively. "I wanted to travel the whole way with him, but he wouldn't let me. He said it would be better if I didn't appear uninvited on their doorstep."

Julianne digested Kimberly's remark. "He's going to tell them about you?" she surmised.

Kimberly nodded. "He's very fond of them, Julianne. They've all gone through a great deal of grief together, and they still think of him as a son. I reckon they're nicer in-laws than my parents will be."

"Don't your parents like Andrew?"

Kimberly snorted. "My parents don't like anyone who harkens from north of the Mason-Dixon line," she commented acerbically. "They don't like my divorce, and they don't like Andrew's politics, and they don't like the fact that he's gone public with his dealings with the C.I.A. Come to think of it, I don't think they like anything at all about the entire situation." Shrugging blithely, she laughed. "Not that that's ever made much of a difference to me. I'm used to their disapproval, and I suppose Andrew will get used to it, too."

"If Andrew's in-laws—the other ones, I mean—if they think of him as a son, then I'm sure they'll be happy to hear that he's getting remarried," Julianne predicted.

"I hope you're right. But he's a veritable wreck about it."

"If he's such a wreck, why is he doing it this weekend?" Julianne inquired. "Hasn't he got enough coming down on him with the committee hearing next week?"

"He couldn't concentrate on the committee hearing with this hanging over his head. He's reconciled to attending the hearing, but he's so worried about Marjorie's parents. They had invited him to visit, and he kept putting it off and putting it off. Then it dawned on him that they would be reading about him in the newspapers soon, and he felt obliged to warn them about that. And since he was going to warn them about that, he also felt obliged to tell them about me." Her smile grew misty as she ruminated. "He's so sensitive, Julianne. These are people who technically have no hold on him, but he's so sensitive about their feelings. I think it's touching that he cares so much about them."

"He's a good man, Kim. We both know that."

Nearing Bergdorf's Julianne contemplated what Kimberly had told her. She, too, thought it was touching that Andrew felt a responsibility toward his first wife's parents. Family was important, even if that family was bound not by blood but by the loss of a loved one.

For Julianne, the concept of family extended beyond her parents and her brother. Numerous relatives lived in and around Meade, Iowa, and even those town residents who weren't related to her were like a large, loose-knit family. Growing up in such a small village, Julianne had known just about every one of Meade's denizens. They had all worshipped at the same church, shopped at the same stores, driven the same downtown streets. The children had all attended the same elementary school and had all been bused to the same regional high school. Julianne's father had delivered most of the town's babies, treated their diseases, set their fractured bones and stitched their gashes. When a citizen of Meade passed away, he or she was buried in the same cemetery where Julianne's brother had delivered the Memorial Day eulogy, and the entire town mourned.

She meditated on Troy's estrangement from his family. No wonder he was able to leave the United States; having already broken with his family, he couldn't have found it as wrenching to break from his country. How rootless he must feel, how unanchored. It was only natural that someone with Troy's background would believe that a mother should turn her back on her criminal son, rather than to offer him the support he might need.

Julianne forced thoughts of Troy from her mind and entered the grand Fifth Avenue foyer of the department store with Kimberly. Craning her neck, Kimberly gawked at the glittering chandelier hanging from the vaulted ceiling. "Well, it's just as lavish as I remember it," she declared. "The last time I was in this store was when my parents came to see me graduate from Barnard. Mother decided to take me here to get some ideas for my trousseau." She giggled at the memory. "Lord, a trousseau.

How bizarre that all seems today. When was the last time you were here, Julianne?"

"My freshman year, I think," Julianne recalled. "I stood outside the door, taking a collection for the starving children of Biafra. I was playing off the guilt of all those monied society matrons."

"You mean, you don't shop here now?" Kimberly asked as they wandered farther inside.

"Once a bargain hunter, always a bargain hunter," Julianne declared with a chuckle. "Some habits are hard to break."

"Don't I know," Kimberly lamented. "I never had to hunt for bargains until Todd and I got divorced. And I imagine that being married to a college professor—one who might get fired by the end of next year—isn't going to mean unlimited charge accounts. Ah, the sacrifices I'm willing to make for Andrew," she concluded with a melodramatic moan. Then she giggled again. "Fortunately he doesn't seem to care much about what I wear. He's much more interested in me when I'm not wearing anything."

"Except sexy underwear?" Julianne posed, remembering what Kimberly had said when they'd spoken on the phone a week ago.

Kimberly colored slightly. "I should never have told you that," she whispered. "Even if it's the truth. But you don't have to cut corners anymore, Julianne. You ought to shop at the best stores. You're a member of the monied class now."

"At least I'm not a society matron," Julianne said.

"No, but I bet those Donna Karan outfits would look wonderful on you. You're so tall and slim. Let's go upstairs and look at them."

An hour later Julianne and Kimberly emerged from the store, blinking in the glare of the sunshine and reeking of perfume. A saleswoman had sprayed their wrists with samples of colognes on their way out. "We smell like a New Orleans cathouse," Kimberly drawled, taking a whiff of her inner arm and wincing. "I can't believe they charge a hundred dollars an ounce for this stuff."

Julianne agreed with a nod. "Pig droppings smell better, and you can get them for free in Iowa. How about some ice cream?" she suggested. "Since I'm a member of the monied class, you can let me treat you to an overpriced sundae at Rumpelmeyer's."

"That's an offer I can't refuse," Kimberly enthused, ambling with Julianne around the Plaza Hotel to Central Park South, where the fashionable ice-cream parlor was located. "Now. Tell me how you've been. I've been prattling on so much I'm beginning to bore myself."

Julianne hadn't been the least bit bored by Kimberly's prattling. She was delighted to hear about the marvelous improvement in Kimberly's spirits since she and Andrew had become a couple. Julianne had devoured everything Kimberly had to tell her about her flourishing love for Andrew, about their evenings spent doing research at the Library of Congress, their outing to an experimental theater at Dupont Circle, their after-dinner constitutionals around Georgetown. She had listened to Kimberly's description of Whitney Brannigan, one of her associates on Senator Milford's staff, whose frustration over Kimberly's having chosen Andrew over him made him petulant and crabby, and to the details of Milford's reelection campaign. The only time Kimberly had stopped talking about herself was when Julianne reluctantly modeled one of Donna Karan's complicated ensembles. Kimberly had joined the saleswoman in exclaiming how much the outfit flattered Julianne, and then had joined Julianne in gasping over the astronomical price attached to the outfit.

Julianne had enjoyed Kimberly's company for the very reason that she wanted to think only of other people, not herself. But now Kimberly turned the spotlight on her. "How have you been?"

"Fine," Julianne replied automatically. Then she pressed her lips together, giving herself a chance to reconsider her answer. Whenever Kimberly asked her how she was, she always answered "Fine." When Kimberly requested specifics, Julianne provided discreet ones. Today she might tell Kimberly about her Memorial Day trip to visit her family, or about her plans for *Dream*'s increased coverage of the Intelligence Committee hearings, or about the increased bickering between Cynthia and Tom on the editorial staff. The two of them sniped at each other as often as Andrew and Kimberly used to snipe at each other when they'd worked together, and Julianne couldn't help but wonder whether an as yet unacknowledged passion was blossoming between her two editors.

She could discuss any of those things with Kimberly. But as she pushed open the door to Rumpelmeyer's and ushered Kimberly to one of the pretty wrought-iron tables inside, Julianne refrained from providing her standard answers to Kimberly's question.

Instead she thought about what Troy had said the previous night: that the reason Julianne didn't confide in others was her fear of being perceived as weak. The most important thing in her life right now was Troy—his return, her emotional turmoil over him, her love and doubt, her confusion and hope, and the gnawing dread of losing him again. If she couldn't reveal her raw vulnerability to Kimberly—if she felt the need to protect her image even with her best friend—then Troy's brutally frank criticism of her was correct.

Smiling anxiously, she opened the menu for Kimberly. "Order something big," she advised. "If you really want to know how I'm doing, we've got a whole lot to talk about."

Eight

"How do I look?" asked Andrew.

"Like you're about to puke," Troy told him. Andrew laughed, and Troy snapped the picture.

The sky above the Capitol dome was slightly overcast, the air muggy and oppressive. Troy had already taken several photos of Andrew in the air-conditioned corridor outside the hearing room, where Andrew had managed to look reasonably fresh and tidy. But once they'd headed outdoors and into the steamy afternoon, Andrew had wilted.

He didn't truly look nauseous. Fatigued, maybe, drained. His collar was unbuttoned, his striped tie loosened. The blazer of his navy-blue suit bore a few faint creases across the back from his having spent upwards of three hours sitting in a high-backed chair in the hearing room, giving his testimony. His once-crisp white shirt lay limp against his chest; his gray-streaked brown hair was tousled. His face reflected a curious blend of resignation and relief.

He was seated on a step halfway up the broad, seemingly endless flight of white stairs that led to the main entrance to the Capitol building, his knees spread and his briefcase balanced between them. About ten yards to his left, a high school glee club stood in a horseshoe formation on the stairs, their conductor leading them in a lusty three-part arrangement of "This Land Is Your Land" for the entertainment of a handful of tourists on the sidewalk below. Troy knelt on a step near Andrew, shooting close-ups to avoid including the chorus in the photos.

"If you want a picture of me puking," Andrew suggested, "I'll see what I can do for you." He pretended to poke his finger down his throat.

Troy chuckled. "No need," he assured Andrew. "You don't really look nauseous. Just wasted."

"I *am* wasted." Andrew eyed the glee club and smiled at the appropriateness of their song selection. "Good choice," he commended them, although they couldn't possibly hear him. "After spending all morning with a bunch of senators, I'm feeling very American."

Troy wondered whether he would ever feel American. Then again, he'd lived in Montreal for fifteen years and didn't feel like a Canadian. Maybe, if he ever had to deal with a group of politicos in close quarters...but he couldn't imagine himself in Andrew's position. As a photographer, Troy tended to separate himself from his surroundings. His camera kept him at a distance.

He snapped another photo. "Did they give you a hard time in there?"

"Not as hard a time as Amherst is sure to give me," Andrew answered.

Troy nodded. Last night after he had checked into his hotel, he had joined Andrew and Kimberly at their Georgetown apartment for dinner. During the meal Andrew had described his precarious position at Amherst College. He expected the school to deny him tenure because of his decision to testify before the Senate Intelligence Committee about his having done research for the

C.I.A. Yet, given the likelihood that he'd find himself unemployed after his contract to teach in the economics department expired the following year, he didn't seem terribly concerned about his future.

That was undoubtedly because Kimberly was destined to be a part of his future—the most significant part of it. She had spent most of the dinner fussing over Andrew, doting on him, reminding him about the many think tanks and research centers in Washington where he would be able to find work if he wanted to remain in the private sector. If he didn't, surely some smart senator or congressman would snatch up for his staff a man with Andrew's impressive credentials, she had maintained.

Troy wished he could feel as secure about his own future. Severing his connection with Bennett-Chartier was turning out to be more complicated than he had anticipated. Claude had been apoplectic when Troy informed him that he wanted to sell his half of the studio, either to Claude, if he wanted to go it alone, or to another photographer, if Claude could find someone interested in entering into a partnership with him. As dismayed as Claude had been about Troy's decision to leave the business, he was even more dismayed by Troy's desire to return to the States. "You want to go back there?" Claude had roared, as if Troy had announced that he wanted to take up residence in Hades. "You want to go back to that pit?"

"Hey, I'm too old to be drafted," Troy had joked. "What can they do to me now?"

"They can screw you. They already did it once," Claude had pointed out. "It's a sick society south of the border."

"People are people," Troy had argued. "Society is society. Anyway, the place doesn't matter. It's Julianne I care about."

Julianne. The real reason Troy was worried about his future was that, unlike Andrew, he wasn't certain the woman he loved was ready to become a part of it. After returning to Montreal Saturday morning, he had telephoned her daily. She had always sounded glad to hear from him, but... She was holding back. He could tell from her tone, from her carefully chosen words, from the complete lack of passion in her delivery, even when he tried to introduce a note of intimacy into their conversations.

When they had been together, when they had made love, when she had astonished Troy with her adventurousness and selflessness in bed—she hadn't been holding anything back then. But the minute he left, she reverted to the cool, detached boss-lady she usually was, providing him with information about the assignment in Washington, revealing nothing of her feelings when he described the hassles he was having with Claude. She hadn't even sounded disappointed when he had told her he'd have to fly directly to Washington without stopping over in New York City and that, unable to find a substitute photographer, he would have to return to Montreal to shoot another wedding the following weekend. "I assumed as much," she had said calmly. "Extricating yourself from a partnership takes more than a little effort."

His thoughts veered to Andrew and Kimberly again. Kimberly was so involved in Andrew's life that she had refused to go to her office that morning, choosing instead to loiter in the hallway outside the hearing room with Troy, Dan Eisner, and an assortment of other reporters. Only after she was sure that Andrew had survived his ordeal did she strand him to attend to her own work. "I'll be inches from my telephone all afternoon if you need me," she had promised. "Just call, or come over."

"I'm all right, Kim," Andrew had sworn.

He was all right. Whatever had occurred in the hearing room, Andrew seemed to have emerged unscathed. As, of course, he would. He had right on his side, and love. The rest was secondary.

The glee club concluded their concert to a smattering of applause and departed from the steps of the Capitol. "Stay put," Troy ordered Andrew as he gathered up his camera bag and loped down the stairs. "I want to get some long shots."

From the sidewalk Andrew appeared isolated to Troy, a solitary figure hunched on the wide white stairs, gazing through his eyeglasses toward the Mall. Troy attached his wide-angle lens to his camera, raised the apparatus to his eye and captured the entire breadth of the stairway, as well as most of the Capitol building, in the frame. He smiled at the scene reduced inside his viewfinder. No matter what happened with Julianne, Troy had this. He had these fine photographs; he had a renewed sense of purpose about his work.

"How much longer are we going to have to be here?" Andrew shouted down to him, his voice sounding thin in the sticky air. "I'm frying alive."

"Just a few more minutes," Troy shouted back, forwarding his film and shooting another wide-angle picture. He worked fast. Like Andrew, he was uncomfortably hot. Perspiration dampened his mustache and his brow and glued his shirt to his back.

He took a final shot, then rewound his film and wedged the camera into his bag. "All done for now," he called to Andrew. "You hungry?"

"I suppose I could use some food," Andrew acknowledged, rising to his feet and gripping his briefcase. "I wouldn't pass up a bit of liquid refreshment, either."

"I got you," Troy agreed with a grin. "Let's go drink some lunch."

They strode down Pennsylvania Avenue to the first café they found, and entered. The dark, chilly interior of the restaurant soothed Troy. He felt the sweat evaporate from his face as he slid into a booth facing Andrew and flagged a waitress to their table. They both ordered beers and burgers, then relaxed in their seats. Troy groped in his shirt pocket for a cigarette and lit it. He had cut down considerably on his smoking since he'd last seen Julianne, but as long as he wasn't in New York, she didn't have to know that he still hadn't conquered the habit.

"So," he said, scrutinizing his friend across the table, "what did they do to you in there?"

"Nothing I wasn't expecting," Andrew answered. "Milford's aides prepped me well. But I don't want to talk about the hearing anymore, Troy. The subject is beginning to bore me. I'd rather talk about you."

"Me?" Troy laughed uncertainly. When the waitress brought their beers to the table, he took a long draught of his, straight from the bottle. "What about me?"

Andrew grinned mischievously. "The real question, Troy, is, what about you and Julianne? What the hell is going on?"

Troy took a deep drag of his cigarette to buy time. What about him and Julianne, indeed? What was there to say? And furthermore, how had Andrew learned about it?

In answer to his unvoiced question, Andrew remarked, "Don't look so shocked, Troy. Julianne's already spilled the beans to Kim, and she passed the word along. I think it's great. Unless you tell me it isn't great. Fill me in, pal."

Again Troy's face registered surprise. *Julianne's already spilled the beans.* Why, after all this time, had she finally gone public with their relationship? Had his observation about her inability to confide in others made that big an impact on her?

Obviously it had. Troy was thrilled to think that no matter how reserved she had seemed with him since he'd left New York, Julianne had taken his well-intended criticism to heart.

"What do you want to know?" he asked Andrew.

"Everything," Andrew replied. "Starting with, why didn't you ever breathe a hint of it when we were in college?"

"She really did spill the beans," Troy said. Apparently Julianne had told Kimberly not just that she and Troy were a couple, but that they had been a couple fifteen years ago.

He gave Andrew another careful perusal. Andrew didn't seem disgruntled about Troy's secretiveness in school. He would have had grounds to be angry; he and Troy were supposed to be close buddies, after all, and their friendship hadn't allowed much room for deception. But Andrew appeared too fascinated to be sore about having been left in the dark for so long.

The waitress delivered their hamburgers, and Troy spent some time hammering ketchup out of the bottle. Sensing Andrew's impatience, he handed over the bottle and shrugged. "If Julianne's told Kimberly the whole story, you probably know everything there is to know."

"All I know is Julianne's version, secondhand," Andrew corrected him.

Troy shrugged again. "Okay. We had a thing going in college. Then I went to Canada. In May, Julianne hired me to do the artwork for an article her magazine is publishing on Laura, and . . . we started up again."

"A 'thing'?" Andrew scoffed at Troy's euphemism. "According to Julianne, it was the love affair of the century."

"She told Kim that?" Troy allowed himself a fleeting instant of joy at Julianne's extravagant description of their relationship. Then he grew sober. If what they'd shared at Columbia was the love affair of the century, then the end of such an affair must have injured Julianne more severely than Troy had guessed. Mending the rift between them might be a more complex project than their one recent night together could accomplish. "It was... it was pretty special," he admitted before taking a bite of his hamburger.

"And what is it now?" Andrew pressed him.

"I don't know," Troy admitted. He ate in silence for a while. "Things were simpler back then. This time around we've got so much baggage to deal with, so much history to overcome. I want to overcome it—and I think Julie does, too. But... I don't know."

"Let me tell you something about that kind of baggage," Andrew proposed. "If you think you and Julianne have a lot of baggage, imagine what Kim and I were lugging around. She and I hated each other in school, remember? We couldn't even have a civil conversation—we were too busy insulting each other all the time. She thought I was an egghead snob, and I thought she was a dimwit."

"How did you turn it around?" Troy asked, eager for advice, any suggestions he could apply to his predicament with Julianne.

Andrew sipped his beer. "Forgive the cliché, Troy, but where there's a will there's a way."

"Sure," Troy grunted.

Undeterred by Troy's obvious disbelief, Andrew went on. "The past is over and done with, Troy. Who we were then, what we felt for each other fifteen years ago—none of that counts in the present. What counts is now, starting new. You can't change the past, but you can accept it and move on. Kim and I laugh about it now."

"Gosh, I'm so happy for you," Troy snorted caustically. "It must be swell, snickering over all the names you used to call each other."

"Actually, that isn't far from the truth," Andrew conceded. "Maybe it isn't swell, maybe we don't snicker about it, but we accept it. We've come to terms with it. We've congratulated ourselves on the fact that we've grown up, that we've overcome it. Our baggage was more than just hating each other, you know."

"You mean, because you've both been married before?"

Andrew nodded. He pulled off his eyeglasses, rubbed the bridge of his nose, then slid the eyeglasses back on. "It's no picnic coming to terms with all that. Kim's divorce really bruised her. And when Marjorie died... well, I don't have to tell you. It was rough. By the time Kim and I started working together on this C.I.A. business, we were both hesitant about trying our luck in another relationship. It seemed so damned risky."

Troy lit another cigarette. "What made you take the risk?" he asked.

"Look at Kim," Andrew responded. "Look at me. We aren't all that exceptional. We haven't got any secret stores of strength. But—" he smiled warmly "—once we'd both considered it, we decided that taking the risk made more sense than not taking it."

"Yes, but you *both* decided to take the risk," Troy contended. "I'm willing, but I don't think Julianne is."

"If she means enough to you, then you've got to make her willing."

"She means enough to me," Troy insisted. Andrew's advice made a great deal of sense—in theory. But Troy needed something concrete, some practical instructions. "You're right, Andrew, your history was pretty rough. How did you put it behind you?"

"I didn't put it behind me," Andrew said quietly. "It's over and done with, but it's still a part of me. I can't pretend I wasn't married to Marjorie. I can't pretend that whole horror didn't happen." He fidgeted with a leftover piece of crust from his hamburger roll, then sighed. "Last Saturday I went up to White Plains to see Marjorie's parents. I couldn't marry Kim without telling them about it first. That's how much a part of me Marjorie still is."

Troy leaned forward, intrigued. "How did that go? How did they take it?"

Andrew smiled crookedly. "I wish I could say they broke out the champagne and celebrated. They didn't. They were polite, but I could tell the news stunned them. We all mouthed a lot of platitudes about how Marjorie would have wanted me to remarry, she would have wanted me to live a full life and find happiness wherever I could. But they were devastated. I know they were."

"What did they think of Kimberly?"

"I didn't bring her with me," Andrew informed him with a tentative grin. "I was afraid they'd resent her. She's...she's so different from Marjorie. She's so—so pretty. Marjorie wasn't pretty, not the way Kim is. And she wasn't polished or rich or..." He exhaled and shook his head. "I loved Marjorie, and I still miss her, and I always will. Edith and Henry believe that if I marry Kim, it means that Marjorie won't be a part of me anymore. But she will be. Forever."

Troy sank back in his seat and mulled over Andrew's words. What had happened between Troy and Julianne fifteen years ago would also be a part of them, no matter where they went from here. Andrew seemed to be saying that you had to accept the past, you couldn't deny it. You simply absorbed it, then put it to rest and moved on.

Troy could never deny the grief he and Julianne had endured so long ago. He couldn't deny that he had broken the law, run away, abandoned Julianne. For that matter, he probably could never compensate Julianne for the pain he'd caused her. He couldn't make it up to her.

All he could do was accept it—and pray that she accepted it, too. It was done, a fact, unalterable. And now it was time to move on.

"You want another beer?" he asked.

"No," Andrew declined. "I'm fully recovered."

"Then let's stop by Kimberly's office. I might get some ideas for additional shots there."

"Okay."

Andrew waved the waitress over, and he and Troy argued over who would cover the tab. Troy won. "If I pay, it goes on my expense report," he explained. "Let's let *Dream* foot the bill."

"Why not?" Andrew concurred, sliding the check over to Troy. "We've both spent our fair share in subscription costs. The least that magazine owes us is a couple of burgers and some brew."

Leaving the restaurant meant reentering the stultifying heat of the Washington afternoon. Troy rolled up his shirt sleeves, and by the time he and Andrew had reached the corner, he was using his unfastened cuffs to mop his brow. "If I lived in D.C., I'd probably get a crew cut," he commented, his hair feeling heavy and woolly on his neck.

"Speaking of which, are you planning to stay in Montreal?" Andrew inquired. "According to Kim—and this is all secondhand, of course—you told Julianne you wanted to move to New York."

"I do."

"You're ready to come back home?" Andrew asked.

Troy shot him a wary look. Laura had also introduced that topic when she'd seen Troy, quizzing him on when he was going to come home. Troy had made the mistake of implying to Laura that he didn't know where home was. It had been an honest answer, but the way she'd reacted made him reluctant to give Andrew the same answer.

"Home is Detroit," he said cautiously. "Or at least, it was Detroit. And I'm not going back there."

"Home is America," Andrew maintained.

"Canada is America, too," Troy argued lightly. "You folks down here tend to forget that."

"You know what I mean," Andrew persisted. "For you, moving back to America means a whole lot more than it would for most people, given the circumstances of your leaving. It's a homecoming, Troy. Don't make light of it."

"Home isn't a place," Troy countered. "I don't care where I live. I care only about being close to Julianne. If she lived in Katmandu I'd move there."

"You're evading the issue, Troy," Andrew chided him. "You didn't flee Katmandu in the dead of the night fifteen years ago."

The sweltering atmosphere bore down on Troy like a weight. He wanted to duck inside the first air-conditioned building they came to and take a few deep breaths. At one time he had found Canada's frigid winters unbearable, even more brutal than Detroit's. But he'd grown inured to the icy air, the bitter winds, the snow that lingered through Easter. His blood had thickened. Now he couldn't abide the humid heat of Washington.

No, it wasn't the climate that was making him uncomfortable. It was Andrew's incisive probing. Just as Troy couldn't deny his past with Julianne, so he couldn't deny his past with the draft board, with the war, with the United States government.

"I'll tell you the truth, Andrew," he said. "Right now, I'm too messed up with the mechanics of closing up shop in Montreal. I'm bargaining with my partner, looking for a replacement, reading the fine print in my apartment lease. That's all I can handle at this point. I'll cope with the heavy stuff later."

"Bad idea," Andrew warned him. "You'd better cope with the heavy stuff now. Once you do, the mechanics will seem trivial." He angled his head toward the Hart Building, where Kimberly's office was located, and they stepped inside. As soon as they had passed through the lobby's metal detector, Andrew drew to a halt. "Come on, Troy. Give it some thought. What does America mean to you? How do you feel about the idea of living here again?"

Troy gazed around him. It was a particularly relevant question for Andrew to be posing in Washington, D.C., of all places. The city was more than just the nation's capital; it was a monument, a shrine to everything the United States stood for. The Stars and Stripes flew over nearly every building. Inside the Capitol, where he'd spent the morning, laws were enacted that helped to shape the identity of the country. Inside that same building, long before Troy was even aware of such things, laws were enacted requiring eighteen-year-old men to register for the draft, and resolutions were passed ordaining that some of those registered men would be denied their freedom and shipped to Southeast Asia.

When he'd stood in the corridor outside the hearing room a few hours ago, he hadn't thought about where he was or what the building represented. He'd thought only about his assignment, the photos, taking enough superlative pictures to win Julianne's love. But Andrew was forcing him to confront something bigger than winning Julianne's love. Troy hadn't understood that there could be anything more important than Julianne. Maybe there was.

He shoved his hands into his pockets and stared at the wall before him. "You want to know the truth, Andrew? Do you really want to know?" He paused, then announced, "I'm mad that Carter gave us amnesty."

His comment clearly startled Andrew. "Why? If he didn't give you amnesty, you couldn't come back at all."

"Giving us amnesty—that's like saying we were wrong but they'll forgive us. The country has no right to forgive us. We *weren't* wrong."

His angry words surprised him. It was one thing to be indignant with Claude, to talk about how their country had screwed them—that was the way all the expatriates talked up in Canada. It was quite another thing to contend with his rage when he was seriously considering what Andrew had aptly labeled a "homecoming." "I don't need some president telling me I did a no-no, but that's all right," Troy fumed. "I don't need people telling me that if I become patriotic, if I stand on Capitol steps and sing 'This Land Is Your Land,' I'll be taken back with open arms. I don't need forgiveness."

Andrew listened to his tirade with a sympathetic smile. "You aren't going to get it, Troy," he noted gently. At Troy's bewildered stare, he elaborated. "I doubt anyone really cares about what you did then. Life goes on. The war is over. Nobody is going to forgive you."

His words cut into Troy, piercing his soul. If he returned to the United States, nobody would embrace him, nobody would pat his head and say, "There, there." The bitterness, the resistance was coming from within, not from without. If anyone had to forgive anything, it was up to Troy to forgive the country. And to forgive himself.

Andrew appeared to sense that Troy didn't want to discuss the subject further. He pressed the elevator button, and when the elevator arrived they rode in silence to Kimberly's office.

Troy remained at Senator Milford's suite for another hour. He took some photos of Kimberly at her desk, and some of her and Andrew together. Then he took some photos of Milford, when the senator arrived at the office, and a few of two fellows named Lee Pappelli and Whitney Brannigan, whom Kimberly introduced as the senator's senior aides. After Troy had taken all the pictures he needed, he bade Kimberly and Andrew farewell, explaining that he had to check out of his hotel and head back to Montreal to get the film developed for Julianne.

He didn't go directly to his hotel, however. Sliding his camera bag higher on his shoulder, he left the Hart Building and marched west, passing the Capitol on his way to the Mall. He ignored the armies of tourists with their Instamatics, the cruising metropolitan police cars, the souvenir vendors, the petition wavers, the religious cultists selling flowers and faith along the grass-lined sidewalks. He paid no attention to the government buildings lining the route, or to the numerous American flags drooping on their flagpoles in the stagnant air. He didn't stop walking until he reached the Vietnam Memorial.

The black gash. That was what a number of displeased critics had called the memorial when the design was approved, years ago. Some people saw its stark black facade as a reproach to the government's policy during the war years. But Troy didn't view it that way. He walked the sloping path along its polished granite surfaces, gazing at the clutter of names carved into it. Each name belonged to a soldier. Each name commemorated a death.

Troy had gone to Canada to preserve his freedom. Other men in his position had relinquished their freedom, some for the term of their service and some for eternity. He felt tears springing to his eyes as he gazed at the densely packed names. So many lives lost, so many men deprived.

What the United States had done to Troy was nothing compared to what it had done to these boys and their loved ones. War was a curse, and in 1972, when Troy's deferment ran out, the nation was functioning under that curse.

As Andrew had said, the war was over. Life went on. Yet, gazing at the mournful wall of names, too tragically numerous to count, Troy wondered whether it was possible to forgive the country for the lives it had sacrificed to some dubious end.

He stepped off the path and onto the grass, backing up until he could view the entire wall. Then he pulled out his camera, affixed the wide-angle lens and snapped the shutter. This was a photo for himself, to remind him of the price too many men had paid for patriotism.

"Is that a Leica you've got there?" a voice broke into his thoughts.

Troy lowered the camera and turned to face the man who had addressed him. The stranger seemed to be a few years Troy's senior. He was nearly as tall as Troy, although skinnier in build, with a receding hairline that he tried to disguise beneath long wisps of brown hair combed across his scalp from his part. He wore a polo shirt and jeans, and the Pentax slung around his neck on a woven strap, to which several canisters of film had been taped, marked him as someone more sophisticated about cameras than all the Instamatic-wielding tourists thronging the Mall.

A fellow photographer, Troy surmised. He smiled and nodded. "Yes, it's a Leica. I use it for my outdoor work."

"Mind if I have a look at it?" the man asked. "I've been tempted to buy one of these babies. I like the Leitz lenses."

Troy handed over the camera. The man examined it thoroughly before lifting it to his eye. "The lenses are good," Troy granted. "I use a Hasselblad for my indoor work, but the Leica makes for better outdoor shots, I think. How do you like the Pentax?"

The man passed Troy's camera back. "This is just for personal use," he explained, lifting his own camera over his head and extending it to Troy. "I used to use it for business, but I'm shopping for something new. You're satisfied with the Leica, then?"

"I haven't got any complaints," Troy said, giving the man's Pentax a cursory once-over and then returning it. "If you ask me, Pentax made better gear ten years ago than it does now."

"I hear you," the man agreed. "What kind of work do you use it for?"

"I'm free-lancing for *Dream* magazine," Troy said, glad that that was an honest answer. He no longer wanted to think of himself as a studio photographer. "How about you?"

"I'm on the staff of the *San Francisco Chronicle*," the man replied. "Just vacationing at the moment. I decided it was time to check out the wall." He gestured toward the memorial.

Troy twisted back to gaze at the angular black monument. "Do you know anyone listed on there?" he asked.

The man exhaled. "Too many of them," he said grimly. "I'm afraid to get too close to the thing. Then I might have to read their names."

"When did you serve?" Troy questioned him.

"I didn't. I was in 'Nam as a stringer for *Newsweek*. They fought and died—" he pointed at the wall again "—and I took pictures of the carnage. God," he muttered. "It still gives me nightmares. I thought I ought to come here, and now I'm here and I can't seem to get within twenty feet of the wall. It's crazy, man, crazy." He eyed Troy curiously. "How about you? Did you get to participate in the fun and games over there?"

Andrew's words flashed through Troy's brain: *Nobody's going to forgive you.* Taking a deep breath, he said, "No. I went to Canada."

"No kidding?" The man examined Troy, searching. "Can't say that I blame you, knowing what I know now."

There it was, then. Neither approval nor disapproval, neither praise nor contempt. Simply acceptance.

"Well." Troy removed his wide-angle lens and slipped it and the camera back into his bag. "I've got things to take care of."

"Nice talking to you," the man said.

Troy took a step away, then called over his shoulder, "Go with the Leica. It's a fine piece of equipment."

"Thanks for the recommendation," the man hollered back to him. "I'll think about it."

With a wave, Troy pivoted and strolled away. Just before he left the Mall, he spun back for a final look at the memorial. He watched as the photographer he'd been chatting with ventured a few paces closer to the wall, then stumbled to a halt. The man scanned the wall, ran his hand across his eyes, moved another stride, halted again.

It must have taken guts to do photojournalism work in Vietnam, Troy thought. It must have taken guts to watch one's friends cut down, to keep one's fear and terror at bay amid all that violence. It had also taken guts to go to Canada. All the survivors had to face their nightmares, had to accept and go on.

"I'M ALL DONE HERE." Troy informed Julianne over the telephone. He was seated on the bed in his hotel room, his suitcase buckled shut on the floor at his feet and his packed camera bag resting on the mattress next to him.

"That was fast," Julianne remarked.

Damn her. Why couldn't she say something like "How wonderful! I'm so glad! Now you can spend a couple of days in New York before you have to do that wedding job this weekend!" Why did she have to sound so subdued, so remote?

If she wouldn't say it, he would. "I'm planning to catch the next shuttle flight back to New York. I should get there by seven or eight. I'd like to see you, Julie."

"Oh."

Oh. That was it? That was all? "What do you mean, oh?" he challenged her. "Can I see you or can't I?"

"I don't know. Something's come up," she explained.

"What's come up?"

"We've had a death in the family."

Chastened, he subsided against the pillow. How dared he allow himself to be angered by Julianne's cool reaction to his impending return when she was confronting such personal sorrow? "I'm sorry, Julianne," he said quickly. "Are you all right?"

"I'm fine," she said with a vague laugh. "It's my Aunt Hazel. My father's aunt, actually. She was ninety-four years old, so it wasn't exactly unexpected."

"I see." He closed his eyes, wishing that he were with Julianne now, wishing that, no matter how expected her great-aunt's death was, he could be beside Julianne, comforting her.

"The funeral's on Thursday," she went on. "I promised my folks I'd fly out to Iowa tomorrow. They're taking it well, but I want to be there. I just saw Aunt Hazel when I was in Meade for the Memorial Day weekend. I guess I'm a little bit in shock. And... I want to be there."

"Of course," Troy agreed. Then he opened his eyes and sat straighter, infused with purpose. "Let me come with you."

"What?"

"Let me come to Iowa with you." As soon as he had verbalized the request, he felt a warm sense of well-being settle over him. He wanted to be with Julianne for her trip home, for her aunt's funeral. He wanted to meet her family. He wanted to see Iowa for himself, to see that pure, clean town of hers and the land that had produced her, the land that had made her what she was today. He wanted to learn from Julianne what home was, what it meant. "Please, Julie," he implored her. "Let me come."

She lapsed into thought, and Troy listened to the scratchy sound of long-distance silence. Then she said, "All right, Troy. Come."

Nine

Troy was staring out the window. Julianne could see only his lush black mop of hair above the broad shelf of his shoulder as he peered down at the earth below them. She wondered what his insistence on flying to Iowa with her meant. She wondered what her having agreed to let him come meant.

They hadn't talked about it last night. Her afternoon had been a hectic series of telephone calls: arranging for a second airline ticket, phoning her father to inform him of her arrival time and to let him know that she was bringing a friend with her, a scramble to fill in the editor who would cover for her during the time she was away from her office, an incoming call from her father, asking if she wanted Nathaniel to pick her and her friend up at the airport in Davenport. Nathaniel would be arriving on an earlier plane from Chicago—Beth and the children were going to stay home, it was decided—and he could meet Julianne if she wished. She had assured her father that she would rather rent a car and drive up to Meade. "You'll probably be needing Nathaniel to take care of things in town," she had pointed out. "We'll get ourselves home. But thanks for the offer." She didn't bother to add that she wanted access to her own transportation during her stay in Iowa, just in case.

Just in case what? Just in case Troy became claustrophobic surrounded by her effusive family and felt the urge to clear out? Just in case the implications of his visit to her family's house sank in and he decided that he didn't like them? Just in case he needed to run away?

She wanted to believe that he understood those implications and that he had chosen to accompany her because of them, not in spite of them. She wanted to believe that everything he had sworn when she'd last seen him would actually come about, that he was determined to have her in his life, that he was never going to run away again. But dreams *didn't* come true; Julianne and Troy both knew that. Believing that they could come true struck her as foolhardy.

Still, he was here now, seated beside her on the plane, winging west through the cloudless sky. Whatever it meant, it meant something. And while last night they had discussed little but the practical details of getting themselves organized, packed and prepared for their trip, once Julianne and Troy had climbed into bed and he'd lovingly enveloped her body with his, Julianne was willing to be foolhardy. She was willing to believe.

A flight attendant leaned over their seats and asked if they wanted to purchase beverages. Troy turned from the window, smiled and shook his head. Julianne also refused a drink. The stewardess left, and Troy directed his smile to Julianne. "Maybe I should have taken some cocktail peanuts."

"I can call her back," Julianne suggested, twisting in her seat to summon the stewardess.

Troy stayed her with his hand on her wrist. "I'm not really hungry," he assured her. "It's just that I'm not used to sitting on a plane without lighting up."

Julianne realized that she hadn't seen Troy take a cigarette since he'd entered her apartment the previous evening. That she had reserved seats for them in the plane's no-smoking section had been a reflex. Troy seemed to have no objections to their seats, however. He honestly intended to quit smoking. That, too, had to mean something.

"Tell me about your aunt," he requested, leaving his hand on the divider between their seats.

Julianne rotated her arm and wove her fingers through his. "She was a neat lady," she related. "Feisty, spunky, as stubborn as all get out."

"Stubbornness runs in the family, huh," Troy joked.

Julianne grinned. "I guess it does. I wouldn't mind taking after Aunt Hazel."

"I hope you inherited her genes for longevity," Troy commented. "Ninety-four is a pretty decent age to reach."

"She was independent to the end, too," said Julianne. "When her husband passed away, about twenty-two, twenty-three years ago, her daughter Milicent tried to talk her into selling her house and moving to Omaha to be near Milicent's family. They wanted Aunt Hazel close by so they could keep an eye on her. She wouldn't hear of it. She loved her house, she was at home in Meade, and she wasn't going to up and move for anyone's sake, not even her daughter's." Julianne chuckled as she reminisced. "The next thing we knew, Aunt Hazel joined the Peace Corps and took off for India."

"The Peace Corps?" Troy repeated incredulously.

Julianne nodded. "She spent a year in a village near New Delhi, teaching classes in hygiene and food preparation. By the time she came back to Iowa, she could speak fluent Hindu and wrap a sari like a pro. God, I miss her already." She sighed wistfully. "When she came to the Memorial Day service this year, Reverend Sykes brought her a folding chair from the church so she wouldn't have to stand at the cemetery like everyone else. She was insulted. She called the reverend a whippersnapper and told him that she had two good feet and intended to use them. She had a cane, too, but she was always forgetting it, leaving it at home. She didn't really need it." Julianne sighed again. "She died in her sleep, apparently. A bunch of people in town used to take turns visiting her every day just to see how she was making out—that used to offend her, too, but she tolerated it. Yesterday morning Janet Munson found her in bed, passed away, looking very peaceful. I imagine it was for the best. If Aunt Hazel had gotten ill, she would have raised hell about it."

"She does sound like a neat lady," Troy concurred. "I wish I could have met her."

"You'll be meeting the rest of my family," Julianne reminded him. "They're just as stubborn and uppity as she was."

"I'd better brace myself," Troy muttered, though his eyes danced with humor. Gradually he grew solemn. "What did you tell your folks about my coming?" he asked.

"Just that you were a friend," Julianne replied. "I'm sure that when they see you..." She meditated for a moment, once again wondering what Troy's presence truly meant. "They'll put two and two together," she concluded.

He opened his mouth, then shut it and gave his words further consideration. "Are they going to give you a hard time?"

Uncertain of what he was getting at, Julianne smiled hesitantly. "If you mean, are they going to put us in separate bedrooms, I'm sure they will."

"That wasn't what I meant," he countered. "What I meant was...have you ever introduced them to any of your other men?"

"What other men?" she blurted out, then laughed sheepishly. "No, I haven't. The people I've dated always lived in New York. My folks don't come to New York very often."

"And you've never brought any of the others with you to visit them?" he half asked.

Julianne assessed his question. He seemed to be seeking confirmation that he was unique in her life, the one special man she was bringing home to meet her family. Perhaps his desire to travel to Meade with her meant exactly what she wanted it to mean: that he was making a commitment; that in meeting her family, he was making a statement about the seriousness of his feelings for Julianne.

"You're it," she told him. "You're the first." She didn't bother to add that her parents were certain to be pleased by the existence of a man in Julianne's life. Although they never probed directly, she suspected that they were concerned about her single status. Not that they thought all women had to pair off with men in order to have full lives, but they were happily married themselves, and they made little effort to hide their desire for their daughter to experience that kind of happiness someday.

Nathaniel wasn't as diplomatic as his parents, of course. He frequently expressed his discontent with Julianne's meager social life. He worried about her single-minded pursuit of professional success. He didn't nag her about it, but he didn't hesitate to make his opinions known.

She hoped that he would approve of Troy. She hoped her parents would approve, as well. Even if they didn't, they never sat in judgment of their children, so Julianne didn't expect any major problems with them regarding Troy. But still, she hoped that they would like him.

Over the loudspeaker, the pilot announced the plane's approach to O'Hare Airport. Troy straightened in his seat and released Julianne's hand in order to buckle his seat belt. His attention returned to the window to watch their descent. Was he nervous about meeting her family? If his intentions were what Julianne assumed them to be, nervousness was probably a natural reaction.

Their connection to Davenport was a tight one, and they managed to board the small commuter plane with only a few minutes to spare. Troy surveyed their fellow passengers and grinned. "I don't see any cowboys," he whispered as the plane taxied away from the terminal.

Cowboys. Julianne recalled the day, back in college, when Troy had complimented her on her tooled Western-style boots and asked if her part of the country was full of cowboys. Given his ignorance about the state, Iowa was bound to be a revelation to him.

Two hours later, after they had retrieved their luggage, picked up their rental car and driven north from Davenport into the farmland, Troy gave voice to his astonishment. "It's so flat here," he observed. "It's so... so *flat*, Julie."

"Of course it's flat," she said with a chuckle. "Welcome to the Great Plains."

"What are they growing?" he asked, scanning the neatly planted rows of green that lined the county route on either side. "Is it corn?"

Julianne glimpsed the acreage to her left, then returned her focus to the road ahead of her. "Soybeans," she told

Troy. "Corn is much taller. I'll point it out to you when we pass some."

He rolled down his window. The air was hot and breezy, comfortably dry. He had brought a suit with him—as he had reminded Julianne the previous night, he'd packed the suit when he'd left Montreal because he had planned to stop over in New York and take Julianne out for dinner at an elegant restaurant once he finished his assignment in Washington. Julianne had also brought a suit appropriate for the funeral. For traveling, they were both dressed casually, Troy in a neat pair of jeans and an oxford shirt, Julianne in pleated cotton slacks and a short-sleeved blouse.

"You never told me how things went in Washington," she commented, easing across the yellow center line to pass a sluggish tractor in her path.

Troy's gaze remained on the tractor as Julianne sped past it. A grizzled old man in a duck-bill cap and weathered denim coveralls bounced in the tractor's seat as he steered half on the road and half on the shoulder, enabling faster-moving vehicles to overtake him. Julianne had seen enough tractors in her life not to be impressed by the huge, deeply treaded tires, the bright yellow color of the chassis, the chugging exhaust stack. But Troy was obviously awed. "That was a farmer," he exclaimed.

"You're catching on," Julianne said with a laugh. "I'm happy to hear you can tell the difference between a farmer and a cowboy."

Troy continued to watch the tractor until it receded into a yellow dot, barely visible through the rear window. Then he faced forward and settled back into his seat.

"Washington," Julianne repeated when she was sure she had his attention again. "How did it go?"

"Fine," Troy answered. "I got some good shots. I was going to see if Peter could borrow that darkroom for me again, so I could get them developed for you right away, but—"

"Don't worry about it," Julianne cut him off. "I won't need them for another couple of weeks. I won't be getting the copy from Dan Eisner until then." She gave Troy a quick glance. "How was Andrew? How did his testimony go?"

"As far as I can gather, it went well," Troy reported. "The senators grilled him for close to three hours, but he was in reasonably good shape afterward."

"Did you get to see Kim?"

"I had dinner with her and Andrew Monday night." He scrutinized Julianne intently. "You told her about us," he declared.

Julianne measured his tone. It wasn't quite accusing, but it contained something more than simple curiosity. "Yes," she admitted softly. "I told her about us. Did she mention it?"

"No, but Andrew did." Troy lapsed into silence for a long moment. "They're good together, Julie. They've got something awfully good going with each other."

Again Julianne struggled to interpret his tone. Was he envious of the joy Kimberly and Andrew had found together? At one time Julianne had almost indulged in envy over her friend's splendid luck in love. She could have been jealous. She should have been. Even now, with Troy beside her, his actions informing her of his desire to forge something lasting with her, she could be jealous of Kimberly and Andrew. Julianne and Troy might be moving toward something awfully good, but they hadn't reached it yet.

"I visited the Vietnam Memorial," Troy announced abruptly, surprising her. "While I was in D.C. I went over and had a look at it."

Julianne recalled what Nathaniel had told her about his trip to view the memorial. He had said that seeing it helped to end the war in his heart. She wondered whether Troy's visit to the memorial had had a similar result. "And?" she prompted him.

Troy's index finger traced an abstract pattern along his leg. He was edgy; he was probably longing for a cigarette. Julianne was proud of him for trying to break the habit, but more than that, she was anxious to hear why thinking about the memorial made him edgy. "I met a guy there," he related. "A fellow photographer. We talked cameras for a while."

He fell silent again, and Julianne cast him a searching look. "And?" she reiterated.

"Ah, Julie." He exhaled, his gaze fastened to the windshield, as if he couldn't bring himself to look at her. "It's a monument to tragedy, you know? It's ghastly. All those names, all those people killed...." He shook his head. "It—it made me glad I went to Canada," he confessed, his voice hushed yet fervent.

A rush of relief flooded Julianne's body. Perhaps Troy had ended the war in his heart, after all. Perhaps he had finally made peace with what he had done.

She wanted to shout her jubilation. She wanted to cry. She wanted to stop the car, wrap her arms around Troy and kiss him. But to do that would probably overwhelm him. So instead she pointed at the dark green stalks pushing up from the soil alongside the road, their narrow leaves reaching toward heaven, and said, "That's corn."

A BROWN PICKUP was parked in the driveway outside her parents' house when Julianne turned onto the elm-lined street a block from Meade's charming business district. Troy had insisted that she cruise around the tiny flower-strewn town square. He had gaped at the shops, housed in one-and-two-story stone-and-shingle buildings bordering the square. "A general store!" he had hooted. "A soda shop! Farm supplies! Cripes, Julianne—this place is like something out of a time warp!"

Julianne pulled to a halt by the strip of grass separating the sidewalk from the street. "My parents must be out," she said, her gaze narrowing on the pickup. "That's not their car." Nor was it Nathaniel's. If he had rented a vehicle at the airport, as she had, he certainly wouldn't have rented a truck.

Troy had already swung out of the car. His gaze took in the tree-shaded street with its well-tended houses. Most of them were modest in size, constructed of clapboard and brick. The Robinson house was the largest on the block, only because Julianne's father had built an extension onto the structure for his medical office.

"This is beautiful," Troy murmured, his eyes widening at the manicured flower beds lining the driveway and the front walk. Julianne's mother was passionate about her flowers. Late-blooming tulips, geraniums, irises and impatiens blazed their showy colors across the yard. Troy inhaled deeply, his smile widening. "It even smells great."

"It smells of fertilizer," Julianne corrected him, smiling. Owing to the expanse of farmland that hemmed in the town on every side, the air in late spring and early summer often held a tangy fragrance that natives recognized as chemical fertilizer. Julianne shut her door and joined Troy at the rear bumper. She unlocked the truck, and Troy removed their bags. They strolled up the front walk, climbed the two steps to the front porch that ran the width of the house and entered through the unlatched screen door. "Hello?" Julianne called out.

"In here," came a woman's voice from the kitchen at the rear of the house. Troy set the suitcases down at the foot of the stairway, then followed Julianne down the hall. The house was redolent with the aromas of baking.

Spotting the woman laboring over a loaf of bread at the table in the center of the spacious kitchen, Julianne raced across the room. "Sally!" she cried, embracing her friend. Sally was, in fact, Julianne's cousin by marriage. They had attended grade school and the regional high school together, and after they'd graduated, Sally had married Julianne's second cousin, Bill, who owned a farm outside town.

Sally set down her knife and returned Julianne's warm hug. Shorter and stockier than Julianne, Sally wore a pair of faded overalls, a T-shirt and canvas sneakers. Her curly hair was tied back from her face with a dark blue bandanna. "Hey, Julianne! How was your trip?"

"It was fine." Julianne turned to the table. Sally had sliced a fresh-baked loaf of bread lengthwise. Ceramic bowls filled with egg salad, tuna salad and deviled ham sat on the table next to the bread. Julianne guffawed. "Don't tell me you're making a sandwich loaf! I haven't seen one of these things since Mrs. Highland's home economics class."

Sally shrugged. "I'm fixing a bunch of stuff. Half the town is going to descend on your parents after the funeral, and they're going to have to feed them something. Your mother's doing a roast for your supper tonight, but there's sure to be leftover for sandwiches tomorrow. I've got deviled eggs and potato salad in the fridge, and Tammy Clinton was over here earlier, making the cakes." Sally gestured toward the stove, where three glazed ring cakes sat cooling. Then she studied her sandwich loaf. "What do you think, Julianne? Should I put some food coloring in the cream cheese frosting? Mrs. Highland always did."

Julianne laughed, and Sally succumbed to a giggle, as well. "She always put in all that red," Julianne recalled, "and the frosting came out shocking pink. Skip it." She peered over her shoulder at Troy, who was hovering in the doorway, evidently not wanting to intrude. Julianne waved him inside. "Sally, this is Troy Bennett, a friend of mine from New York. Troy, Sally Traynor—one of my cousins."

After dusting the bread crumbs from her palm on the seat of her overalls, Sally extended her hand to Troy, who stepped into the kitchen and shook it politely. Sally gave him a quick but comprehensive inspection, then smiled. "Nice meeting you," she said before spinning back to Julianne. "Your mom said you were bringing someone with you. She and your dad are over at the church right now, by the way."

"Did Nathaniel get here yet?"

Sally dipped her knife into the tuna salad and began to spread it evenly over the bread. She nodded. "He's at Hazel's house with Milicent and her husband. They flew in last night."

"How's Milicent?"

"Bearing up. She's been expecting it for some time. Everyone was expecting it," Sally commented pensively, "but it's still a big shock. Hazel was such a fixture around here, you know?"

"I know."

"She was a tough bird, right up to the end. Remember how she kicked up that godawful fuss about the chair on Memorial Day?"

Julianne's eyes met Sally's. The tears glistening along Sally's pale lashes heightened Julianne's awareness of the dampness rimming her own eyes. She wiped them with her hand, then forced a smile. "How are you and Bill doing?" she asked, eager to change the subject before they both became maudlin.

"Don't ask," Sally grumbled, setting a second layer of bread on top of the tuna salad and smearing egg salad across it. "You know what the farm scene is like these days. We're hanging on by a thread."

"At least you're still hanging on," Julianne encouraged her.

Sally shrugged. "It ain't easy, I'll tell you. Up until the end of February, we didn't even know if we were going to get the money to plant this year. But the bank came through for us, God bless 'em." She set down the knife and grinned. "Everybody's helping everybody. We're all in it together. Your dad has been something else, Julianne. This past winter, Robin developed chronic bronchitis. She had a horrible cough—it sounded like a car backfiring. Your dad drove out three times just to check on her. Refused to send us a bill, even when I begged him to."

"That's his idea of retirement," Julianne explained. "He keeps working just as hard, only he stops taking money for it."

"He's a wonder," Sally said. "He's been trying to find someone to take over for him, you know? Combing the medical schools, running ads in all the papers. Nobody wants to come. They think it's a dead end. They'd all rather be in New York, making money." She eyed Julianne admiringly. "Speaking of which, you look like a million bucks, as usual. Troy's treating you right, I take it?" She tossed a playful look Troy's way.

"Doing my best," he conceded with a shy smile. That he wasn't disconcerted by Sally's teasing reassured Julianne. Evidently Troy was ready to accept the assumptions people were bound to make about his having accompanied Julianne to Iowa.

"I tell you what, Sally," Julianne proposed. "Give us a few minutes to take our things upstairs and freshen up, and then we'll give you a hand here in the kitchen."

"Forget it," Sally rebuffed her, pointing toward the door. "I'm almost all done with this loaf, and I don't want you hanging around and reminding me of Mrs. Highland's shocking pink frosting."

Chuckling, Julianne ushered Troy out of the kitchen. Halfway down the hall, they halted at the sound of footsteps clomping across the front porch. The screen door flew open and Julianne's parents entered the house. They were both large people—which wasn't surprising, given Julianne's height—with clean, wholesome looks. Julianne's mother wore a lightweight floral dress that downplayed her thick middle, and her silver-streaked hair was drawn back from her relatively unlined face in a girlish ponytail. Dr. Robinson wore a suit minus a tie. His ruddy, handsome facial features and thick gray crop of hair made him appear far younger than his sixty-eight years.

"Julianne!" her mother roared, waltzing down the hallway with her arms outstretched. Within an instant, Julianne was engulfed in her mother's adoring embrace. "Darling! I'm so glad you're here." She delivered Julianne over to Dr. Robinson, who swaddled her in another smothering hug.

Julianne's mother turned to Troy. "You must be Troy Bennett," she said gathering Troy's hand in both of hers and clasping it with genuine affection. "It was so kind of you to come."

Dr. Robinson released Julianne to shake hands with Troy. "How do you do?" Troy said courteously.

"It's our pleasure, Troy, our pleasure." Julianne's father gripped Troy's hand and pumped it up and down energetically. "I'm only sorry the occasion isn't a happier one."

Noticing the suitcases, Julianne's mother nudged her husband. "They've just barely arrived, Tom. Why don't you take their things upstairs while I get them something to drink?"

"We'll take them up," Julianne insisted, lifting one of the bags. She suddenly wanted to get Troy alone for a minute. He seemed contemplative, absorbing everything but revealing little. She was dying to find out what he was thinking.

"All right," Mrs. Robinson acquiesced. "I'd better go give Sally some help in the kitchen. We're putting Troy up in the attic room, darling."

Nodding, Julianne relinquished her bag to Troy, who gathered up the other one, as well, and trailed her up the stairs. She led him into her old bedroom. Her parents hadn't altered the furnishings since Julianne had moved out nearly twenty years ago. The heavy oak dresser, desk and matching headboard had all been recently polished, and the lace-trimmed runner on the dresser was clean and starched. Julianne crossed to the window and opened it to let some fresh air into the room. Then she spun around to Troy.

He was gazing at the twin bed, with its eyelet spread and two plump pillows. When Julianne approached him, he lifted his eyes. They glittered enigmatically. "Hello," she whispered.

He drew her into his arms and kissed her forehead. "Hello."

"They're a bit effusive, I know," she said, referring to her parents. "But once things settle down here—"

"They're wonderful," he cut her off. Pulling her close, he rested his chin against the crown of her head. "I used to wonder how you got to be so strong and sure of yourself. Now I know."

Julianne puzzled over his words. When it came to her parents, yes, she was sure of herself. She was sure of their love and of the pride they took in her, sure that no matter what she did, she would always be welcome in their home.

But when it came to Troy...she still wasn't sure. The insecurity she felt about him was an alien emotion, but she couldn't seem to shake it. She had hoped that by seeing him together with her family, she would find the confidence she needed to believe in his love for her. Yet even with his arms closed around her, even with his body pressed to hers, she was doubtful and afraid. She had never lost her parents, but she had lost Troy. She had loved him and she had lost him, and even after all this time the wounds hadn't healed completely.

THEY ATE DINNER at six, just Julianne's immediate family. Sally had returned to her farm an hour ago, and Nathaniel had announced that Milicent and her husband were going to have supper at another cousin's house. The Robinsons and Troy feasted on roast beef, a hearty potato-and-cheese casserole, bread, salad and wine at the long linen-covered table in the dining room.

Julianne's parents were diplomatic in their questioning of Troy. She knew they were interested in learning about him, but they posed their questions judiciously and exhibited general pleasure with his answers. When he revealed that he lived in Montreal, they didn't ask how he had wound up living in Canada, but instead inquired about the city. "Is there really as much strife between the English and the French as we read about?" Dr. Robinson asked. "Are there really people agitating for separation?"

They asked Troy about his photography, and in particular his recent work for *Dream*. Their delight at the success of Julianne's magazine was palpable, and Troy granted that he was honored to be working for it.

After dinner Julianne's parents ordered her, Troy and Nathaniel out onto the porch to polish off the wine. "You've all traveled so far today," Julianne's mother remarked when Julianne asked if she could help with the dishes. "We've got plenty to do here, but you young folks should relax. All I ask is that you steer clear of us for a while."

Nathaniel didn't protest. He gleefully lifted the half-full bottle of burgundy and his wineglass and headed for the porch. Recognizing the futility of arguing with her mother, Julianne slipped her hand through the bend in Troy's arm and guided him outside.

Nathaniel was already lounging in one of the redwood chairs on the porch. The sky was dark blue, and crickets chirped their cacophony into the descending night. As soon as Troy and Julianne settled onto the upholstered outdoor love seat, Nathaniel topped off their glasses with wine and set the empty bottle on the plank flooring at his feet. "So, you're Troy," he said, zeroing in on Julianne's guest. "Pardon me if I'm mistaken, but aren't you the guy who jilted my sister after college?"

"Nathaniel!" Julianne socked her brother's arm. She understood that he was only kidding around, but Troy couldn't know that. Indeed, Troy's grim frown indicated that Nathaniel had succeeded in putting him on the defensive.

Nathaniel grinned. "Excuse me, Troy, but I've got a memory like an elephant's. The only time I ever saw Julianne broken up over a guy, the name she mentioned was yours. I take it you're planning to make it up to her?"

"I am," Troy vowed solemnly.

"Ignore him," Julianne advised Troy. "Don't let him give you a hard time. He's just playing the role of big brother to his baby sister."

"He's right," Troy contradicted her. "I didn't exactly jilt you, but..."

"Montreal," Nathaniel plowed ahead, leaning forward and resting his forearms on his spread knees. He sipped his wine, studying Troy speculatively. "Did you really have to go that far away to break up with Julianne?"

"Stop it, Nathaniel," Julianne demanded sternly. Kidding was kidding, but she wasn't going to let him draw and quarter Troy for his own amusement.

Troy silenced her with a searing look. Then he met Nathaniel's inquisitive gaze and said, "I didn't go far away because I wanted to break up with Julianne, Nathaniel. I went to Canada to avoid getting drafted."

Julianne held her breath. She hadn't expected Troy to reveal that fact about himself, especially to Nathaniel. Troy knew that her brother was a Vietnam veteran. But if Nathaniel had been testing Troy with his tactless jokes, now Troy was testing Nathaniel. He stared steadily at Nathaniel, awaiting a response.

At Troy's blunt statement, Nathaniel flinched. He inspected Troy, his flinty blue eyes shuttling from Troy to Julianne and back to Troy again. Julianne watched him, alert for any change in his demeanor, alert for signs of rage.

She sensed more than saw the hardening of his jaw, the tensing of his lips. "You did what?" he asked, his voice taut.

Troy's gaze remained unwavering on Nathaniel. "I went to Canada to evade the draft. I was earmarked for Vietnam, and I went to Canada, instead."

Nathaniel muttered an oath. Averting his eyes, he took a long swig of wine. Julianne braced herself against his building anger. She expected to be the object of it, for having brought home a man who had done what Troy had just confessed to doing. But Nathaniel ignored her and bore down on Troy. "You left Julianne for—for that?" His mouth was twisted into a grimace; his gaze was venomous. "You broke my sister's heart for that?"

Now it was Troy's turn to be startled. The cause of Nathaniel's fury seemed to be less that Troy had dodged the draft than that Julianne had been injured in the process. "I never wanted to hurt Julianne," he maintained, his voice as low as Nathaniel's. "Going to Vietnam would have meant leaving her, too."

Nathaniel cursed again. He stood, prowled to the porch railing and gazed up into the starry sky. Then he pivoted and stared down at Troy. "I served over there. I risked my life so bastards like you would have the freedom to cross the border," he fumed. "I went over and fought so you could walk away from it."

"No," Troy said, his voice hushed but even. "You served because you chose to. You did what you had to do, Nathaniel. I did what I had to do. We both made our choices." He reached for Julianne's hand, and only the fierceness of his grip communicated his own tension to her. "And if Julianne wasn't lying to me all those years ago, the choice you made broke her heart, too."

Julianne felt awkward listening to herself being spoken of in the third person, as if she weren't sitting right there. Yet she was too transfixed to move, or even to speak. She was too mesmerized by Troy's powerful conviction, by his failure to bend before Nathaniel's blistering fury.

Nathaniel turned to her. His eyes were no longer filled with disgust. They radiated confusion, a strange beseechment. "I know you didn't want me to go, Julianne, but—but it didn't break your heart. It was something we begged to differ on, that was all."

"That wasn't all," Julianne argued gently. "I thought I had lost you, too."

"I promised I'd come back—"

"As if that was a promise you could have made," she chided him. "But it didn't matter. I thought I had lost you because you decided to do something I considered wrong."

"Why...? Why didn't we ever talk about this, Julianne? Why didn't you tell me?"

"You knew how I felt," she claimed. "I hated you for going, but I respected that you'd reached your decision after careful deliberation. It was the same thing with Troy. I hated that he went, but I understood his reasons."

"My going—it did break your heart, then, didn't it?" Nathaniel's shock gave way to rue.

She nodded. "But you went, and you came back. And Troy went, and he came back."

Nathaniel fell silent. The only sound was the constant screeching of the crickets. The only movement was the light summer breeze wafting across the dark porch, ruffling Julianne's fine hair. After an interminable minute, Nathaniel moved to the empty bottle, lifted it and stalked into the house.

Troy turned to her. "I'm sorry, Julie—"

"No. Don't be."

He peered into her eyes. "I wasn't going to bring it up, but he asked."

She leaned toward Troy and touched her lips to his. The strength he had just revealed told her everything she needed to know about his resolution, about his feelings for her, about his having come to terms with the war.

Troy drew back. He left his arm around her, but his eyes drifted past her to the screen door through which Nathaniel had just vanished. "I am sorry, Julianne," he persisted. "I want your family to like me. It was wrong of me to attack him that way—"

"If he survived the Vietcong, he can certainly survive attacks by you," Julianne reassured Troy. "You weren't wrong. He was wrong, standing there and saying that it was just something we begged to differ on. It was much more than that, Troy. We fought long and hard about it. I was demolished when he went."

"He doesn't know that."

"But he should," she asserted. "I told him at the time—"

"Did you?" Troy interrupted. His eyes returned to her, glittering with wisdom, with profound comprehension. "You're too damned good at containing your misery, Julie. You're too damned good at being calm and rational, keeping it all under wraps." He stroked her cheek, brushing a strand of hair behind her ear. "Did you ever let your brother see you cry?" he asked, his voice muted. "Did you ever really let him know how you felt?"

No. She hadn't cried in front of Nathaniel. She had debated with him, quarreled with him, engaged in heated arguments about the validity of the war. It had all been an intellectual exercise, though. As devastated as she had been, she hadn't fallen apart in front of Nathaniel.

Once again Troy was right about her. She had spent too much of her life being strong and unflappable, too much of her life being sensible, fighting for principles but not for people, not even for the people who meant the most to her. It wasn't a crime to have been hurt. It wasn't a crime to acknowledge her pain. But perhaps it had been a crime to hide her pain.

She leaned toward Troy again, and this time when her lips found his he didn't back away. He arched his arm around her and bound her to himself, his tongue sliding deep into her mouth and his fingers raveling through her hair to the nape of her neck. Her breath became trapped in her throat, but she gave herself fully to his kiss. She loved him enough not to contain herself or conceal her emotions. She loved him enough to let him know.

The muffled sound of the telephone ringing inside her parents' house hardly made an impression on her. Nor did her mother's voice, calling through the screen door. "Julianne?" When Julianne didn't respond, her mother cleared her throat and commanded, "Um—Julianne, may I speak with you for a minute?"

Reluctantly Troy broke from her. "You'd better find out what she wants," he whispered hoarsely, managing a crooked grin. "It's bad enough your brother despises me. I don't want to have your parents on my case, too."

Sighing, Julianne rose on trembling legs and entered the house. Her mother was standing by the stairs, trying to suppress a chuckle but not doing a particularly good job of it. "I just got a call from Nell Delaney across the street," Mrs. Robinson confided. "She said she thought I ought to know that on the eve of her great-aunt's funeral, my daughter and her boyfriend were necking shamelessly on the front porch."

Chagrined, Julianne rolled her eyes. "Lord save me from small-town busybodies!" she gasped.

Her mother gave in to a rollicking laugh. "You're a big girl, darling. If you and Troy want to let the sparks fly, I have no objections. But since Nell does, I think you ought to relocate to the backyard."

Sharing her mother's laughter, Julianne shook her head. "Now I know why I live in New York City. Tell Nell to put away her binoculars. The show's over." Still grinning, Julianne marched outside, grabbed Troy's hand and hauled him out of the love seat. "All right," she declared brusquely, to Troy's bewilderment. "I don't mind making myself vulnerable, but I'll only do it in front of a very select audience." With that she escorted him into the house.

NOBODY IS GOING to forgive you.

Andrew's warning resounded inside Troy. Sitting up, he shoved back the covers and groped for his watch, which he'd left on the nightstand beside the bed. He squinted at its dial. Midnight. One o'clock eastern time. He was exhausted, but he couldn't sleep.

He swung his legs over the side of the bed, felt for the braided area rug with his bare feet and stood. He bent over to tug on his jeans, and when he straightened up his head banged against the sloping attic roof. Grunting, he stooped slightly and padded to the dormer window to gaze out at the backyard. It was vast, a rolling stretch of grass interrupted by several apple trees in bloom. A vegetable garden had been carved into one corner of the lawn, which was fenced by a towering stand of pine trees. Given his high vantage, Troy was able to glimpse an overgrown meadow behind the trees. A curving splinter of moon hung low above the horizon.

The song of the crickets had died down, but the wind offered a tuneless melody, soughing through the trees. Despite the close ceiling of the attic bedroom and its lack of air conditioning, Troy wasn't hot. He leaned against the window sill and tried to imagine what it must have been like growing up in a rural town like Meade, in a house like this, with a family like the Robinsons.

He marveled at them. Julianne's parents were so basically nice, so decent and warm and openly affectionate. The miles separating New York from Iowa couldn't separate Julianne from her loved ones. Nor could differences of opinion.

He liked Nathaniel, too. When Troy and Julianne had rejoined her family, offering their assistance in readying the house for the deluge of visitors they expected after the funeral the following morning, Troy and Nathaniel had managed to talk congenially, to joke about the quantity of mismatched vases Mrs. Robinson owned and to help each other lug borrowed chairs over from a neighbor's house. They didn't mention Vietnam—enough had been said on that subject for now. But Nathaniel's rancor about Troy's flight to Canada had obviously dissipated.

What Troy really liked about Nathaniel, as he reassessed their fiery encounter on the porch, was the love Nathaniel exuded toward Julianne. The war itself hadn't been at issue. Nathaniel had grilled Troy about Canada not because he abhorred Troy's actions, but because he ached for his sister. He had stormed away from the porch not because he was horrified by what he himself had chosen to do, but because he had never before realized how much his own actions had hurt her.

Troy had never seen so much genuine caring in a family, so much respect and concern. So much love. So much forgiveness.

He heard a light tap on his door, and then a barely audible whisper. "Troy? Are you awake?"

Spinning around, he bumped his head on the ceiling again. Stifling a curse, he said, "Come on in."

The door edged open, and Julianne stepped across the threshold. She was dressed in a flowing floor-length nightgown, its translucent peach-colored fabric revealing the silhouette of her willowy legs and its narrow straps and scooped neck exposing more of her slender throat and her breasts than Troy's temperament could handle. When she glided across the room to him, he gathered her in his arms and kissed her hungrily. His hands slid from her shoulder blades forward, caressing her breasts through the thin cloth. Shuddering, she buried her face against his chest and moaned. "This isn't why I came up here," she murmured breathlessly.

He let his hands roam down to her waist and held her. "Why did you come up?"

"I heard you banging around," she explained. "My bedroom is right below you."

He tilted his head to view the angled ceiling and snorted softly. "This room wasn't designed for anyone taller than five feet."

"Five feet four, actually," she informed him, her lips moving with unintended sensuality against his throat as she spoke. "My grandmother lived here for a while when I was a little girl. She was pretty short—for a Robinson, anyway."

Groaning, Troy tucked his thumb beneath her chin and lifted her lips to his again. Julianne melted into his kiss for a moment, then resolutely pulled away. "We can't, Troy," she whispered. "Not here. For all I know, Nell Delaney is hiding in the hedges, spying on us."

"Who?"

"Never mind," Julianne said with a hushed laugh. Then she grew sober. "It's my parents' house, Troy. I know they wouldn't feel comfortable with us making love. If they did, they wouldn't have put you in the attic."

Nodding, Troy dropped his hands from her and took a safe step backward. "I don't want to do anything that would make them uncomfortable," he conceded. "They're such good people, Julie."

"They are, aren't they," she agreed.

"Your brother, too."

She eyed Troy dubiously. "You like Nathaniel?"

"Very much." He turned to stare out at the yard again. Ogling the trees was easier than ogling Julianne when she was so alluring, and so damnably unattainable. "You have a wonderful family, Julie. Do you know how lucky you are?"

She stepped closer, sharing the windowsill with him, sharing the panorama beyond. "I have an inkling," she allowed.

"I wish I—" Faltering, he pressed his lips together. It was impossible; why drive himself crazy wishing for something that couldn't be?

Julianne tore her eyes from the window to study him. "You wish what, Troy?"

"I wish I had a family like yours. I wish I could see them, talk to them, explain who I am and why... and beg to differ with them." Admitting to such a yearning made it seem even more powerful to him. He tried to cast off the idea, but it had already been uttered. It was the truth. He couldn't retract it.

Julianne sighed. "I wish you could, too."

"I will," he said. His eyes remained fixed on the stars dotting the sky. Stars were for dreamers, for making wishes on. "I'll try. I have to. That's the other war, Julie, and I can't keep evading it forever. That's the one I've got to fight."

Julianne circled his waist with her arm and hugged him. She said nothing. Together they stared at the stars.

Ten

Just when Julianne was ready for everything to be right between them, something was wrong.

The few days they'd spent together in Iowa had proved what she hadn't dared to believe: that Troy had finally confronted his past and made his peace. He wouldn't have been able to stand up to Julianne's brother if he hadn't. He wouldn't have been able to speak so resolutely about what he had done. He had been neither defensive about his own decision nor offensive about Nathaniel's. Troy had come to Meade to meet her family—and to meet, head-on, the truth about what had happened between Julianne and himself so many years ago.

She was ready to welcome him home. Yet all of a sudden, it seemed, he was in retreat.

His excuse for not being able to leave Montreal and visit her in New York was valid enough: he and Claude were interviewing potential replacements for Troy. They had found a young photographer who exhibited immense talent and with whom Claude felt comfortable, but the fellow was short on funds and didn't know whether he could afford to buy Troy's share of the business. They were talking to lawyers and bankers, discussing possible loan arrangements. "It's all very complicated right now," Troy told her whenever she asked, during their telephone calls, whether he would be able to skip down to Manhattan for a quick visit. "I'm up to my ears in this thing. The kid's great, but the finances are a major tangle. We've got a lot of working out to do."

"What about *your* finances?" she asked, forgoing tact. "Is it that you can't afford a trip to New York right now? Because I'd be happy to cover the cost, Troy."

"It isn't money," he swore. "It's just... like I said, things are complicated. I can't do a disappearing act on Claude while we're trying to hammer out a settlement here."

On another evening, Julianne mentioned to Troy that he didn't have to worry about trying to find a place to live in the city. "I want you living here, with me," she told him.

He didn't respond immediately. "That isn't necessary, Julie," he assured her. "I know rentals are hard to come by, but I'm sure I'll find something."

"I don't want you to find something," she insisted. "I want you with me."

"That's... a big commitment," he allowed.

"One I'm willing to make."

He sighed. "I want to do things right this time, Julianne," he said quietly. "I thought I made it clear that I don't want to be your charity case."

As if that was why she had invited him to move in with her. As if she had made the offer only to smooth the way back home for him. Didn't he understand that she wanted him to live with her because she was finally prepared to make that big commitment?

It wasn't as though he didn't intend to come to New York eventually. Obviously he did. He wouldn't be so busy trying to sell his half of Bennett-Chartier if he didn't plan to return to the United States.

But his subtle withdrawal from Julianne vexed her. She missed him. Over a week had elapsed since they had parted ways at O'Hare Airport and Troy had flown off to Montreal while she had returned to New York. They spoke often on the telephone, but still... Before their journey to Iowa, Troy had been willing to turn somersaults in order to see her. He had traveled to Washington with a dress suit in his bag because he planned to stop over in New York on his way back to Canada, just to take Julianne out for dinner.

But now, now that she had conquered her own demons, had faced up to her own past pain and vanquished it, Troy was backing off. Just when she was positive that he had ended the war in his heart he was running away again.

And she wasn't going to beg him to come to her. She simply wasn't going to beg.

A second week passed, a week of hot, sticky days as spring slid into summer. A week of challenging work at the magazine. At one time, such work would have been enough to satisfy Julianne. But lately she found herself attending to her responsibilities with an uncharacteristic listlessness. She proofread articles, negotiated contracts with writers, took advertisers to lunch at the Four Seasons and imagined taking Troy there with her, instead. She imagined gazing into the crystalline fountain at the center of the dining room with him, admiring how handsome he looked in his suit, trading tastes of their appetizers and entrées and skipping dessert for the much sweeter conclusion to their meal that they would find in her bedroom.

"June ends this week," she reminded him during a phone conversation one night. "Does that mean the wedding season will taper off for your studio?"

"Yes," he said.

"Then maybe..." *Don't beg*, she cautioned herself. "Maybe," she continued brightly, "you could take a weekend off from work."

He offered a noncommittal grunt.

Refusing to beg was fine, but Julianne wasn't going to remain passive. If something was amiss between them, if Troy had an authentic reason for avoiding her, she deserved to know about it. "We haven't seen each other in two weeks, Troy," she noted, doing her best not to come across as plaintive.

"I know that, Julie. I know that." He sounded impatient.

She took a deep breath for fortitude. "Talk to me, Troy," she implored him. "Tell me what's wrong."

"Nothing's wrong," he claimed.

She wasn't persuaded. "Why don't you want to see me?" she asked, choosing directness. She wasn't begging, she consoled herself; she wasn't pleading. She was only demanding the explanation he owed her.

"I do want to see you," he swore, sounding more impassioned than he had in any of their talks since the trip to Iowa. "I want to see you so badly...."

"Then why—"

"I will," he promised. "I'll have it all worked out soon. I want everything settled, Julie. Before I see you. I want to be free before I come back to you."

He wanted to be free. He had chosen freedom when he'd left her fifteen years ago. Today he was choosing freedom again. She knew how much freedom meant to Troy, and she respected his yearning for it. More than respected it, she considered his love of freedom one of his finest attributes.

But what did that have to do with visiting her? How could he equate the dissolving of his business partnership with something as significant as freedom?

It wasn't his business that was chaining him. Julianne recognized that. It was something else. "What do you have to work out, Troy? Tell me the truth."

He was silent for several minutes. Julianne listened to the hum of static on the long-distance line and tried to fend off the dread that was slowly creeping over her. What could be troubling him so much, what could be standing in his way?

"I have to go to Detroit," he said at last. His tone was tense and gravelly, as if he were trying to conceal his apprehension—and failing.

Detroit. His parents. Of course.

He had confessed to Julianne that tranquil starlit midnight in the Robinsons' attic room that he wanted to see his parents again. He had confessed that he wanted to fight the one remaining battle, and that he would. When he had revealed his wish to Julianne, she had understood that it had arisen from his astonishment at the abundant love he felt in her family. Viewing her easy interaction with her parents and even with her brother—most importantly, with her brother—had instilled in him a longing to make amends with his own family.

"When are you going to go?" she inquired. She was asking not because she assumed that once he had gone to Detroit she would have him all to herself, but because she was worried for him, because she cared.

"This weekend," he informed her. "You're right. The wedding scene has slowed down, and Matt—the new guy—is going to cover for me."

"Let me come with you."

"No." His answer was swift and sharp.

She refused to be discouraged. "I let you come with me to Aunt Hazel's funeral."

"That was different," he asserted.

Yes, that had been different. But one thing about it was the same: she and Troy belonged together. They had belonged together then and they belonged together now.

"I want to meet your parents, too," she said straightforwardly, refusing to resort to wheedling. "If we're going to make a go of it, Troy, I've got a right to meet your family, just as you met mine."

"This isn't going to be a happy reunion," Troy snapped. "It's going to be a disaster."

"What makes you so sure of that?"

He hesitated before answering. "I've already called them to let them know I was coming," he said. "They told me to stay away."

Her heart ached in sympathy for him. How painful it must be to hear one's parents reject one so coldly. But if she were with Troy, she could help him cope with his sorrow. She could lend him her love and support. She could console him. She had stood by his decision to flee the draft. She could stand by him in this crisis, too.

"You're planning to go, anyway?" she asked, seeking confirmation.

"Yes."

"Then I'm coming, too." It was no longer a question. She had made up her mind.

Troy was apparently able to sense her resolve. He laughed wryly. "You're the most stubborn woman I've ever met," he complained.

"You knew that from the start, Troy. When are you going? I can meet you there."

He issued a mild curse. "If you're really going to be so pigheaded about this—"

"I grew up in pig country," she joked. "Of course I'm pigheaded."

He relented with a sigh. "All right. You can meet me at the hotel, if it means all that much to you. But I'm not going to bring you with me to their house. It's going to be awful, Julie. I don't want you to have to witness it."

Julianne almost argued that she did have to witness it. She almost blurted out that far from wanting Troy to protect her from the likely ugliness of his confrontation with his parents, she wanted to be present in order to protect him. But she held her words in check and calmly asked him for the name of the hotel where he'd made his reservation. "I'll meet you there sometime Saturday," she promised. "I love you."

"I love you, too," he said. "Even if you're being a pain about this."

Smiling, she bade him good-night and hung up.

A CAB delivered her to the Holiday Inn. Unable to book an earlier flight on such short notice, she'd arrived in Detroit after seven o'clock. She didn't get to see much of the city during the cab drive from the airport, but she didn't mind. As with her trip to Montreal, her only concern was Troy. Sight-seeing was the last thing she was interested in.

The motel's desk clerk rang Troy's room, announced Julianne's arrival and listened. Then he hung up his console phone. "Mr. Bennett will be with you in a minute," he informed Julianne.

Nodding, she stepped away from the desk and surveyed the impersonal lobby of the motel. She couldn't really concentrate on the furnishings, the stark plate-glass front wall of the motel, the potted plants and vending machines, the people milling in and out of the cocktail lounge off the lobby. Her entire nervous system was focused on the fact that Troy was somewhere in the building, right this minute, leaving his room, locking the door, strolling down the hall, nearing her. She was going to be with him. She hadn't done much to help him through his battle fifteen years ago, but she was going to help him through this one.

She saw him walking from the hallway into the lobby, his footsteps silenced by the patterned green carpet. Clad in faded blue jeans and an open-necked polo shirt, he was dressed more casually than she was. An anxious smile flickered across his face as his eyes met hers.

He drew to a halt beside her, then bent and shyly kissed her cheek. "Hello," he murmured.

She hadn't expected an X-rated welcome from him in the public environment of the motel lobby, but even at that, she could tell from his restrained greeting that he was nervous. She sensed the tension knotting his shoulders and darkening his brow. Smiling gently, hoping that he understood why she was there, she returned his light kiss and squeezed his hand.

He laced his fingers through hers, lifted her bag and escorted her down the hall. Neither of them spoke until they were inside his room and the door was shut behind them. "How are you?" Julianne questioned him, her tone brimming with compassion.

"Don't ask," he muttered.

"Too late," she said. "I already did."

His smile widened slightly, his eyes sparkling and his mustache enhancing the curve of his lips. "Do you really want to know how I am?" he asked, crossing to the laminated dresser and lifting a pack of cigarettes, which he displayed for her. "I bought these a half-hour ago. The first smokes I've bought since Iowa."

She stared at the cigarettes. "You haven't opened the pack yet," she observed.

He lowered his eyes to the cellophane-wrapped package in his hand. After a moment's silent debate, he tightened his fingers into a fist, crushing the pack. Then he tossed it into the garbage pail, straightened and turned back to Julianne.

"I got here in the nick of time," she concluded with a laugh. She didn't want to bowl Troy over with her delight at his having quit smoking—her particular delight that he hadn't succumbed during what was surely one of the most trying evenings of his life. Instead she glided across the room to him and gathered him to herself in a warm embrace. "You're going to be fine," she whispered as his arms closed around her, returning her hug. "No matter what happens tomorrow, you're going to be fine."

"You've got an awful lot of faith in me," he commented uncertainly.

"That's right. I do."

His lips found hers, no longer shy. He drank her in, his tongue filling her mouth, his hold on her unbreakable. There was more than love in his kiss, more than lust. Julianne sensed aching need in it, desperation, fear...and strength. As frightened as Troy was, his kiss told her that, whatever occurred at his parent's home tomorrow, he *was* going to be fine.

"I want you," he groaned, yanking at her blouse and pulling it from the waistband of her slacks.

She kissed the angle of his jaw. "You have me," she assured him. "I'm here."

"Against my better judgment," he grumbled, although his hands continued to move on her, stripping off her blouse and flinging it away, tugging imperatively on the zipper of her slacks. His harsh, jerky motions conveyed his want to Julianne as clearly as his powerful kiss had. There was nothing overtly seductive about his actions, nothing slow and provocative, but that didn't bother Julianne. She wanted him, too. She wanted to give him everything and to take whatever he was able to give her. She had come to Detroit to share herself with him in any way—in every way—she could.

As soon as she was undressed, he turned his attention to himself, spurning her assistance as he writhed out of his shirt, as he stepped out of his jeans. Although they had only kissed, he was already fully aroused as he ushered her to the king-size bed and fell across it, carrying her down with him. His mouth devoured hers, his body bore down on hers, and he shuddered as her fingers roamed over his back, digging into the clenched muscles along his spine, attempting to massage the stress out of them.

His hands skimmed the length of her, barely pausing at her breasts and her belly. He reached between her legs, rubbing her with his palm and then his fingers, sending shafts of sensation through her. "I want you," he repeated, his voice ragged. "I want you, Julianne."

"I want you, too," she vowed, rising from the pillow to kiss him, brushing her hand over his hard flesh.

He issued a broken moan, an inchoate word, and abruptly slipped away from her. Lying on his back, he stared at the ceiling for an instant, then shut his eyes and covered them with his arm. His chest pumped fiercely as he wrestled with his breath.

She rolled onto her side, propped her head in her hand and peered down at him. His forearm hid his expressive eyes from her. She ran her index finger gently over his mustache. "Troy?"

"I can't do this," he confessed. "I want to, Julie, but... I can't."

"It's all right," she whispered, letting her finger dance across his lower lip, trying to soften his frown. She eased his arm from his face and gazed into his eyes, easily reading his anguish in their shadowed depths. "It's all right."

"I thought..." He inhaled steadily, regulating his lungs. His voice was hoarse, and he had difficulty shaping his words. "I thought going to Canada was frightening. That was a cakewalk compared to this, Julie."

"I know."

"I can't—I can't make love knowing what's waiting for me tomorrow. I want to. I want you so much—"

"You have me," she insisted, stroking his cheek, pushing back the damp black waves of his hair. "I'm not going to go away. You have me, Troy."

His gaze absorbed her face above his, taking in her smooth brow, her piercing blue eyes, her delicate cheeks and tender smile. She detected a glimmer of hope in his expression, but he doused it with a shake of his head. "What are you doing here?" he grumbled. "Why did I say you could come?"

"You didn't," she reminded him. "I came anyway."

"Why?" he asked, that glimmer of hope returning, eradicating the bitterness in his eyes, relaxing the set of his mouth.

Julianne continued to stroke his head, winding her fingers through the hair at his temple in a soothing pattern. "Why did you come?" she countered. "Your parents told you not to."

The anger returned to his features in a brief flare, then subsided. He gave her question careful reflection. "That's different," he responded.

"Oh? How is it different, Troy?"

He appeared momentarily exasperated by her inquiry. His gaze shifted back to the ceiling as he struggled through his thoughts. "I'm here to force the issue with them. I'm here because they're my family and we've got to work things out, one way or the other. I can't keep it dangling forever. I want to put that part of my life back together again, to see it through. Maybe I won't be able to, but that's what I want. That's why I'm here."

"And that's why I'm here," Julianne explained, her voice velvet soft in the room's waning light. "I'm here to see things through with you, Troy. I'm here because you're my family and we've got to work things out."

"What do you mean, I'm your family?" He appeared bewildered. "You've got a family, Julie. You've got the nicest family I've ever encountered."

"I've got parents and a brother," she distinguished. "I've got a sister-in-law and a niece and a nephew, and dozens of aunts, uncles and cousins. But I'm here because I want you, because we're also trying to put ourselves back together." Her hand came to rest against the side of his head. "You've been running away from me, Troy. I let you go once, but I'm not going to let you go again."

"I haven't been running away from you," he protested. "I've only..." He sighed. "I wanted this behind me when we got back together. I wanted to come to you whole."

"Whole? You're already whole," she argued. Then she contradicted herself. "No, you aren't. Neither am I. The day a person becomes whole is the day he dies. As long as we're still living, we'll always be incomplete. That's part of the adventure of life, don't you think?"

"Don't get philosophical with me," Troy objected, though he was grinning. His expression became solemn as he added, "When I see my folks, I'll probably wind up badly hurt. I don't want you to think of me that way, Julie. I'm a man. I want you to think of me as strong and tough and able to take it. Tomorrow... I may not be able to take it."

"Oh, Troy." She bowed to kiss his lips. "Troy, you were the one who told me it was all right to let other people see that you're not always strong. You were the one who said it was all right to break down sometimes, to let someone you love see you cry." She kissed him again, a light brush of her mouth against his. "Just coming to Detroit means that you're strong. Just being willing to take a chance and face your parents means that you're as strong as you'll ever have to be."

"I'm not as strong as you," Troy mumbled, his gaze drifting from her once more.

"You're stronger," she assured him.

"I ran away," he asserted. "Isn't that a sign of weakness?"

"Not when you're guided by principles," she argued. "You were strong enough to shoulder the decision, to take it out of my hands. You were strong enough to do what you had to do and not to let me sway you. Of course I wanted you to choose jail over Canada—it would have been better for me. I even might have considered going to Canada with you. But that wouldn't have been right for me, then. You knew that. You were strong enough to leave me behind, to let me build my own life and make my own choices."

"Julie." He turned back to her, and his eyes locked with hers. "You're great for my ego, you know?"

"I'm not telling you this to boost your ego," she declared. "I'm just being sensible."

"You're just being a boss," he teased, arching his arm around her and pulling her to himself. He held her snugly, nestling her head into his shoulder. "Thanks, boss," he whispered. "Thank you for coming."

He thanked her again, later. Much later. She was lost in a deep slumber, hours after midnight, and then the dream began. A dream of his lips on hers, of his hands coaxing her body awake even as her mind remained locked in oblivion. A dream of his sweet touch, his gentle mouth, his magnificent body rising onto her. When she opened her eyes, she found the room awash in darkness, so she closed them again and trusted her other senses to carry her off. Trusted her senses, and trusted Troy.

She had awakened to him the first time, too. He had barged into her dreams then, and proved them paltry when compared to the real thing. Loving Troy had been an awakening. It still was.

He surged inside her, his breath rough against her cheek, his body hard and dynamic as it drew her out of the dream and forced her to accept the reality of him. She responded by instinct, by reflex. She had come to Detroit with only one thought: to give of herself. But Troy was doing all of the giving. Julianne took.

His thrusts became faster, surer. She arched to him, feeling the escalating pressure inside her, the rising tide rushing through her, breaking over her, releasing her. She moaned, clinging to Troy as his body wrenched free of passion's grip. Gasping, he sank onto her with a weary shudder.

They didn't speak. They didn't have to. They had each other; no words were needed.

They had each other. There would be no more running away.

THE HOUSE was empty. It was a narrow brick row house, nearly identical to every other narrow brick row house crowding the block. The neighborhood seemed gloomy to Julianne, despite the cloudless sky overhead and the brilliant midday sun. The crumbling sidewalks were lined with battered aluminum garbage pails, and the house across the street was obviously deserted, some of its windows boarded up and others cracked. A thin veneer of soot spread across every surface, every wall and every car parked along the curb.

Down the street in one direction, two young girls were playing hopscotch. Not far from them, a boy rode his skateboard in lopsided circles, apparently trying to attract the girls' attention. Down the street in the other direction, two teenagers were hunched over the engine of a pickup truck, its hood propped up. The street was filled with the muffled noise of a television program issuing from an open window nearby.

Julianne and Troy sat on the concrete steps that led to his parents' front door. The locked screen door featured an aluminum frame with a large *B* centered on it. The frame sparkled from a recent cleaning. Beside the door stood a stone flowerpot filled with gladioluses. Julianne appreciated their cheerful color. Maybe Troy's mother adored flowers as much as Julianne's mother did. Julianne took the flowers as a good omen.

Having lived in Manhattan for so long, she was accustomed to the grime and clutter of city neighborhoods. But this wasn't just a city neighborhood; this was Troy's childhood home. He had grown up on this dreary block, closed in by brick, breathing the stale scent of automobile fumes. He might have been shocked to learn that Iowa wasn't overrun with cowboys, but Julianne was similarly startled to see for herself the grim boundaries of his youth. For some reason this street didn't seem like the sort of place that would breed a committed pacifist or a talented photographer.

"Maybe they'll be home soon," she suggested.

Troy peered at her. Once again he was dressed more casually than she. As befitted a first meeting with the parents of one's lover, she had chosen a summery cotton dress of a conservative cut, with bright flowers flocked across its crisp fabric. Her hair was neat, her makeup subdued, her feet shod in white leather sandals. Troy was dressed in jeans, a white oxford shirt with the sleeves turned up and his sneakers.

He shrugged. "We'll wait a while."

"Does it feel strange?" she inquired. "Sitting here like this, I mean. Are you anxious?"

He attempted a smile. "Sure, I'm anxious." He stiffened suddenly, his gaze narrowing on a yellow sedan that had just turned the corner and was cruising down the road. "There they are," he mouthed.

Julianne refused to turn from Troy. She would have a chance to look at his parents soon enough. Right now, gauging Troy's reaction to their arrival was more important.

If he was anxious, he hid it well. His jaw was rigid, his dark eyes fixed to the car as it slowed, as it coasted to a halt in front of the house. Julianne knew he was nervous, but he was doing an admirable job of maintaining a stoical facade.

The car idled in the center of the street before the house, its occupants evidently sizing up the two uninvited visitors seated on the front steps. Then it accelerated and vanished up the driveway separating the Bennett house from the one next door.

Julianne and Troy listened to the sound of car doors opening and slamming shut. Then he stood, took her hand and helped her to her feet. "Now I know what soldiers must feel like when they march off to face the fire," he muttered.

"You've got all the arms you need," Julianne placated him.

He shot her a tense smile. "All the arms I need are your two," he punned in a whisper, brushing her cheek with a brief kiss and then standing at attention as the front door opened.

A woman glowered at them through the interwoven bars of the screen door's frame. Clad in a pair of baggy cotton shorts and a sleeveless blouse, her gray hair forming a frizzy cloud of curls about her face, she was thin but soft, her arms dotted with freckles and her hands roughened by years spent immersed in dishwater.

"I thought I told you not to come" were her first words, addressed to Troy, although her eyes were fastened to Julianne. They were as dark and penetrating as his.

"I want you to meet Julianne," he said, his tone low and surprisingly even. "I believe it's customary for a son to bring his lady home to meet his parents."

Troy's mother gave Julianne a skeptical study. "You're his lady? What's that supposed to mean? He hasn't done right by you yet, is that it?"

"Troy has done very right by me," Julianne declared, hooking her hand around Troy's elbow. "I'm so glad to meet you, Mrs. Bennett."

"He isn't welcome here!" Troy's father bellowed from somewhere inside the house. "Tell him to go away!"

Mrs. Bennett appeared to be of two minds. When her gaze narrowed on Troy, it glinted with fury. But when it returned to Julianne, she wavered. If Troy were doing something as chivalrous as introducing his girlfriend to his parents, then perhaps Mrs. Bennett had to match his courtesy by allowing them to enter.

After an internal debate, she glanced over her shoulder and hollered, "It's his lady or something. He's brought her home to meet us."

An explosive curse emanated from the interior of the house.

"Come on, Mom," Troy said firmly. "This has gone on long enough. Let us in."

Casting her son a dubious look, Mrs. Bennett released the lock on the screen door. As a final act of resistance, she refused to open the door for them. Troy pulled it open and urged Julianne inside ahead of himself.

The entry foyer led into a compact living room overwhelmed by huge furniture—overstuffed chairs and a couch, a cabinet television set, a large circular coffee table that consumed much of the available floor space. A framed portrait of a bride and groom—undoubtedly Troy's sister and her husband—stood on a shelf, surrounded by smaller framed photos of a young boy—Troy's nephew, Julianne surmised. Above the shelf, a patriotic brass eagle wearing a red-white-and-blue breast shield hung on the wall.

Troy's father was willfully studying a copy of *TV Guide*. He was almost as tall as Troy, and his hair, while shorter, was full and dark. He didn't look up at their entrance.

"It's his girlfriend," Mrs. Bennett said almost apologetically.

"Fine," Mr. Bennett grunted, still without looking up. "Hi. Nice to meet you. Now get out of here."

"George," Mrs. Bennett scolded him. When he didn't respond, she turned hopelessly to Julianne. "What is this, you getting married or something?"

"Yes," Troy said before Julianne could reply.

Not exactly a romantic marriage proposal, but she felt an indescribable elation at his terse statement. Yes. They were going to get married. They belonged together, in good times and bad, for better or worse. Clearly this was one of the bad times. But they would see it through together.

"You a Canadian?" Mrs. Bennett asked.

Julianne was gratified by the woman's attempt, however minimal, at hospitality. "No," she answered. "I live in New York."

Mrs. Bennett turned to Troy, who nodded. "I'm moving there," he explained.

"They ought to lock you up," Mr. Bennett snorted, his nose still buried in his magazine.

"Give me some time alone with him, Mom," Troy murmured, nudging his mother toward the doorway leading to the foyer.

Mrs. Bennett's gaze shuttled between her husband and her son, and she shrugged. "You're still a fool, Troy," she concluded, spinning on her heel and stalking out of the room. Not knowing what else to do, Julianne followed.

They ended up in the kitchen at the rear of the house. The back door was open. Peeking through it, Julianne spotted the yellow sedan parked in front of a detached garage at the end of the rutted driveway. A line of freshly laundered clothes fluttered in the breeze above the vest-pocket backyard, which was paved in except for a mangy strip of unmowed grass bordering the high wood fence at the rear.

Mrs. Bennett moved to the refrigerator. "You want something to drink?" she asked.

"No, thank you."

"I'm having some iced tea. It's a scorcher out there," Mrs. Bennett noted. She seemed high-strung, the words tumbling out of her mouth as she pulled a glass bottle of already mixed iced tea from a shelf of the refrigerator. "I'm not offering Troy any. His pop would as soon poison it as let him drink it straight." She filled a glass, gulped some down and refilled it. "You know him long?"

"Since college," Julianne replied.

His mother coughed. "That damned college of his. Filled his head with all sorts of garbage. He wanted to go to college—he should've gone to Wayne State, like his sister. But no, he had to run off to some fancy Ivy League place and turn into a rebel."

Julianne refrained from pointing out that Troy was already a rebel by the time he'd gotten to college. He'd made his break from his father on a hunting trip, when he was a teenager.

"You really want to marry him?" Mrs. Bennett posed. She sized Julianne up with a skeptical look. "You look like a nice girl. And he's a criminal."

"A criminal of conscience," Julianne corrected her. "And he isn't anymore. The war ended a long time ago, Mrs. Bennett."

"Not around here it didn't," Mrs. Bennett muttered astutely. She gathered a plastic bag of string beans from the refrigerator and an aluminum pot from the gas range and set them on the kitchen table at the center of the room. "I got work to do," she said, sitting at the table and pulling a bean from the bag. She snapped it briskly, then tossed it into the pot.

"Can I help?" Julianne offered, taking a seat beside Mrs. Bennett.

Mrs. Bennett glared at her but said nothing. Julianne engrossed herself in breaking the beans into the pot.

The rumbling voices of the men spilled into the kitchen from the living room, along with the babble of a televised baseball game. Julianne tried to decipher what Troy and his father were saying, but she could make out only a few heated words. Mrs. Bennett's face was impassive; if she was trying to eavesdrop, she gave no indication of what she thought about the altercation in the other room.

Mr. Bennett cursed a lot. Occasionally Troy let loose with an expletive of his own. If this was making peace, Julianne mused, it wasn't turning out to be a peaceful procedure.

After fifteen minutes the beans were all broken. Without a word Mrs. Bennett rose and rinsed them at the sink. Then she occupied herself seasoning a roast.

Julianne studied the room. The appliances weren't new, but they were clean. A crude crayon drawing was fastened to the refrigerator with four fruit-shaped magnets, obviously a gift from Troy's nephew. A bulletin board attached to the wall near the telephone was adorned with numerous papers: a mimeographed invitation to a Ford company picnic, a calendar, a postcard displaying a mountain scene, a flyer announcing outdoor band concerts in a neighborhood park, a reminder note from a dentist. A church-key bottle opener hung on a string from a drawer knob.

Nothing about the room told Julianne what she wanted to know. Nothing informed her of the kind of home this was, the kind of home that had produced a man like Troy. Her journalistic instincts compelled her to search for clues, but she came up blank. All she had to go on was the increasing pitch of the battle in the living room and the things Troy had told her about himself. "He hated hunting," she announced.

Mrs. Bennett rotated to face her. "What?"

"The one time Troy's father took him hunting, he got sick to his stomach. How could you have expected him to fight in a war?"

Mrs. Bennett's jaw went slack. "Sick to his stomach?" she exclaimed.

Evidently neither Troy nor his father had ever told Mrs. Bennett about their hunting expedition to the Minnesota wilderness. But Julianne wasn't sorry she'd broached the subject. She wanted to break through to these people, to force them to acknowledge the son they had created.

"He hated killing," Julianne explained. "He hated the idea of it. He's a loving man, a gentle man. You have to accept that."

"Sick to his stomach," Mrs. Bennett repeated, mulling over Julianne's revelation. "He never got sick. Half the kids in school would be out with the flu, or the chicken pox. But not Troy. He never got sick."

"Violence makes him sick," said Julianne.

Mrs. Bennett leaned against the chipped Formica counter and perused Julianne. "Why did he come here?" she asked. "What does he hope to get out of it? His father's never going to forgive him."

"I don't want forgiveness," Troy said, suddenly appearing in the doorway. He looked fatigued, his eyes distant, his mouth expressionless.

"Then what do you want?" his mother asked.

"I want him to accept me. I want him to say, 'Yes, you're my son.'"

Mrs. Bennett pursed her lips and averted her eyes. "It'll be a cold day in hell before he says that."

"So I've discovered," Troy admitted, his gaze traveling to Julianne and remaining on her.

She longed to run to him, to comfort him. She longed to demand that he tell her everything that had transpired in the other room, everything he'd said, everything his father had said. But she couldn't, not now. Troy would tell her when he was able. She was patient; she could wait. When he needed her to listen, she would be ready.

"Not all dreams can come true, Mom," he murmured. "But if you're lucky, sometimes one or two might. I've got Julianne. That one came true. I'll count my blessings."

He strode across the room to his mother and kissed her cheek. Mrs. Bennett flinched, and Troy backed off before she could push him away. His father's rejection was hard enough to take. He wasn't about to give his mother a chance to reject him, too.

Sighing, he turned to Julianne. He grabbed her hand and helped her to her feet. "Let's go," he said. "Let's go home and get married and make a dream come true."

A cease-fire wasn't a peace, but it was better than war. As Troy led Julianne through the house and out the front door, she understood that even if his dream of reconciliation with his family hadn't come completely true, he wasn't about to abandon it. He would accept the dream that had come true, and continue to dream about the rest.

And that, she decided, was a very good reason to love him.

Epilogue

"The thing about telling people you've climbed Mount Everett," Andrew explained, "is that if you slur your words, you can dupe people into believing you climbed Mount Everest."

"I could never dupe anyone into believing that!" Kimberly disputed him before dissolving in laughter.

The truth was, they hadn't actually climbed Mount Everett, either. They'd driven most of the distance up the rounded peak located in the Massachusetts Berkshires not far from Amherst College. All six of them had converged on Amherst for the three-day July Fourth weekend. Laura and Seth had dropped off Laura's daughter in Brooklyn so she could visit with her best friend there, and then they had met up with Troy and Julianne in Manhattan, piled into Troy's car and headed north to see Andrew and Kimberly. Laura and Seth had spent much of the four-hour drive regaling Julianne and Troy with a description of their flight east, and the Dramamine Seth had force-fed Laura over her protests about the danger of relying on drugs. Even with the Dramamine, she reported almost boastfully, she'd felt queasy during most of the flight to the East Coast.

Because Andrew's apartment was so small, Julianne, Troy, Seth and Laura had spent Friday night at the Lord

Jeffrey Inn. Saturday morning, armed with an enormous picnic basket heaped with goodies, they'd driven west and valiantly scaled the last few hundred feet of Mount Everett.

It was a glorious day, sunny but not too hot, the air clean and fragrant, the few clouds scattered across the crisp blue sky appearing too cottony to be real. The mountain's summit was a flat, grassy field dotted with shade trees and evergreens. As soon as Kimberly picked a level spot beneath a broad-limbed maple and spread out the blanket for their picnic, Andrew produced a Frisbee from the basket. As enthusiastic as children, the three men raced into the field to play catch.

Julianne appropriated a corner of the blanket to sit on and leaned back against the sturdy trunk of the maple tree. Her thoughts wandered to a July Fourth fifteen years ago, a day engraved in her memory. She wanted this day engraved in her memory, too. It was a day of reunions and joy, not a day of departure and grief. "Are there going to be fireworks up here?" she asked Kimberly.

"Not that I know of," Kimberly replied. "They'll probably have some down in Great Barrington or Stockbridge, but not until nightfall. And there's no way I'm staying on top of a mountain after dark."

"A mountain!" Laura hooted. "I'll tell you one thing. California has definitely changed my opinion of mountains. You know what they'd call this place out west? An anthill."

"I knew it," Kimberly taunted her. "I knew you'd turn into a California girl on us."

"I'm not a California girl," Laura refuted her with a laugh. She shoved a long, kinky lock of hair from her face and refastened her barrette. "All I'm saying is, easterners tend to be pretty provincial. I've learned a lot about geography by living in Topanga Canyon."

"You'll learn a lot more once the big earthquake hits and you fall into the ocean," Julianne warned.

"Fortunately we all know how to swim," Laura responded placidly. "Even Barney, the dog. We'll survive."

Kimberly proceeded to unpack the basket, arranging wedges of cheese on a wide cutting board, filling wicker trays with crackers, trying to catch the apples before they rolled off the blanket. "What are you all doing with yourself these days?" she asked Laura. "Has unemployment started to wear on you yet?"

Laura laughed. "I love unemployment. Isn't that shameful? I love not having to hustle through the rush hour and fuss over a bunch of girls who wish I'd leave them alone. Instead I fuss over Rita. She probably wishes I'd leave her alone, too."

"Does she like California?"

"Does she ever," Laura replied. "There are more gorgeous men per square inch out there than anywhere else in the world."

"Mount Everett excluded," Julianne commented, gazing affectionately at Seth, Andrew and Troy as they flung the Frisbee around. They were showing off, if not for the women, then for each other. Seth tried to catch the Frisbee behind his back and wound up tripping and falling. Troy succeeded in catching it on the tip of his index finger, but when he tossed it between his legs it arced off course, forcing Andrew to chase it across the field.

"What a bunch of babies," Laura joked lovingly, her eyes also on the game of catch.

"Mmm, but gorgeous babies," Julianne emphasized.

"Gorgeous babies," Kimberly echoed vaguely, her gaze growing misty. Then her smile returned, dazzling in its beauty, and she rummaged through the basket for the plastic wineglasses she'd packed. "I hope this wine's still cold," she said as she slid the bottle from its built-in slot. "It's—" she read from the label "—a Johannesburg Riesling, if anyone cares."

"Johannesburg? South Africa?" Laura quipped. "Shouldn't we be boycotting that?"

Julianne laughed. "What did we use to drink in college? Almaden Chablis, right?"

"Boone's Farm Apple Wine," Kimberly reminded her.

Laughing harder, Julianne wrinkled her nose. "Oh, Lord, remember that stuff? It was vile!"

"It was cheap," Laura recalled, helping herself to one of the glasses. "Now that I'm a Hollywood wife, I expect the best. Fill me up, Kim."

Kimberly dutifully filled Laura's glass and filled a second for Julianne. Then she recorked the bottle. "Aren't you having any?" Julianne asked.

Kimberly smiled enigmatically. "No, I don't think I will."

Julianne's gaze hardened on Kimberly. Her Cheshire-cat grin provoked Julianne to blurt out, "Since when did you turn into a teetotaler? Are you pregnant or something?"

Kimberly lowered her eyes and giggled. "It appears that way."

"Kimberly!" Laura and Julianne screamed in unison. When Laura recovered from her shock, she examined Kimberly's petite figure closely. "It definitely does *not* appear that way at all. How far along are you?"

"I've hardly begun," she revealed. "I haven't even had a test yet. But..." Her smile grew warm, and her eyes glistened with tears of pleasure. "I'm sure I am. I can just feel it. Ever since the night—well..." She blushed modestly. "It was the night after Andrew testified. It was such a burden off us, and we were so glad that he'd gotten through it, and... well, we celebrated." Her blush deepened. "I felt it then, right away. Everything was changed. I felt all different."

"Does Andrew know?" Julianne asked.

"Oh, yes," Kimberly swore. "He felt it, too. He said he could tell, just by looking into my eyes."

Laura set down her wineglass and gave Kimberly a congratulatory hug. "I'm so happy for you, Kim! That's wonderful!"

"Please!" Kimberly extricated herself from Laura's exuberant embrace. "I'm happy, too, but it's still a long way off. Things could go wrong. Given my age, I'll probably have amniocentesis. I'm afraid to think too much about the baby, because that might jinx everything." She allowed herself a whimsical grin. "But I'm awfully happy for me, too."

"Now Andrew's going to have to marry you," Julianne ribbed her.

"There's poetic justice in it, don't you think?" Kimberly mused. "Me, proper Kimberly Belmont, conceiving out of wedlock. Once my parents find out they'll surely have a fit."

"They'll get over it," Laura predicted. "I've been there, Kim. Parents love to be grandparents. It mellows them. Your folks are going to be thrilled."

"I've met your mother," Kimberly remarked. "She seems far more capable of handling these things than mine."

"But you'll be married by the time the baby arrives," Julianne pointed out.

Kimberly nodded. "August eighth. We've got our tickets to London, and I'm still enough of a traditionalist to believe we ought to get married before we go on our honeymoon. So we finally set a date. But my parents are sure to count backward after the baby arrives." She chuckled gleefully. "I hope they do have a fit. It would please me no end."

"Help!" Troy roared. The women glanced across the field to see him lying flat on his back, with Seth racing toward him, preparing to jump on him. "Truce!" Troy begged, waving his arms in the air. "Surrender!"

Seth leaped gracefully over Troy's prostrate body, then playfully whacked his belly with the Frisbee.

"Whatever are they up to?" Kimberly asked before succumbing to a guffaw.

"I don't know," Julianne muttered. "We're the ones guzzling all the wine and they're acting drunk."

"Wine?" Andrew boomed, approaching the blanket, out of breath from their rowdy game. "Did somebody say wine?" He pulled off his eyeglasses to mop the perspiration from his brow, then set them back on his nose and knelt beside Kimberly. She poured a glass for him, and he kissed her cheek.

"Lovebirds," Laura muttered to Julianne. "Doesn't it just make you sick?"

"If it makes you sick, then take a Dramamine," Julianne ordered her before convulsing in laughter.

Soon Troy and Seth joined them on the blanket, grabbing at the bottle and the crackers. "I'm starving," Seth declared, shoving his long blond hair out of his eyes and wolfing down a chunk of cheese. "Is this all we've got? Didn't anyone bring any hamburgers?"

"As you can see, we're back to Ax Man," Laura confided. "All he thinks about these days is red meat dripping blood."

"Are you really going to write another Ax Man flick?" Andrew asked him.

"Now that I've found an independent producer for *Good Fences*, I can devote myself to my real vocation—schlock movies."

"You found a producer?" Julianne exclaimed. Seth had been trying to peddle his serious screenplay for so long without success, she'd assumed that he had given up on ever seeing *Good Fences* made into a film.

"Last week," Laura crowed. "I knew someone would option it someday."

"That's all it is—optioned," Seth cautioned. "These things take years to reach fruition. Whether it'll ever appear on the screen is anybody's guess."

"My guess is, it will," Julianne said. "I've got faith in you, Seth."

"Julianne has faith in everybody," Troy commented quietly, stretching out on the blanket and resting his head in her lap. He gazed up into her face and smiled. "She had enough faith to rope us into writing that dumb newspaper for a class assignment. And look what she's done with it."

"Dumb?" Julianne pounced on the word. "You think *The Dream* was dumb?"

"I thought the idea was... questionable," he admitted, choosing a tactful word. "Why did you even ask me to join the staff?"

"You know why I did," she chided him. "We needed a photographer. You had a camera."

"How did you know I had a camera?"

"I was teamed up with Andrew by the professor," she explained. "Andrew was your buddy. He told me you were an ace photographer."

Troy turned quizzically to Andrew. "Did you really tell her that?"

Andrew's eyes met Julianne's, and he chuckled. "If you want to know the truth—"

"He doesn't," Julianne said quickly.

Troy twisted back to Julianne, then sat up to face her squarely. "I do want to know the truth, boss. Here I am, still working for you, taking pictures for your dumb magazine—"

"It isn't dumb!" she argued, trying unsuccessfully to smother her laughter.

"So tell me the truth." When Julianne refused to provide the answer Troy demanded, he spun back to Andrew. "Come on, Dr. Collins. Spit it out."

Andrew shrugged and swallowed a cracker. "The truth was, we were paired up, and we got to talking, and Julianne mentioned her newspaper idea—*I* didn't think it was dumb, by the way," he noted, shooting Julianne an ameliorating look. She scowled, knowing full well what Andrew was about to disclose to her friends. "Anyway, we were talking about whether we should invite a few other classmates to join us in this enterprise, and Julianne said, 'You seem to be buddy-buddy with that guy with the mustache. Can we ask him?' "

"That's all he has to know," Julianne said hurriedly, clamping her hands over Troy's ears to prevent him from hearing any more.

He easily pried her hands from him. His attention was fully on Andrew. "All right," he said, awaiting a more earth-shattering revelation. "So she guessed that you and I were pals. So what?"

"So..." Andrew deliberately drew out the telling to build suspense. "So, I said, 'Why do you want me to ask Troy to join us?' And she said, 'Because he's really good-looking.' "

Troy gaped at Julianne. "You didn't!"

Abashed, Julianne nodded. "I'm not going to call Andrew a liar."

"You? Sensible, logical Julianne? You were gaga over me?"

"I wasn't gaga," she defended herself. "I was merely sensible and logical enough to notice that you were an attractive man."

Troy mulled over her rationalization and shook his head. "And all this time I thought you were after my camera," he murmured.

"That was a handy excuse," she explained. "It worked out well, didn't it?"

Troy seemed on the verge of teasing her, but he didn't. Instead he smiled and touched his lips to hers. "It did work out well," he whispered. "Very well."

"What I meant was, you were a good photographer," she hastened to clarify.

But her shimmering blue eyes gave her away, and her breathtaking smile, and the love flooding from her to wash over Troy. She was indeed quite pleased with the way things had worked out.